MOBILE SUIT

GUNDAM

THE ORIGIN

VII

—BATTLE OF LOUM—

YOSHIKAZU YASUHIKO

ORIGINAL STORY BY:
YOSHIYUKI TOMINO • HAJIME YATATE

MECHANICAL DESIGN BY:
KUNIO OKAWARA

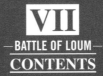

Collector's Edition

Mobile Suit Gundam
THE ORIGIN

VII

—BATTLE OF LOUM—

CONTENTS

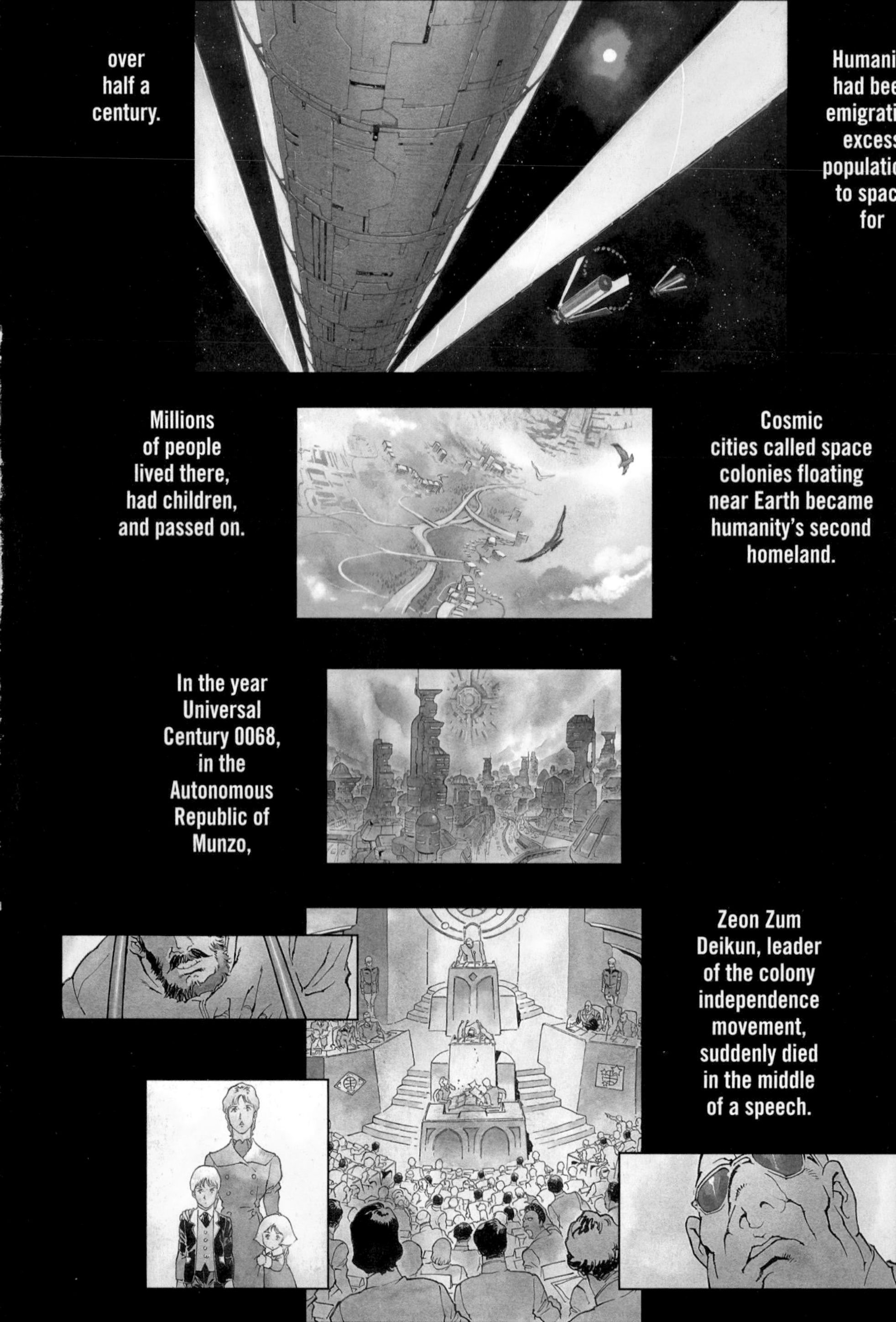
Humani
had bee
emigrati
excess
populatio
to spac
for
over half a century.
Cosmic cities called space colonies floating near Earth became humanity's second homeland.
Millions of people lived there, had children, and passed on.
In the year Universal Century 0068, in the Autonomous Republic of Munzo,
Zeon Zum Deikun, leader of the colony independence movement, suddenly died in the middle of a speech.

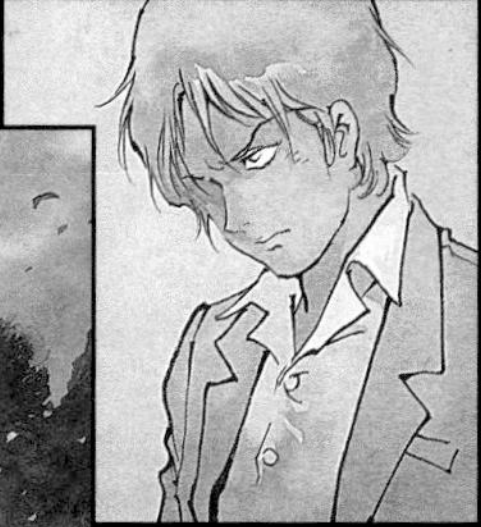

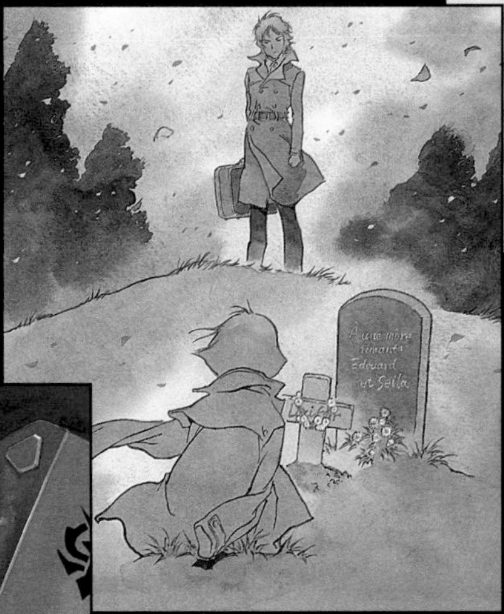

Deikun's children, who had fled the ensuing political clashes and lived in hiding on the Texas Colony, received word of their mother's death.

Bent on avenging their mother, elder brother Casval bid farewell to his sister Artesia and left for Side 3.

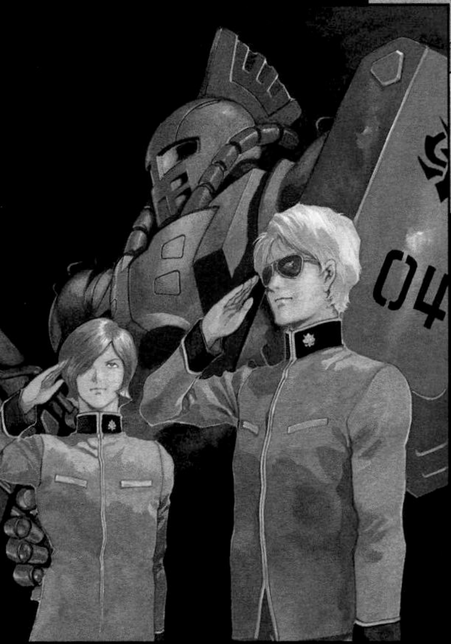
04

Casval assumed the identity of his friend Char Aznable—who died in an "accident" arranged by House Zabi—and entered the military academy. While training there, he became a close friend to Garma, the youngest Zabi son.

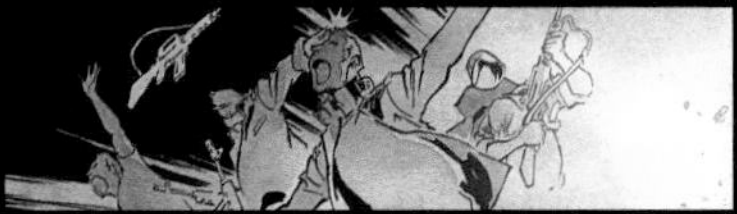

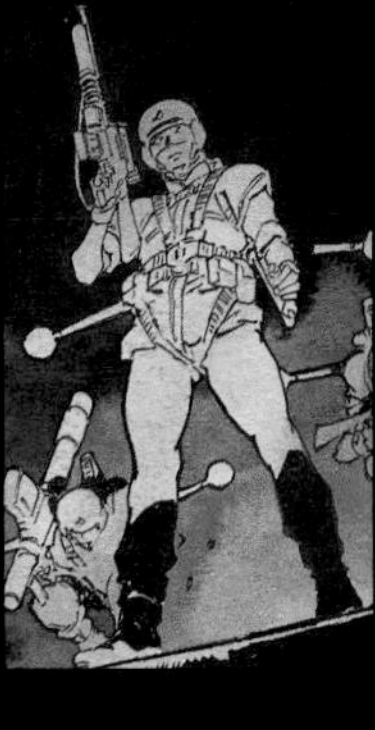

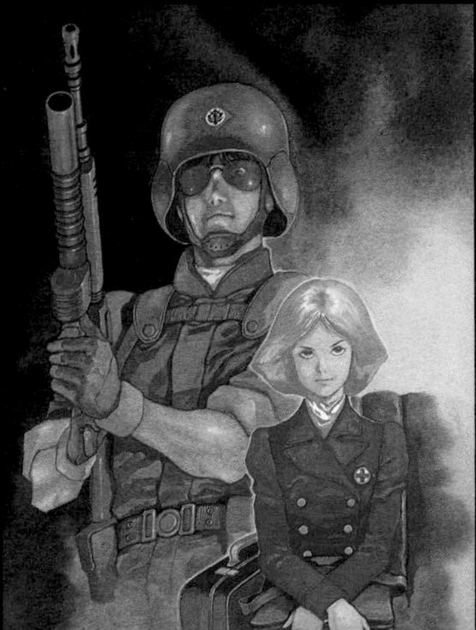

After earning his commission, Char deftly manipulated Garma into leading their fellow graduates in an uprising. They attacked and seized the barracks of the Federation's colonial garrison, disarming its troops.

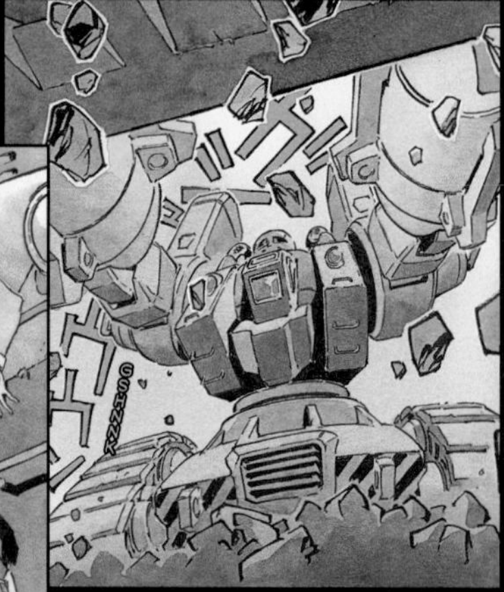
GSHNNK

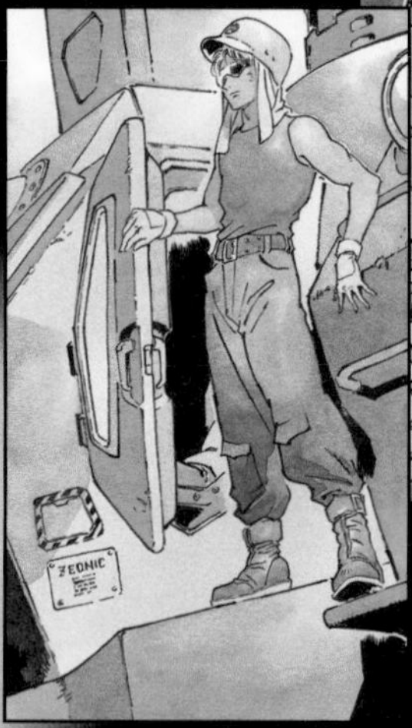
ZEONIC

Char, stripped of his rank for his role in the uprising, went down alone to Earth.

He operated a mobile worker at the construction site of a new Federation defense facility in Jaburo, South America. There, he crossed paths with an Indian girl named Lalah.

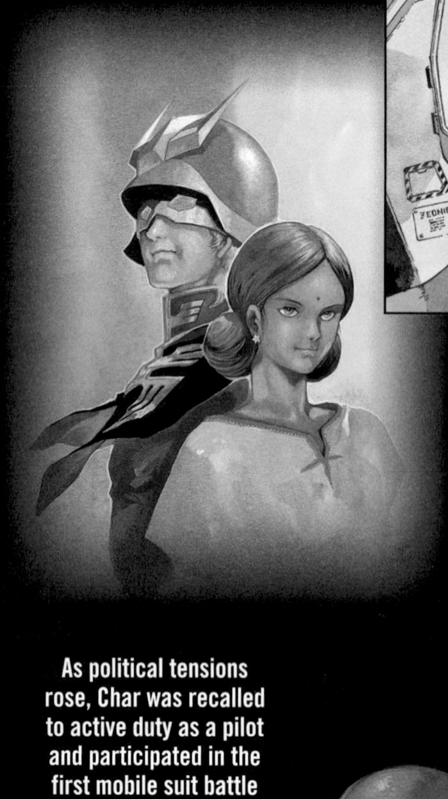

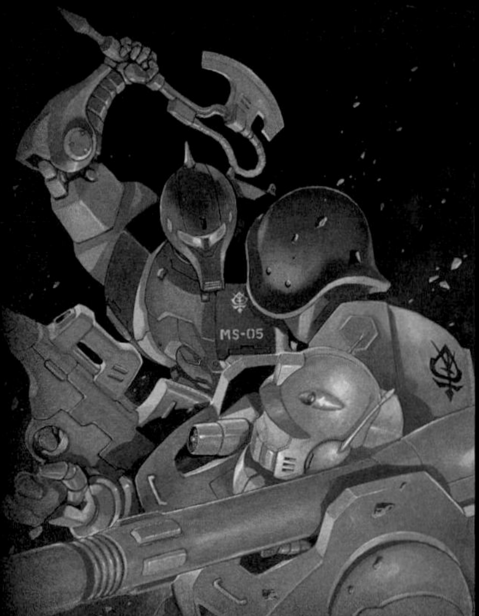
MS-05

As political tensions rose, Char was recalled to active duty as a pilot and participated in the first mobile suit battle in history, demolishing a detachment of the Federation's Guncannons.

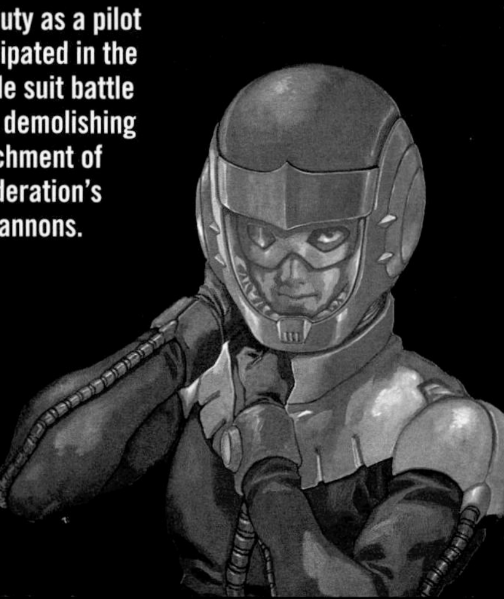

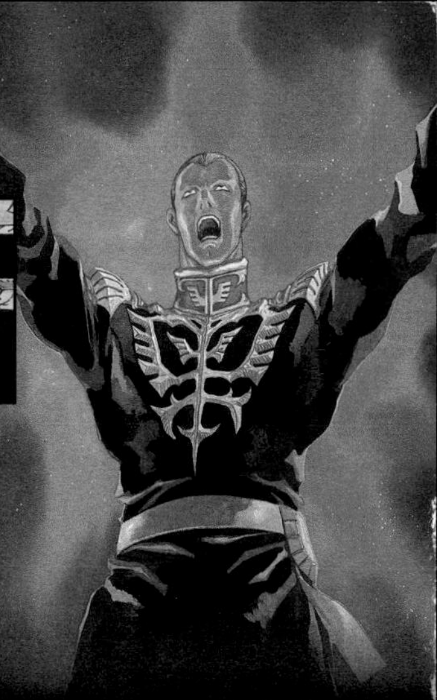

Guided by House Zabi, Side 3 proclaimed itself the Principality of Zeon and declared war against the Earth Federation.

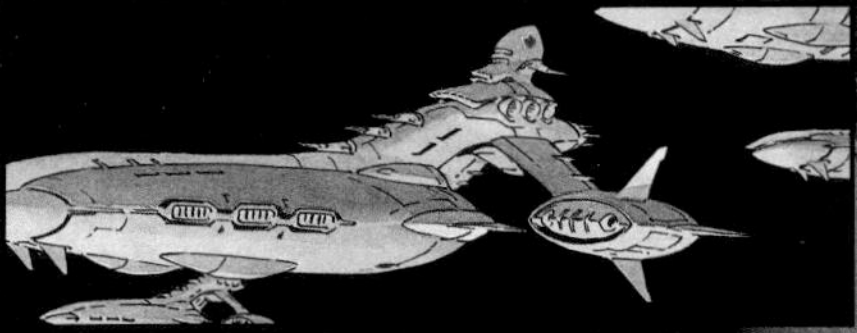

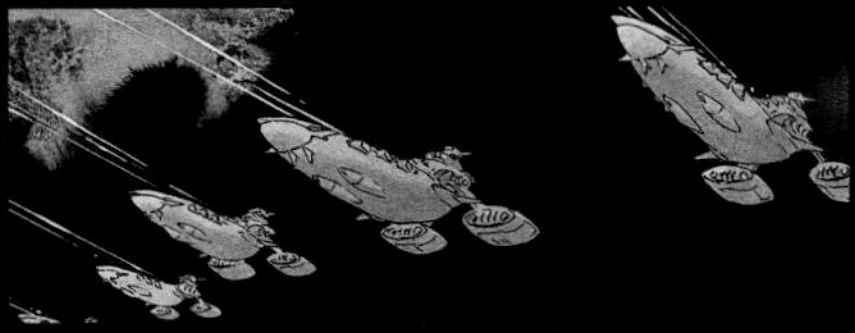

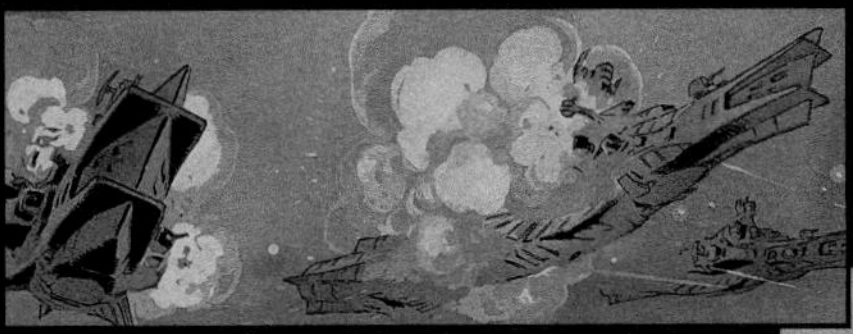

Thanks to a fleet built in utmost secrecy and the new armament Zaku's overwhelming capabilities, Zeon routed the Federation's space forces.

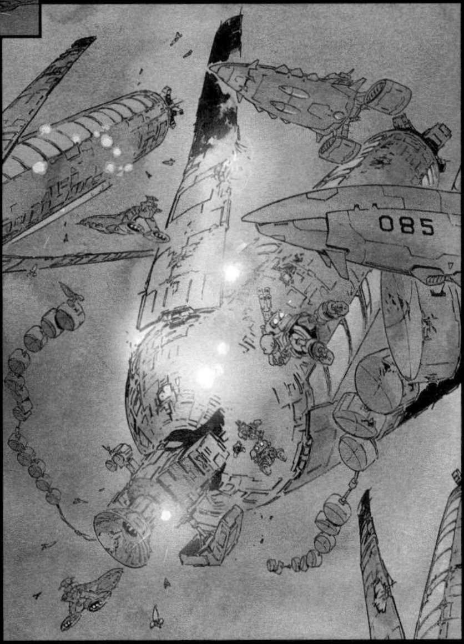
085

Aiming for a brief and decisive end to the war, Supreme Commander Gihren Zabi ordered the massacre of the citizens of Side 2, which stood hostile. The lifeless colony was then itself used as a mass weapon and dropped on Earth.

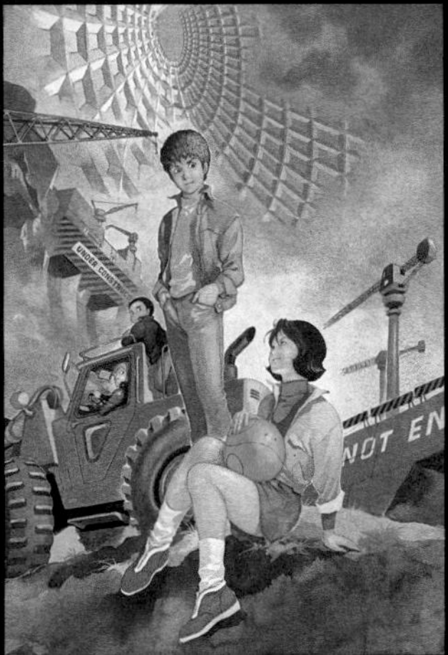

In just over one month, half the human population was lost. But still the war rages on.

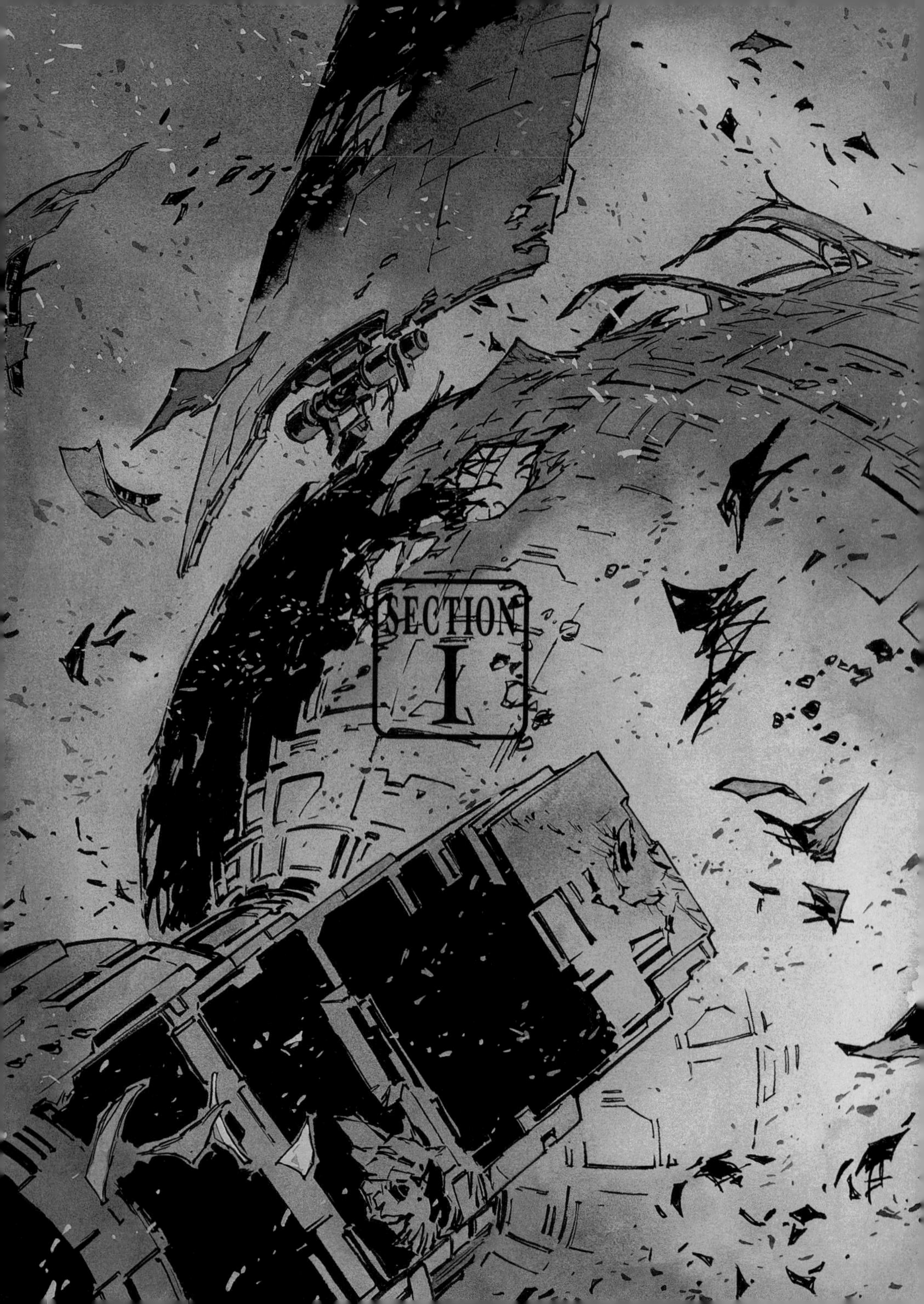
SECTION
I

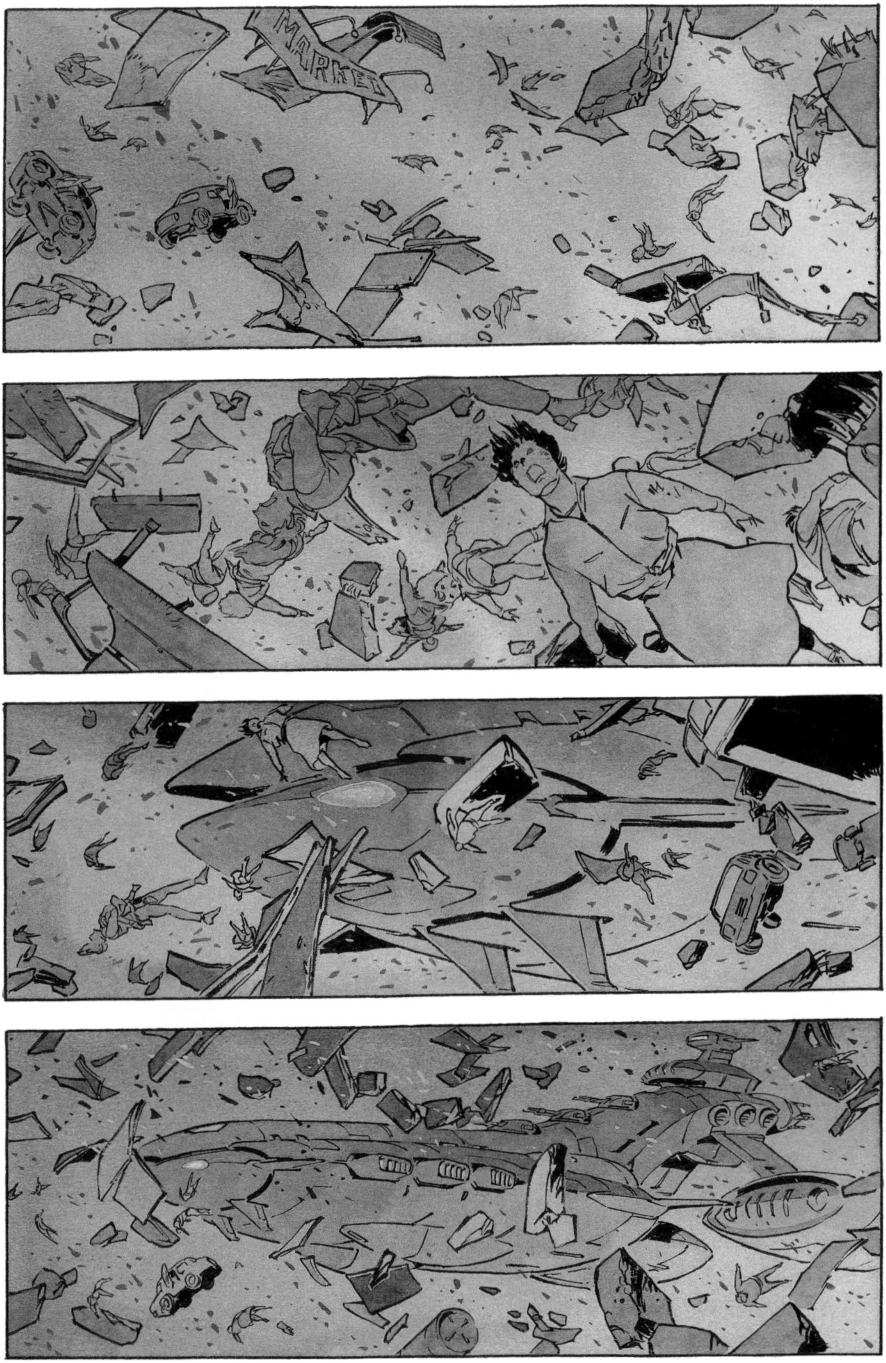
MARKET

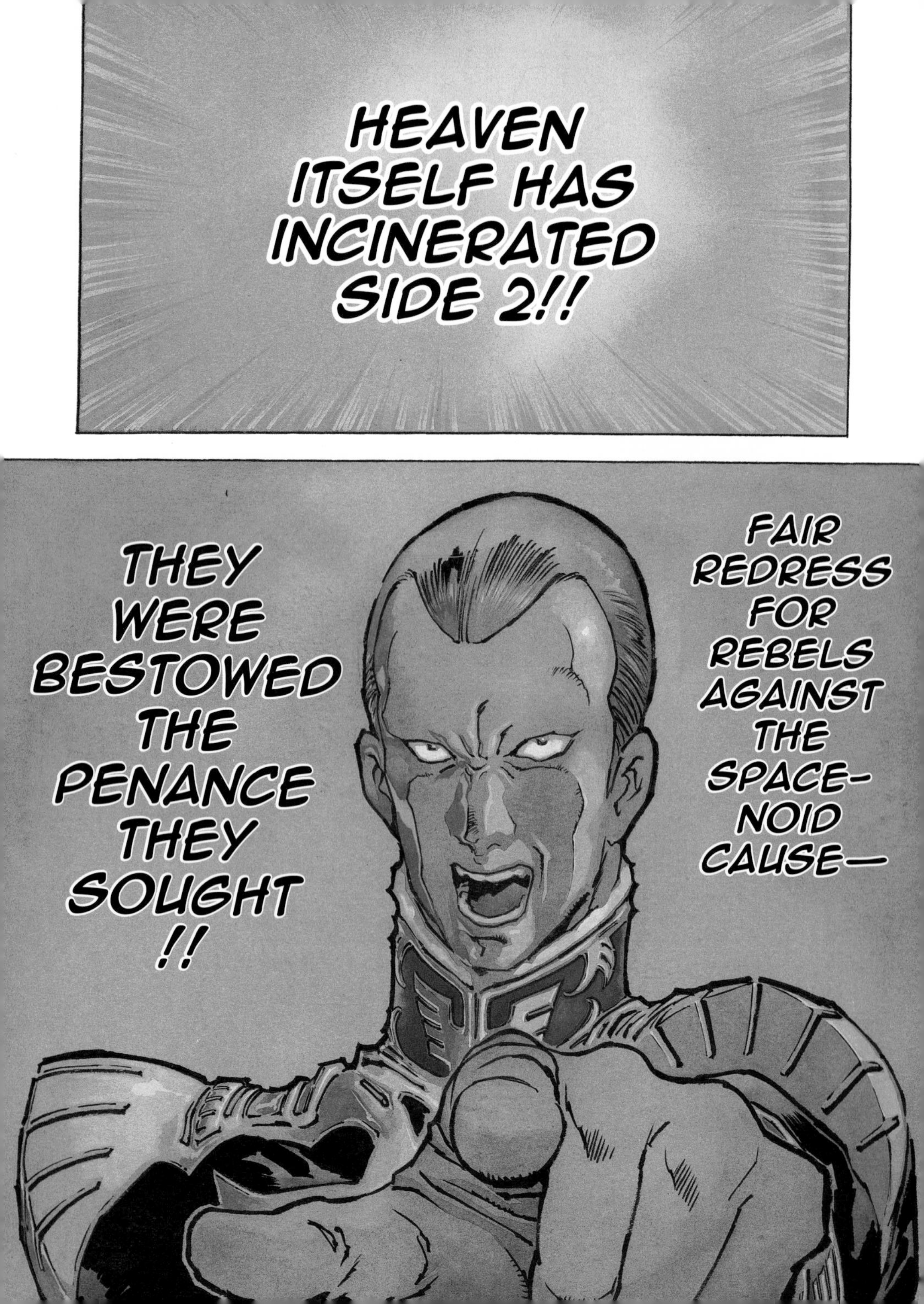
HEAVEN ITSELF HAS INCINERATED SIDE 2!!
FAIR REDRESS FOR REBELS AGAINST THE SPACE-NOID CAUSE—
THEY WERE BESTOWED THE PENANCE THEY SOUGHT!!

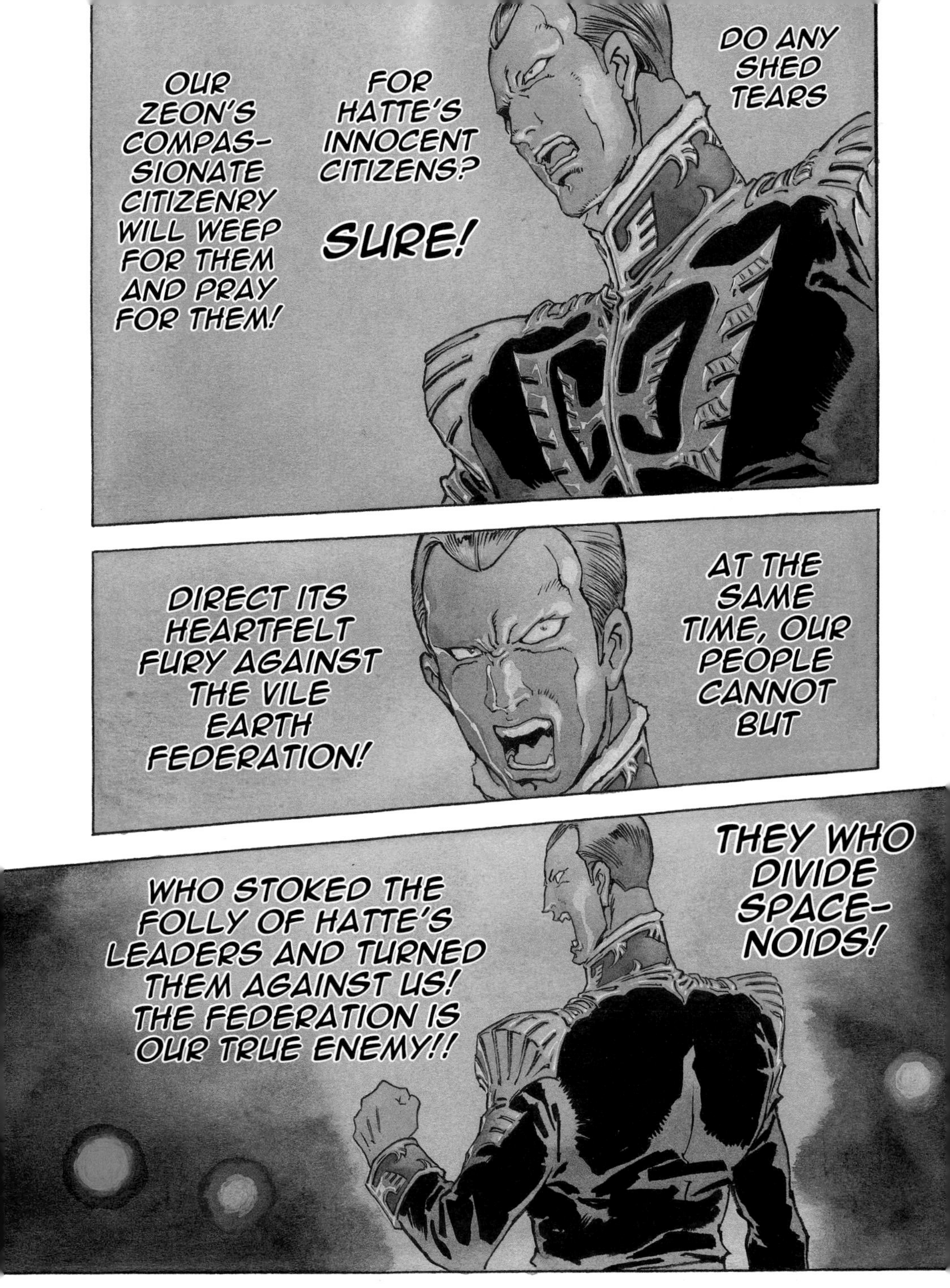
DO ANY SHED TEARS
FOR HATTE'S INNOCENT CITIZENS?
SURE!
OUR ZEON'S COMPAS-SIONATE CITIZENRY WILL WEEP FOR THEM AND PRAY FOR THEM!
AT THE SAME TIME, OUR PEOPLE CANNOT BUT
DIRECT ITS HEARTFELT FURY AGAINST THE VILE EARTH FEDERATION!
THEY WHO DIVIDE SPACE-NOIDS!
WHO STOKED THE FOLLY OF HATTE'S LEADERS AND TURNED THEM AGAINST US! THE FEDERATION IS OUR TRUE ENEMY!!

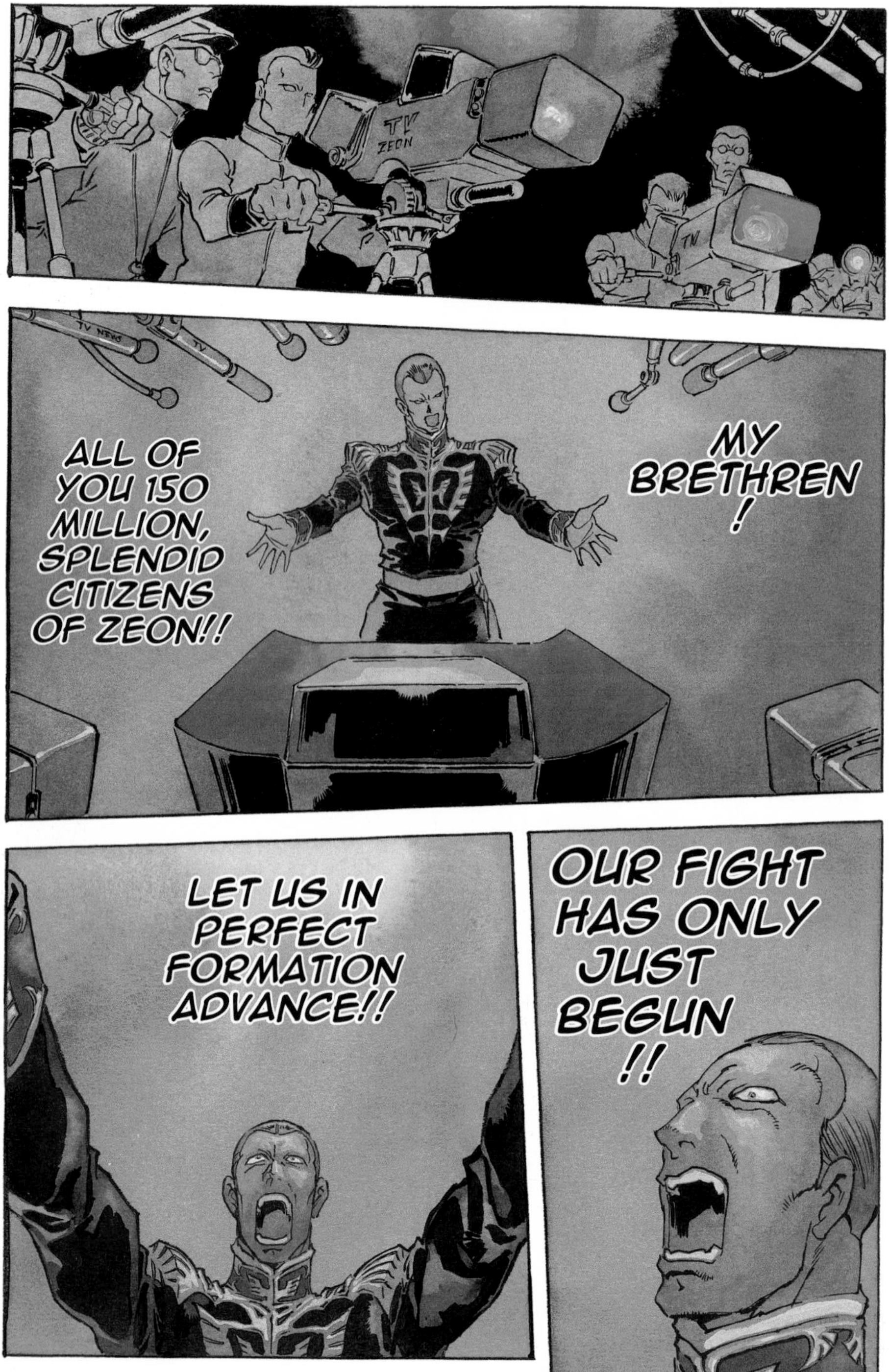
MY BRETHREN!
ALL OF YOU 150 MILLION, SPLENDID CITIZENS OF ZEON!!
OUR FIGHT HAS ONLY JUST BEGUN!!
LET US IN PERFECT FORMATION ADVANCE!!

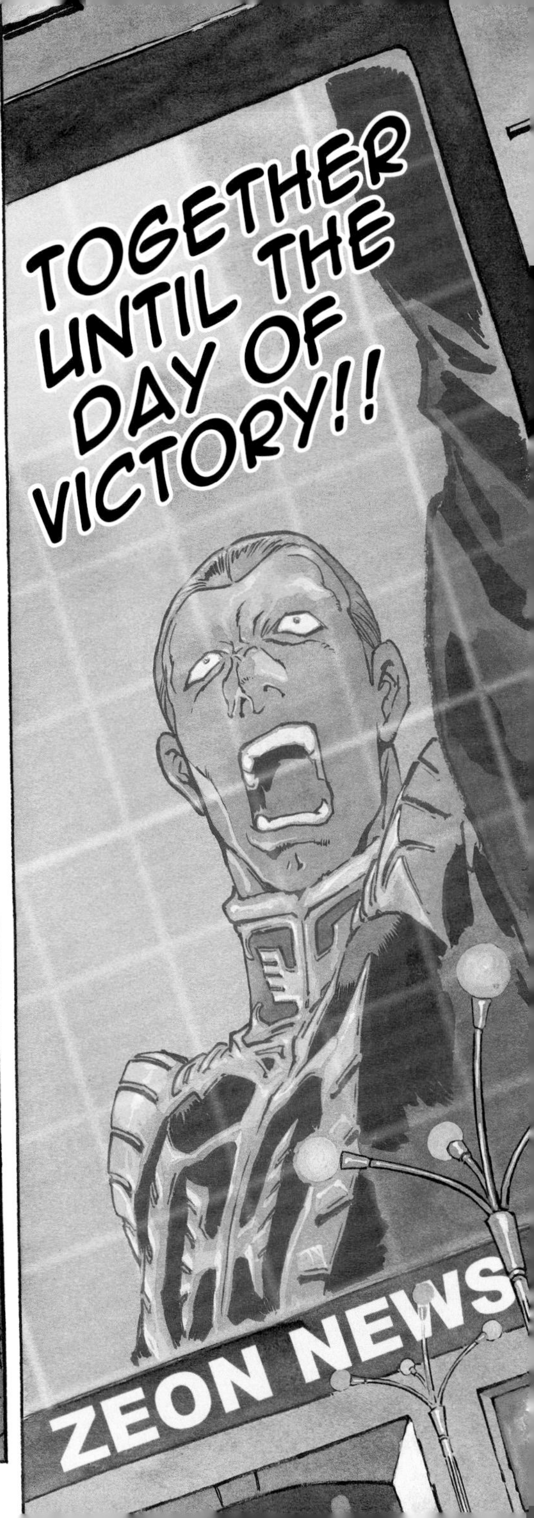
TOGETHER UNTIL THE DAY OF VICTORY!!
ZEON NEWS

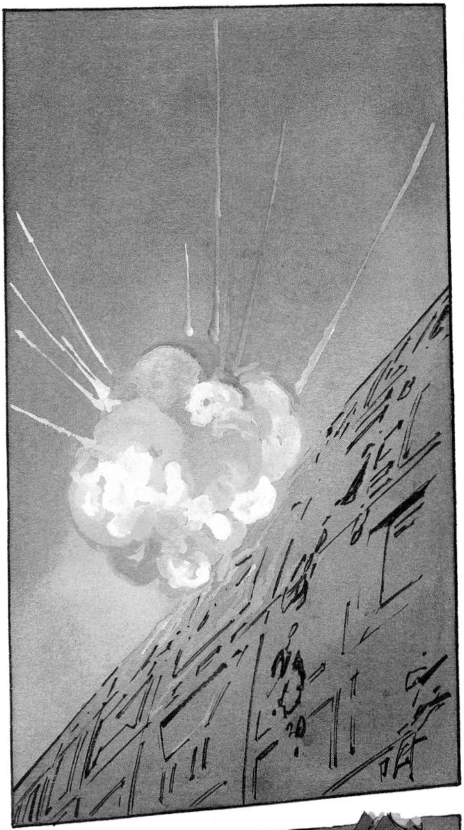

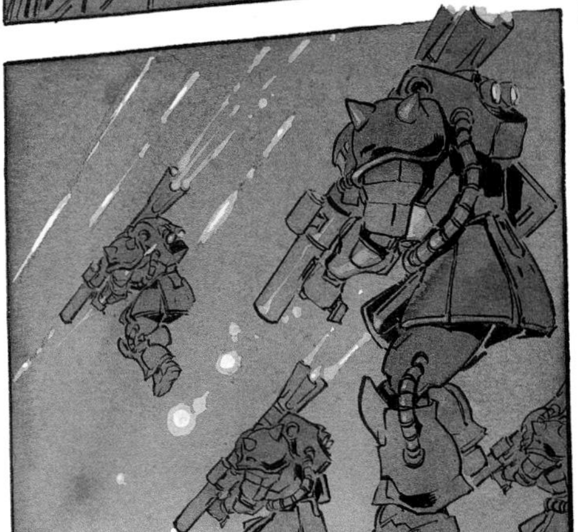

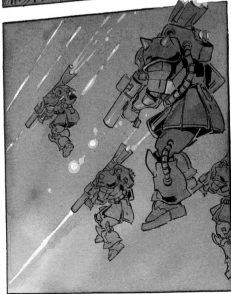

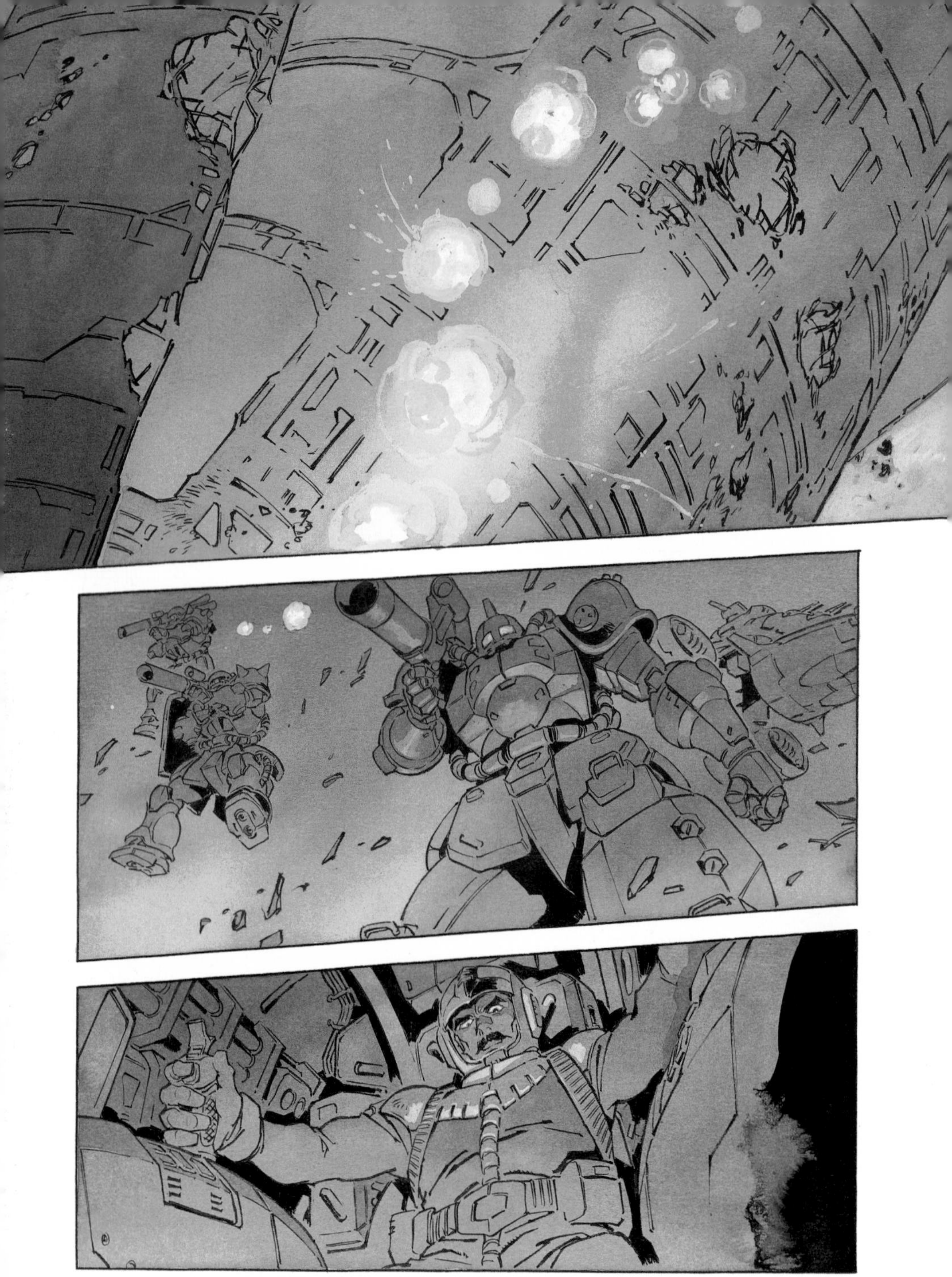

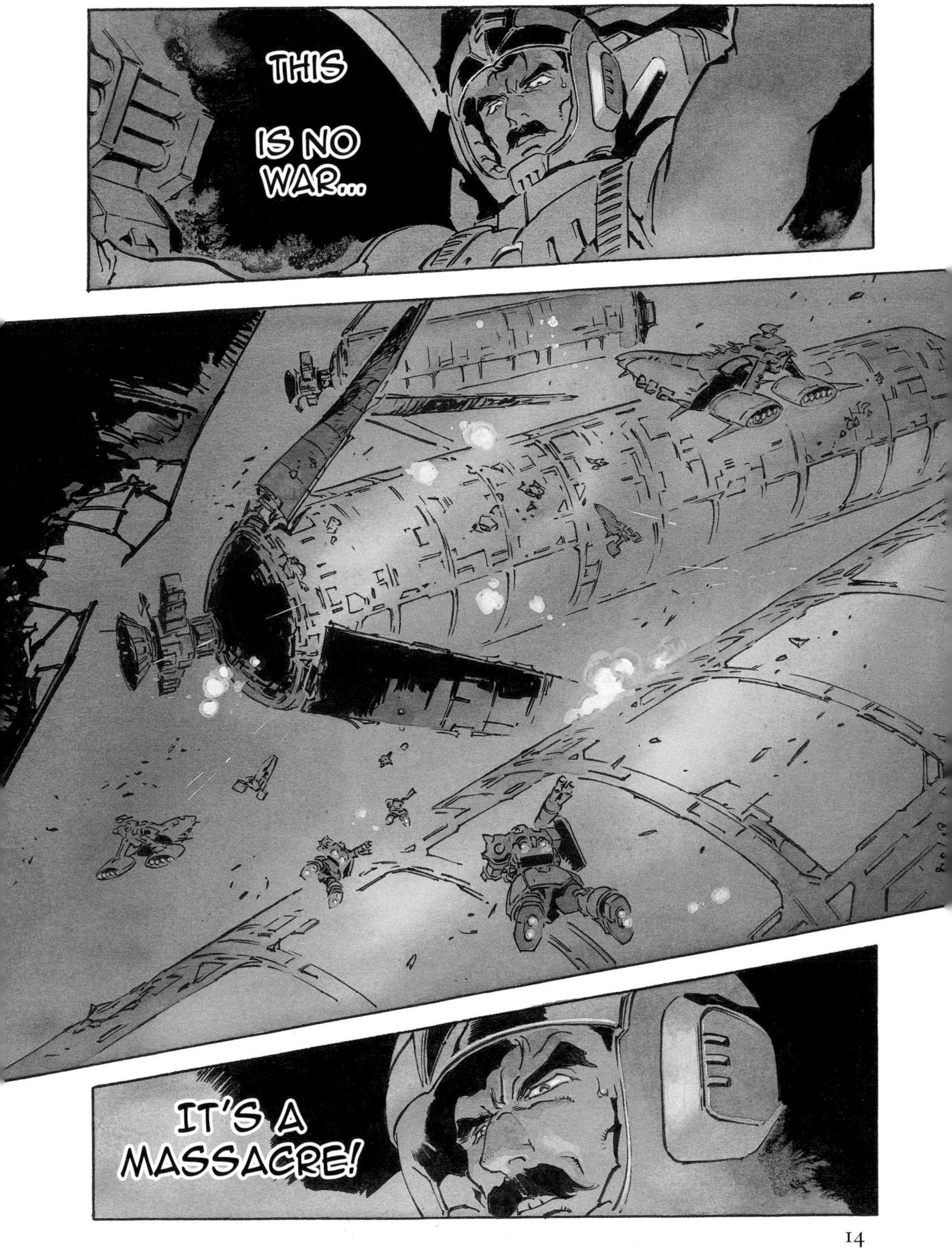
THIS
IS NO WAR...
IT'S A MASSACRE!

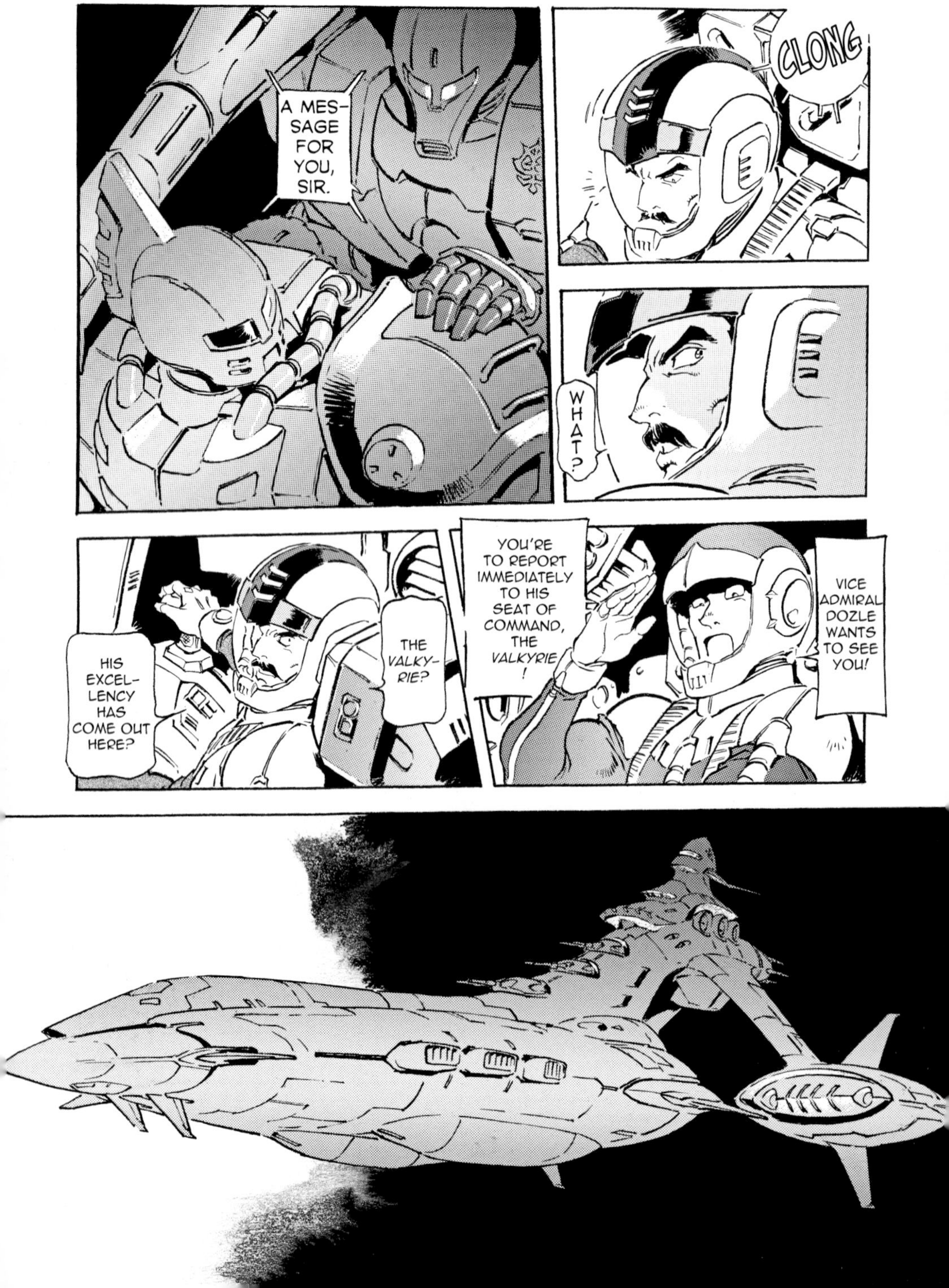
CLONG
WHAT?
A MESSAGE FOR YOU, SIR.
VICE ADMIRAL DOZLE WANTS TO SEE YOU!
YOU'RE TO REPORT IMMEDIATELY TO HIS SEAT OF COMMAND, THE *VALKYRIE*!
THE *VALKYRIE*?
HIS EXCELLENCY HAS COME OUT HERE?

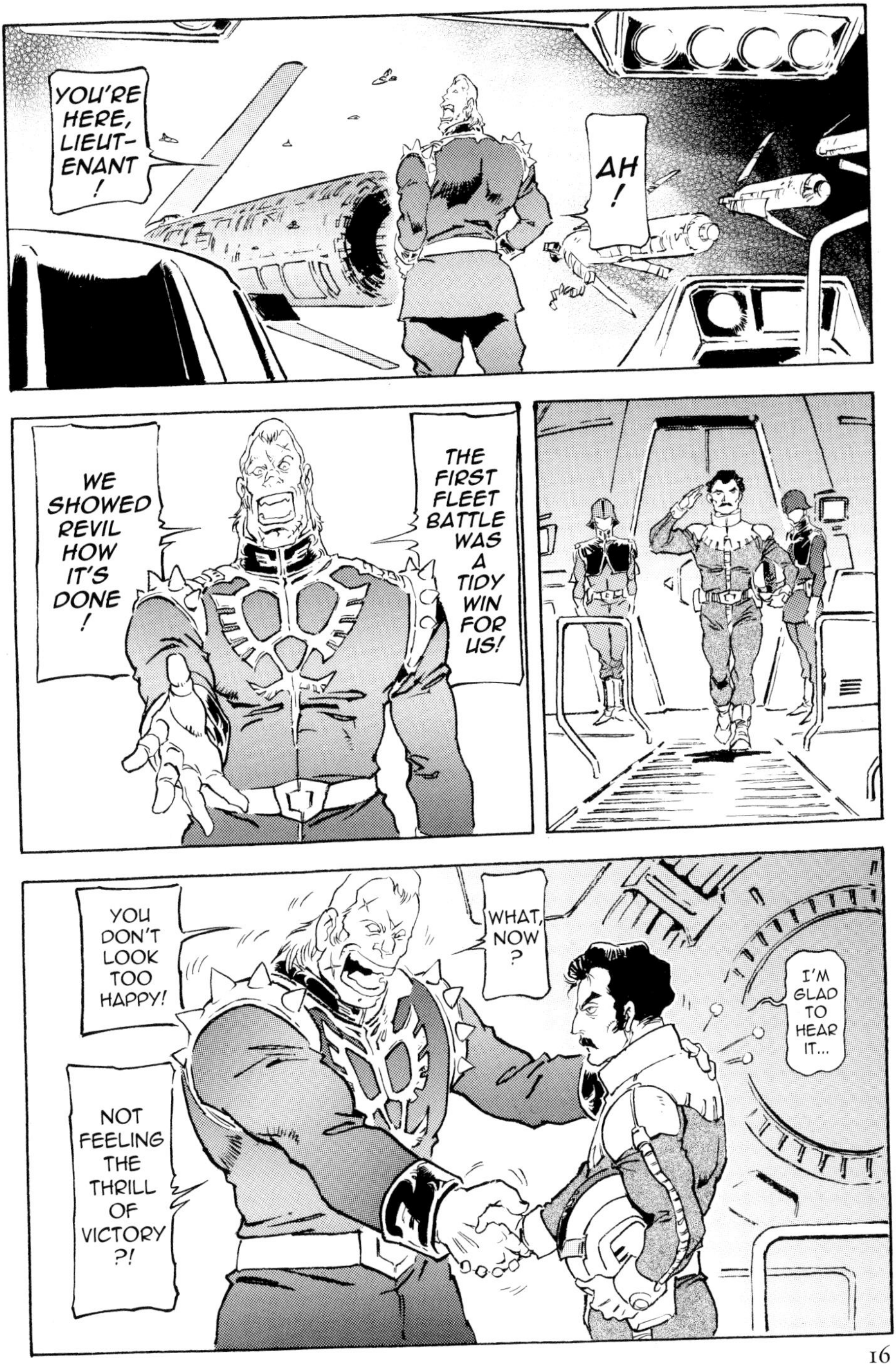
AH!
YOU'RE HERE, LIEUT-ENANT!
THE FIRST FLEET BATTLE WAS A TIDY WIN FOR US!
WE SHOWED REVIL HOW IT'S DONE!
I'M GLAD TO HEAR IT...
WHAT, NOW?
YOU DON'T LOOK TOO HAPPY!
NOT FEELING THE THRILL OF VICTORY?!

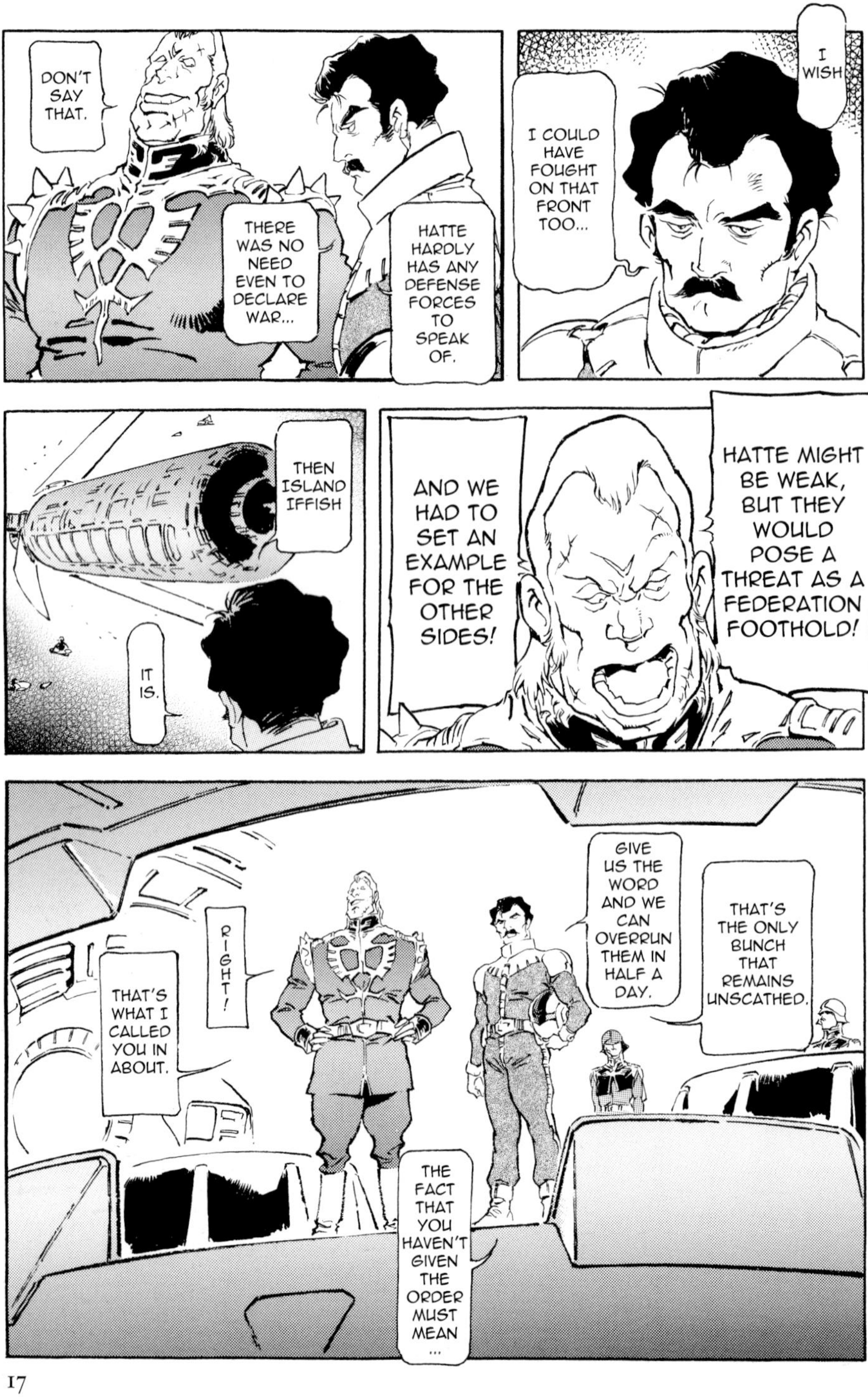
I WISH
I COULD HAVE FOUGHT ON THAT FRONT TOO...
DON'T SAY THAT.
HATTE HARDLY HAS ANY DEFENSE FORCES TO SPEAK OF.
THERE WAS NO NEED EVEN TO DECLARE WAR...
HATTE MIGHT BE WEAK, BUT THEY WOULD POSE A THREAT AS A FEDERATION FOOTHOLD!
AND WE HAD TO SET AN EXAMPLE FOR THE OTHER SIDES!
THEN ISLAND IFFISH
IT IS.
THAT'S THE ONLY BUNCH THAT REMAINS UNSCATHED.
GIVE US THE WORD AND WE CAN OVERRUN THEM IN HALF A DAY.
RIGHT!
THAT'S WHAT I CALLED YOU IN ABOUT.
THE FACT THAT YOU HAVEN'T GIVEN THE ORDER MUST MEAN...

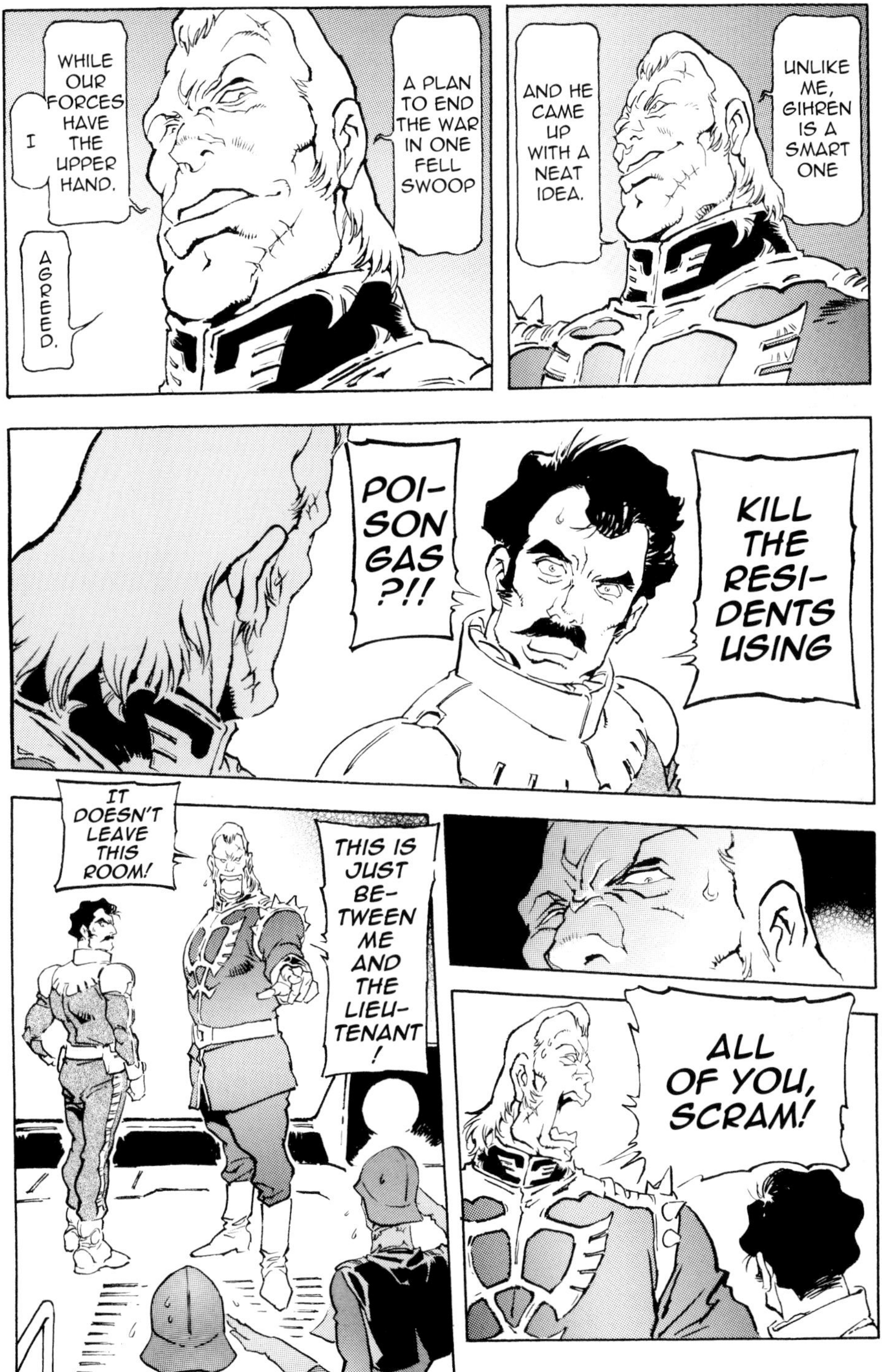
UNLIKE ME, GIHREN IS A SMART ONE
AND HE CAME UP WITH A NEAT IDEA.
A PLAN TO END THE WAR IN ONE FELL SWOOP
WHILE OUR FORCES HAVE THE UPPER HAND.
I
AGREED.
KILL THE RESIDENTS USING
POISON GAS?!!
ALL OF YOU, SCRAM!
THIS IS JUST BETWEEN ME AND THE LIEUTENANT!
IT DOESN'T LEAVE THIS ROOM!

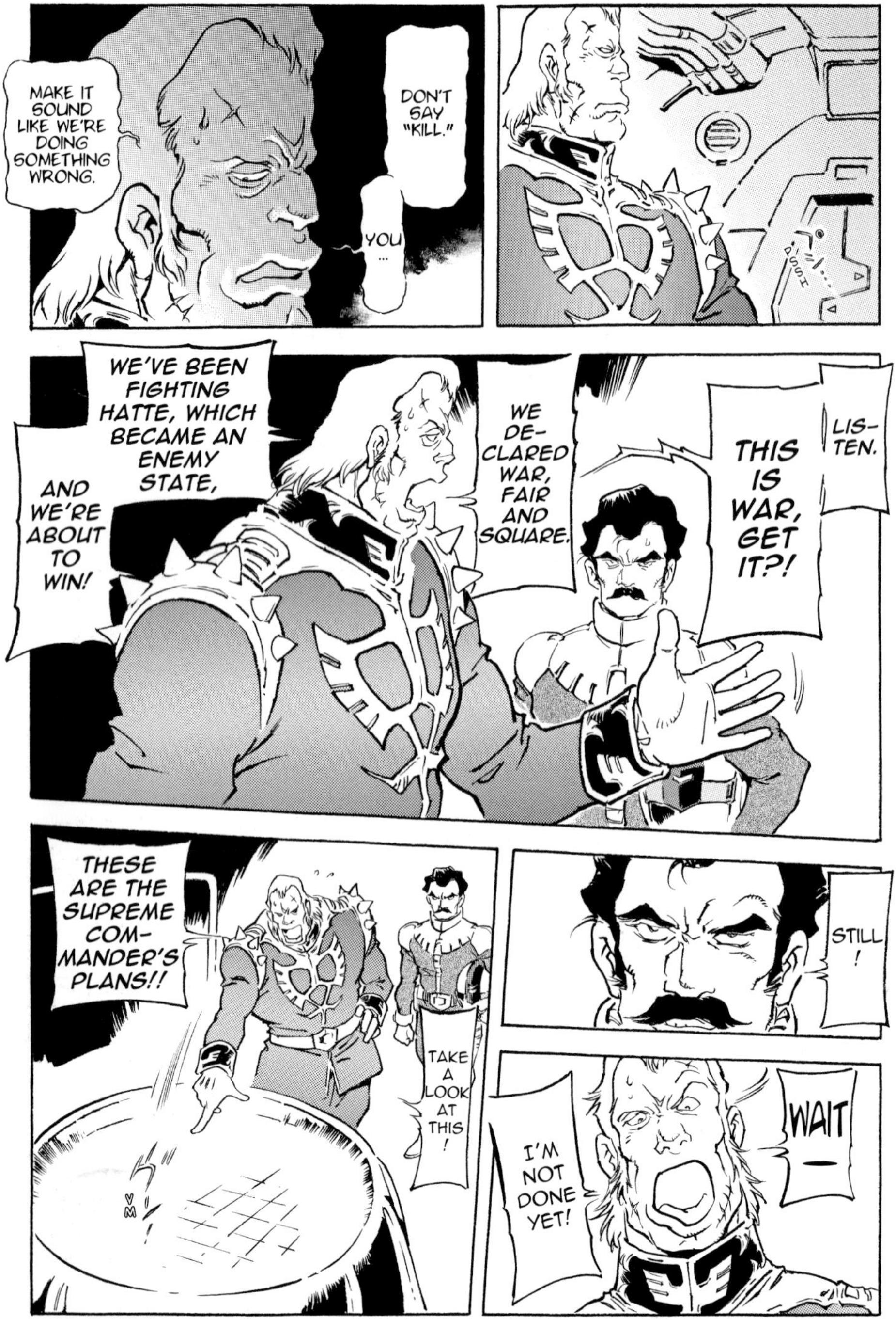
DON'T SAY "KILL."
YOU ...
MAKE IT SOUND LIKE WE'RE DOING SOMETHING WRONG.
LIS-TEN.
THIS IS WAR, GET IT?!
WE DE-CLARED WAR, FAIR AND SQUARE.
WE'VE BEEN FIGHTING HATTE, WHICH BECAME AN ENEMY STATE,
AND WE'RE ABOUT TO WIN!
STILL !
WAIT —
I'M NOT DONE YET!
THESE ARE THE SUPREME COM-MANDER'S PLANS!!
TAKE A LOOK AT THIS !

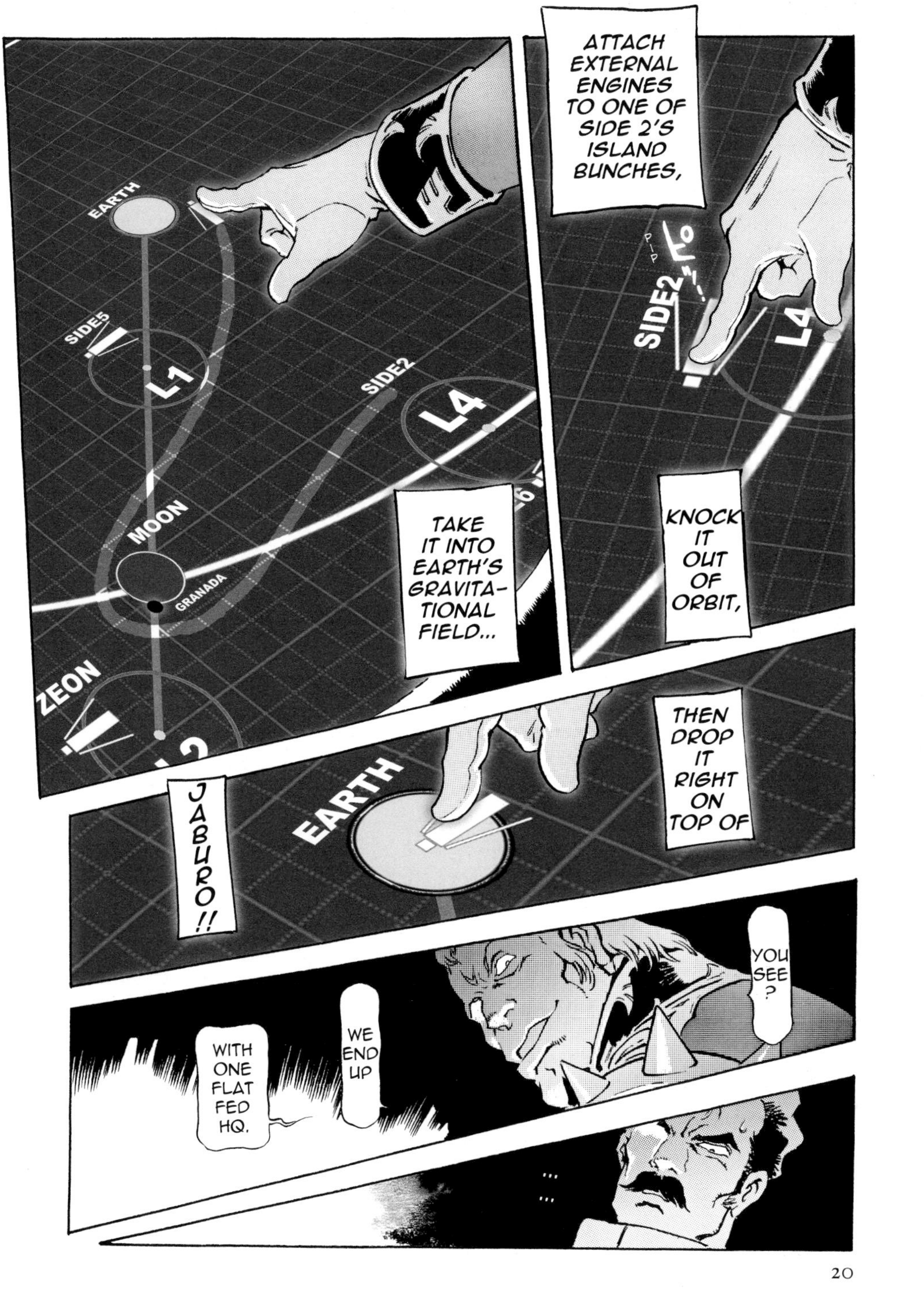

ATTACH EXTERNAL ENGINES TO ONE OF SIDE 2'S ISLAND BUNCHES,
PIP
SIDE2
L4
KNOCK IT OUT OF ORBIT,
EARTH
SIDE5
L1
SIDE2
L4
MOON
GRANADA
ZEON
TAKE IT INTO EARTH'S GRAVITA-TIONAL FIELD...
THEN DROP IT RIGHT ON TOP OF
EARTH
JABURO!!
YOU SEE?
WE END UP
WITH ONE FLAT FED HQ.
...
...

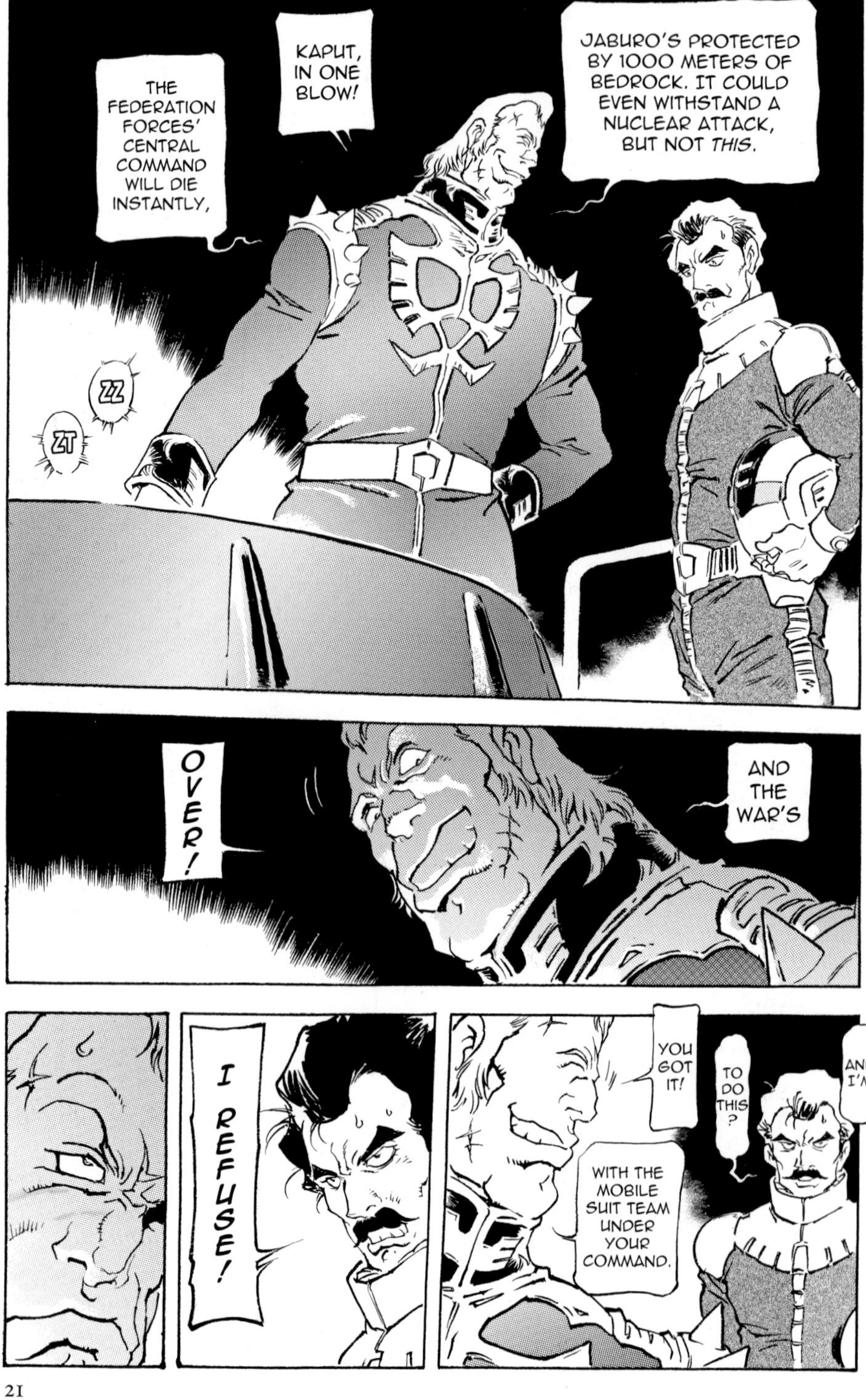
JABURO'S PROTECTED BY 1000 METERS OF BEDROCK. IT COULD EVEN WITHSTAND A NUCLEAR ATTACK, BUT NOT *THIS*.
KAPUT, IN ONE BLOW!
THE FEDERATION FORCES' CENTRAL COMMAND WILL DIE INSTANTLY,
ZZ
ZT
AND THE WAR'S
OVER!
AND I'M
TO DO THIS?
YOU GOT IT!
WITH THE MOBILE SUIT TEAM UNDER YOUR COMMAND.
I REFUSE!

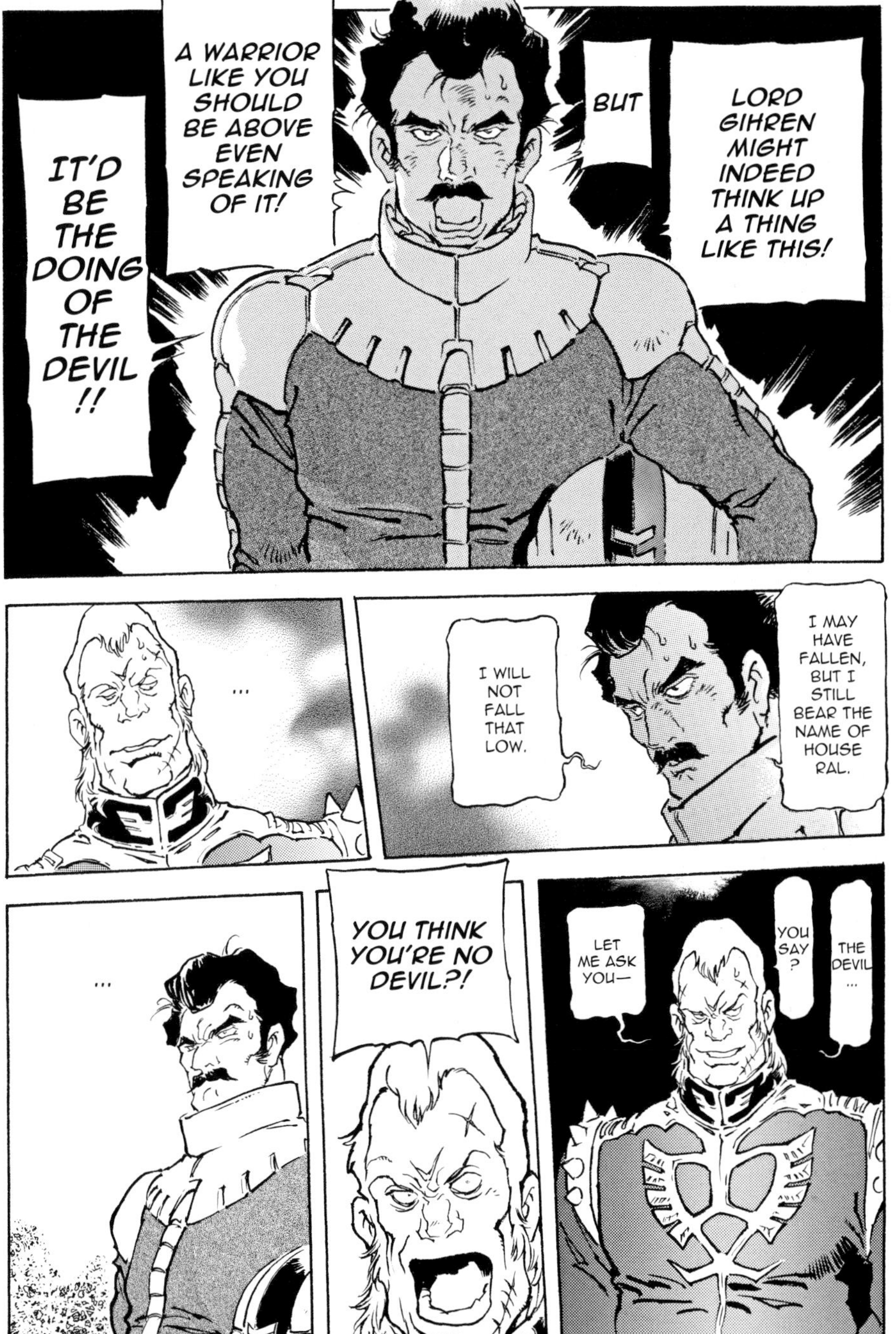
LORD GIHREN MIGHT INDEED THINK UP A THING LIKE THIS!
BUT
A WARRIOR LIKE YOU SHOULD BE ABOVE EVEN SPEAKING OF IT!
IT'D BE THE DOING OF THE DEVIL!!
I MAY HAVE FALLEN, BUT I STILL BEAR THE NAME OF HOUSE RAL.
I WILL NOT FALL THAT LOW.
...
THE DEVIL...
YOU SAY?
LET ME ASK YOU—
YOU THINK YOU'RE NO DEVIL?!
...

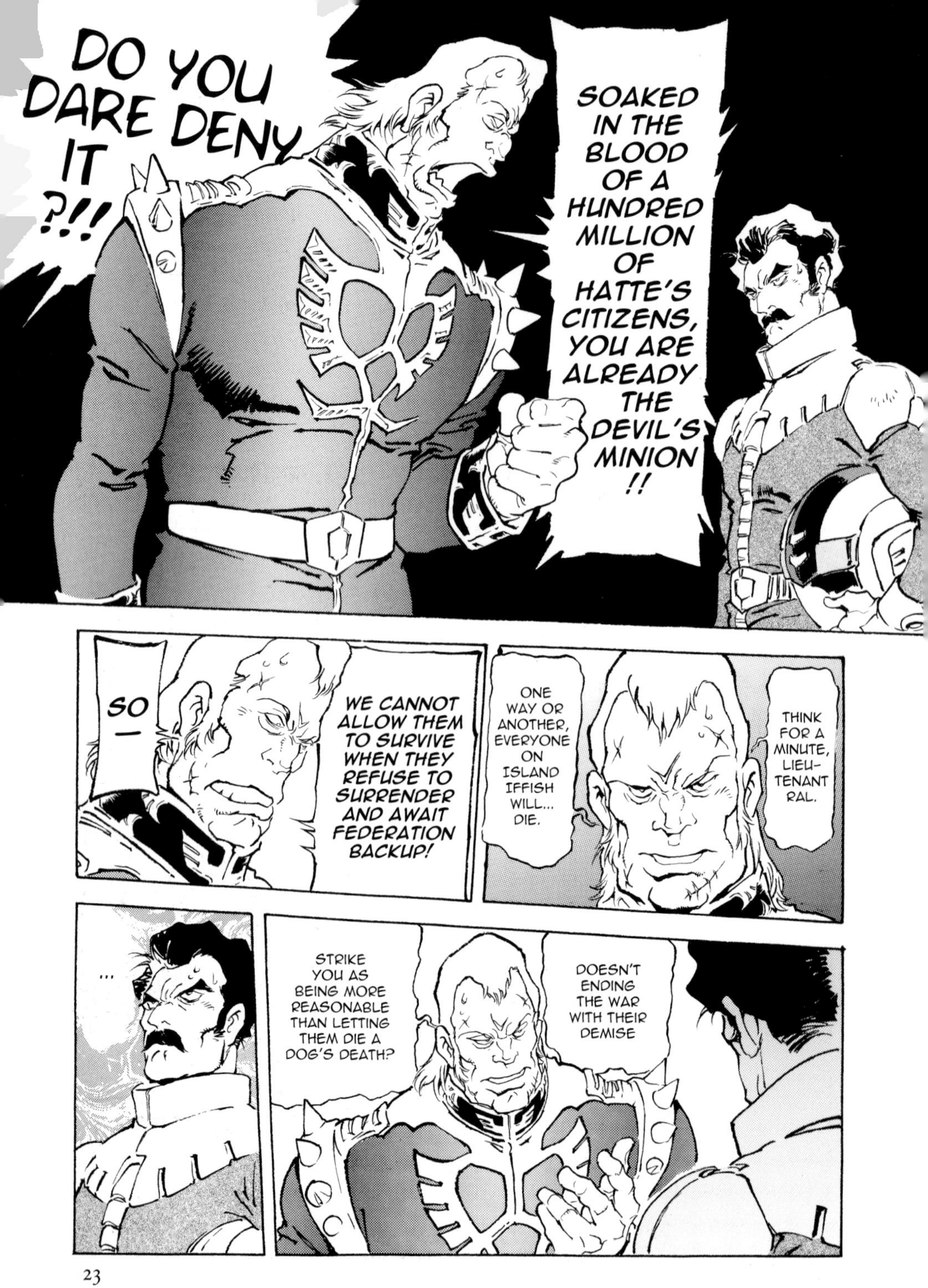
SOAKED IN THE BLOOD OF A HUNDRED MILLION OF HATTE'S CITIZENS, YOU ARE ALREADY THE DEVIL'S MINION !!
DO YOU DARE DENY IT ?!!
THINK FOR A MINUTE, LIEU-TENANT RAL.
ONE WAY OR ANOTHER, EVERYONE ON ISLAND IFFISH WILL... DIE.
WE CANNOT ALLOW THEM TO SURVIVE WHEN THEY REFUSE TO SURRENDER AND AWAIT FEDERATION BACKUP!
SO —
DOESN'T ENDING THE WAR WITH THEIR DEMISE
STRIKE YOU AS BEING MORE REASONABLE THAN LETTING THEM DIE A DOG'S DEATH?
...

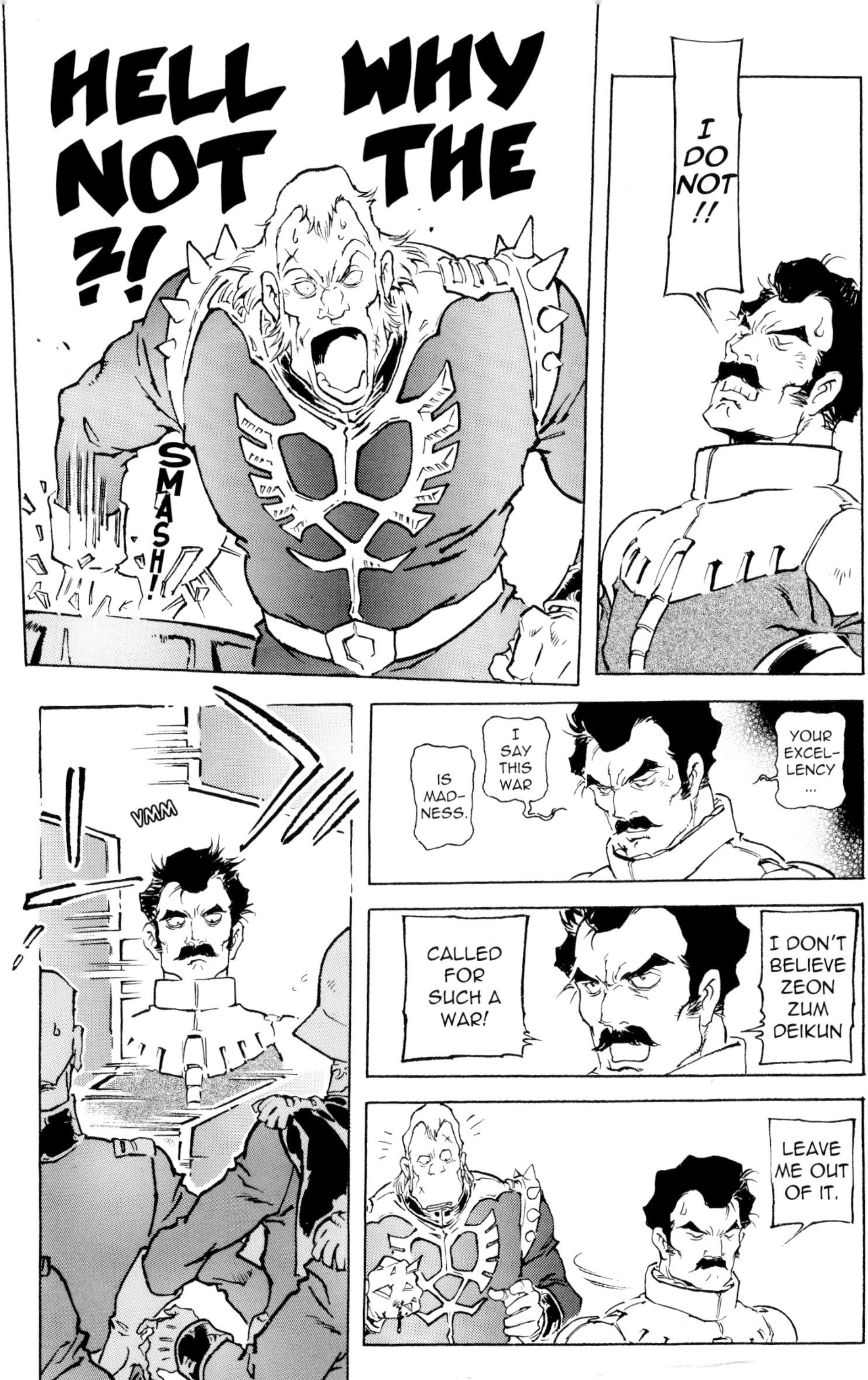
I DO NOT!!
WHY THE HELL NOT?!
SMASH!
YOUR EXCEL-LENCY...
I SAY THIS WAR
IS MAD-NESS.
I DON'T BELIEVE ZEON ZUM DEIKUN
CALLED FOR SUCH A WAR!
LEAVE ME OUT OF IT.
VMM

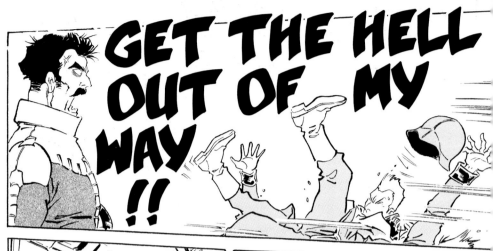

GET THE HELL OUT OF MY WAY !!

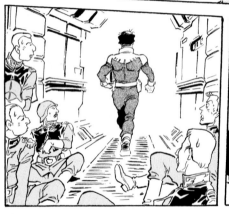

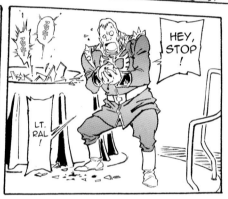

HEY, STOP!

LT. RAL!

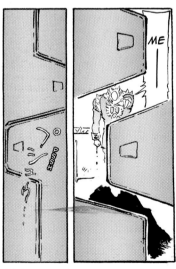

ME

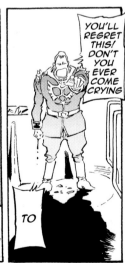

YOU'LL REGRET THIS! DON'T YOU EVER COME CRYING

TO

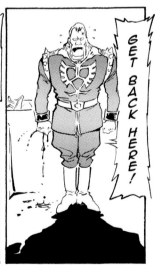

GET BACK HERE!

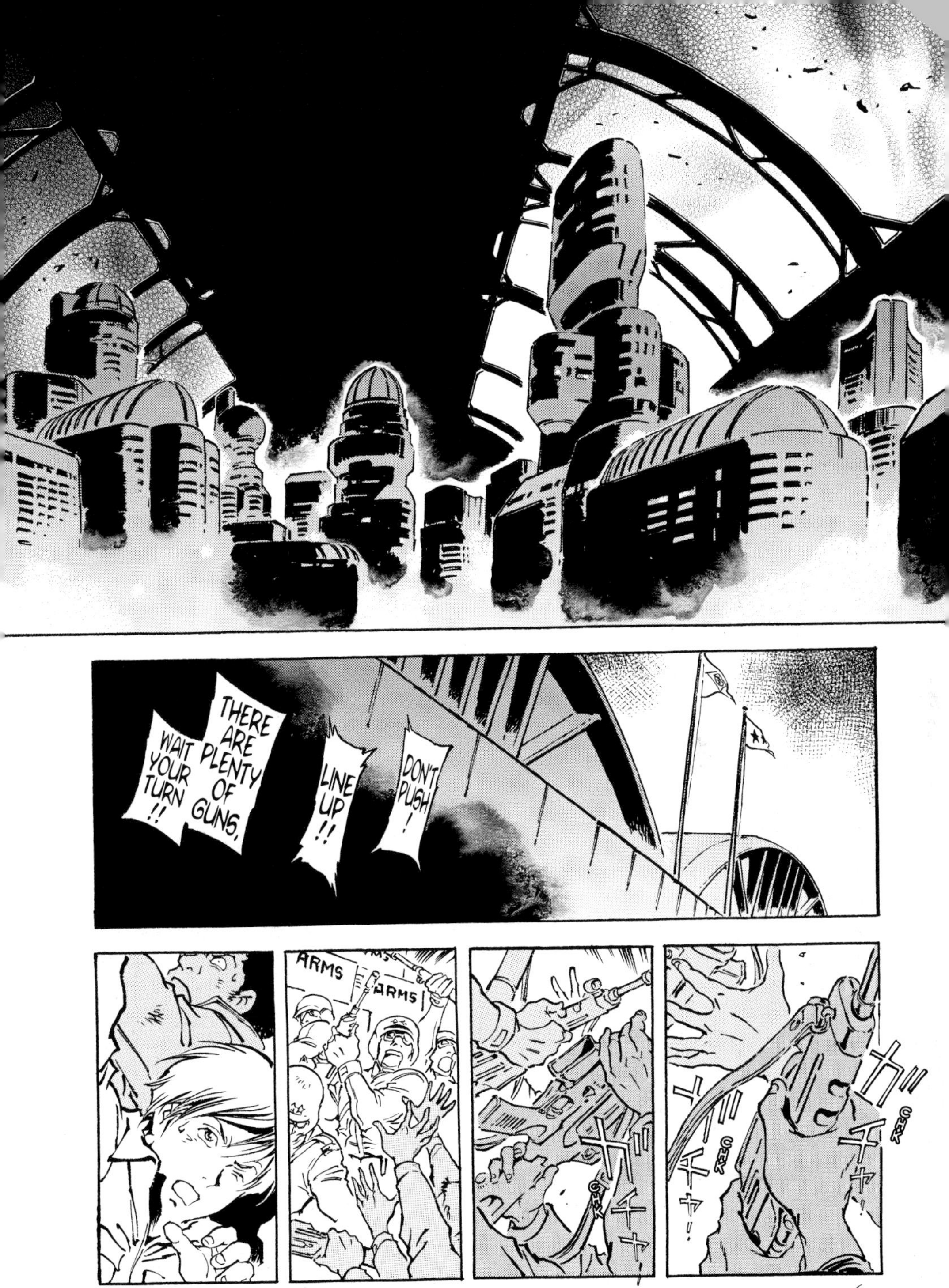
DON'T PUSH!
LINE UP!!
THERE ARE PLENTY OF GUNS. WAIT YOUR TURN!!
CHK
CHK
CHK
ARMS
ARMS

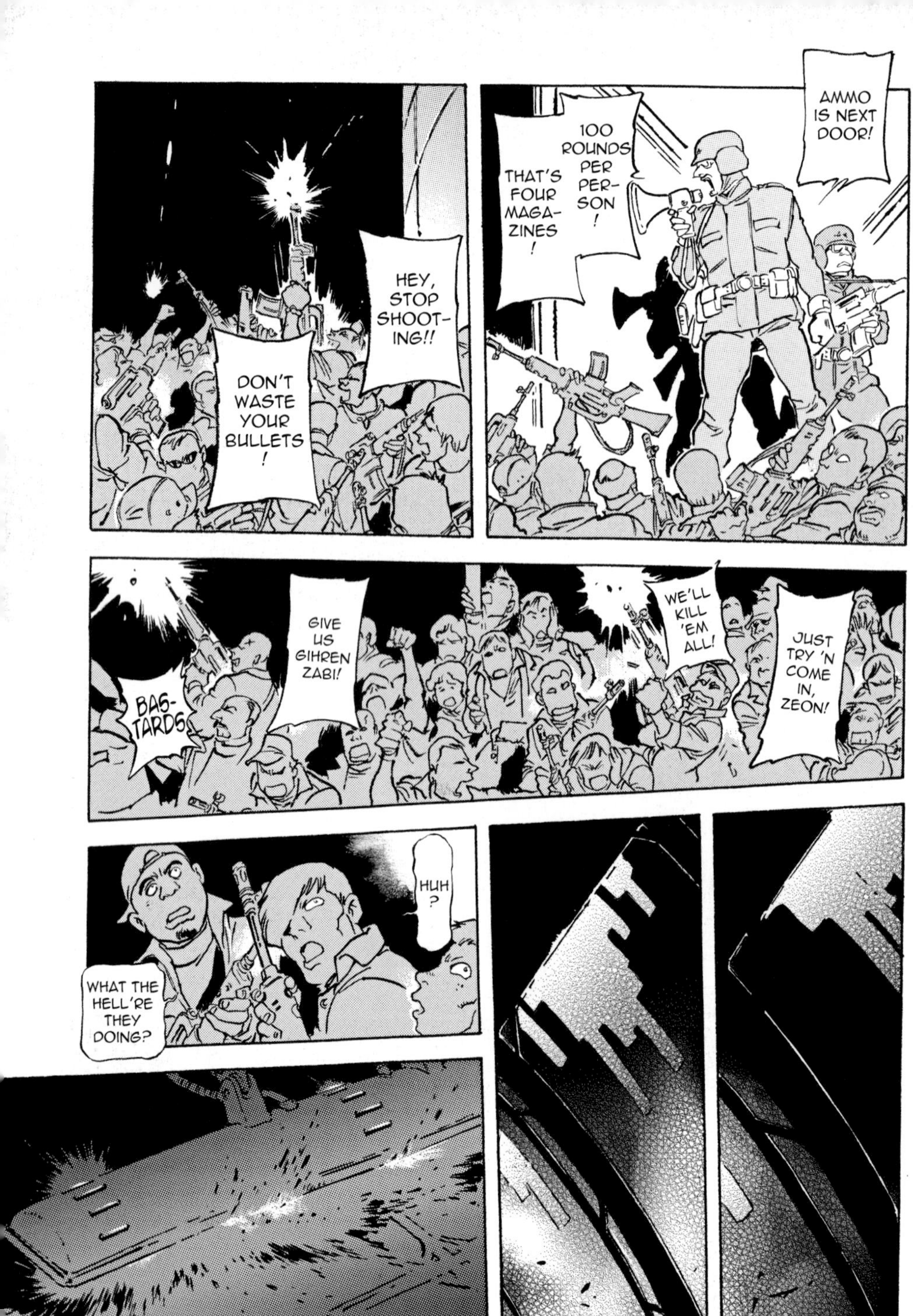
AMMO IS NEXT DOOR!
100 ROUNDS PER PERSON!
THAT'S FOUR MAGAZINES!
HEY, STOP SHOOTING!!
DON'T WASTE YOUR BULLETS!
JUST TRY 'N COME IN, ZEON!
WE'LL KILL 'EM ALL!
GIVE US GIHREN ZABI!
BASTARDS
HUH?
WHAT THE HELL'RE THEY DOING?

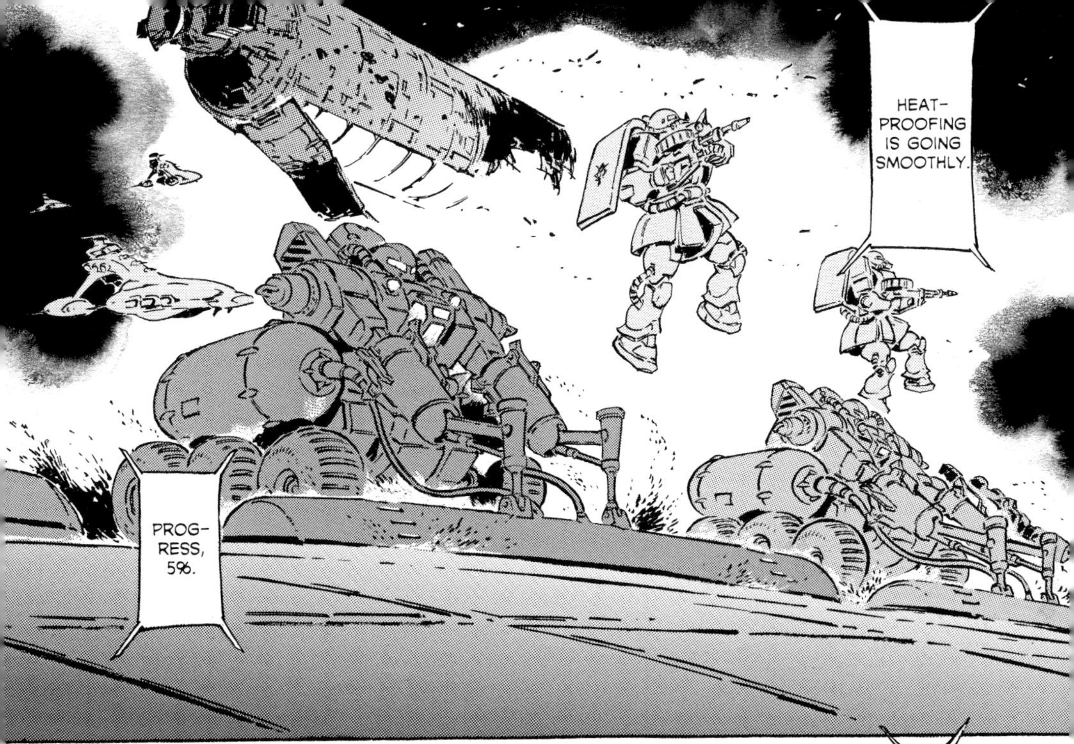
HEAT-PROOFING IS GOING SMOOTHLY.
PROG-RESS, 5%.

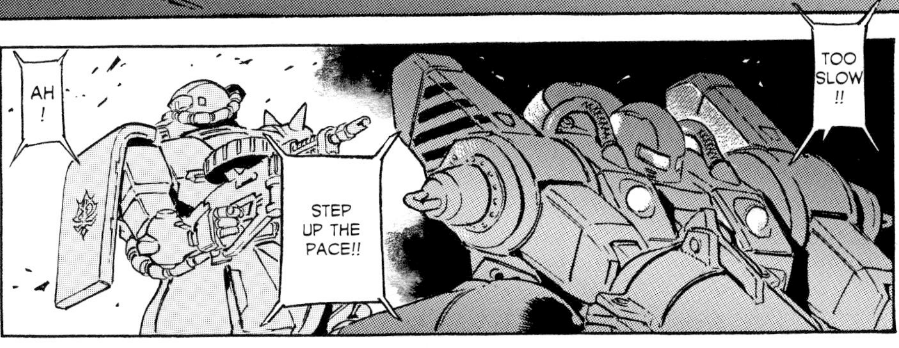
TOO SLOW!!
STEP UP THE PACE!!
AH!

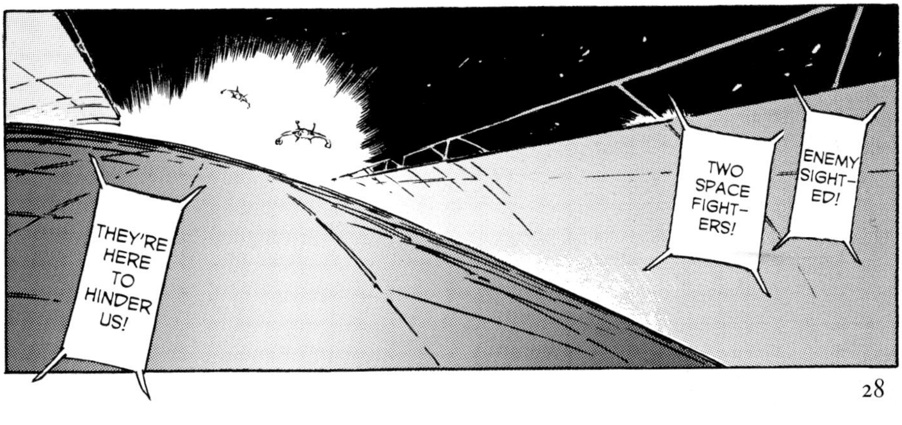
ENEMY SIGHT-ED!
TWO SPACE FIGHT-ERS!
THEY'RE HERE TO HINDER US!

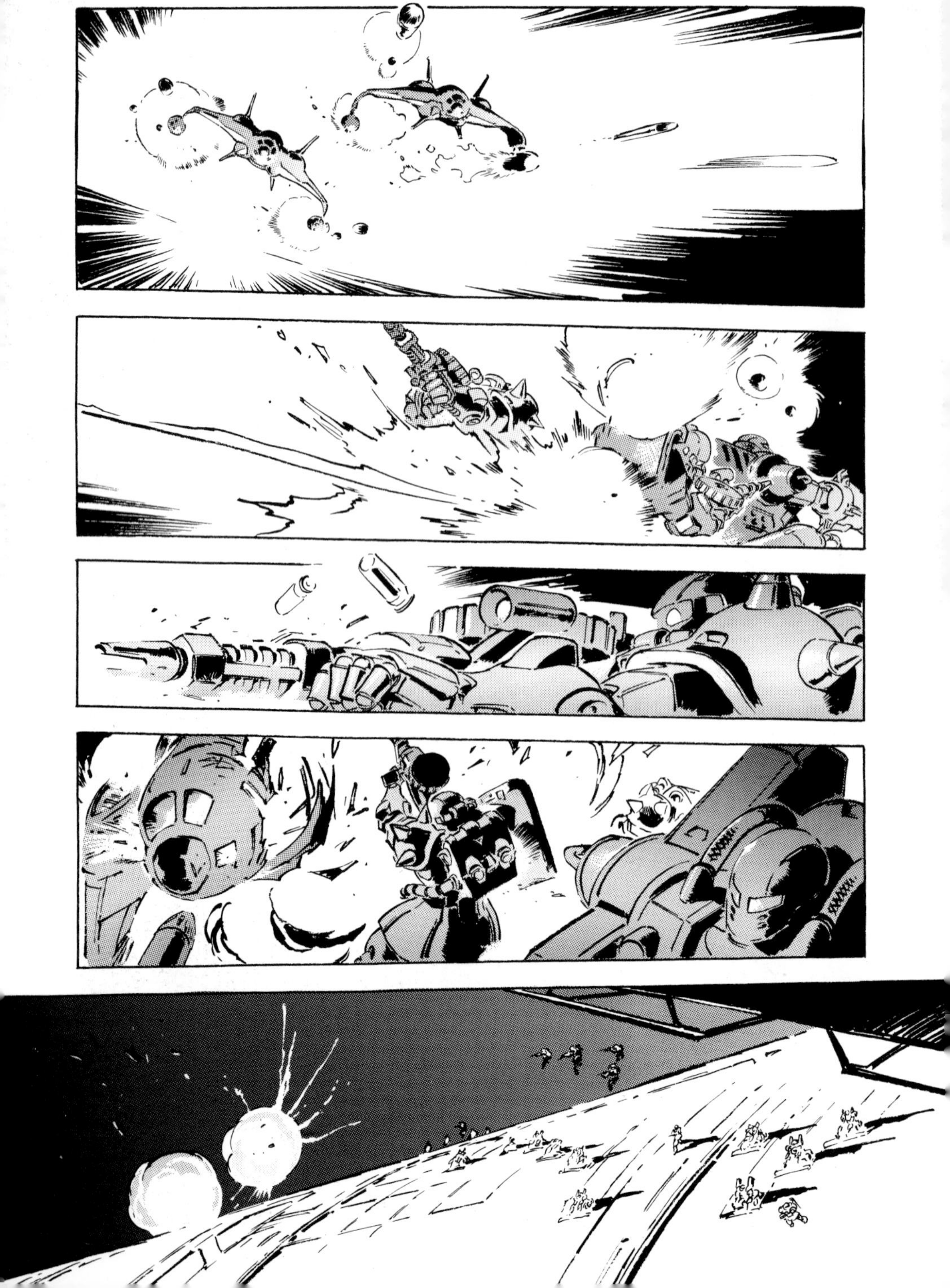

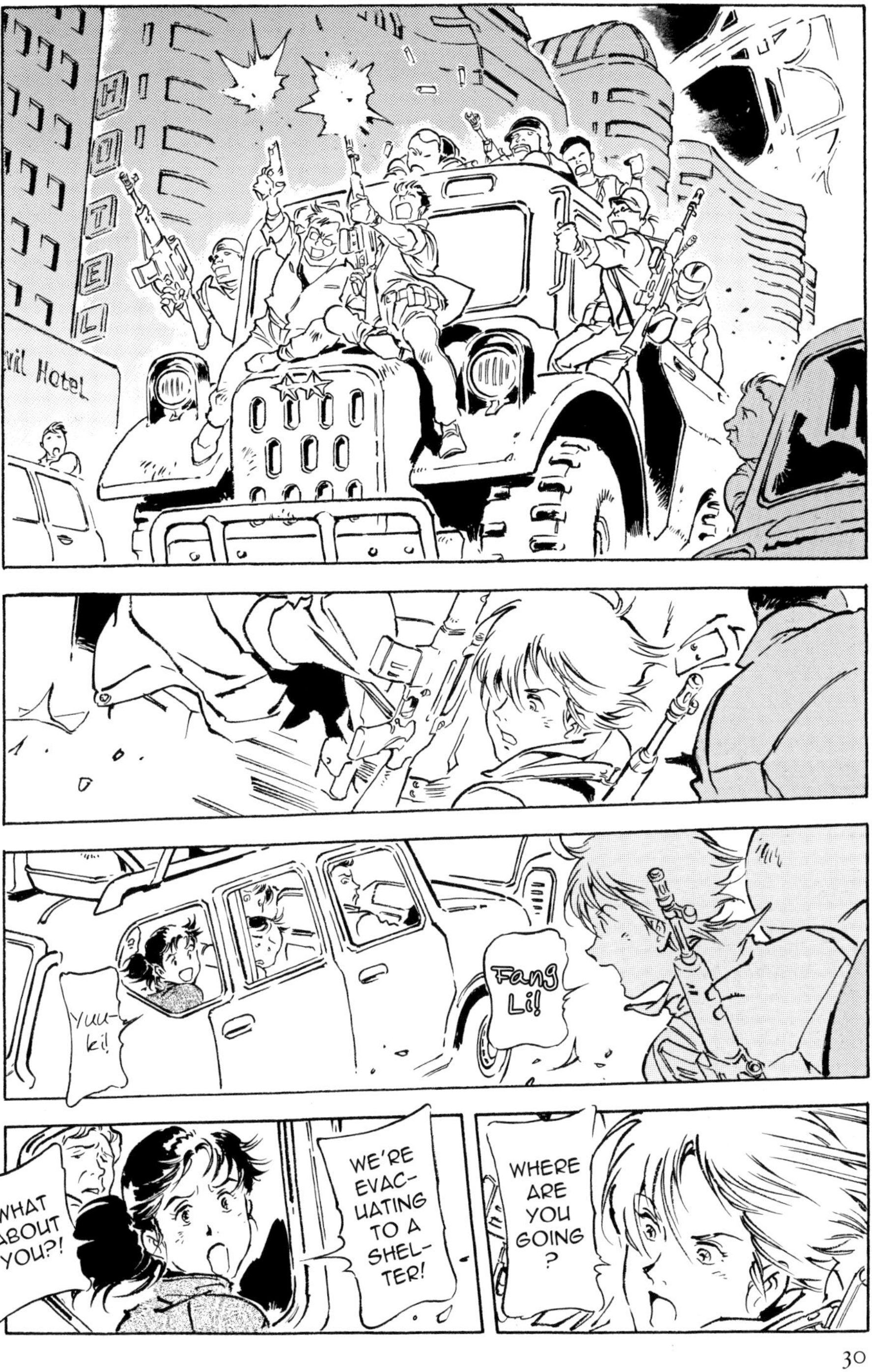
HOTEL
vil HoteL
Fang Li!
Yuu-ki!
WHERE ARE YOU GOING?
WE'RE EVAC-UATING TO A SHEL-TER!
WHAT ABOUT YOU?!

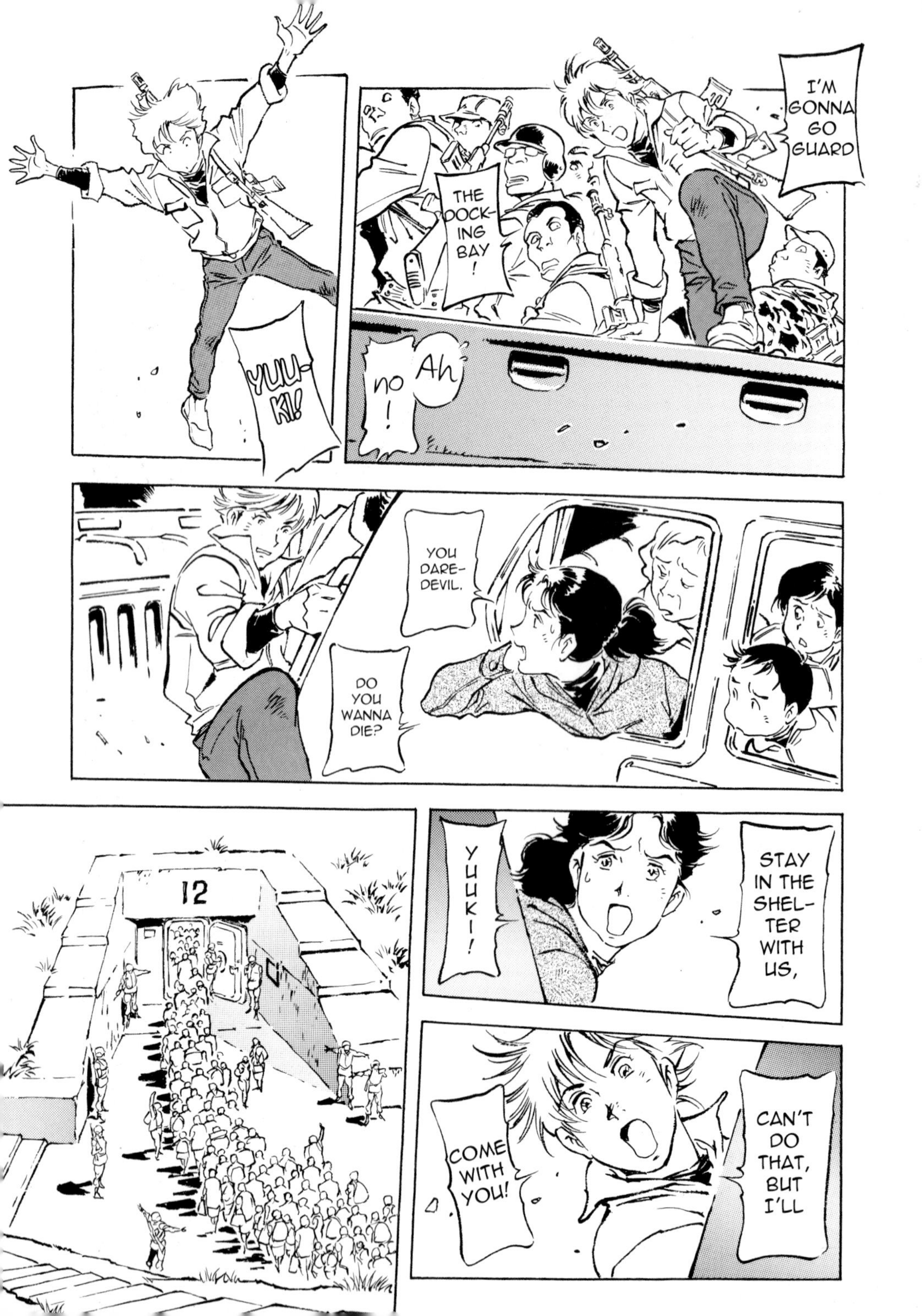
I'M GONNA GO GUARD
THE DOCK-ING BAY!
Ah
no!
YUU-KI!
YOU DARE-DEVIL.
DO YOU WANNA DIE?
STAY IN THE SHEL-TER WITH US,
YUUKI!
CAN'T DO THAT, BUT I'LL
COME WITH YOU!
12

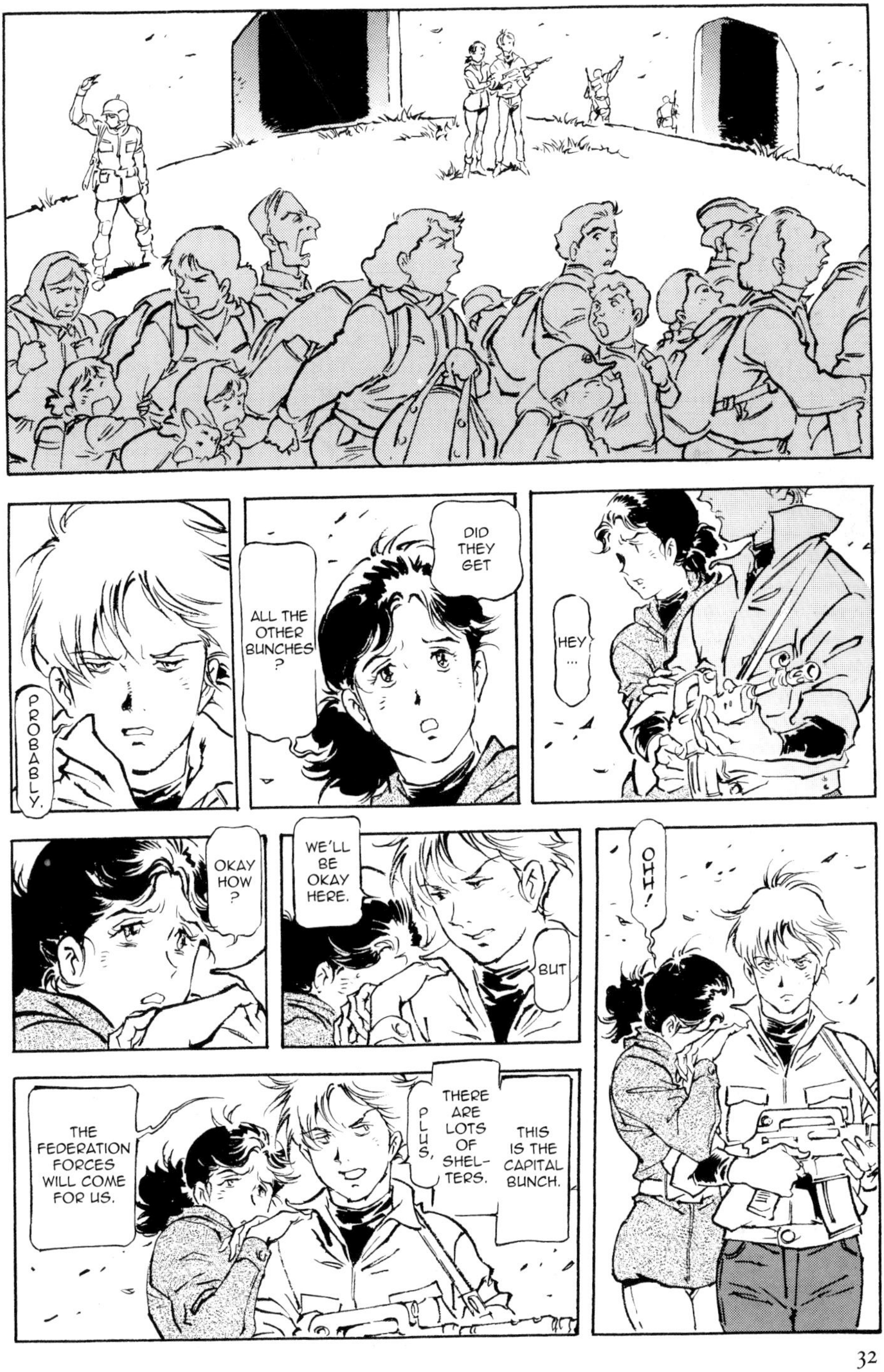
HEY ...
DID THEY GET
ALL THE OTHER BUNCHES ?
PROBABLY.
OHH!
WE'LL BE OKAY HERE.
BUT
OKAY HOW ?
THIS IS THE CAPITAL BUNCH.
PLUS,
THERE ARE LOTS OF SHEL- TERS.
THE FEDERATION FORCES WILL COME FOR US.

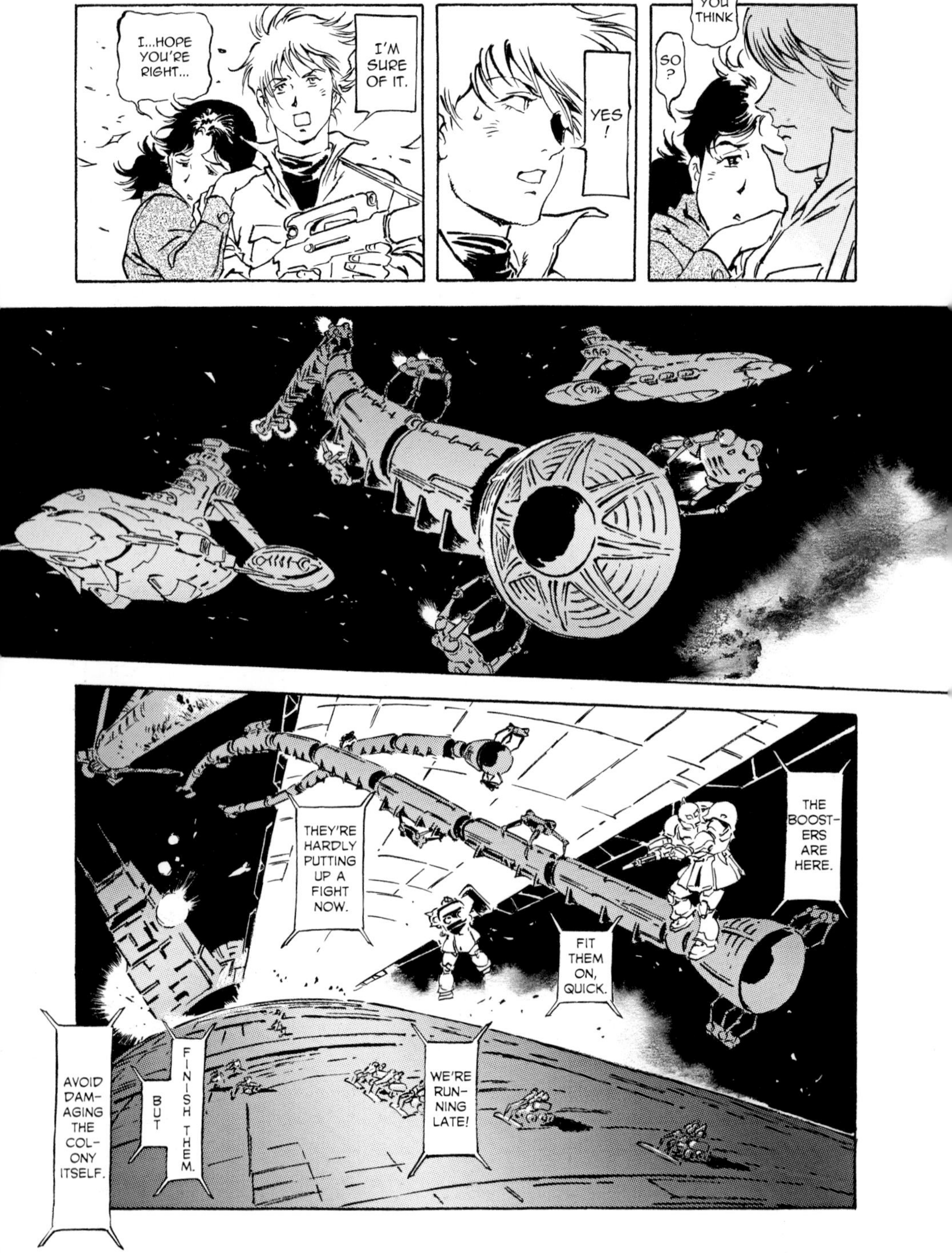
YOU THINK SO?
YES!
I'M SURE OF IT.
I...HOPE YOU'RE RIGHT...
THE BOOSTERS ARE HERE.
THEY'RE HARDLY PUTTING UP A FIGHT NOW.
FIT THEM ON, QUICK.
WE'RE RUNNING LATE!
FINISH THEM.
BUT
AVOID DAMAGING THE COLONY ITSELF.

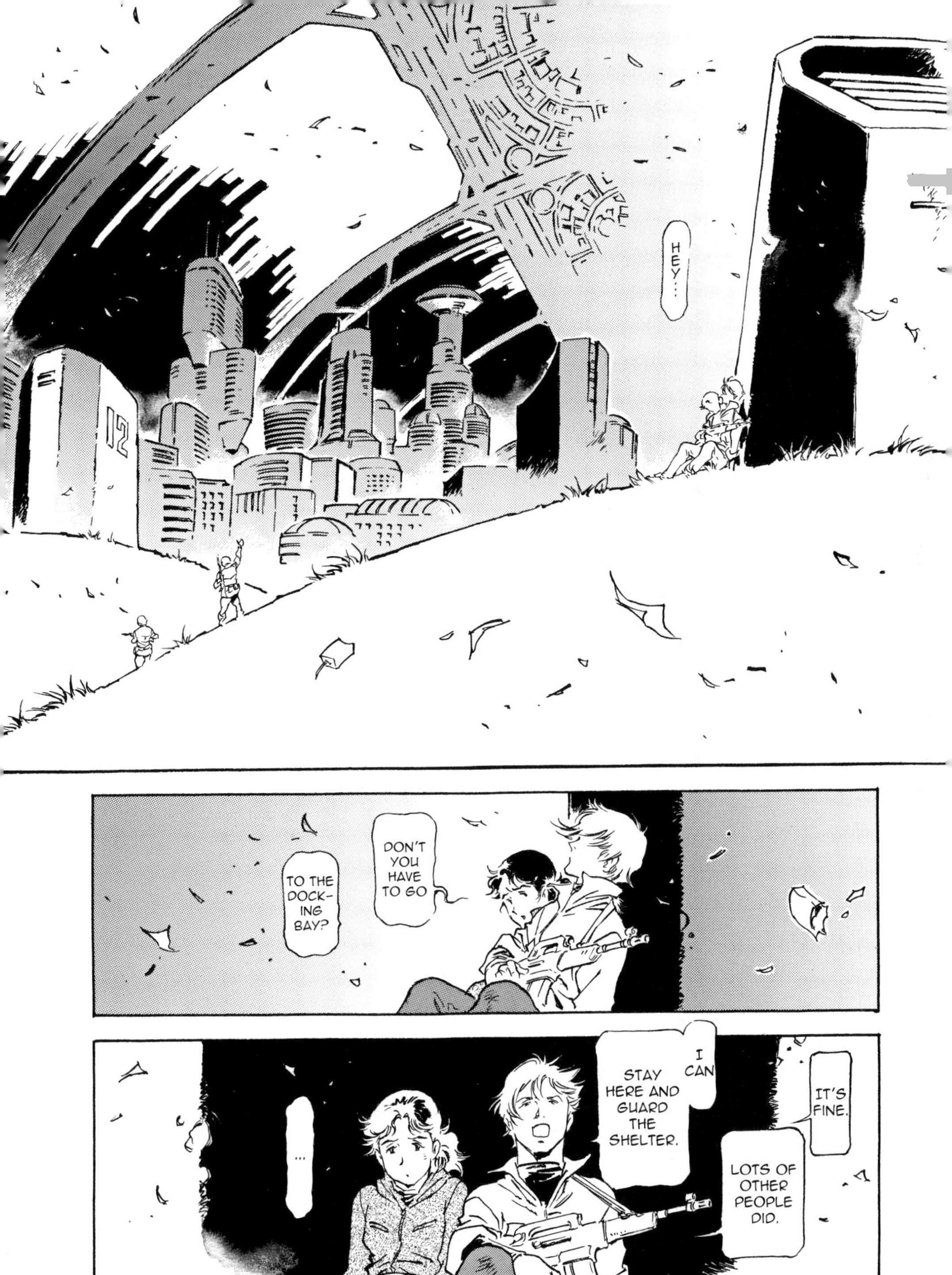
HEY…
DON'T YOU HAVE TO GO
TO THE DOCK-ING BAY?
IT'S FINE.
I CAN STAY HERE AND GUARD THE SHELTER.
LOTS OF OTHER PEOPLE DID.
…

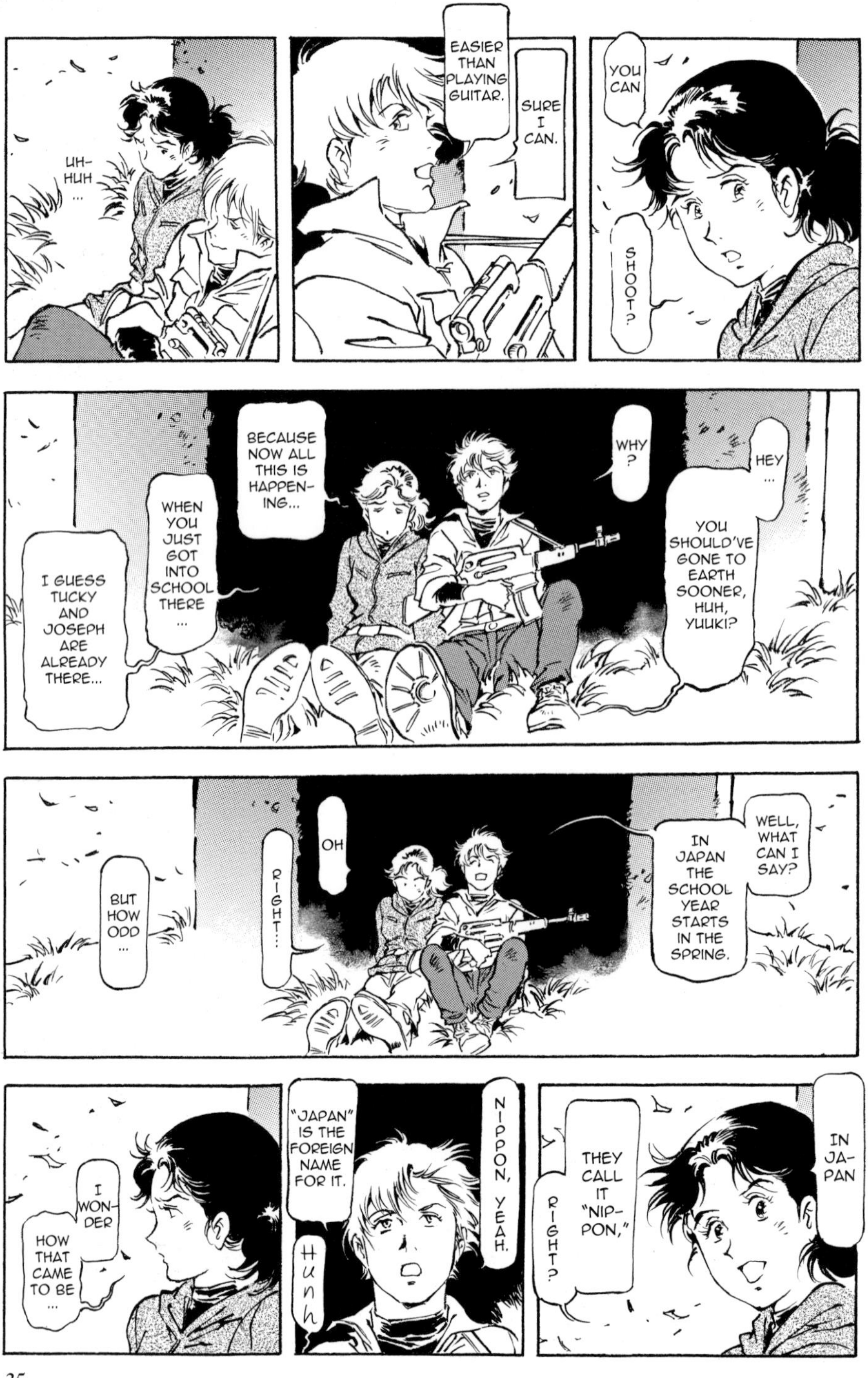

YOU CAN
SHOOT?
SURE I CAN.
EASIER THAN PLAYING GUITAR.
UH-HUH ...
HEY ...
YOU SHOULD'VE GONE TO EARTH SOONER, HUH, YUUKI?
WHY?
BECAUSE NOW ALL THIS IS HAPPEN-ING...
WHEN YOU JUST GOT INTO SCHOOL THERE ...
I GUESS TUCKY AND JOSEPH ARE ALREADY THERE...
WELL, WHAT CAN I SAY?
IN JAPAN THE SCHOOL YEAR STARTS IN THE SPRING.
OH
RIGHT...
BUT HOW ODD ...
IN JA-PAN
THEY CALL IT "NIP-PON,"
RIGHT?
NIPPON, YEAH.
"JAPAN" IS THE FOREIGN NAME FOR IT.
Hunh
I WON-DER
HOW THAT CAME TO BE ...

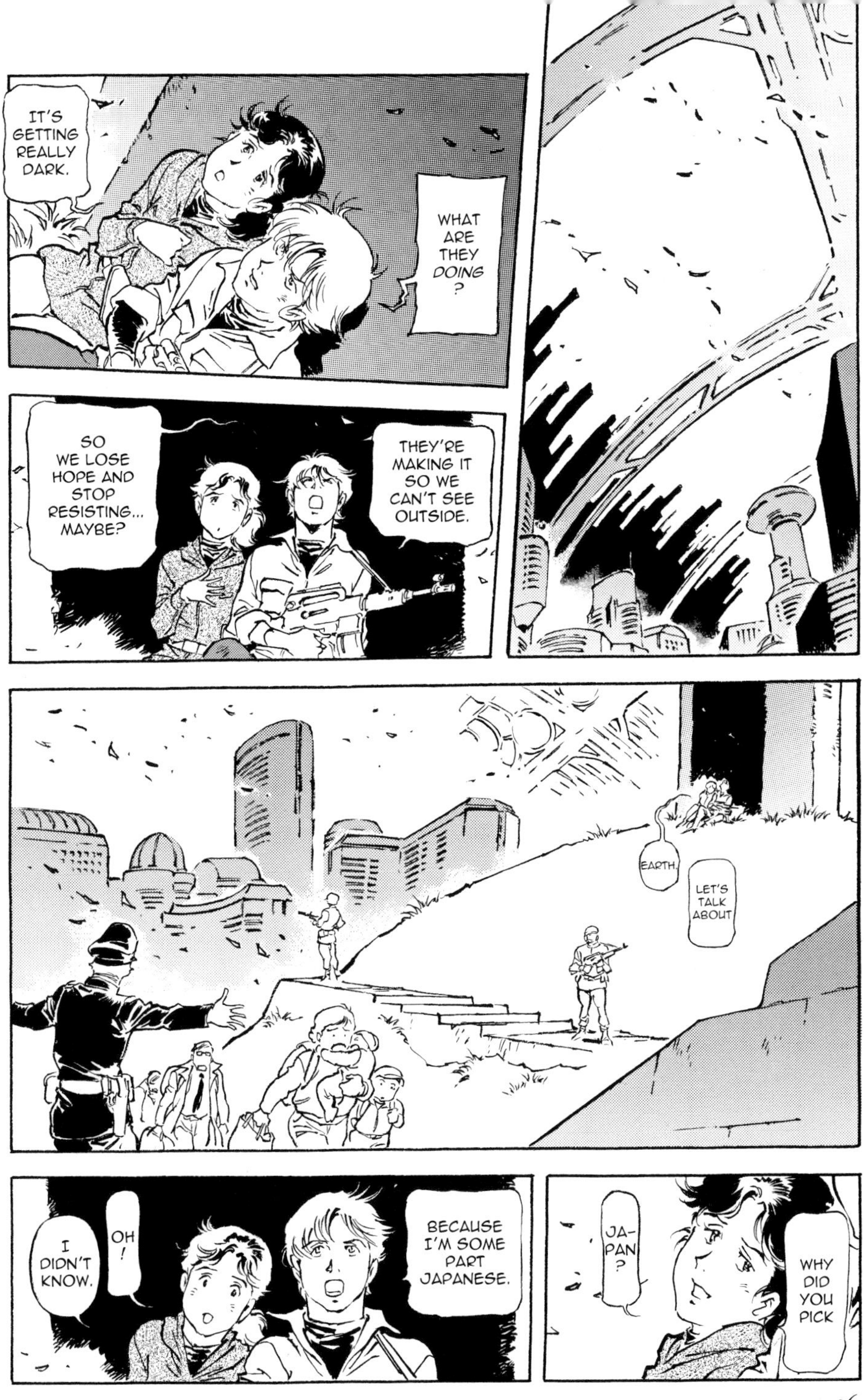
IT'S GETTING REALLY DARK.
WHAT ARE THEY DOING?
THEY'RE MAKING IT SO WE CAN'T SEE OUTSIDE.
SO WE LOSE HOPE AND STOP RESISTING... MAYBE?
LET'S TALK ABOUT
EARTH.
WHY DID YOU PICK
JA-PAN?
BECAUSE I'M SOME PART JAPANESE.
OH!
I DIDN'T KNOW.

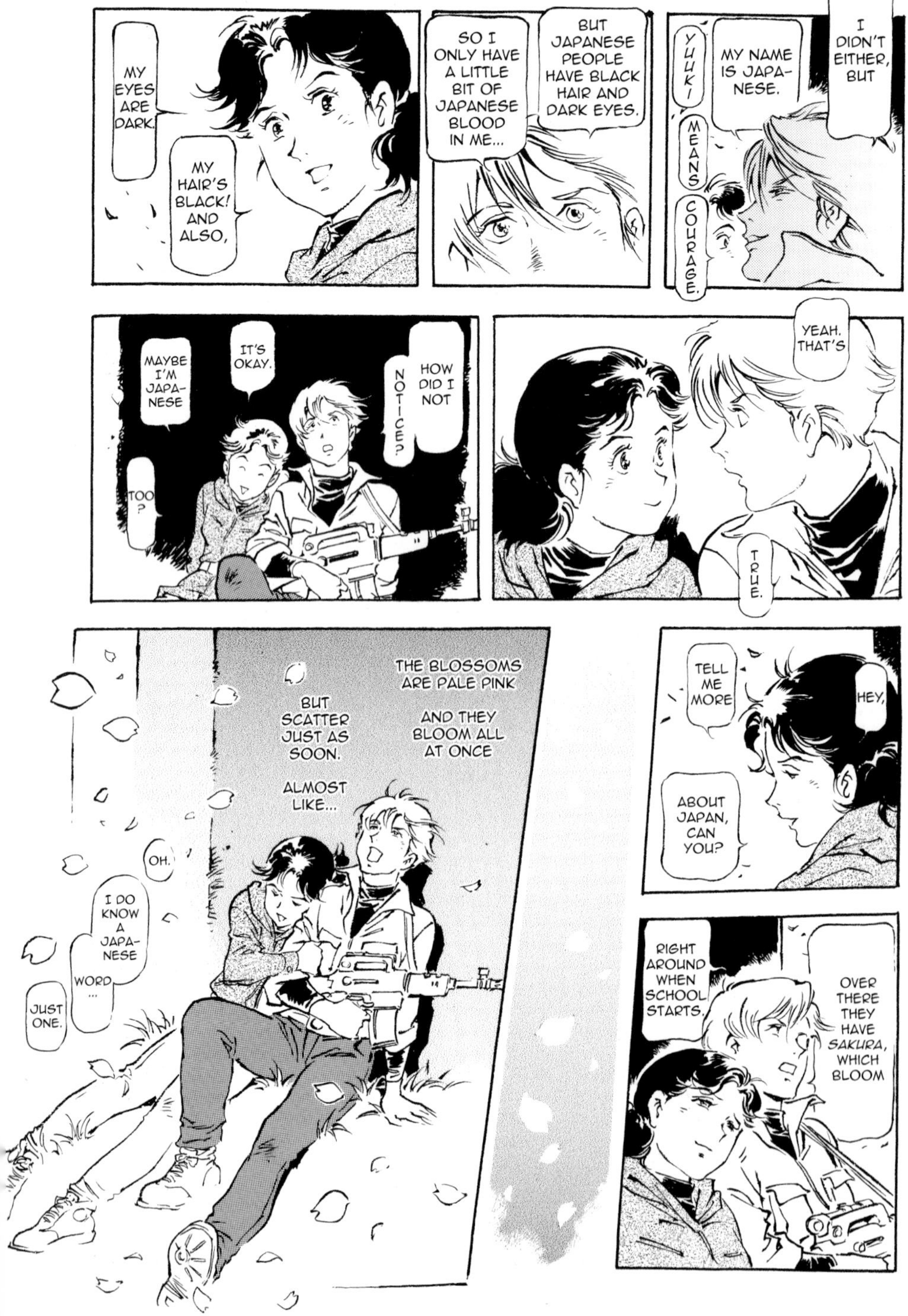
I DIDN'T EITHER, BUT
MY NAME IS JAPANESE.
YUUKI MEANS COURAGE.
BUT JAPANESE PEOPLE HAVE BLACK HAIR AND DARK EYES.
SO I ONLY HAVE A LITTLE BIT OF JAPANESE BLOOD IN ME...
MY HAIR'S BLACK! AND ALSO,
MY EYES ARE DARK.
YEAH. THAT'S
TRUE.
HOW DID I NOT NOTICE?
IT'S OKAY.
MAYBE I'M JAPANESE
TOO?
HEY,
TELL ME MORE
ABOUT JAPAN, CAN YOU?
OVER THERE THEY HAVE SAKURA, WHICH BLOOM
RIGHT AROUND WHEN SCHOOL STARTS.
THE BLOSSOMS ARE PALE PINK
AND THEY BLOOM ALL AT ONCE
BUT SCATTER JUST AS SOON.
ALMOST LIKE...
OH.
I DO KNOW A JAPANESE
WORD...
JUST ONE.

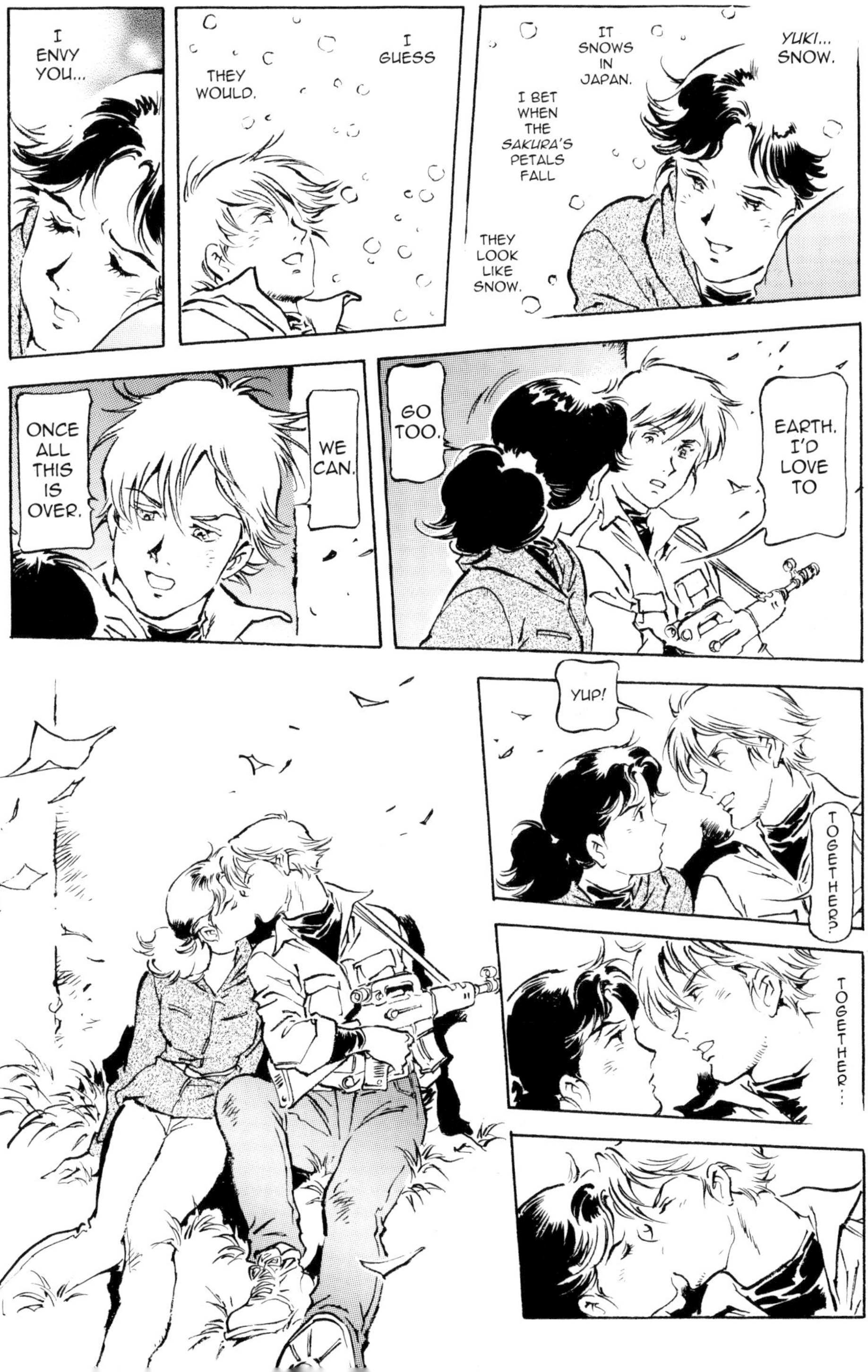
YUKI... SNOW.
IT SNOWS IN JAPAN.
I BET WHEN THE SAKURA'S PETALS FALL
THEY LOOK LIKE SNOW.
I GUESS
THEY WOULD.
I ENVY YOU...
EARTH. I'D LOVE TO
GO TOO.
WE CAN.
ONCE ALL THIS IS OVER.
YUP!
TOGETHER?
TOGETHER...

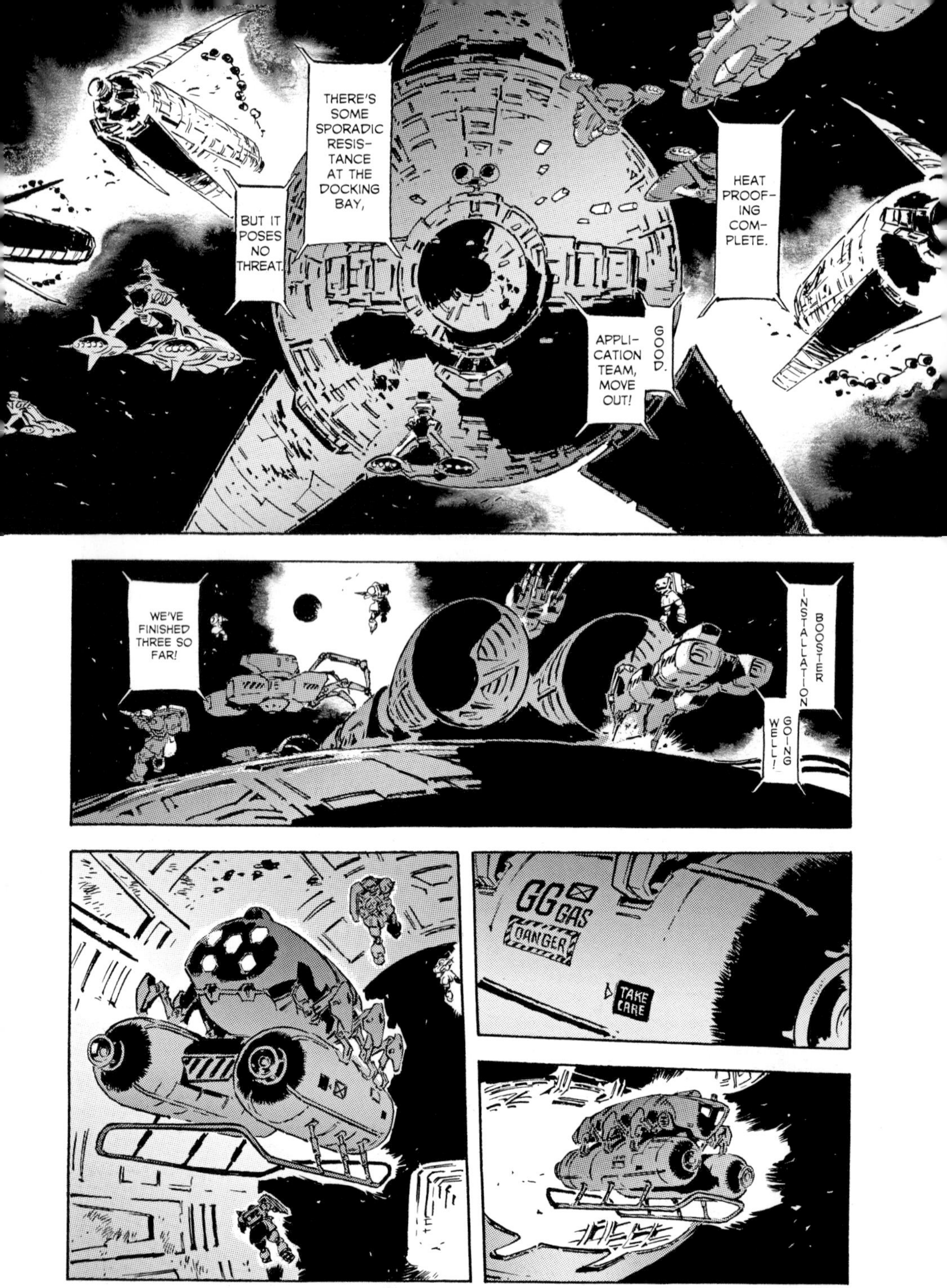
HEAT PROOF-ING COM-PLETE.
THERE'S SOME SPORADIC RESIS-TANCE AT THE DOCKING BAY,
BUT IT POSES NO THREAT.
GOOD.
APPLI-CATION TEAM, MOVE OUT!
BOOSTER INSTALLATION GOING WELL!
WE'VE FINISHED THREE SO FAR!
GG GAS
DANGER
TAKE CARE

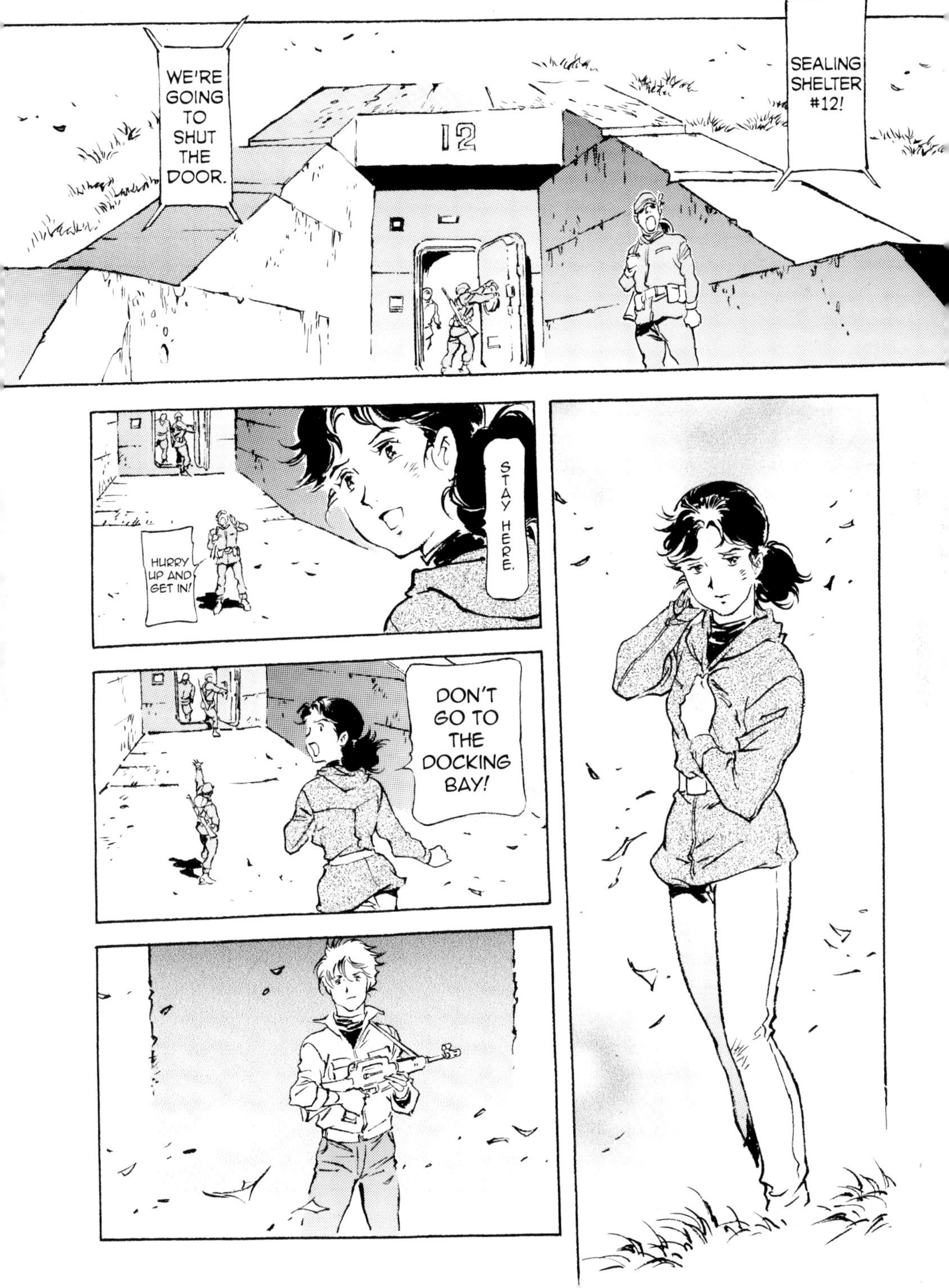

SEALING SHELTER #12!
WE'RE GOING TO SHUT THE DOOR.
12
STAY HERE.
HURRY UP AND GET IN!
DON'T GO TO THE DOCKING BAY!

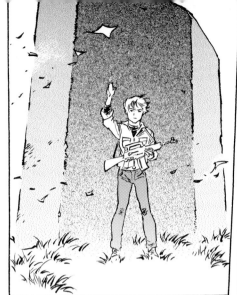

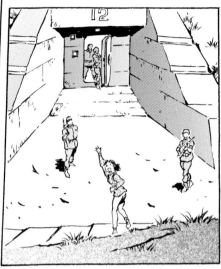

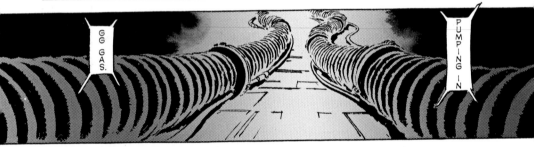

GG GAS.

PUMPING IN

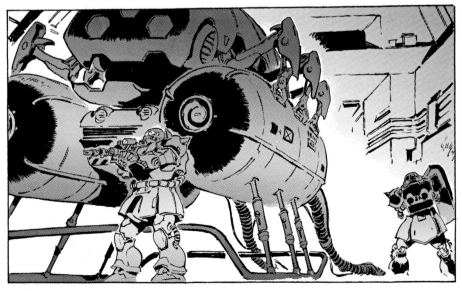

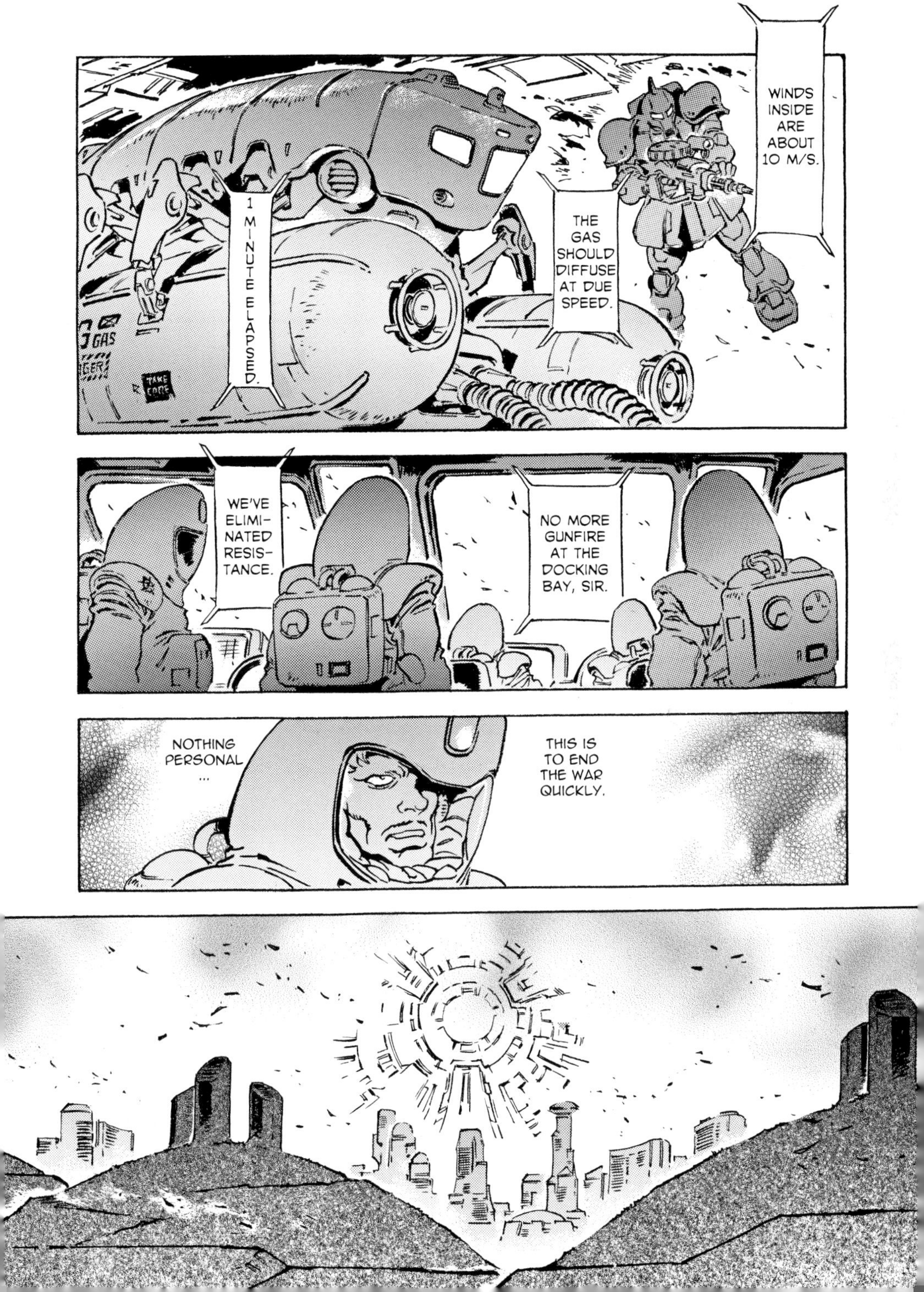
WINDS INSIDE ARE ABOUT 10 M/S.
THE GAS SHOULD DIFFUSE AT DUE SPEED.
1 MINUTE ELAPSED.
NO MORE GUNFIRE AT THE DOCKING BAY, SIR.
WE'VE ELIMI-NATED RESIS-TANCE.
THIS IS TO END THE WAR QUICKLY.
NOTHING PERSONAL ...

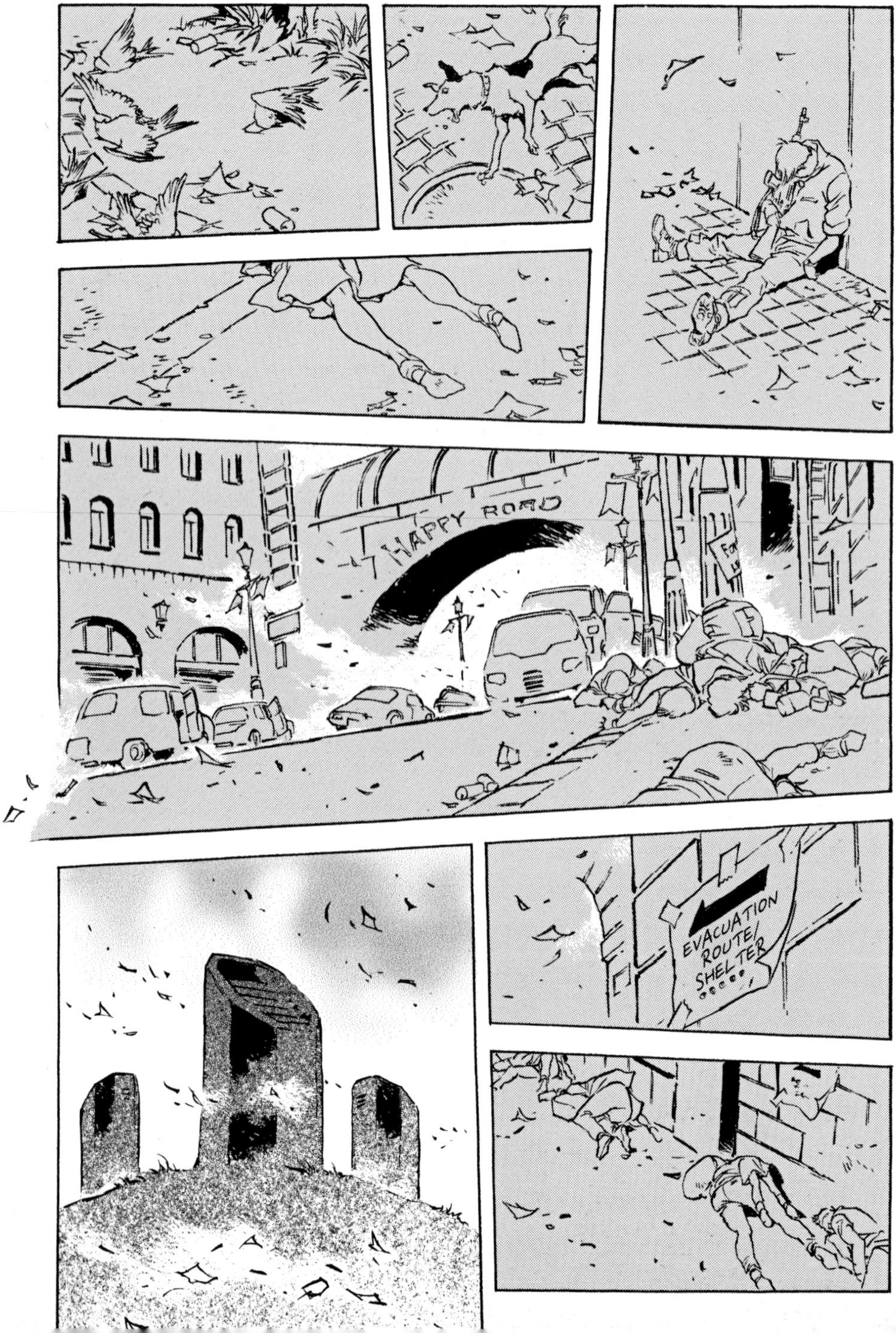
HAPPY ROAD
EVACUATION ROUTE/ SHELTER

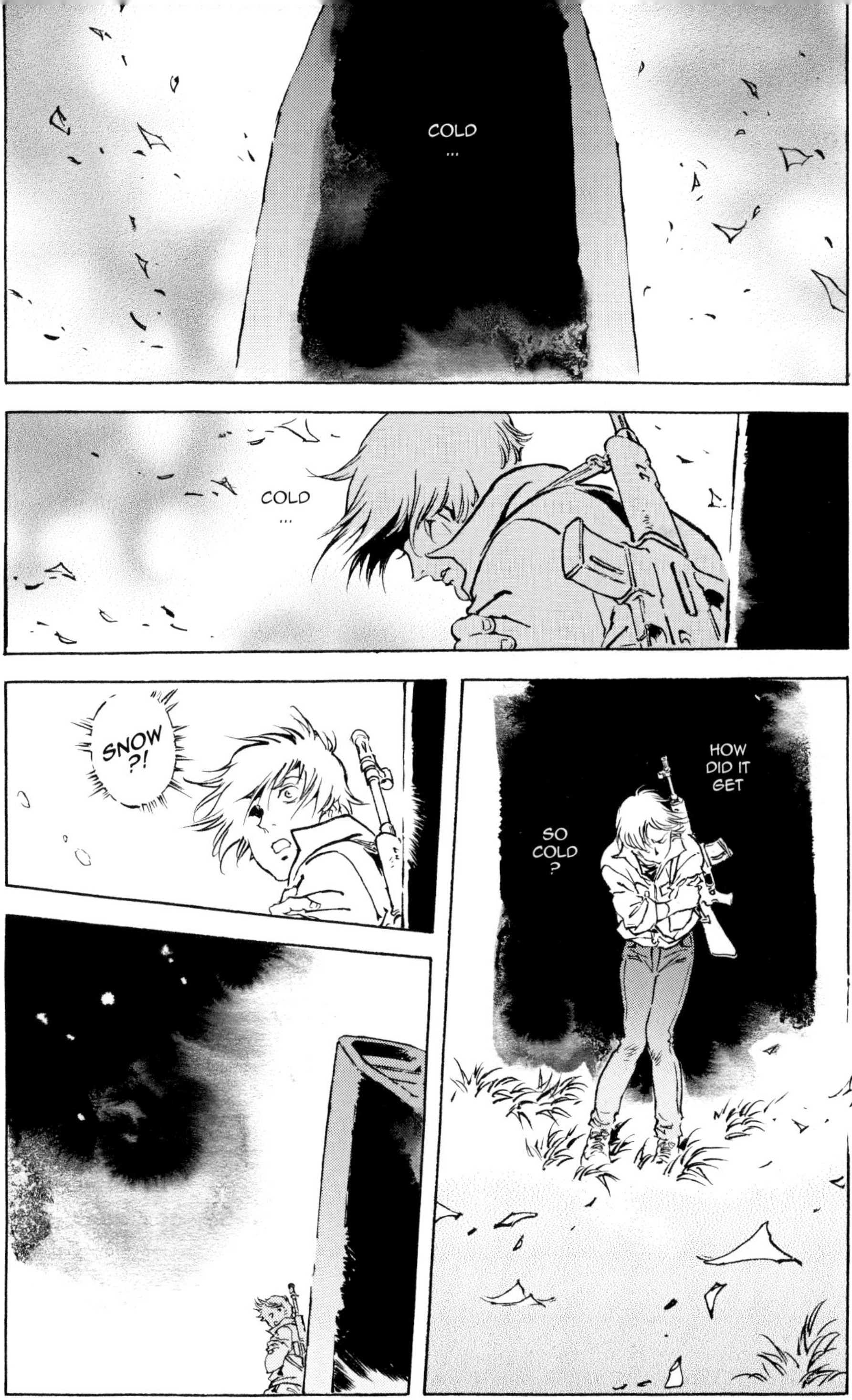
COLD ...
COLD ...
HOW DID IT GET
SO COLD ?
SNOW ?!

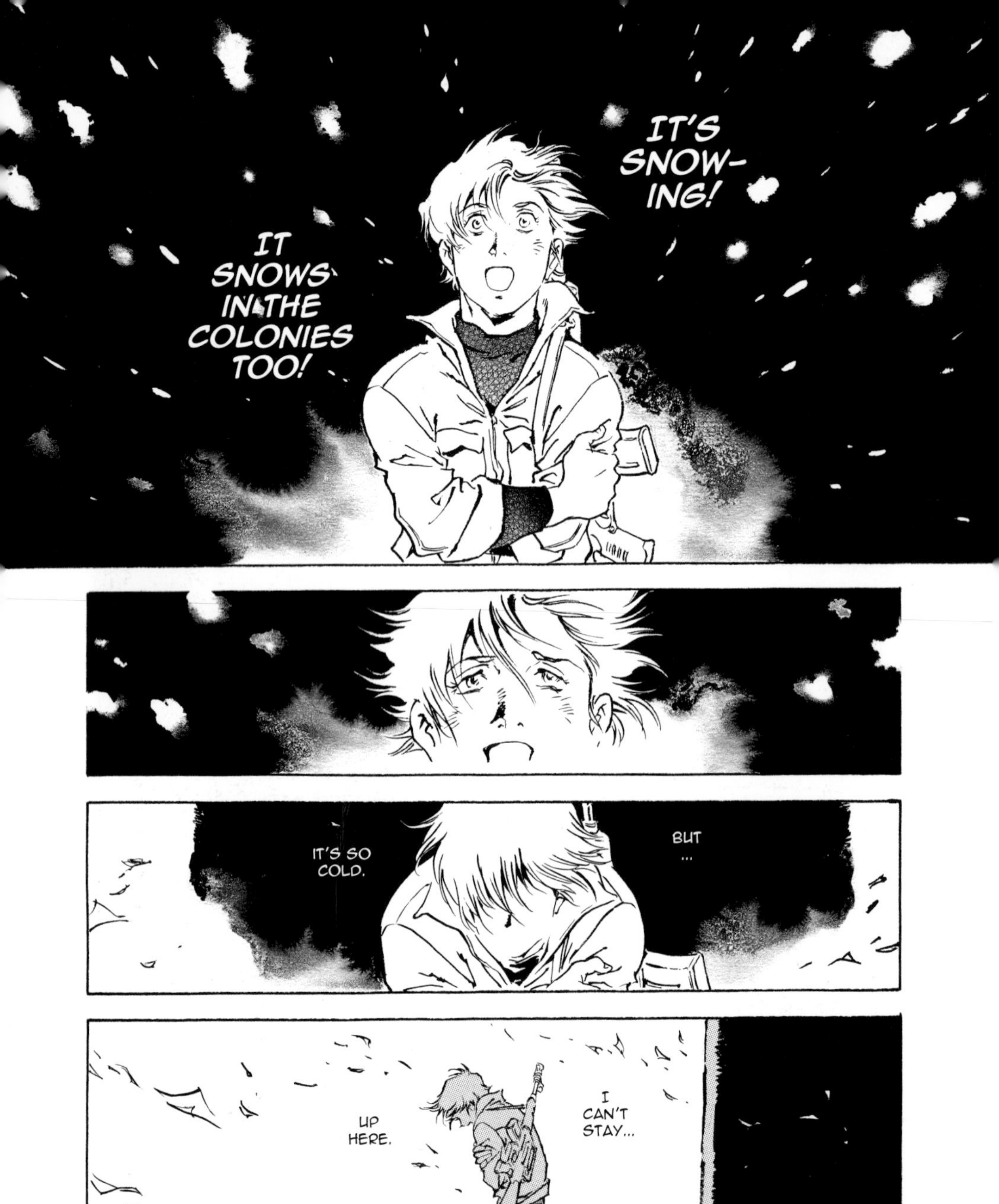
IT'S SNOWING!
IT SNOWS IN THE COLONIES TOO!
BUT ...
IT'S SO COLD.
I CAN'T STAY...
UP HERE.

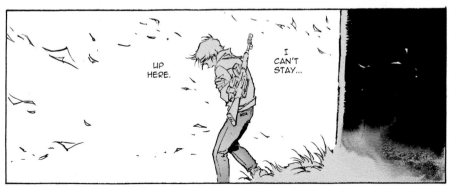

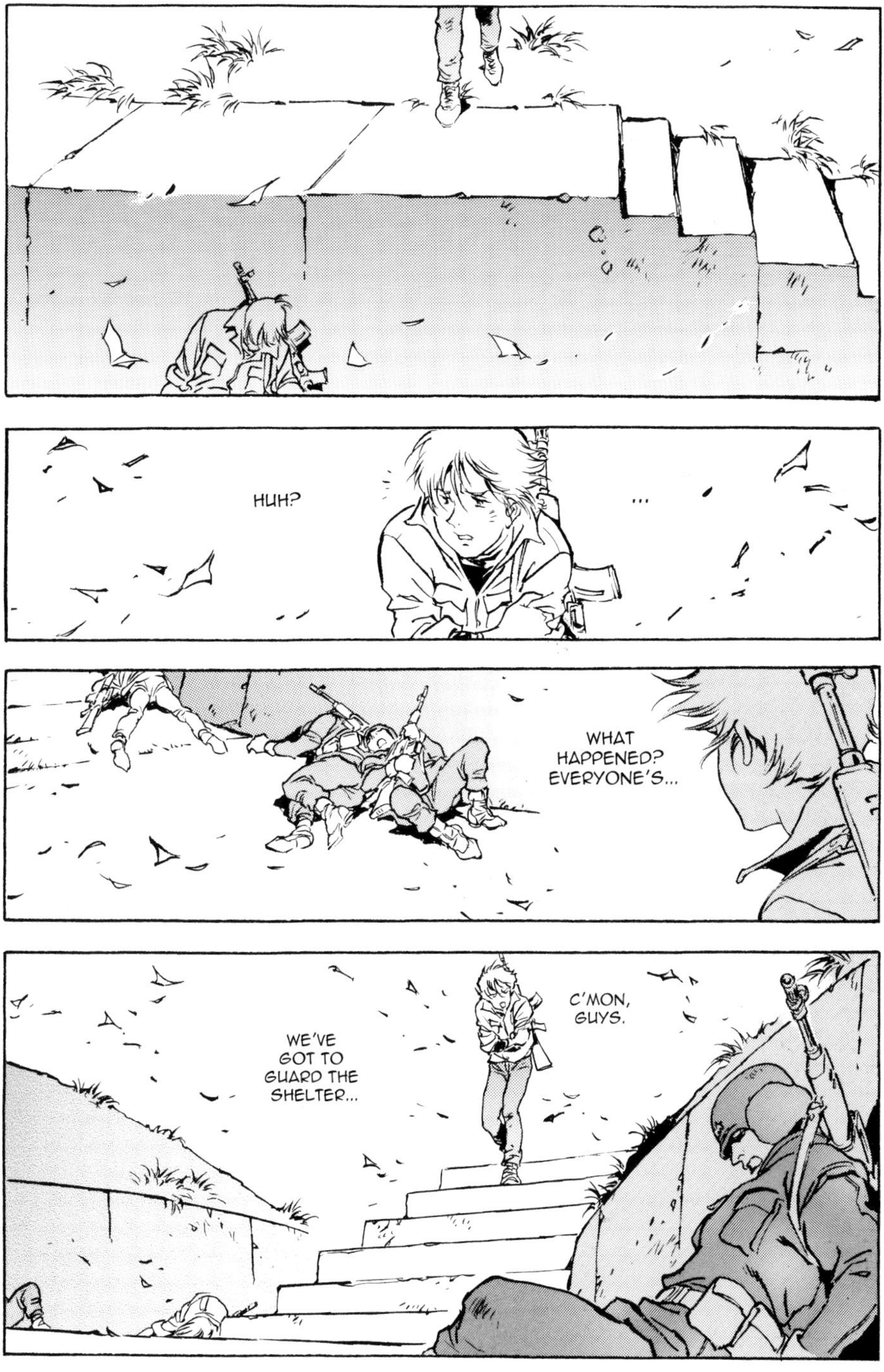
...
HUH?
WHAT HAPPENED? EVERYONE'S...
C'MON, GUYS.
WE'VE GOT TO GUARD THE SHELTER...

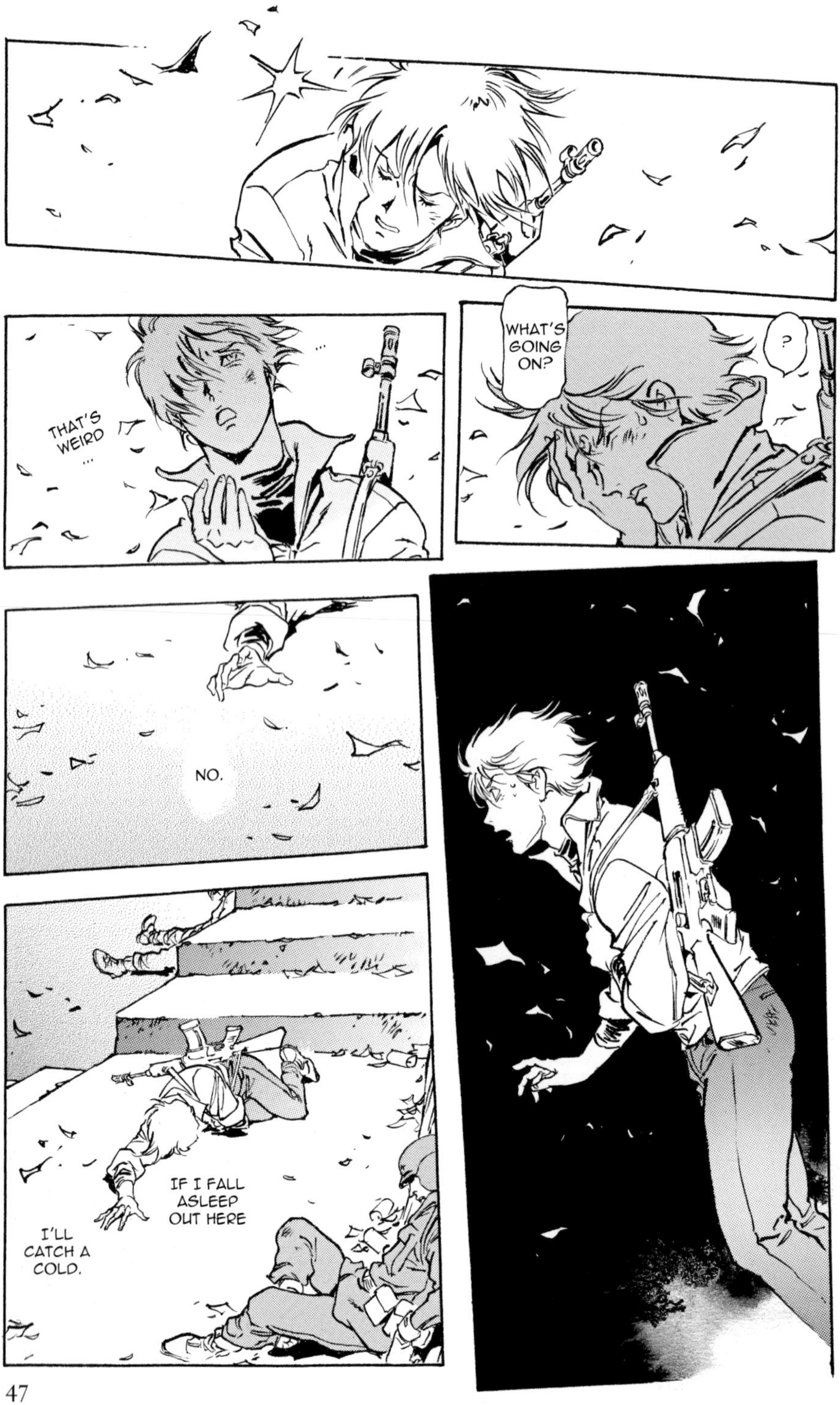
?
WHAT'S GOING ON?
...
THAT'S WEIRD ...
NO.
IF I FALL ASLEEP OUT HERE
I'LL CATCH A COLD.

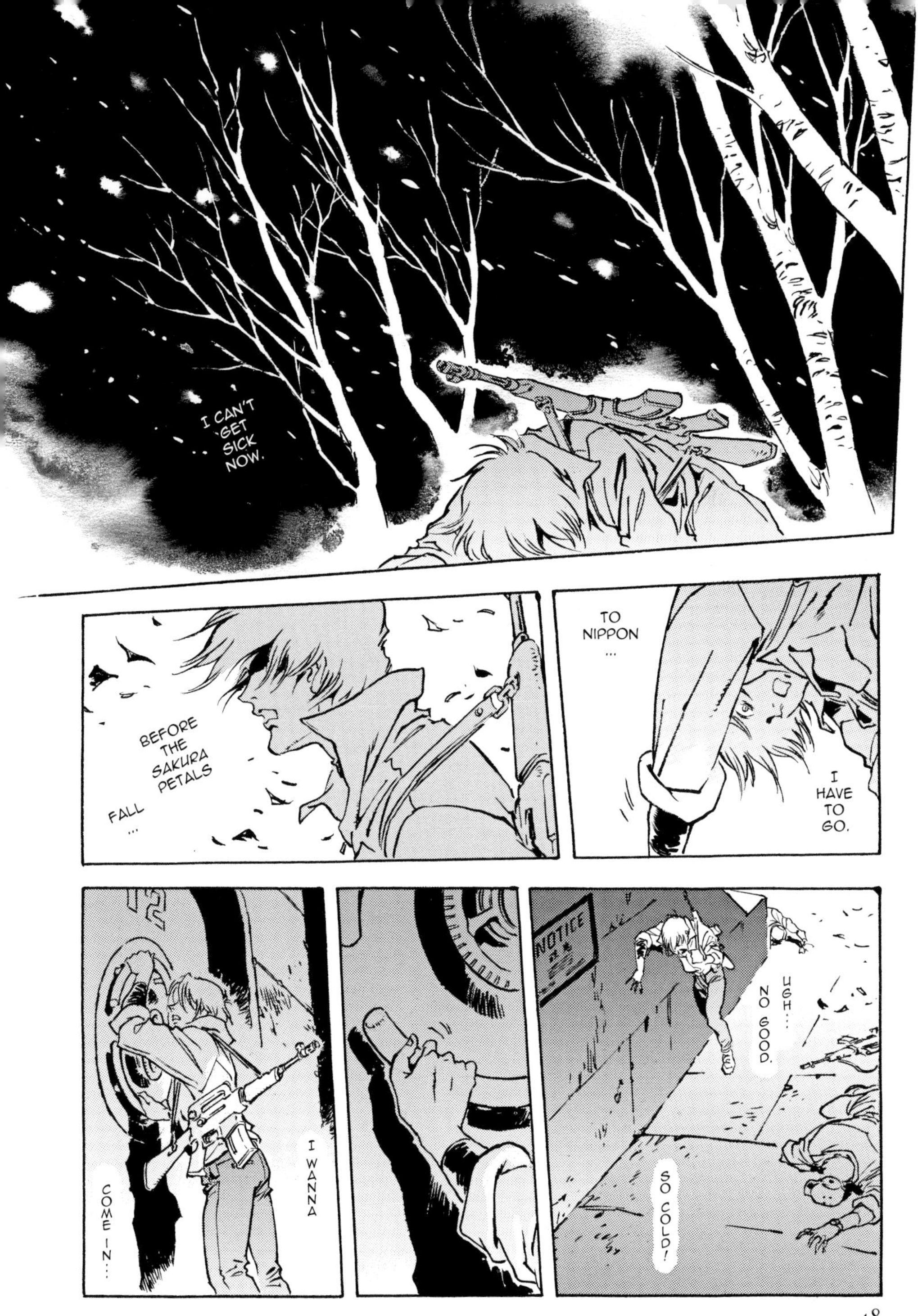
I CAN'T GET SICK NOW.
TO NIPPON ...
I HAVE TO GO.
BEFORE THE SAKURA PETALS FALL ...
UGH... NO GOOD.
SO COLD!
I WANNA COME IN...

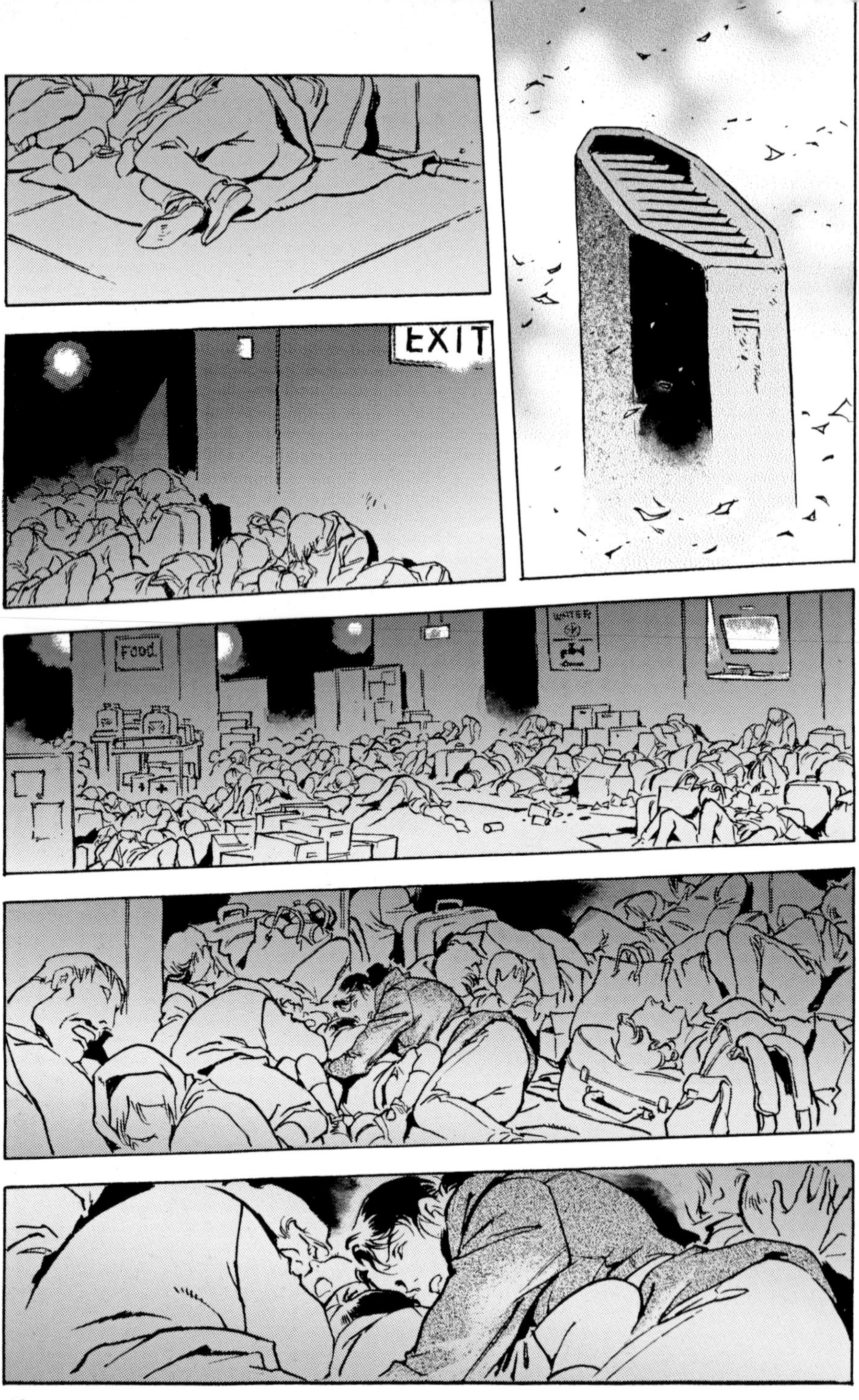
EXIT
WATER
Food

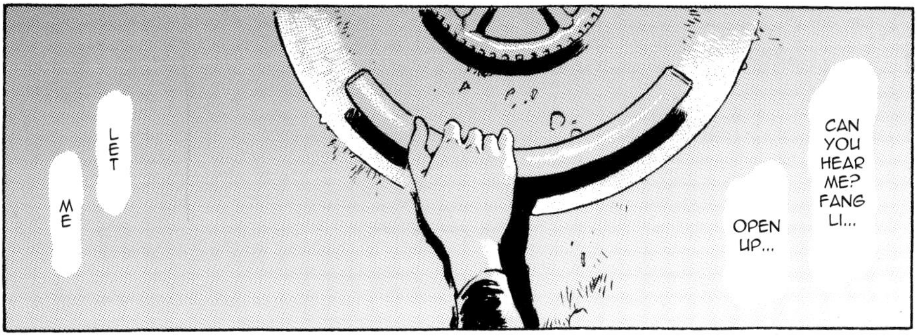
CAN YOU HEAR ME? FANG LI...
OPEN UP...
LET
ME

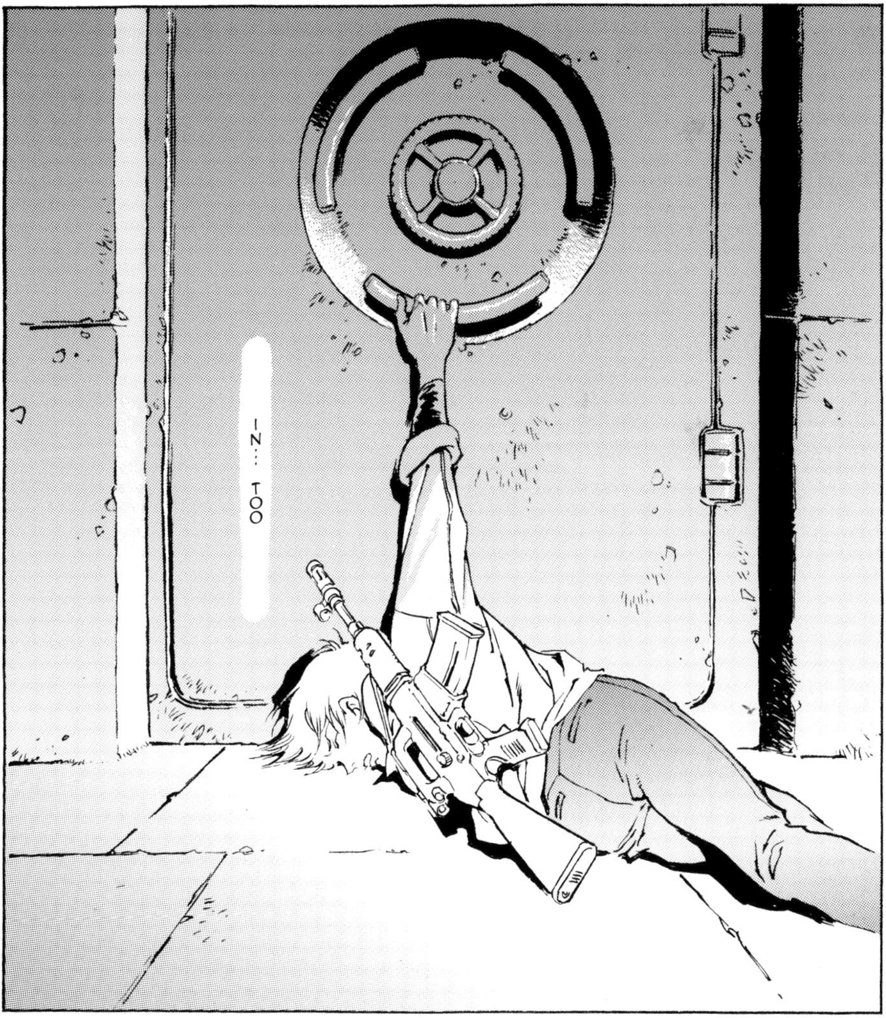
IN... TOO

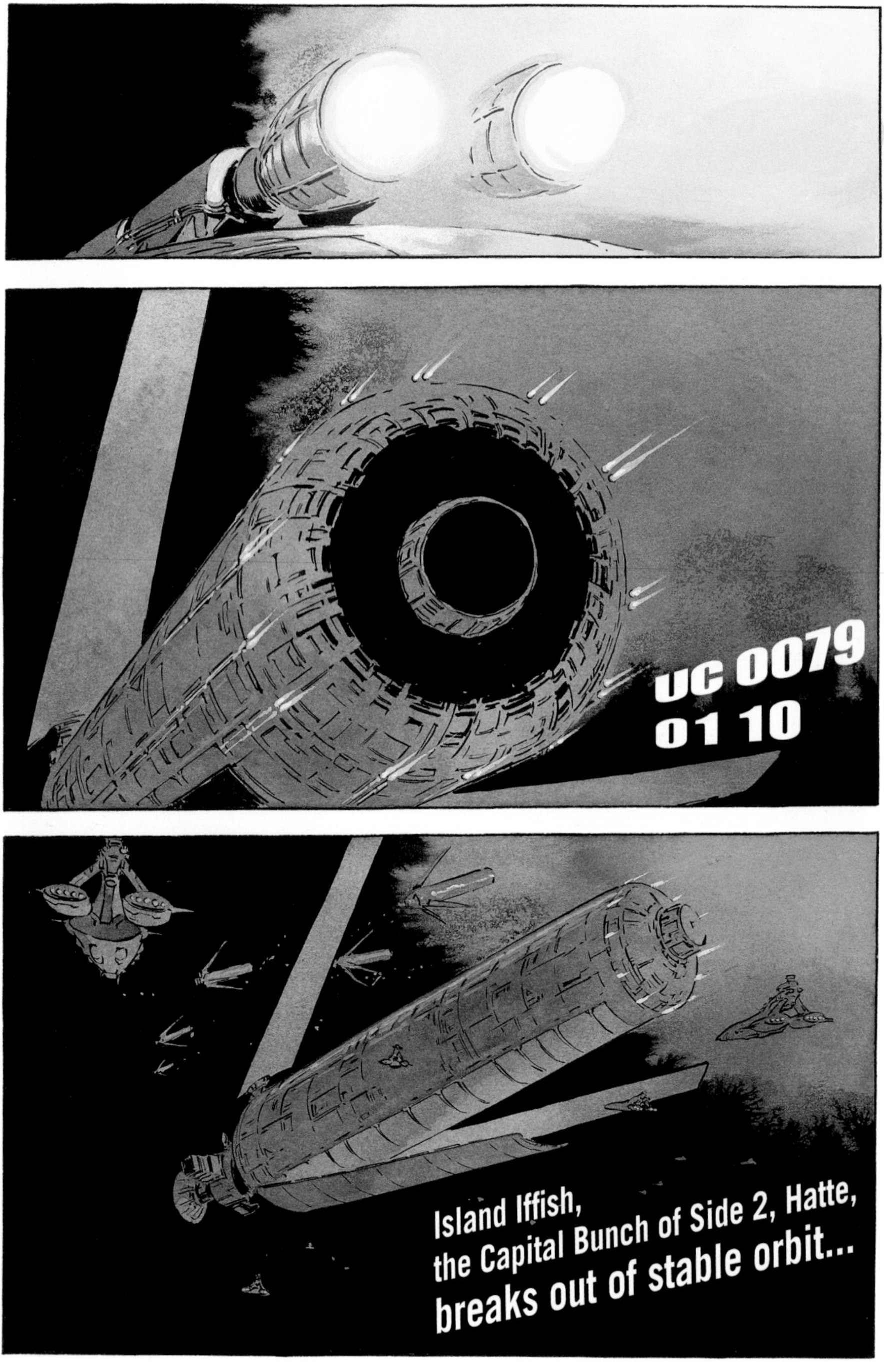
UC 0079
01 10
Island Iffish,
the Capital Bunch of Side 2, Hatte,
breaks out of stable orbit...

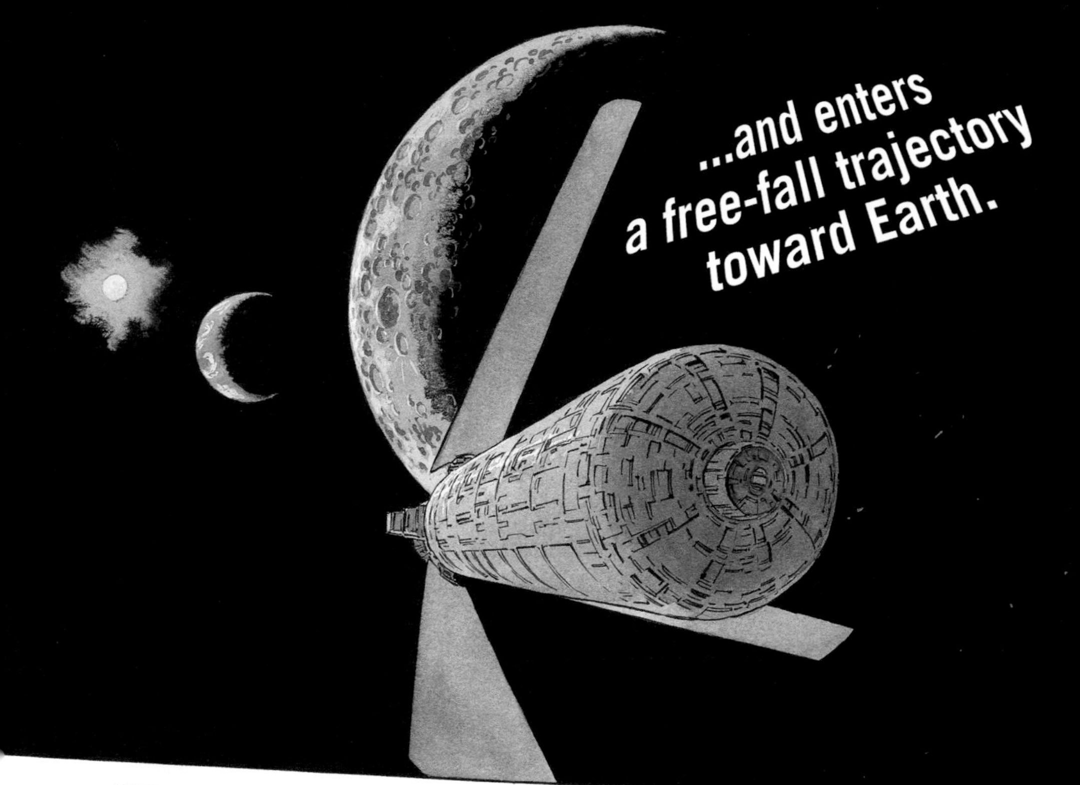
...and enters
a free-fall trajectory
toward Earth.
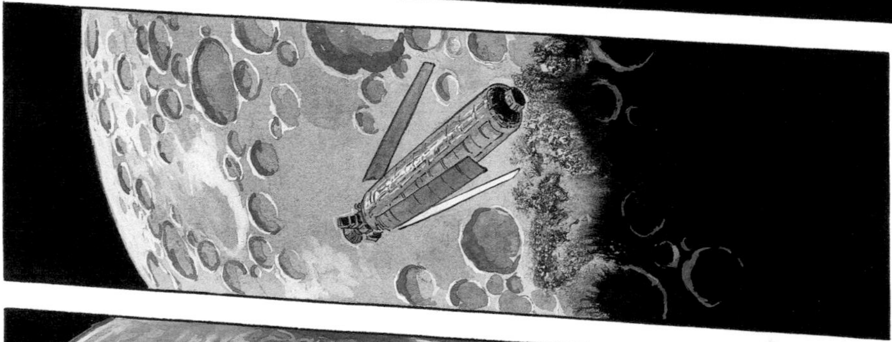
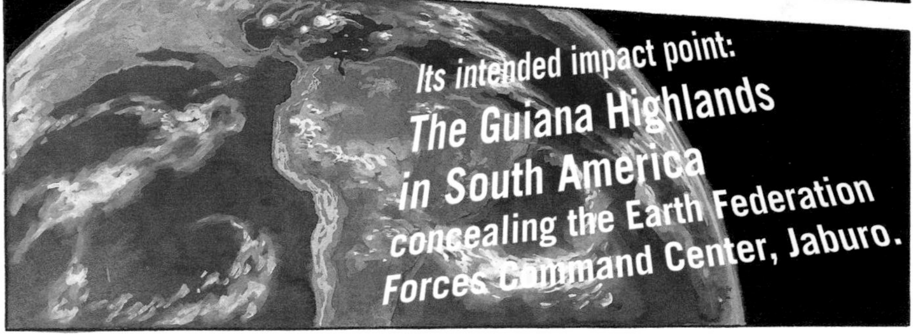
Its intended impact point:
The Guiana Highlands
in South America
concealing the Earth Federation
Forces Command Center, Jaburo.

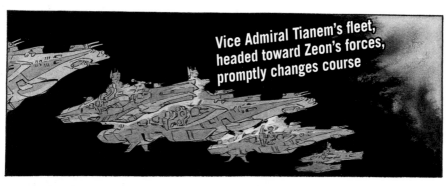

Vice Admiral Tianem's fleet, headed toward Zeon's forces, promptly changes course

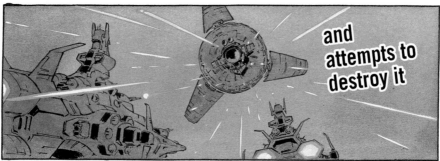

and attempts to destroy it

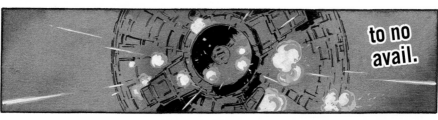

to no avail.

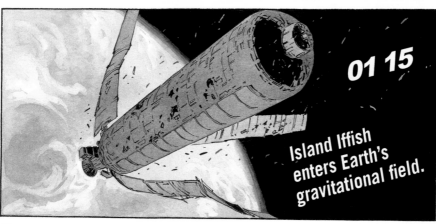

01 15

Island Iffish enters Earth's gravitational field.

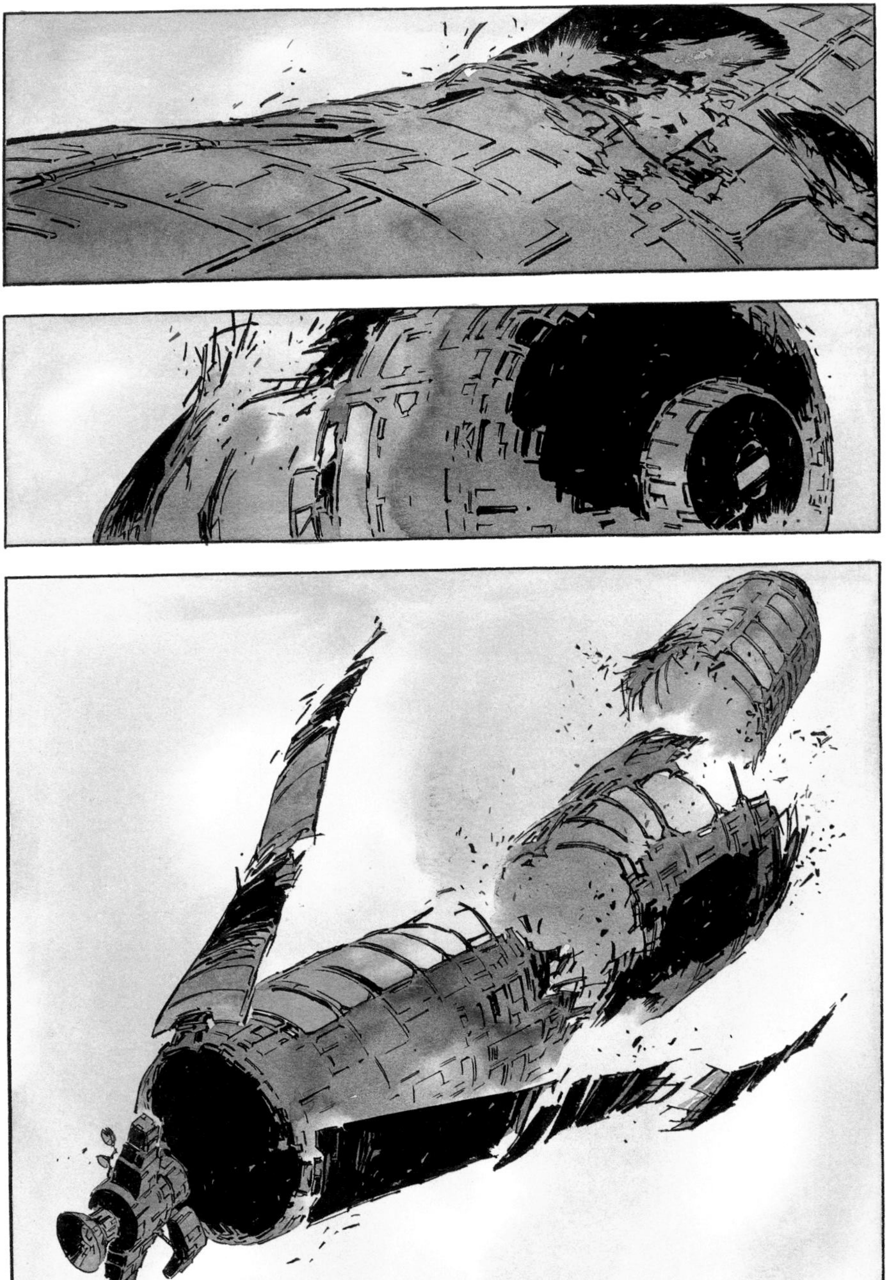

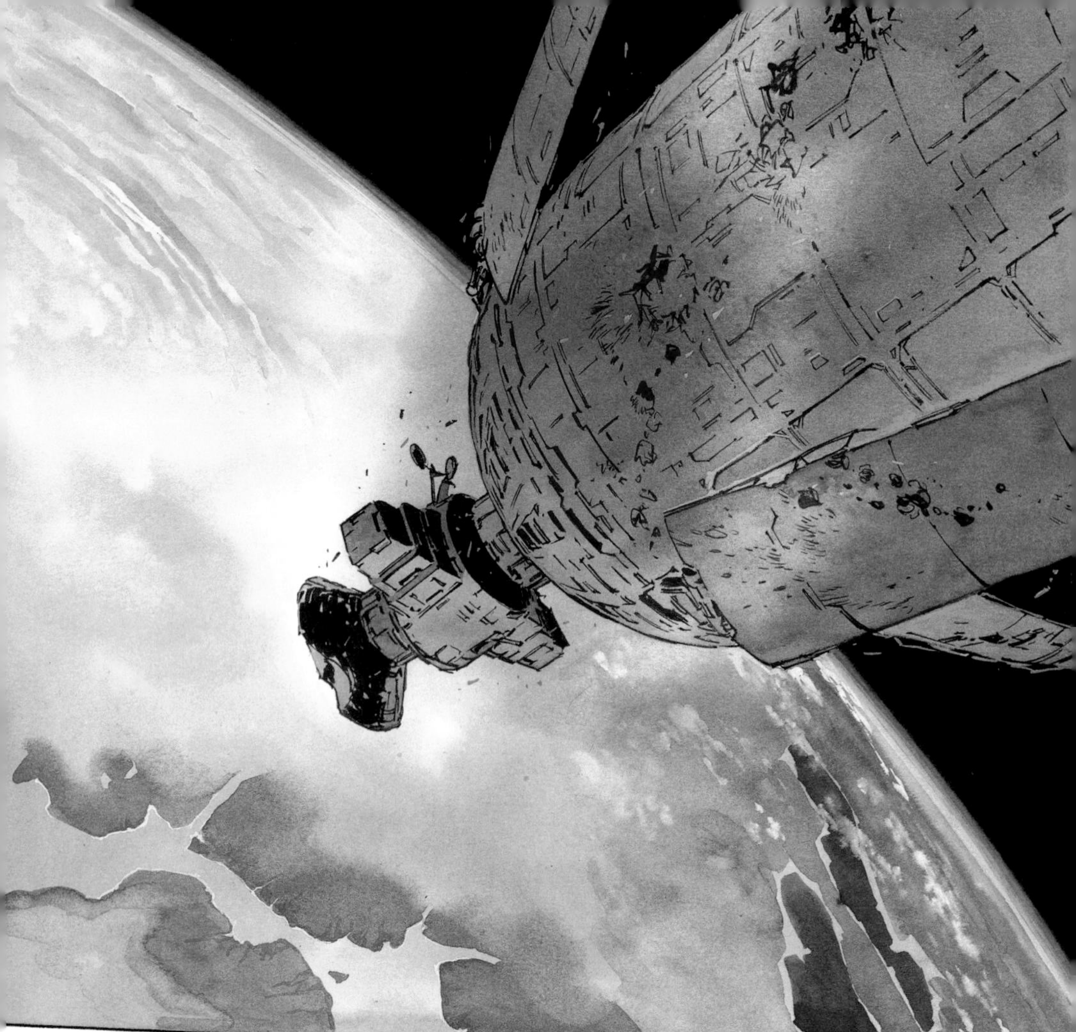
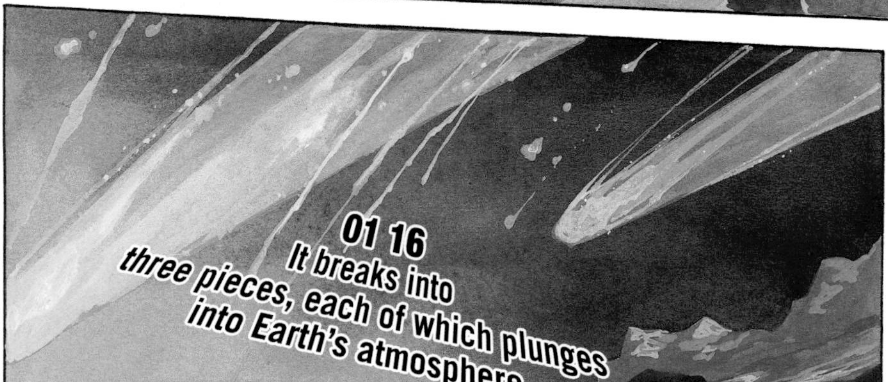
01 16
It breaks into three pieces, each of which plunges into Earth's atmosphere.

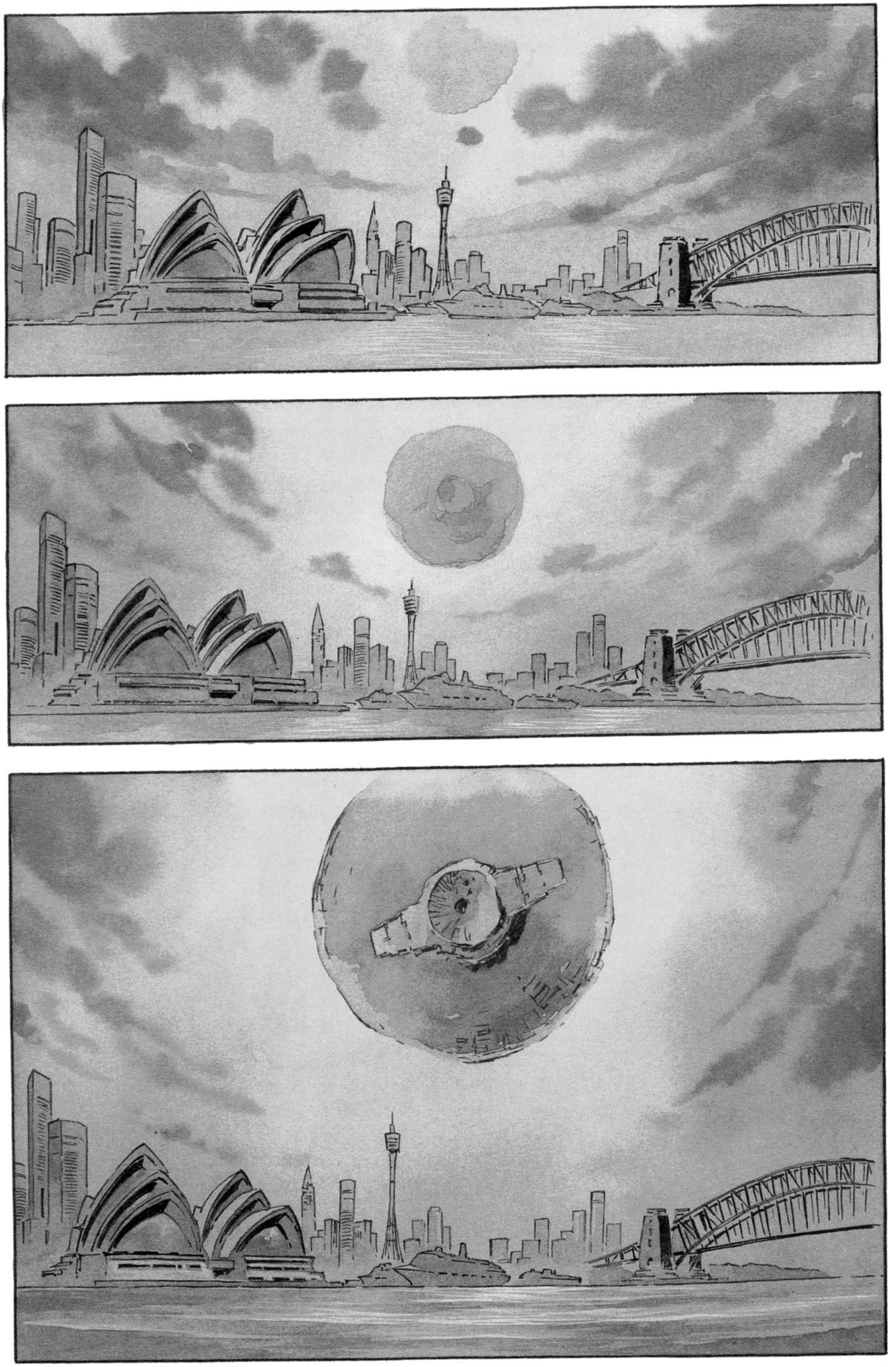

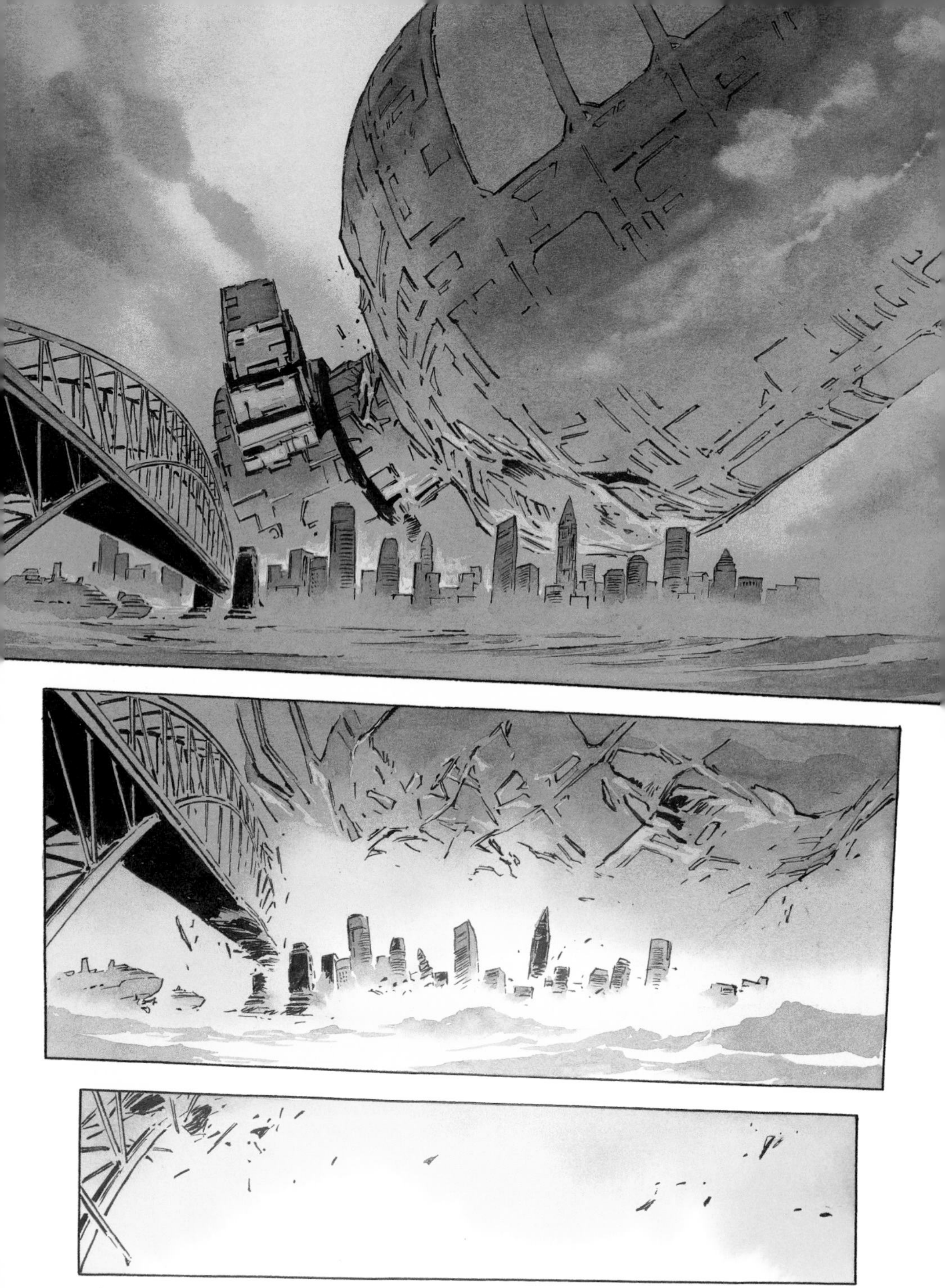

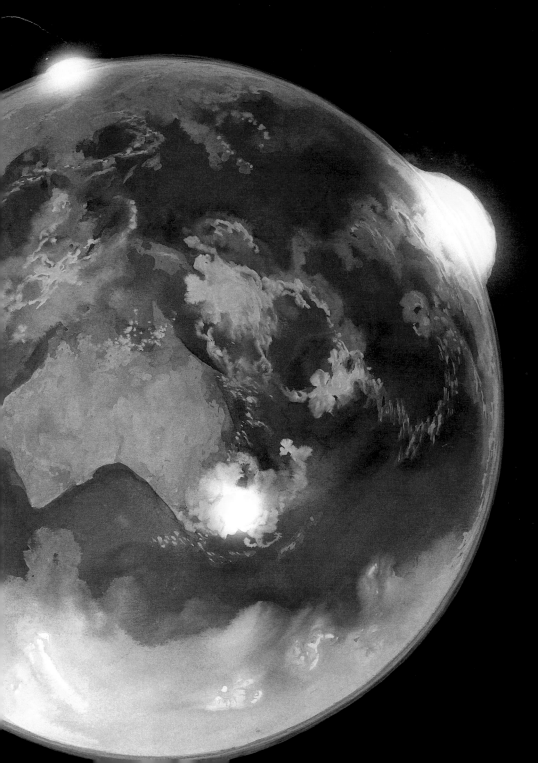

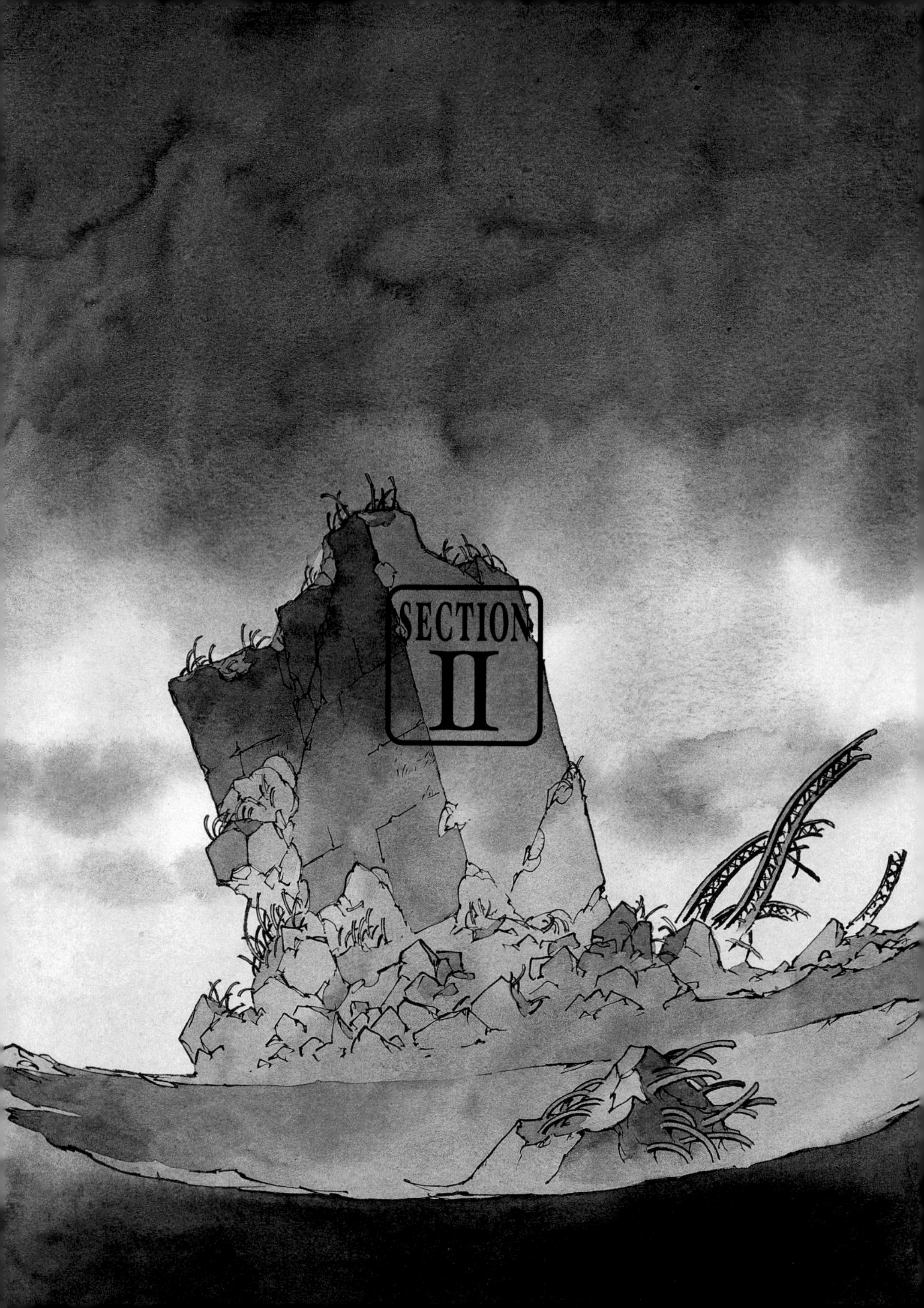
SECTION
II

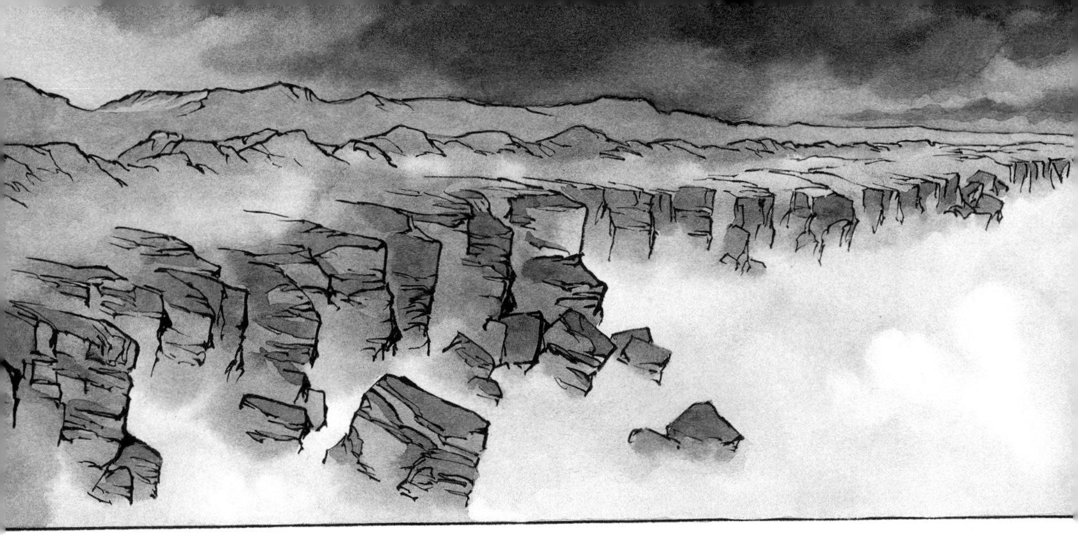

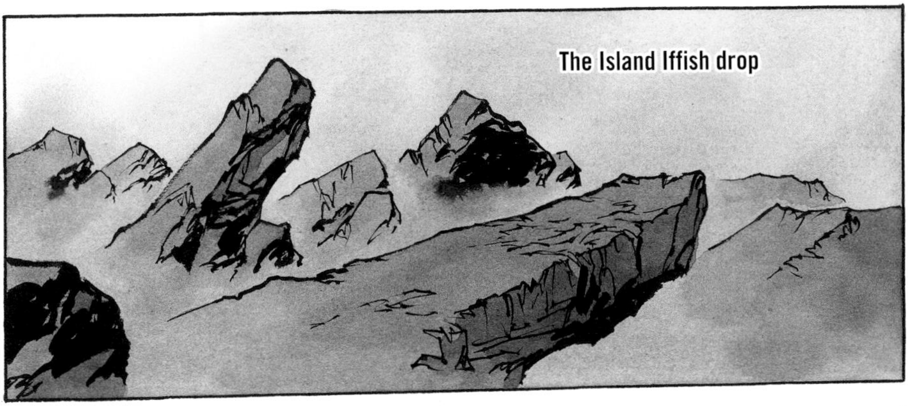
The Island Iffish drop

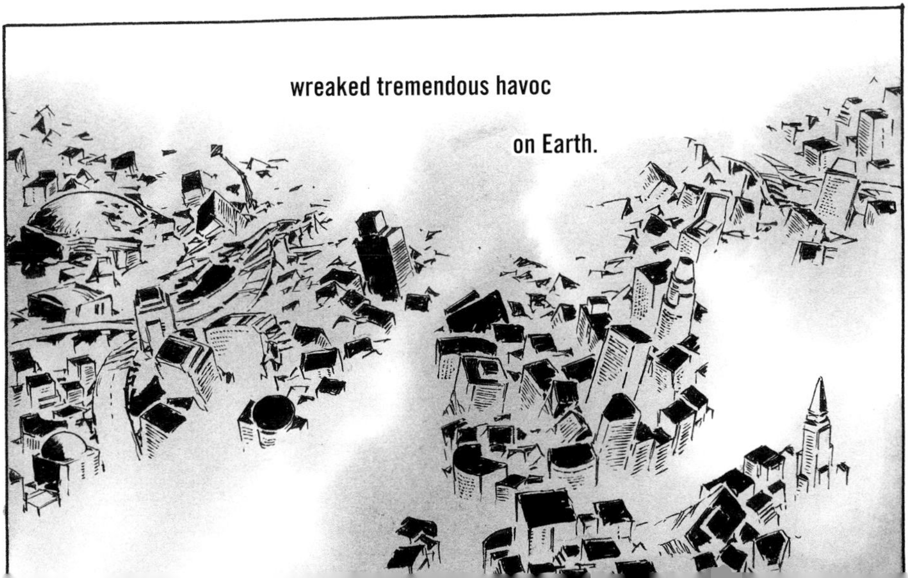
wreaked tremendous havoc
on Earth.

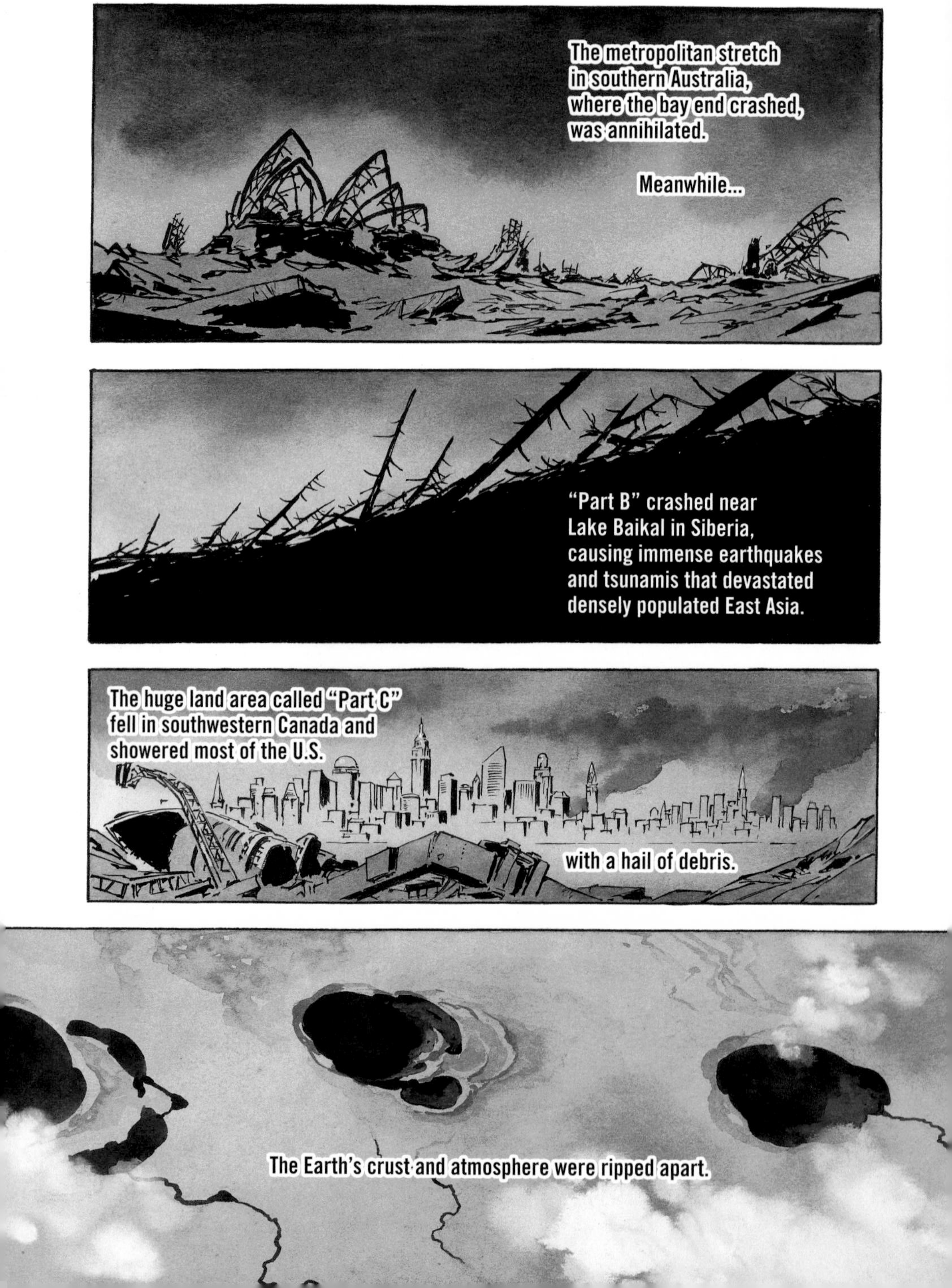
The metropolitan stretch in southern Australia, where the bay end crashed, was annihilated.
Meanwhile...
"Part B" crashed near Lake Baikal in Siberia, causing immense earthquakes and tsunamis that devastated densely populated East Asia.
The huge land area called "Part C" fell in southwestern Canada and showered most of the U.S.
with a hail of debris.
The Earth's crust and atmosphere were ripped apart.

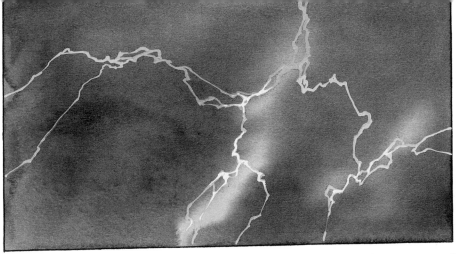
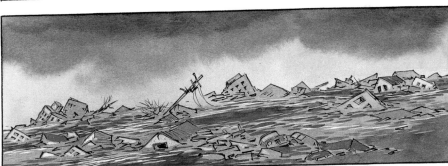
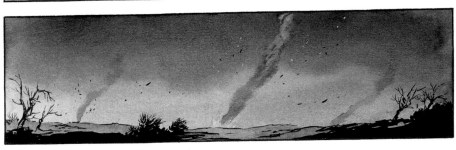
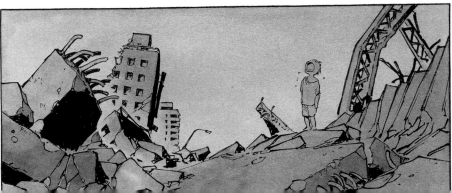

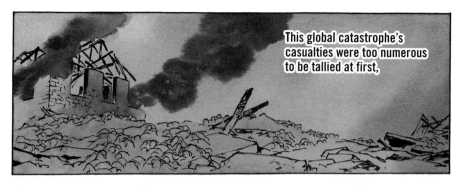

This global catastrophe's casualties were too numerous to be tallied at first,

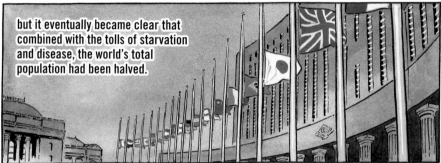

but it eventually became clear that combined with the tolls of starvation and disease, the world's total population had been halved.

The war, however, had only begun. The first stages, from its declaration to the destruction of Hatte, later came to be called the "One Week War."

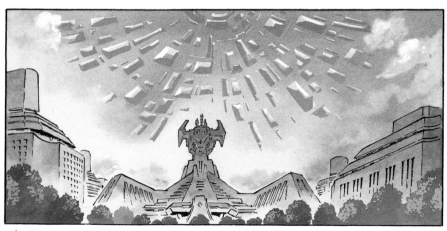

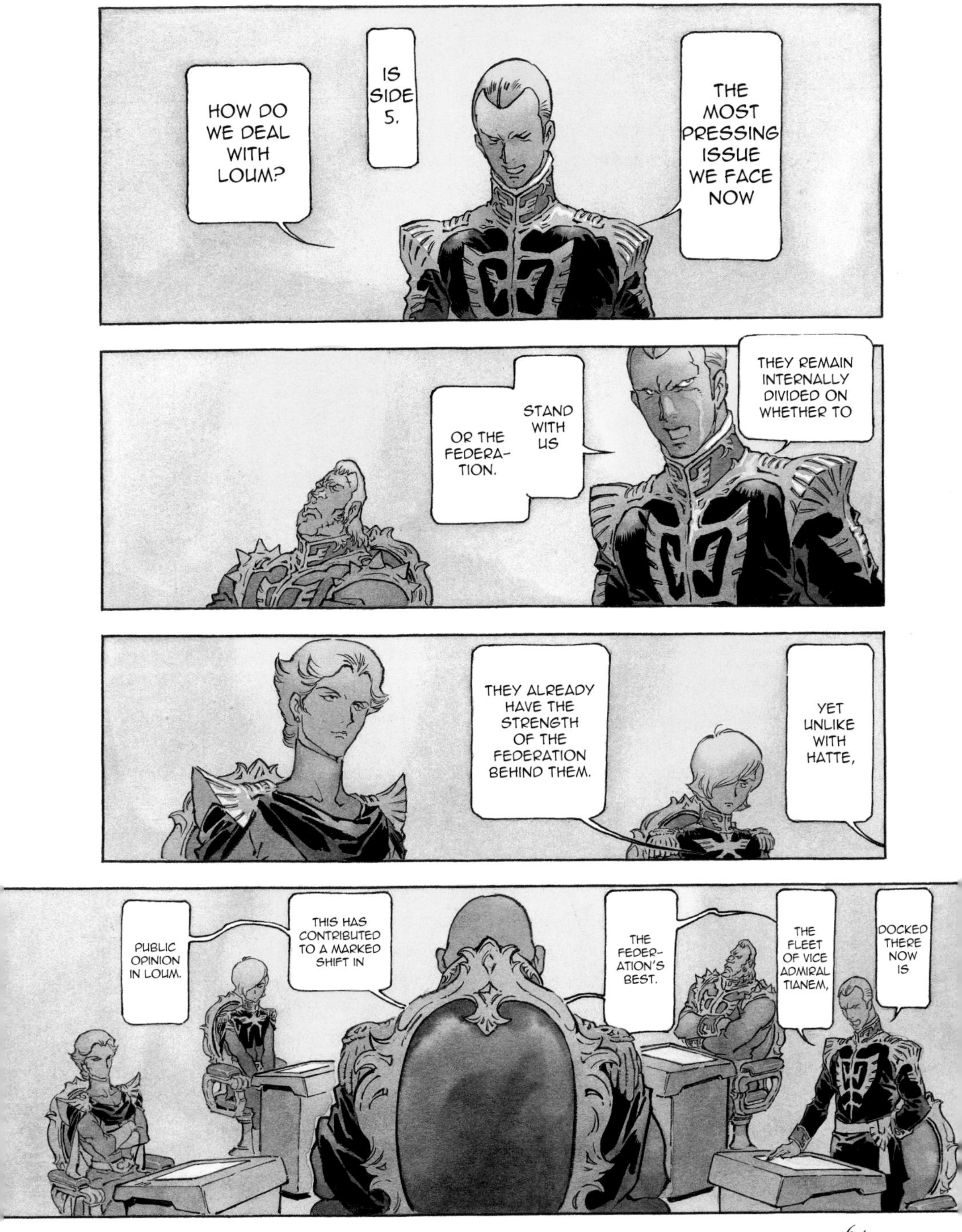
THE MOST PRESSING ISSUE WE FACE NOW
IS SIDE 5.
HOW DO WE DEAL WITH LOUM?
THEY REMAIN INTERNALLY DIVIDED ON WHETHER TO
STAND WITH US
OR THE FEDERA-TION.
YET UNLIKE WITH HATTE,
THEY ALREADY HAVE THE STRENGTH OF THE FEDERATION BEHIND THEM.
DOCKED THERE NOW IS
THE FLEET OF VICE ADMIRAL TIANEM,
THE FEDER-ATION'S BEST.
THIS HAS CONTRIBUTED TO A MARKED SHIFT IN
PUBLIC OPINION IN LOUM.

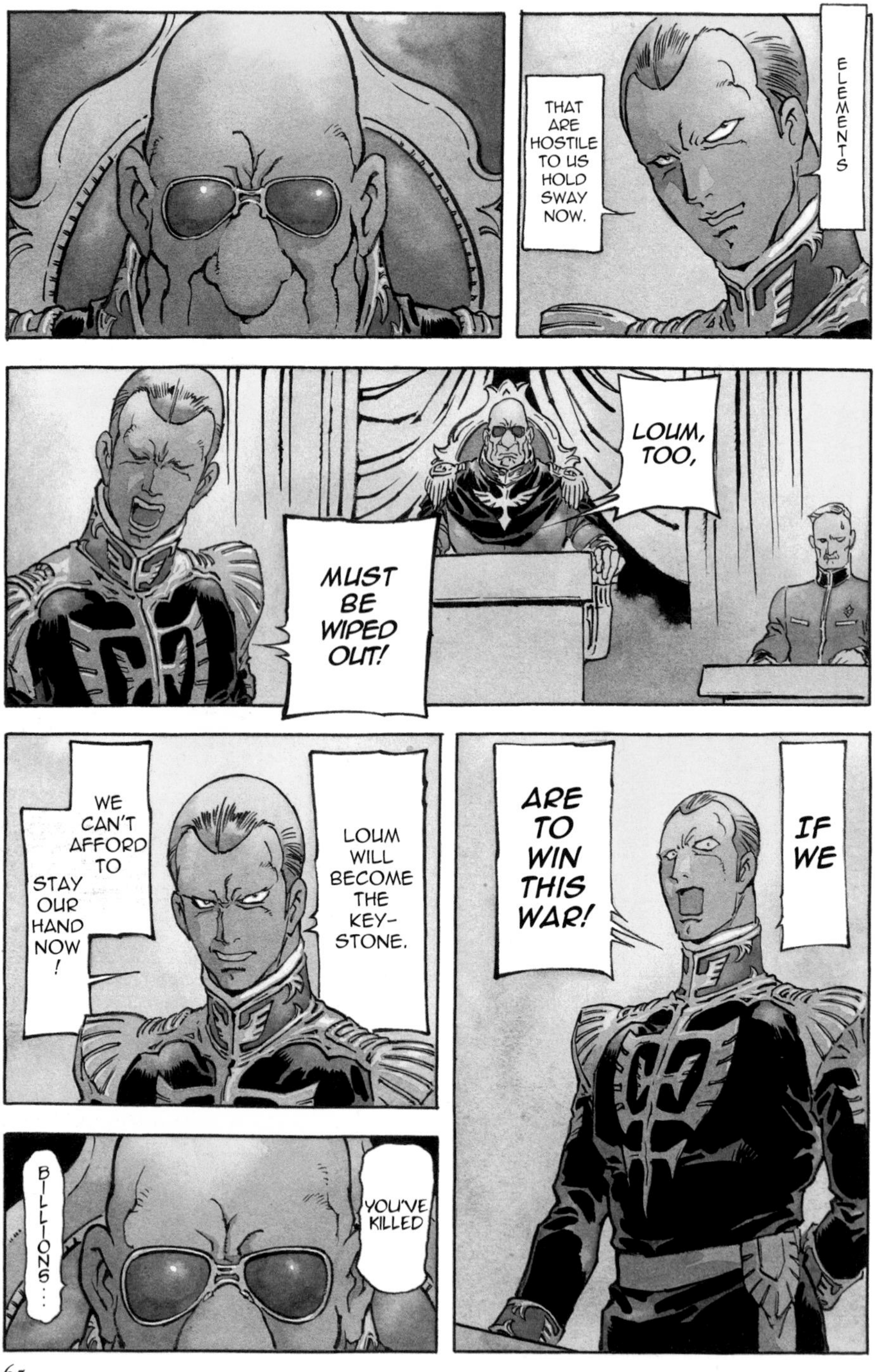
ELEMENTS
THAT ARE HOSTILE TO US HOLD SWAY NOW.
LOUM, TOO,
MUST BE WIPED OUT!
IF WE
ARE TO WIN THIS WAR!
LOUM WILL BECOME THE KEYSTONE.
WE CAN'T AFFORD TO STAY OUR HAND NOW!
YOU'VE KILLED
BILLIONS...

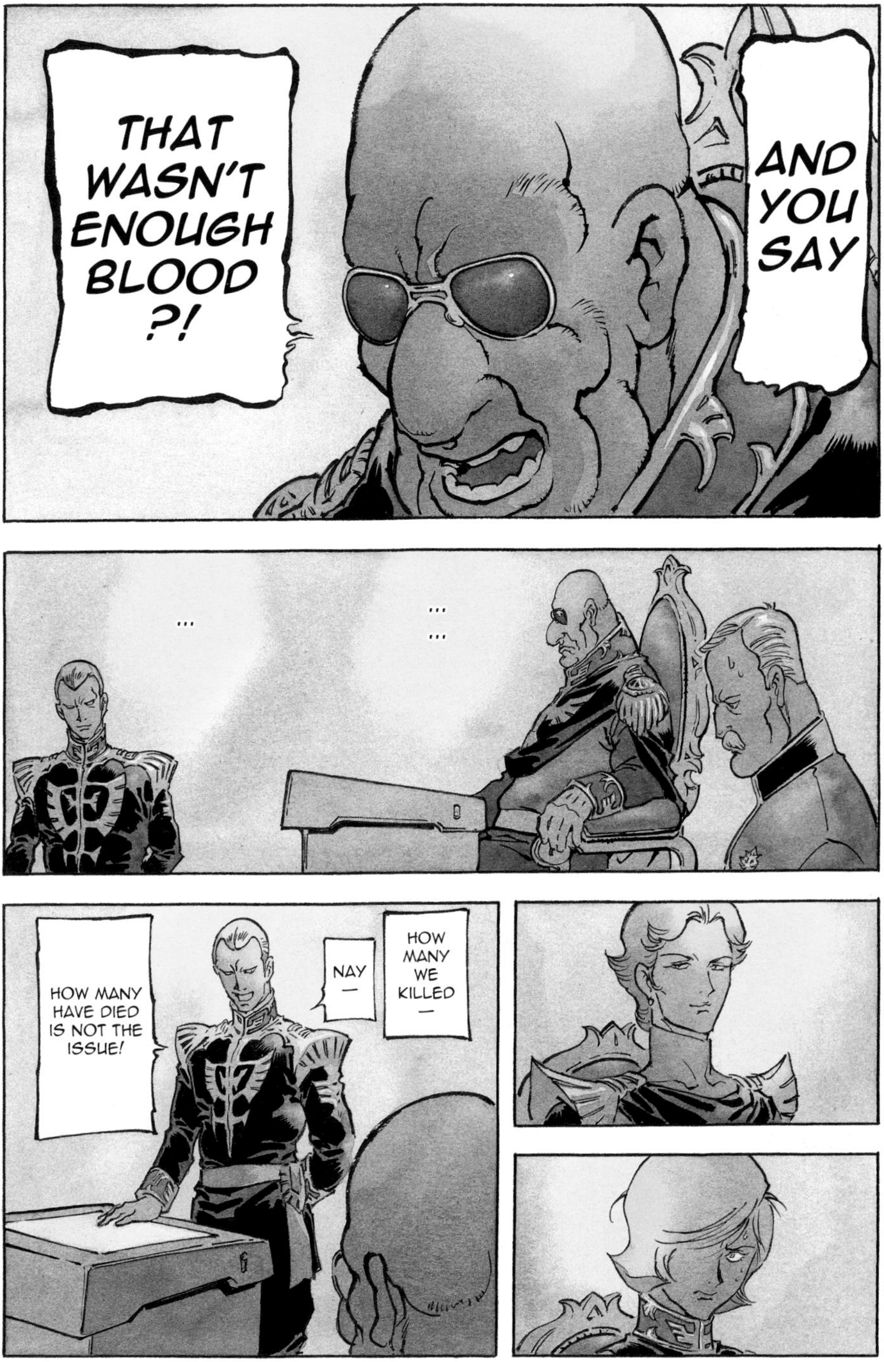
AND YOU SAY
THAT WASN'T ENOUGH BLOOD ?!
... ...
...
HOW MANY WE KILLED —
NAY —
HOW MANY HAVE DIED IS NOT THE ISSUE!

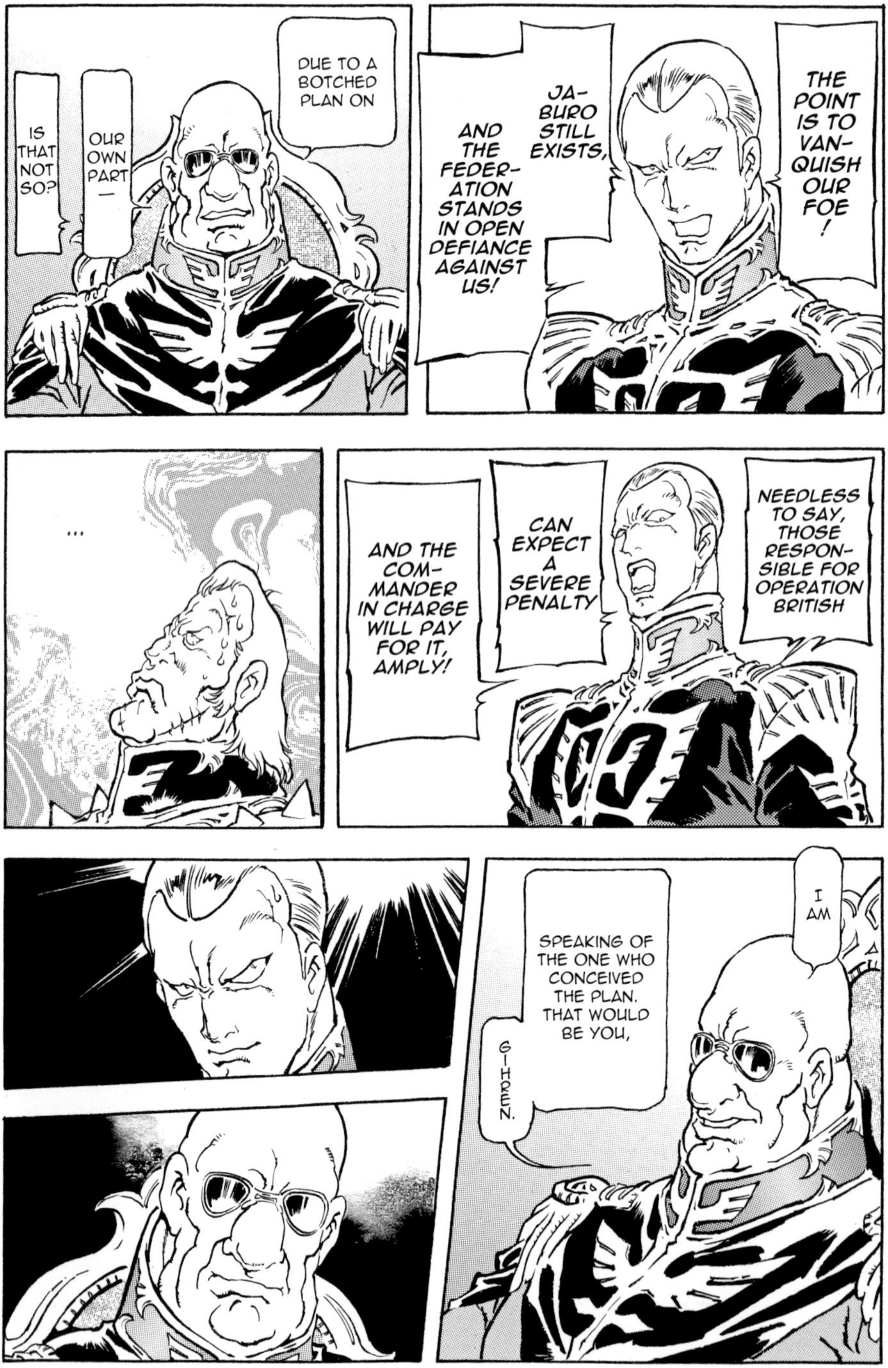
THE POINT IS TO VAN-QUISH OUR FOE!
JA-BURO STILL EXISTS,
AND THE FEDER-ATION STANDS IN OPEN DEFIANCE AGAINST US!
DUE TO A BOTCHED PLAN ON
OUR OWN PART —
IS THAT NOT SO?
NEEDLESS TO SAY, THOSE RESPON-SIBLE FOR OPERATION BRITISH
CAN EXPECT A SEVERE PENALTY
AND THE COM-MANDER IN CHARGE WILL PAY FOR IT, AMPLY!
...
I AM
SPEAKING OF THE ONE WHO CONCEIVED THE PLAN. THAT WOULD BE YOU,
GIHREN.

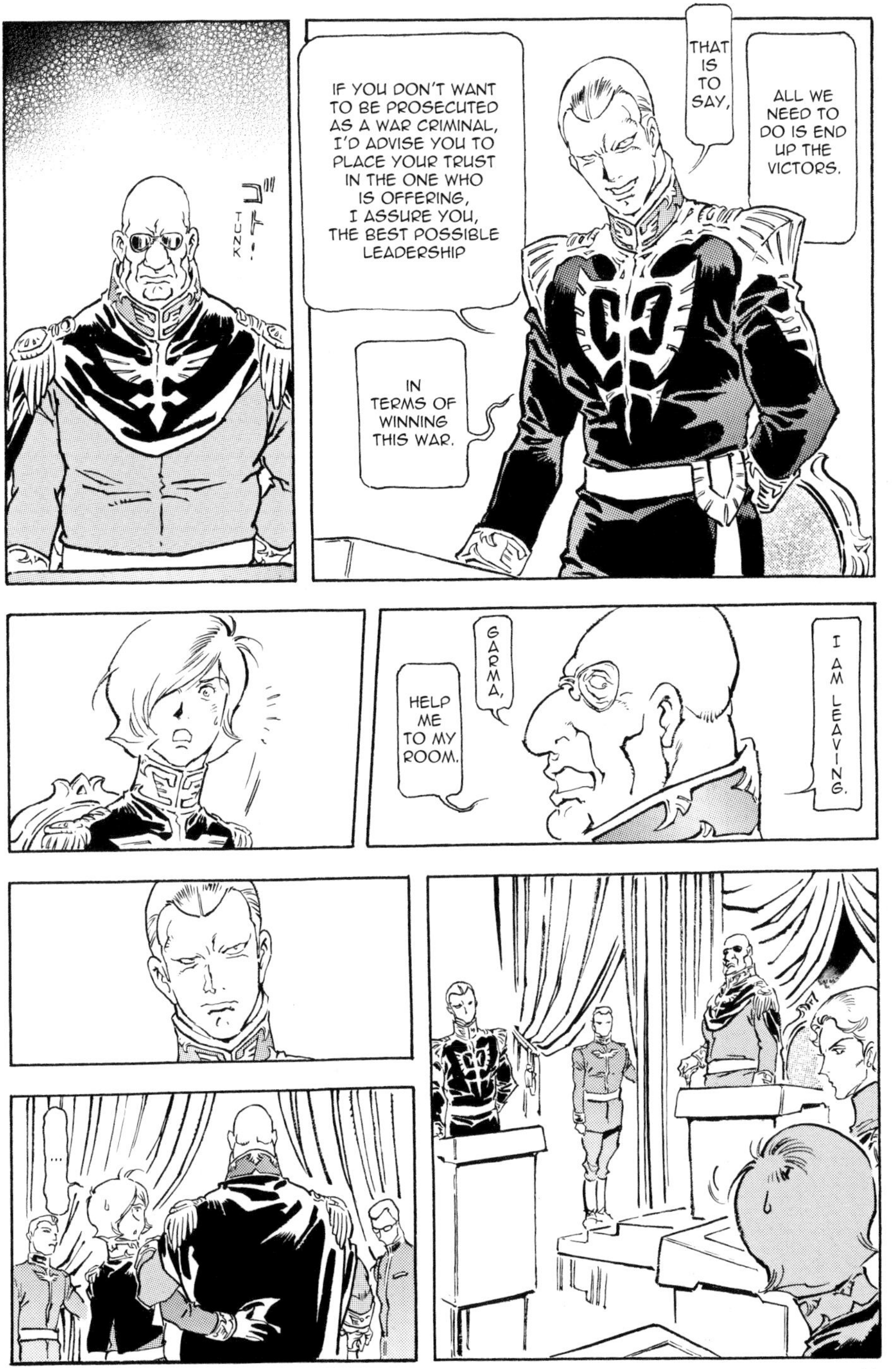
THAT IS TO SAY,
ALL WE NEED TO DO IS END UP THE VICTORS.
IF YOU DON'T WANT TO BE PROSECUTED AS A WAR CRIMINAL, I'D ADVISE YOU TO PLACE YOUR TRUST IN THE ONE WHO IS OFFERING, I ASSURE YOU, THE BEST POSSIBLE LEADERSHIP
IN TERMS OF WINNING THIS WAR.
ゴト…
TUNK
I AM LEAVING.
GARMA,
HELP ME TO MY ROOM.
…

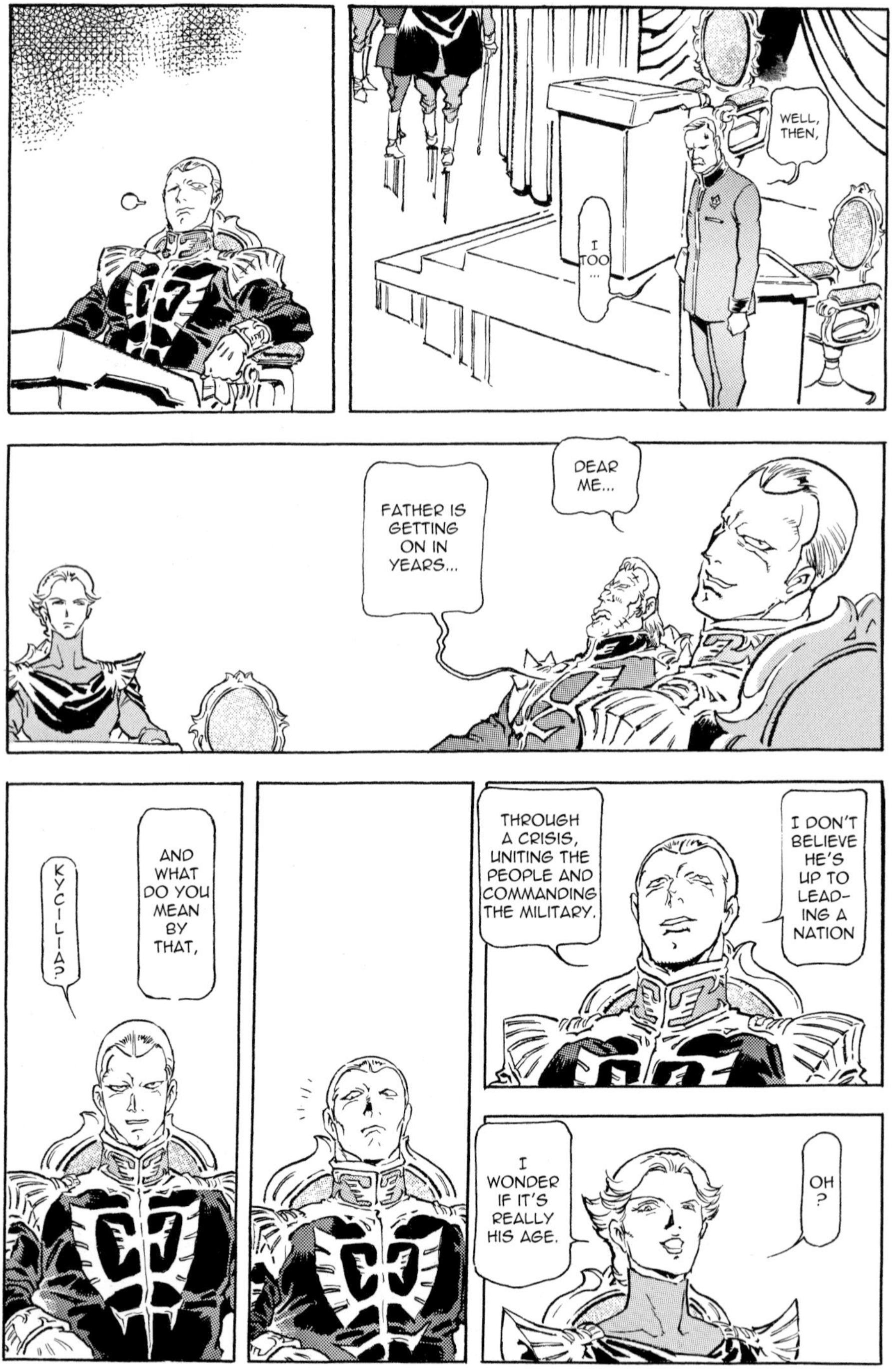
WELL, THEN,
I TOO...
DEAR ME...
FATHER IS GETTING ON IN YEARS...
I DON'T BELIEVE HE'S UP TO LEAD-ING A NATION
THROUGH A CRISIS, UNITING THE PEOPLE AND COMMANDING THE MILITARY.
OH?
I WONDER IF IT'S REALLY HIS AGE.
AND WHAT DO YOU MEAN BY THAT,
KYCILIA?

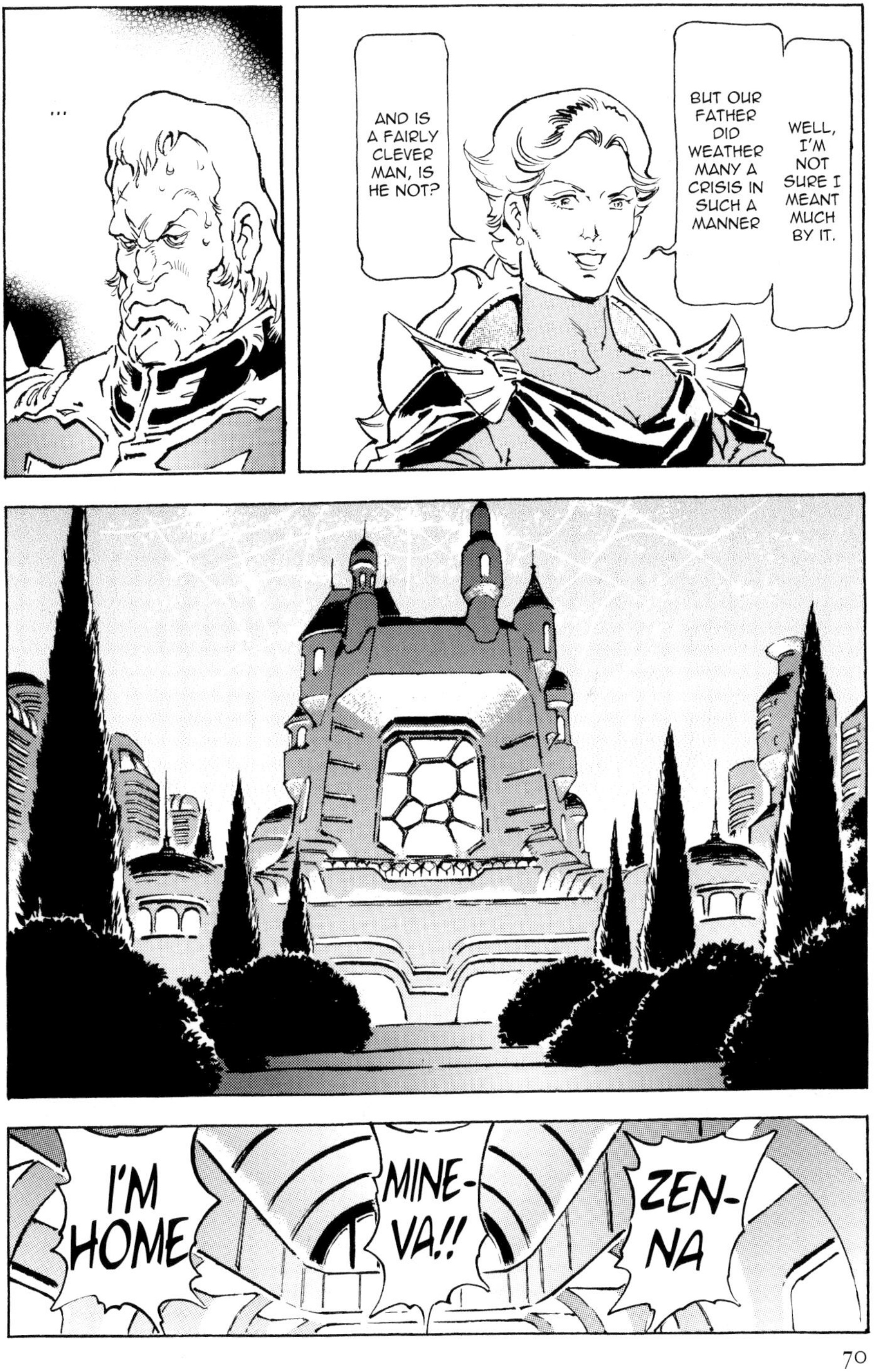
WELL, I'M NOT SURE I MEANT MUCH BY IT.
BUT OUR FATHER DID WEATHER MANY A CRISIS IN SUCH A MANNER
AND IS A FAIRLY CLEVER MAN, IS HE NOT?
...
ZEN-NA
MINE-VA!!
I'M HOME

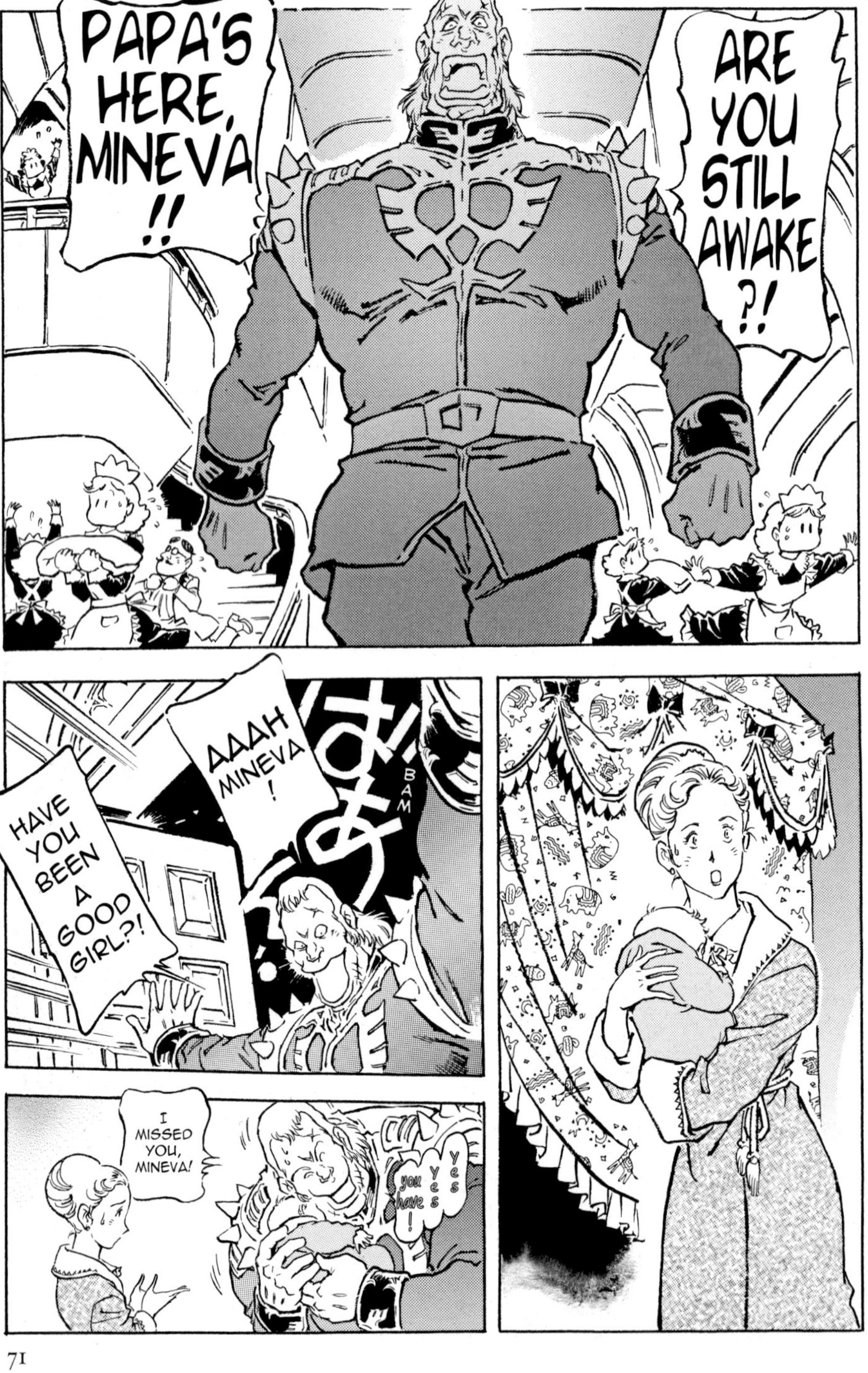
ARE YOU STILL AWAKE?!
PAPA'S HERE, MINEVA!!
AAAH MINEVA!
BAM
HAVE YOU BEEN A GOOD GIRL?!
Yes yes
you have!
I MISSED YOU, MINEVA!

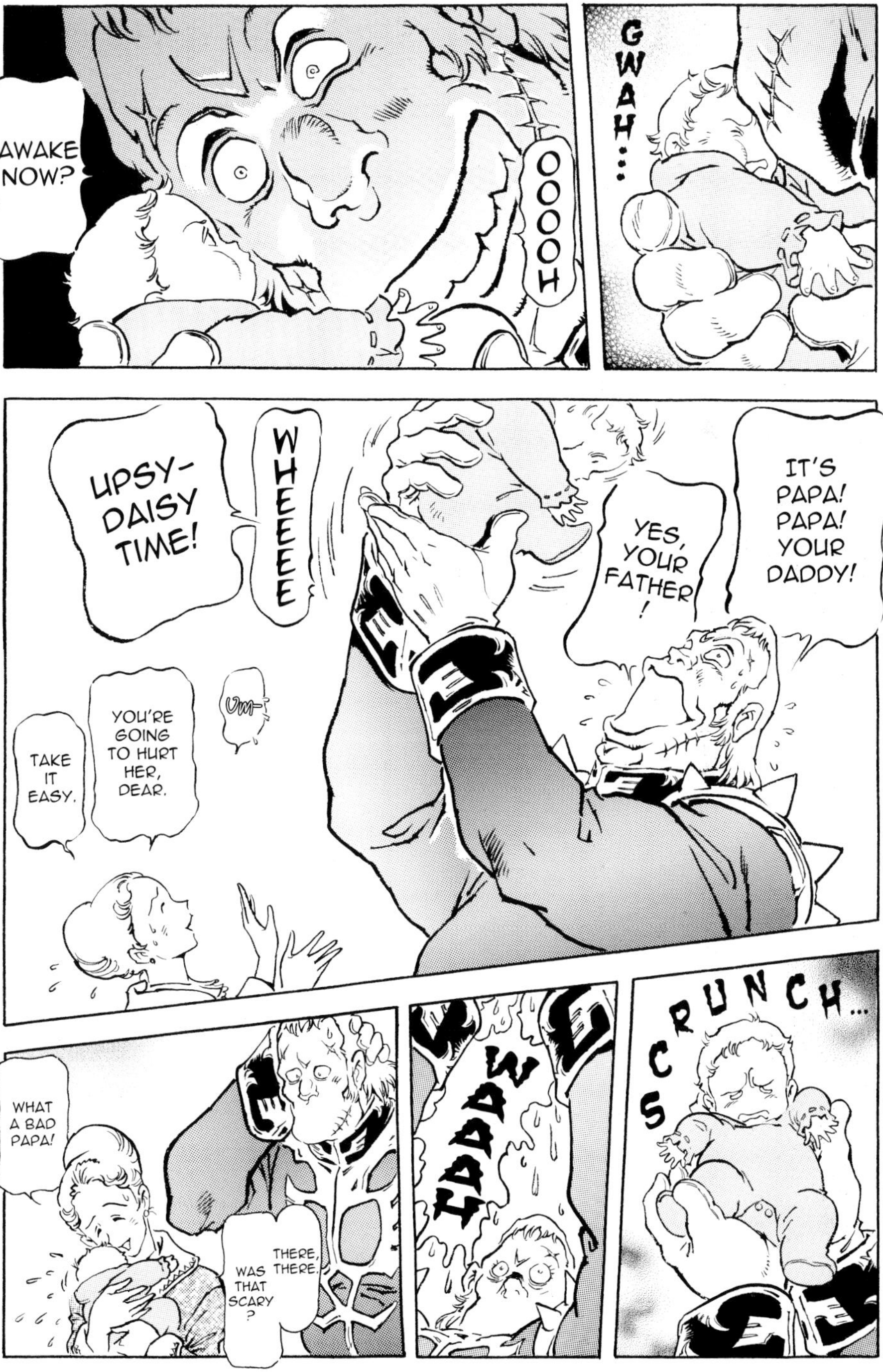
GWAH...
OOOOH
AWAKE NOW?
IT'S PAPA! PAPA! YOUR DADDY!
YES, YOUR FATHER!
WHEEEEE
UPSY-DAISY TIME!
UM-
YOU'RE GOING TO HURT HER, DEAR.
TAKE IT EASY.
SCRUNCH...
WAAAAH
THERE, THERE.
WAS THAT SCARY?
WHAT A BAD PAPA!

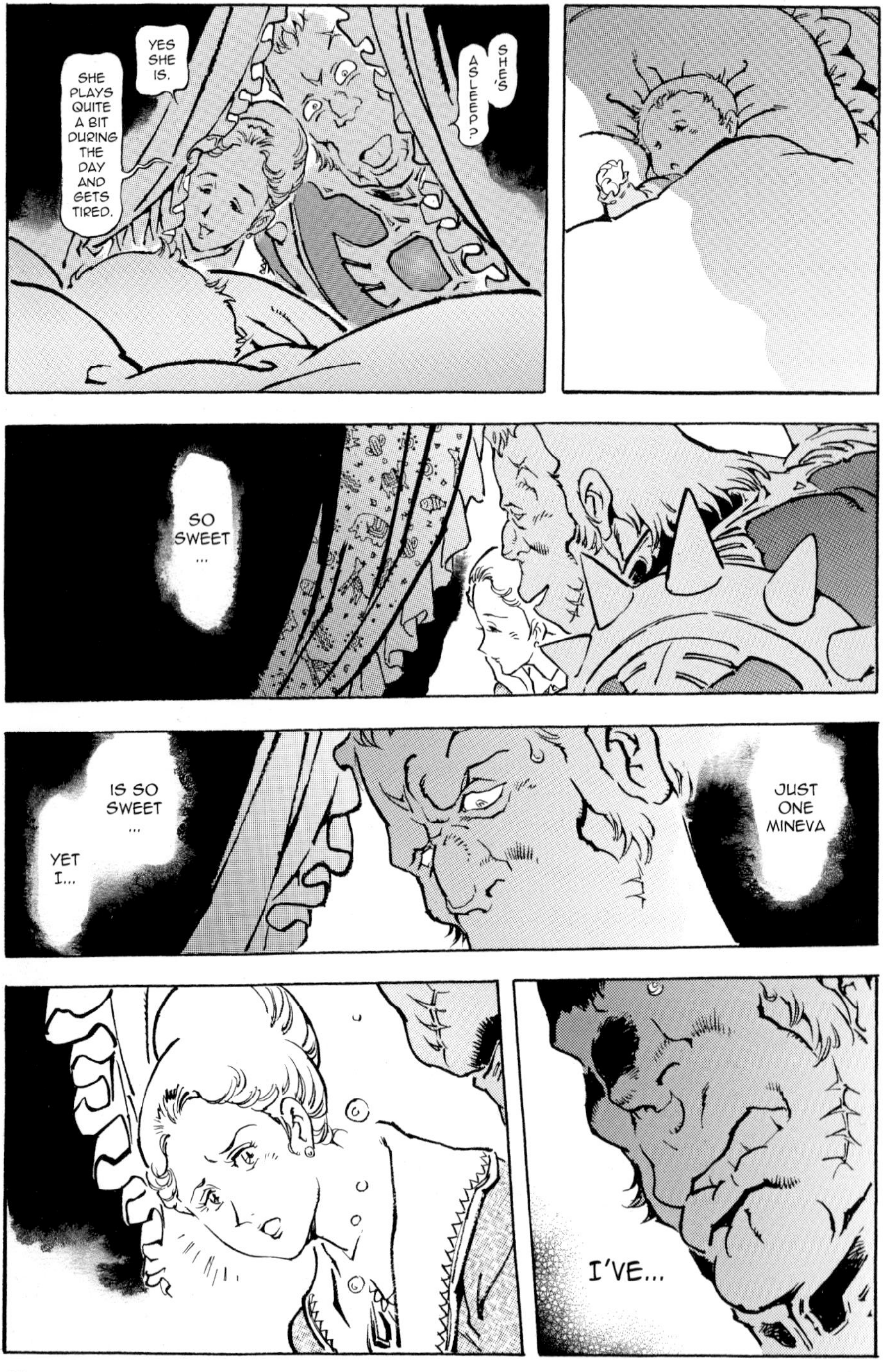
SHE'S ASLEEP?
YES SHE IS.
SHE PLAYS QUITE A BIT DURING THE DAY AND GETS TIRED.
SO SWEET ...
JUST ONE MINEVA
IS SO SWEET ...
YET I...
I'VE...

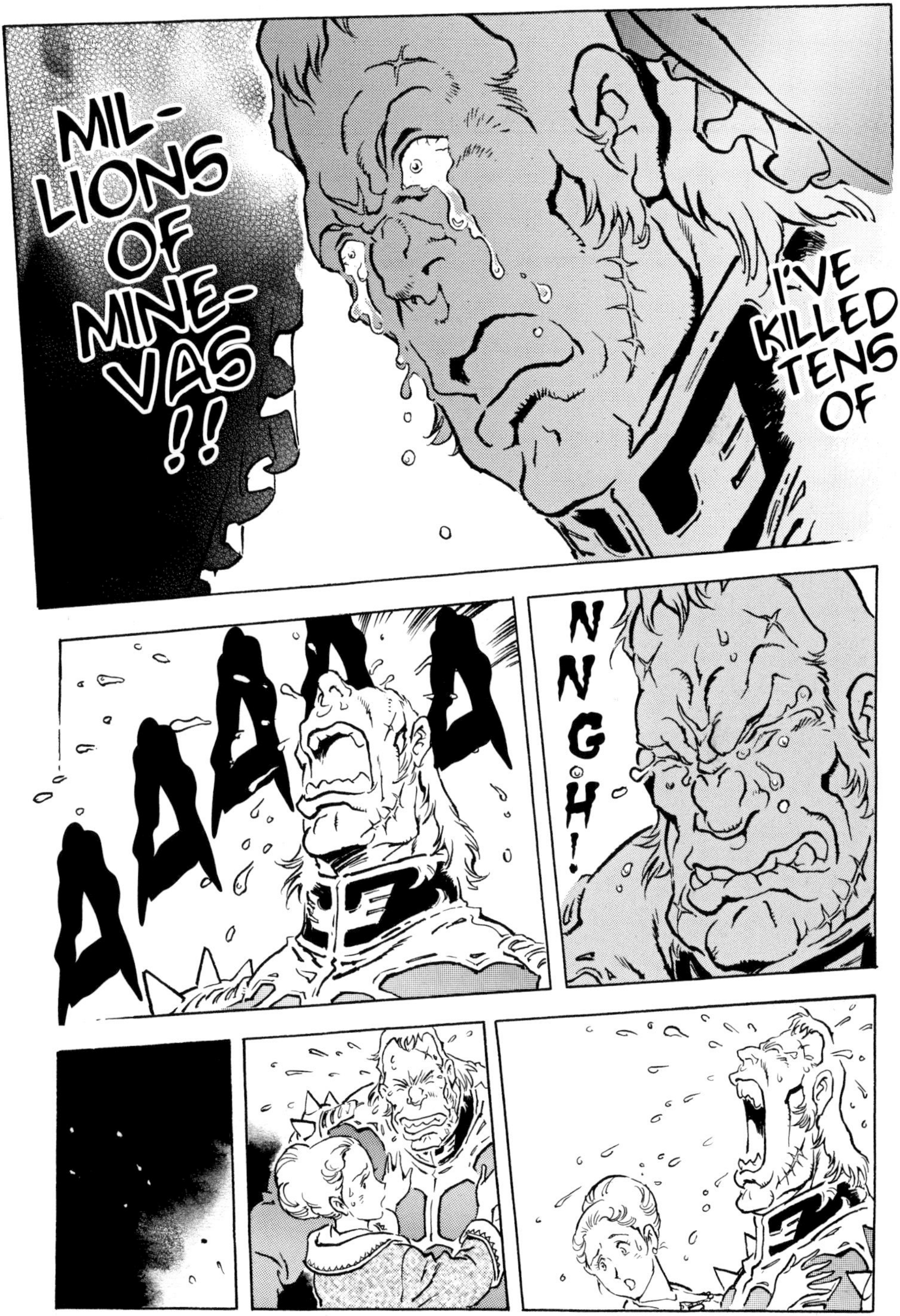
I'VE KILLED TENS OF
MIL-LIONS OF MINE-VAS!!
NNGH!
AAAAAAAA

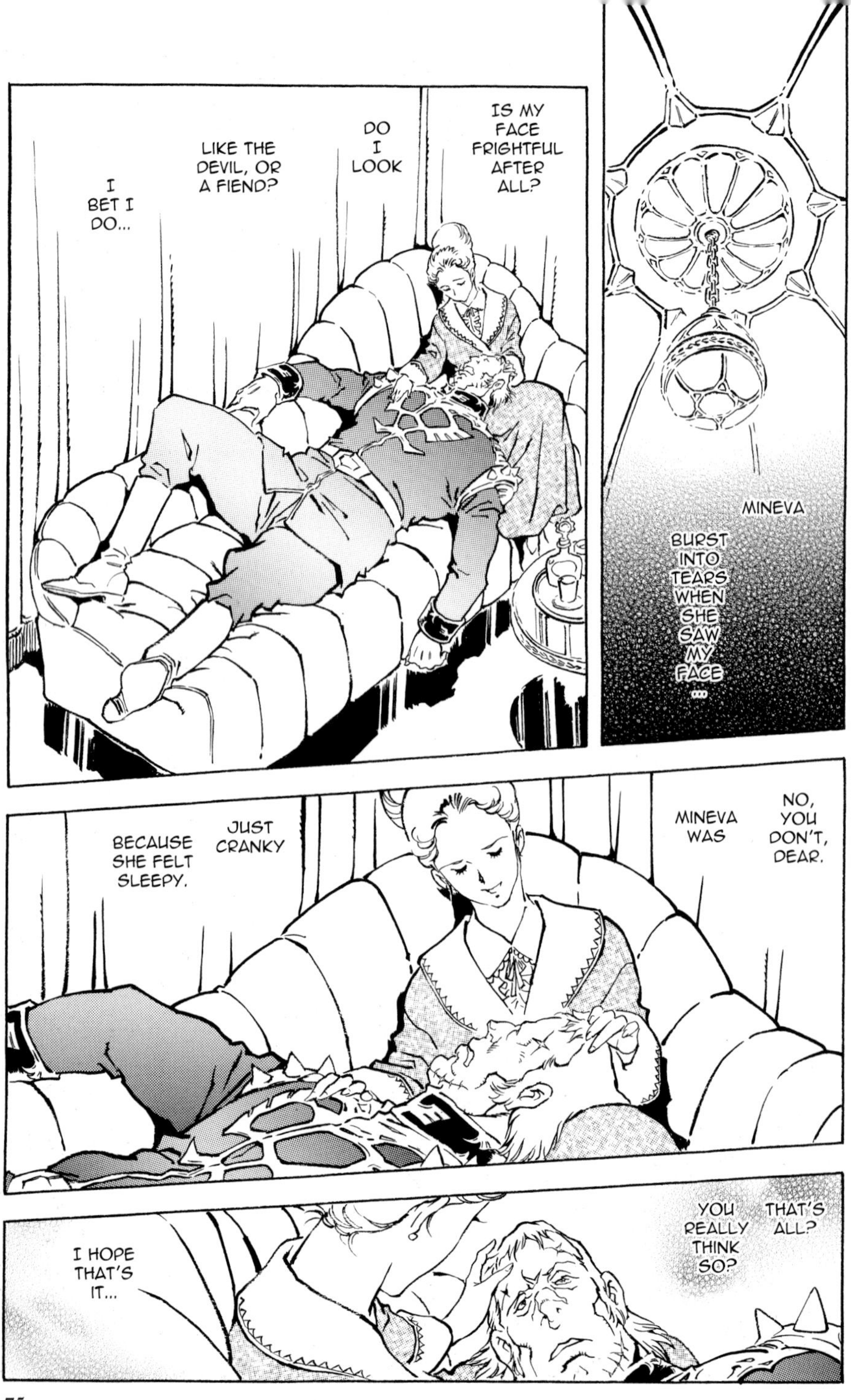
MINEVA
BURST INTO TEARS WHEN SHE SAW MY FACE...
IS MY FACE FRIGHTFUL AFTER ALL?
DO I LOOK
LIKE THE DEVIL, OR A FIEND?
I BET I DO...
NO, YOU DON'T, DEAR.
MINEVA WAS
JUST CRANKY
BECAUSE SHE FELT SLEEPY.
THAT'S ALL?
YOU REALLY THINK SO?
I HOPE THAT'S IT...

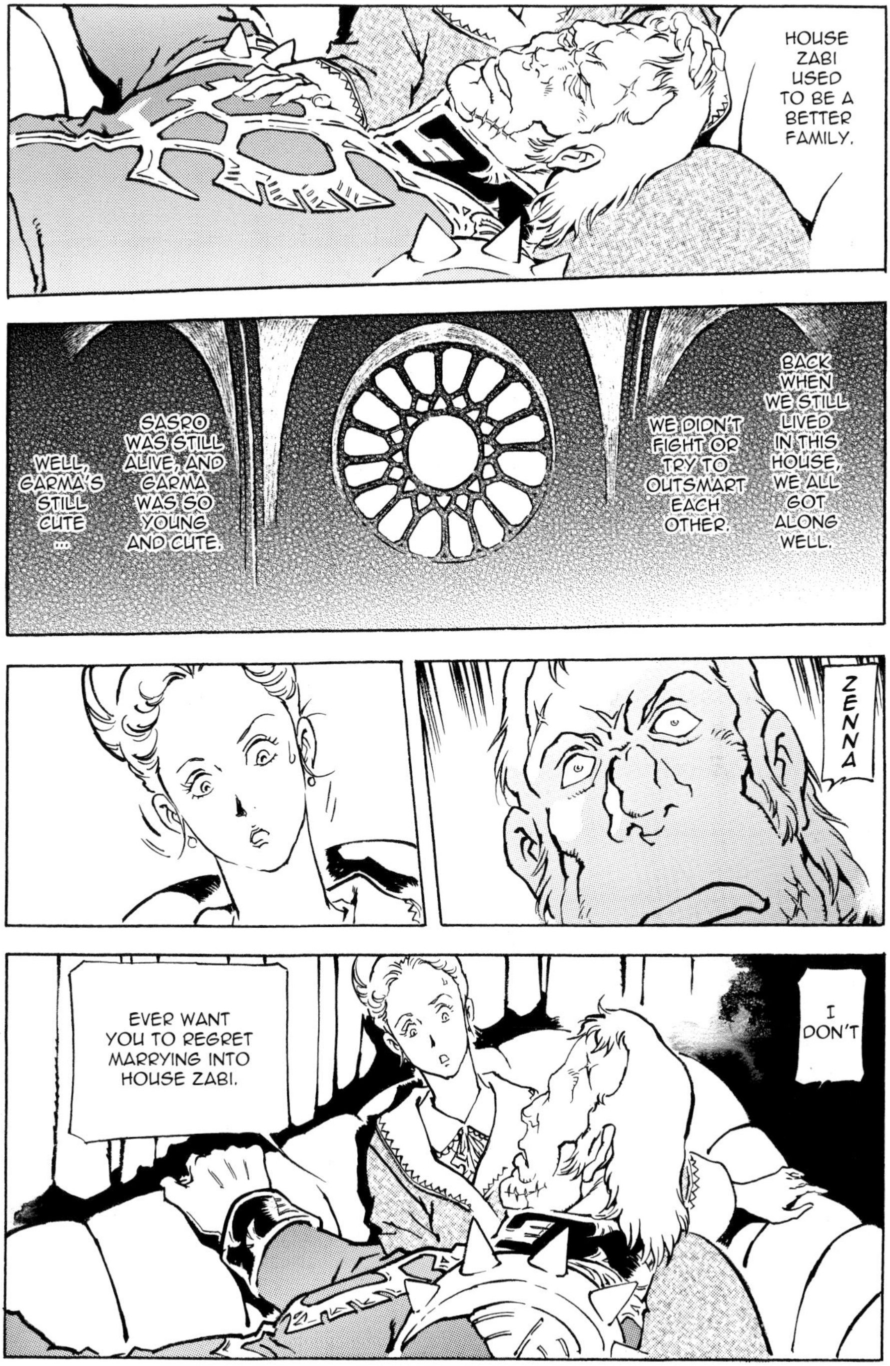
HOUSE ZABI USED TO BE A BETTER FAMILY.
BACK WHEN WE STILL LIVED IN THIS HOUSE, WE ALL GOT ALONG WELL.
WE DIDN'T FIGHT OR TRY TO OUTSMART EACH OTHER.
SASRO WAS STILL ALIVE, AND GARMA WAS SO YOUNG AND CUTE.
WELL, GARMA'S STILL CUTE ...
ZENNA
I DON'T
EVER WANT YOU TO REGRET MARRYING INTO HOUSE ZABI.

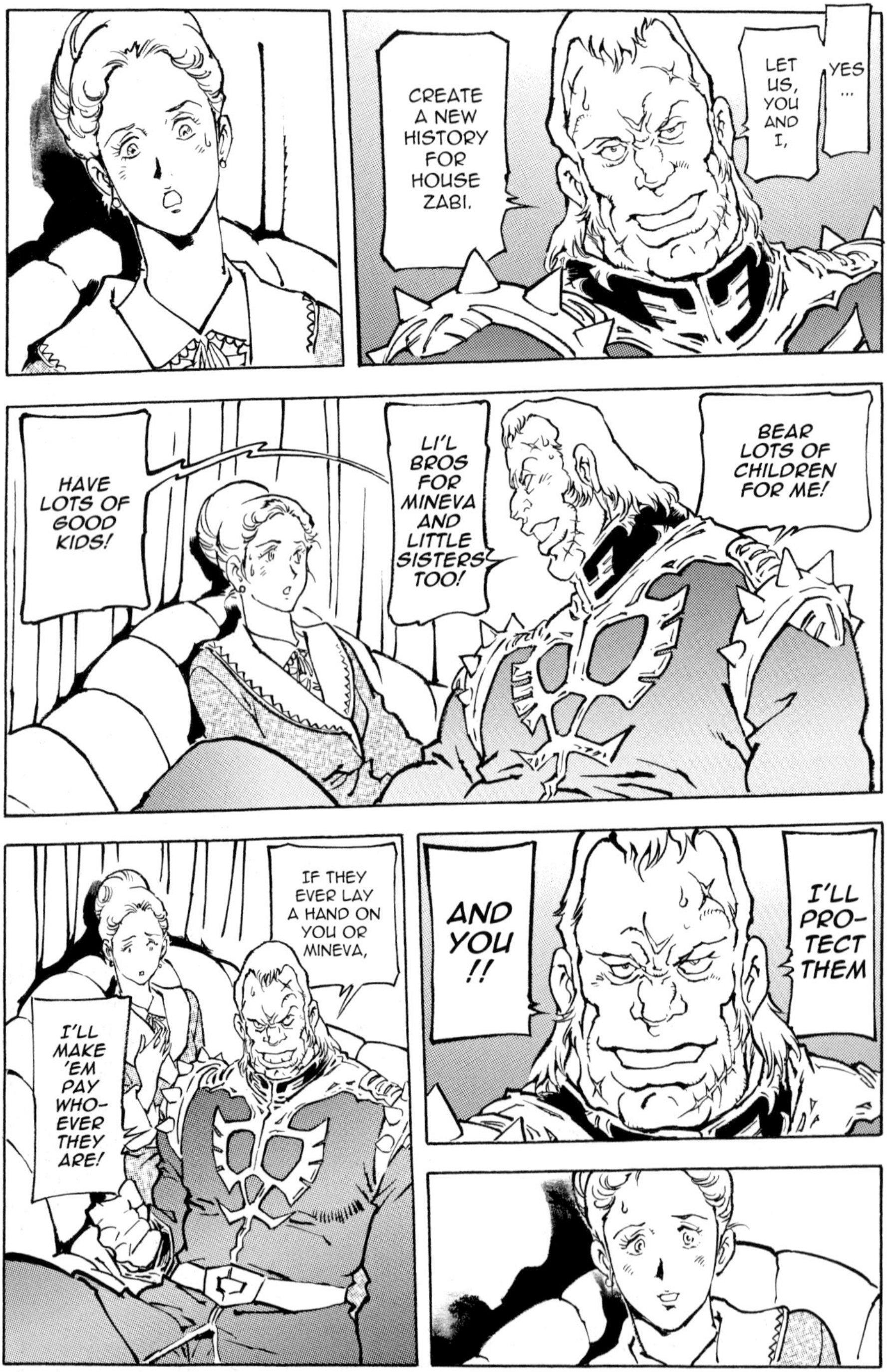
YES ...
LET US, YOU AND I,
CREATE A NEW HISTORY FOR HOUSE ZABI.
BEAR LOTS OF CHILDREN FOR ME!
LI'L BROS FOR MINEVA AND LITTLE SISTERS TOO!
HAVE LOTS OF GOOD KIDS!
I'LL PROTECT THEM
AND YOU !!
IF THEY EVER LAY A HAND ON YOU OR MINEVA,
I'LL MAKE 'EM PAY WHO-EVER THEY ARE!

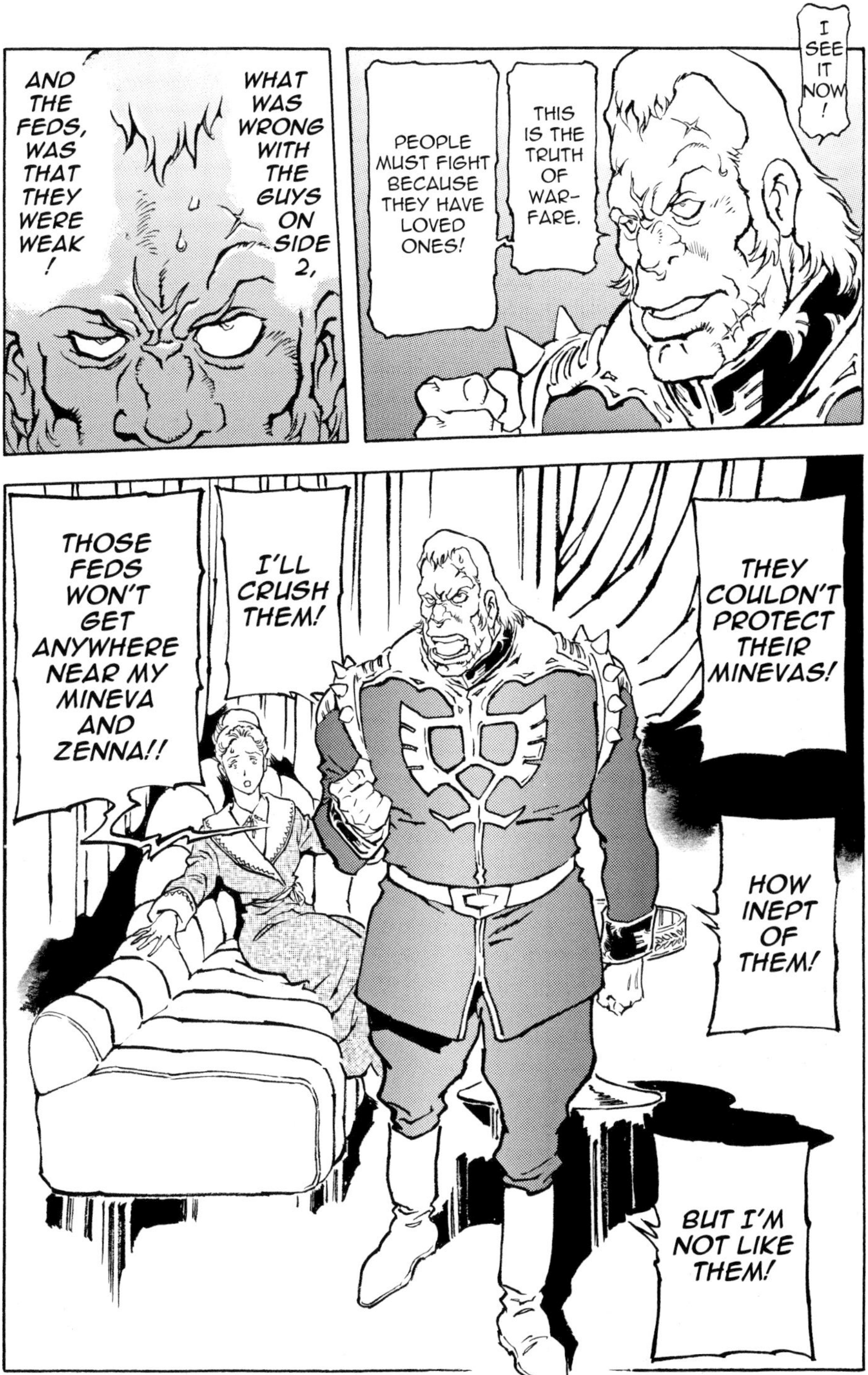
I SEE IT NOW!
THIS IS THE TRUTH OF WARFARE.
PEOPLE MUST FIGHT BECAUSE THEY HAVE LOVED ONES!
WHAT WAS WRONG WITH THE GUYS ON SIDE 2,
AND THE FEDS, WAS THAT THEY WERE WEAK!
THEY COULDN'T PROTECT THEIR MINEVAS!
HOW INEPT OF THEM!
BUT I'M NOT LIKE THEM!
I'LL CRUSH THEM!
THOSE FEDS WON'T GET ANYWHERE NEAR MY MINEVA AND ZENNA!!

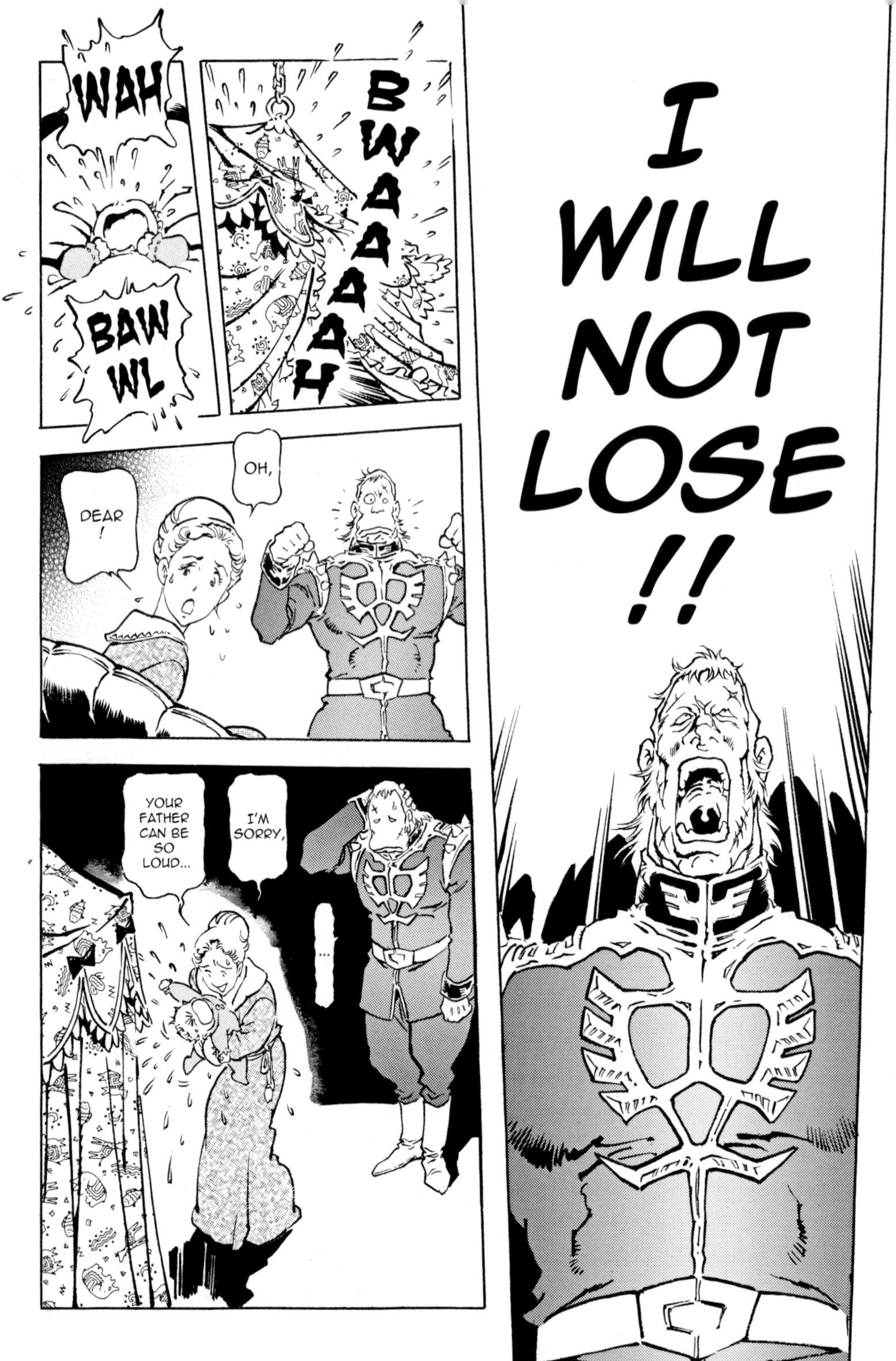
I WILL NOT LOSE!!
BWAAAAAH
WAH
BAWWL
OH,
DEAR!
I'M SORRY,
YOUR FATHER CAN BE SO LOUD...
...

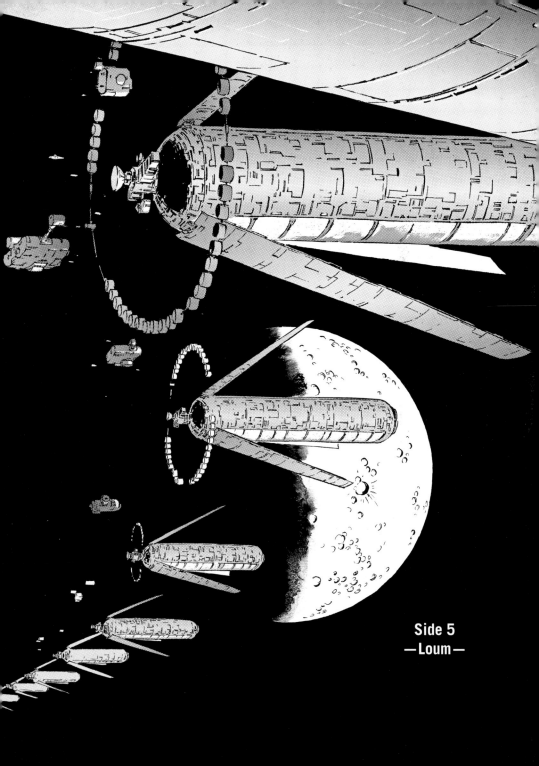

Side 5
—Loum—

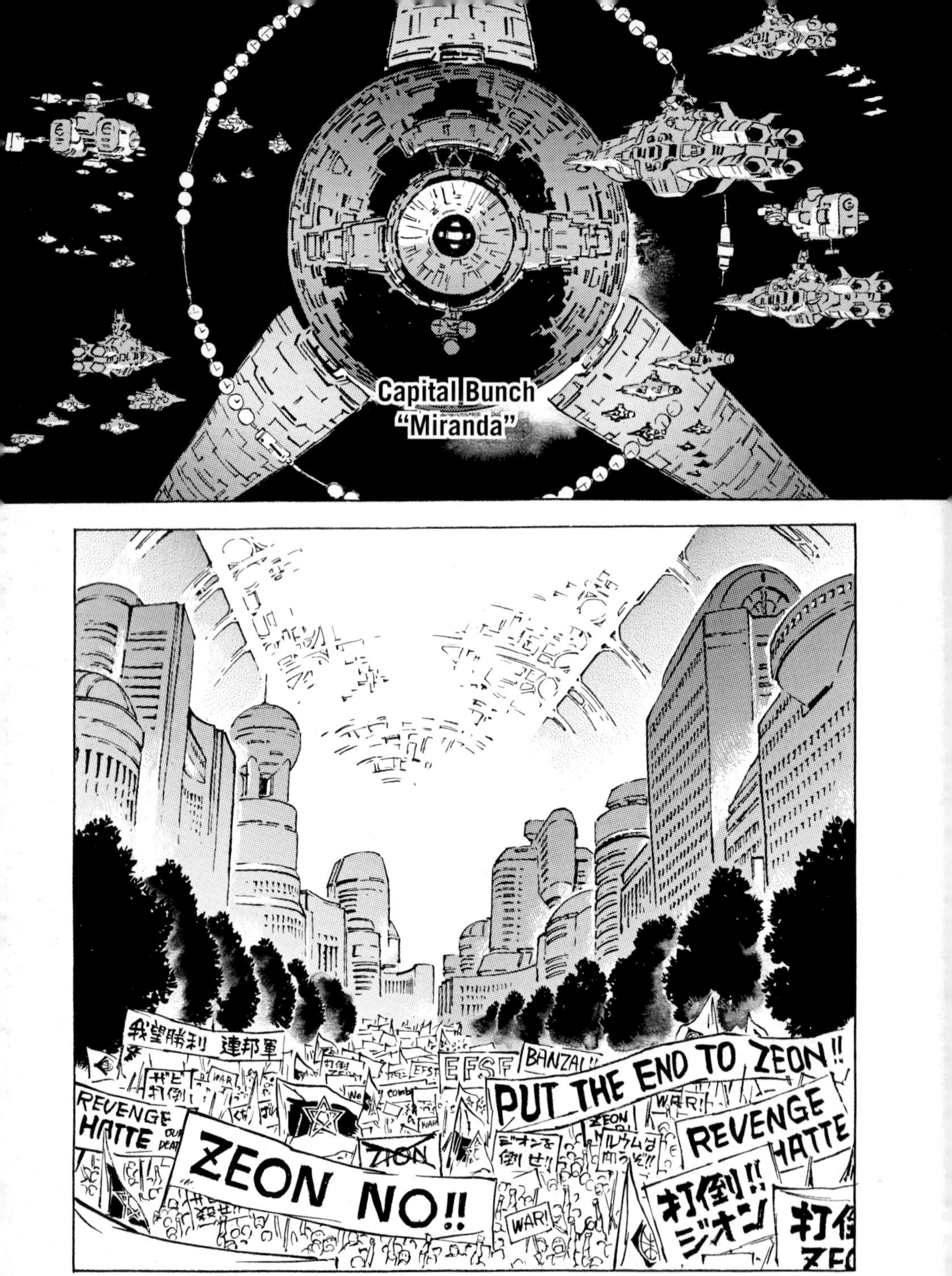
Capital Bunch
“Miranda”
PUT THE END TO ZEON!!
REVENGE
HATTE
打倒!!
ジオン
WAR!
BANZAI!!
EFSF
ジオンを
倒せ!!
我望勝利 連邦軍
REVENGE
HATTE
ZEON NO!!
WAR!

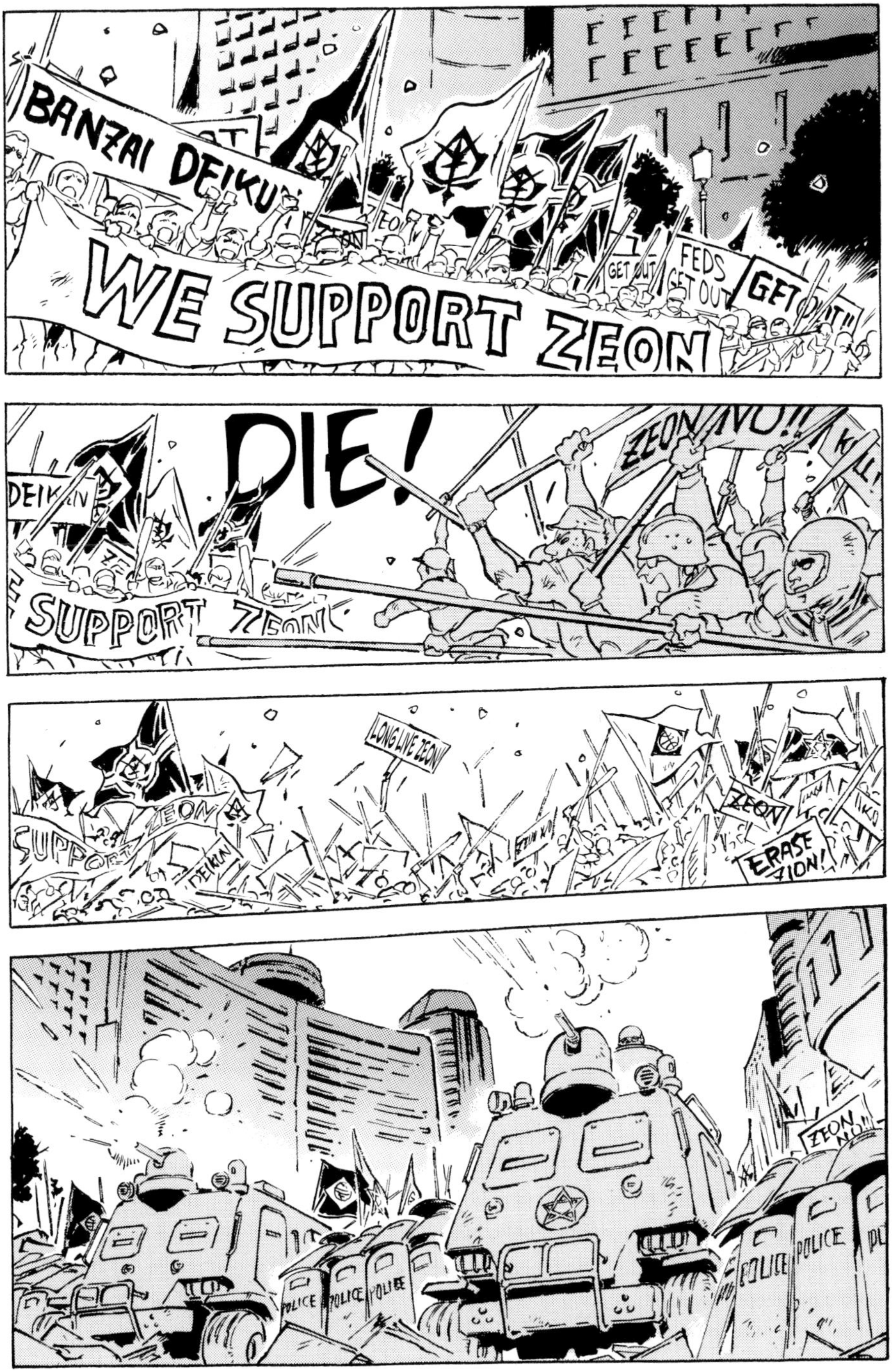
GET OUT!!
FEDS GET OUT
GET OUT
BANZAI DEIKU
WE SUPPORT ZEON
ZEON NO!!
DIE!
DEIKUN
SUPPORT ZEON
ERASE ZEON!
ZEON
LONG LIVE ZEON
SUPPORT ZEON
DEIKUN
ZEON NO
POLICE
POLICE
POLICE
POLICE
POLICE

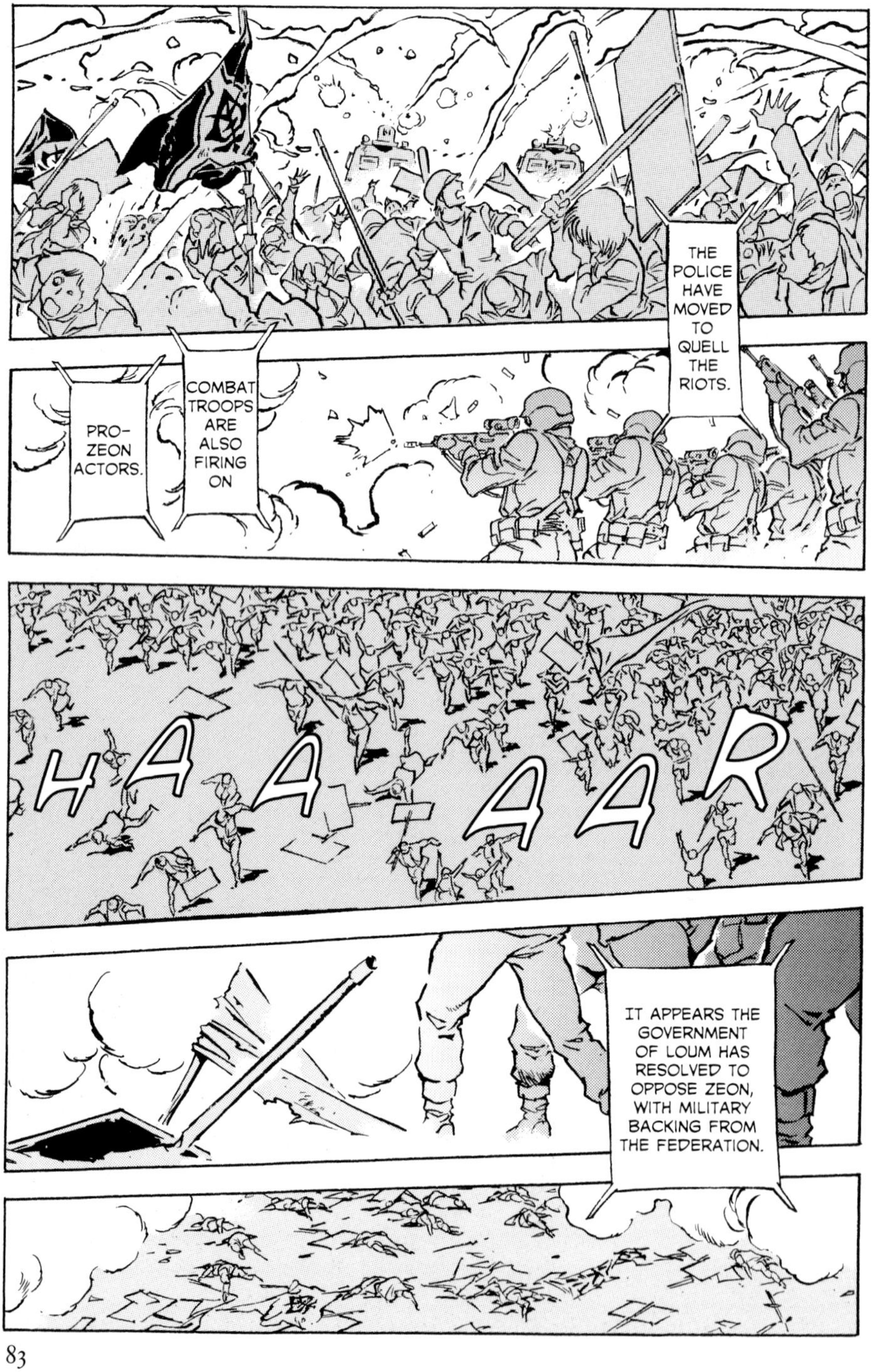
THE POLICE HAVE MOVED TO QUELL THE RIOTS.
COMBAT TROOPS ARE ALSO FIRING ON
PRO-ZEON ACTORS.
HAAA-AAR
IT APPEARS THE GOVERNMENT OF LOUM HAS RESOLVED TO OPPOSE ZEON, WITH MILITARY BACKING FROM THE FEDERATION.

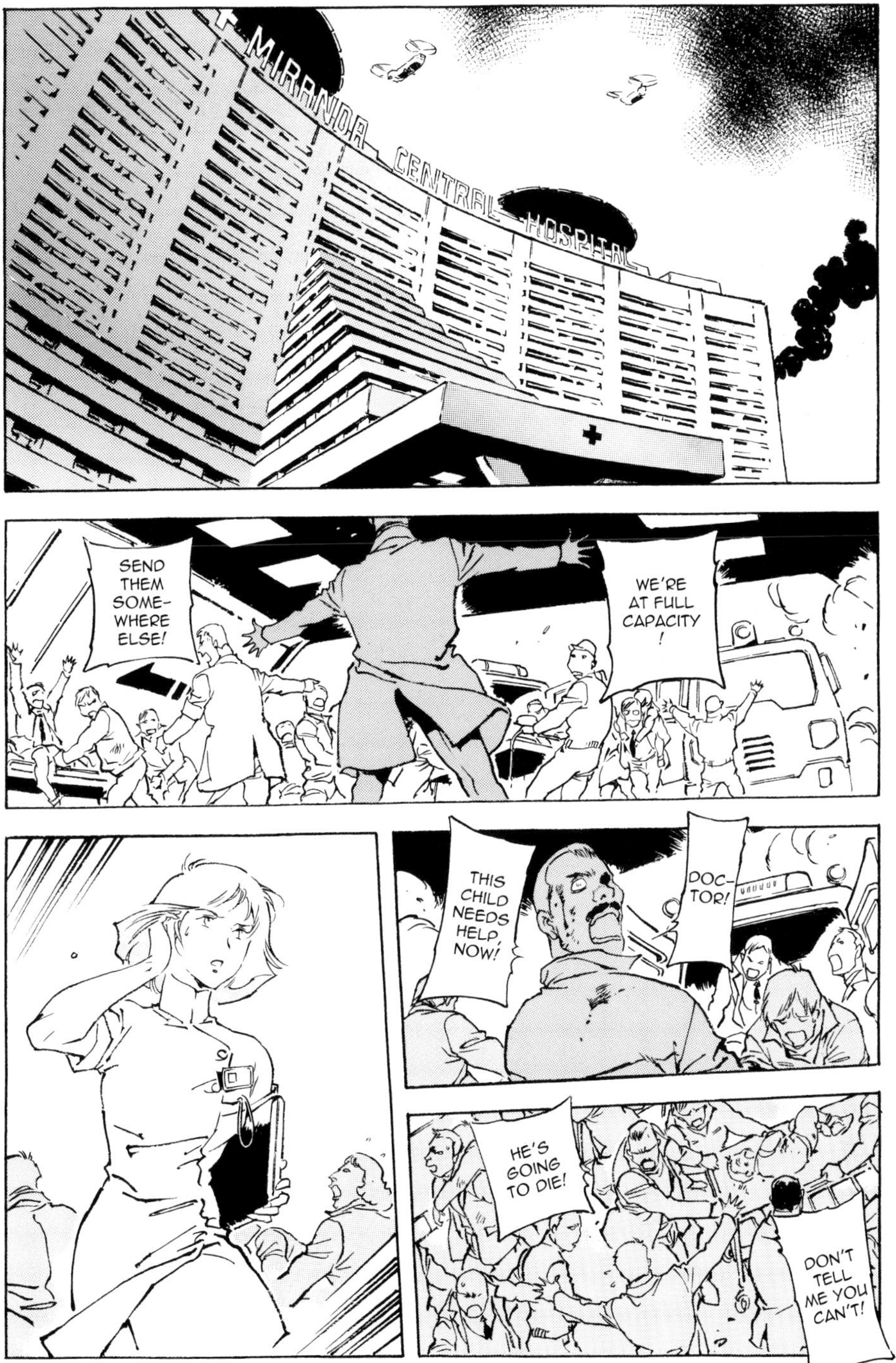
MIRANDA CENTRAL HOSPITAL
WE'RE AT FULL CAPACITY!
SEND THEM SOME-WHERE ELSE!
DOC-TOR!
THIS CHILD NEEDS HELP NOW!
HE'S GOING TO DIE!
DON'T TELL ME YOU CAN'T!

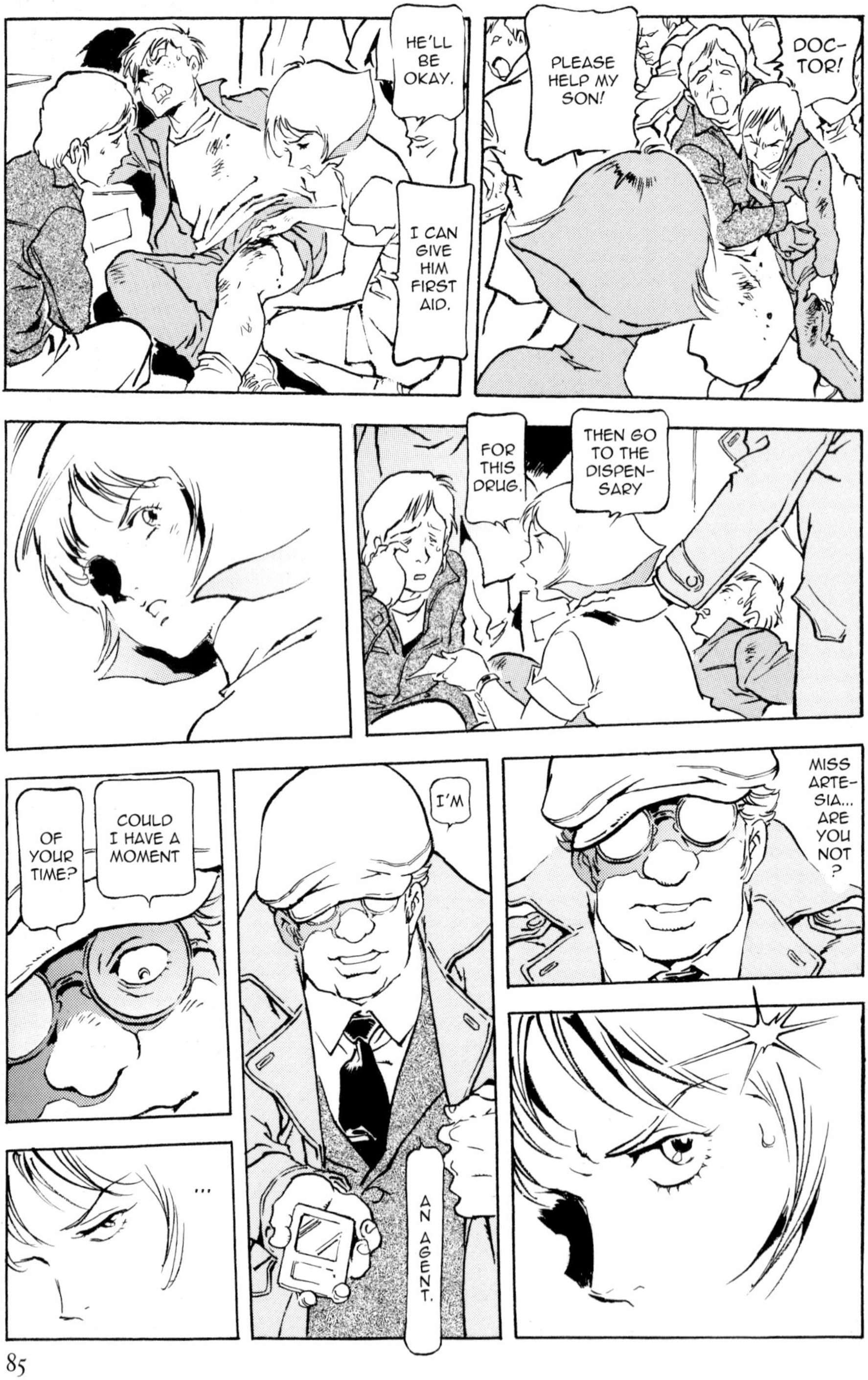
DOC-TOR!
PLEASE HELP MY SON!
HE'LL BE OKAY.
I CAN GIVE HIM FIRST AID.
THEN GO TO THE DISPEN-SARY
FOR THIS DRUG.
MISS ARTE-SIA... ARE YOU NOT ?
I'M
AN AGENT.
COULD I HAVE A MOMENT
OF YOUR TIME?
...

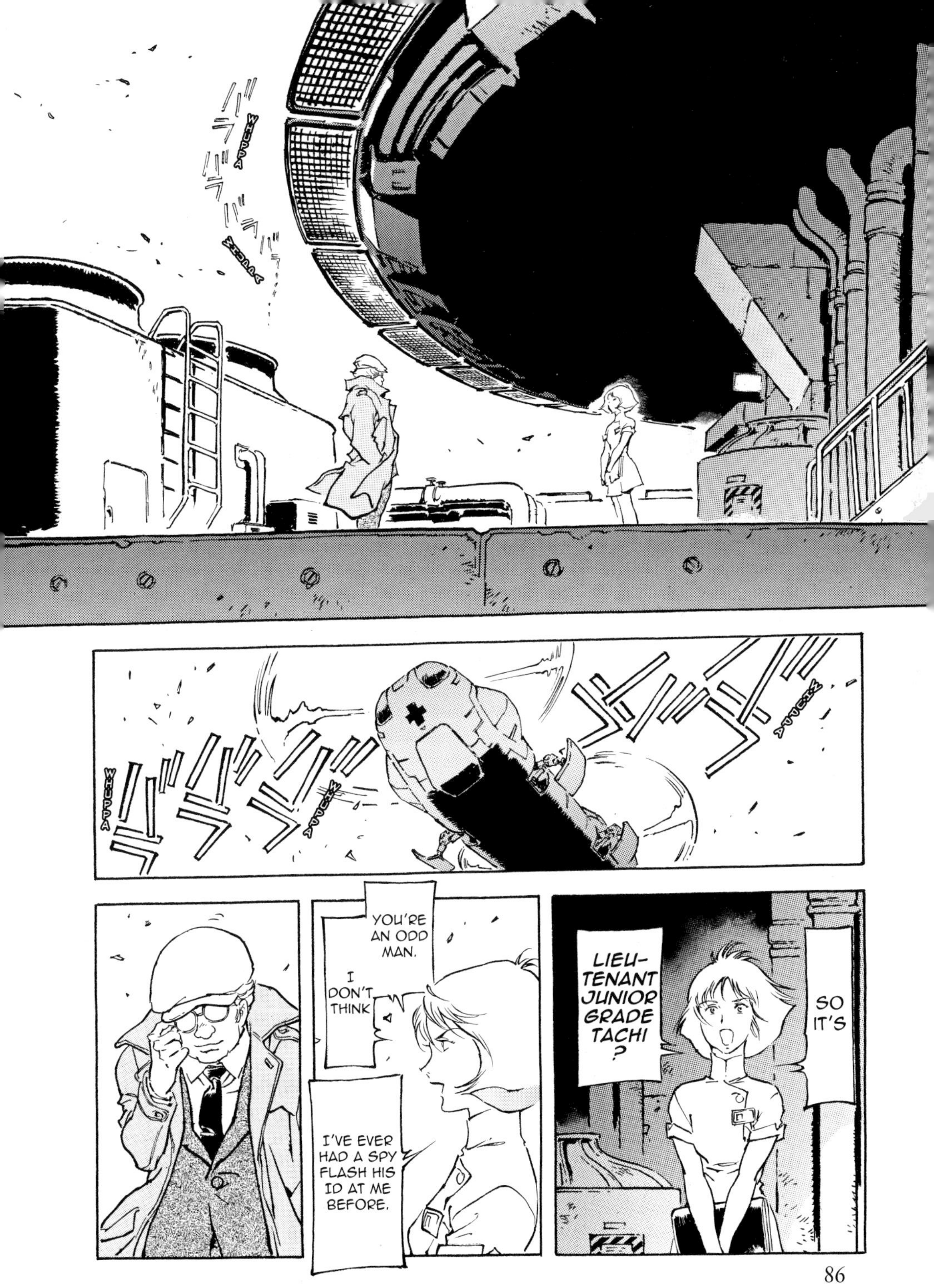
WHUPPA
WHUPPA
WHUPPA
WHUPPA
WHUPPA
SO IT'S
LIEU-TENANT JUNIOR GRADE TACHI?
YOU'RE AN ODD MAN.
I DON'T THINK
I'VE EVER HAD A SPY FLASH HIS ID AT ME BEFORE.

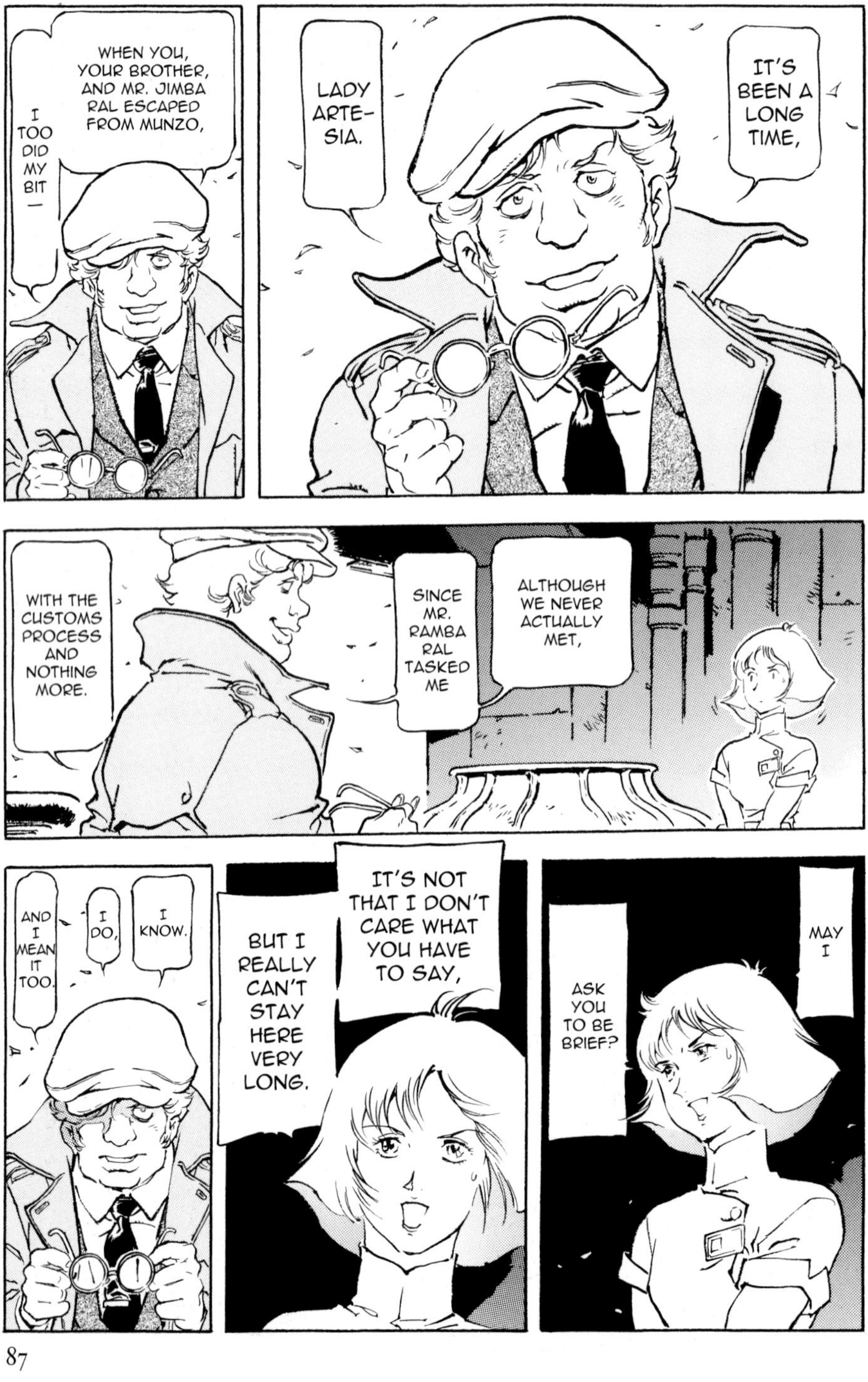
IT'S BEEN A LONG TIME,
LADY ARTESIA.
WHEN YOU, YOUR BROTHER, AND MR. JIMBA RAL ESCAPED FROM MUNZO,
I TOO DID MY BIT —
ALTHOUGH WE NEVER ACTUALLY MET,
SINCE MR. RAMBA RAL TASKED ME
WITH THE CUSTOMS PROCESS AND NOTHING MORE.
MAY I
ASK YOU TO BE BRIEF?
IT'S NOT THAT I DON'T CARE WHAT YOU HAVE TO SAY,
BUT I REALLY CAN'T STAY HERE VERY LONG.
I KNOW.
I DO,
AND I MEAN IT TOO.

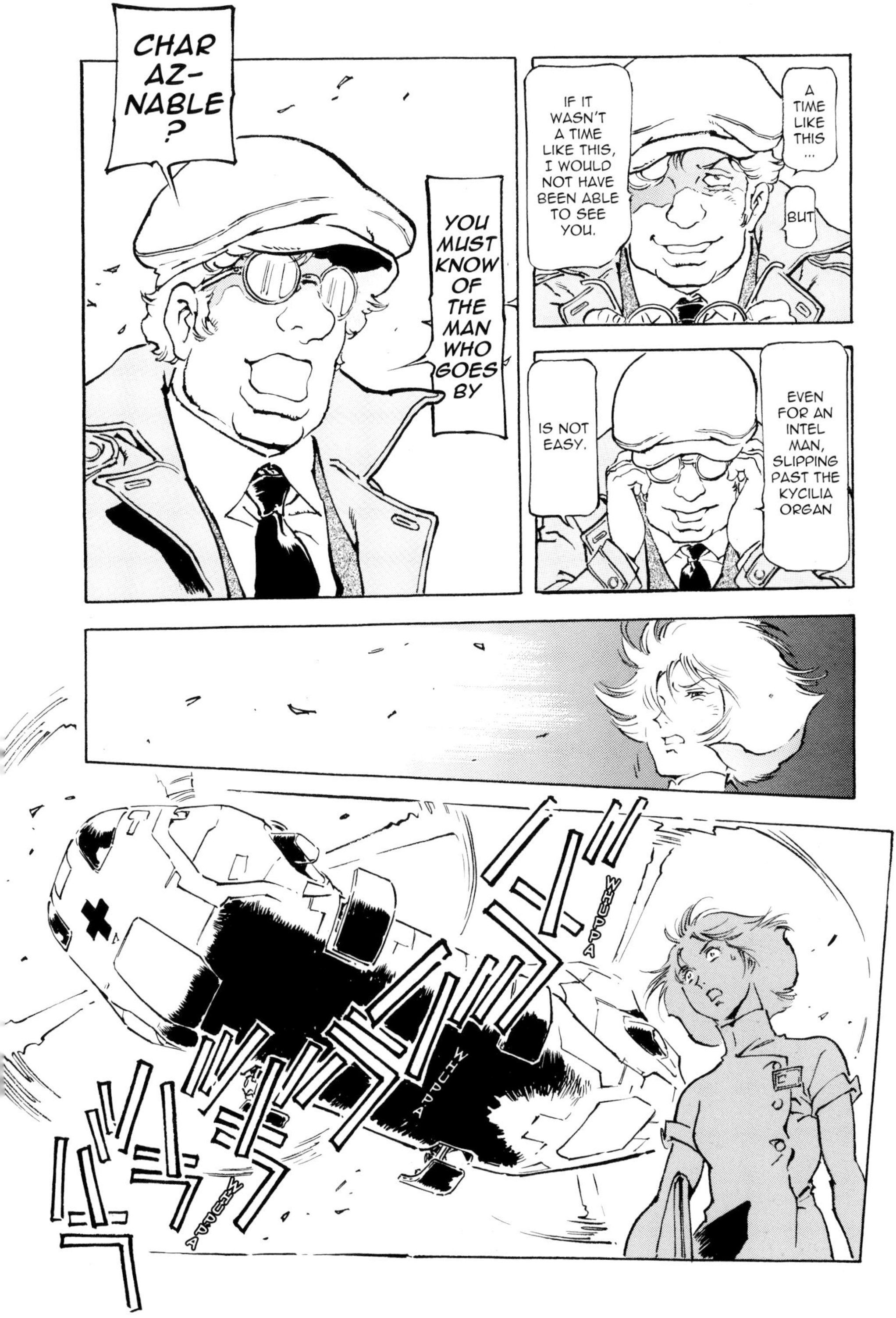
A TIME LIKE THIS ...
BUT
IF IT WASN'T A TIME LIKE THIS, I WOULD NOT HAVE BEEN ABLE TO SEE YOU.
EVEN FOR AN INTEL MAN, SLIPPING PAST THE KYCILIA ORGAN
IS NOT EASY.
YOU MUST KNOW OF THE MAN WHO GOES BY
CHAR AZ-NABLE?
WHUPPA
WHUPPA
WHUPPA

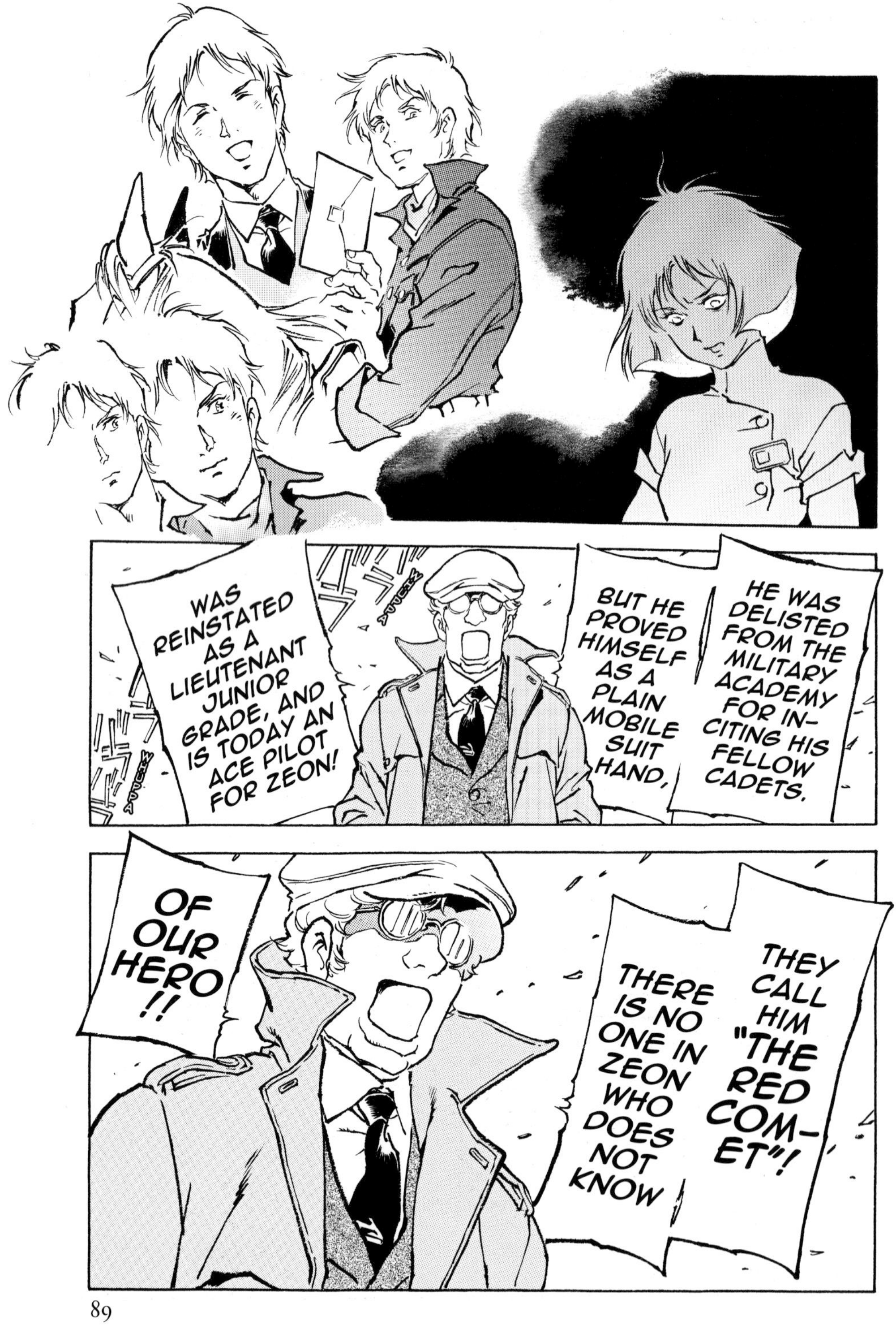
HE WAS DELISTED FROM THE MILITARY ACADEMY FOR IN-CITING HIS FELLOW CADETS.
BUT HE PROVED HIMSELF AS A PLAIN MOBILE SUIT HAND,
WAS REINSTATED AS A LIEUTENANT JUNIOR GRADE, AND IS TODAY AN ACE PILOT FOR ZEON!
THEY CALL HIM "THE RED COM-ET"!
THERE IS NO ONE IN ZEON WHO DOES NOT KNOW
OF OUR HERO!!

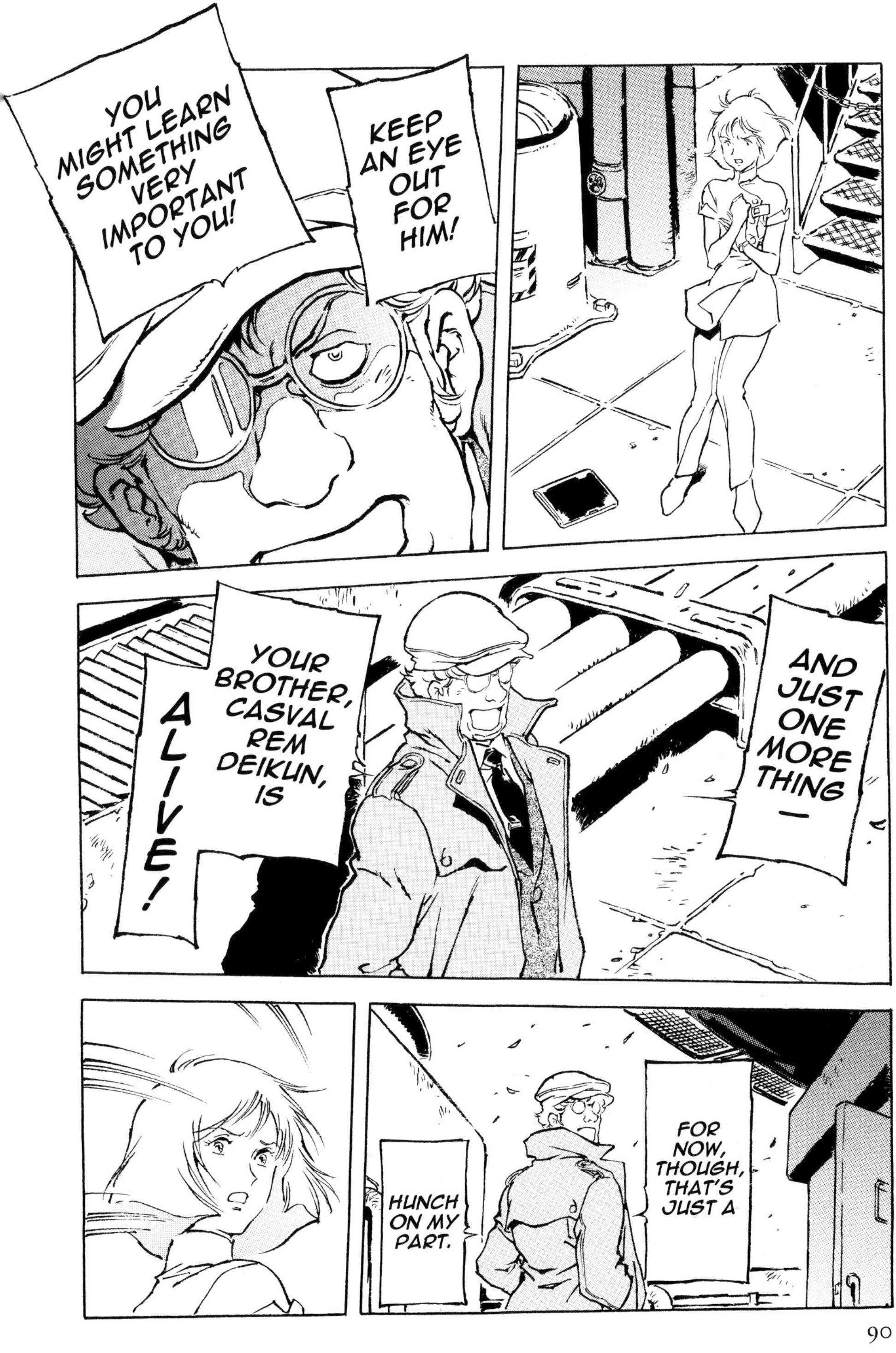
KEEP AN EYE OUT FOR HIM!
YOU MIGHT LEARN SOMETHING VERY IMPORTANT TO YOU!
AND JUST ONE MORE THING —
YOUR BROTHER, CASVAL REM DEIKUN, IS
ALIVE!
FOR NOW, THOUGH, THAT'S JUST A
HUNCH ON MY PART.

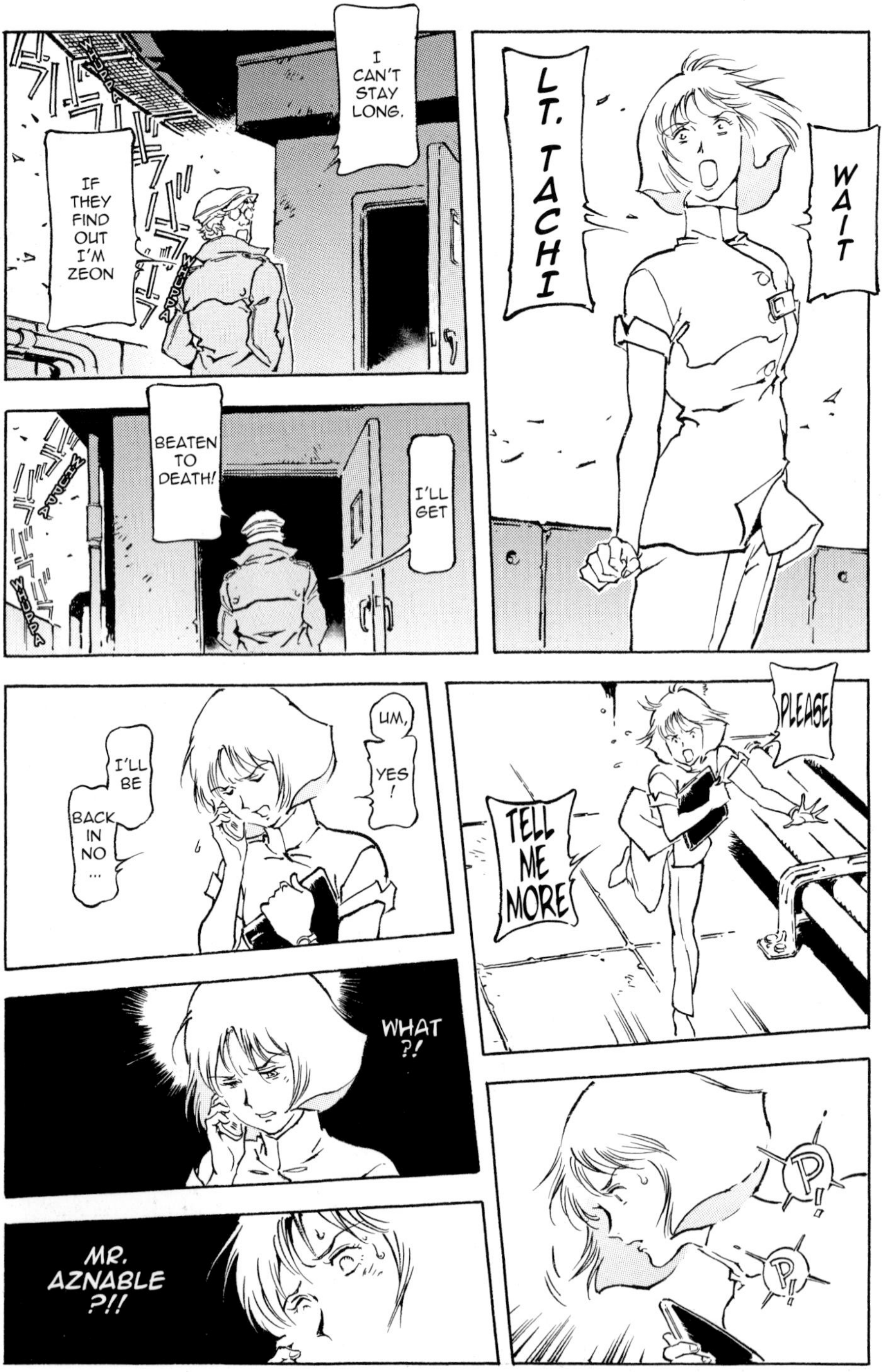
WAIT
LT. TACHI
I CAN'T STAY LONG.
IF THEY FIND OUT I'M ZEON
I'LL GET
BEATEN TO DEATH!
PLEASE
TELL ME MORE
UM, YES!
I'LL BE
BACK IN NO ...
WHAT ?!
MR. AZNABLE ?!!

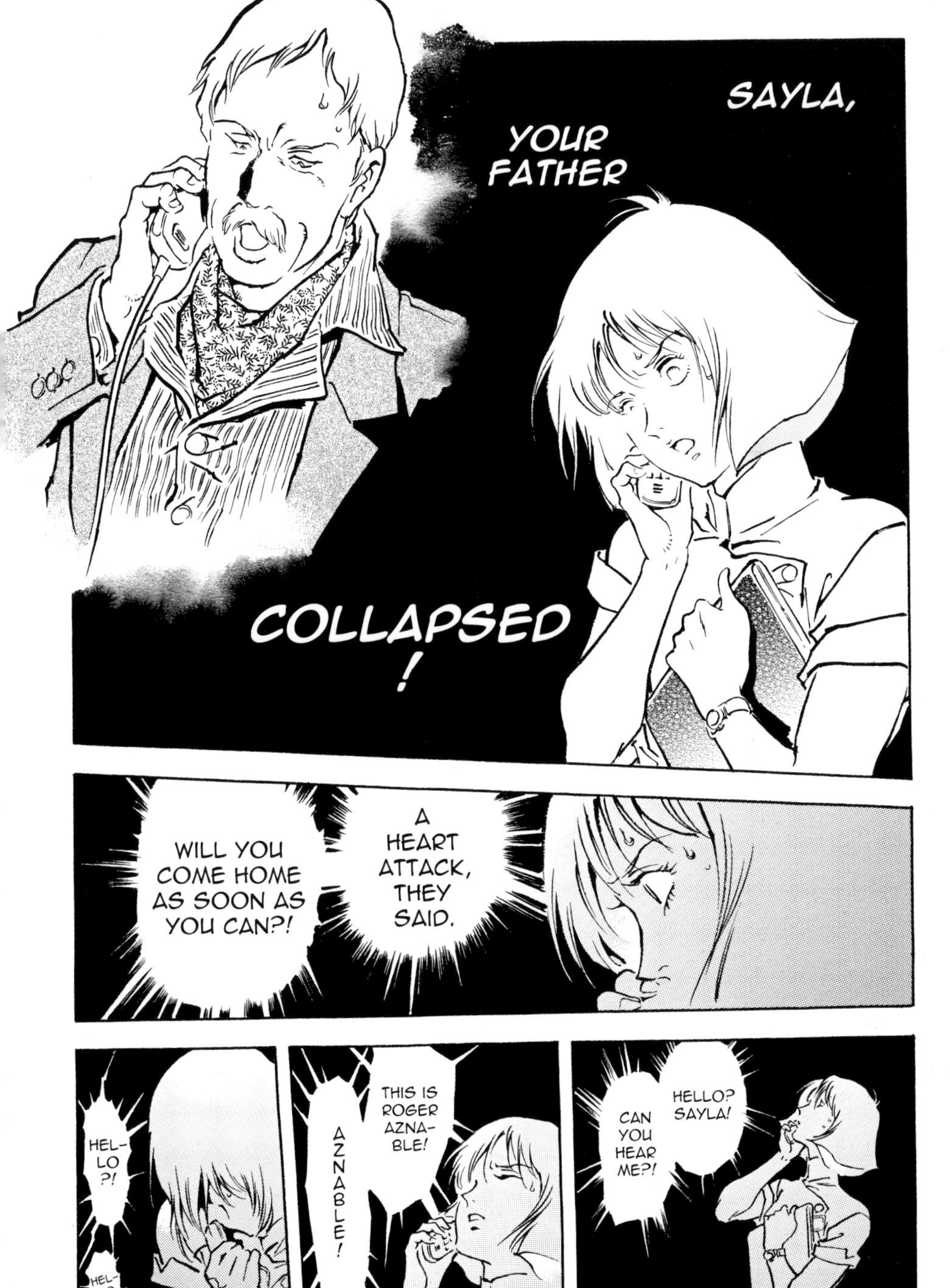
SAYLA,
YOUR FATHER
COLLAPSED !
A HEART ATTACK, THEY SAID.
WILL YOU COME HOME AS SOON AS YOU CAN?!
HELLO? SAYLA!
CAN YOU HEAR ME?!
THIS IS ROGER AZNABLE!
AZNABLE!
HELLO?!
HELLO...

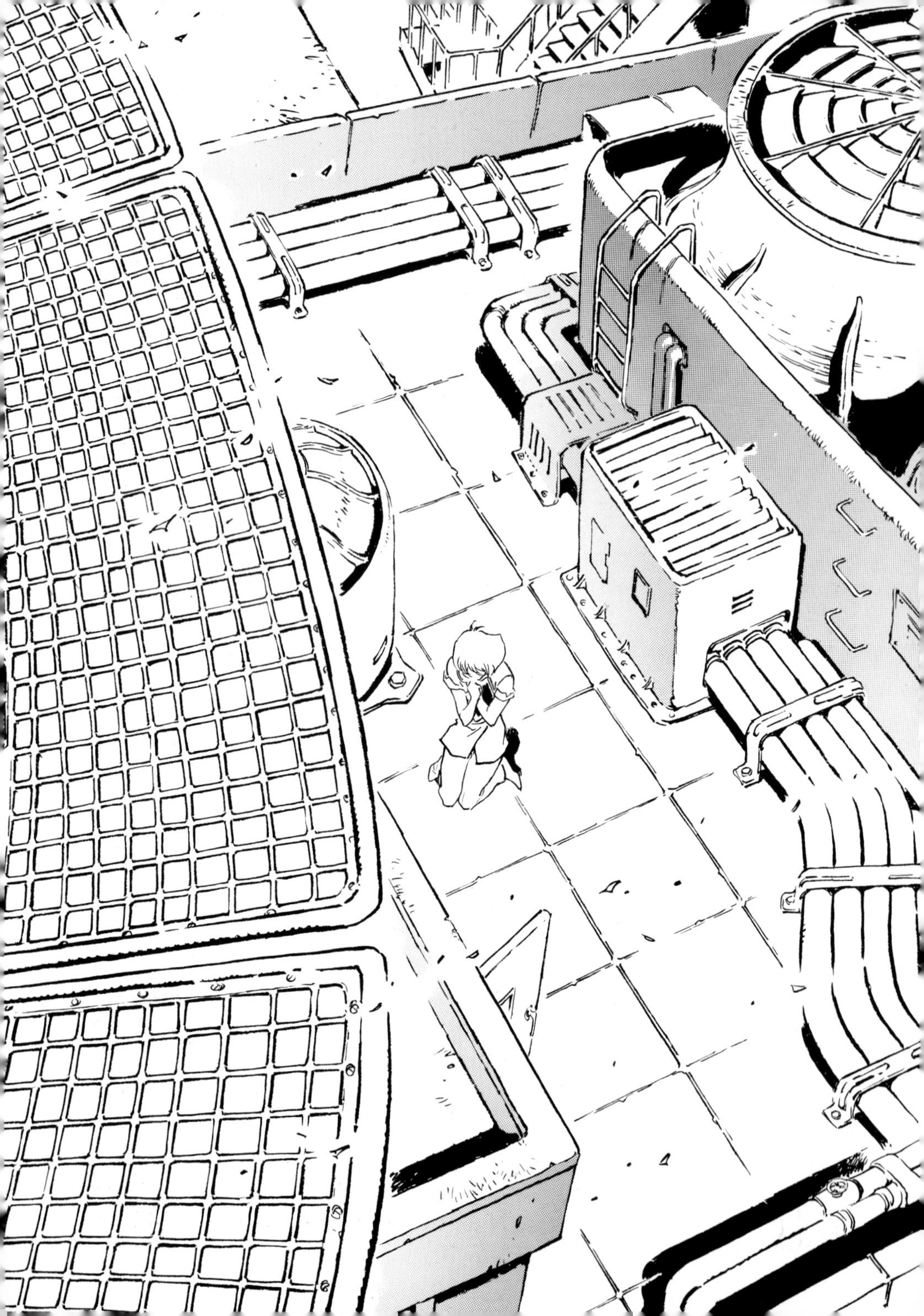

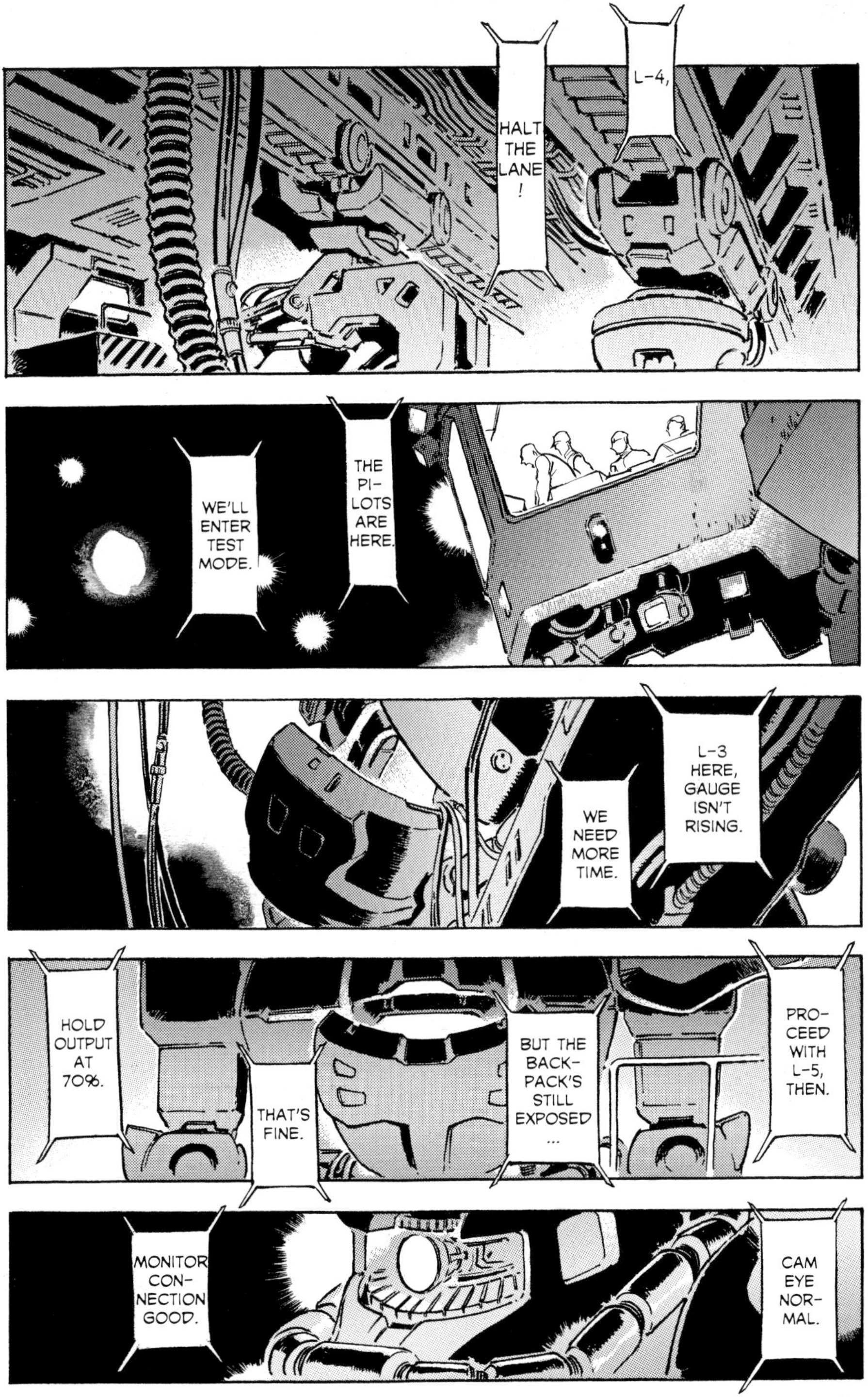
L-4,
HALT THE LANE!
THE PI-LOTS ARE HERE.
WE'LL ENTER TEST MODE.
L-3 HERE, GAUGE ISN'T RISING.
WE NEED MORE TIME.
PRO-CEED WITH L-5, THEN.
BUT THE BACK-PACK'S STILL EXPOSED...
THAT'S FINE.
HOLD OUTPUT AT 70%.
CAM EYE NOR-MAL.
MONITOR CON-NECTION GOOD.

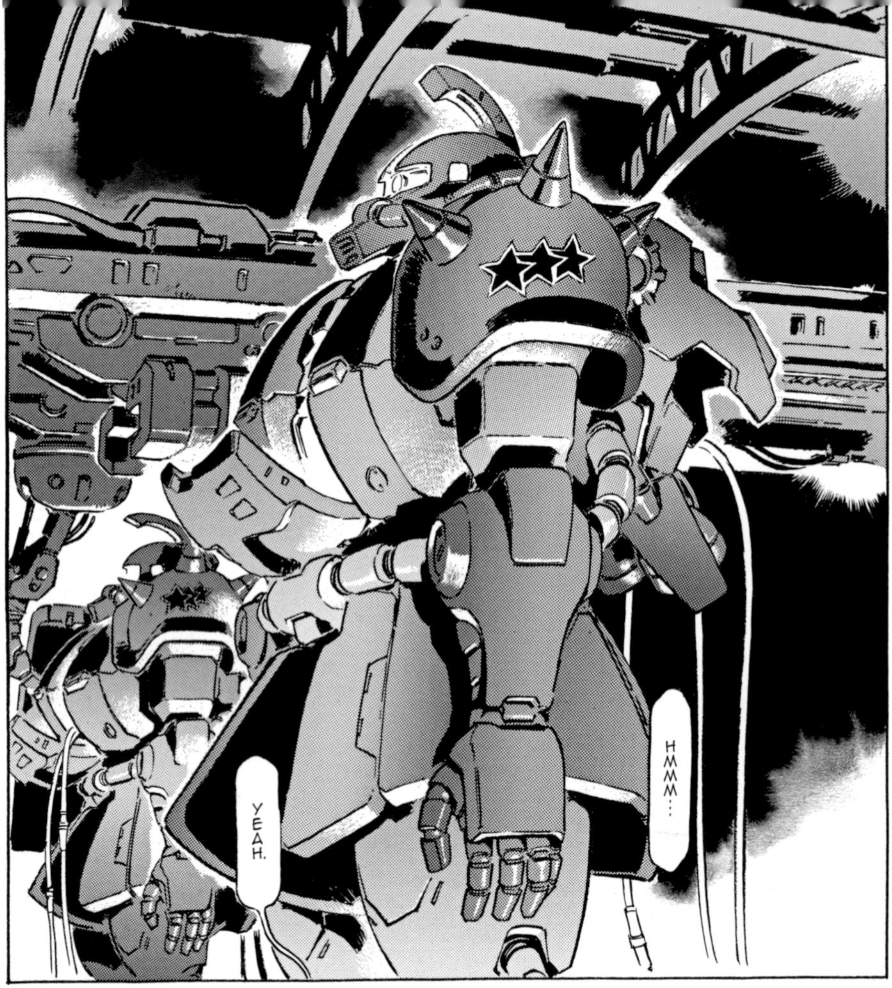
HMMM...
YEAH.
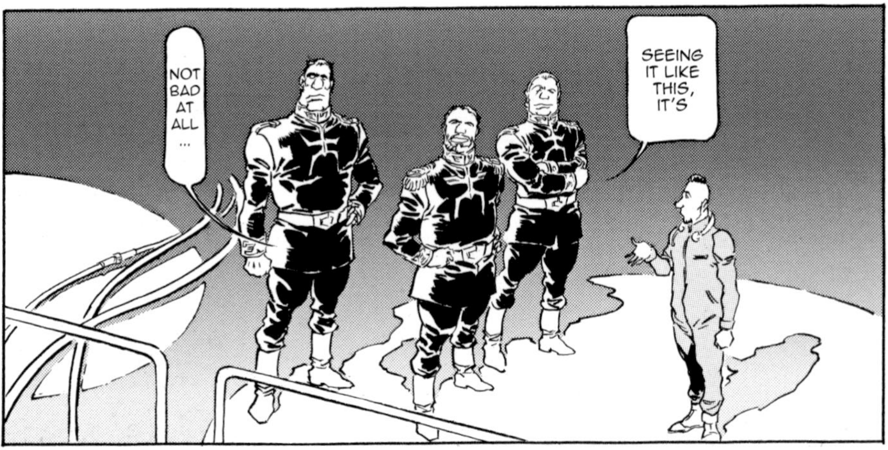
SEEING IT LIKE THIS, IT'S
NOT BAD AT ALL...

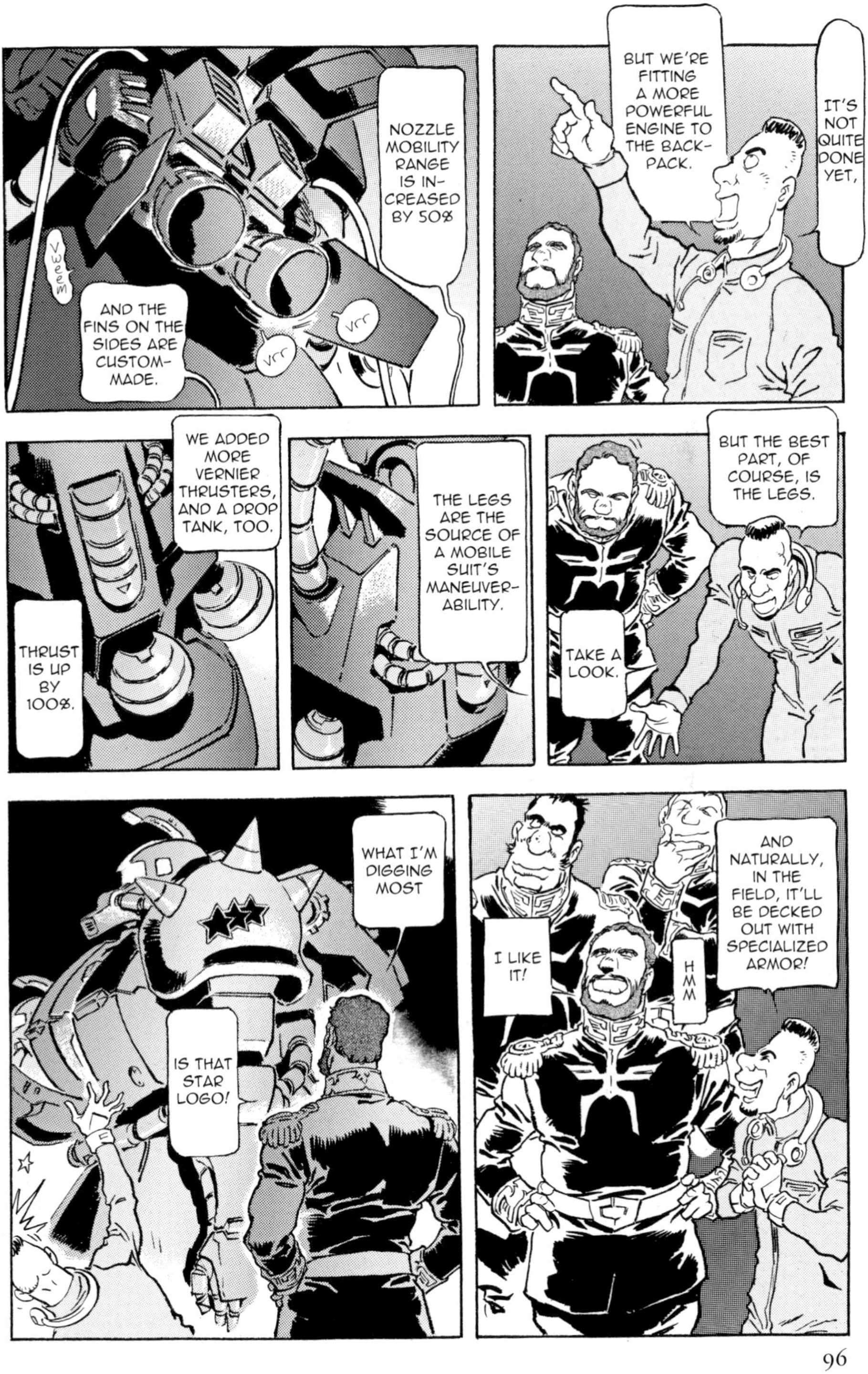
IT'S NOT QUITE DONE YET,
BUT WE'RE FITTING A MORE POWERFUL ENGINE TO THE BACK-PACK.
NOZZLE MOBILITY RANGE IS INCREASED BY 50%
Vweem
vrr
vrr
AND THE FINS ON THE SIDES ARE CUSTOM-MADE.
BUT THE BEST PART, OF COURSE, IS THE LEGS.
TAKE A LOOK.
THE LEGS ARE THE SOURCE OF A MOBILE SUIT'S MANEUVER-ABILITY.
WE ADDED MORE VERNIER THRUSTERS, AND A DROP TANK, TOO.
THRUST IS UP BY 100%.
AND NATURALLY, IN THE FIELD, IT'LL BE DECKED OUT WITH SPECIALIZED ARMOR!
HMM
I LIKE IT!
WHAT I'M DIGGING MOST
IS THAT STAR LOGO!

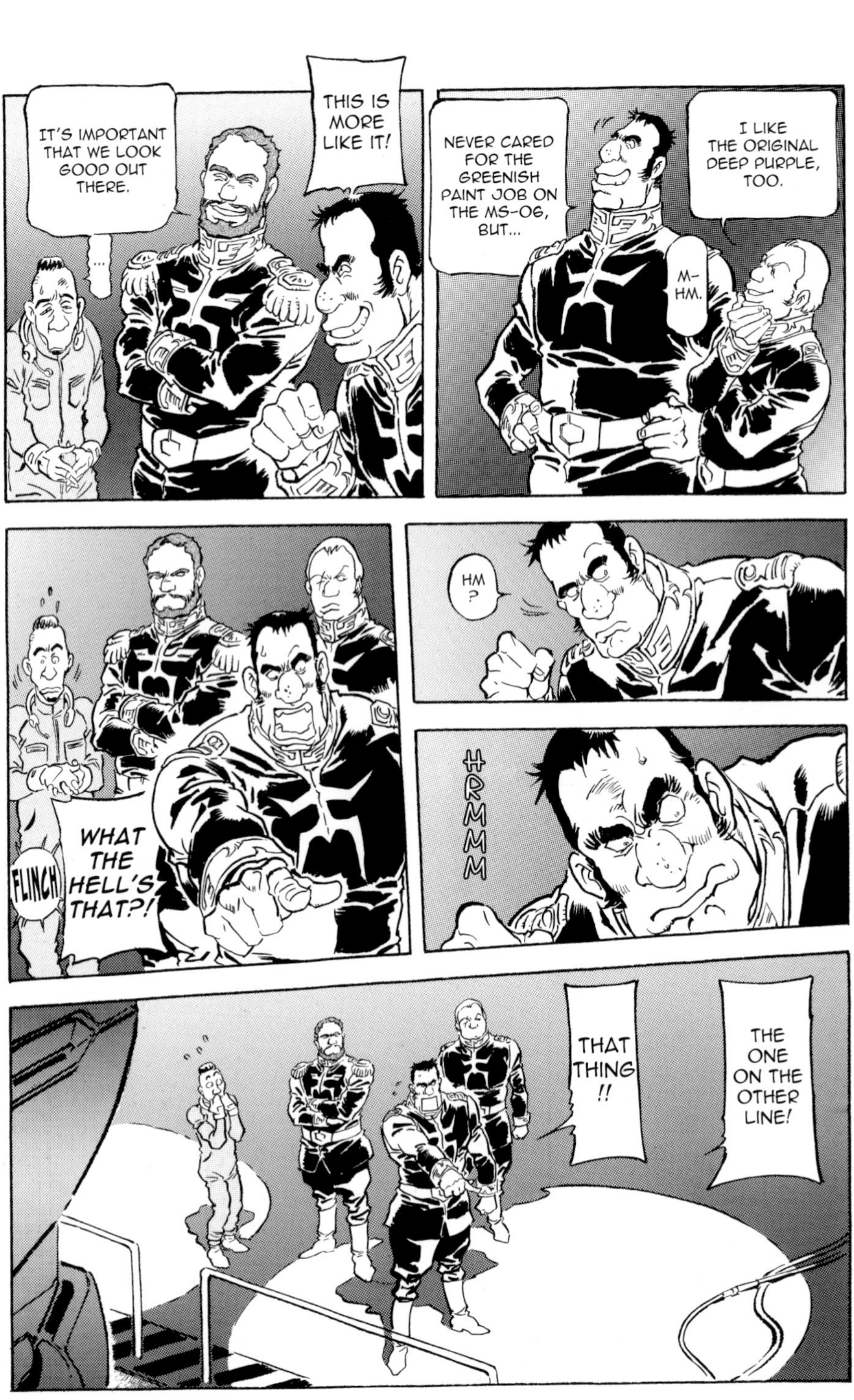
I LIKE THE ORIGINAL DEEP PURPLE, TOO.
NEVER CARED FOR THE GREENISH PAINT JOB ON THE MS-06, BUT...
M-HM.
THIS IS MORE LIKE IT!
IT'S IMPORTANT THAT WE LOOK GOOD OUT THERE.
...
HM?
HRMMMM
WHAT THE HELL'S THAT?!
FLINCH
THE ONE ON THE OTHER LINE!
THAT THING!!

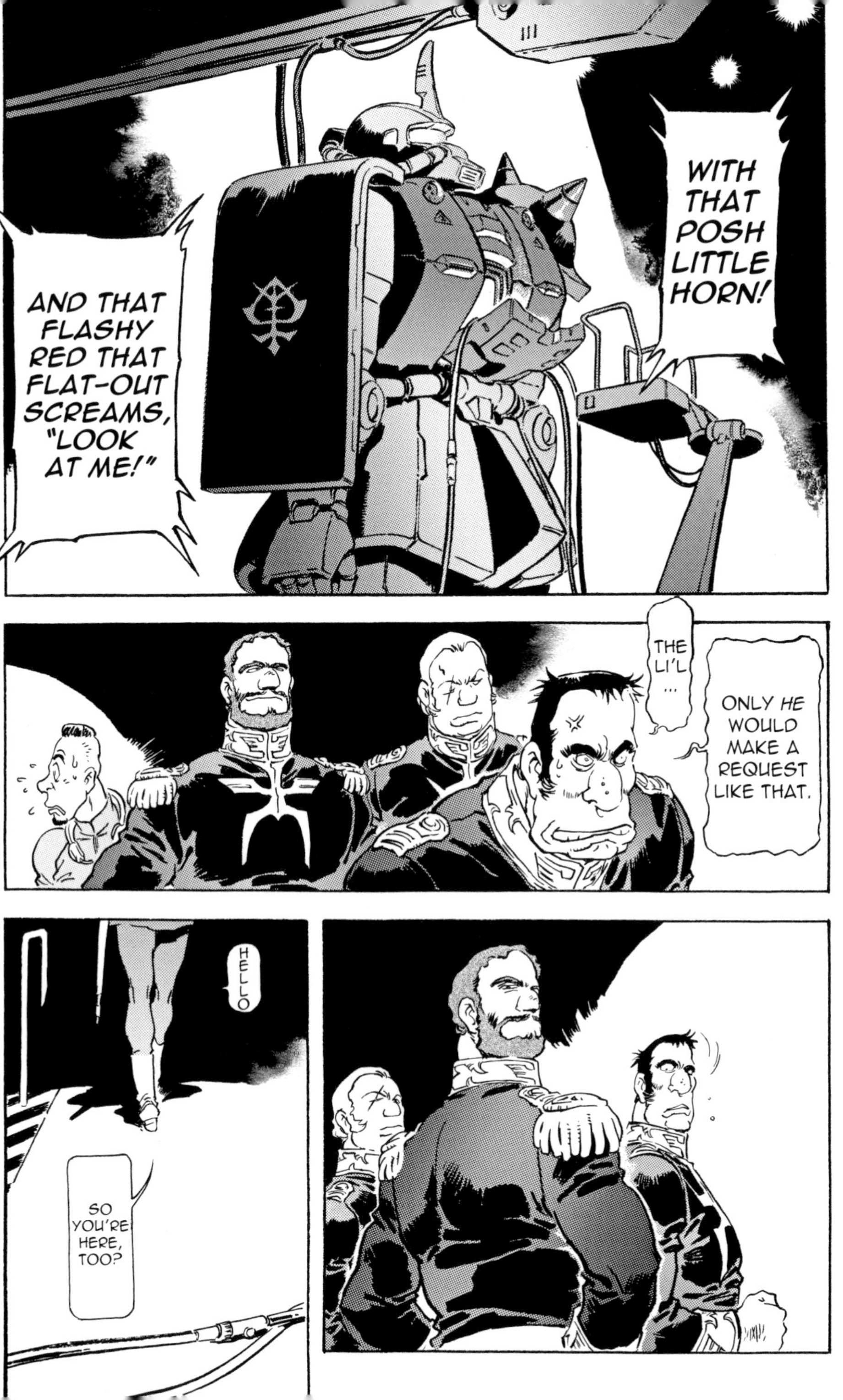
WITH THAT POSH LITTLE HORN!
AND THAT FLASHY RED THAT FLAT-OUT SCREAMS, "LOOK AT ME!"
THE LI'L ...
ONLY HE WOULD MAKE A REQUEST LIKE THAT.
HELLO
SO YOU'RE HERE, TOO?

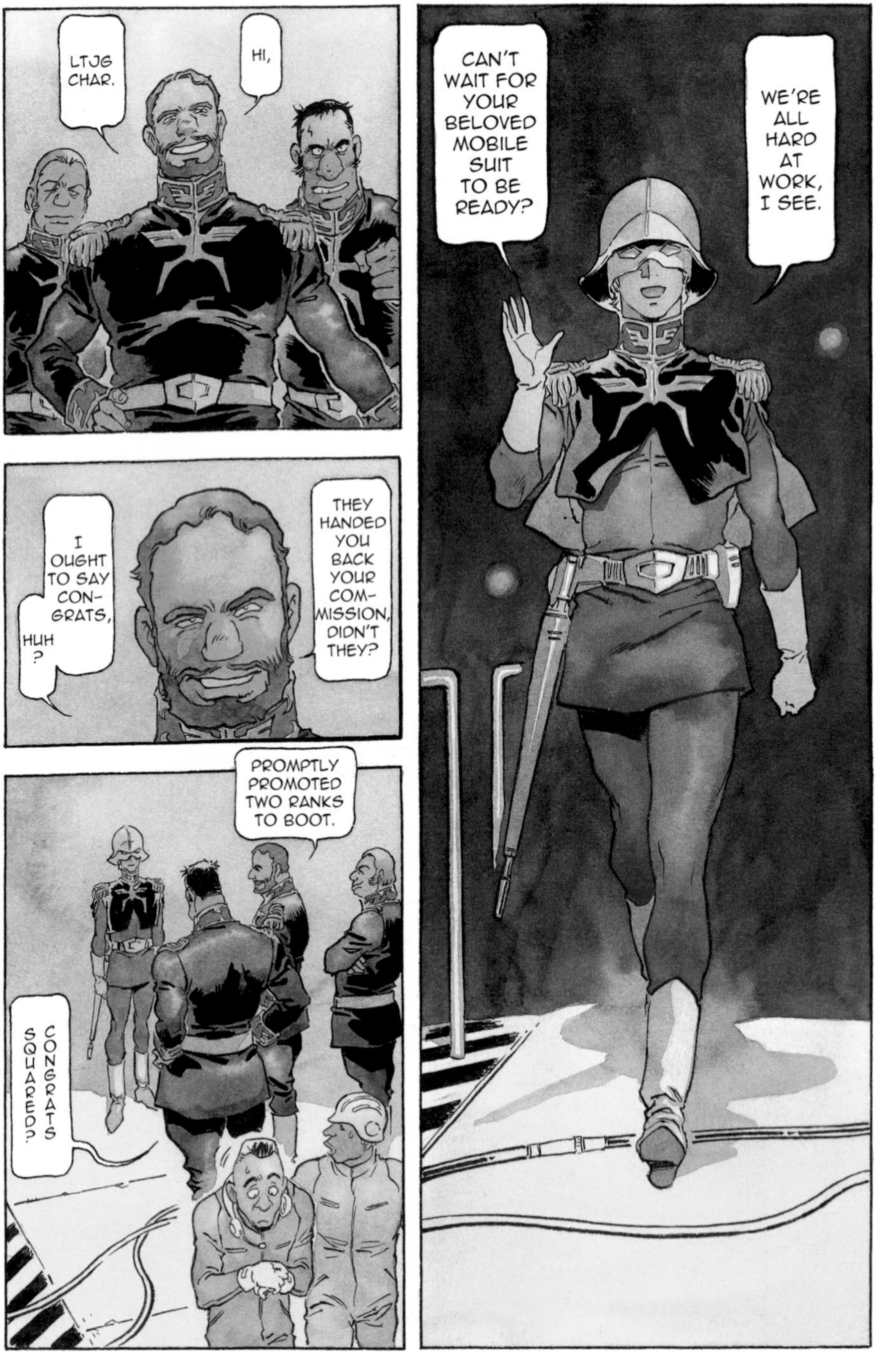
WE'RE ALL HARD AT WORK, I SEE.
CAN'T WAIT FOR YOUR BELOVED MOBILE SUIT TO BE READY?
HI,
LTJG CHAR.
THEY HANDED YOU BACK YOUR COM-MISSION, DIDN'T THEY?
I OUGHT TO SAY CON-GRATS,
HUH?
PROMPTLY PROMOTED TWO RANKS TO BOOT.
CONGRATS SQUARED?

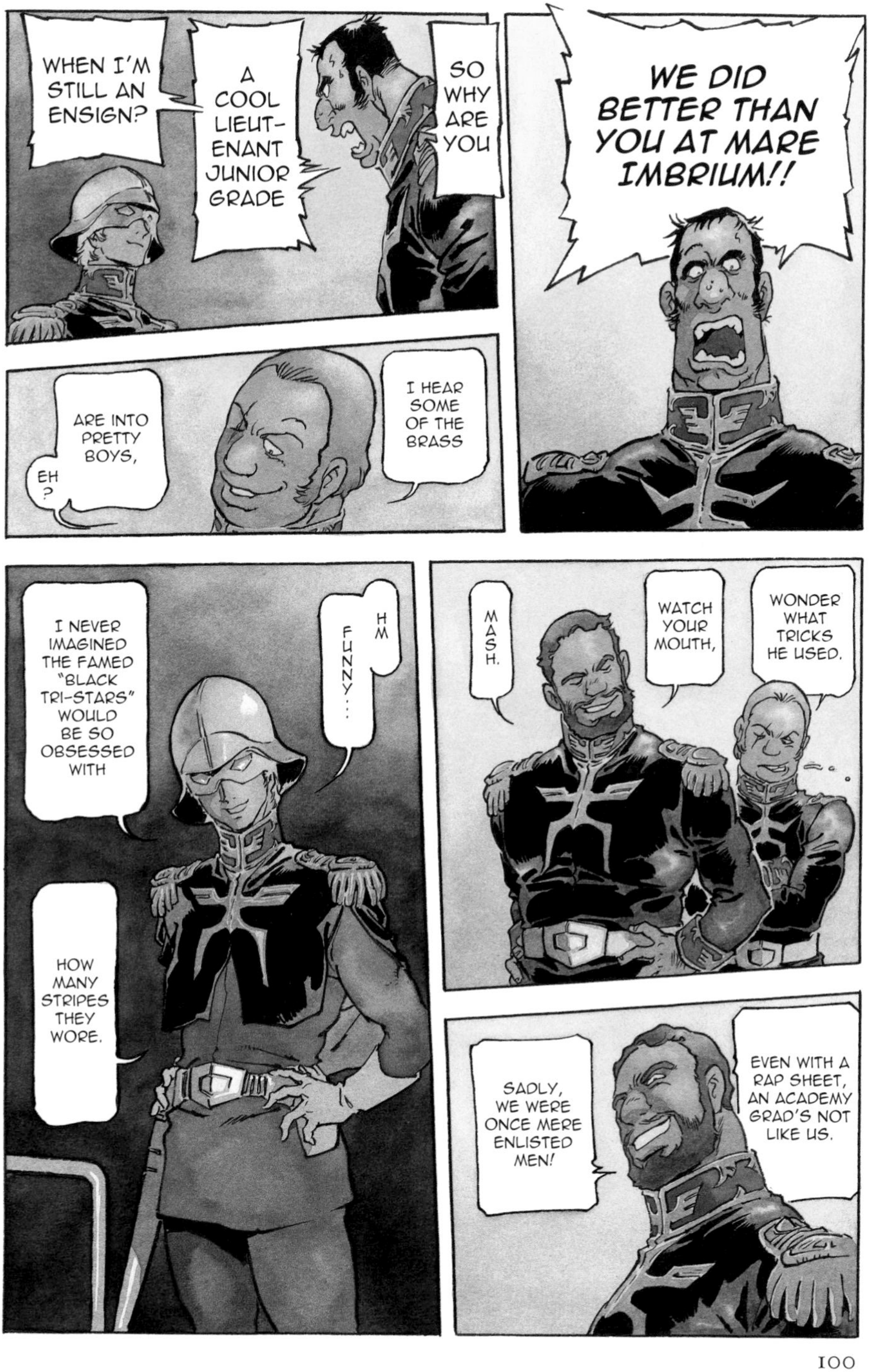
WE DID BETTER THAN YOU AT MARE IMBRIUM!!
SO WHY ARE YOU
A COOL LIEUT-ENANT JUNIOR GRADE
WHEN I'M STILL AN ENSIGN?
I HEAR SOME OF THE BRASS
ARE INTO PRETTY BOYS,
EH?
WONDER WHAT TRICKS HE USED.
WATCH YOUR MOUTH,
MASH.
EVEN WITH A RAP SHEET, AN ACADEMY GRAD'S NOT LIKE US.
SADLY, WE WERE ONCE MERE ENLISTED MEN!
HM
FUNNY...
I NEVER IMAGINED THE FAMED "BLACK TRI-STARS" WOULD BE SO OBSESSED WITH
HOW MANY STRIPES THEY WORE.

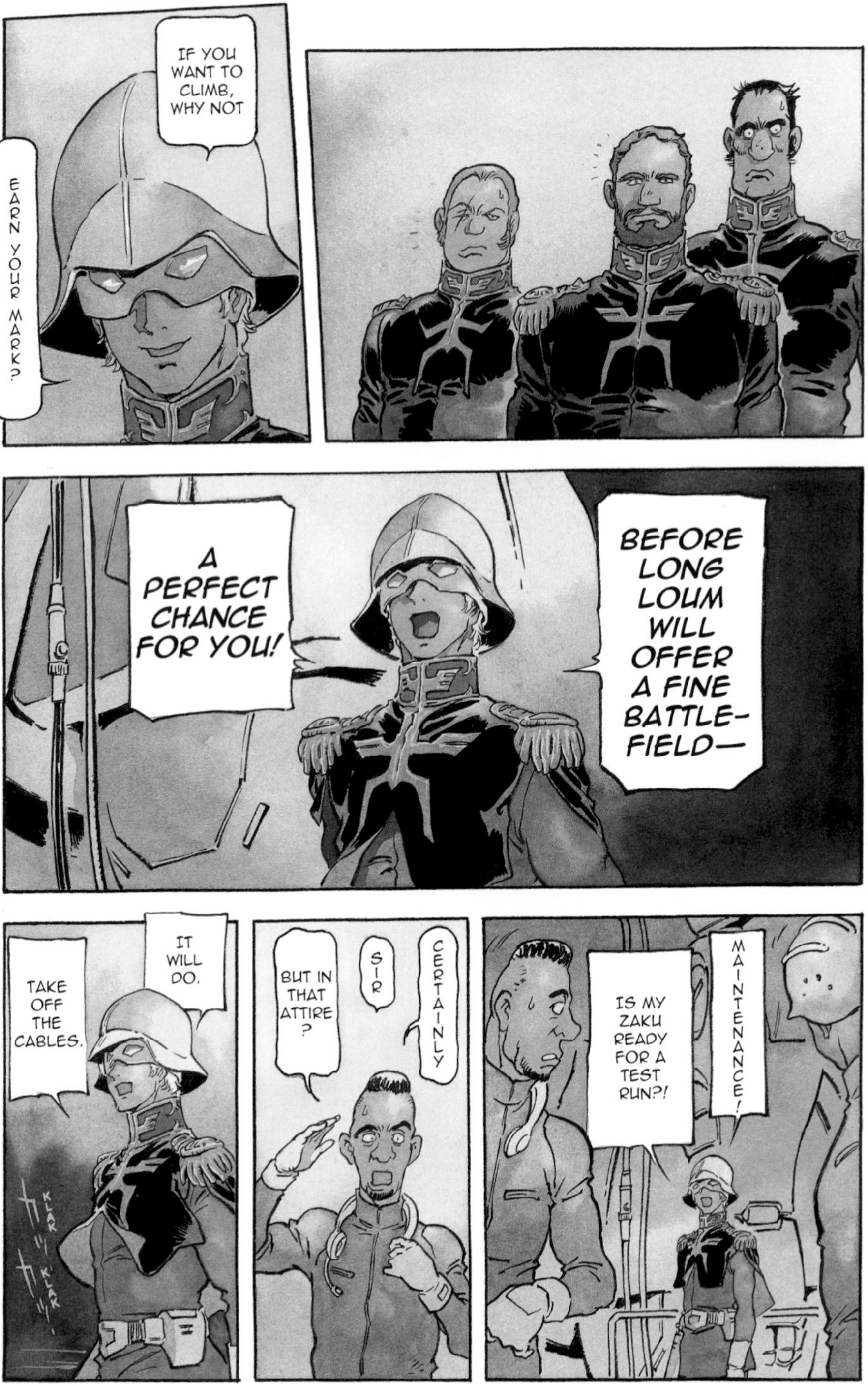
IF YOU WANT TO CLIMB, WHY NOT
EARN YOUR MARK?
BEFORE LONG LOUM WILL OFFER A FINE BATTLE-FIELD—
A PERFECT CHANCE FOR YOU!
MAINTENANCE!
IS MY ZAKU READY FOR A TEST RUN?!
CERTAINLY
SIR
BUT IN THAT ATTIRE?
IT WILL DO.
TAKE OFF THE CABLES.
KLAK
KLAK

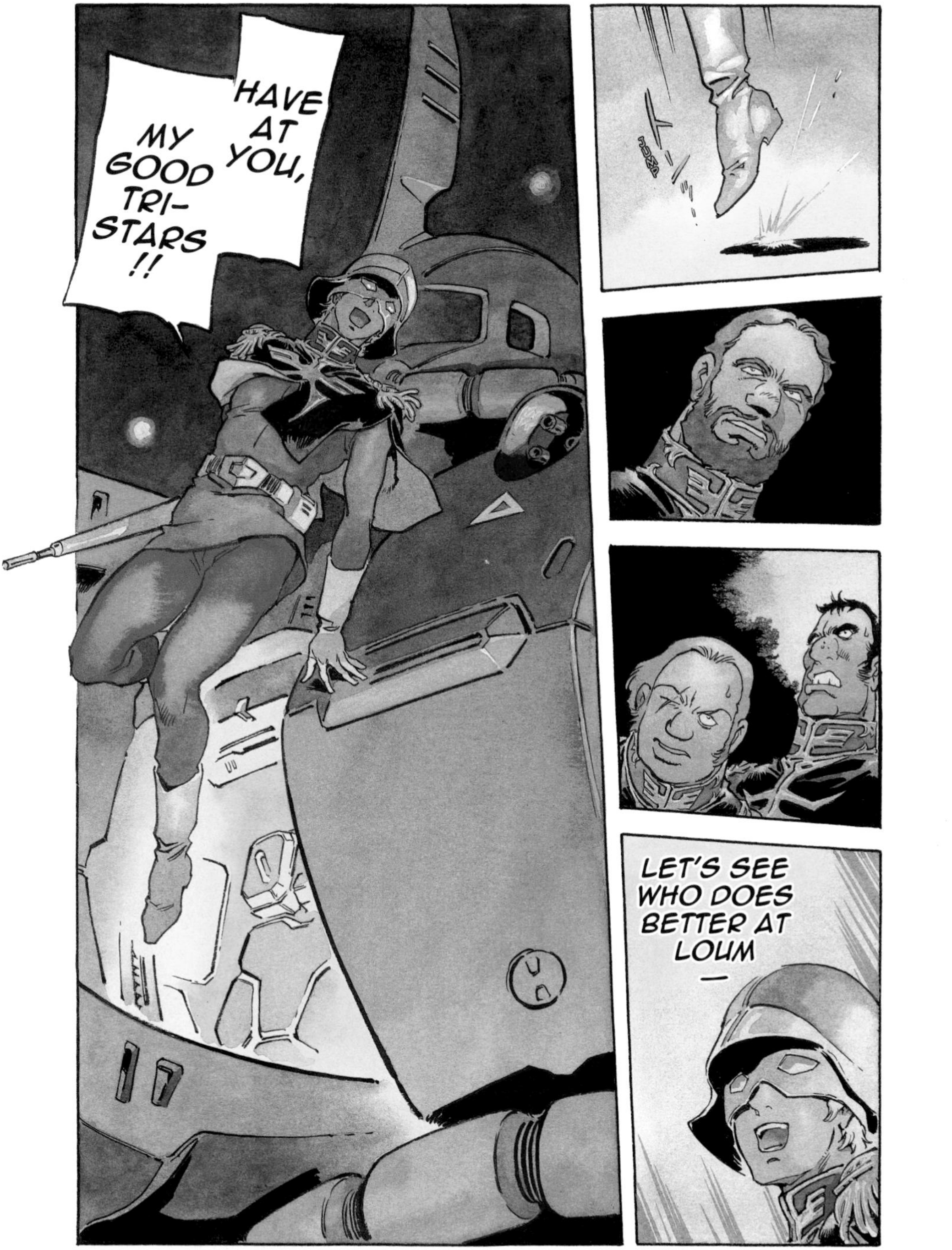
LET'S SEE WHO DOES BETTER AT LOUM
—
HAVE AT YOU,
MY GOOD TRI-STARS!!

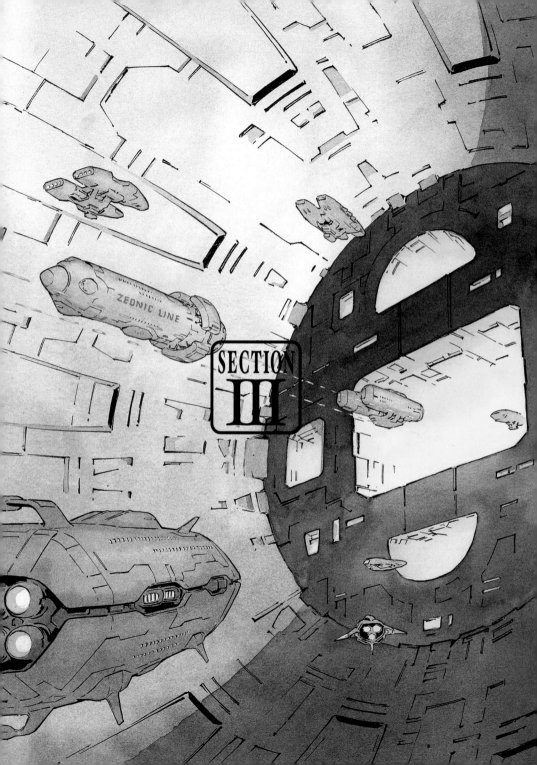

SECTION
III

ZEONIC LINE

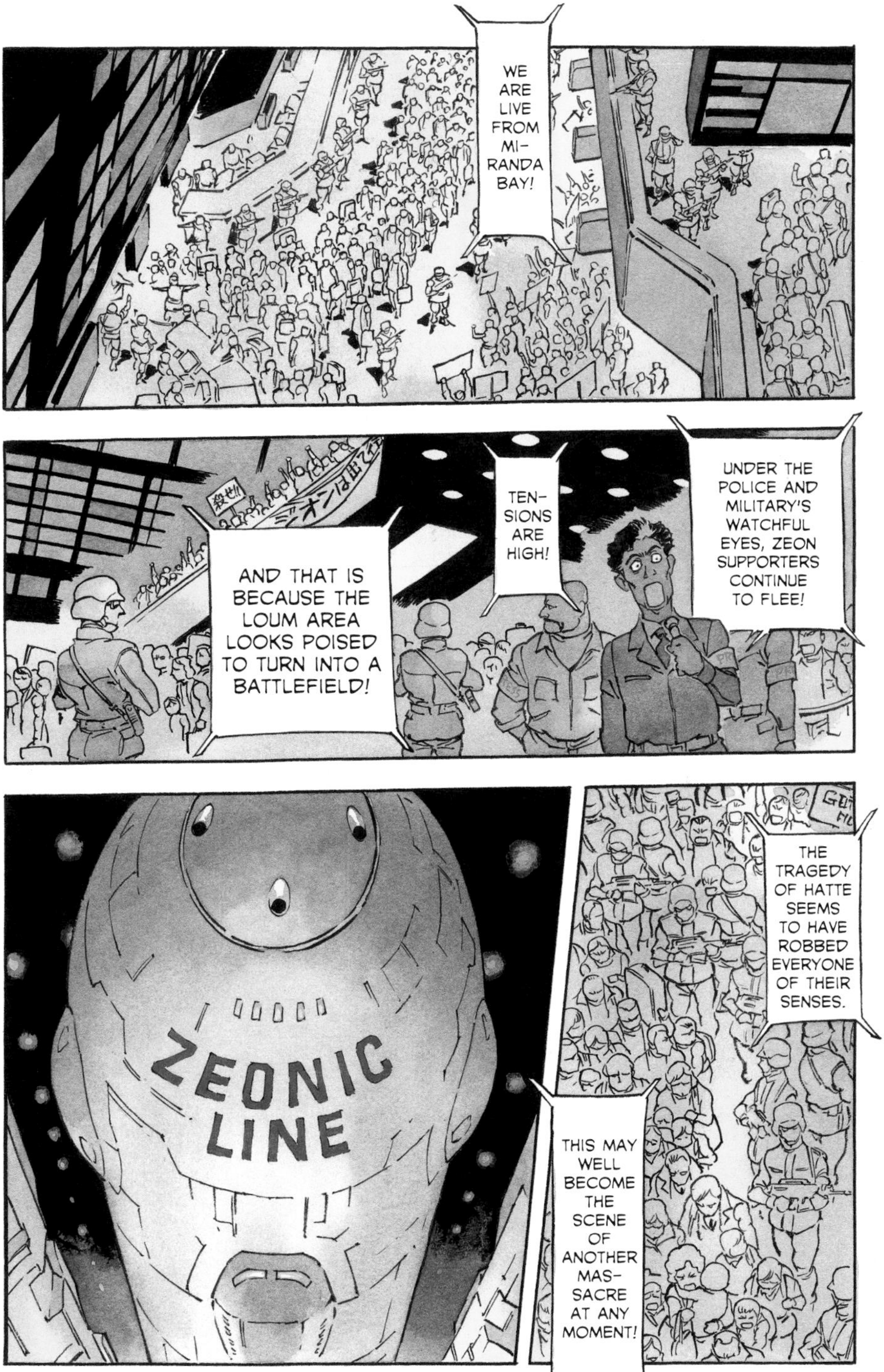
WE ARE LIVE FROM MI-RANDA BAY!
UNDER THE POLICE AND MILITARY'S WATCHFUL EYES, ZEON SUPPORTERS CONTINUE TO FLEE!
TEN-SIONS ARE HIGH!
AND THAT IS BECAUSE THE LOUM AREA LOOKS POISED TO TURN INTO A BATTLEFIELD!
THE TRAGEDY OF HATTE SEEMS TO HAVE ROBBED EVERYONE OF THEIR SENSES.
THIS MAY WELL BECOME THE SCENE OF ANOTHER MAS-SACRE AT ANY MOMENT!
ZEONIC LINE

ZEONIC LINE
ZEONIC LINE

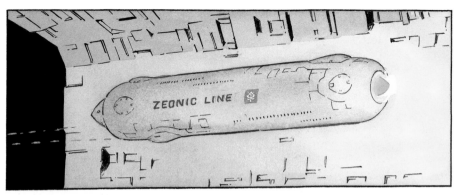

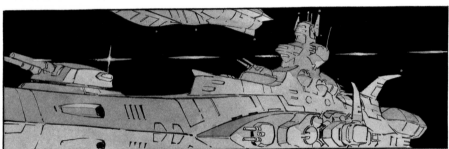

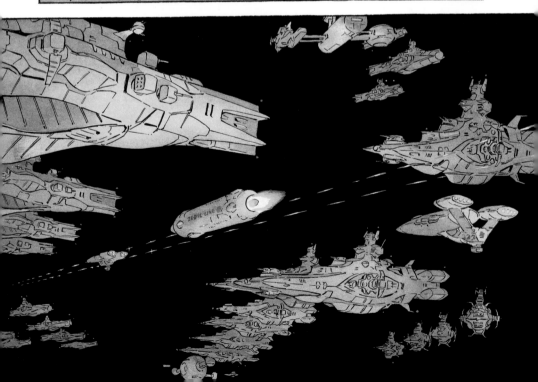

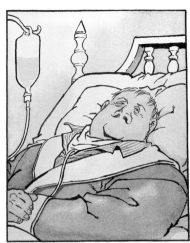

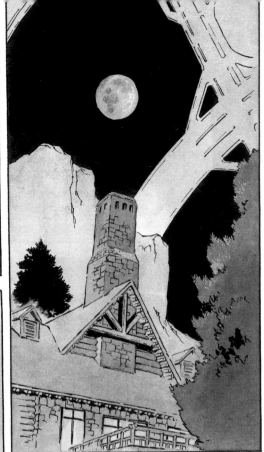

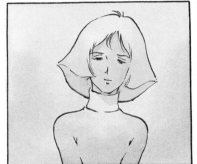

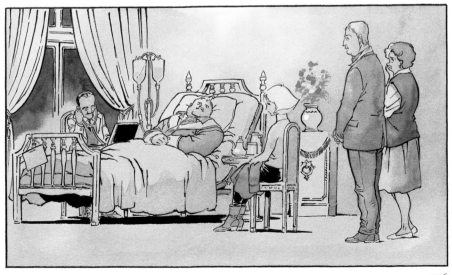

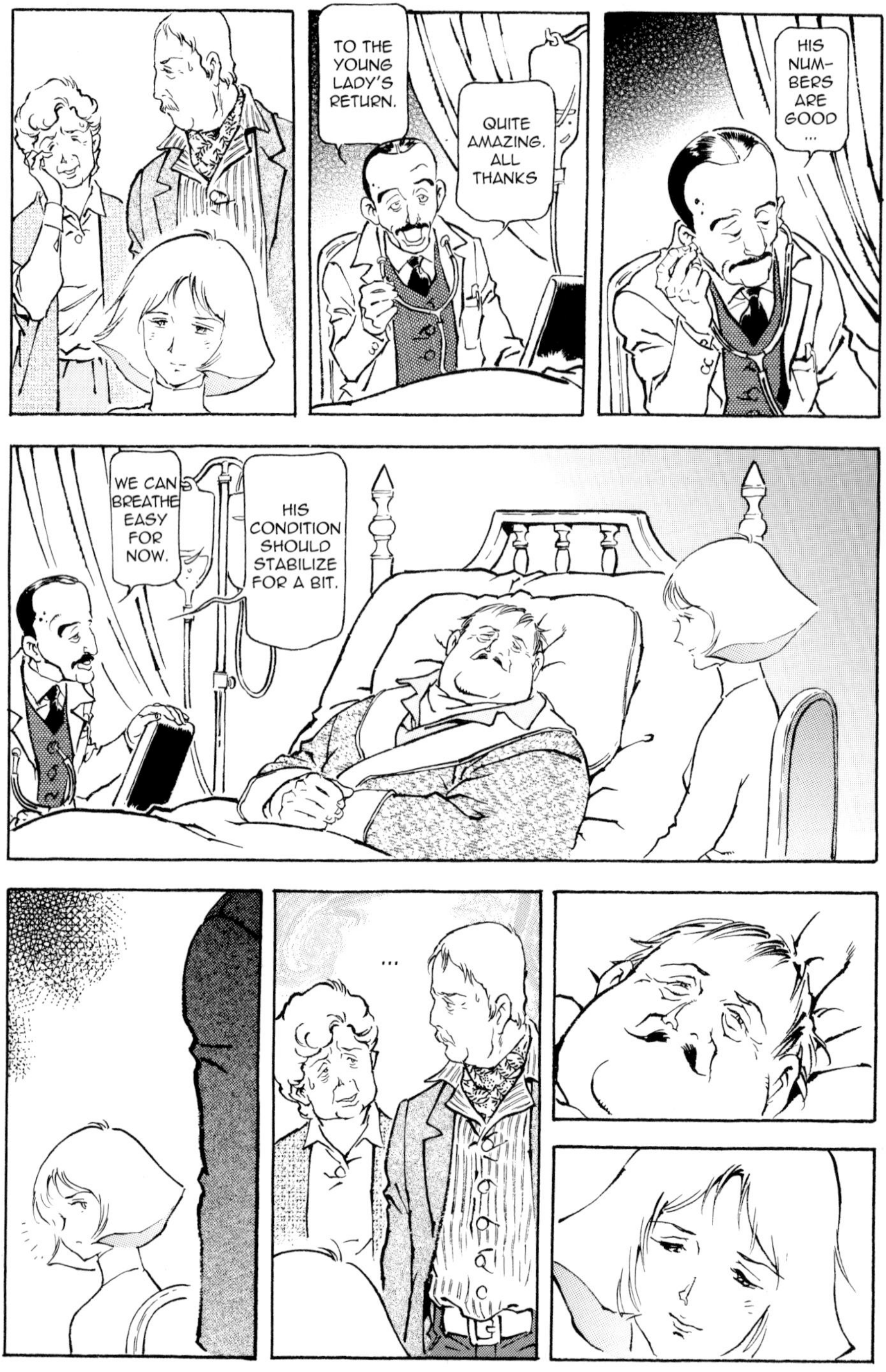
HIS NUM-BERS ARE GOOD ...
QUITE AMAZING. ALL THANKS
TO THE YOUNG LADY'S RETURN.
HIS CONDITION SHOULD STABILIZE FOR A BIT.
WE CAN BREATHE EASY FOR NOW.
...

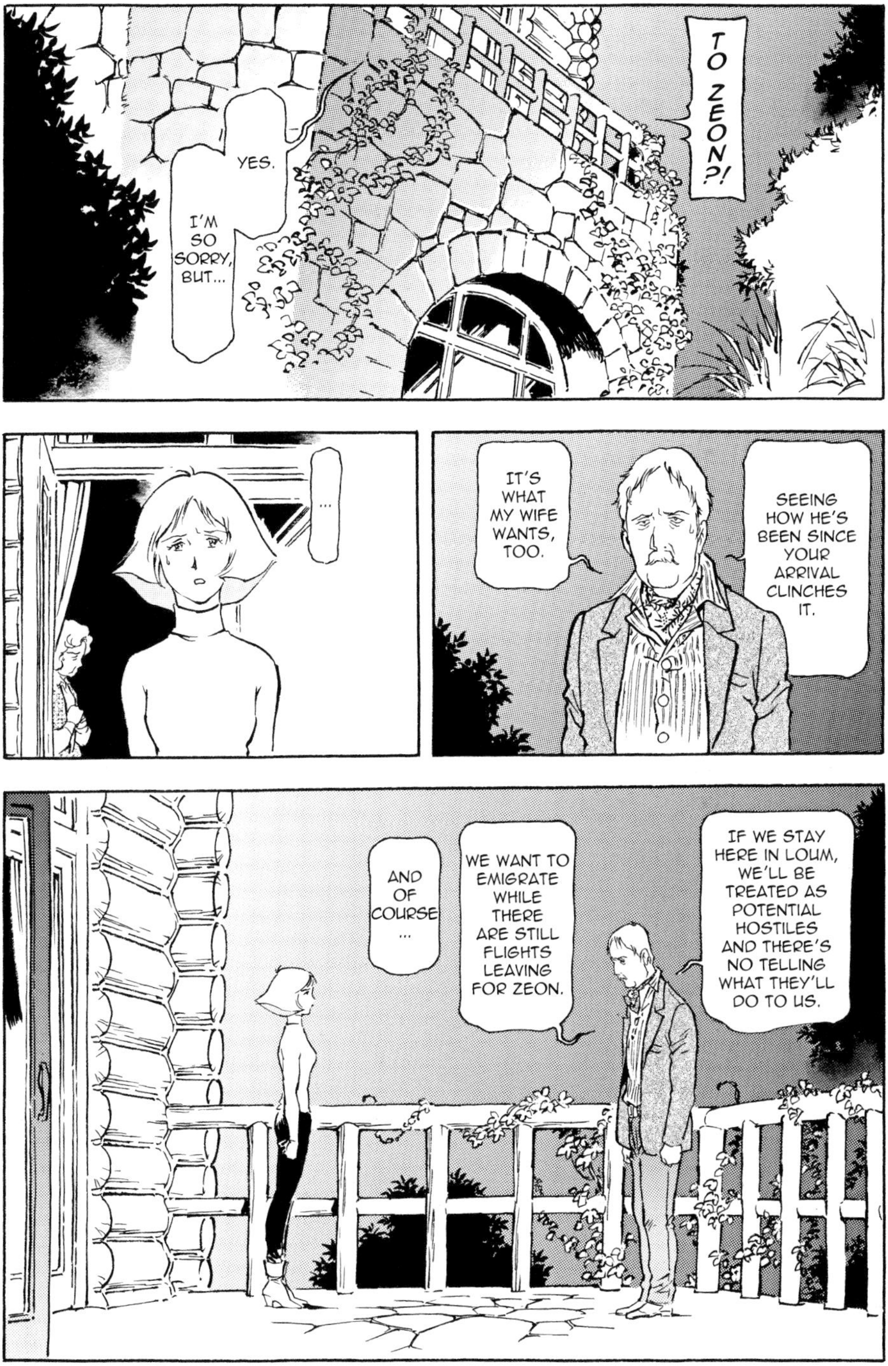
TO ZEON?!
YES.
I'M SO SORRY, BUT...
SEEING HOW HE'S BEEN SINCE YOUR ARRIVAL CLINCHES IT.
IT'S WHAT MY WIFE WANTS, TOO.
...
IF WE STAY HERE IN LOUM, WE'LL BE TREATED AS POTENTIAL HOSTILES AND THERE'S NO TELLING WHAT THEY'LL DO TO US.
WE WANT TO EMIGRATE WHILE THERE ARE STILL FLIGHTS LEAVING FOR ZEON.
AND OF COURSE...

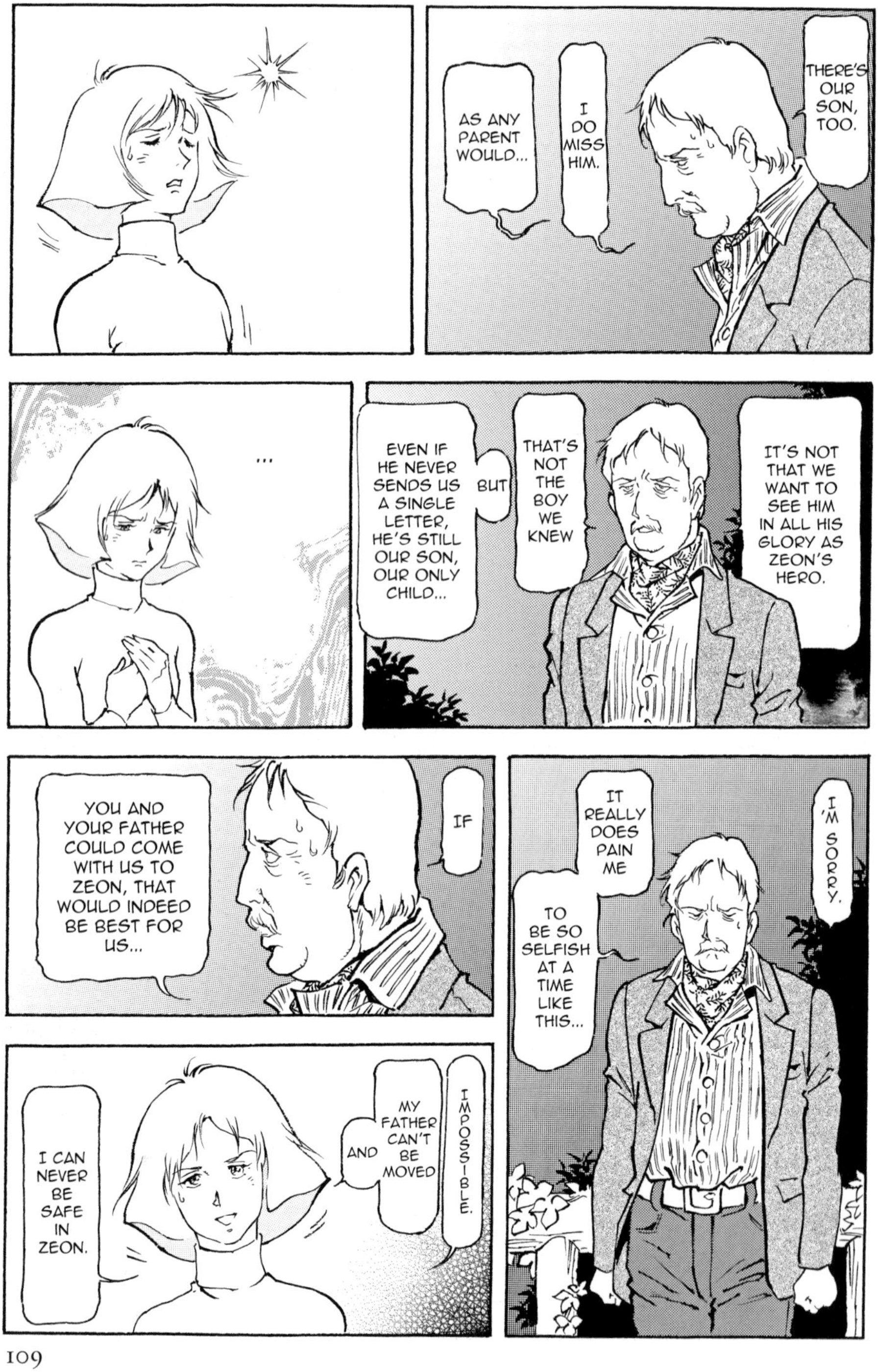
THERE'S OUR SON, TOO.
I DO MISS HIM.
AS ANY PARENT WOULD...
IT'S NOT THAT WE WANT TO SEE HIM IN ALL HIS GLORY AS ZEON'S HERO.
THAT'S NOT THE BOY WE KNEW
BUT
EVEN IF HE NEVER SENDS US A SINGLE LETTER, HE'S STILL OUR SON, OUR ONLY CHILD...
...
I'M SORRY.
IT REALLY DOES PAIN ME
TO BE SO SELFISH AT A TIME LIKE THIS...
IF
YOU AND YOUR FATHER COULD COME WITH US TO ZEON, THAT WOULD INDEED BE BEST FOR US...
IMPOSSIBLE.
MY FATHER CAN'T BE MOVED
AND
I CAN NEVER BE SAFE IN ZEON.

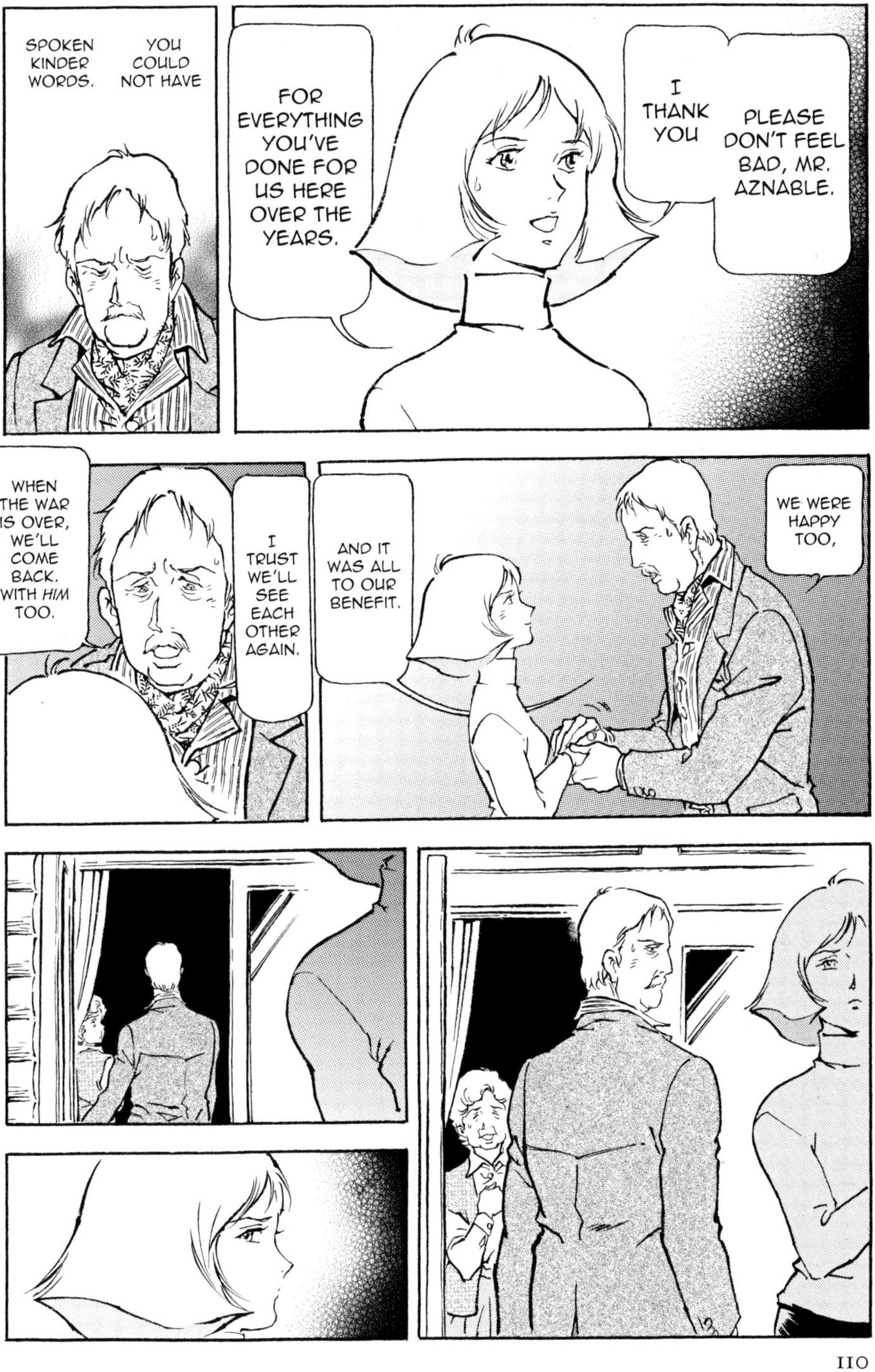
PLEASE DON'T FEEL BAD, MR. AZNABLE.
I THANK YOU
FOR EVERYTHING YOU'VE DONE FOR US HERE OVER THE YEARS.
YOU COULD NOT HAVE
SPOKEN KINDER WORDS.
WE WERE HAPPY TOO,
AND IT WAS ALL TO OUR BENEFIT.
I TRUST WE'LL SEE EACH OTHER AGAIN.
WHEN THE WAR IS OVER, WE'LL COME BACK. WITH *HIM* TOO.

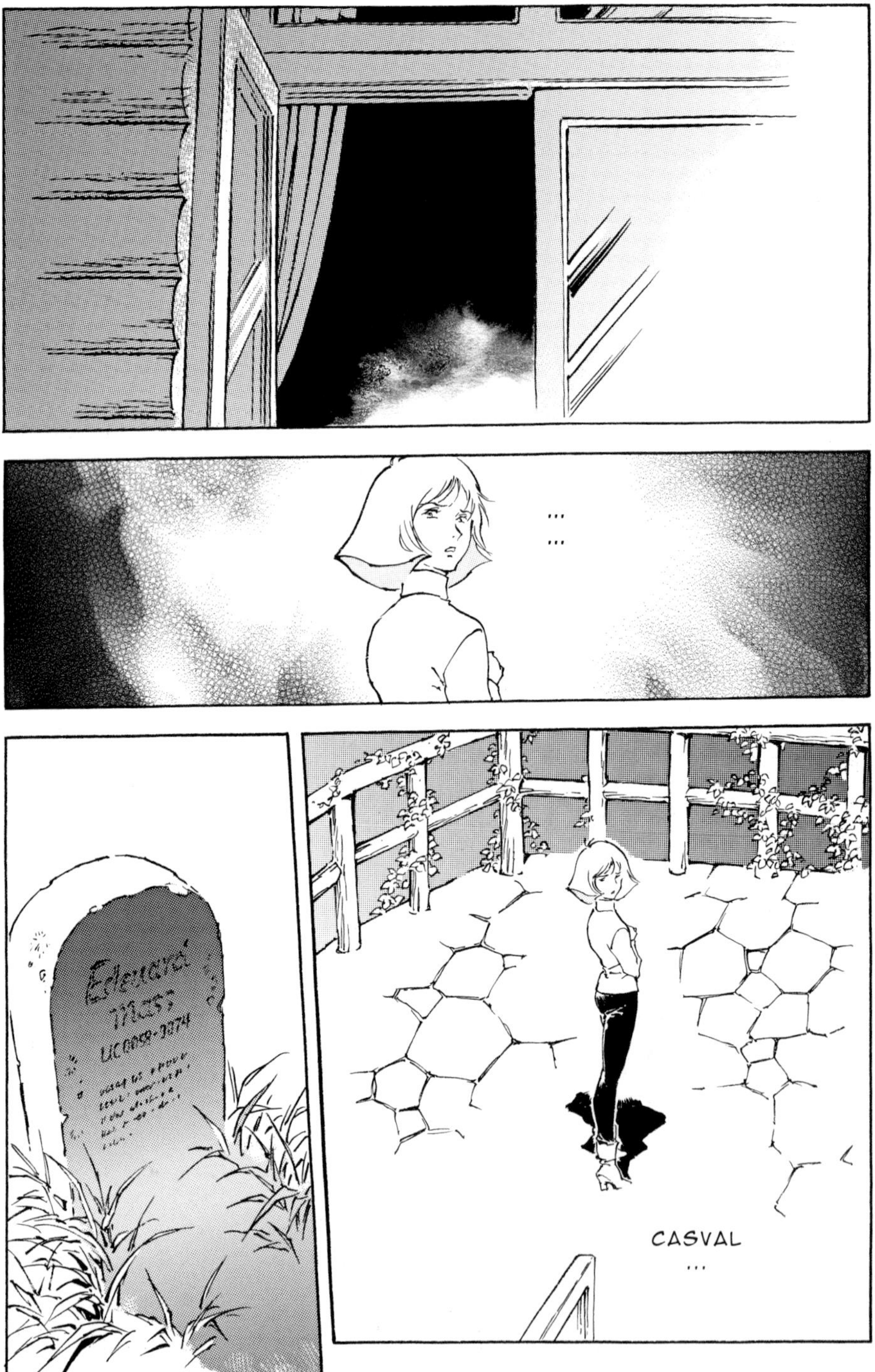
...
...
CASVAL
...

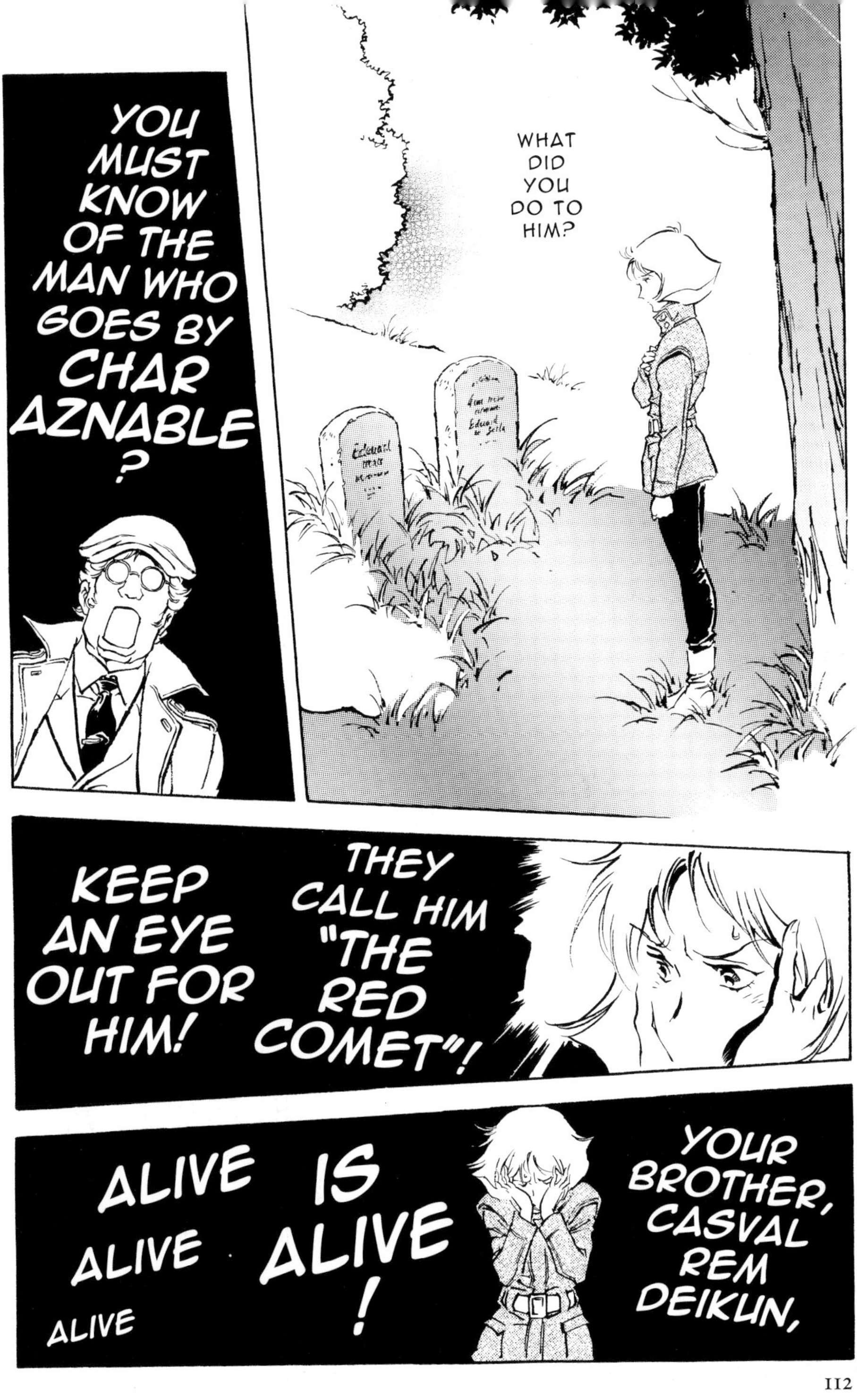
WHAT DID YOU DO TO HIM?
YOU MUST KNOW OF THE MAN WHO GOES BY CHAR AZNABLE?
THEY CALL HIM "THE RED COMET"!
KEEP AN EYE OUT FOR HIM!
YOUR BROTHER, CASVAL REM DEIKUN,
IS ALIVE!
ALIVE
ALIVE
ALIVE

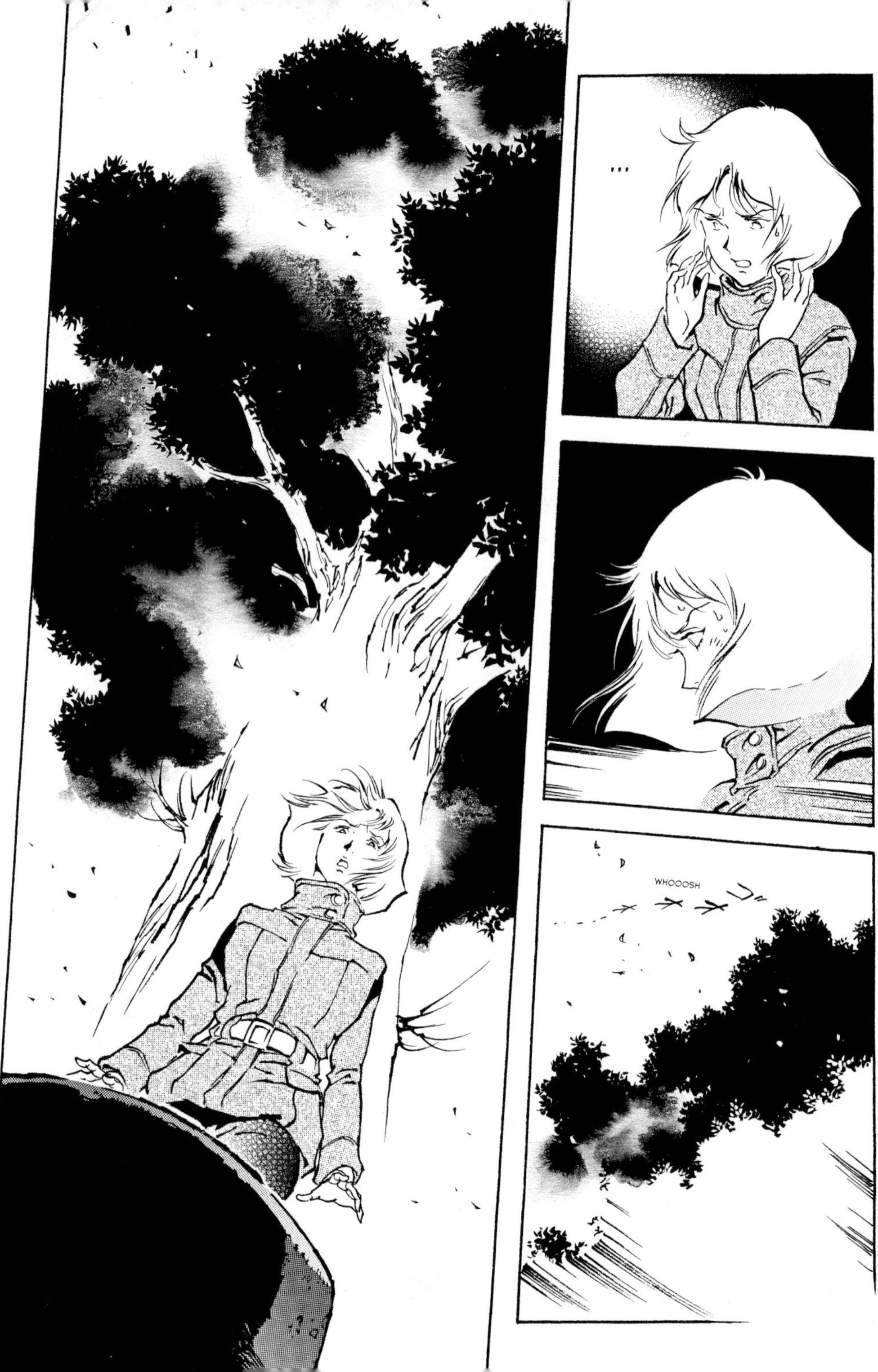
...
WHOOOSH

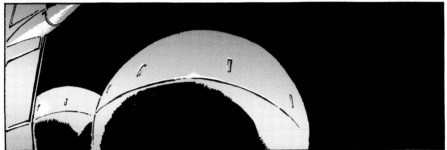

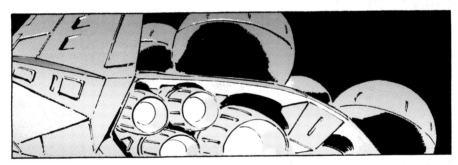

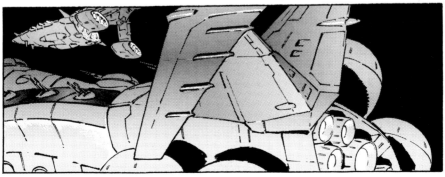

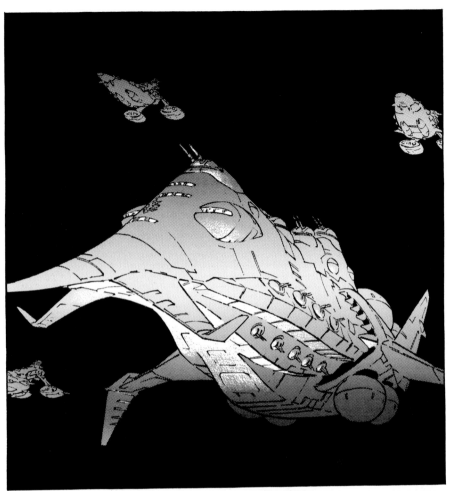

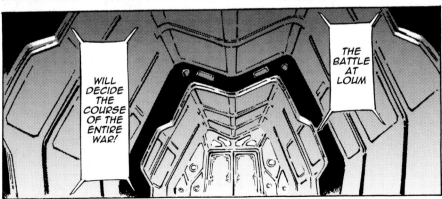

THE BATTLE AT LOUM

WILL DECIDE THE COURSE OF THE ENTIRE WAR!

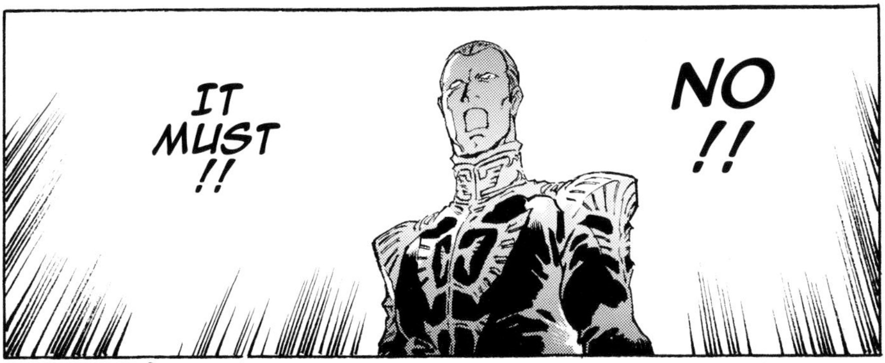
NO!!
IT MUST!!

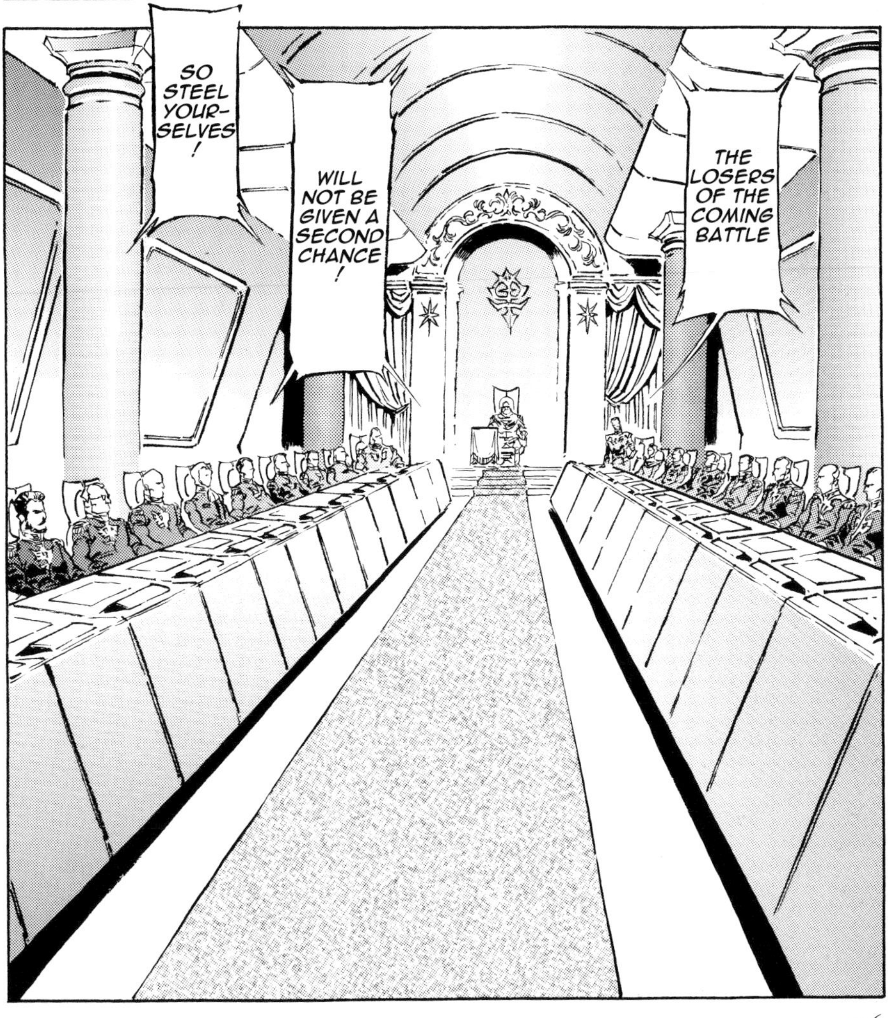
THE LOSERS OF THE COMING BATTLE
WILL NOT BE GIVEN A SECOND CHANCE!
SO STEEL YOUR-SELVES!

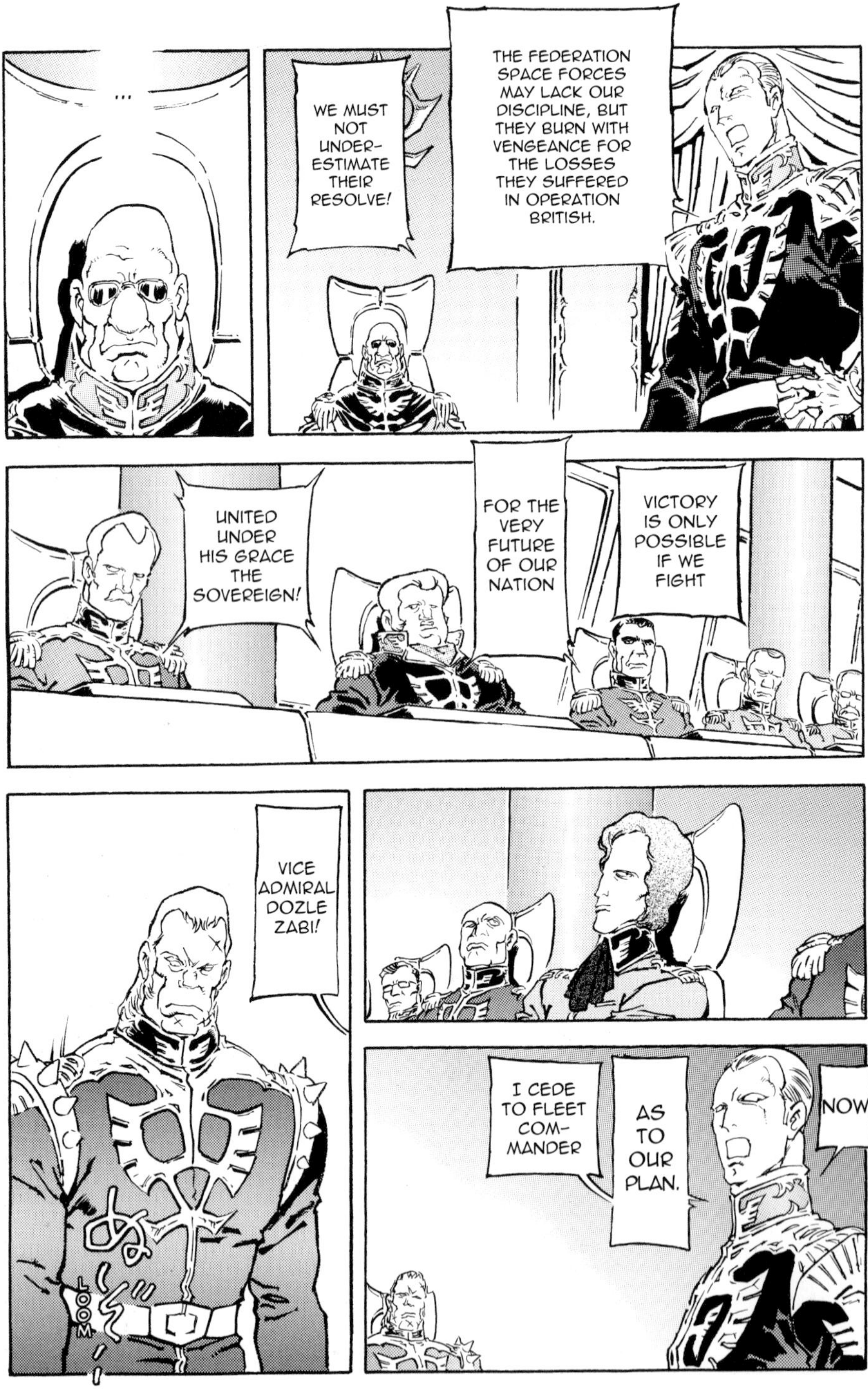
THE FEDERATION SPACE FORCES MAY LACK OUR DISCIPLINE, BUT THEY BURN WITH VENGEANCE FOR THE LOSSES THEY SUFFERED IN OPERATION BRITISH.
WE MUST NOT UNDER-ESTIMATE THEIR RESOLVE!
...
VICTORY IS ONLY POSSIBLE IF WE FIGHT
FOR THE VERY FUTURE OF OUR NATION
UNITED UNDER HIS GRACE THE SOVEREIGN!
NOW
AS TO OUR PLAN.
I CEDE TO FLEET COM-MANDER
VICE ADMIRAL DOZLE ZABI!
ぬぅ
LOOM

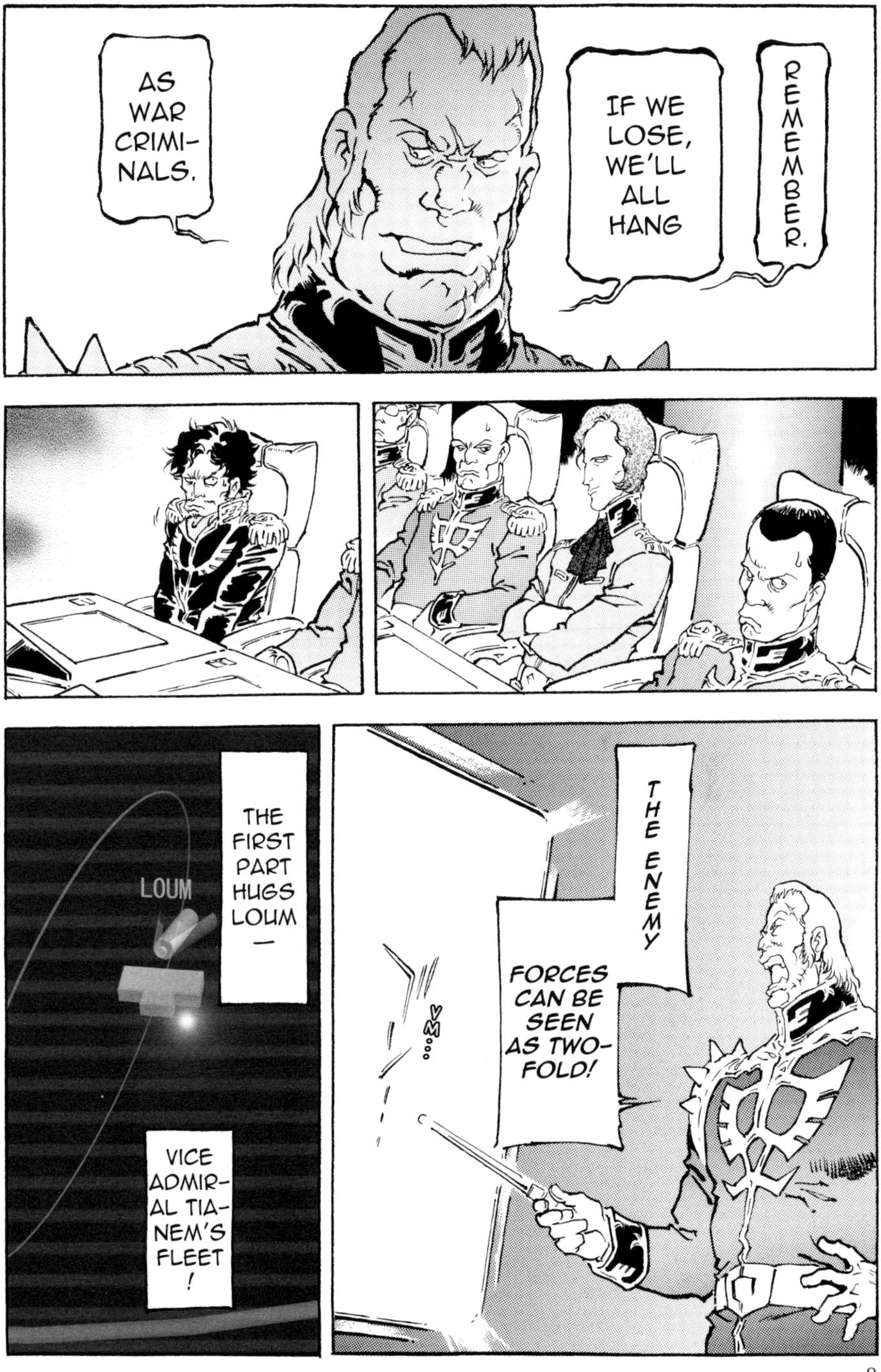
REMEMBER.
IF WE LOSE, WE'LL ALL HANG
AS WAR CRIMI-NALS.
THE ENEMY
FORCES CAN BE SEEN AS TWO-FOLD!
VM...
THE FIRST PART HUGS LOUM —
LOUM
VICE ADMIR-AL TIA-NEM'S FLEET !

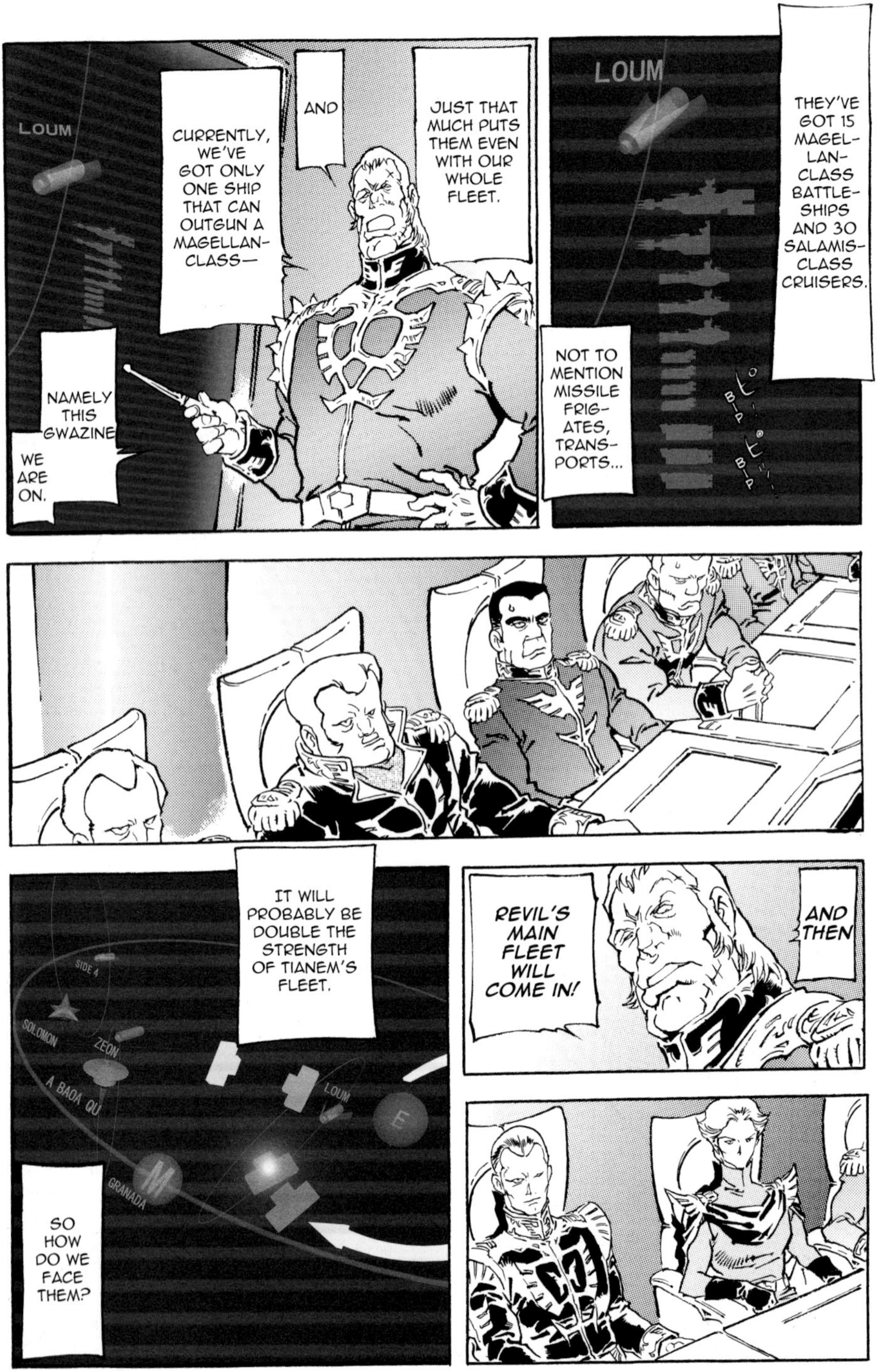
LOUM
THEY'VE GOT 15 MAGELLAN-CLASS BATTLESHIPS AND 30 SALAMIS-CLASS CRUISERS.
NOT TO MENTION MISSILE FRIGATES, TRANSPORTS...
BIP BIP
JUST THAT MUCH PUTS THEM EVEN WITH OUR WHOLE FLEET.
AND
CURRENTLY, WE'VE GOT ONLY ONE SHIP THAT CAN OUTGUN A MAGELLAN-CLASS—
LOUM
NAMELY THIS GWAZINE
WE ARE ON.
AND THEN
REVIL'S MAIN FLEET WILL COME IN!
IT WILL PROBABLY BE DOUBLE THE STRENGTH OF TIANEM'S FLEET.
SIDE 4
SOLOMON
ZEON
A BAOA QU
LOUM
E
M
GRANADA
SO HOW DO WE FACE THEM?

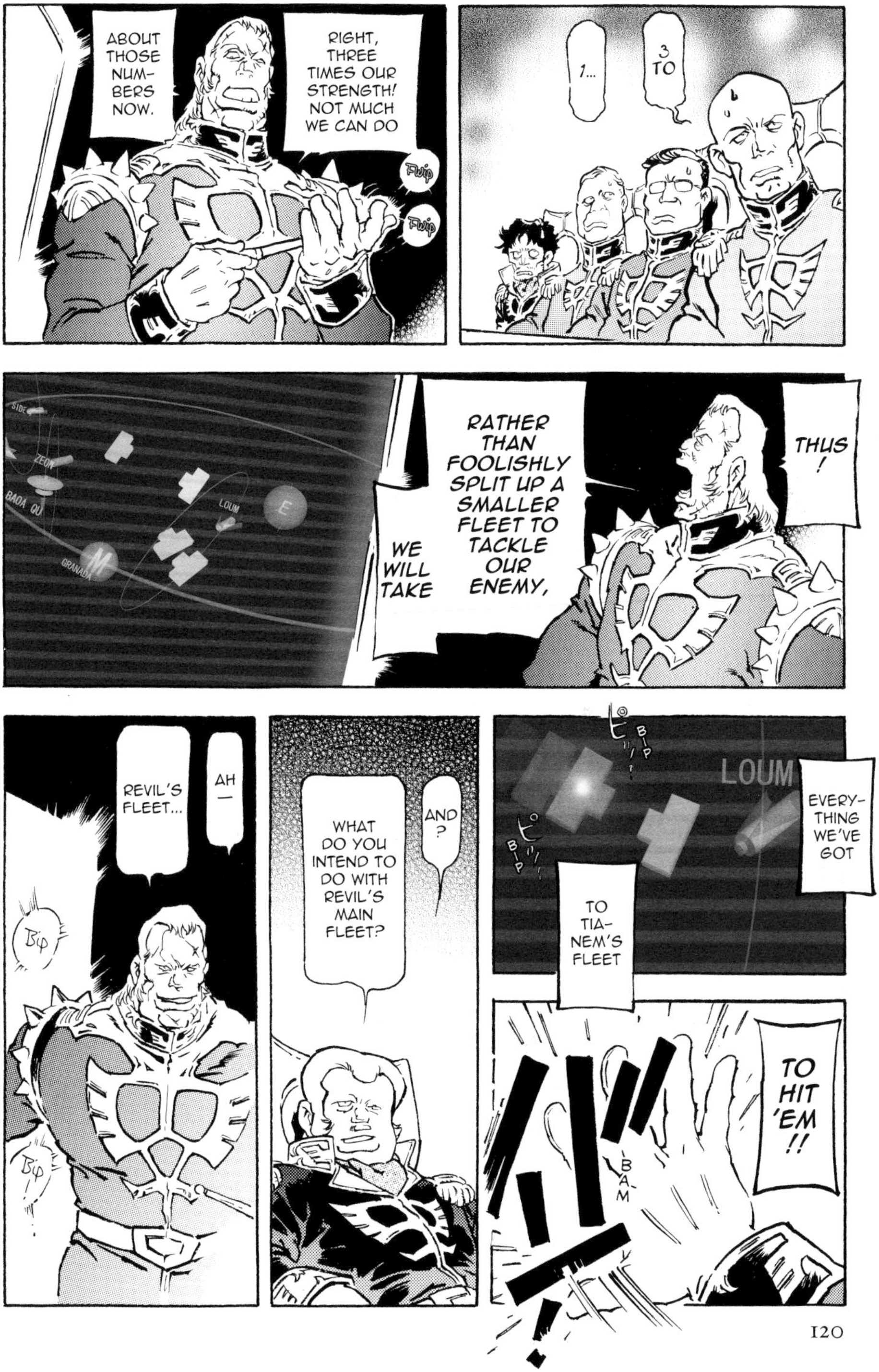
3 TO
1...
RIGHT, THREE TIMES OUR STRENGTH! NOT MUCH WE CAN DO
ABOUT THOSE NUM-BERS NOW.
Fwip
Fwip
THUS!
RATHER THAN FOOLISHLY SPLIT UP A SMALLER FLEET TO TACKLE OUR ENEMY,
WE WILL TAKE
SIDE
ZEON
BAOA QU
LOUM
E
M
GRANADA
EVERY-THING WE'VE GOT
LOUM
BIP
BIP
TO TIA-NEM'S FLEET
TO HIT 'EM!!
BAM
AND?
WHAT DO YOU INTEND TO DO WITH REVIL'S MAIN FLEET?
AH—
REVIL'S FLEET...
Bip
Bip

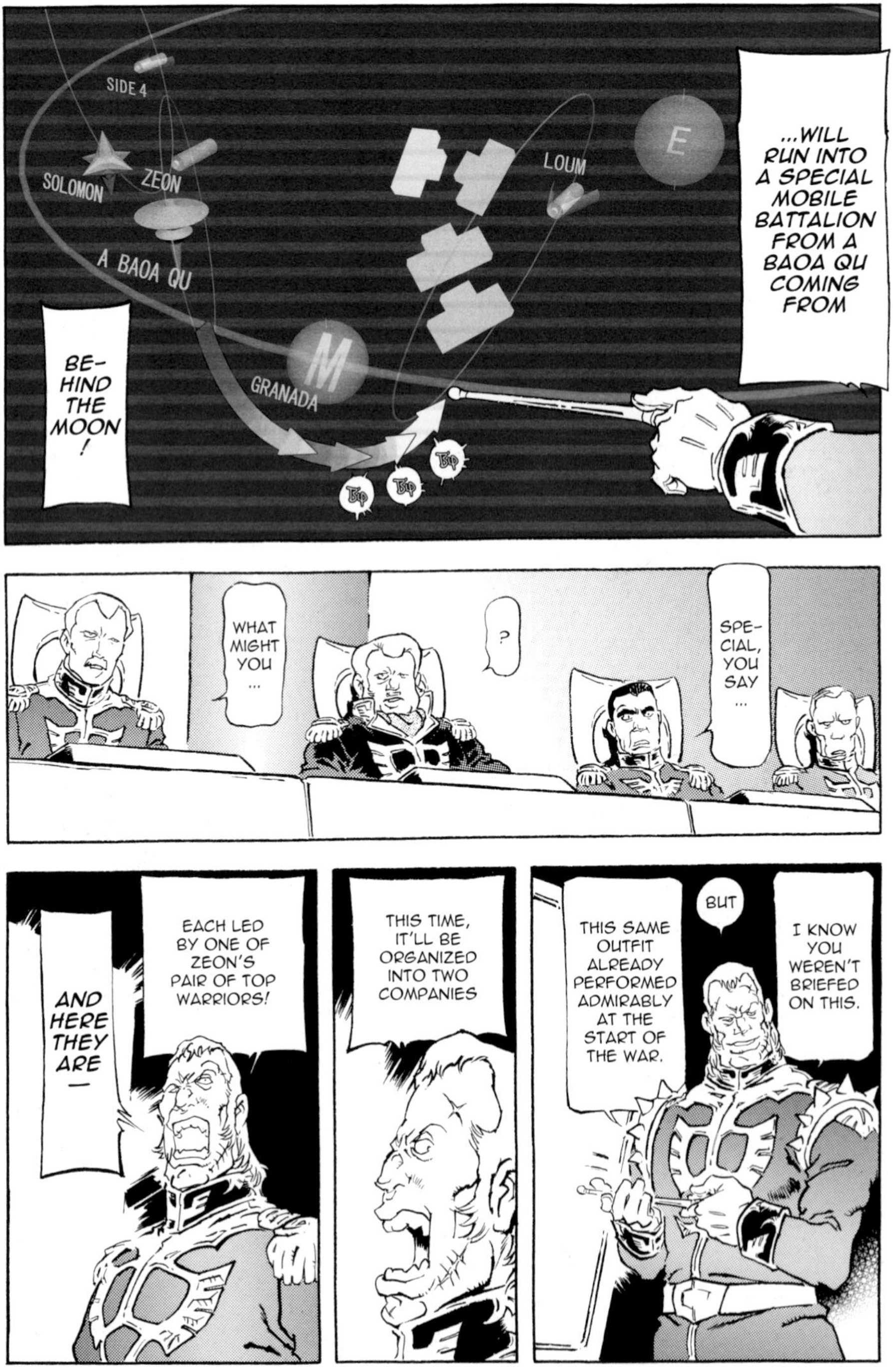
...WILL RUN INTO A SPECIAL MOBILE BATTALION FROM A BAOA QU COMING FROM
E
LOUM
SIDE 4
ZEON
SOLOMON
A BAOA QU
M
GRANADA
BEHIND THE MOON!
SPECIAL, YOU SAY ...
?
WHAT MIGHT YOU ...
I KNOW YOU WEREN'T BRIEFED ON THIS.
BUT
THIS SAME OUTFIT ALREADY PERFORMED ADMIRABLY AT THE START OF THE WAR.
THIS TIME, IT'LL BE ORGANIZED INTO TWO COMPANIES
EACH LED BY ONE OF ZEON'S PAIR OF TOP WARRIORS!
AND HERE THEY ARE—

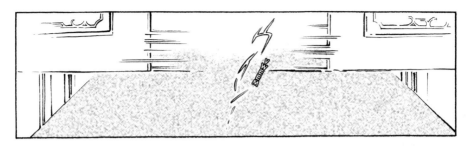

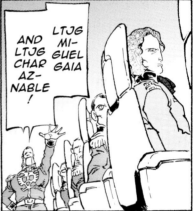

AND LTJG CHAR AZ-NABLE!

LTJG MI-GUEL GAIA

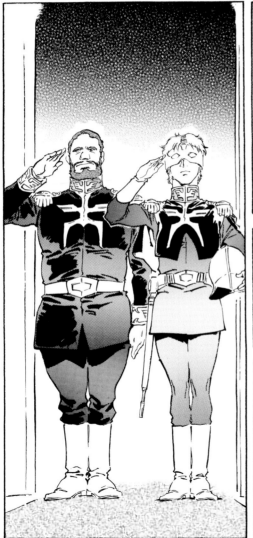

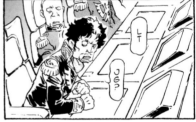

LT
JG?

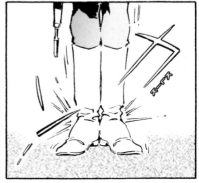

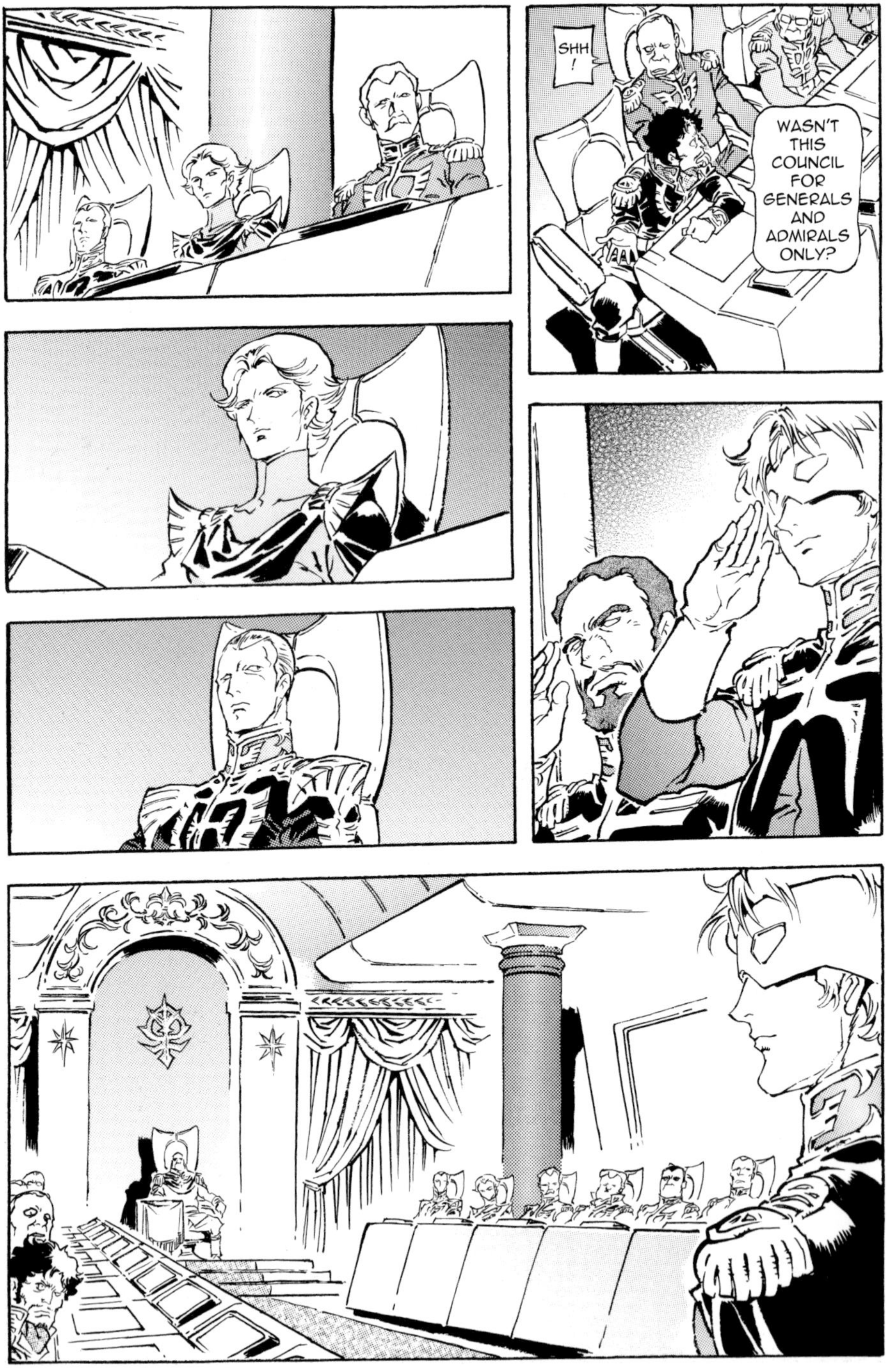
SHH!
WASN'T THIS COUNCIL FOR GENERALS AND ADMIRALS ONLY?

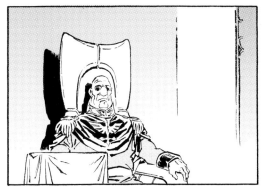

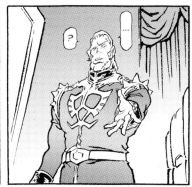

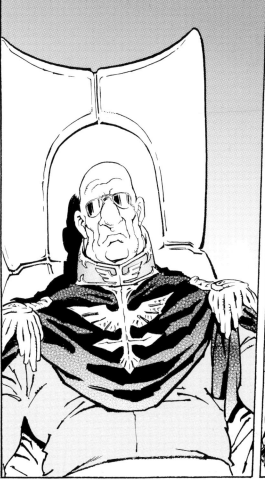

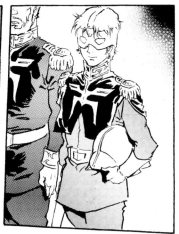

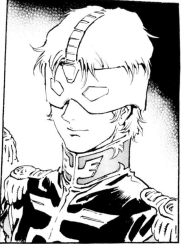

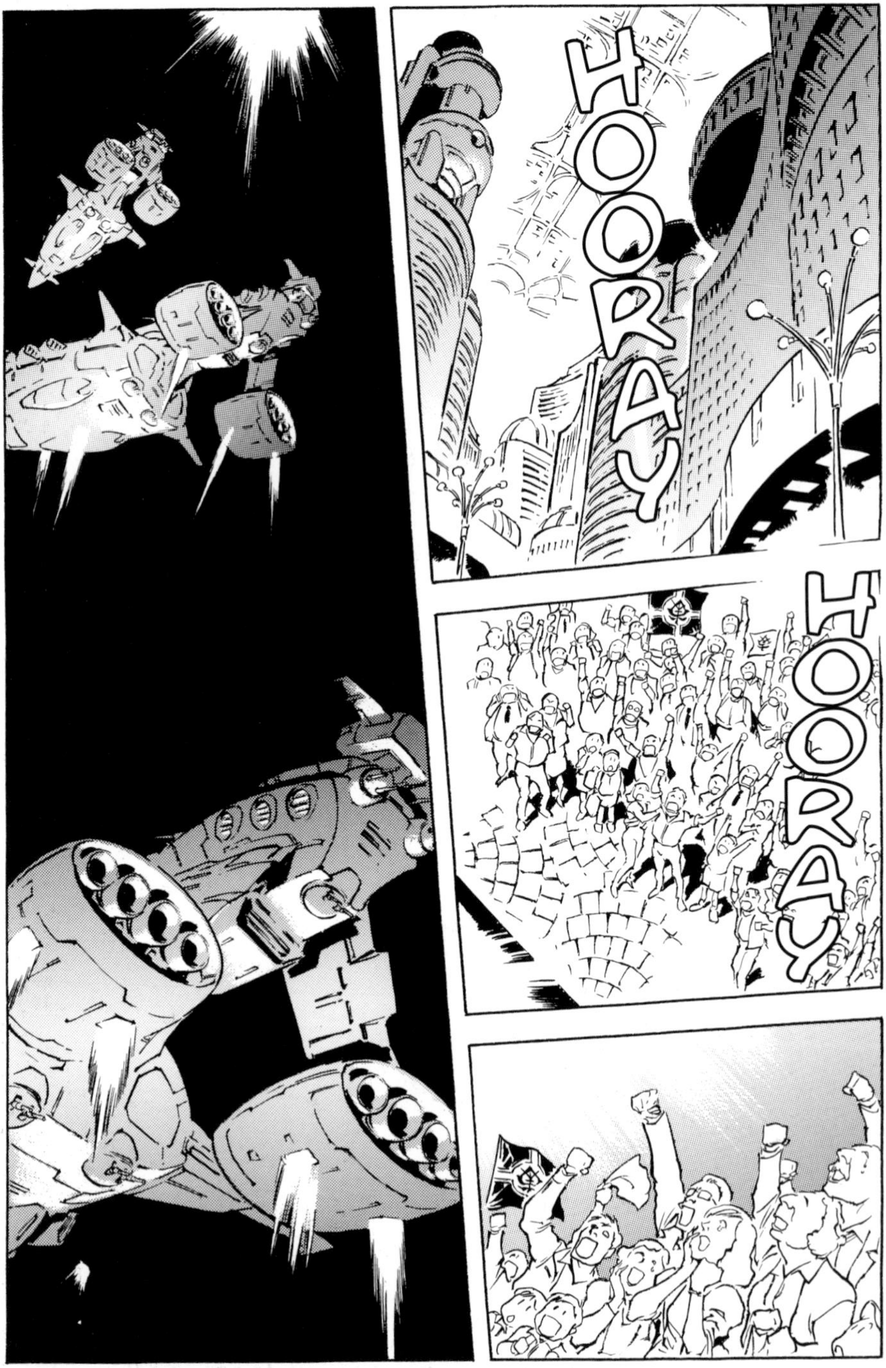
HOORAY
HOORAY

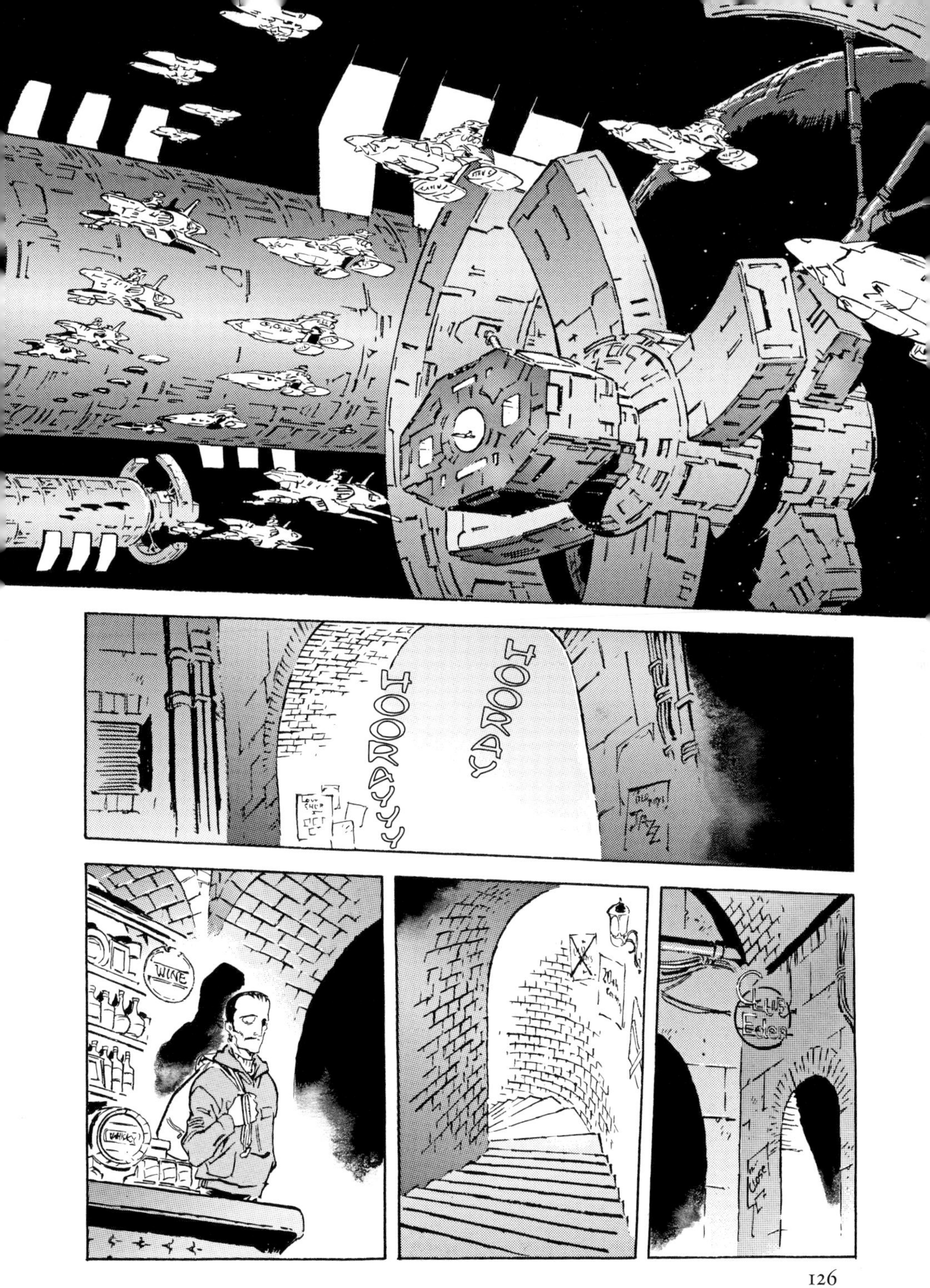
HOORAY
HOORAYYY
JAZZ
WINE

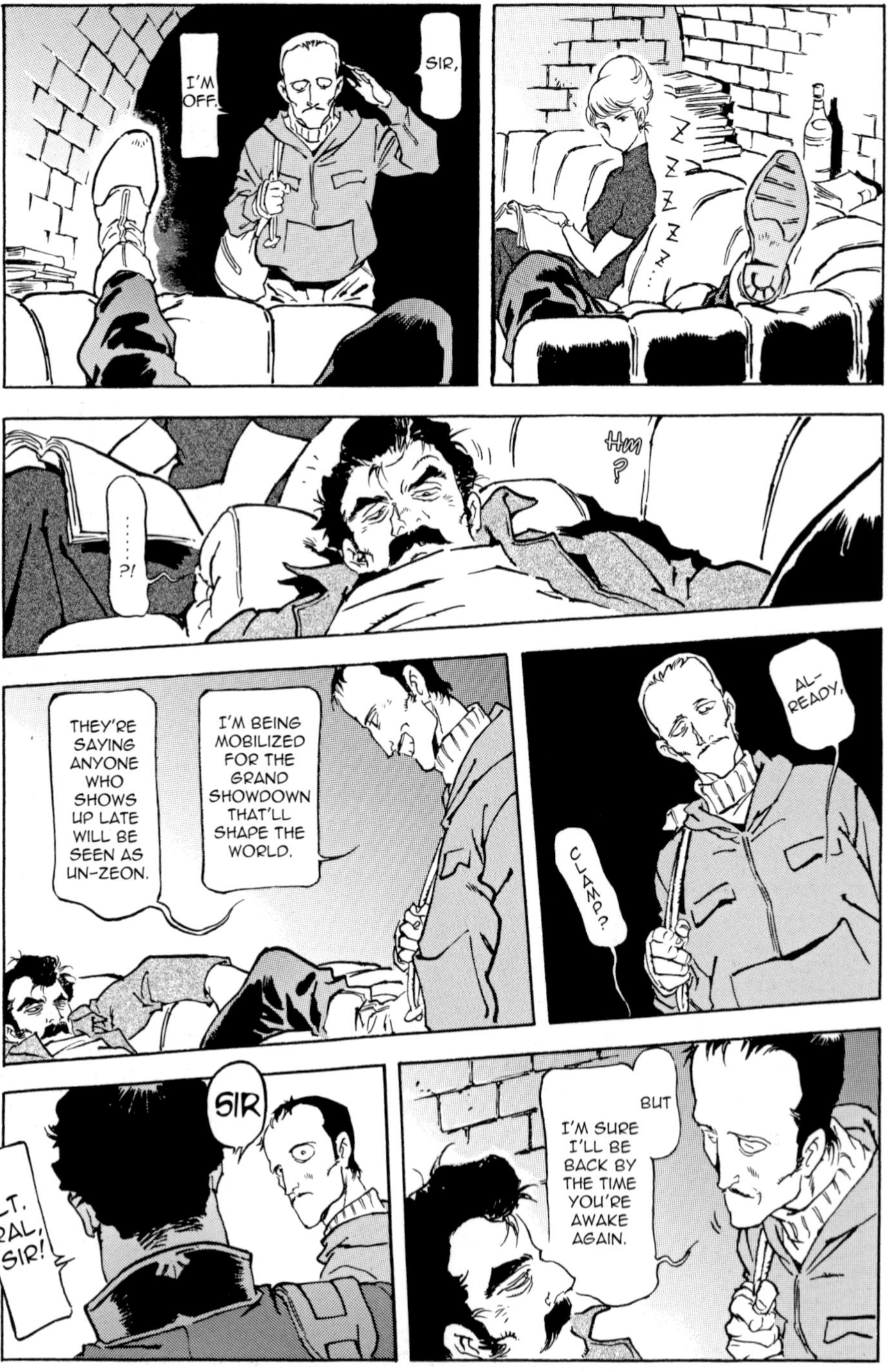

ZZZZZZ...
SIR,
I'M OFF.
HM ?
......?!
AL-READY,
CLAMP?
I'M BEING MOBILIZED FOR THE GRAND SHOWDOWN THAT'LL SHAPE THE WORLD.
THEY'RE SAYING ANYONE WHO SHOWS UP LATE WILL BE SEEN AS UN-ZEON.
BUT I'M SURE I'LL BE BACK BY THE TIME YOU'RE AWAKE AGAIN.
SIR
LT. RAL, SIR!

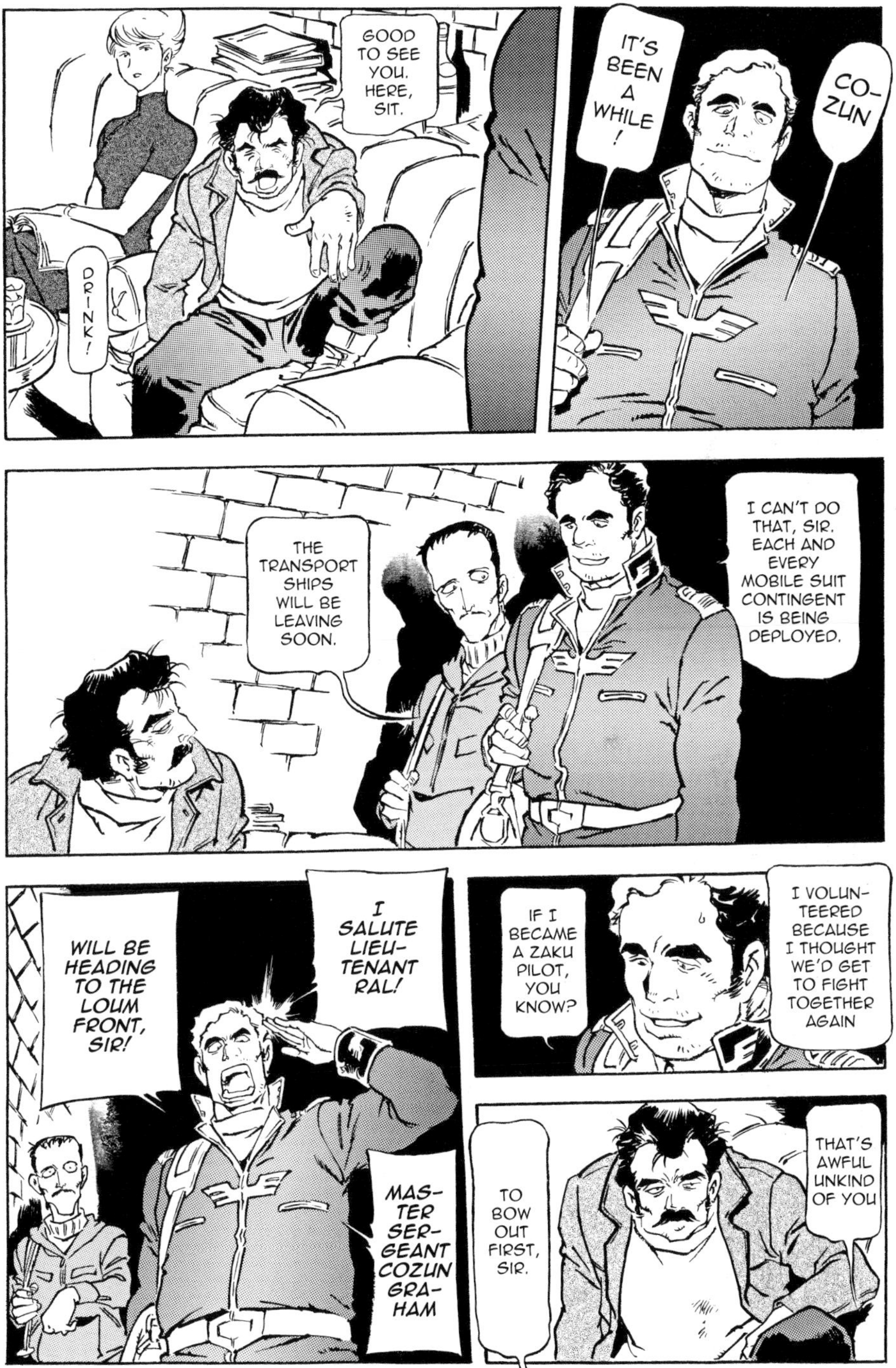
CO-ZUN
IT'S BEEN A WHILE!
GOOD TO SEE YOU. HERE, SIT.
DRINK!
I CAN'T DO THAT, SIR. EACH AND EVERY MOBILE SUIT CONTINGENT IS BEING DEPLOYED.
THE TRANSPORT SHIPS WILL BE LEAVING SOON.
I VOLUNTEERED BECAUSE I THOUGHT WE'D GET TO FIGHT TOGETHER AGAIN
IF I BECAME A ZAKU PILOT, YOU KNOW?
THAT'S AWFUL UNKIND OF YOU
TO BOW OUT FIRST, SIR.
I SALUTE LIEUTENANT RAL!
WILL BE HEADING TO THE LOUM FRONT, SIR!
MASTER SERGEANT COZUN GRAHAM

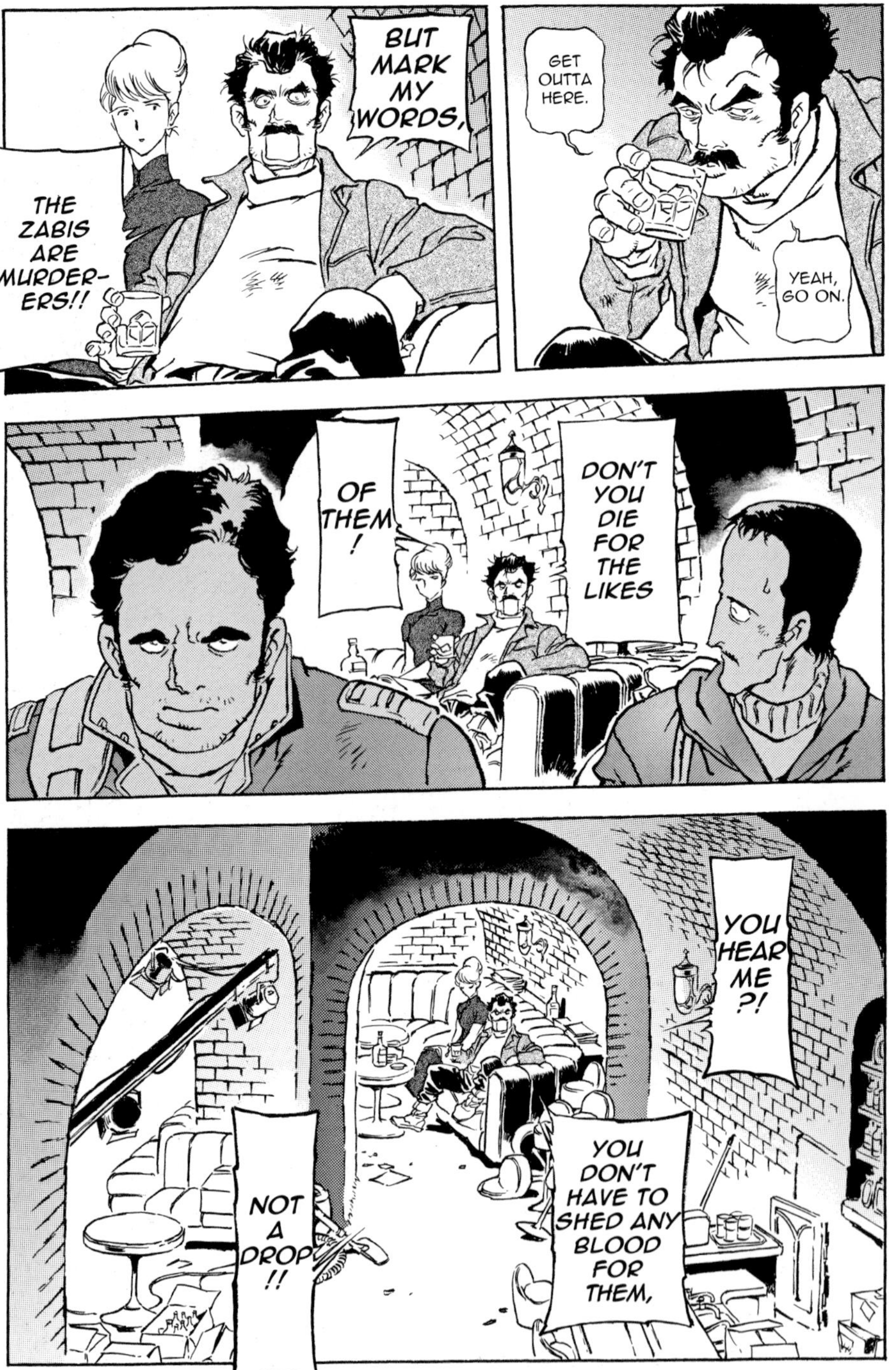
GET OUTTA HERE.
YEAH, GO ON.
BUT MARK MY WORDS,
THE ZABIS ARE MURDERERS!!
DON'T YOU DIE FOR THE LIKES
OF THEM!
YOU HEAR ME?!
YOU DON'T HAVE TO SHED ANY BLOOD FOR THEM,
NOT A DROP!!

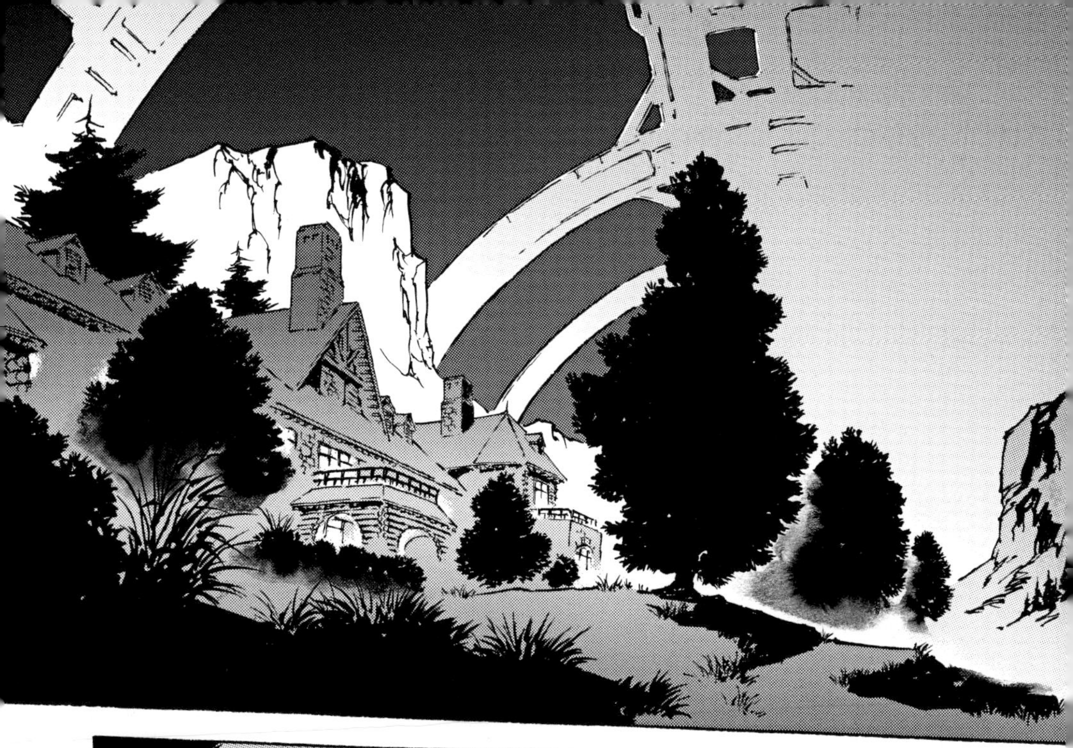

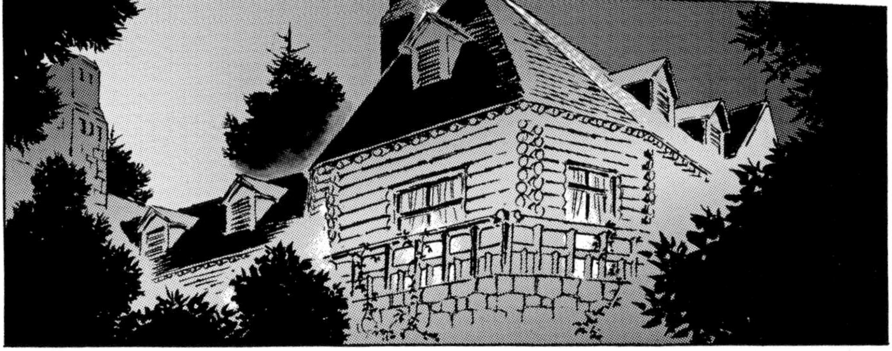

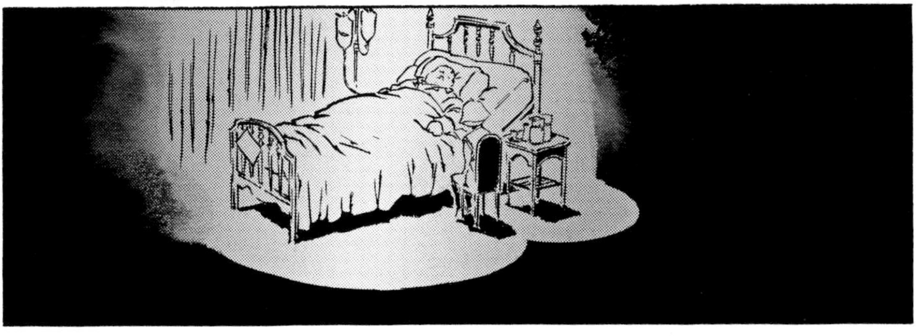

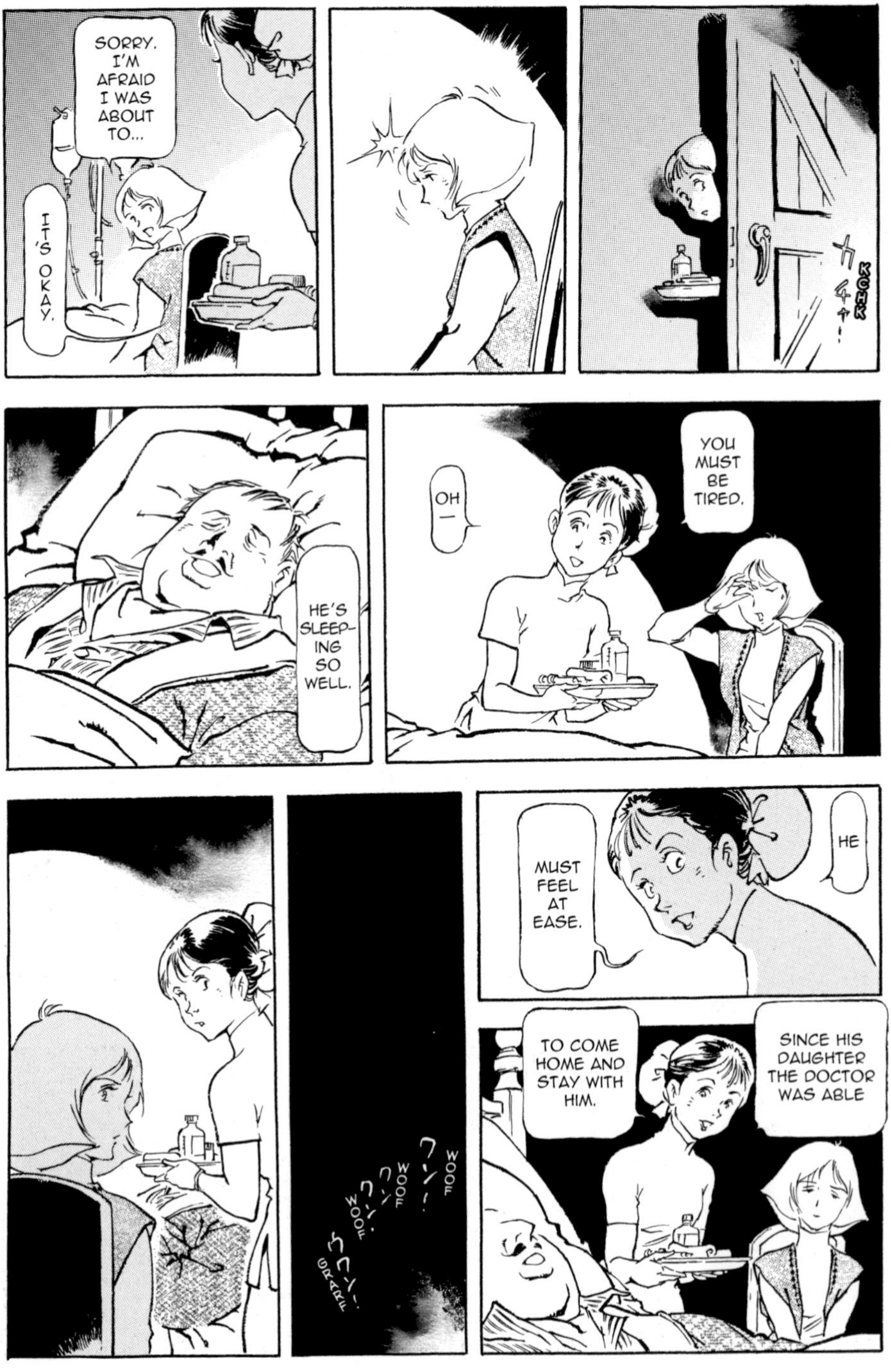

カチャ…
KCHK
SORRY. I'M AFRAID I WAS ABOUT TO...
IT'S OKAY.
YOU MUST BE TIRED.
OH—
HE'S SLEEPING SO WELL.
HE
MUST FEEL AT EASE.
SINCE HIS DAUGHTER THE DOCTOR WAS ABLE
TO COME HOME AND STAY WITH HIM.
ワン!
WOOF
ワン
WOOF
ワン!
WOOF
ウワン!
GRARF

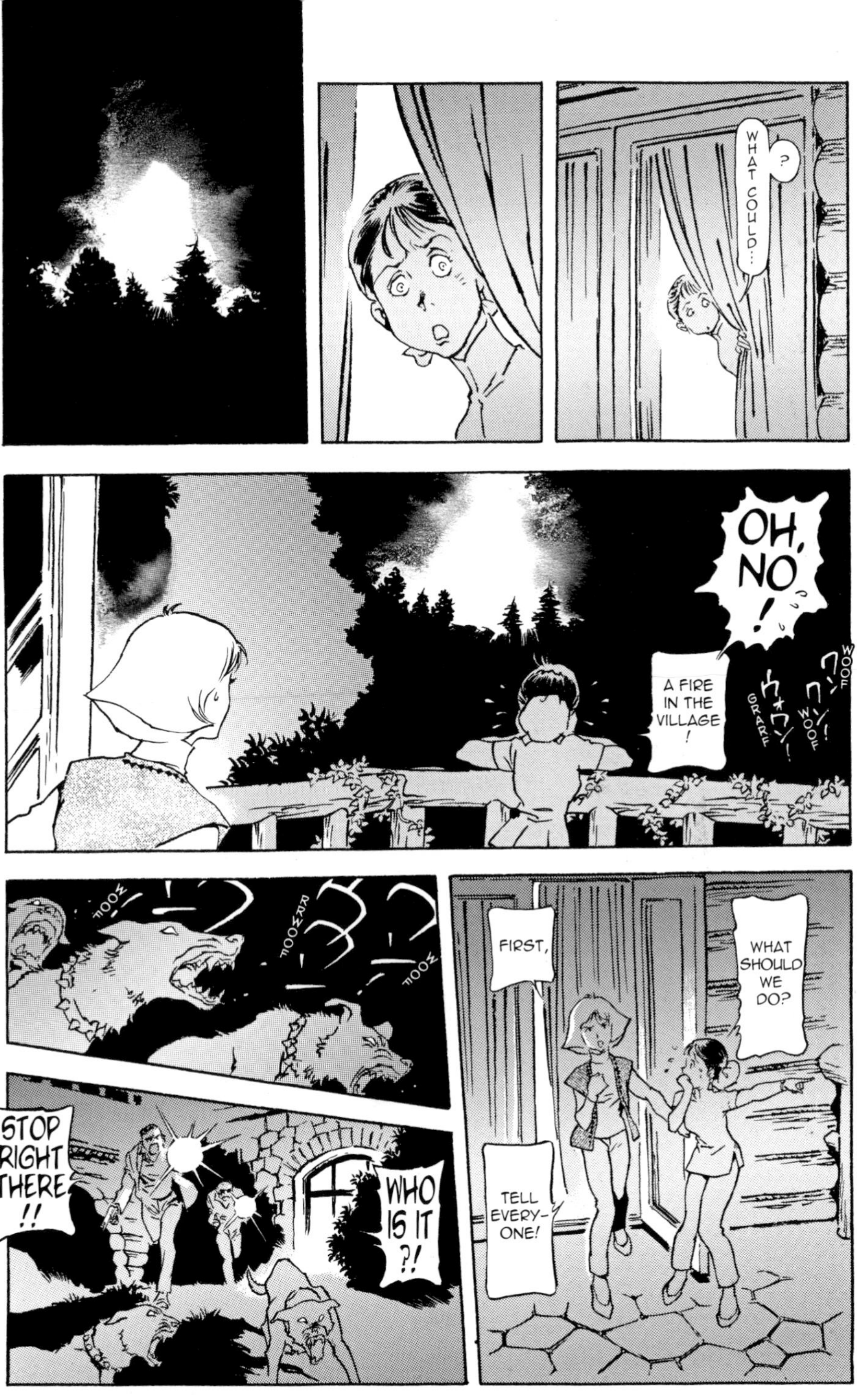
?
WHAT COULD...
OH, NO!
A FIRE IN THE VILLAGE!
WOOF WOOF
GRARF
WHAT SHOULD WE DO?
FIRST,
TELL EVERY-ONE!
WOOF
RAWOOF
WOOF
WHO IS IT?!
STOP RIGHT THERE!!

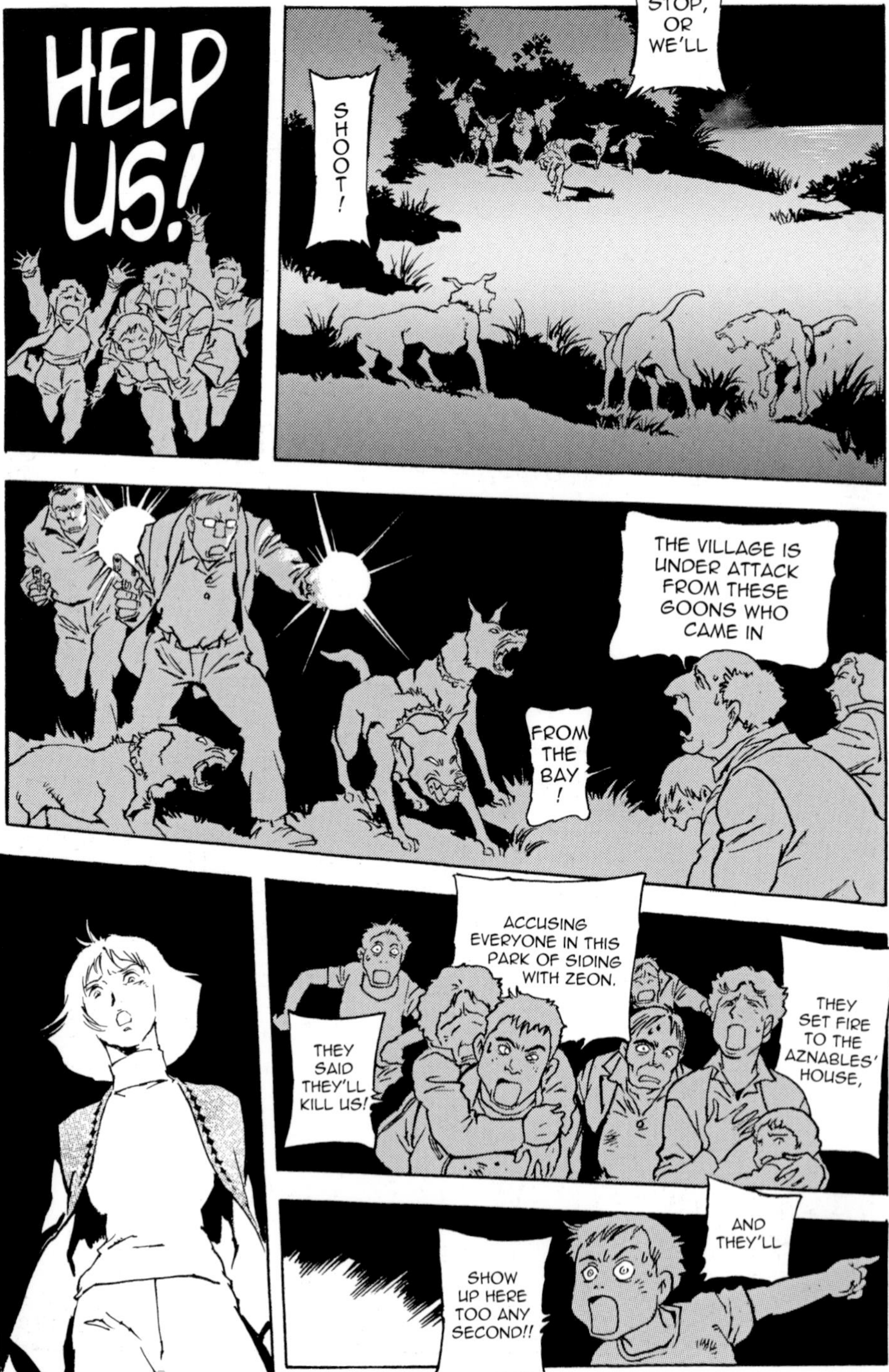
STOP, OR WE'LL
SHOOT!
HELP US!
THE VILLAGE IS UNDER ATTACK FROM THESE GOONS WHO CAME IN
FROM THE BAY!
THEY SET FIRE TO THE AZNABLES' HOUSE,
ACCUSING EVERYONE IN THIS PARK OF SIDING WITH ZEON.
THEY SAID THEY'LL KILL US!
AND THEY'LL
SHOW UP HERE TOO ANY SECOND!!

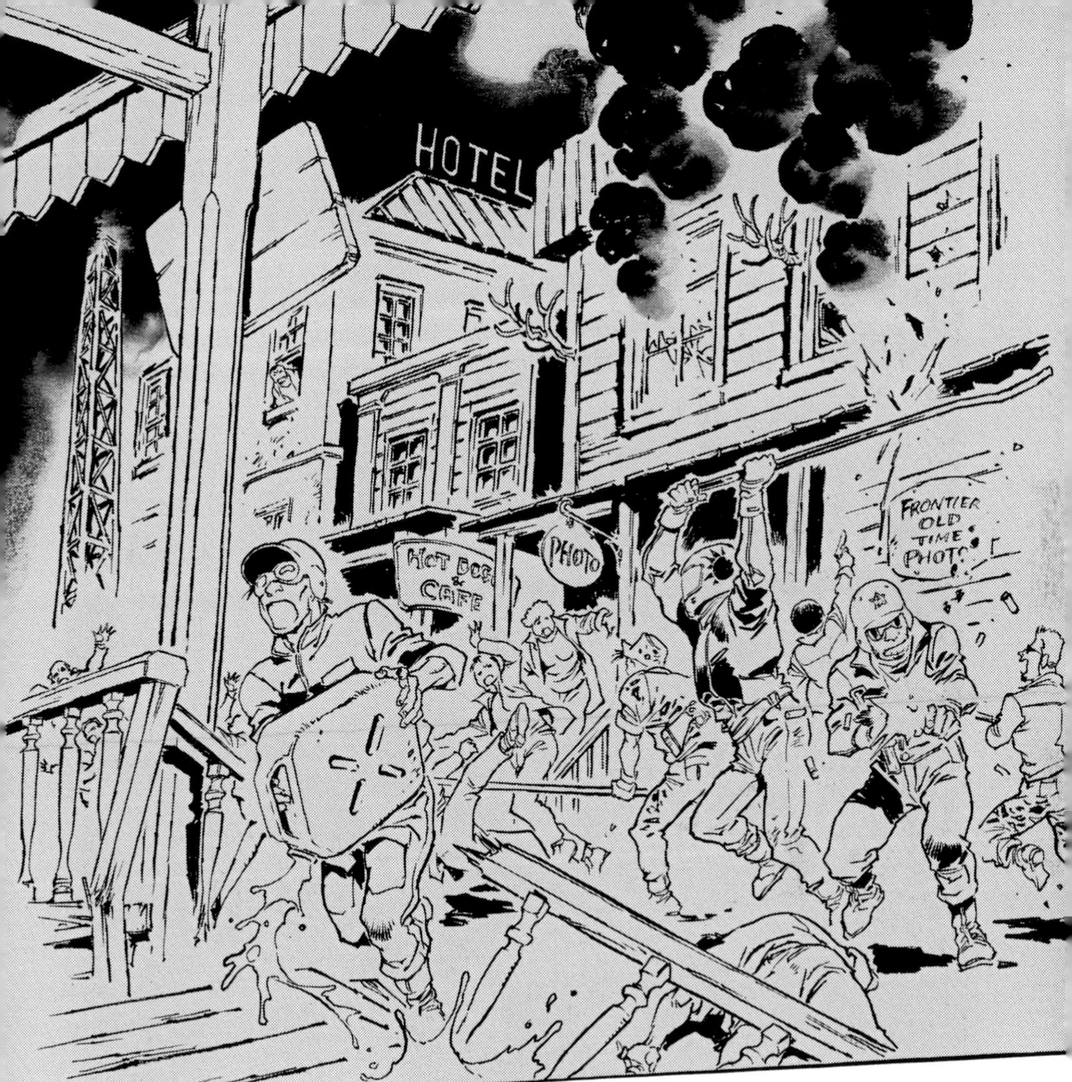
HOTEL
HOT DOG & CAFE
PHOTO
FRONTIER OLD TIME PHOTO
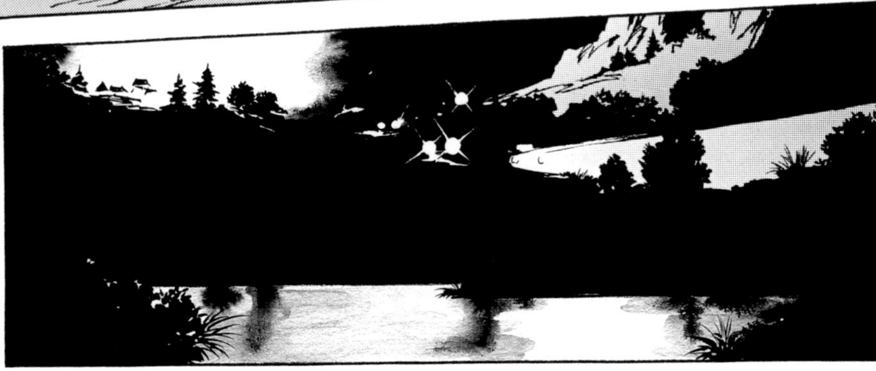

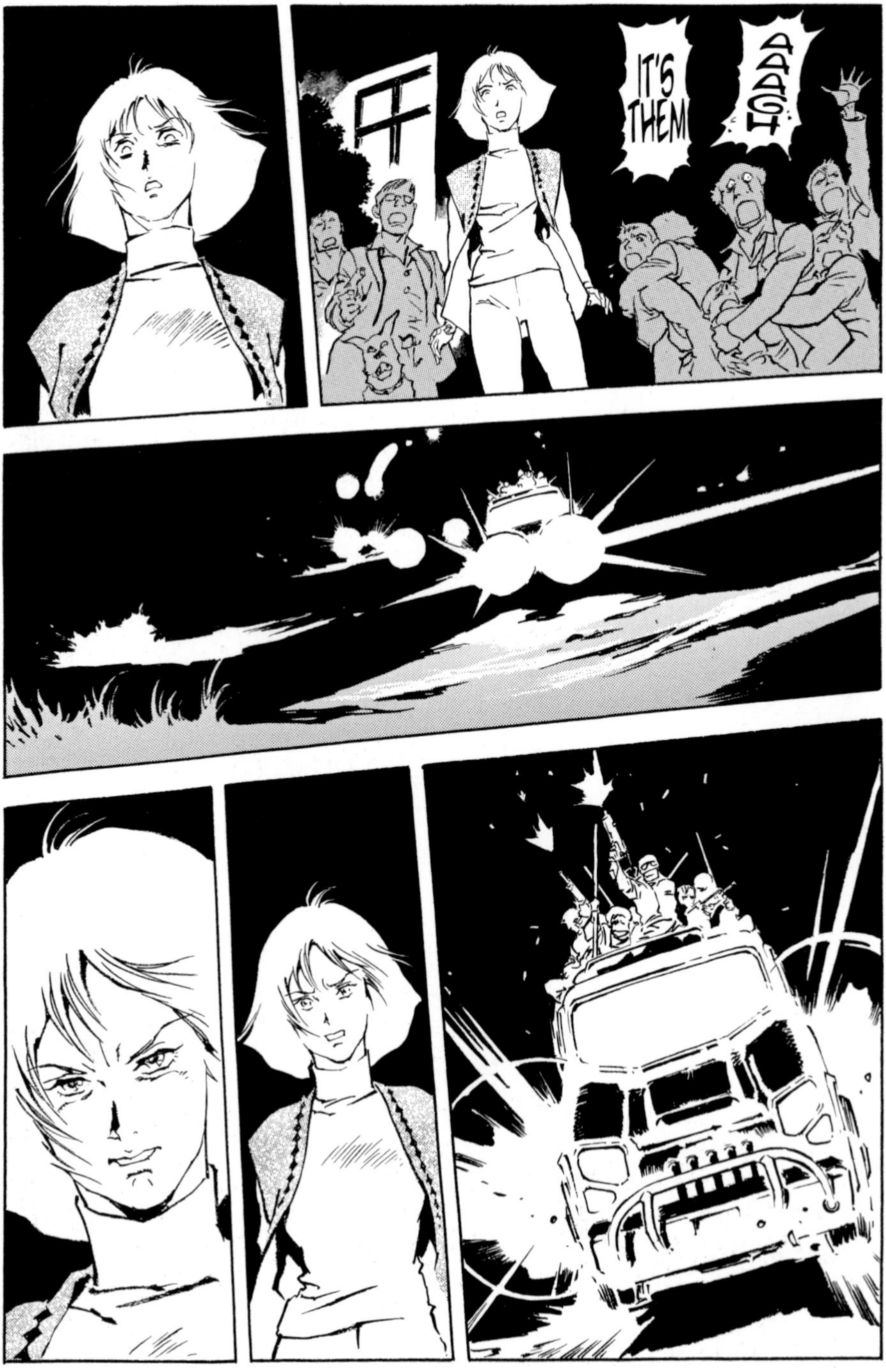
AAAGH
IT'S THEM

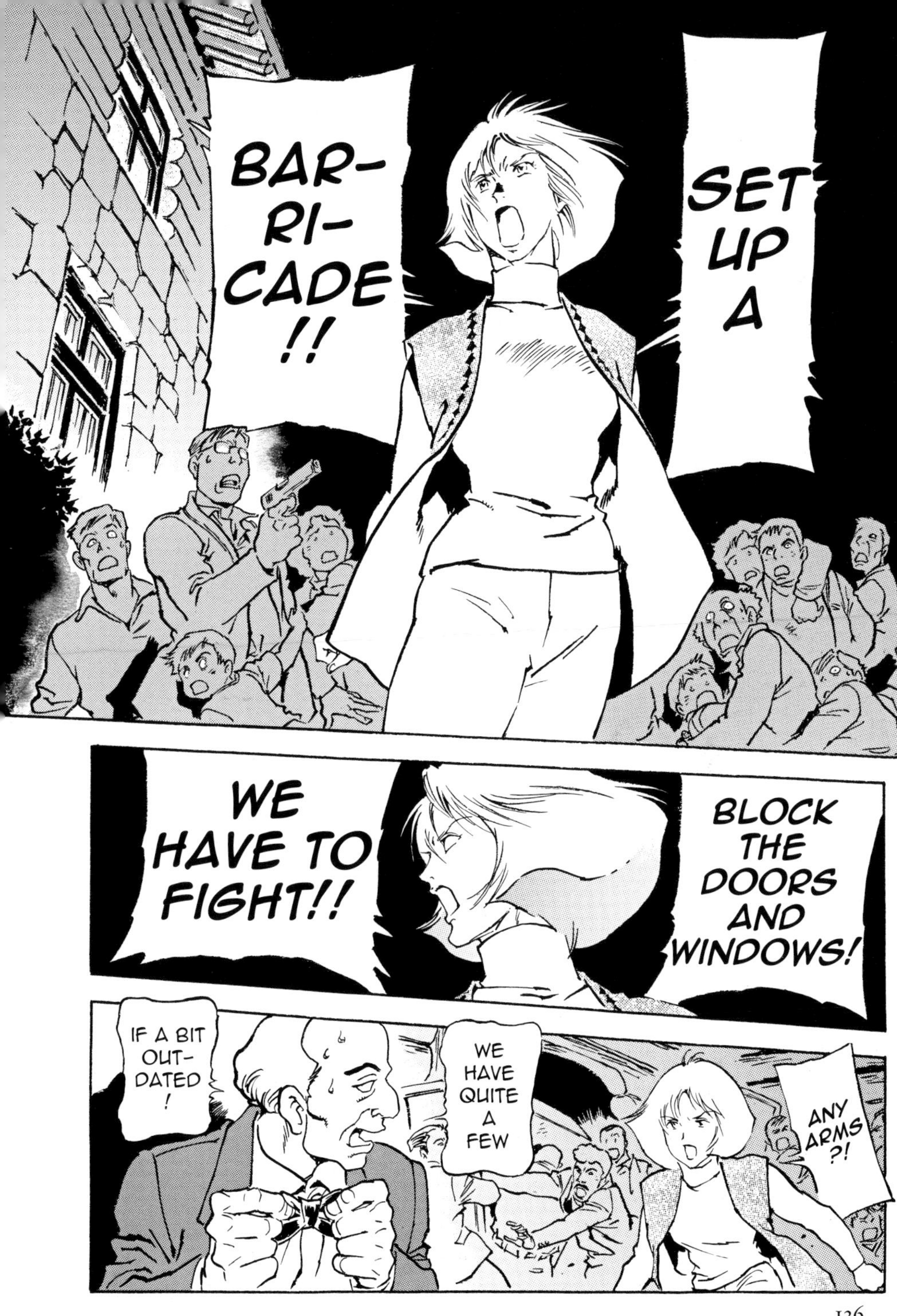
SET UP A
BAR-RI-CADE!!
BLOCK THE DOORS AND WINDOWS!
WE HAVE TO FIGHT!!
ANY ARMS?!
WE HAVE QUITE A FEW
IF A BIT OUT-DATED!

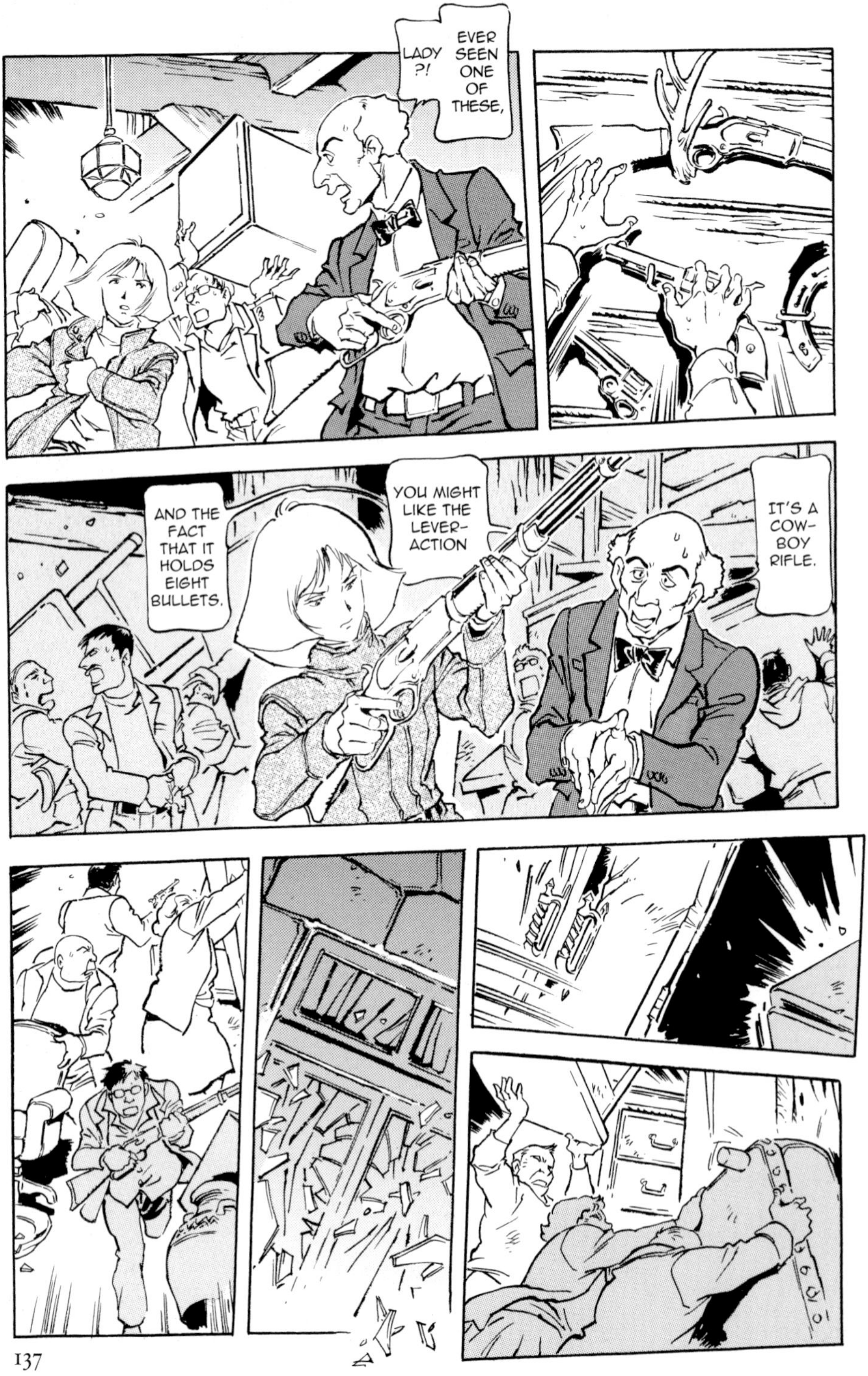
EVER SEEN ONE OF THESE,
LADY?!
IT'S A COWBOY RIFLE.
YOU MIGHT LIKE THE LEVER-ACTION
AND THE FACT THAT IT HOLDS EIGHT BULLETS.

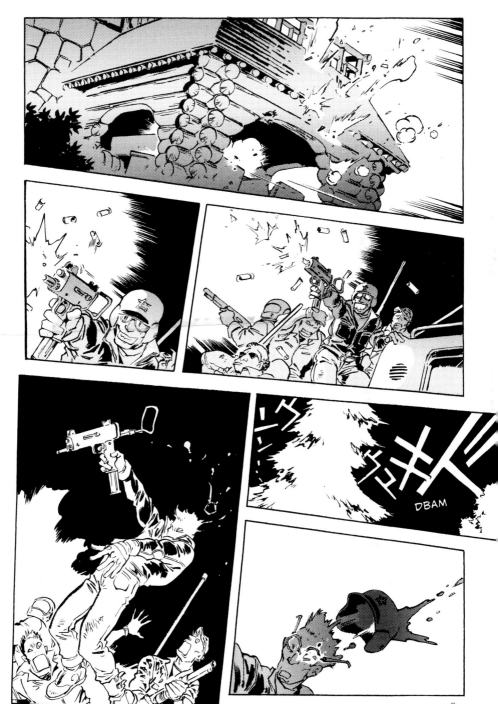

DBAM

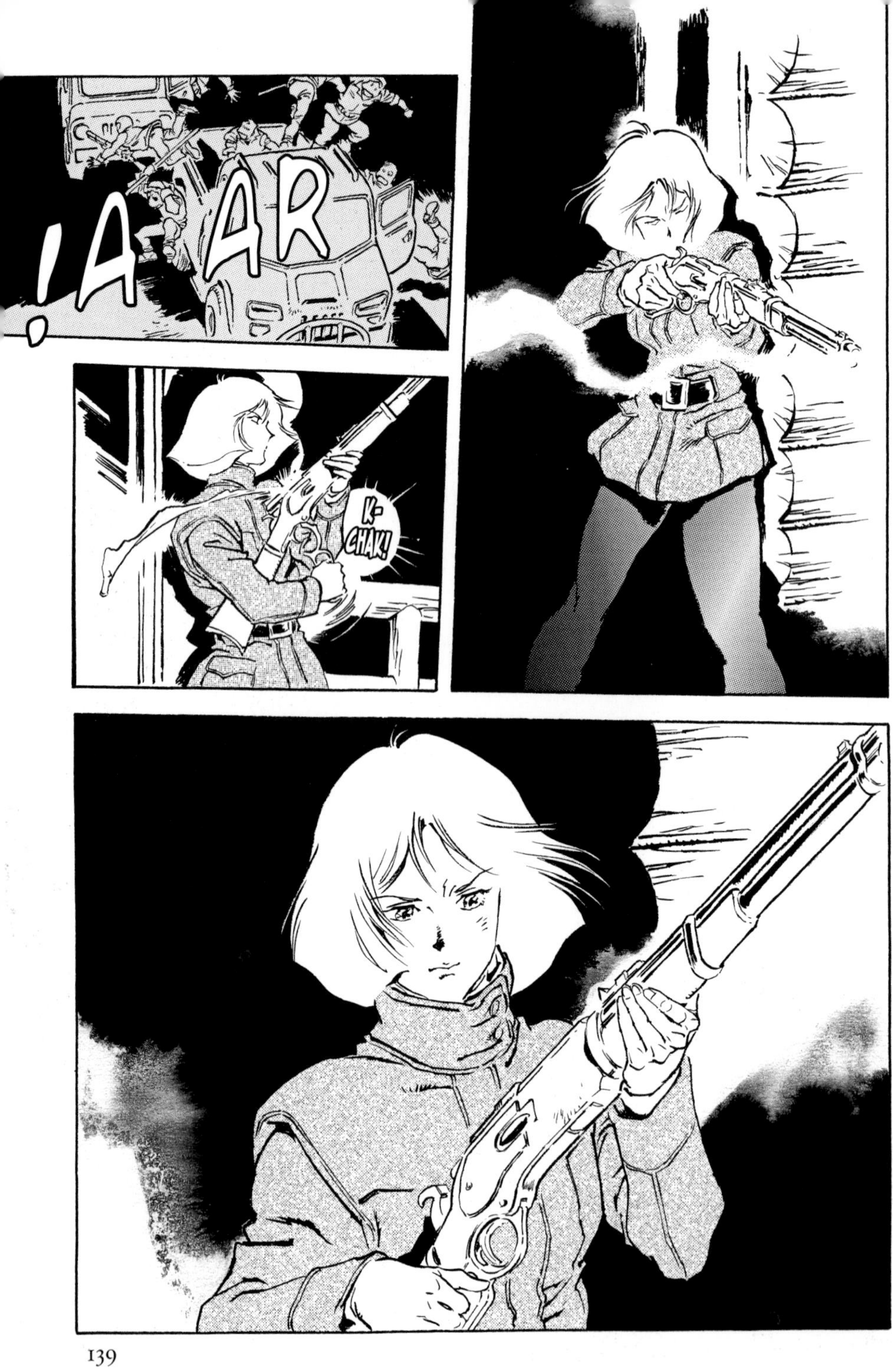

!A AR
K-CHAK!

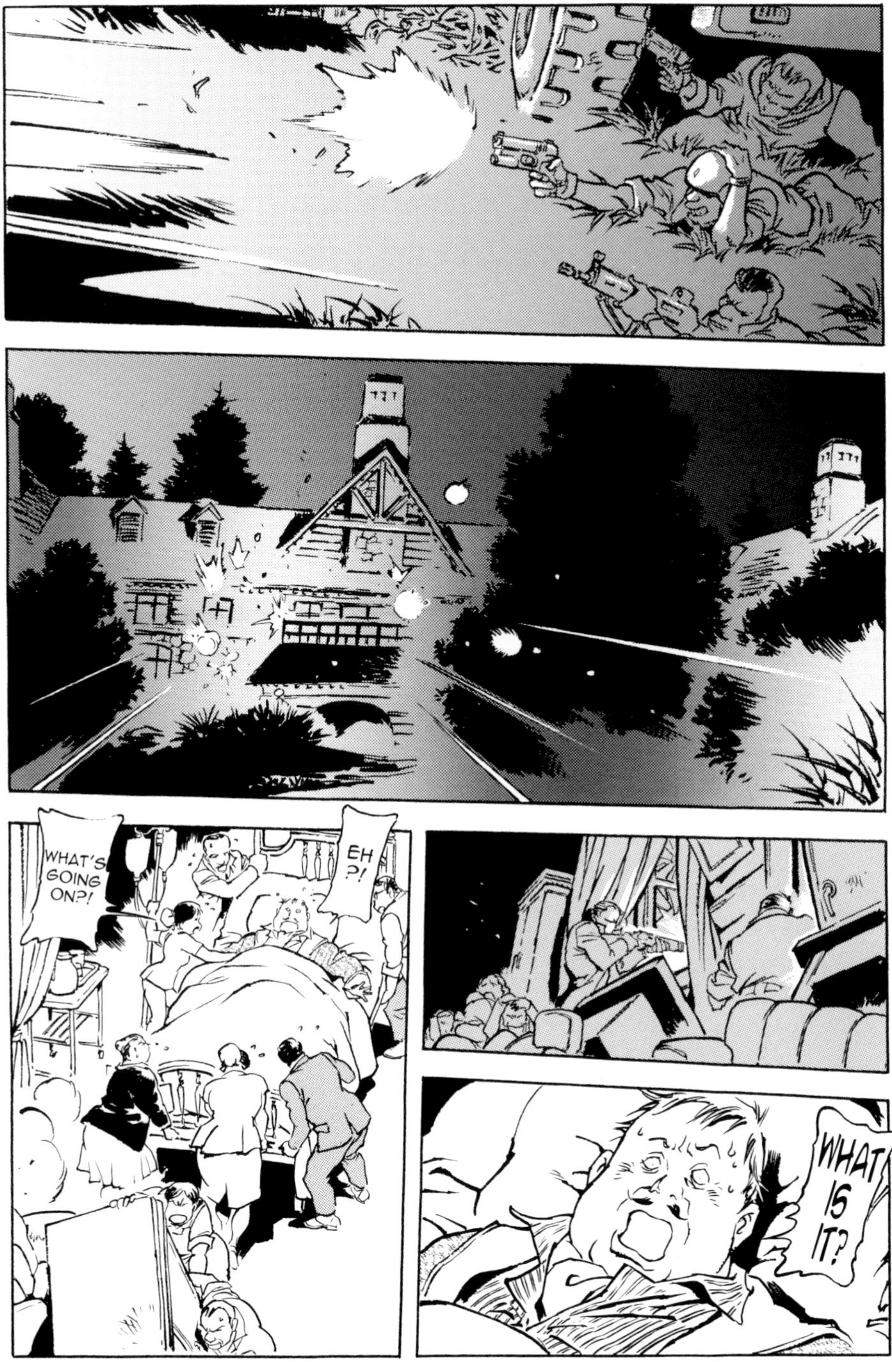
WHAT IS IT?
EH?!
WHAT'S GOING ON?!

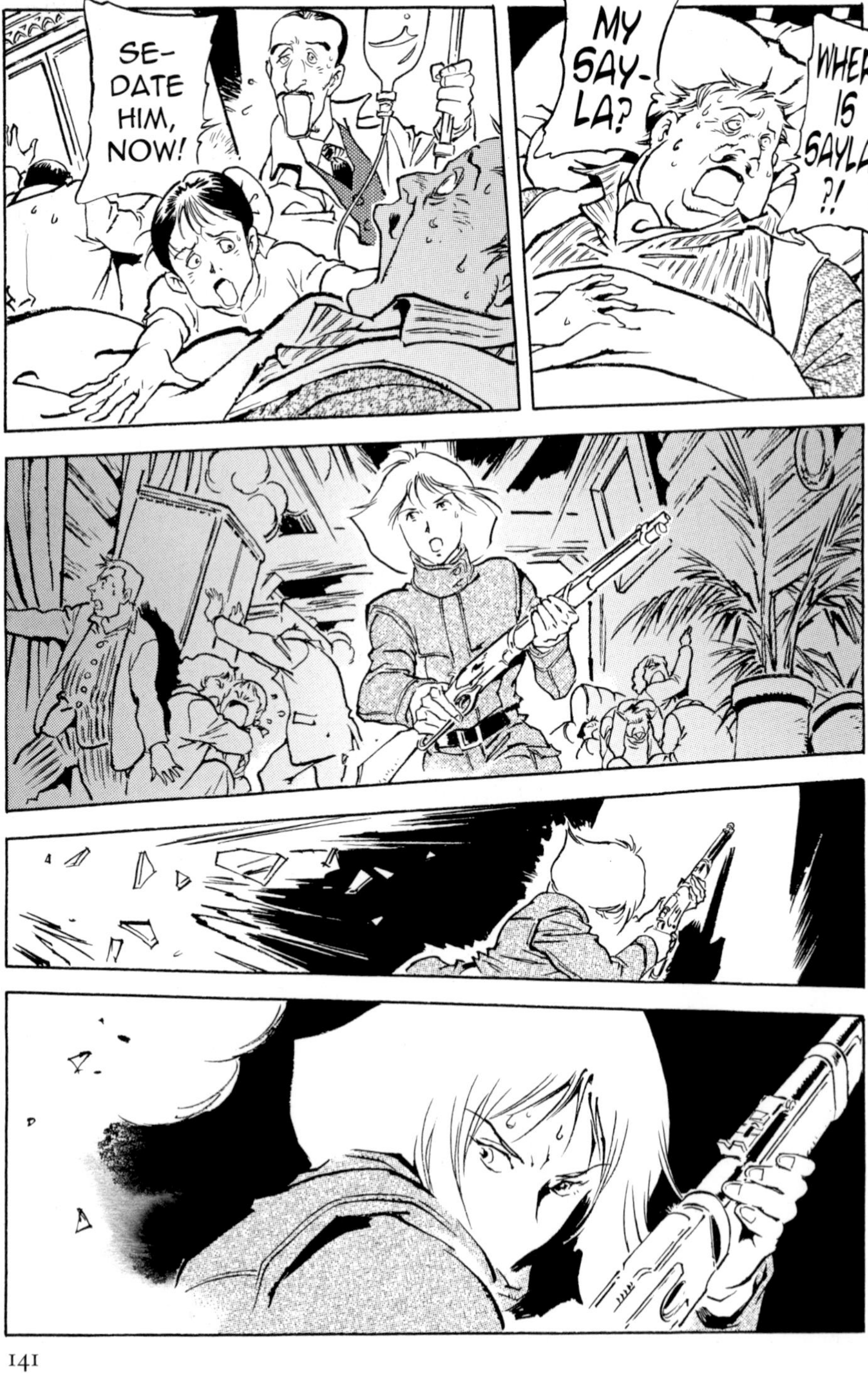
WHERE IS SAYLA?!
MY SAYLA?
SEDATE HIM, NOW!

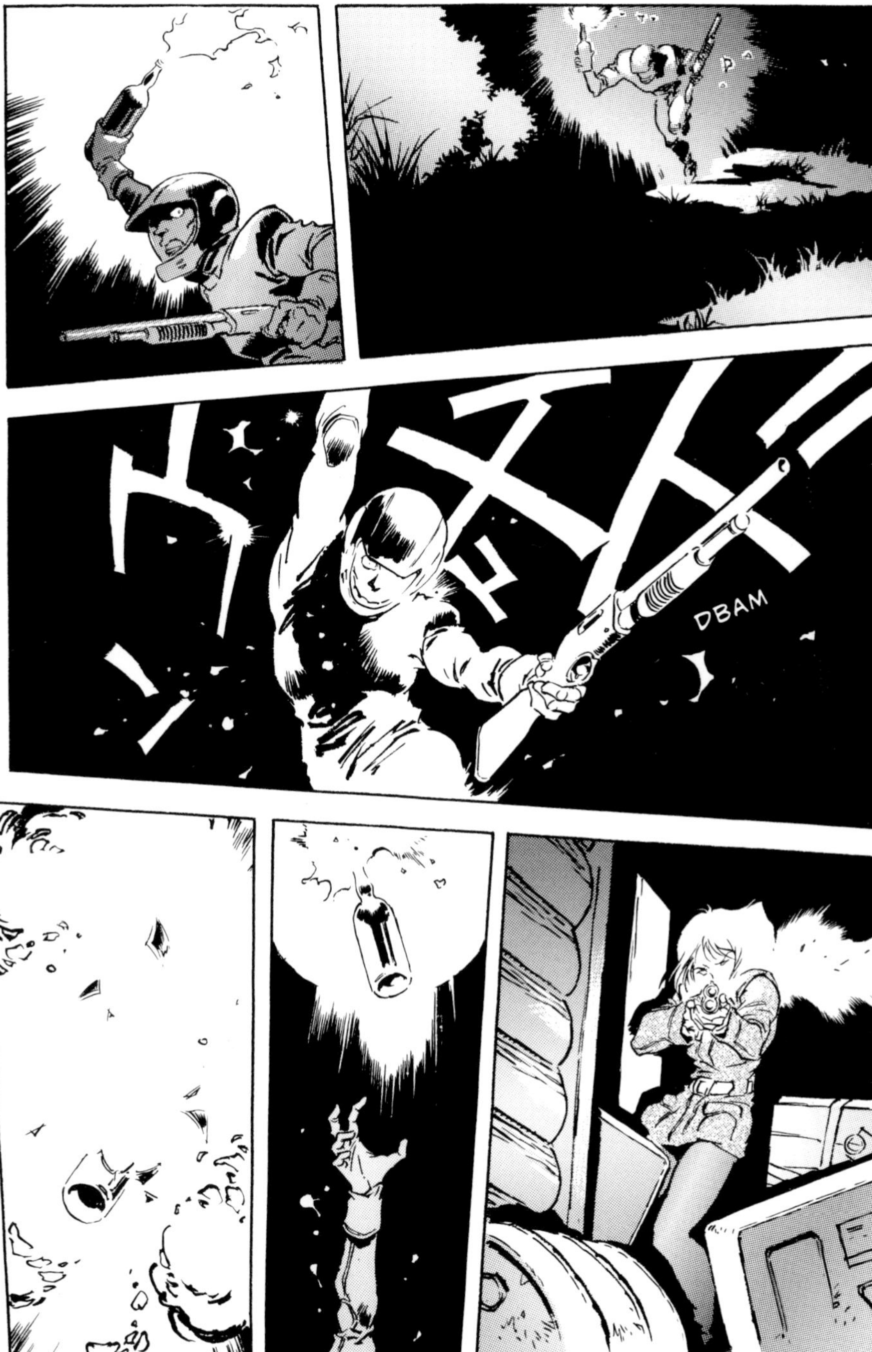
DBAM

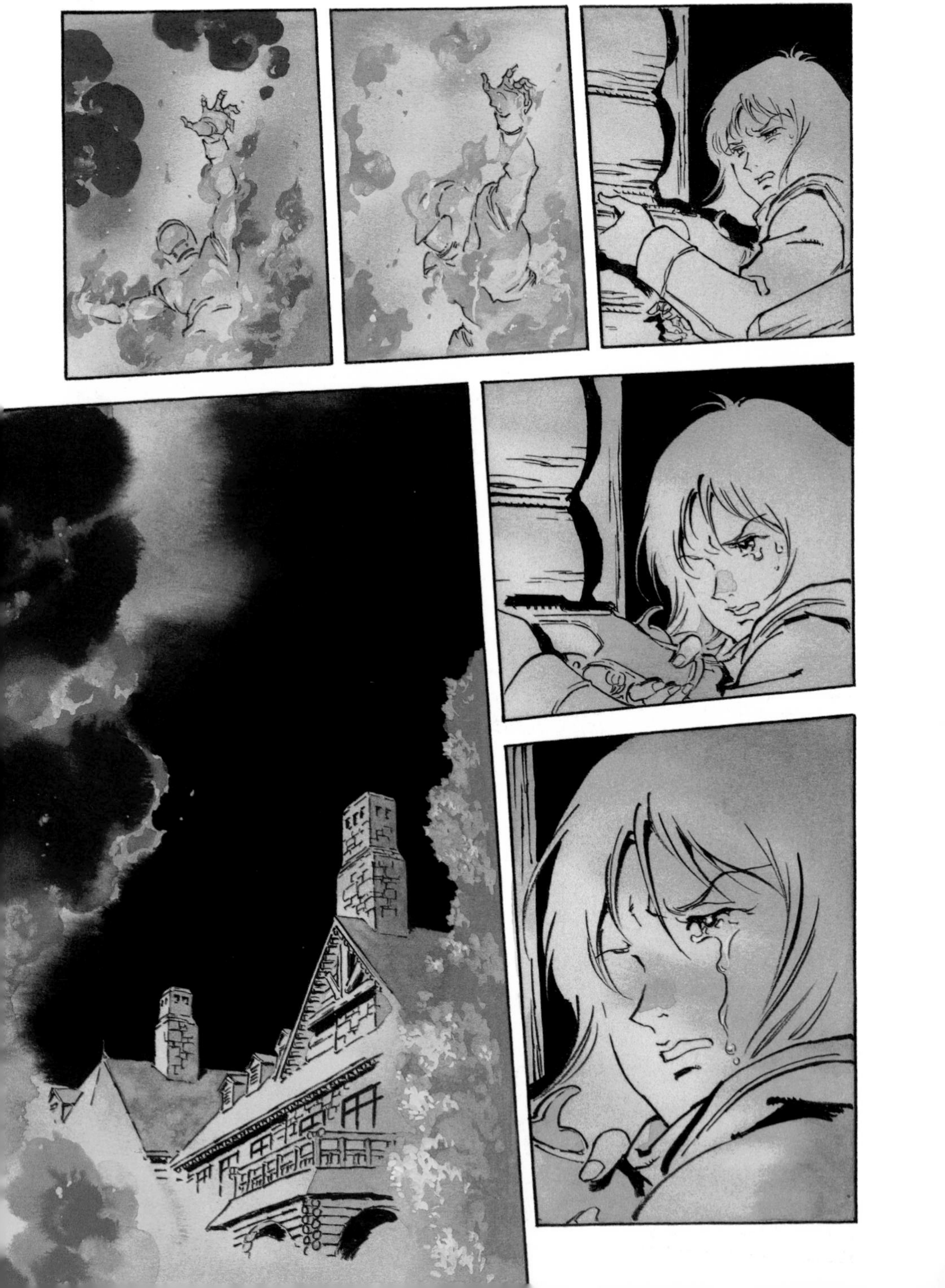

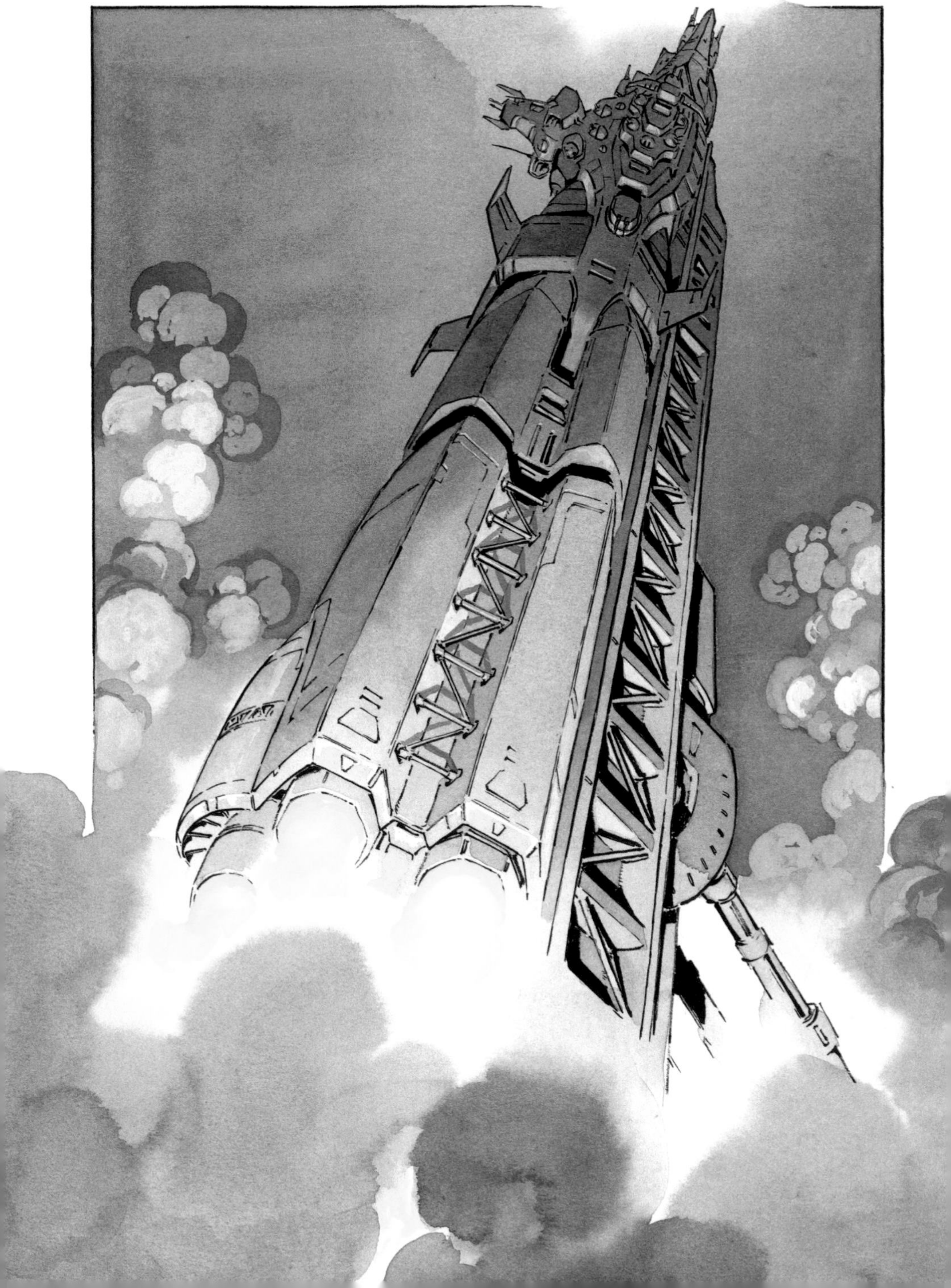

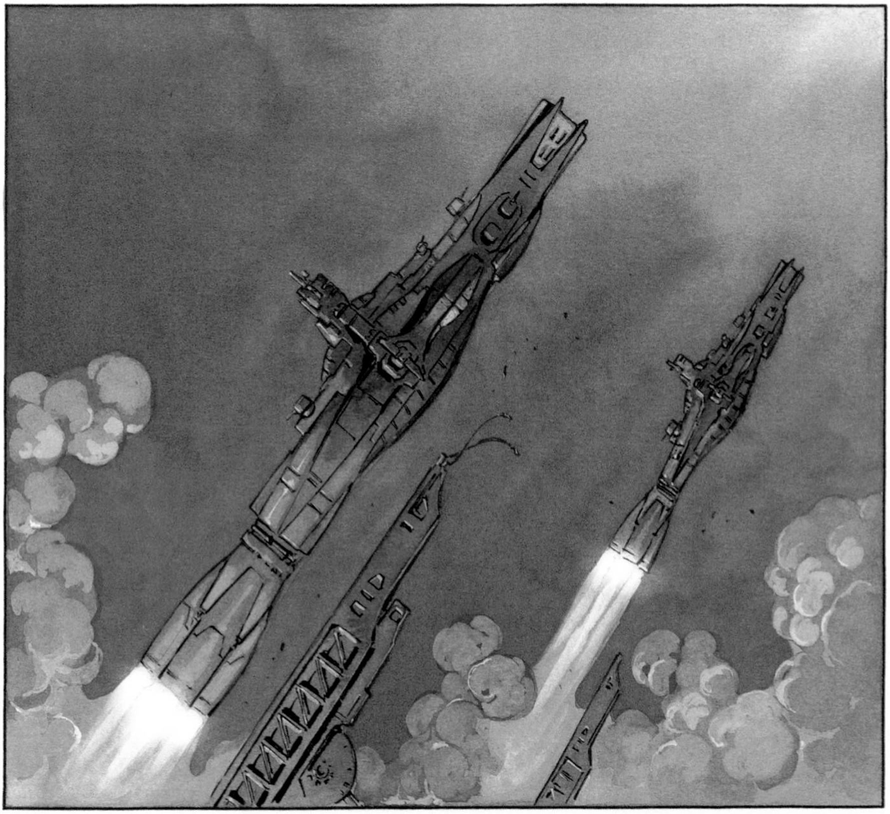
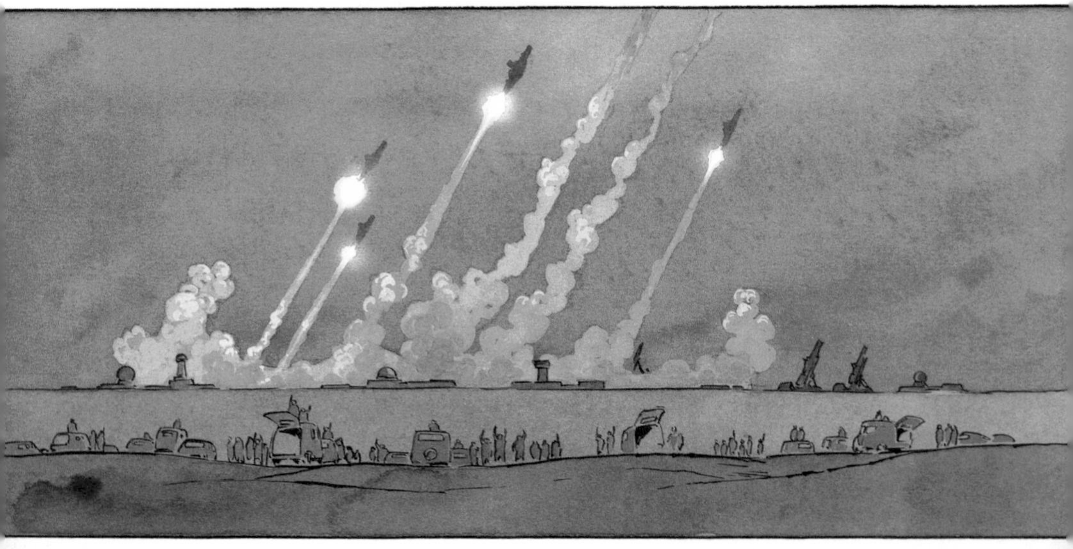

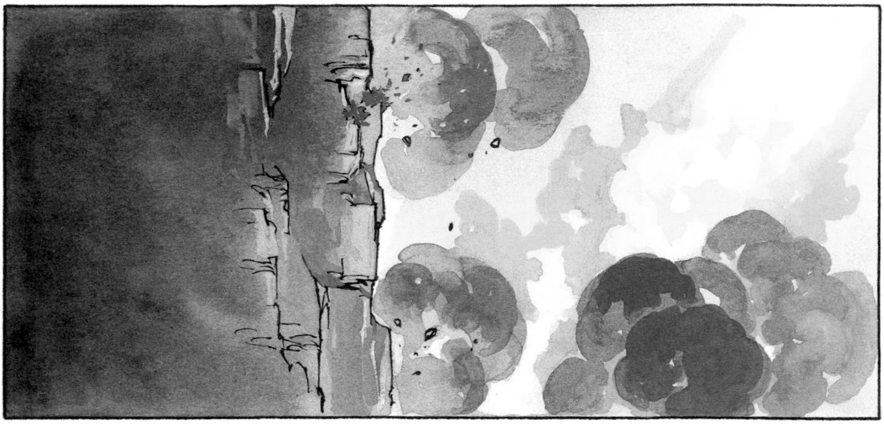
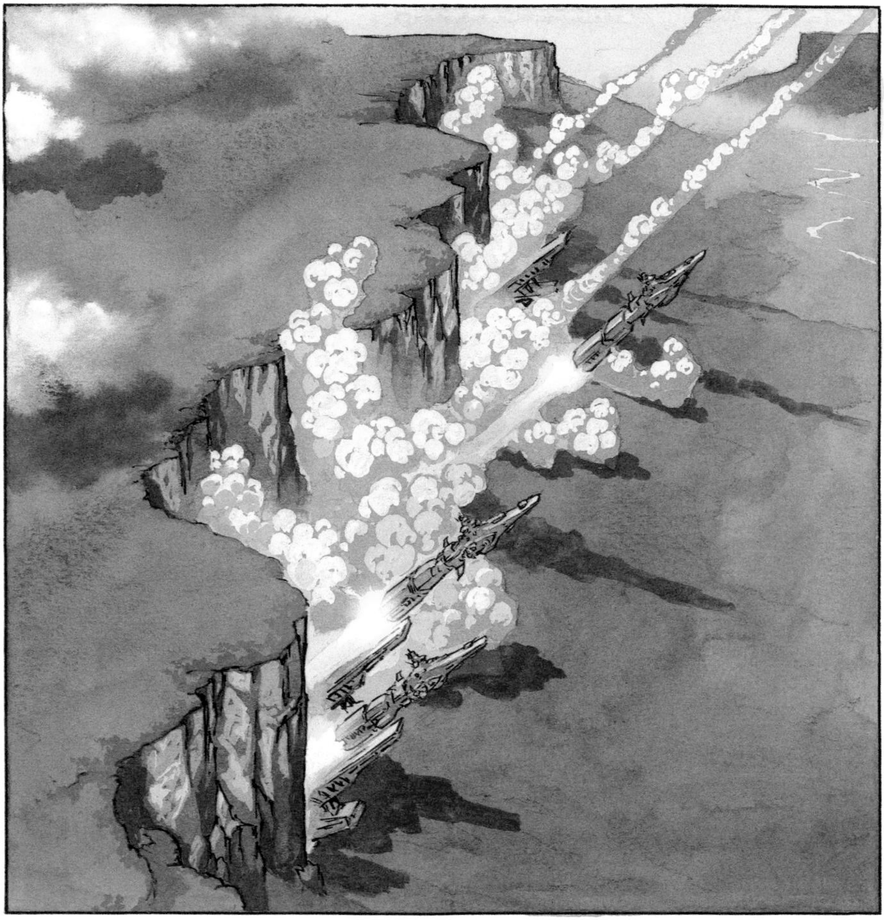

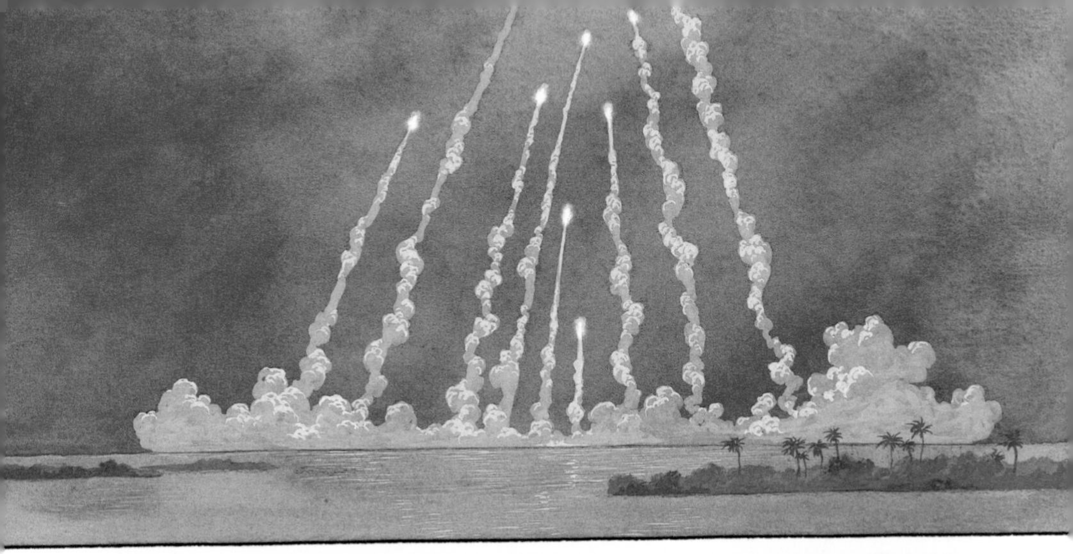
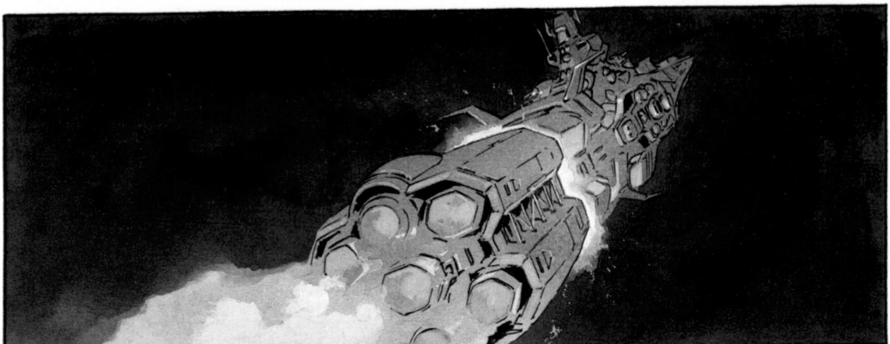
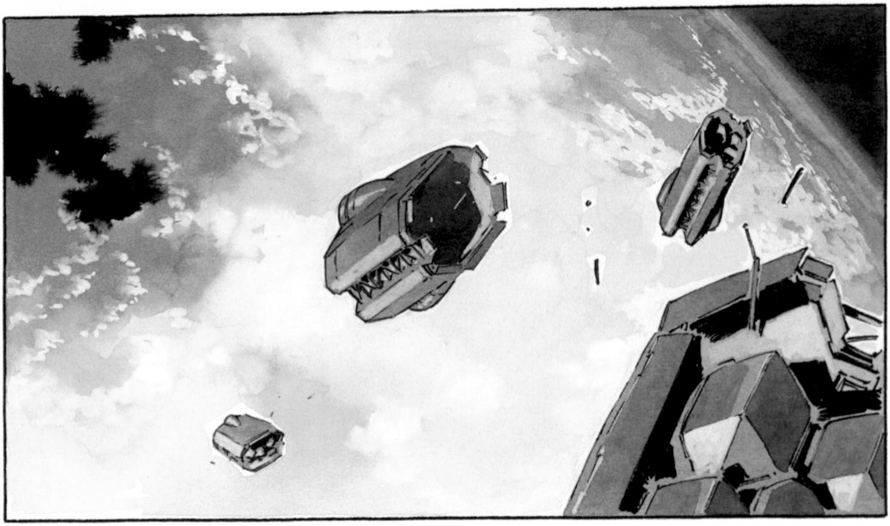

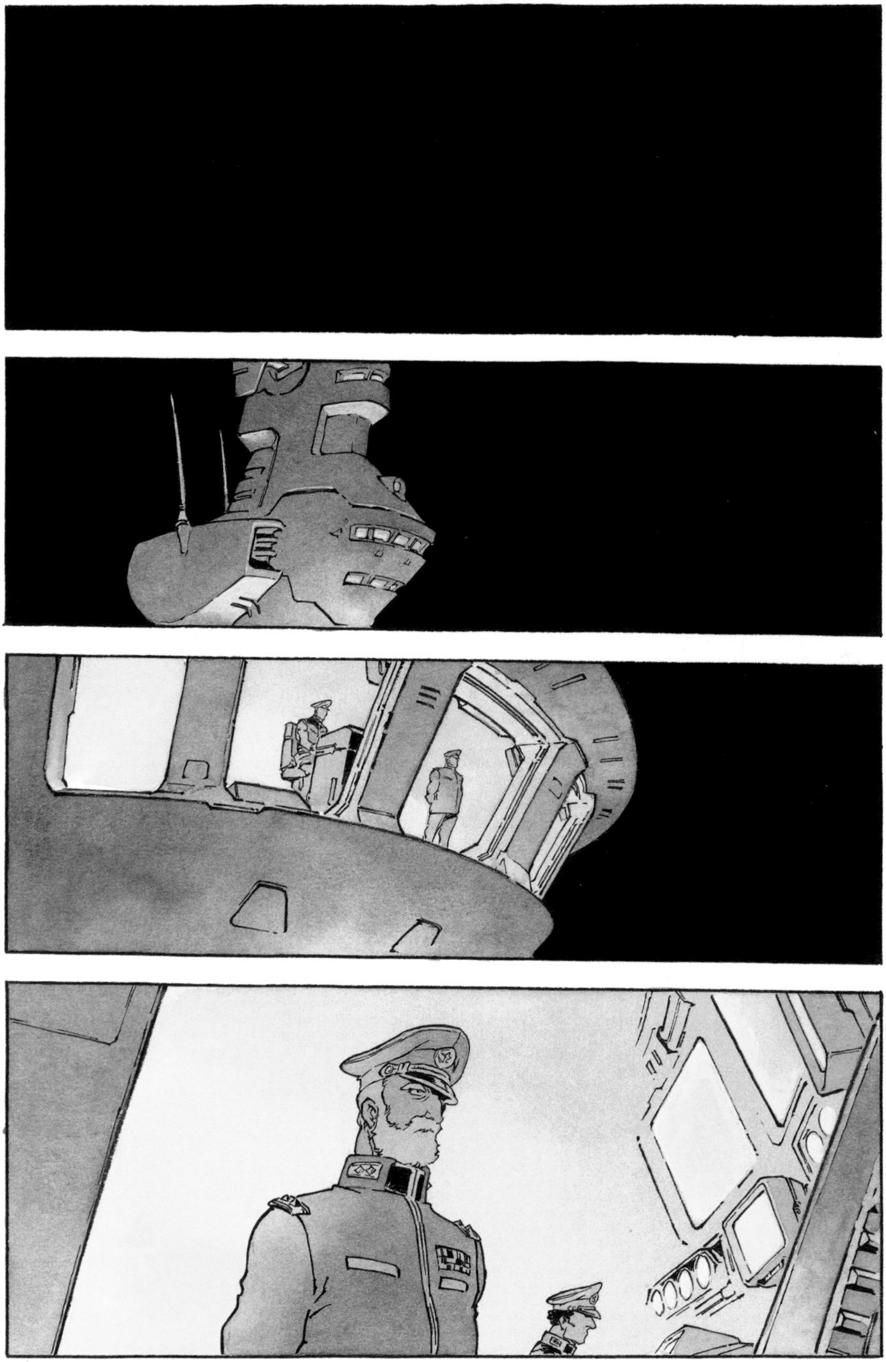

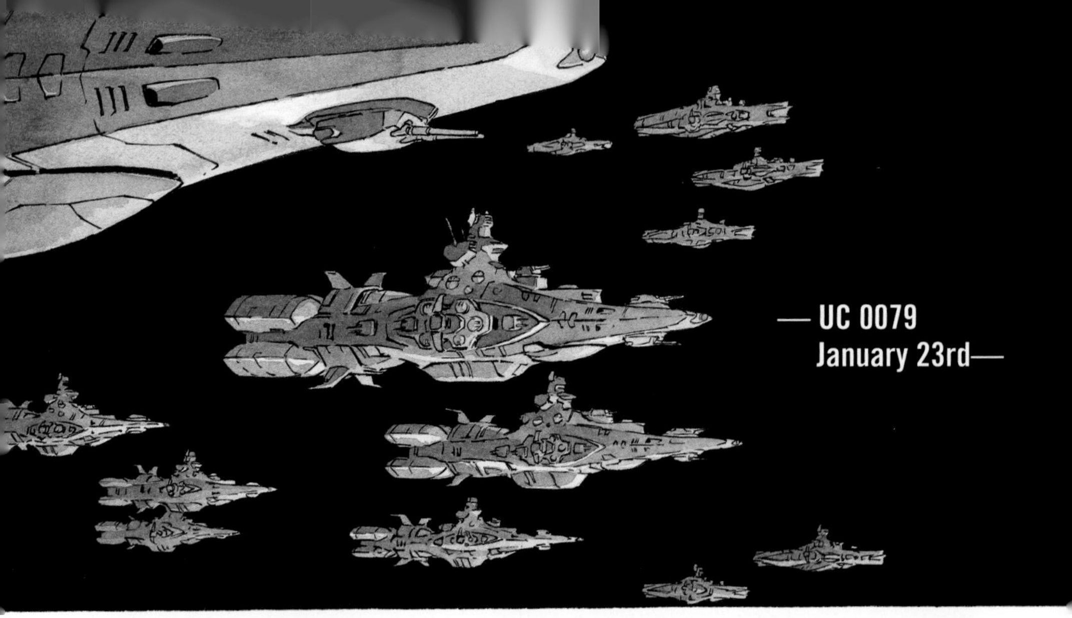
—UC 0079
January 23rd—

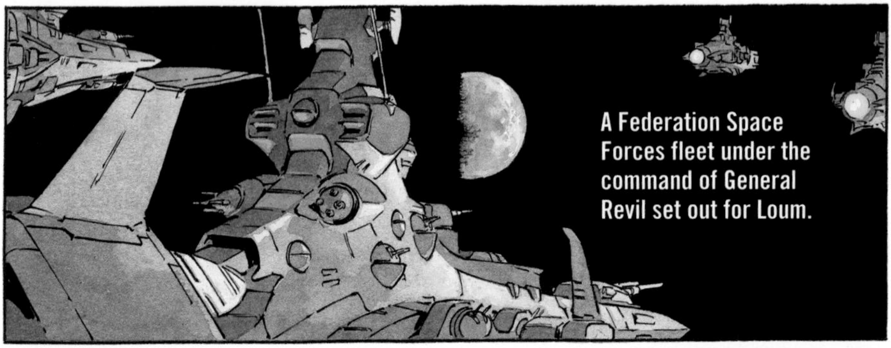
A Federation Space Forces fleet under the command of General Revil set out for Loum.

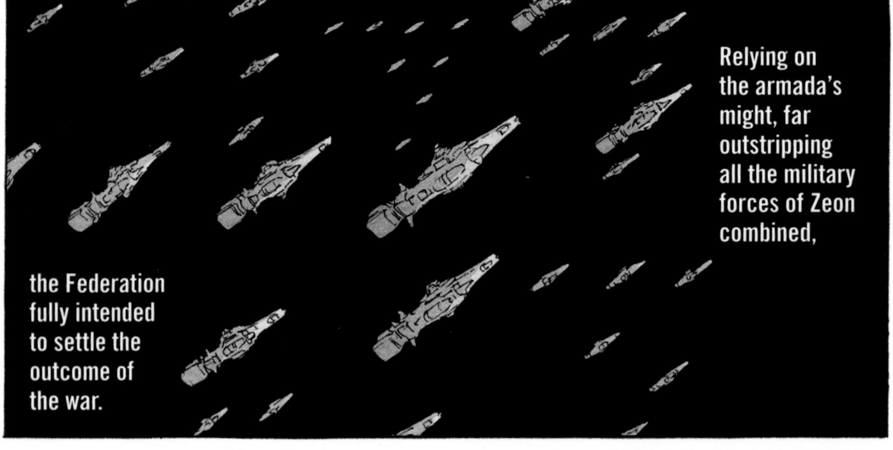
Relying on the armada's might, far outstripping all the military forces of Zeon combined,
the Federation fully intended to settle the outcome of the war.

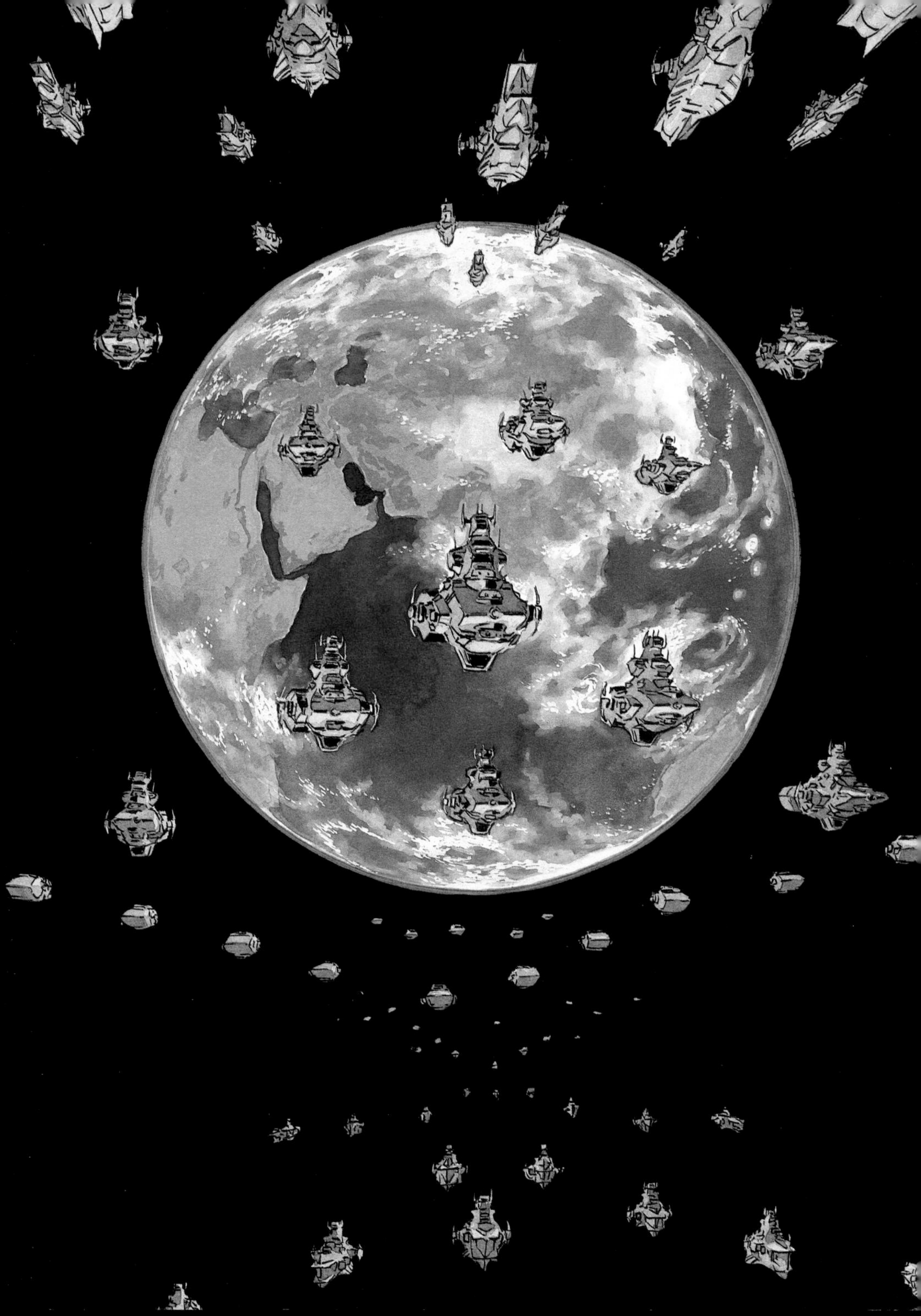

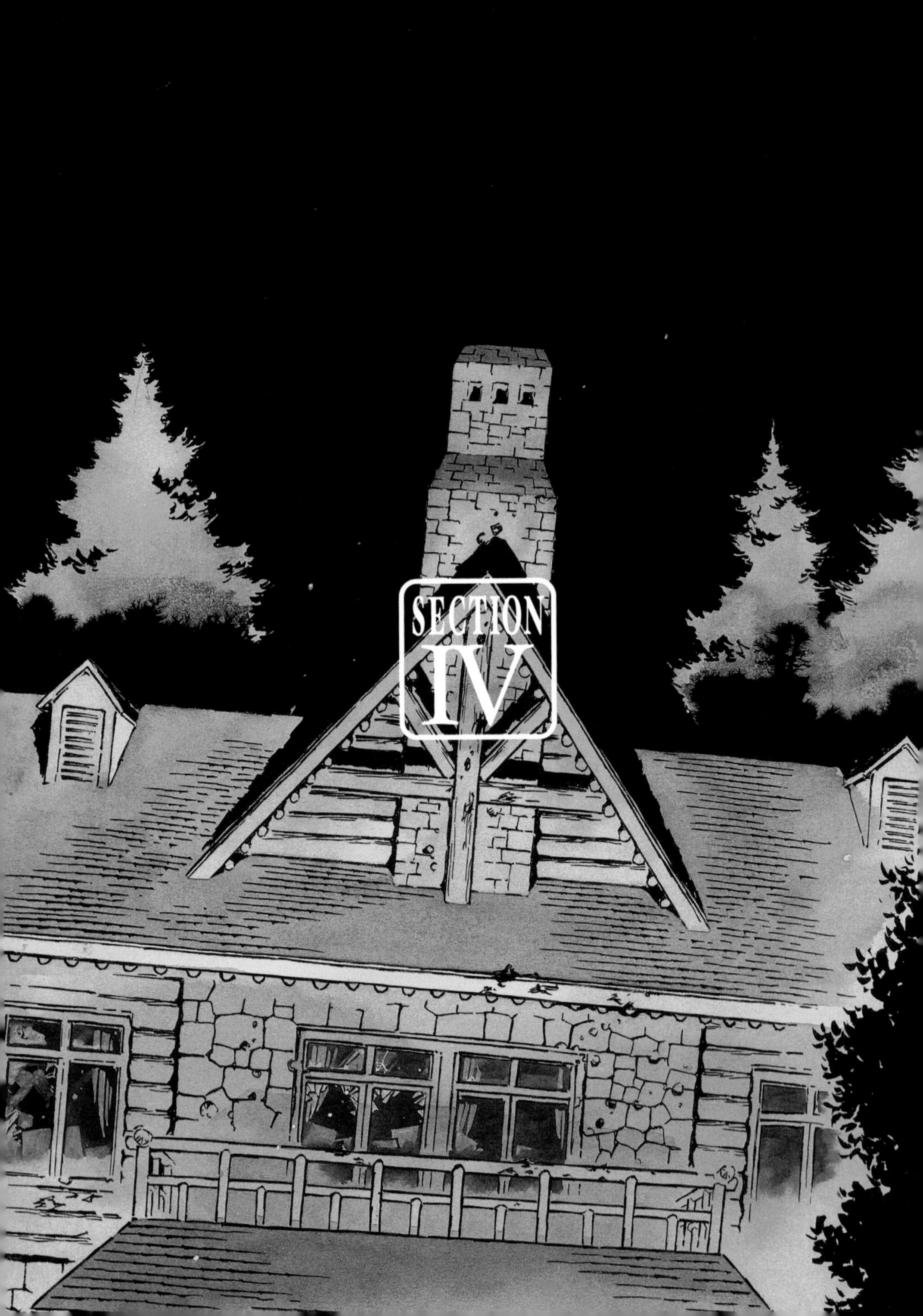
SECTION
IV

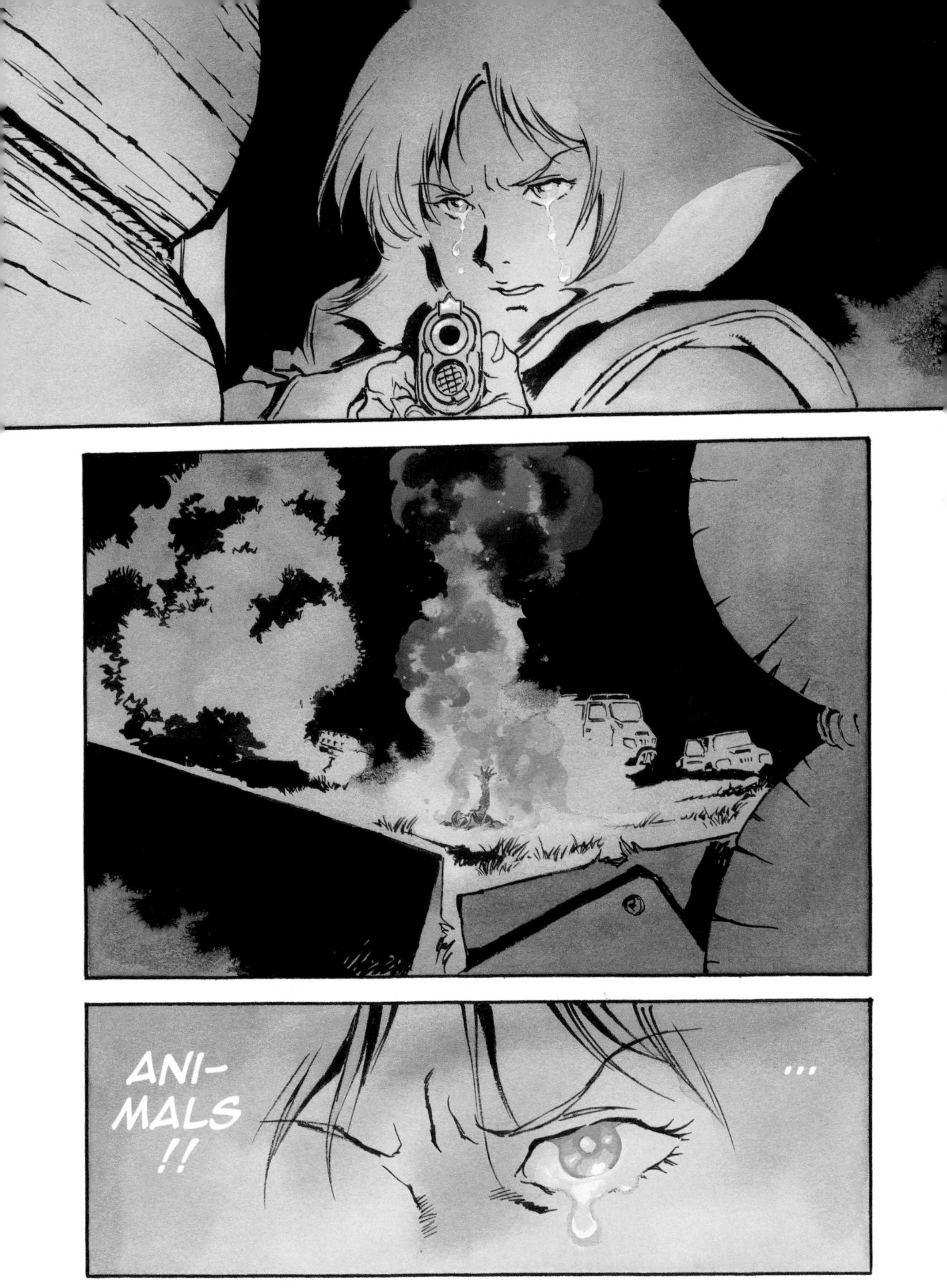
...
ANI-
MALS
!!

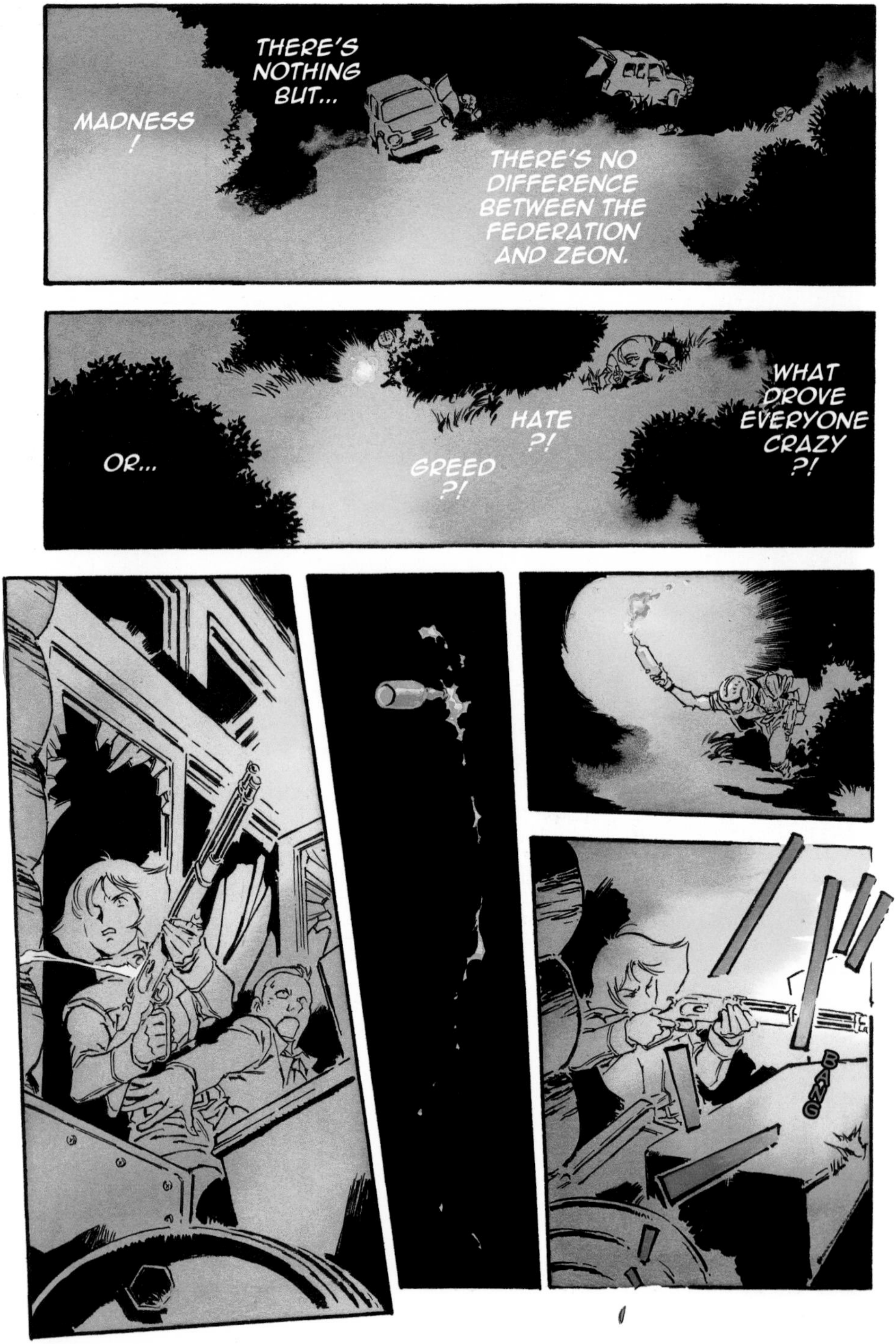
THERE'S NO DIFFERENCE BETWEEN THE FEDERATION AND ZEON.
THERE'S NOTHING BUT...
MADNESS!
WHAT DROVE EVERYONE CRAZY?!
HATE?!
GREED?!
OR...
BANG

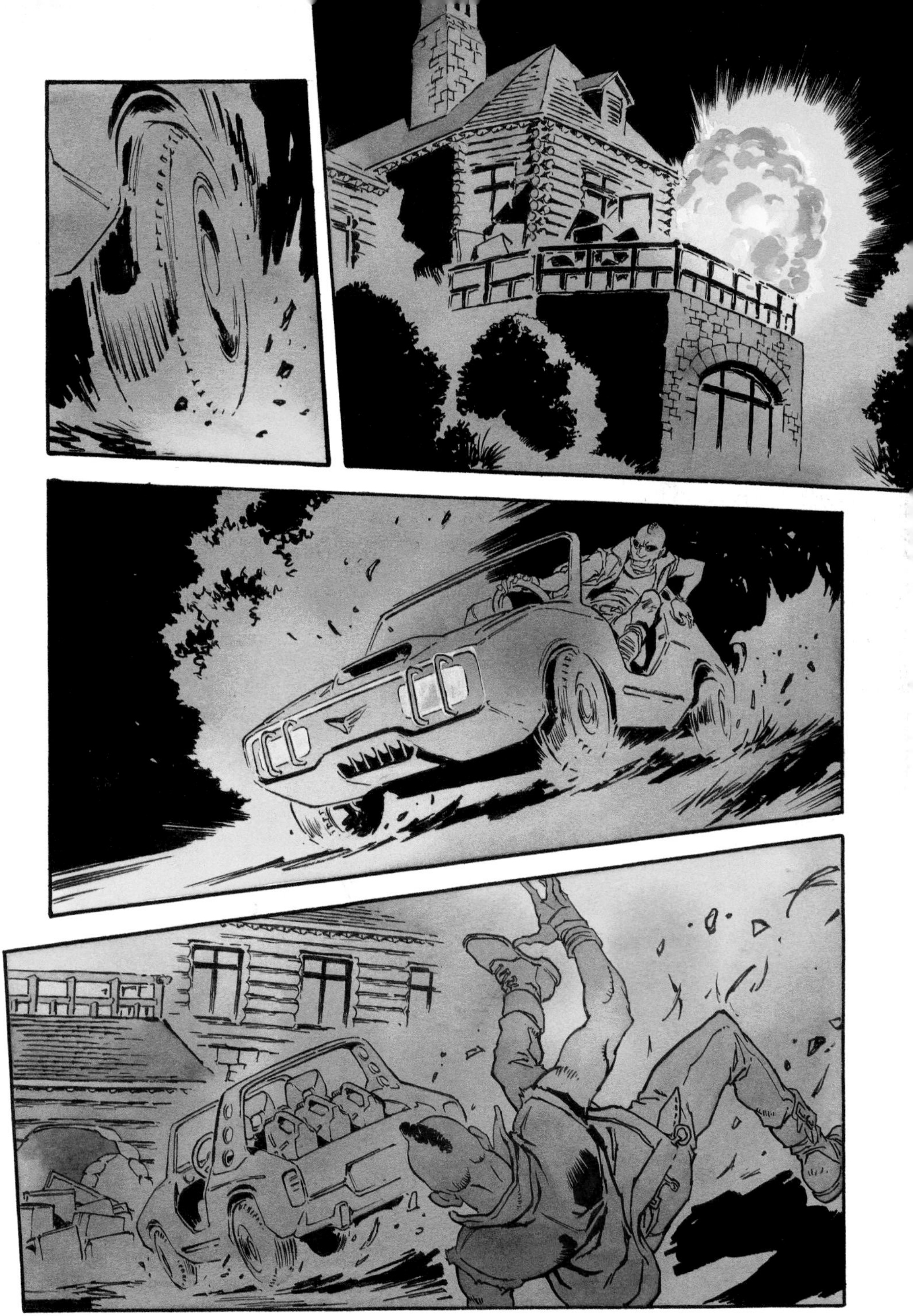

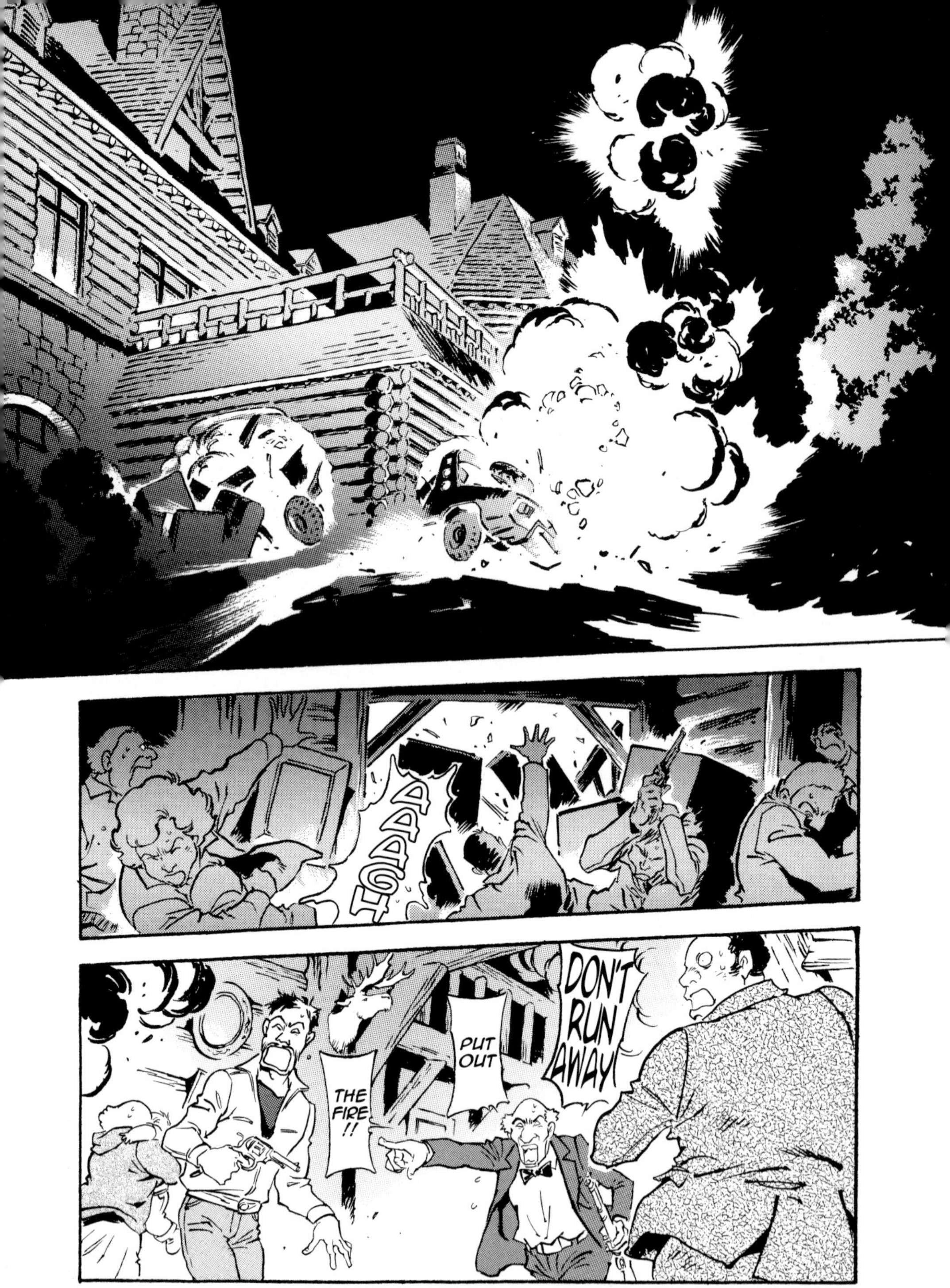
AAAGH
DON'T RUN AWAY!
PUT OUT
THE FIRE!!

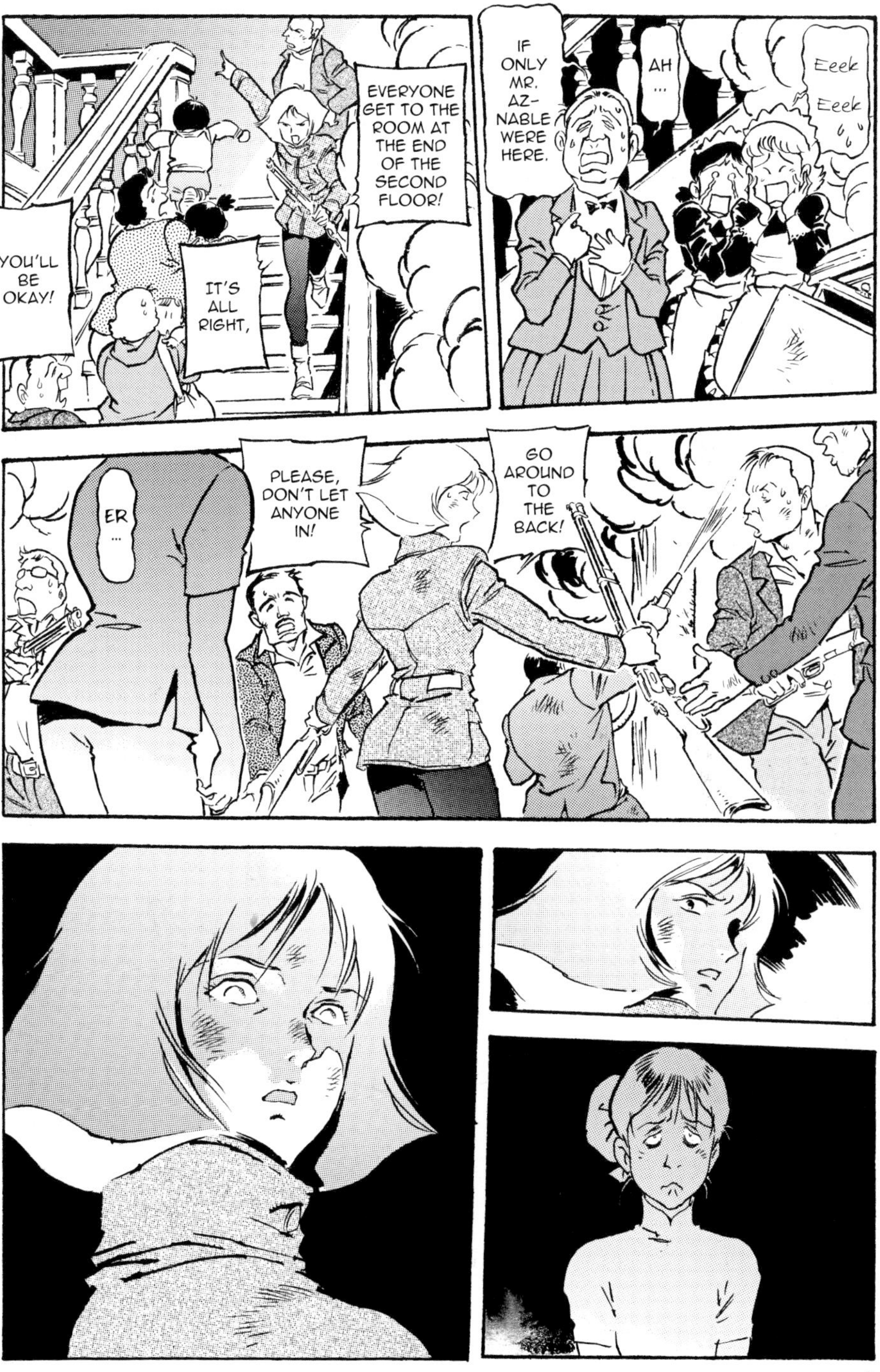
Eeek
Eeek
AH ...
IF ONLY MR. AZ-NABLE WERE HERE.
EVERYONE GET TO THE ROOM AT THE END OF THE SECOND FLOOR!
IT'S ALL RIGHT,
YOU'LL BE OKAY!
GO AROUND TO THE BACK!
PLEASE, DON'T LET ANYONE IN!
ER ...

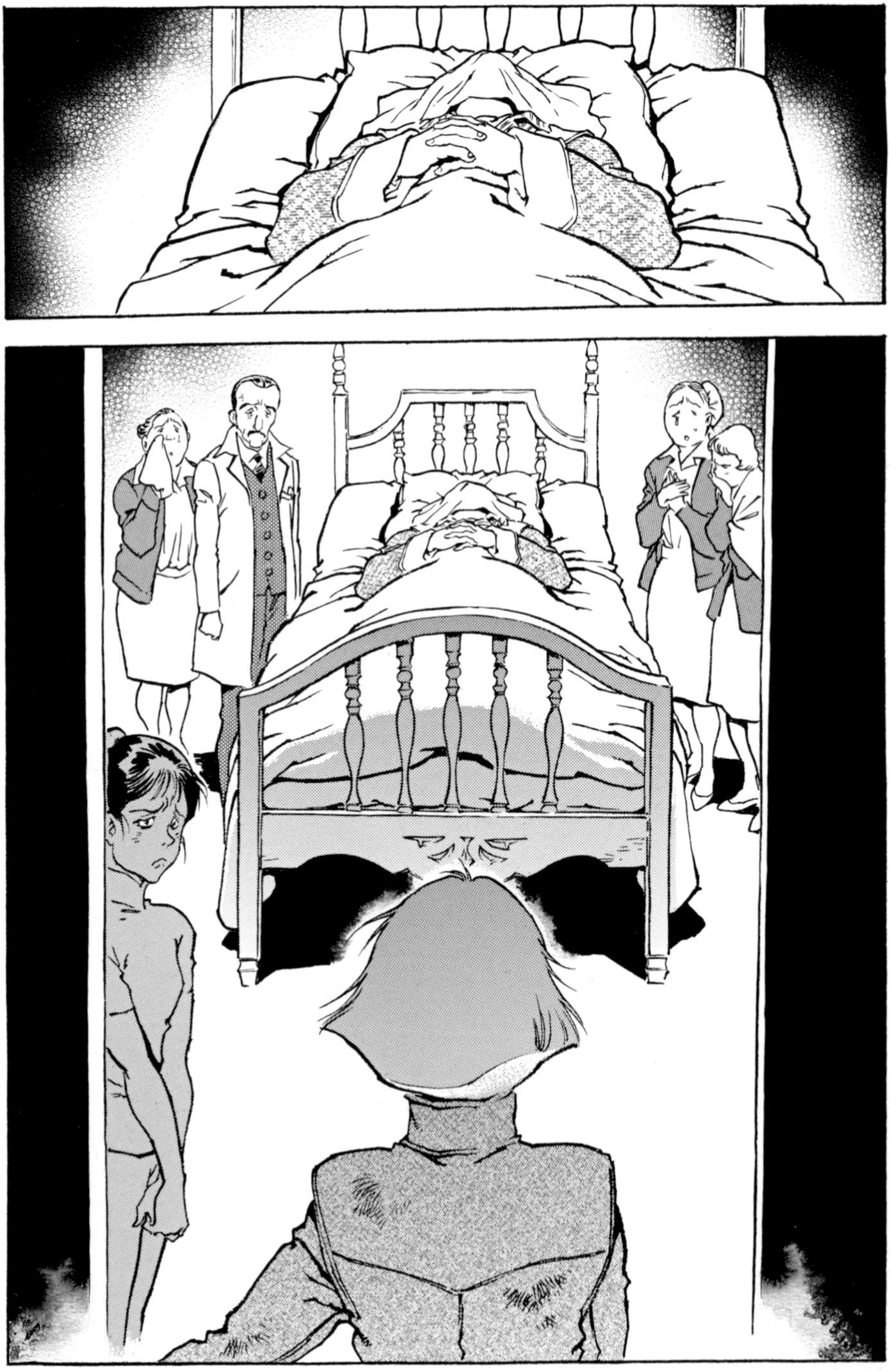

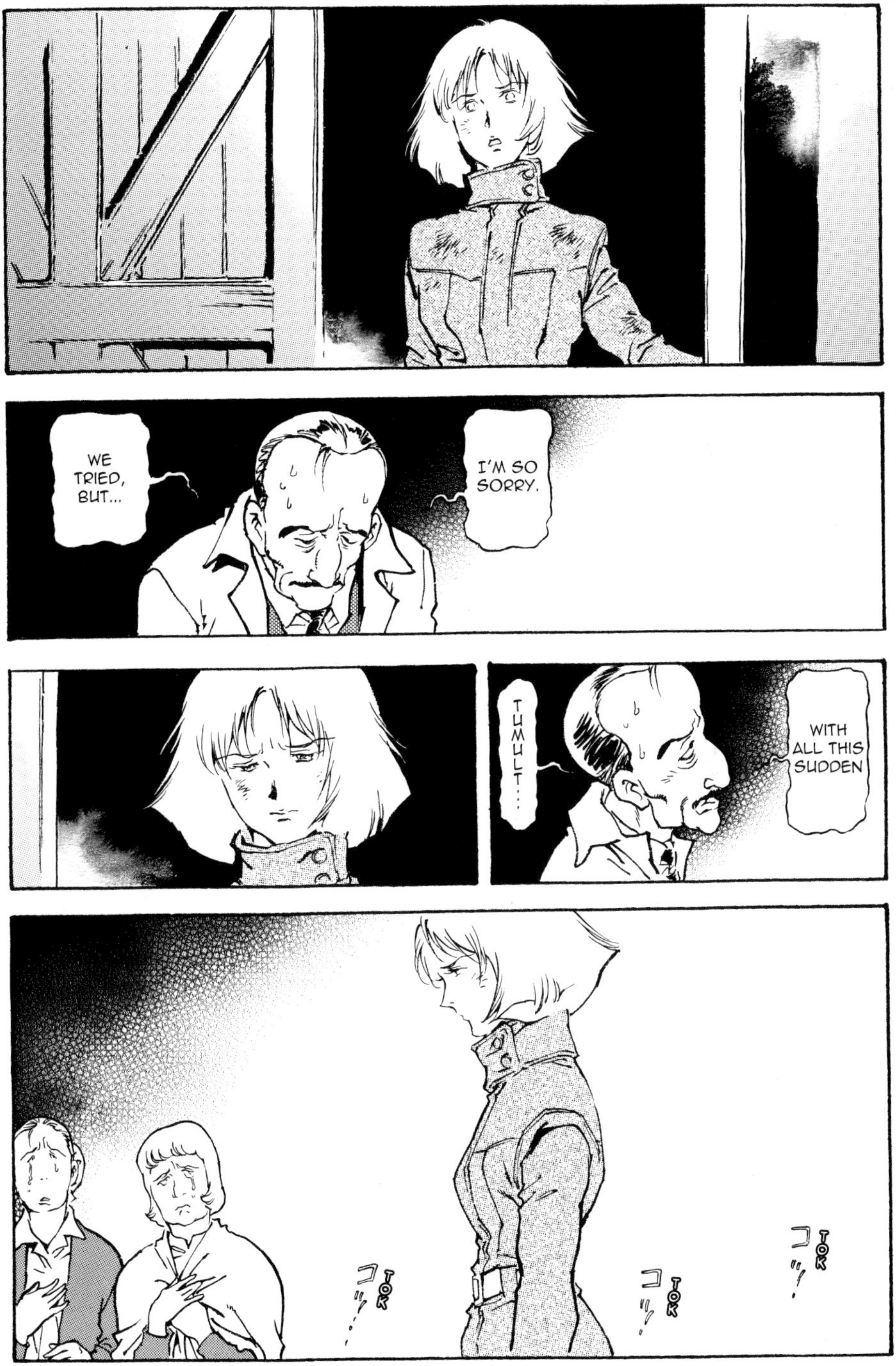
I'M SO SORRY.
WE TRIED, BUT...
WITH ALL THIS SUDDEN
TUMULT...
TOK
TOK
TOK

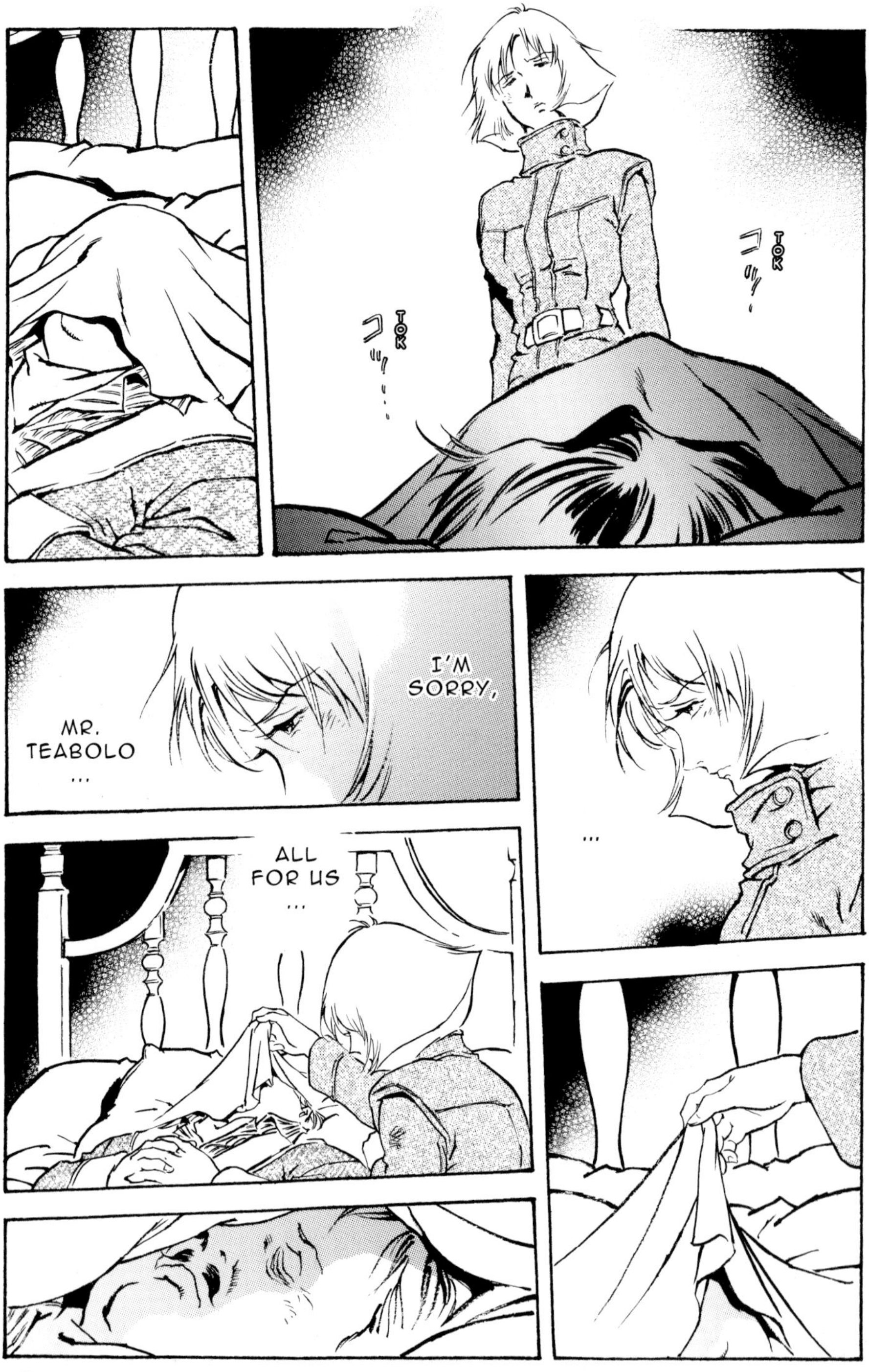
TOK
TOK
...
I'M SORRY,
MR. TEABOLO ...
ALL FOR US ...

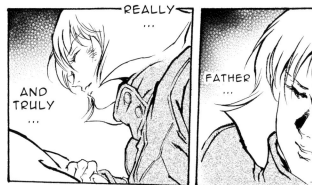

REALLY
...

AND
TRULY
...

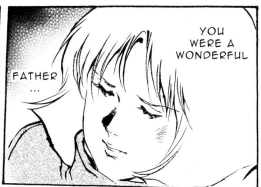

YOU
WERE A
WONDERFUL

FATHER
...

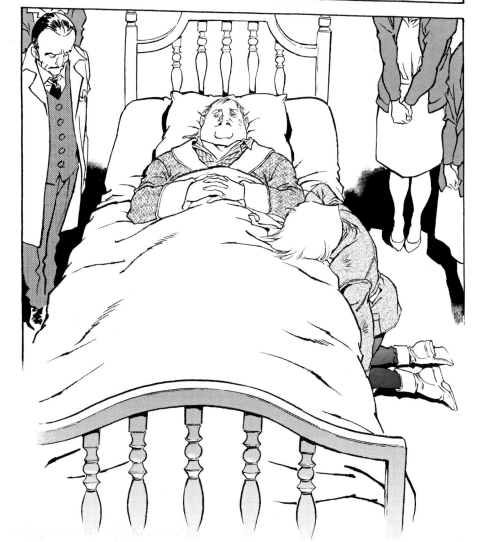

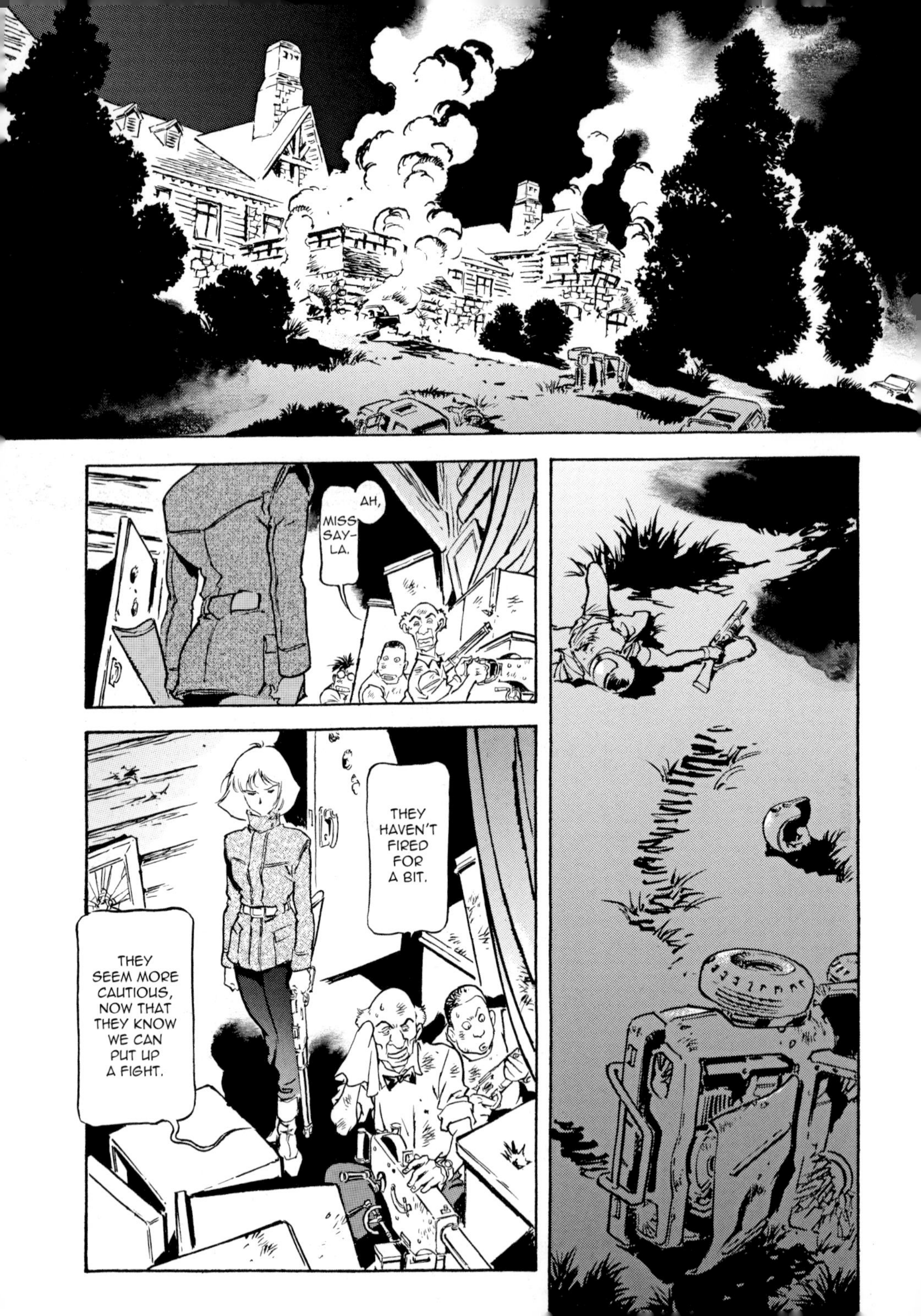
AH, MISS SAY-LA.
THEY HAVEN'T FIRED FOR A BIT.
THEY SEEM MORE CAUTIOUS, NOW THAT THEY KNOW WE CAN PUT UP A FIGHT.

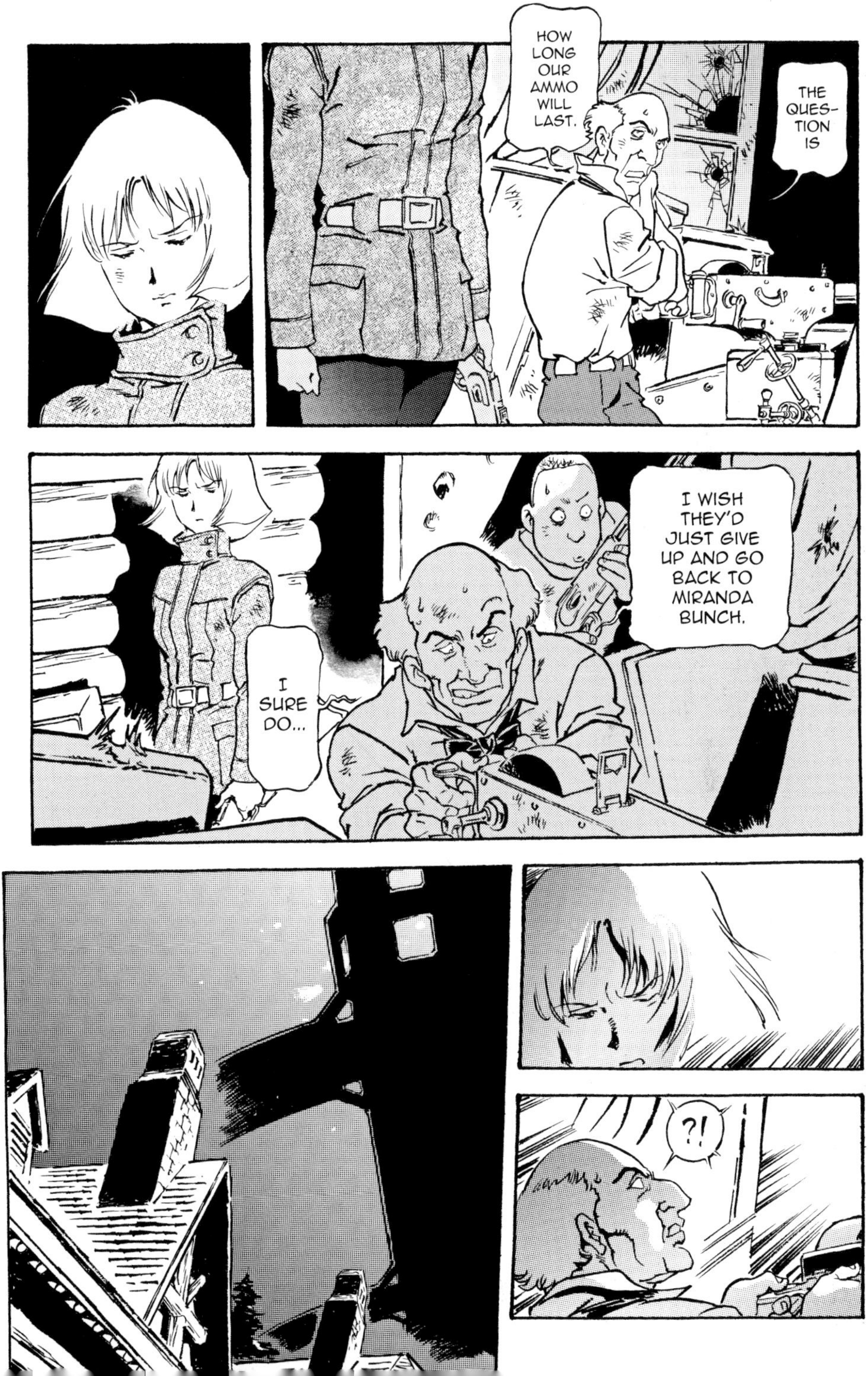
THE QUES-TION IS
HOW LONG OUR AMMO WILL LAST.
I WISH THEY'D JUST GIVE UP AND GO BACK TO MIRANDA BUNCH.
I SURE DO...
?!

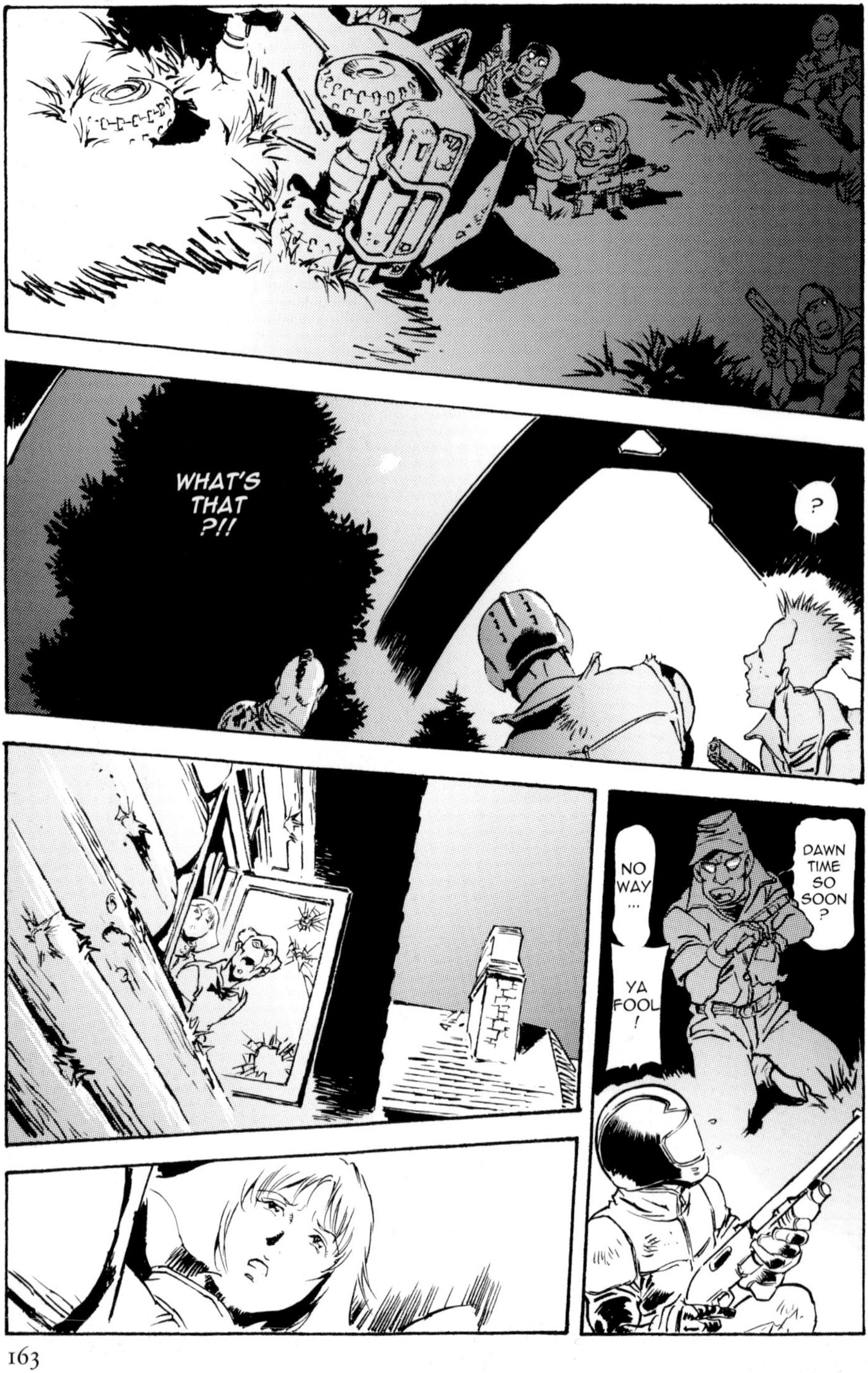
?
WHAT'S THAT ?!!
DAWN TIME SO SOON ?
NO WAY ... YA FOOL !

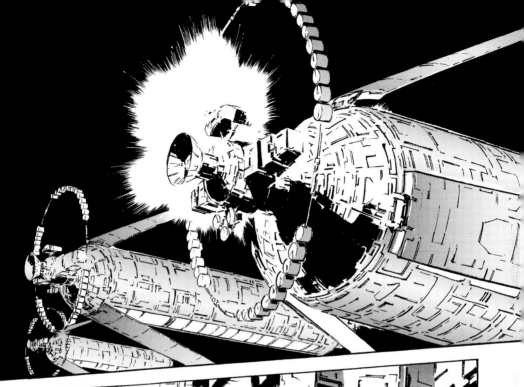

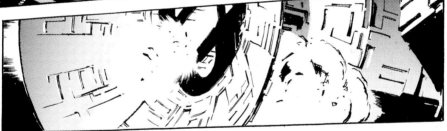

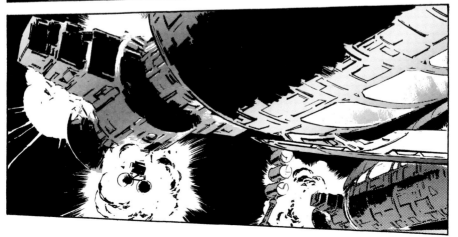

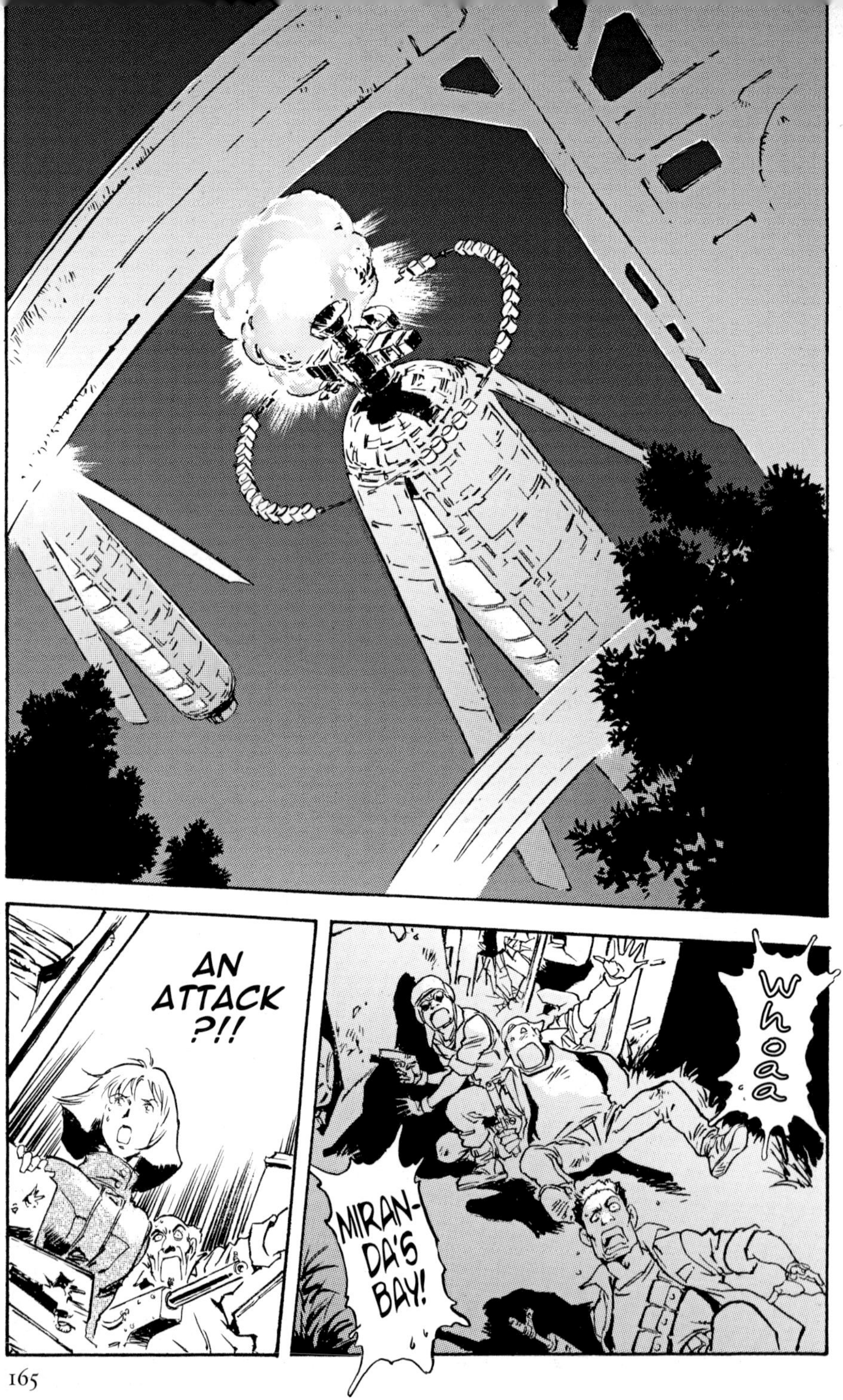
Whoaa
MIRAN-DA'S BAY!
AN ATTACK ?!!

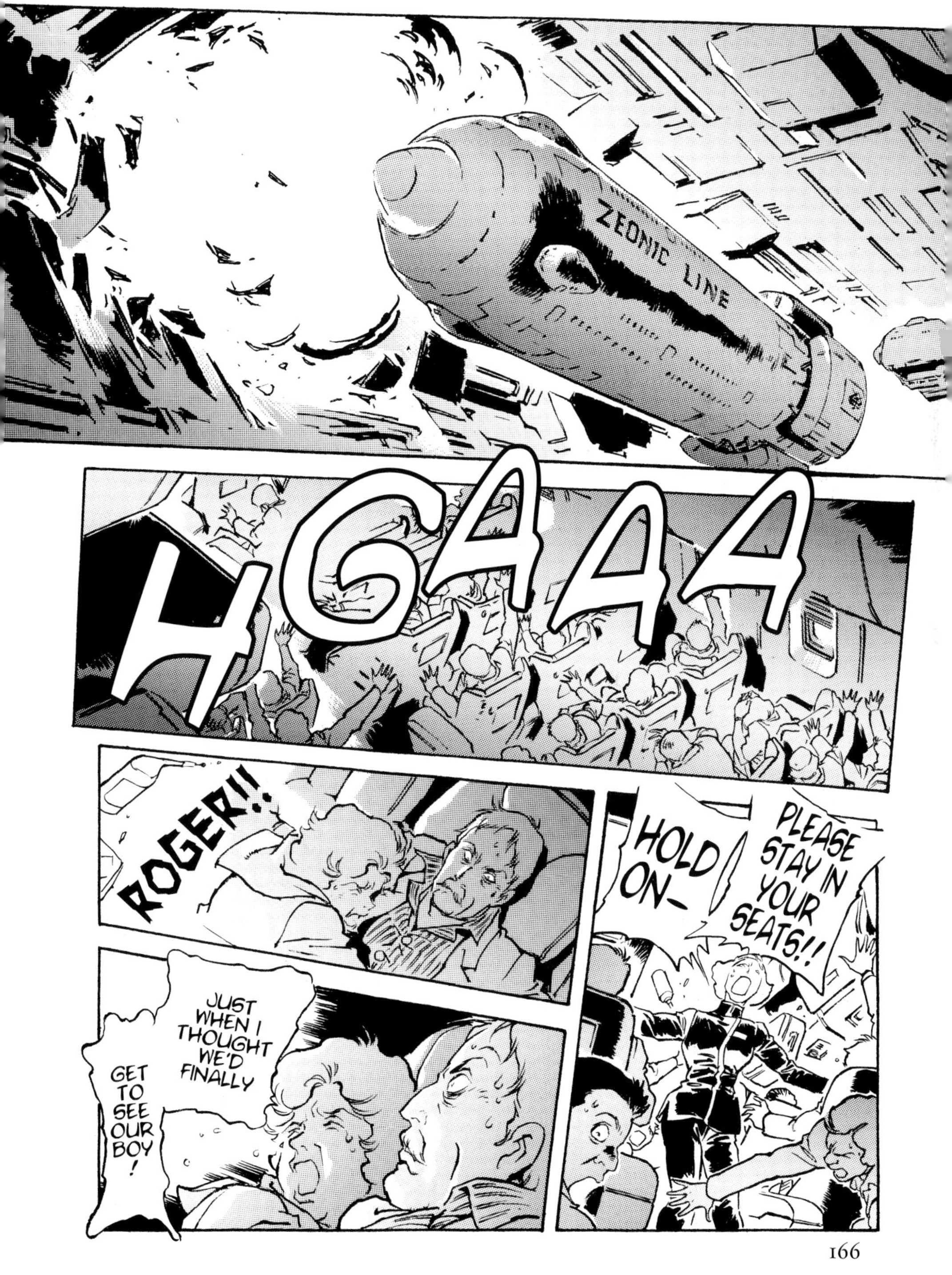
ZEONIC LINE
HGAAA
PLEASE STAY IN YOUR SEATS!!
HOLD ON-
ROGER!!
JUST WHEN I THOUGHT WE'D FINALLY
GET TO SEE OUR BOY!

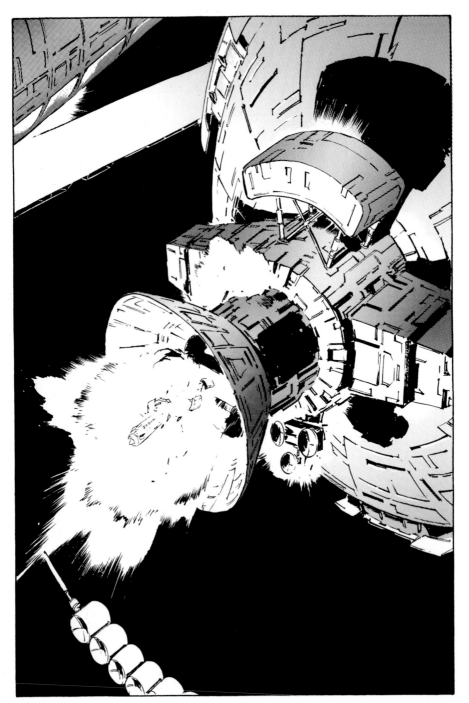

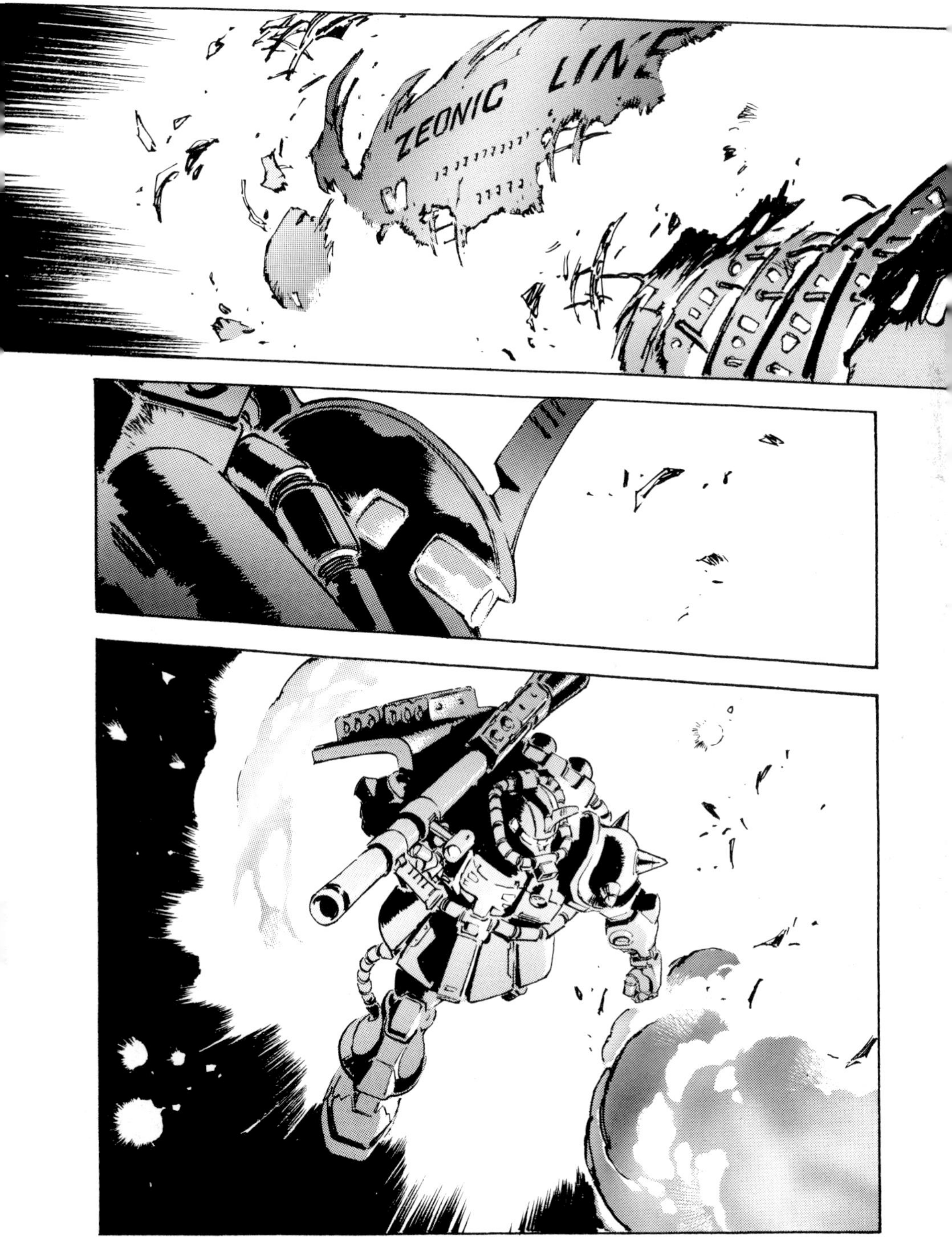
ZEONIC LINE

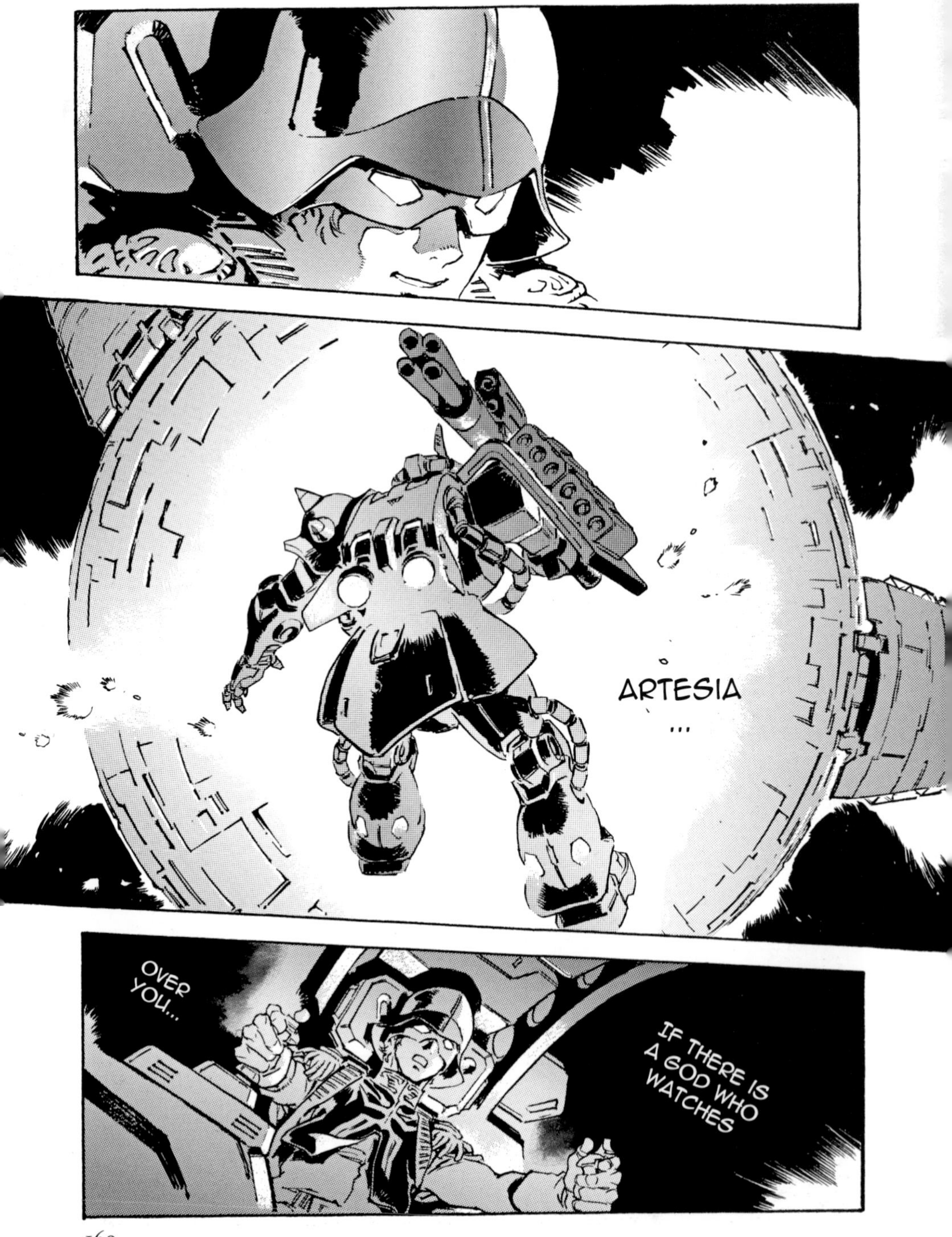
ARTESIA ...
IF THERE IS A GOD WHO WATCHES
OVER YOU...

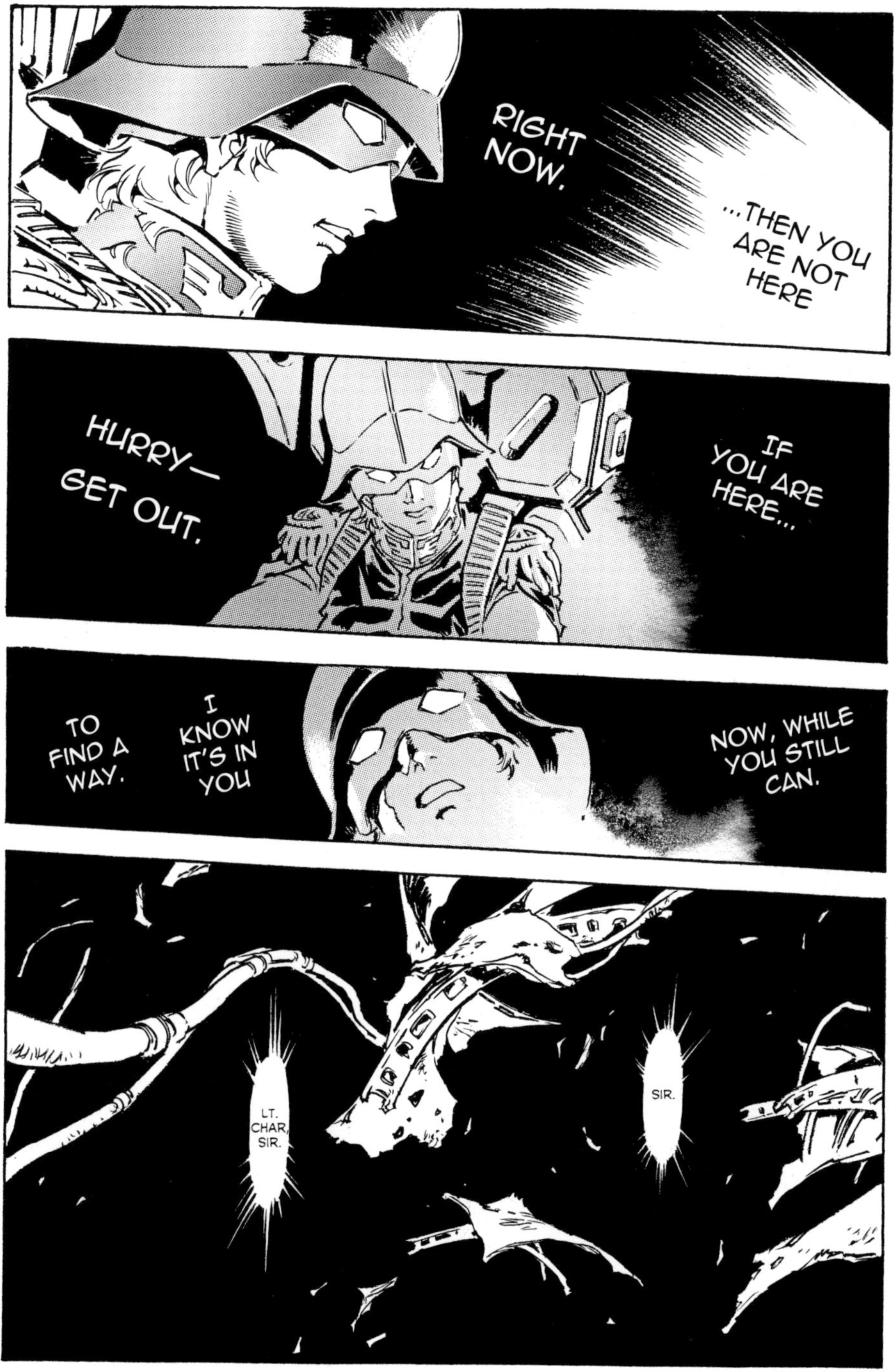
...THEN YOU ARE NOT HERE
RIGHT NOW.
IF YOU ARE HERE...
HURRY— GET OUT.
NOW, WHILE YOU STILL CAN.
I KNOW IT'S IN YOU
TO FIND A WAY.
SIR.
LT. CHAR, SIR.

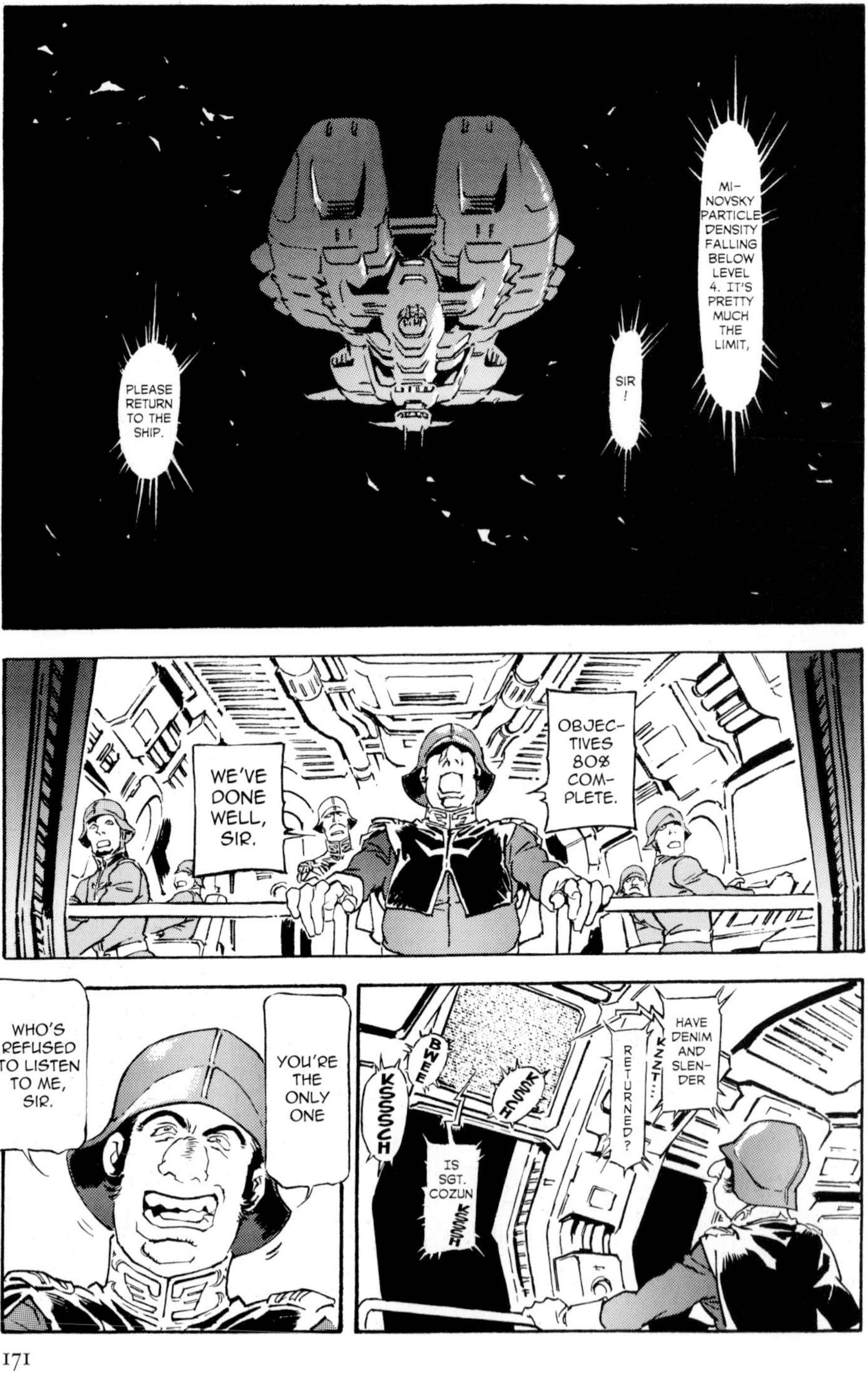

MI-NOVSKY PARTICLE DENSITY FALLING BELOW LEVEL 4. IT'S PRETTY MUCH THE LIMIT,
SIR!
PLEASE RETURN TO THE SHIP.
OBJEC-TIVES 80% COM-PLETE.
WE'VE DONE WELL, SIR.
HAVE DENIM AND SLEN-DER
KZZT...
RETURNED?
BWEE
KSSSCH
KSSCH
IS SGT. COZUN
KSSSCH
YOU'RE THE ONLY ONE
WHO'S REFUSED TO LISTEN TO ME, SIR.

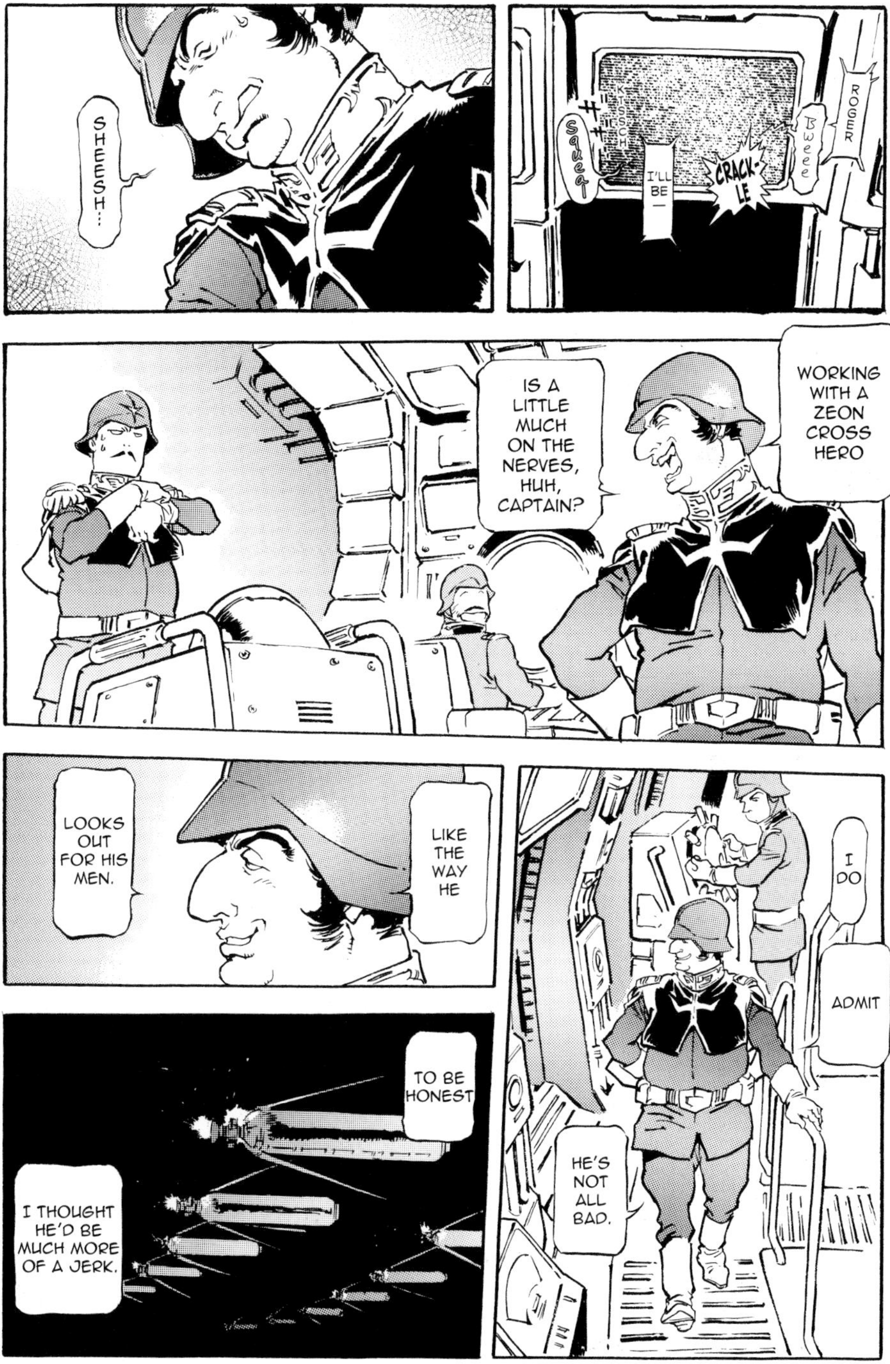
ROGER
Bweee
CRACK-LE
I'LL BE —
KISSCH
Squeal
SHEESH...
WORKING WITH A ZEON CROSS HERO
IS A LITTLE MUCH ON THE NERVES, HUH, CAPTAIN?
I DO
ADMIT
HE'S NOT ALL BAD.
LIKE THE WAY HE
LOOKS OUT FOR HIS MEN.
TO BE HONEST
I THOUGHT HE'D BE MUCH MORE OF A JERK.

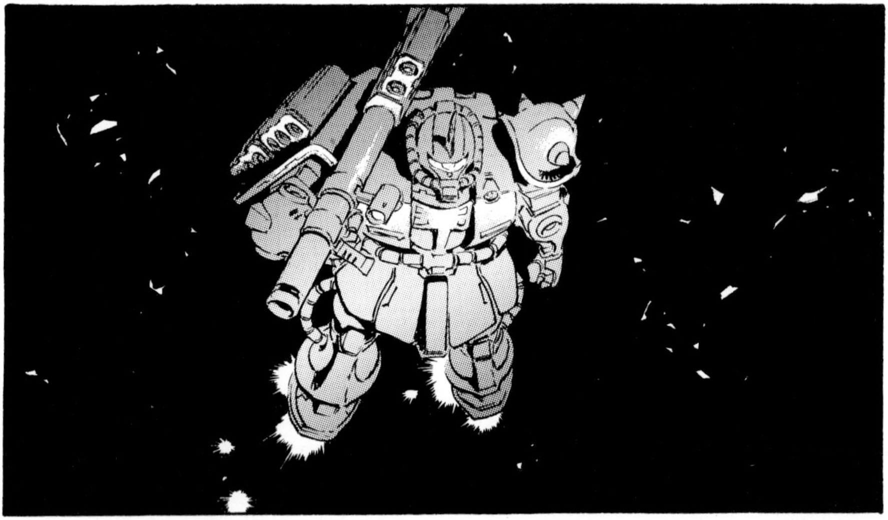

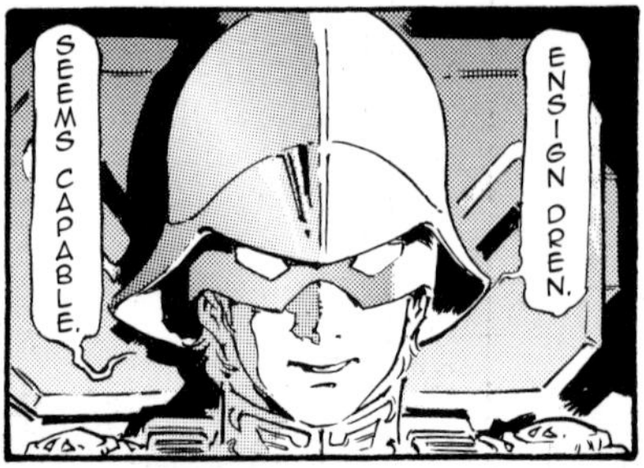
ENSIGN DREN.
SEEMS CAPABLE.

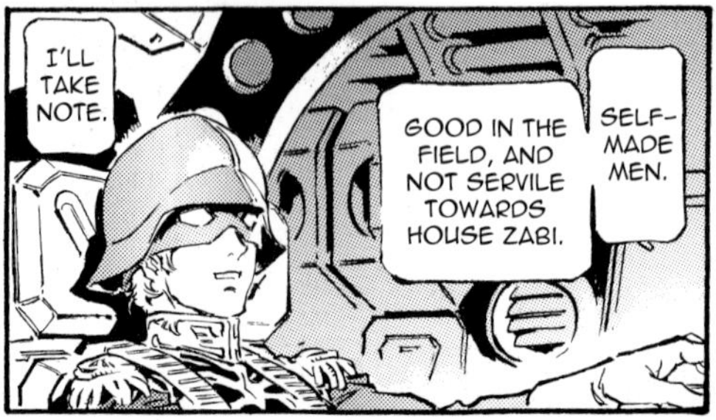
SELF-MADE MEN.
GOOD IN THE FIELD, AND NOT SERVILE TOWARDS HOUSE ZABI.
I'LL TAKE NOTE.

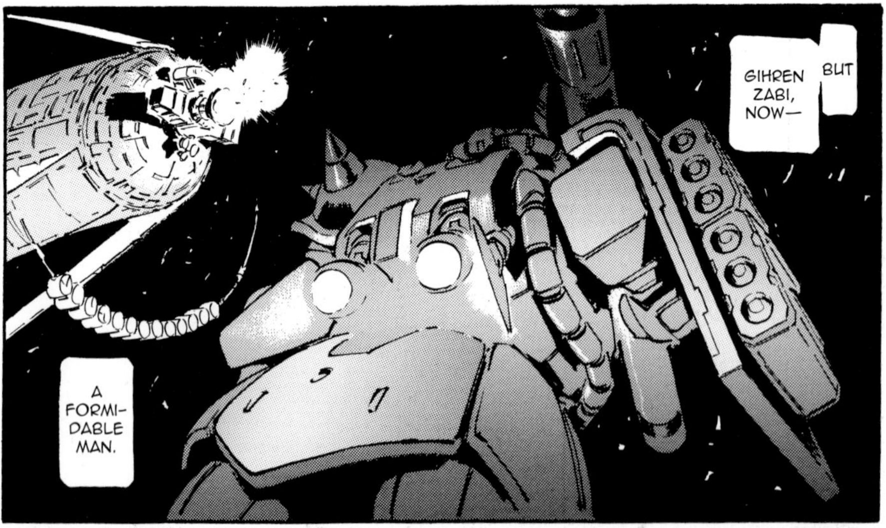
BUT
GIHREN ZABI, NOW—
A FORMIDABLE MAN.

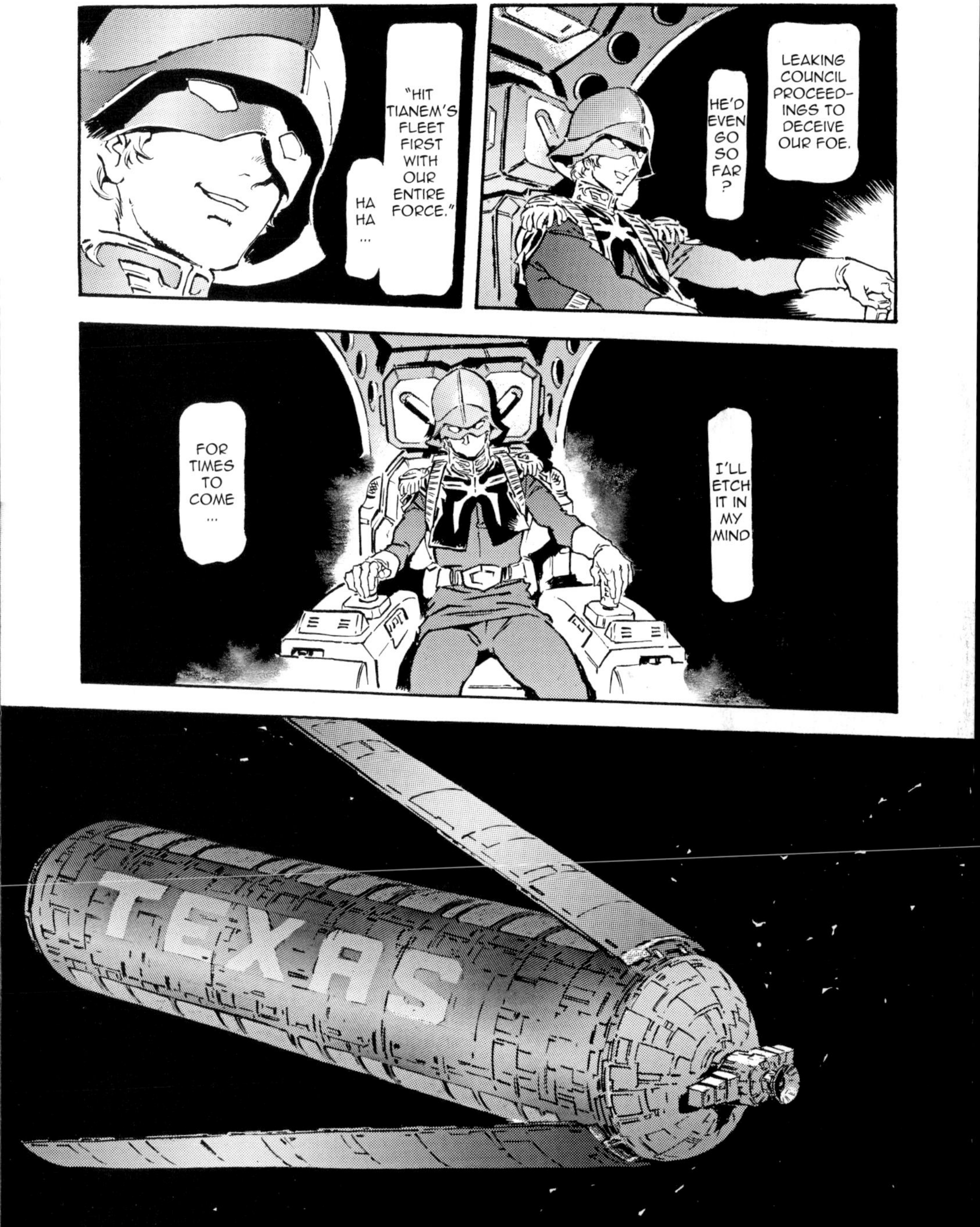
LEAKING COUNCIL PROCEED-INGS TO DECEIVE OUR FOE.
HE'D EVEN GO SO FAR?
"HIT TIANEM'S FLEET FIRST WITH OUR ENTIRE FORCE."
HA HA...
I'LL ETCH IT IN MY MIND
FOR TIMES TO COME...
TEXAS

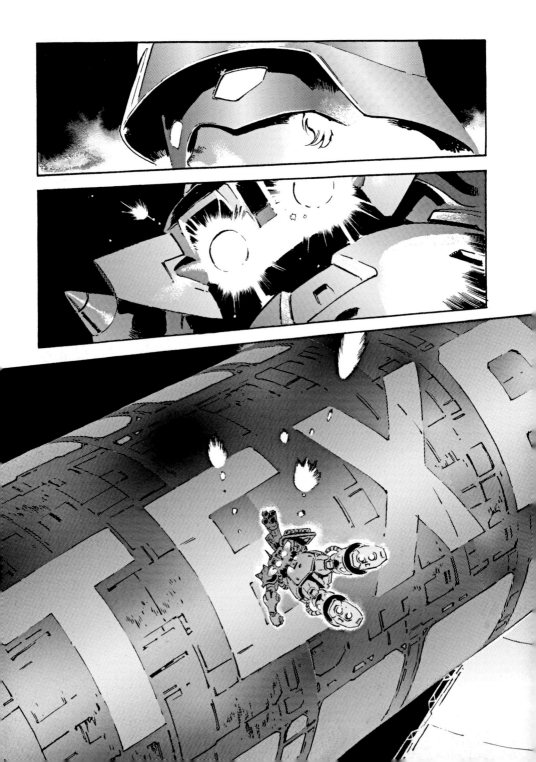

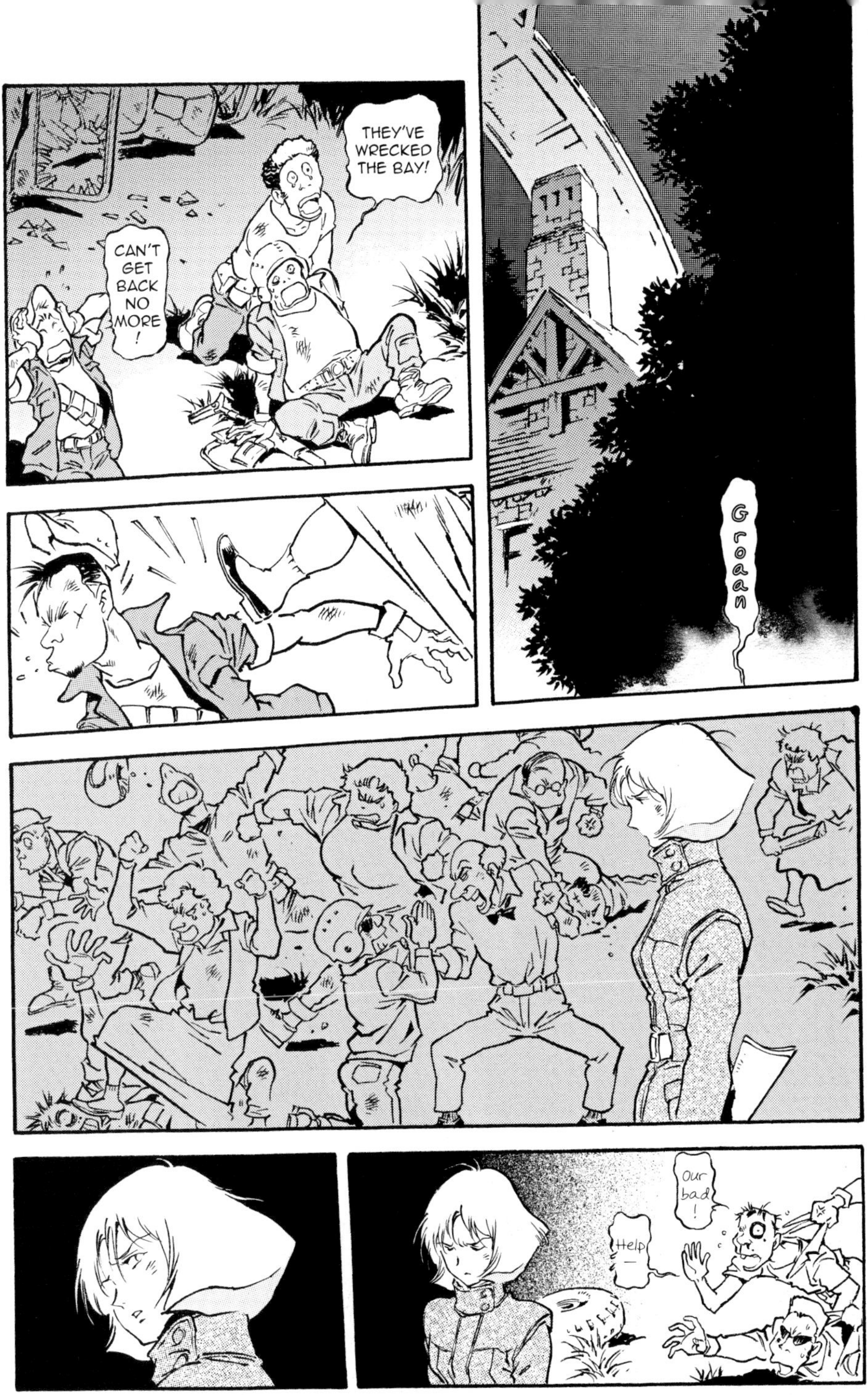
Groaan
THEY'VE WRECKED THE BAY!
CAN'T GET BACK NO MORE!
Our bad!
Help—

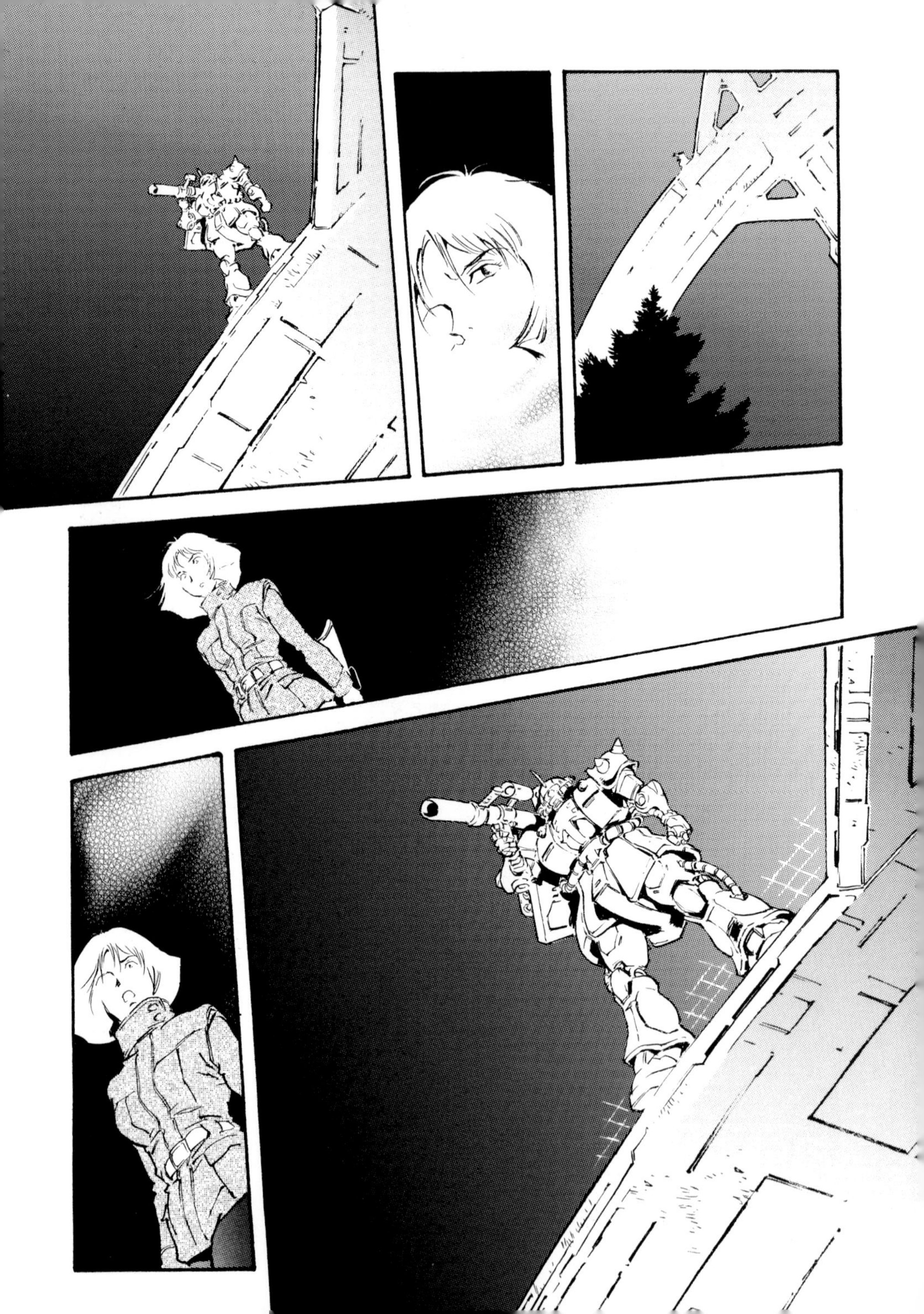

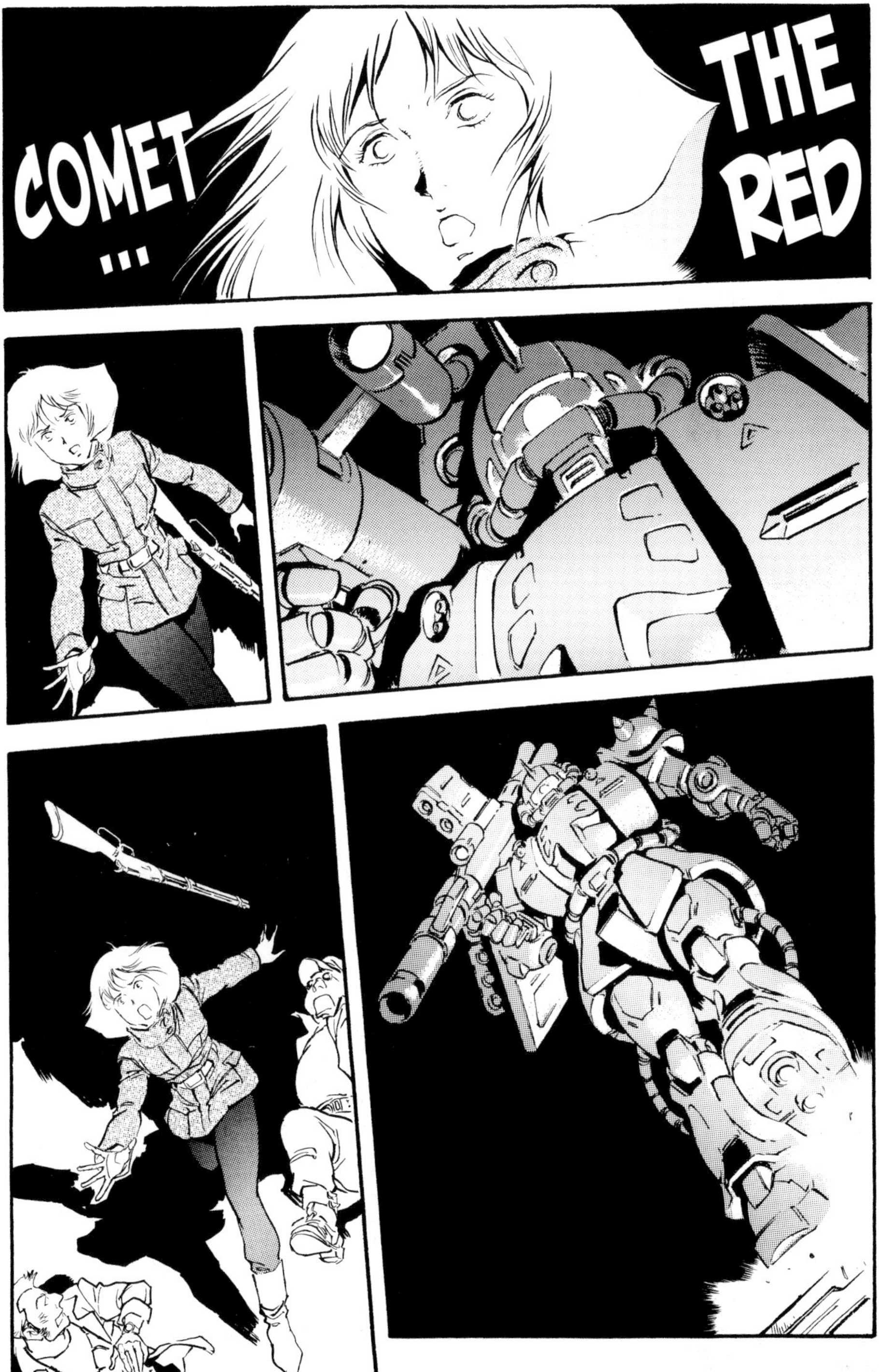
THE RED
COMET ...

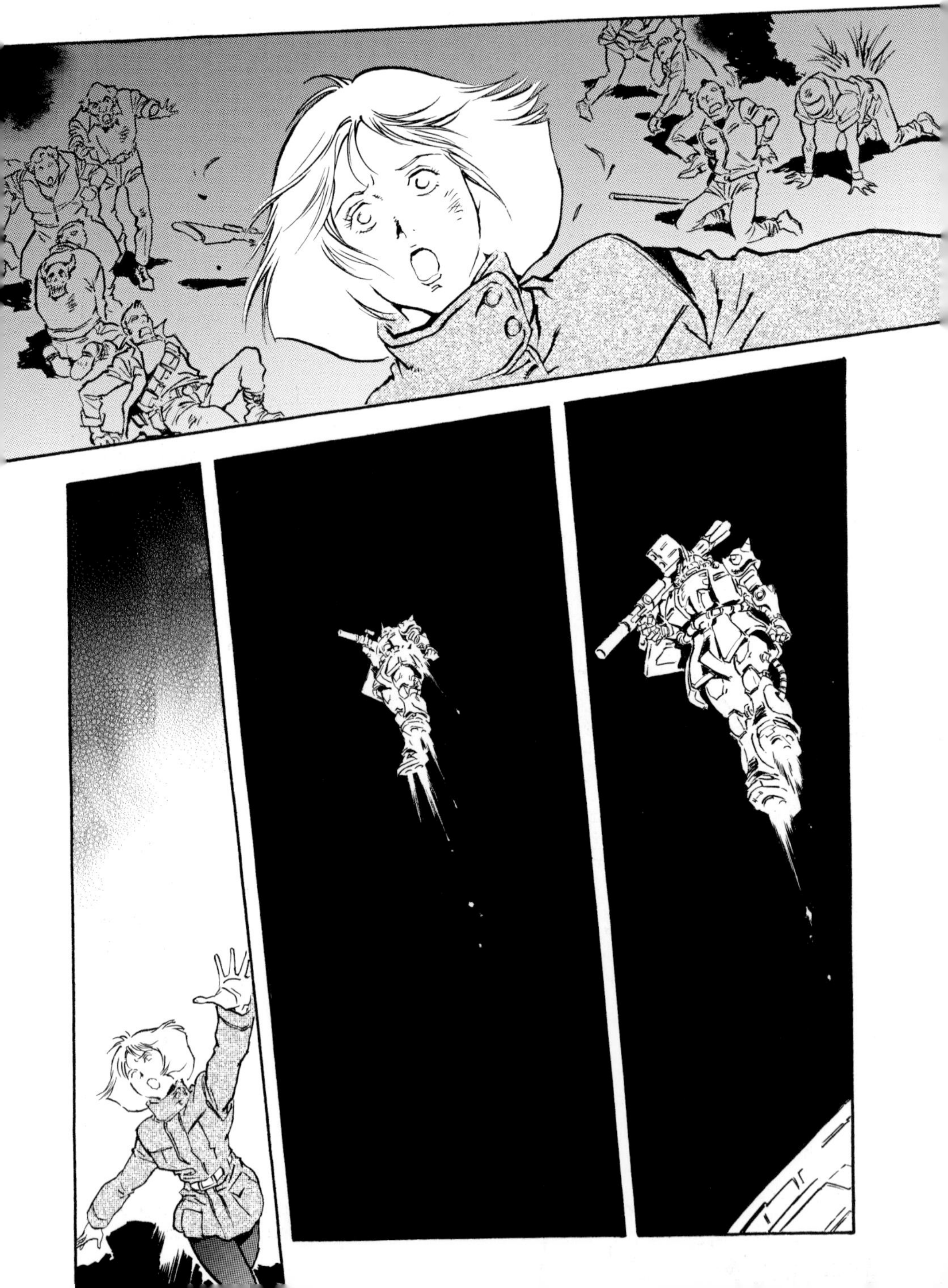

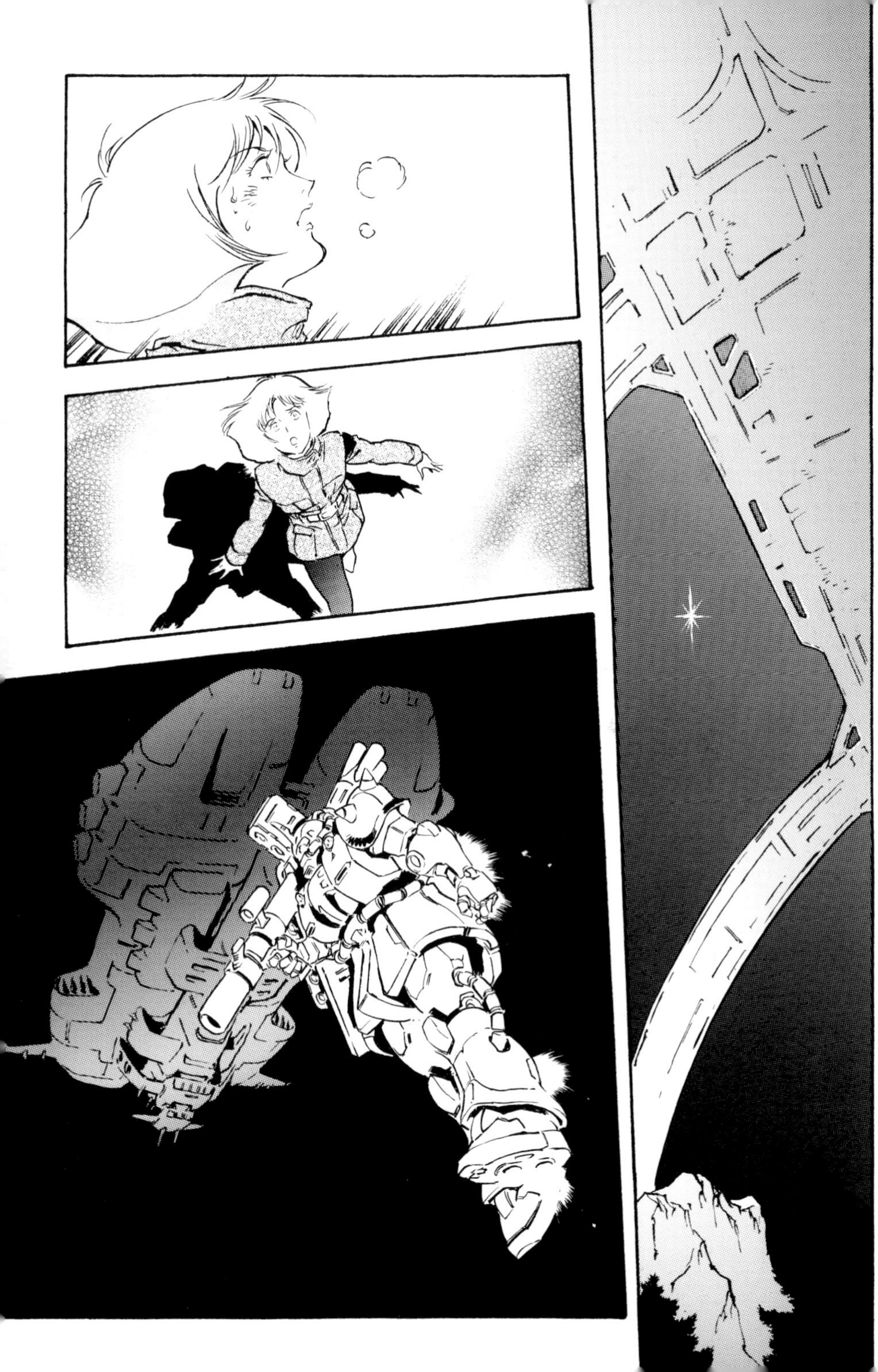

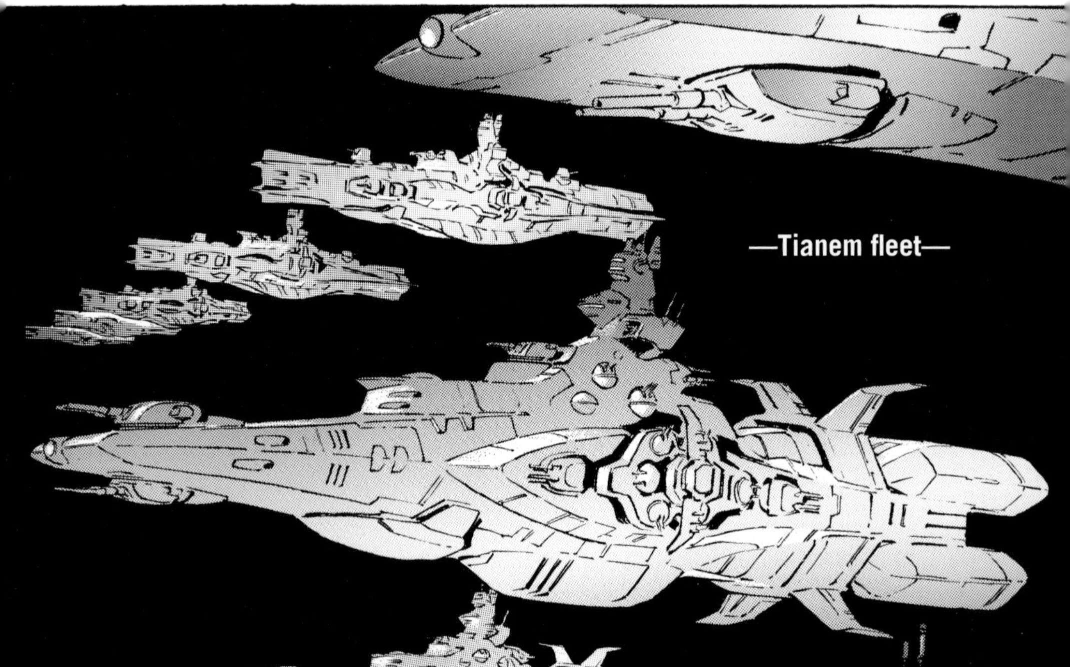
—Tianem fleet—

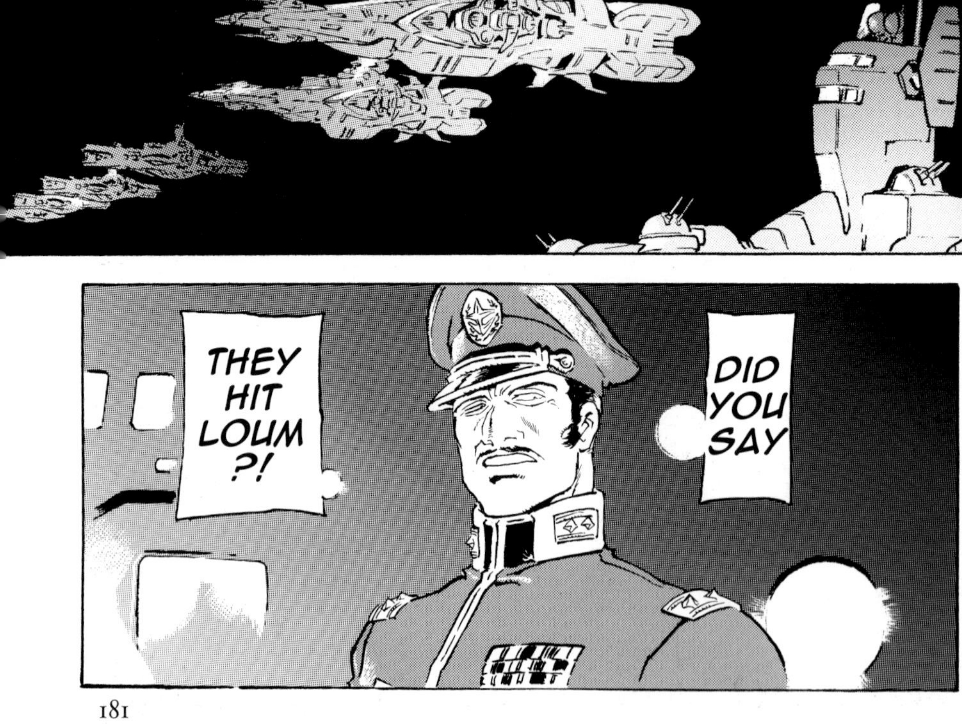
DID YOU SAY
THEY HIT LOUM ?!

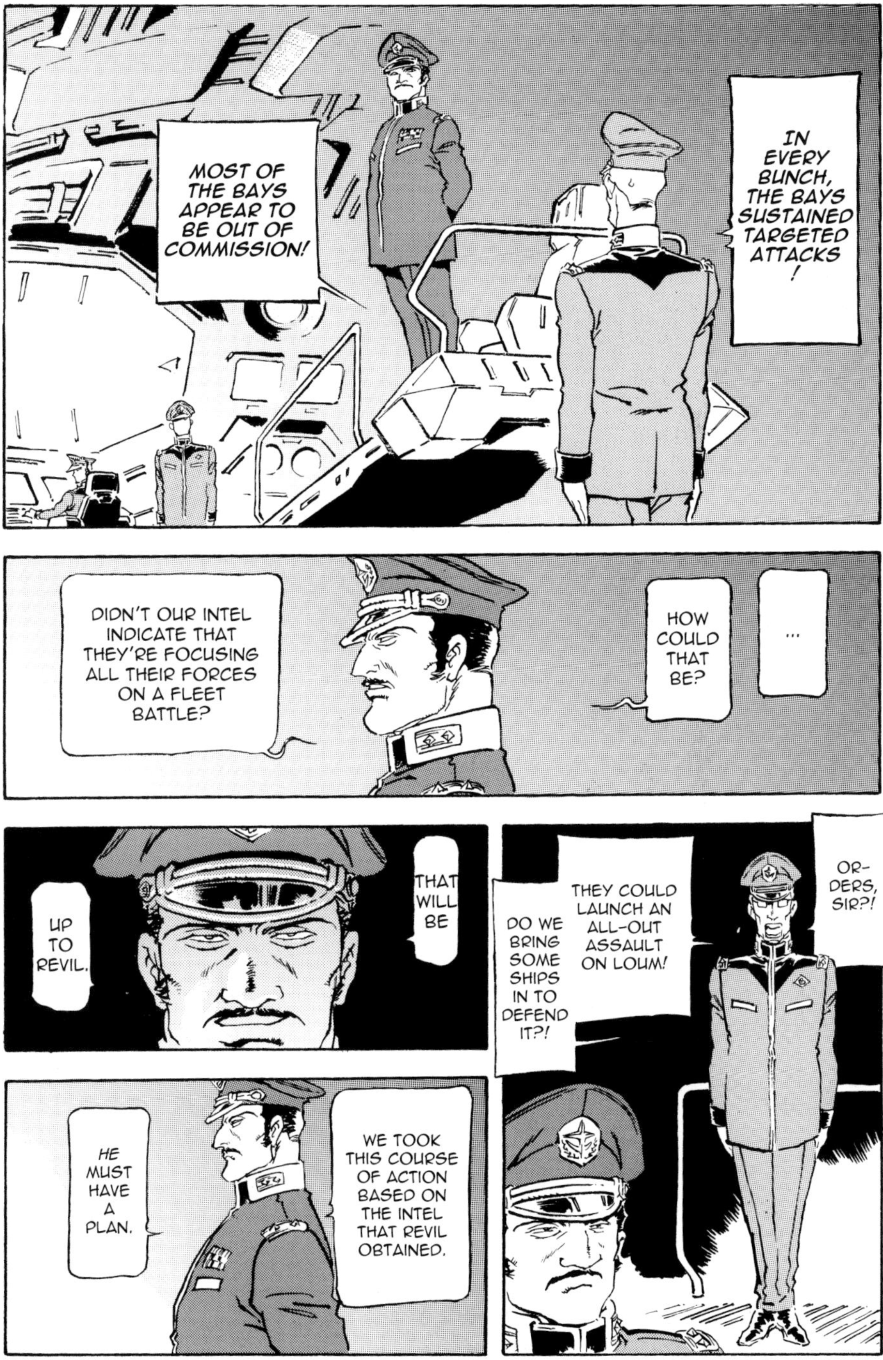
IN EVERY BUNCH, THE BAYS SUSTAINED TARGETED ATTACKS!
MOST OF THE BAYS APPEAR TO BE OUT OF COMMISSION!
...
HOW COULD THAT BE?
DIDN'T OUR INTEL INDICATE THAT THEY'RE FOCUSING ALL THEIR FORCES ON A FLEET BATTLE?
ORDERS, SIR?!
THEY COULD LAUNCH AN ALL-OUT ASSAULT ON LOUM!
DO WE BRING SOME SHIPS IN TO DEFEND IT?!
THAT WILL BE
UP TO REVIL.
WE TOOK THIS COURSE OF ACTION BASED ON THE INTEL THAT REVIL OBTAINED.
HE MUST HAVE A PLAN.

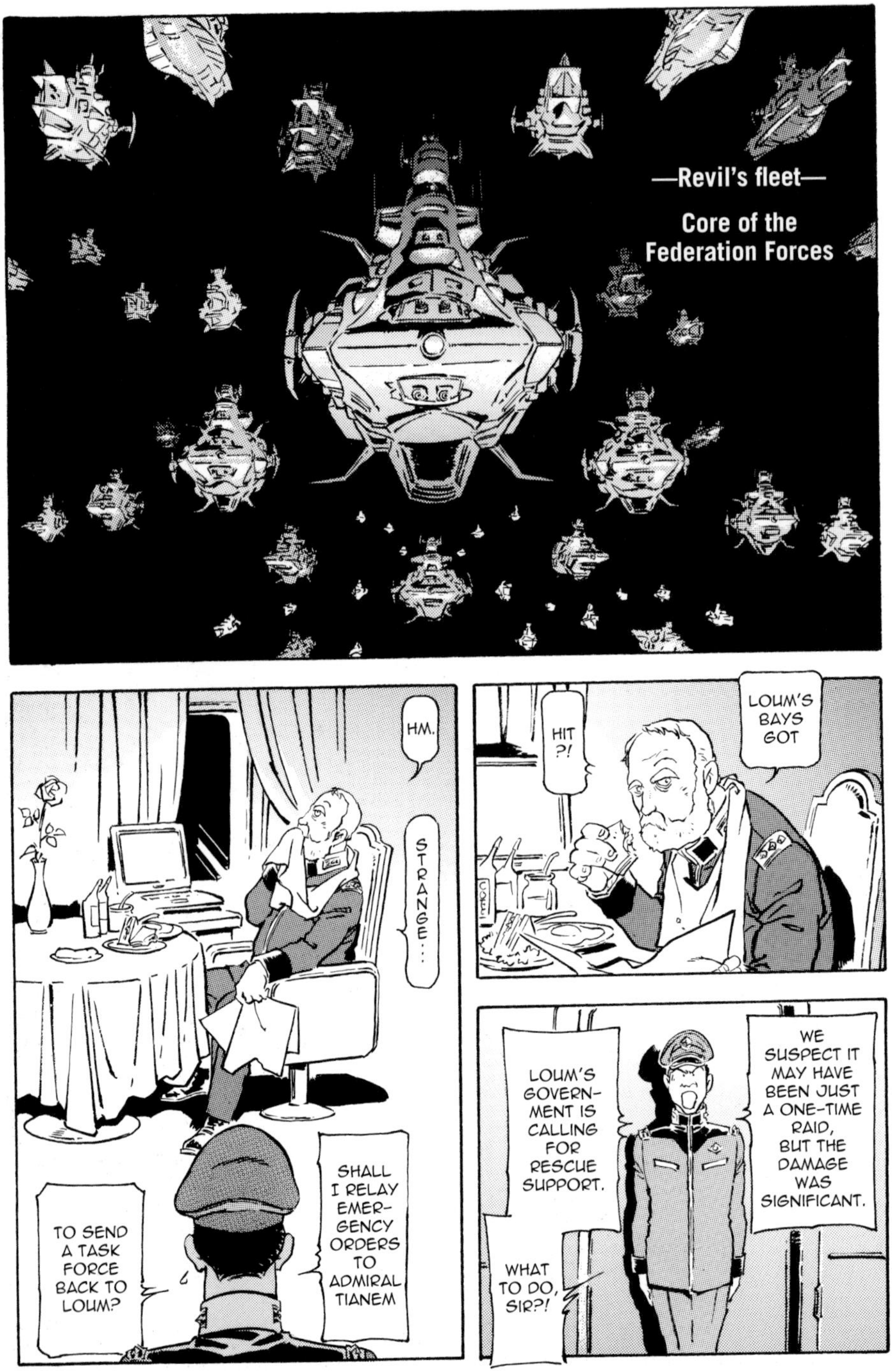
—Revil's fleet—
Core of the Federation Forces
LOUM'S BAYS GOT
HIT?!
WE SUSPECT IT MAY HAVE BEEN JUST A ONE-TIME RAID, BUT THE DAMAGE WAS SIGNIFICANT.
LOUM'S GOVERNMENT IS CALLING FOR RESCUE SUPPORT.
WHAT TO DO, SIR?!
HM.
STRANGE...
SHALL I RELAY EMERGENCY ORDERS TO ADMIRAL TIANEM
TO SEND A TASK FORCE BACK TO LOUM?

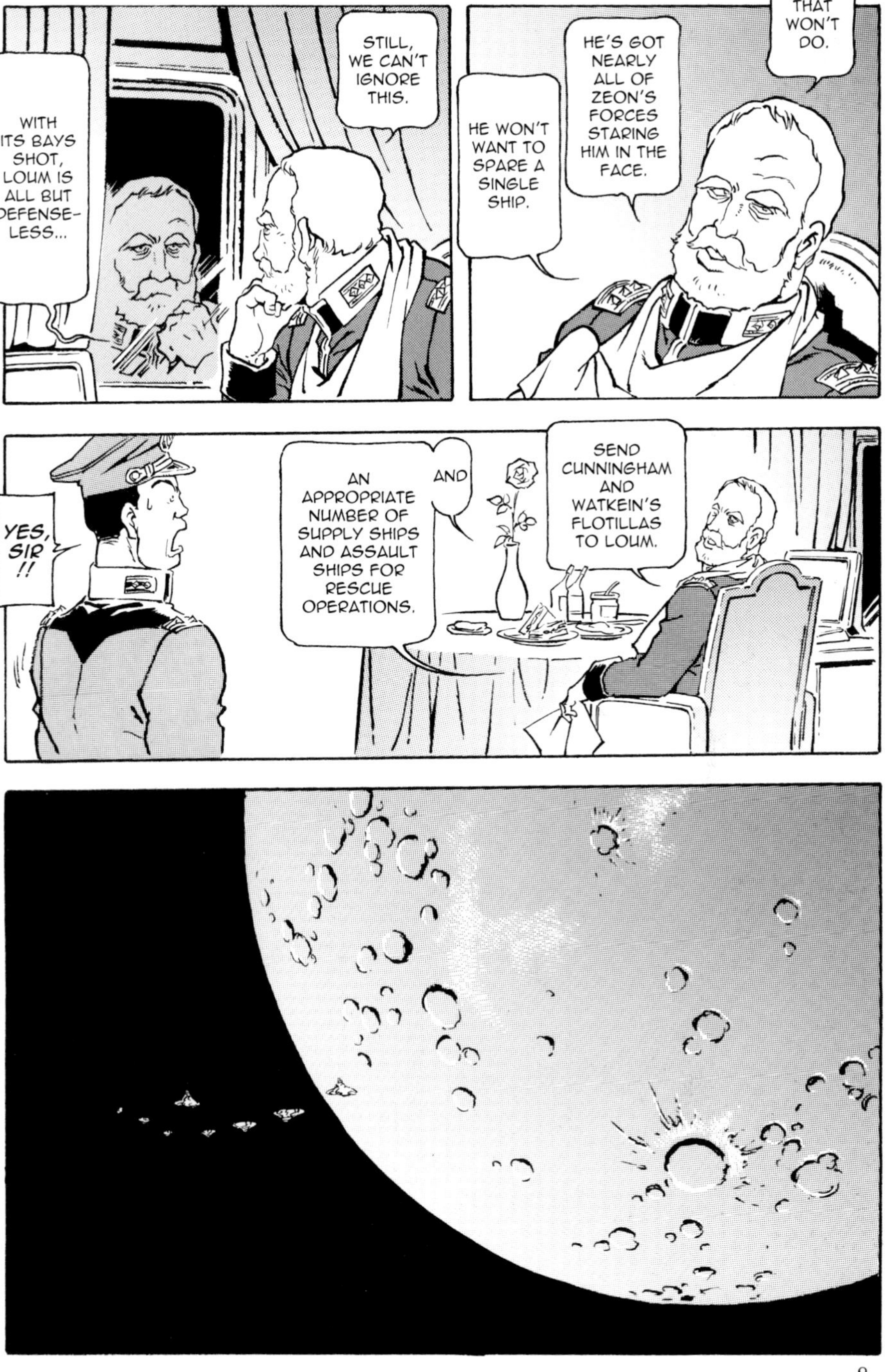
THAT WON'T DO.
HE'S GOT NEARLY ALL OF ZEON'S FORCES STARING HIM IN THE FACE.
HE WON'T WANT TO SPARE A SINGLE SHIP.
STILL, WE CAN'T IGNORE THIS.
WITH ITS BAYS SHOT, LOUM IS ALL BUT DEFENSE-LESS...
SEND CUNNINGHAM AND WATKEIN'S FLOTILLAS TO LOUM.
AND
AN APPROPRIATE NUMBER OF SUPPLY SHIPS AND ASSAULT SHIPS FOR RESCUE OPERATIONS.
YES, SIR!!

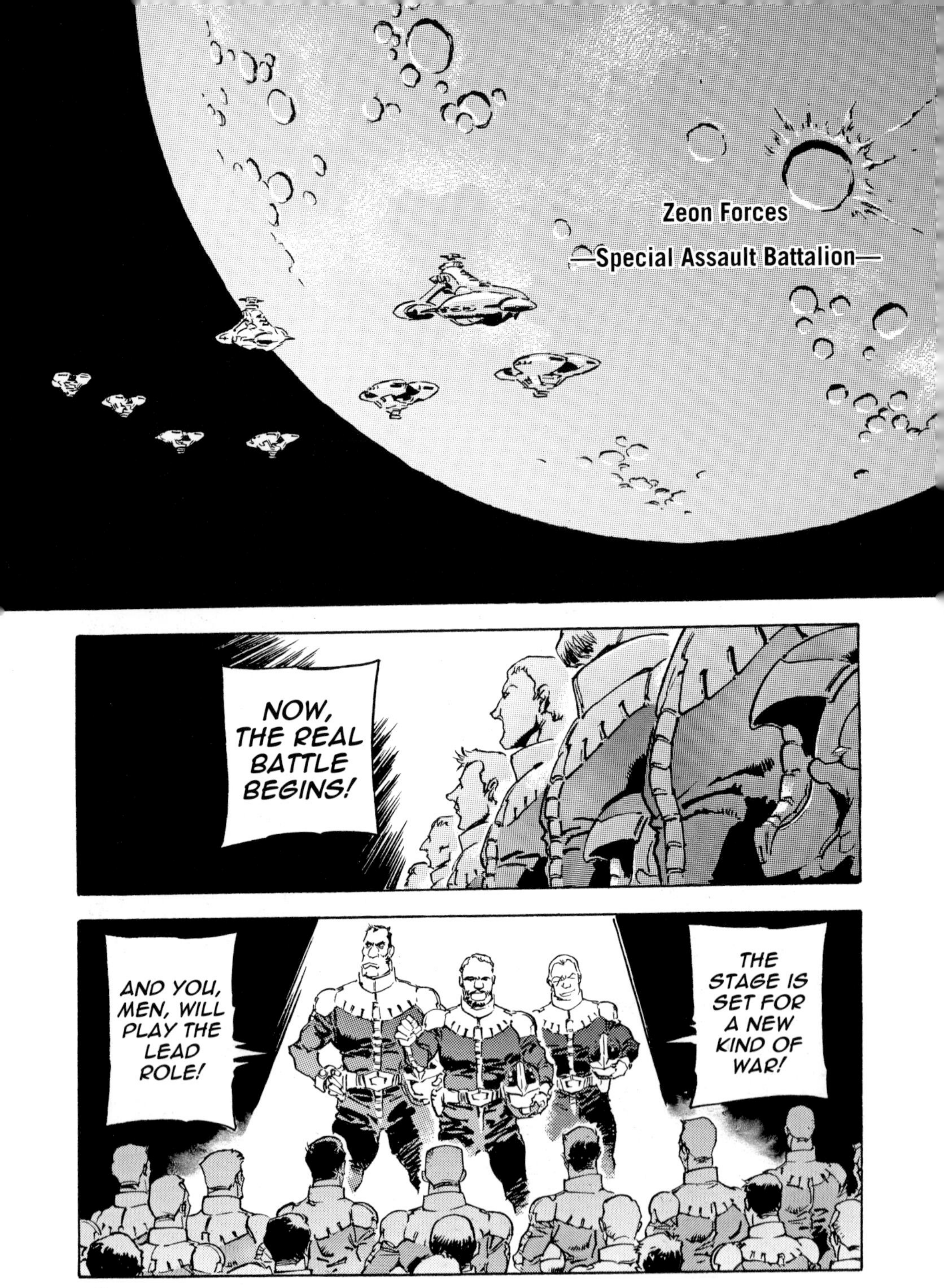
Zeon Forces
—Special Assault Battalion—
NOW, THE REAL BATTLE BEGINS!
THE STAGE IS SET FOR A NEW KIND OF WAR!
AND YOU, MEN, WILL PLAY THE LEAD ROLE!

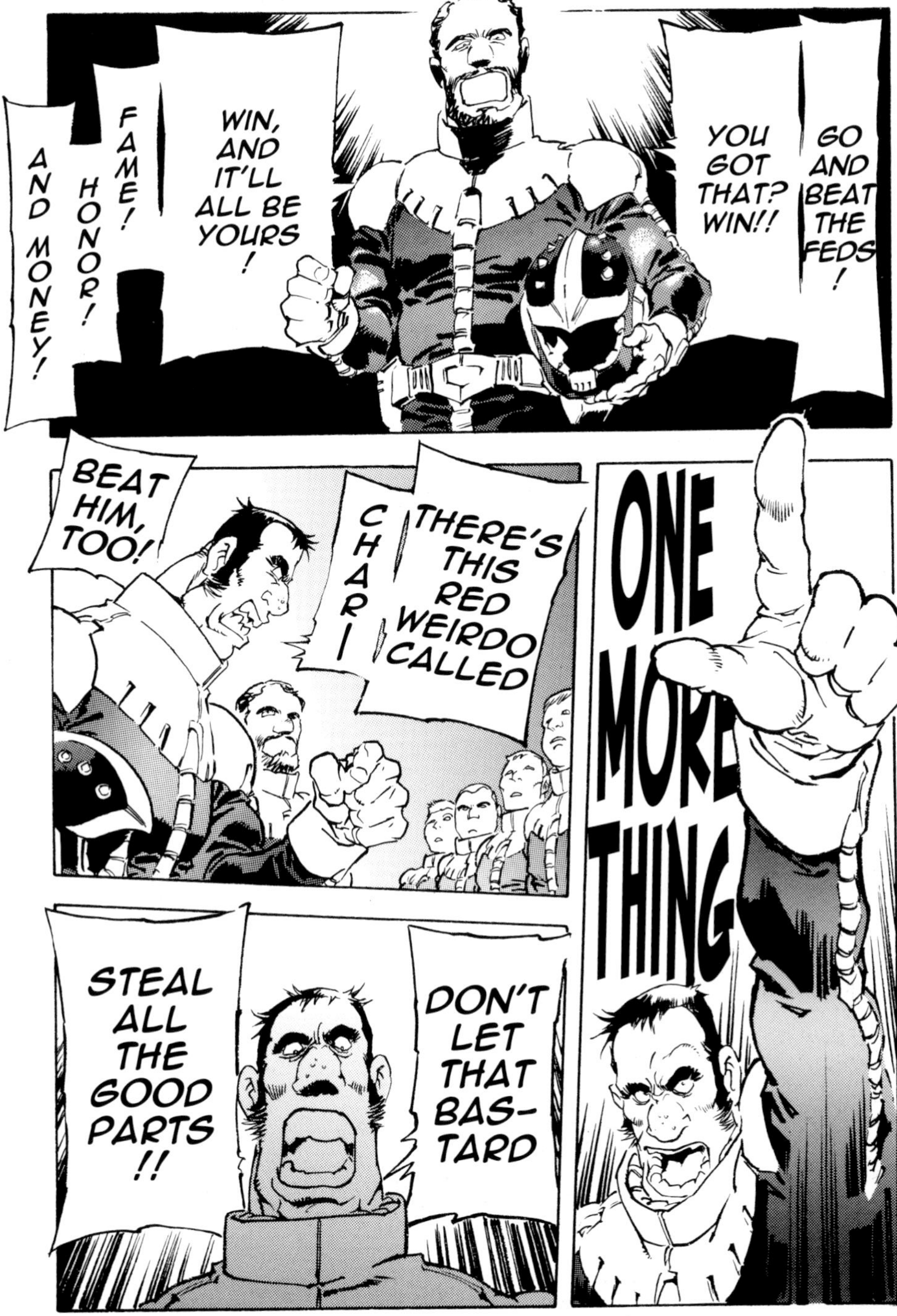
GO AND BEAT THE FEDS!
YOU GOT THAT? WIN!!
WIN, AND IT'LL ALL BE YOURS!
FAME!
HONOR!
AND MONEY!
ONE MORE THING
THERE'S THIS RED WEIRDO CALLED
CHAR!
BEAT HIM, TOO!
DON'T LET THAT BAS-TARD
STEAL ALL THE GOOD PARTS!!

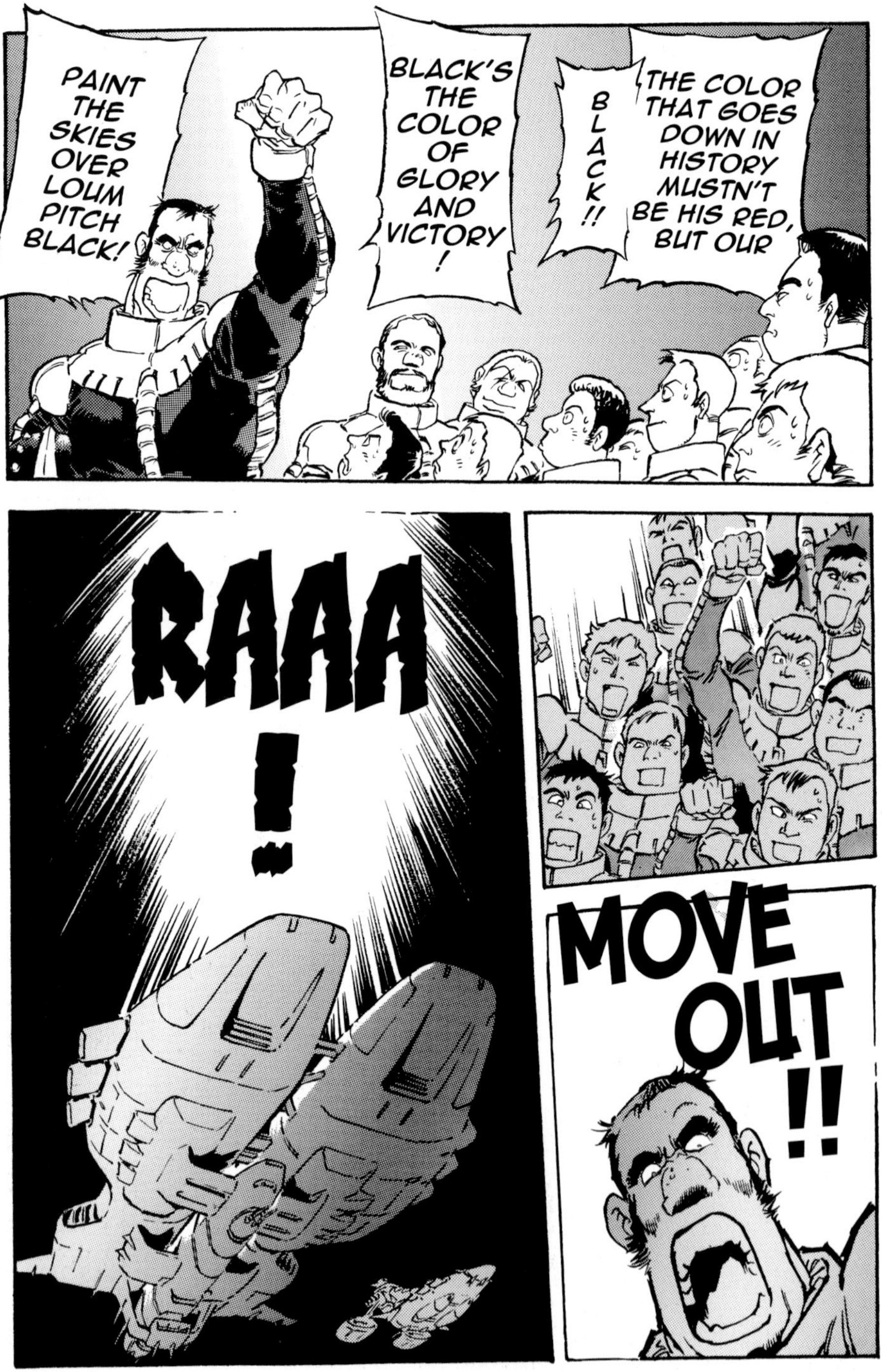
THE COLOR THAT GOES DOWN IN HISTORY MUSTN'T BE HIS RED, BUT OUR
BLACK!!
BLACK'S THE COLOR OF GLORY AND VICTORY!
PAINT THE SKIES OVER LOUM PITCH BLACK!
MOVE OUT!!
RAAA!!

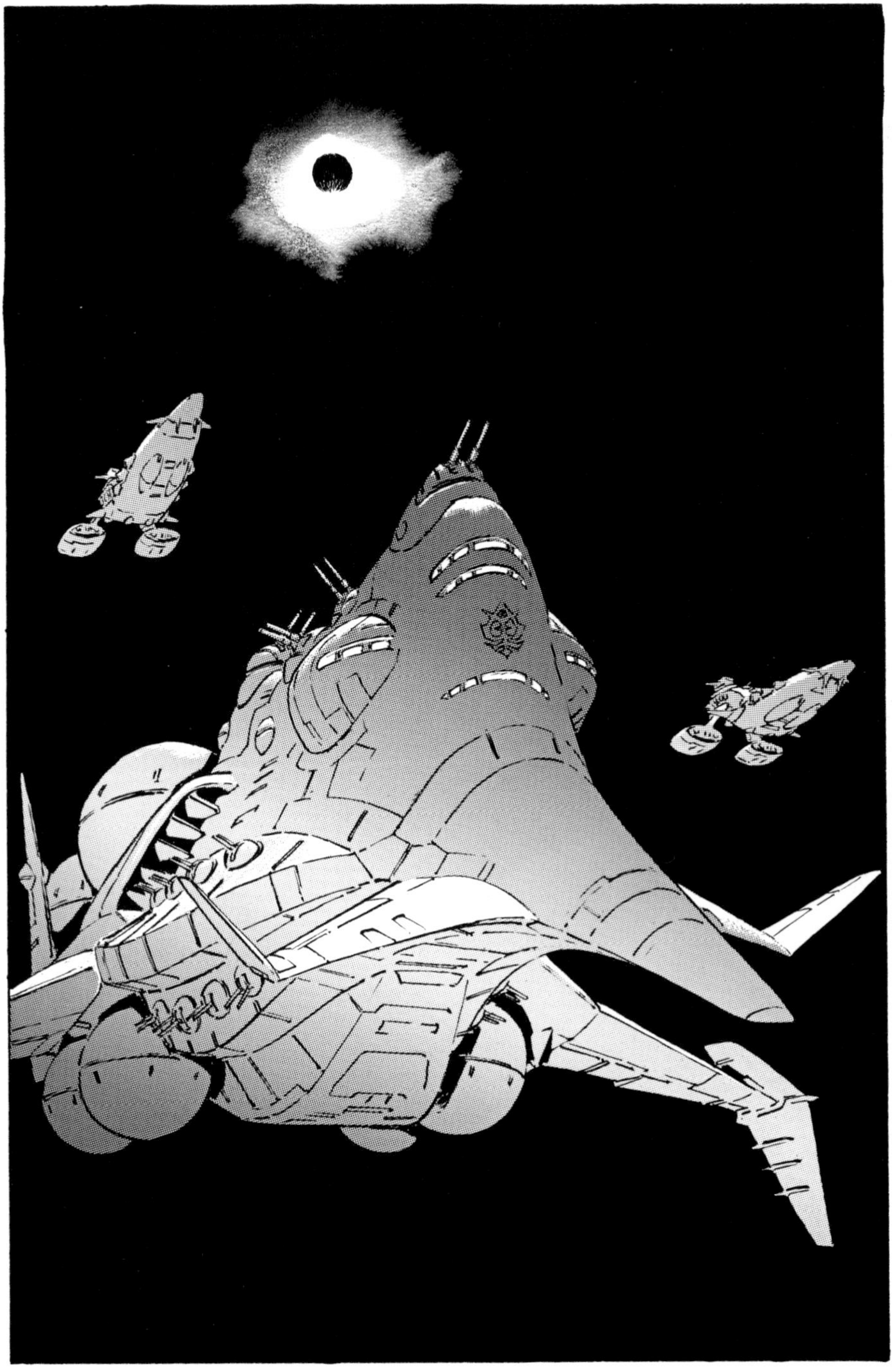

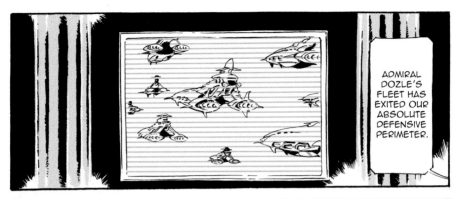

ADMIRAL DOZLE'S FLEET HAS EXITED OUR ABSOLUTE DEFENSIVE PERIMETER.

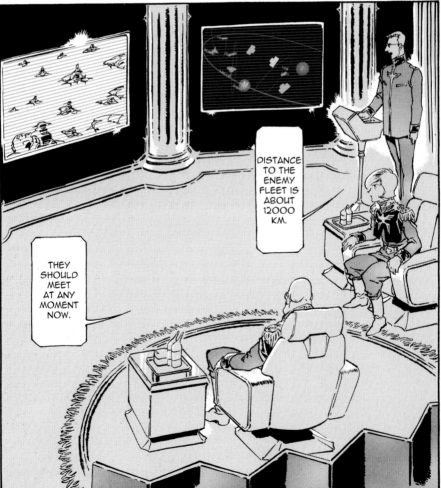

DISTANCE TO THE ENEMY FLEET IS ABOUT 12000 KM.

THEY SHOULD MEET AT ANY MOMENT NOW.

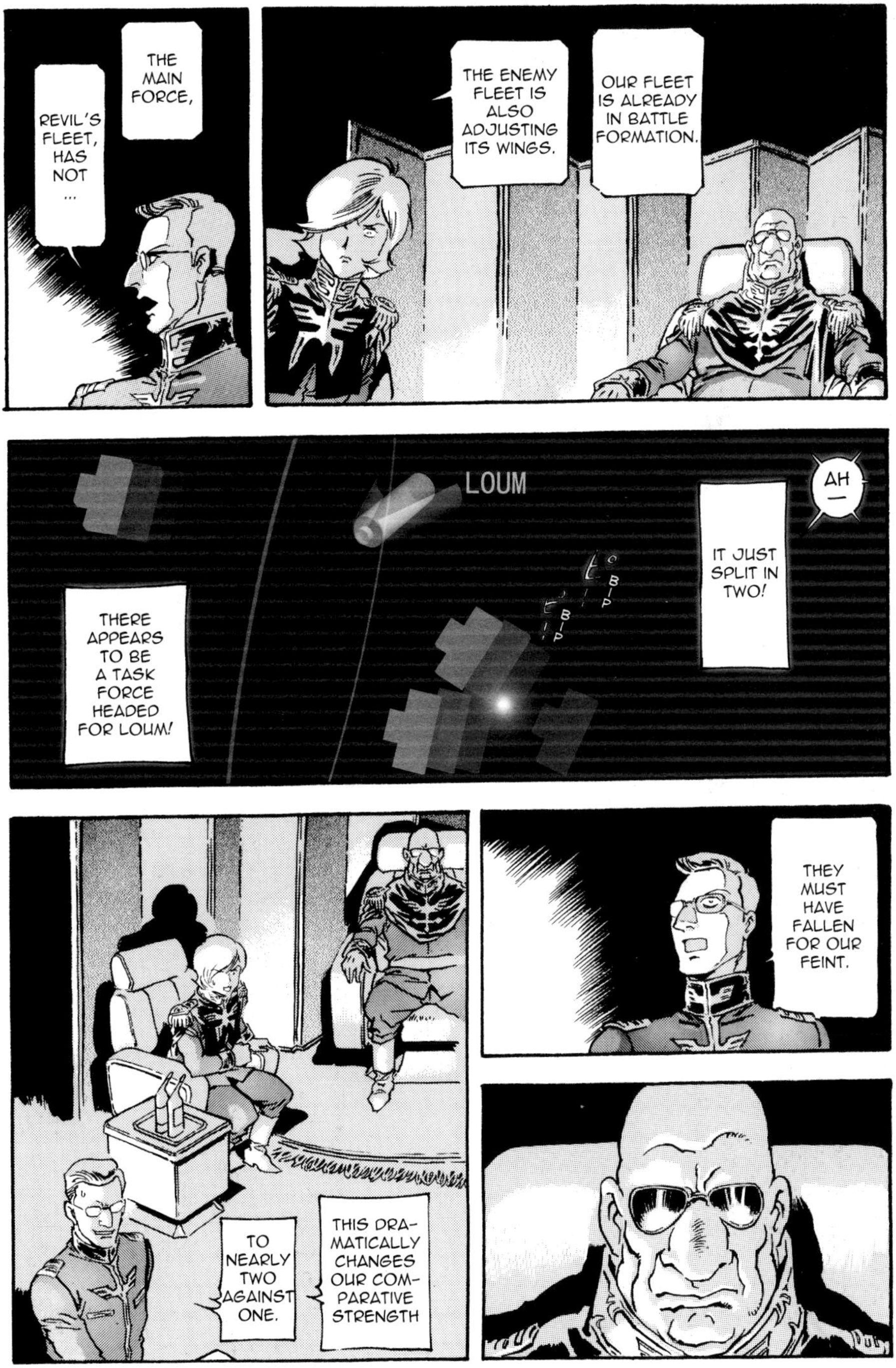
OUR FLEET IS ALREADY IN BATTLE FORMATION.
THE ENEMY FLEET IS ALSO ADJUSTING ITS WINGS.
THE MAIN FORCE,
REVIL'S FLEET, HAS NOT ...
AH—
IT JUST SPLIT IN TWO!
BIP
BIP
LOUM
THERE APPEARS TO BE A TASK FORCE HEADED FOR LOUM!
THEY MUST HAVE FALLEN FOR OUR FEINT.
THIS DRAMATICALLY CHANGES OUR COMPARATIVE STRENGTH
TO NEARLY TWO AGAINST ONE.

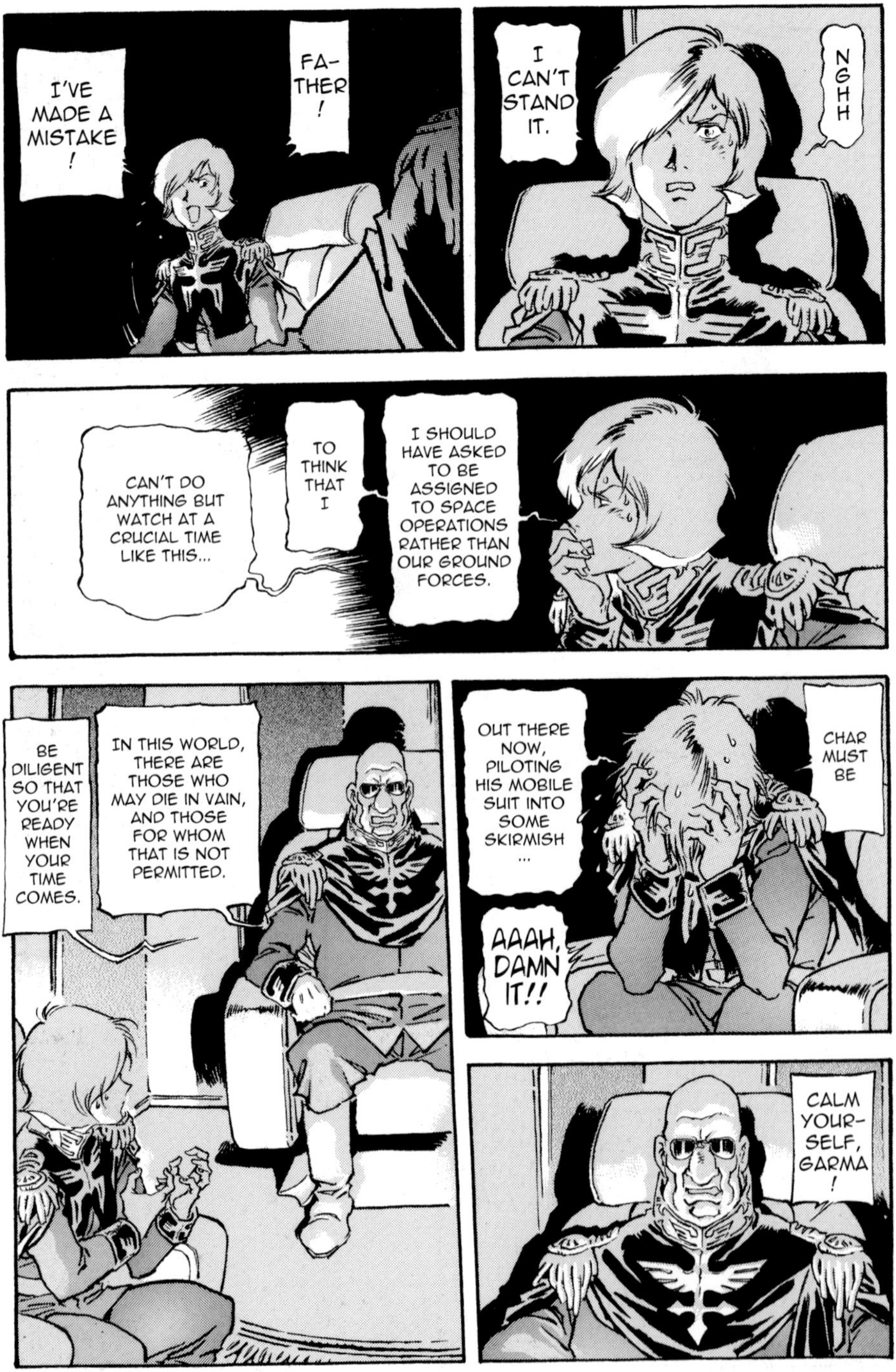
NGHH
I CAN'T STAND IT.
FA-THER!
I'VE MADE A MISTAKE!
I SHOULD HAVE ASKED TO BE ASSIGNED TO SPACE OPERATIONS RATHER THAN OUR GROUND FORCES.
TO THINK THAT I
CAN'T DO ANYTHING BUT WATCH AT A CRUCIAL TIME LIKE THIS...
CHAR MUST BE
OUT THERE NOW, PILOTING HIS MOBILE SUIT INTO SOME SKIRMISH ...
AAAH, DAMN IT!!
CALM YOURSELF, GARMA!
IN THIS WORLD, THERE ARE THOSE WHO MAY DIE IN VAIN, AND THOSE FOR WHOM THAT IS NOT PERMITTED.
BE DILIGENT SO THAT YOU'RE READY WHEN YOUR TIME COMES.

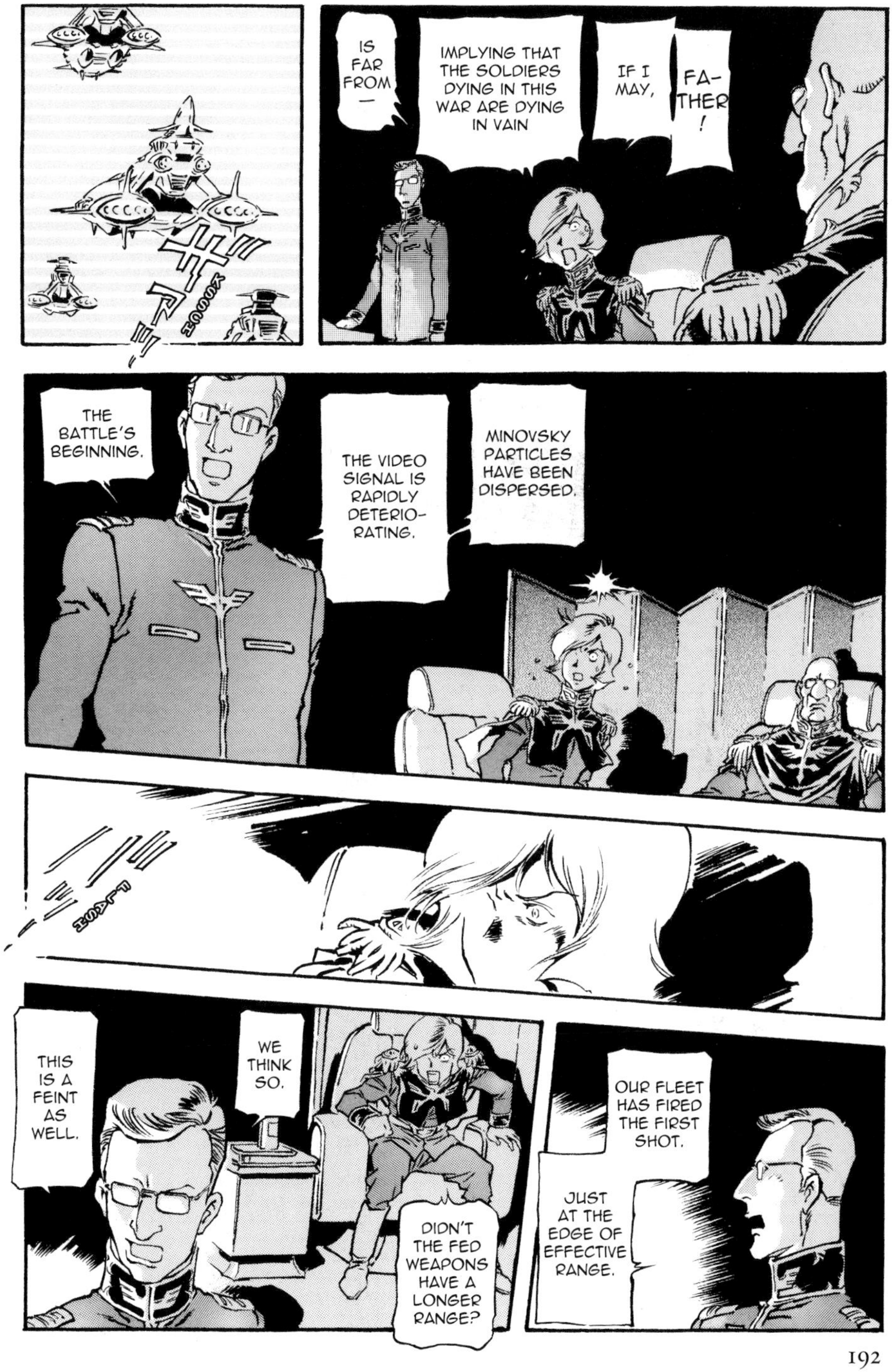
FA-
THER
!
IF I MAY,
IMPLYING THAT THE SOLDIERS DYING IN THIS WAR ARE DYING IN VAIN
IS FAR FROM
—
MINOVSKY PARTICLES HAVE BEEN DISPERSED.
THE VIDEO SIGNAL IS RAPIDLY DETERIO-RATING.
THE BATTLE'S BEGINNING.
OUR FLEET HAS FIRED THE FIRST SHOT.
JUST AT THE EDGE OF EFFECTIVE RANGE.
DIDN'T THE FED WEAPONS HAVE A LONGER RANGE?
WE THINK SO.
THIS IS A FEINT AS WELL.

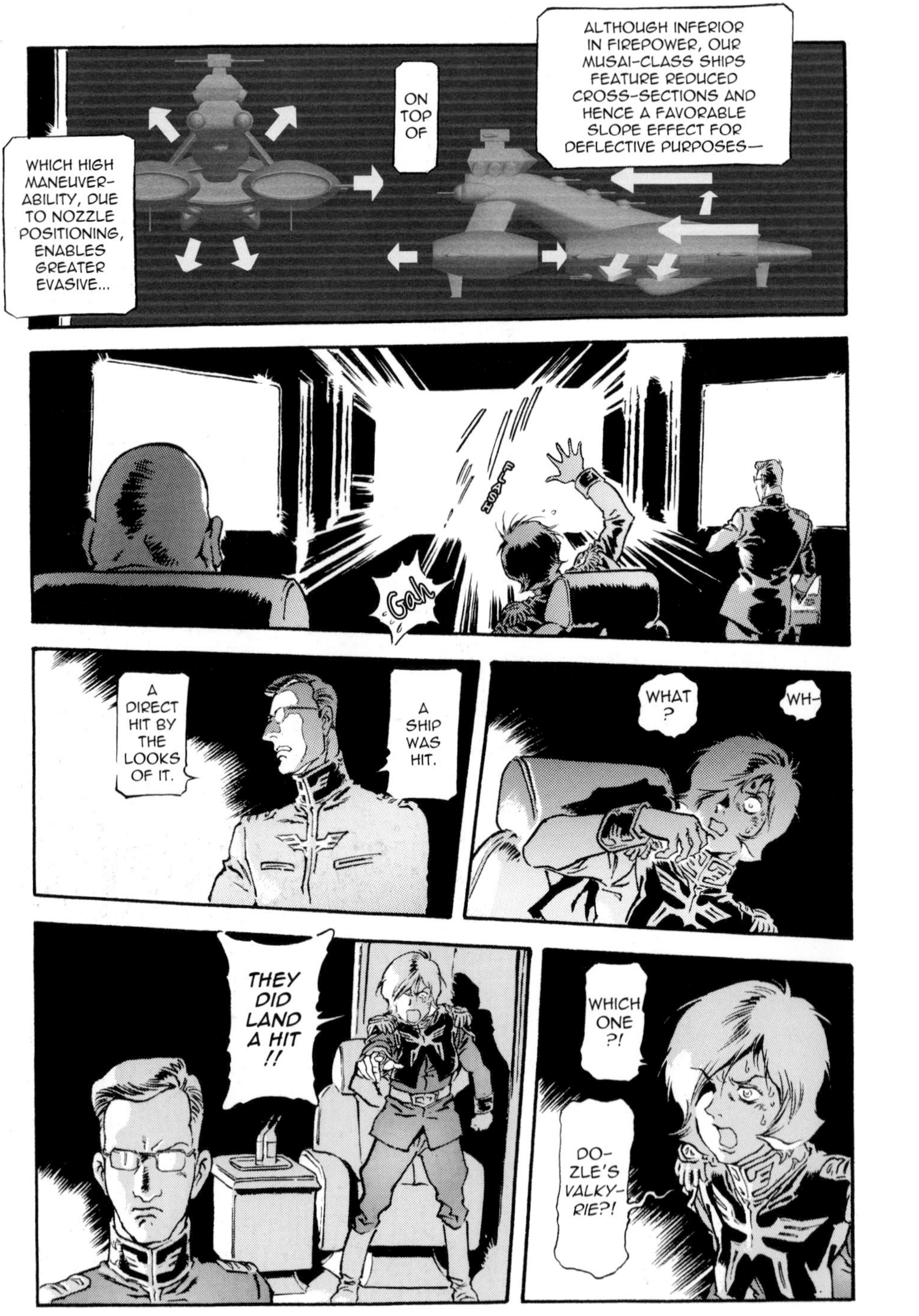
ALTHOUGH INFERIOR IN FIREPOWER, OUR MUSAI-CLASS SHIPS FEATURE REDUCED CROSS-SECTIONS AND HENCE A FAVORABLE SLOPE EFFECT FOR DEFLECTIVE PURPOSES—
ON TOP OF
WHICH HIGH MANEUVER-ABILITY, DUE TO NOZZLE POSITIONING, ENABLES GREATER EVASIVE...
Gah
WH-
WHAT?
A SHIP WAS HIT.
A DIRECT HIT BY THE LOOKS OF IT.
WHICH ONE?!
DO-ZLE'S VALKY-RIE?!
THEY DID LAND A HIT!!

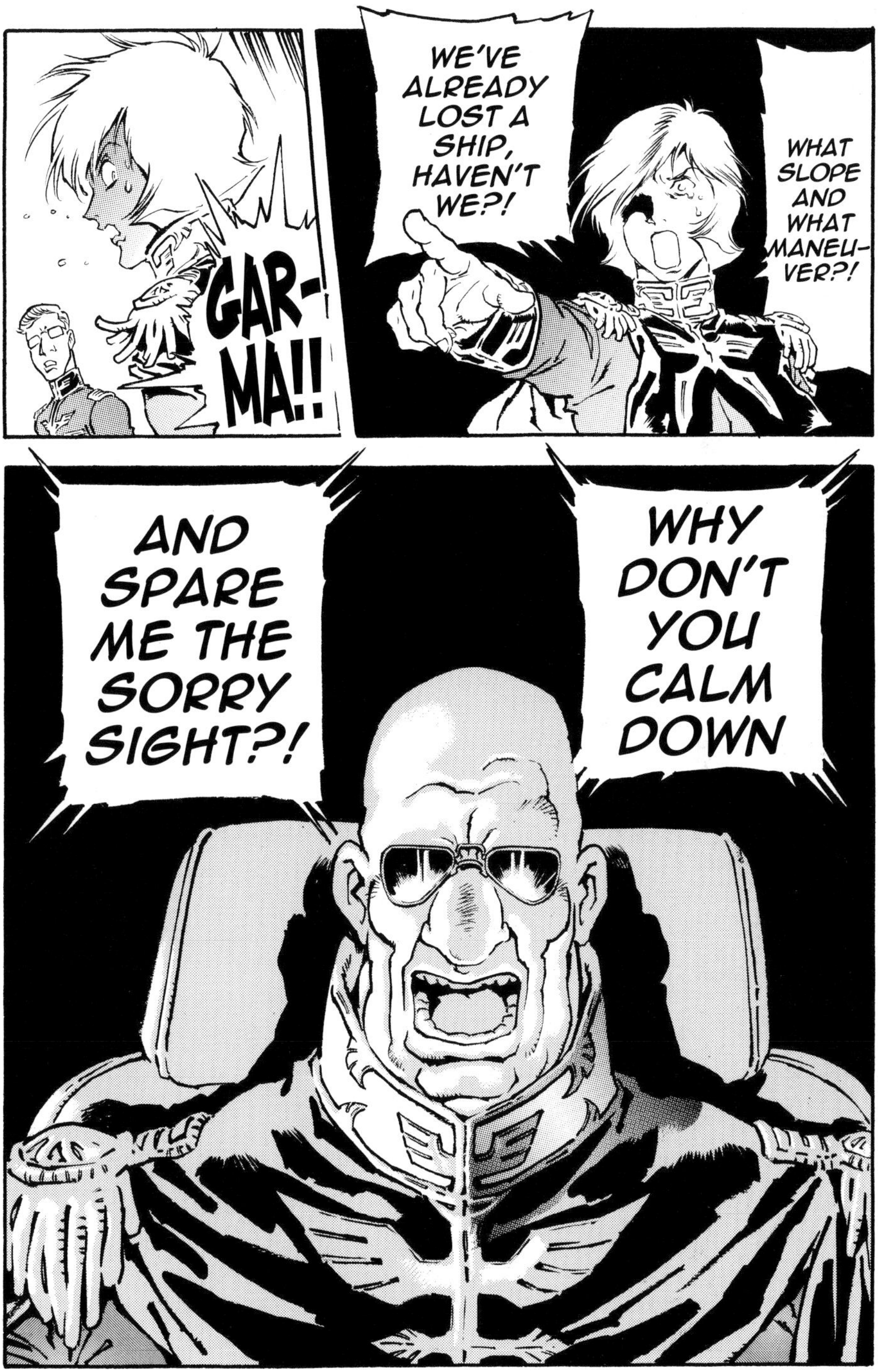
WHAT SLOPE AND WHAT MANEU-VER?!
WE'VE ALREADY LOST A SHIP, HAVEN'T WE?!
GAR-MA!!
WHY DON'T YOU CALM DOWN
AND SPARE ME THE SORRY SIGHT?!

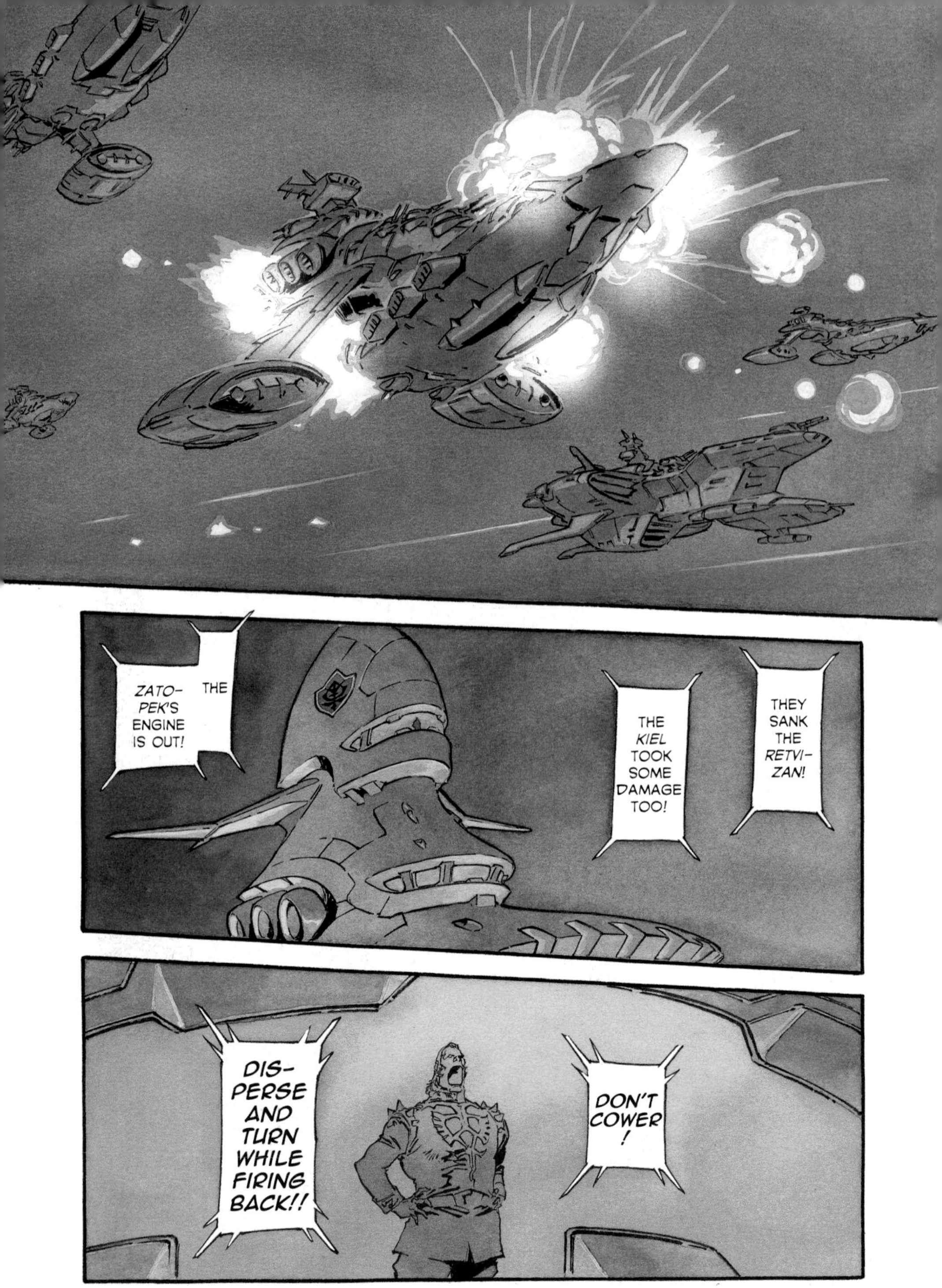
THEY SANK THE *RETVIZAN*!
THE *KIEL* TOOK SOME DAMAGE TOO!
THE *ZATOPEK*'S ENGINE IS OUT!
DON'T COWER!
DISPERSE AND TURN WHILE FIRING BACK!!

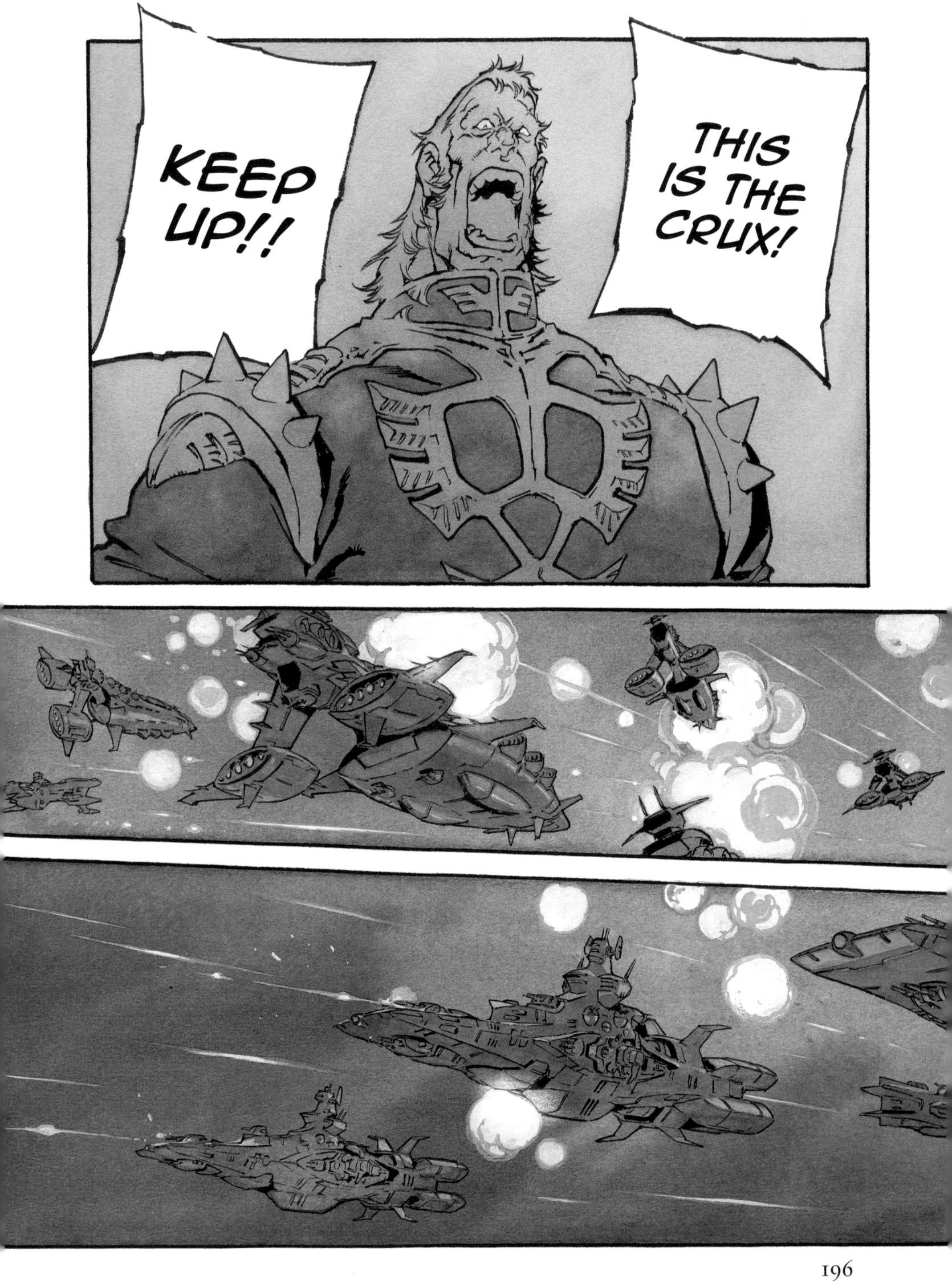
THIS IS THE CRUX!
KEEP UP!!

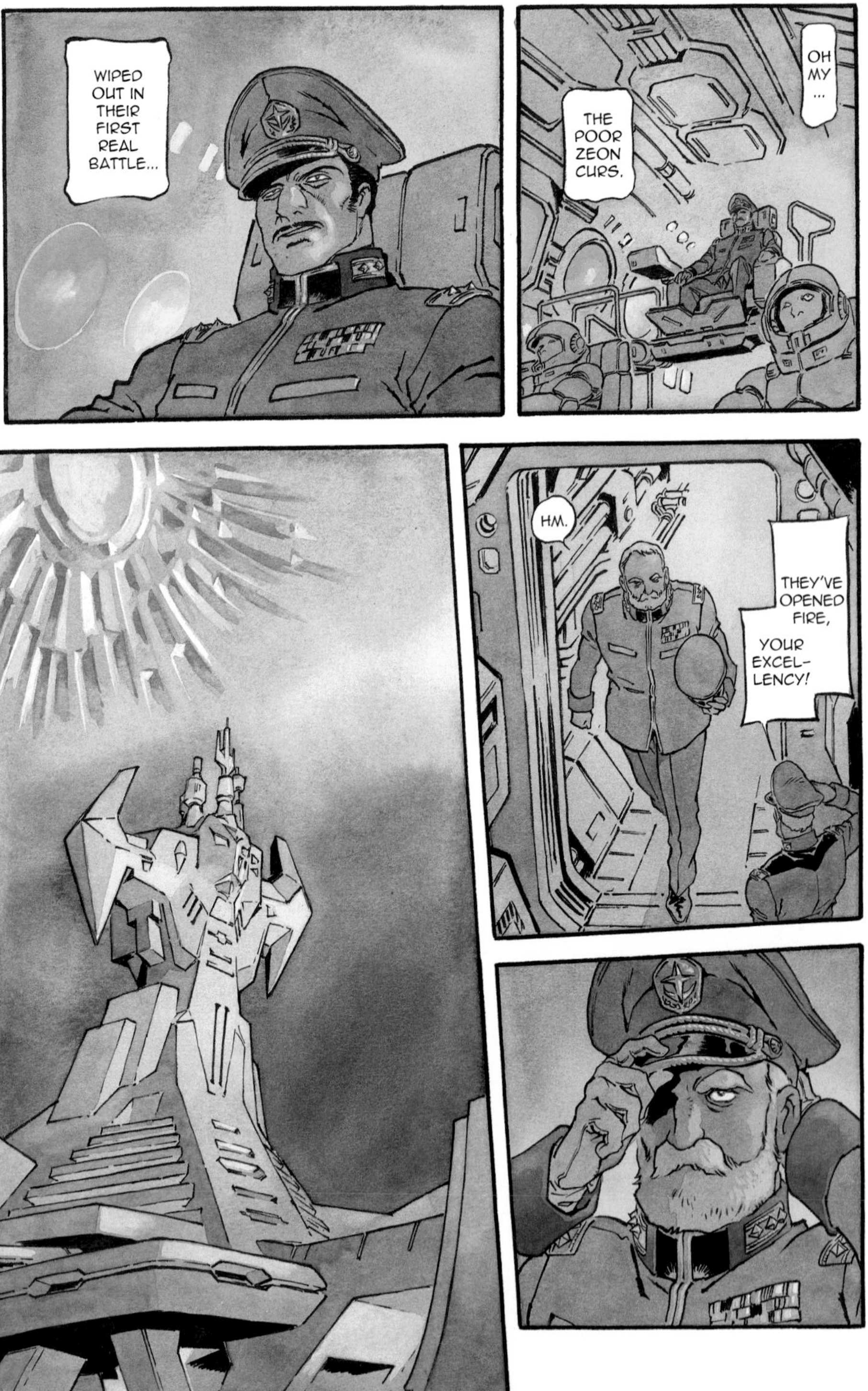
OH MY ...
THE POOR ZEON CURS.
WIPED OUT IN THEIR FIRST REAL BATTLE...
THEY'VE OPENED FIRE,
YOUR EXCEL-LENCY!
HM.

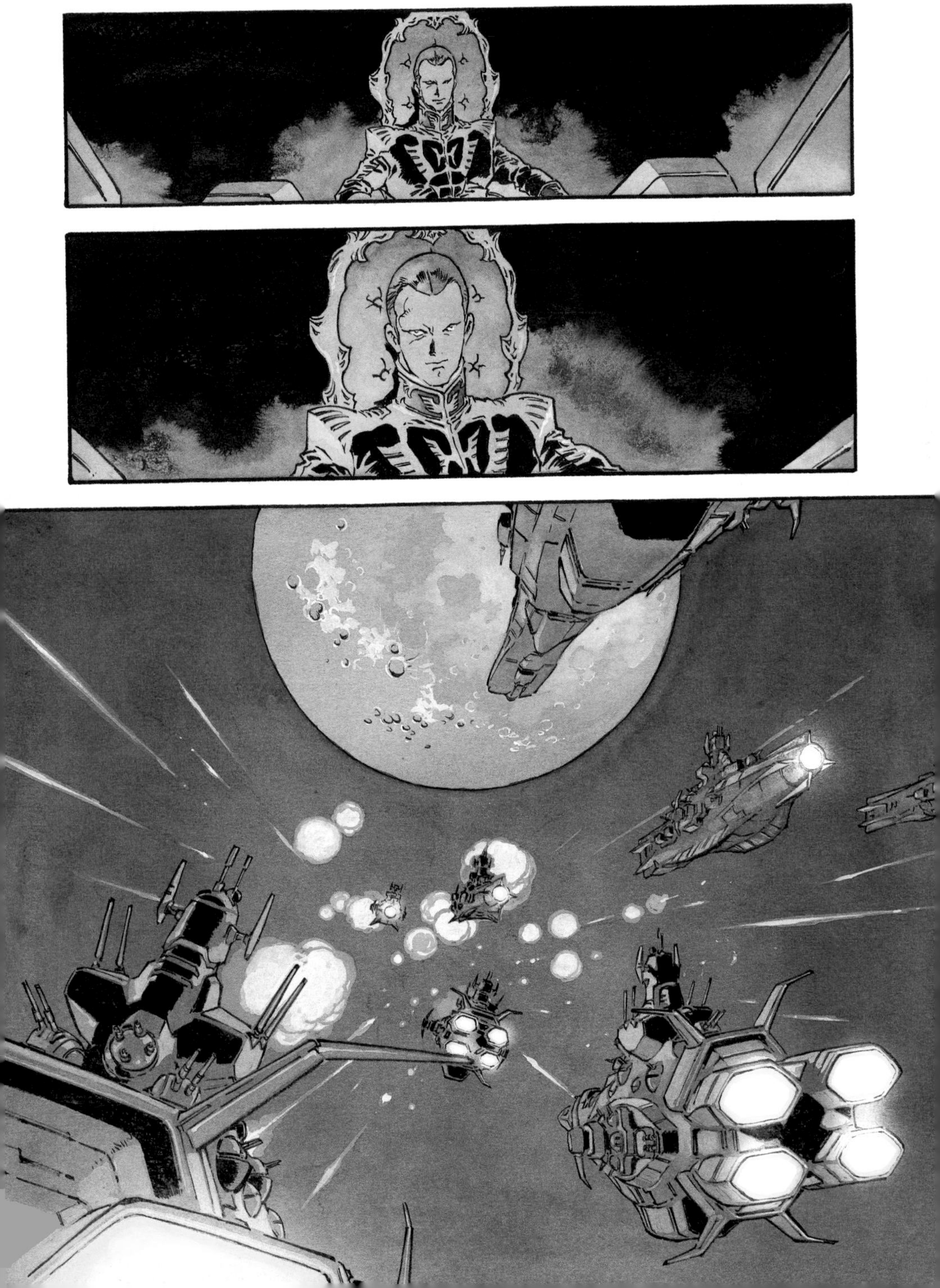

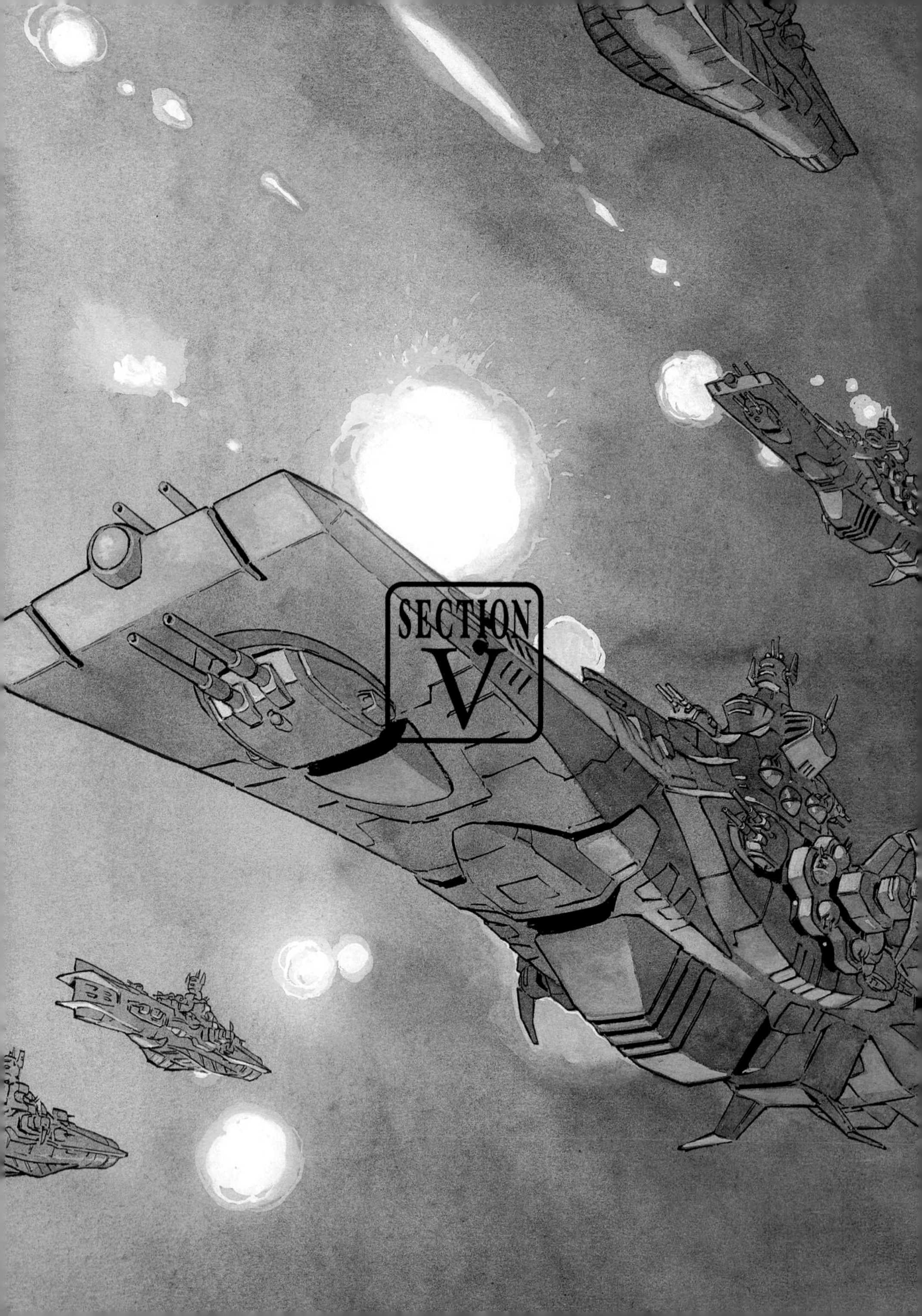
SECTION
V

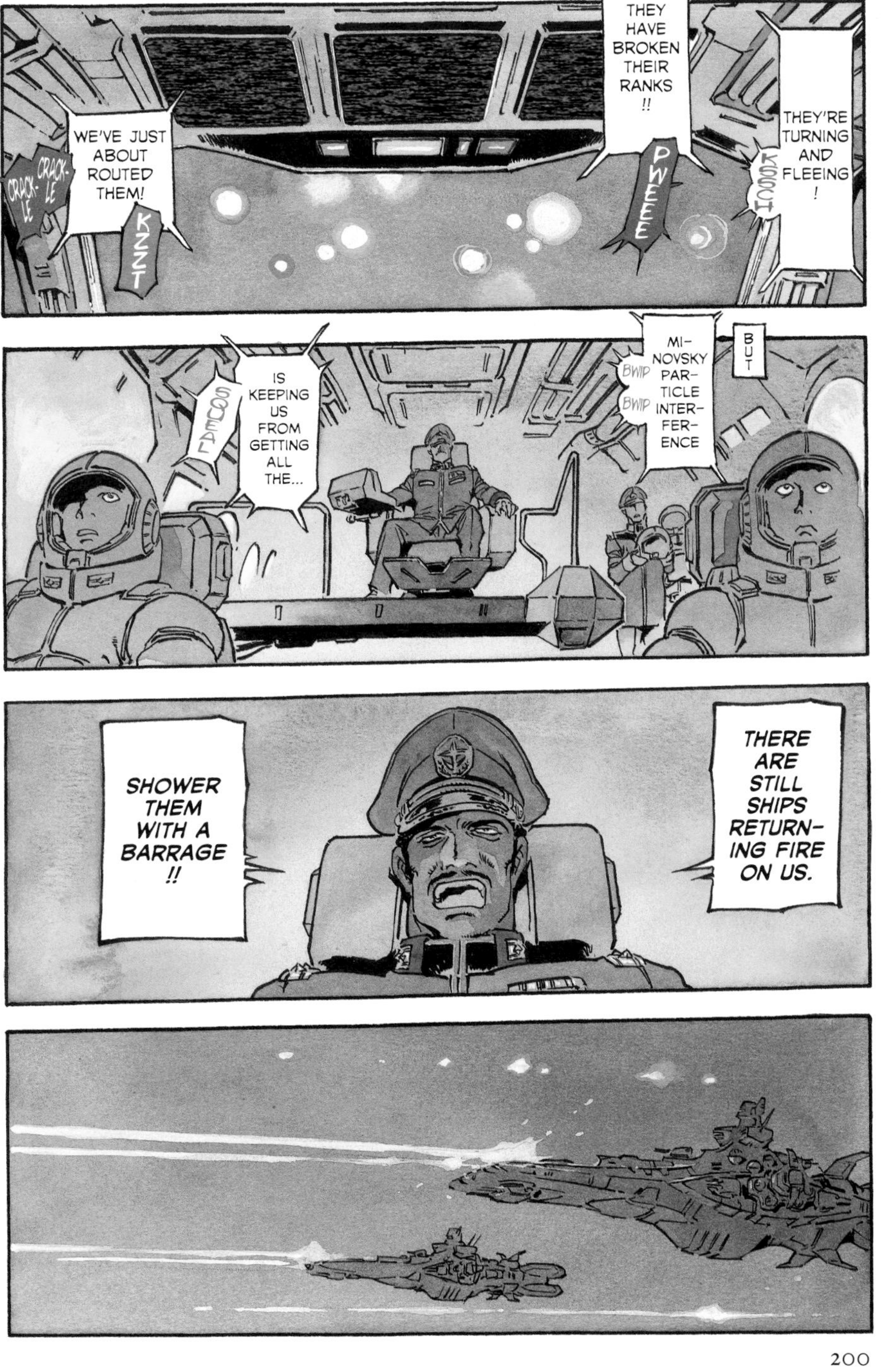
KSSCH
THEY'RE TURNING AND FLEEING!
PWEEE
THEY HAVE BROKEN THEIR RANKS!!
KZZT
WE'VE JUST ABOUT ROUTED THEM!
CRACK-LE
CRACK-LE
BUT
MINOVSKY PARTICLE INTERFERENCE
BWIP
BWIP
IS KEEPING US FROM GETTING ALL THE...
SQUEAL
THERE ARE STILL SHIPS RETURNING FIRE ON US.
SHOWER THEM WITH A BARRAGE!!

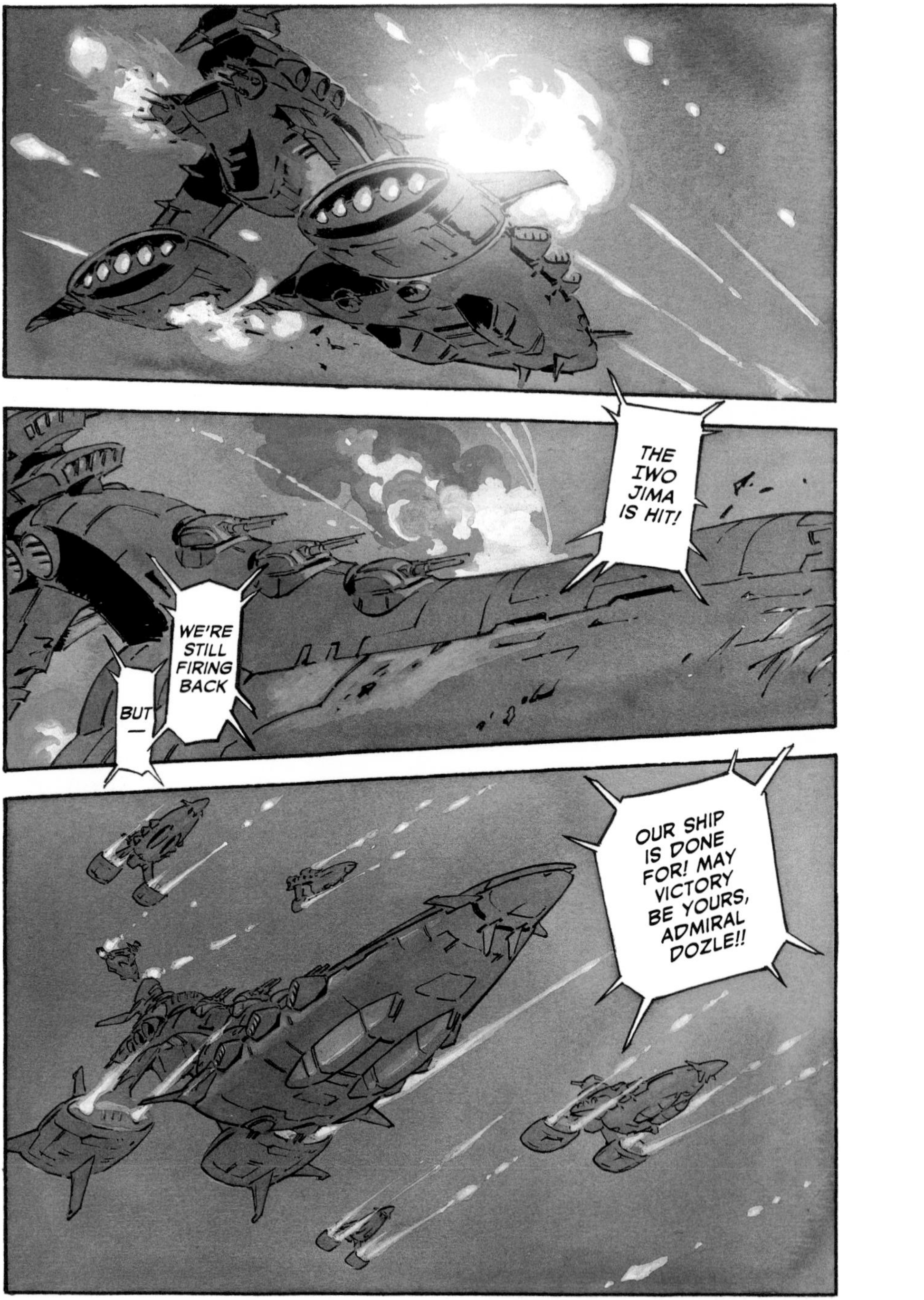
THE IWO JIMA IS HIT!
WE'RE STILL FIRING BACK
BUT—
OUR SHIP IS DONE FOR! MAY VICTORY BE YOURS, ADMIRAL DOZLE!!

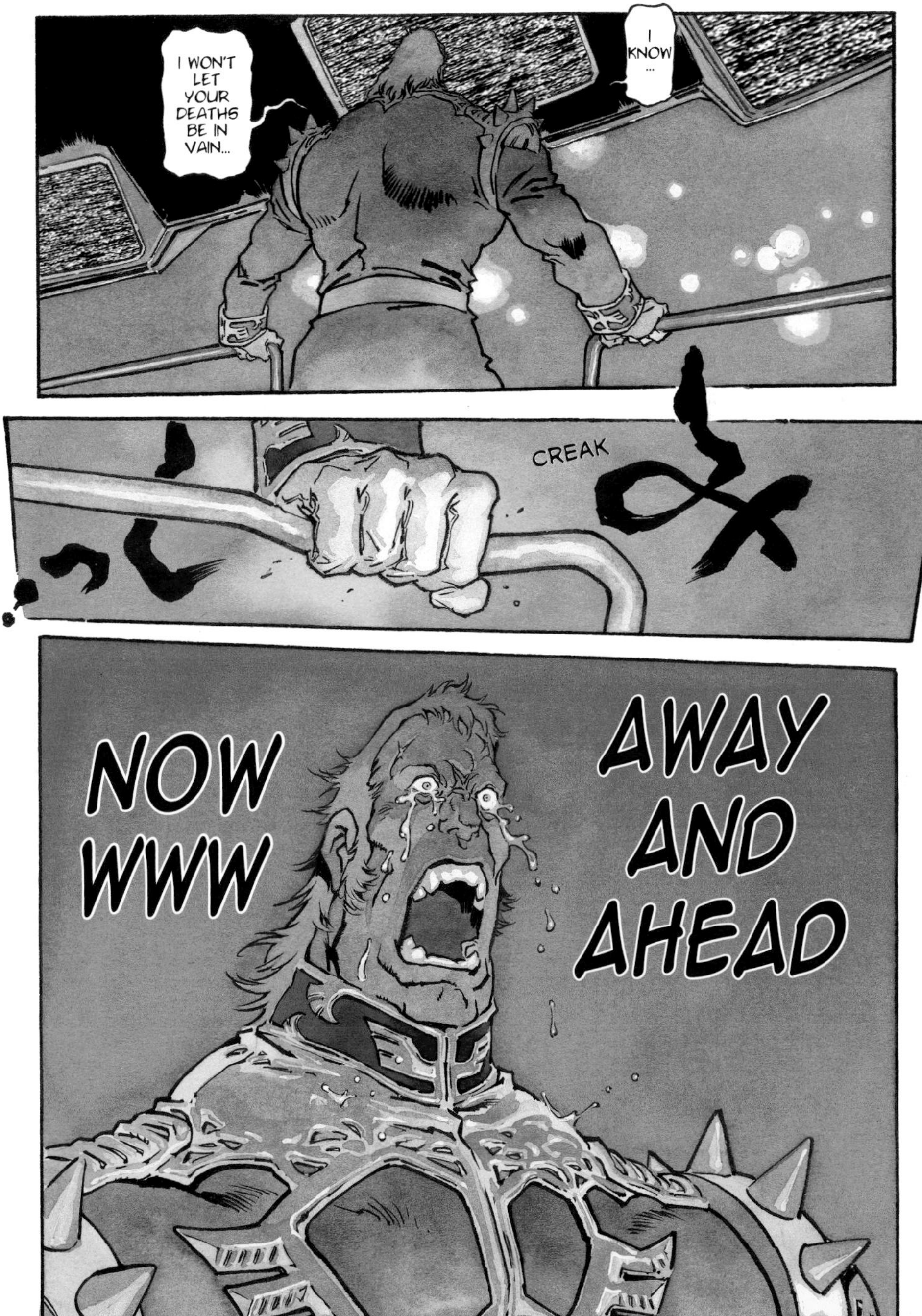
I KNOW ...
I WON'T LET YOUR DEATHS BE IN VAIN...
CREAK
AWAY AND AHEAD
NOW WWW

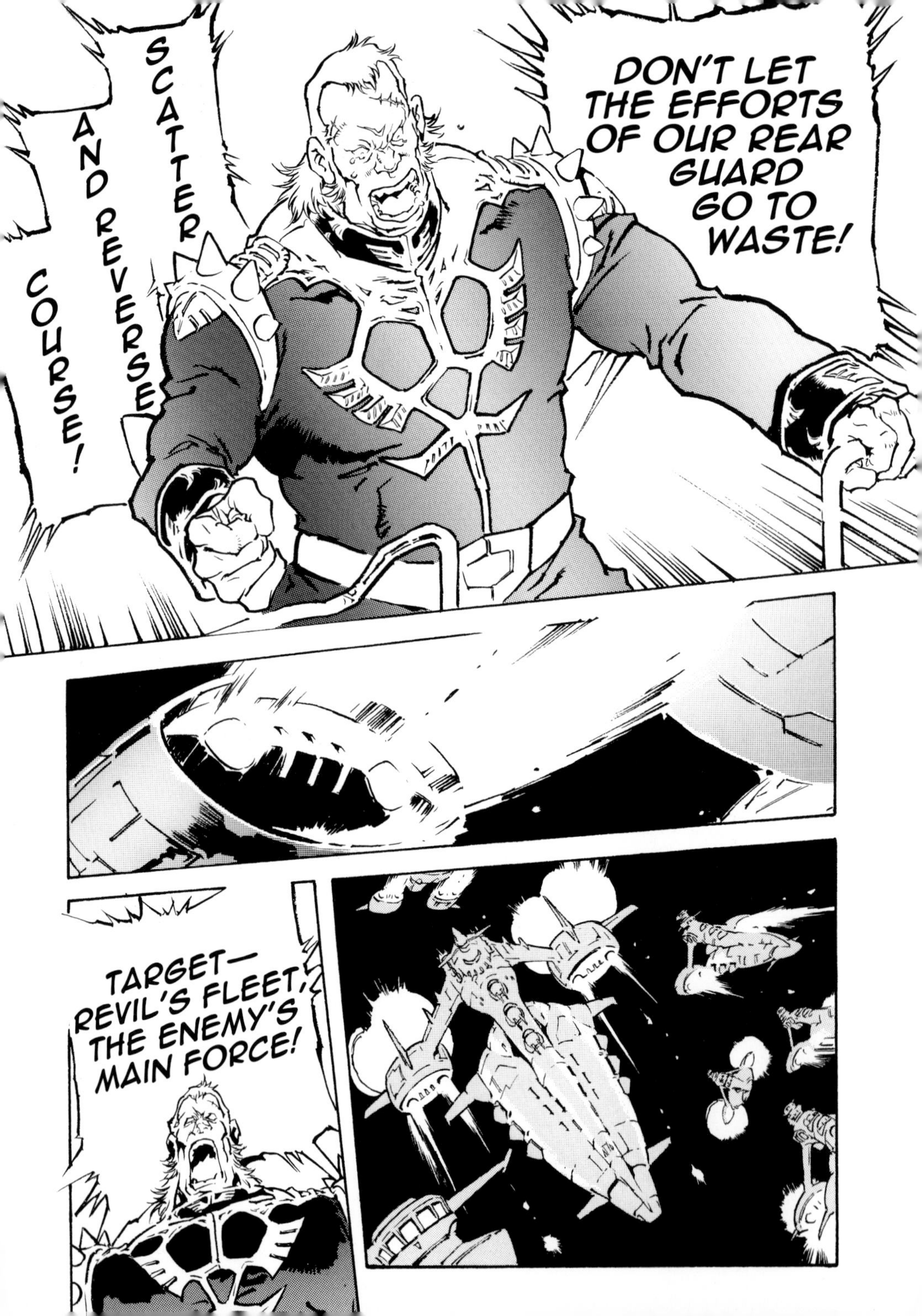
DON'T LET THE EFFORTS OF OUR REAR GUARD GO TO WASTE!
SCATTER AND REVERSE COURSE!
TARGET—REVIL'S FLEET, THE ENEMY'S MAIN FORCE!

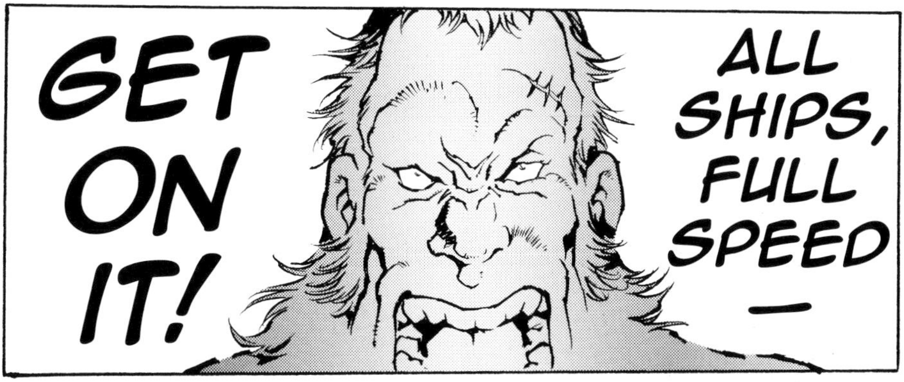
ALL SHIPS, FULL SPEED —
GET ON IT!
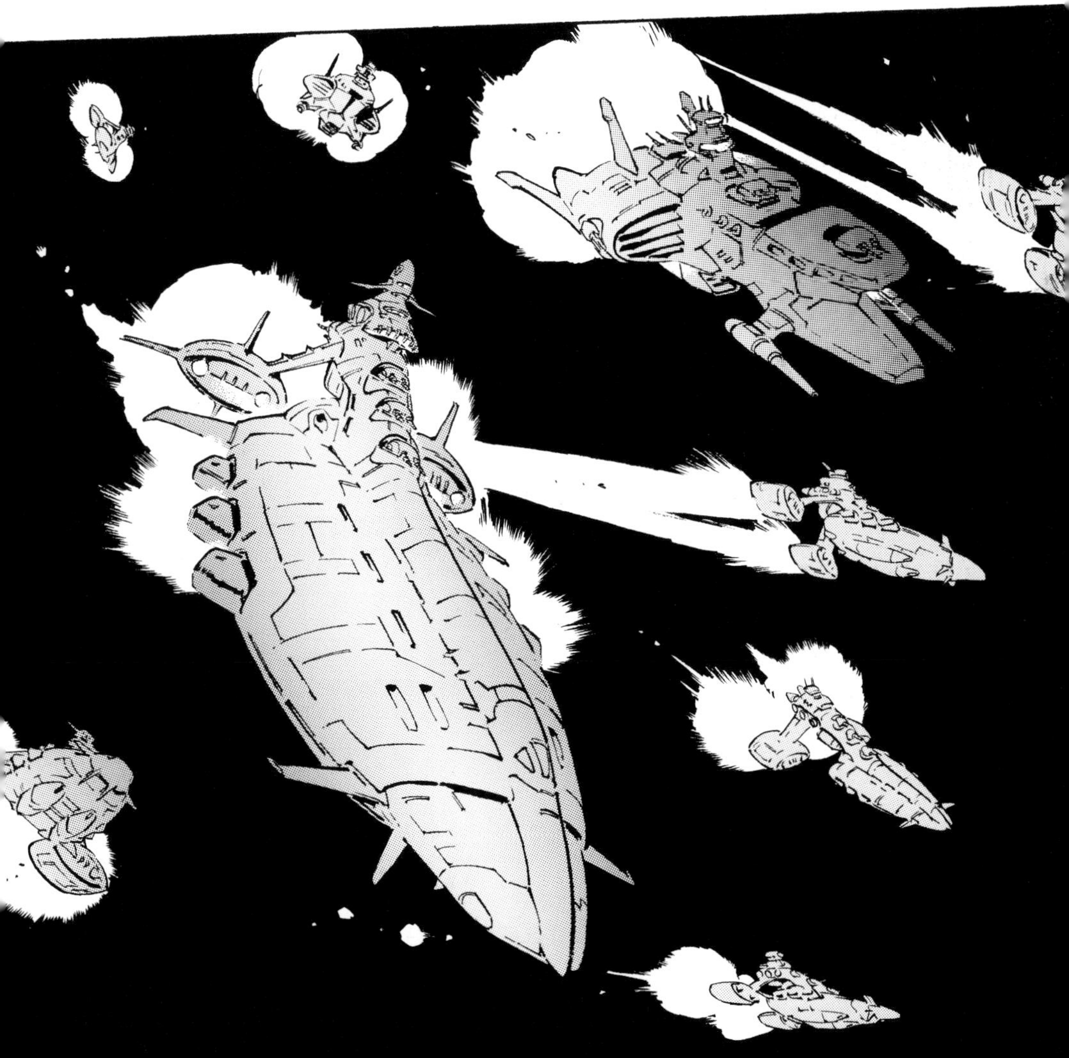

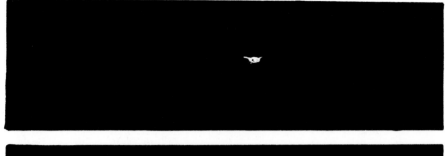

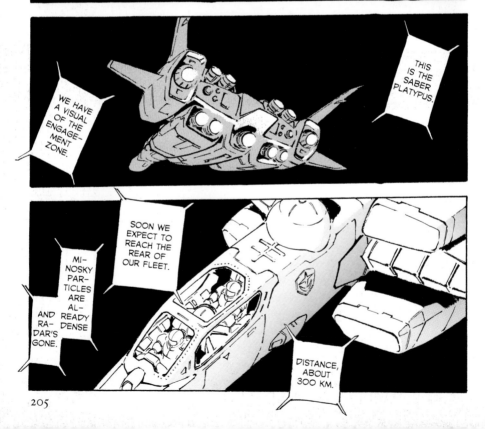

THIS IS THE SABER PLATYPUS.

WE HAVE A VISUAL OF THE ENGAGEMENT ZONE.

SOON WE EXPECT TO REACH THE REAR OF OUR FLEET.

MINOSKY PARTICLES ARE ALREADY DENSE

AND RADAR'S GONE.

DISTANCE, ABOUT 300 KM.

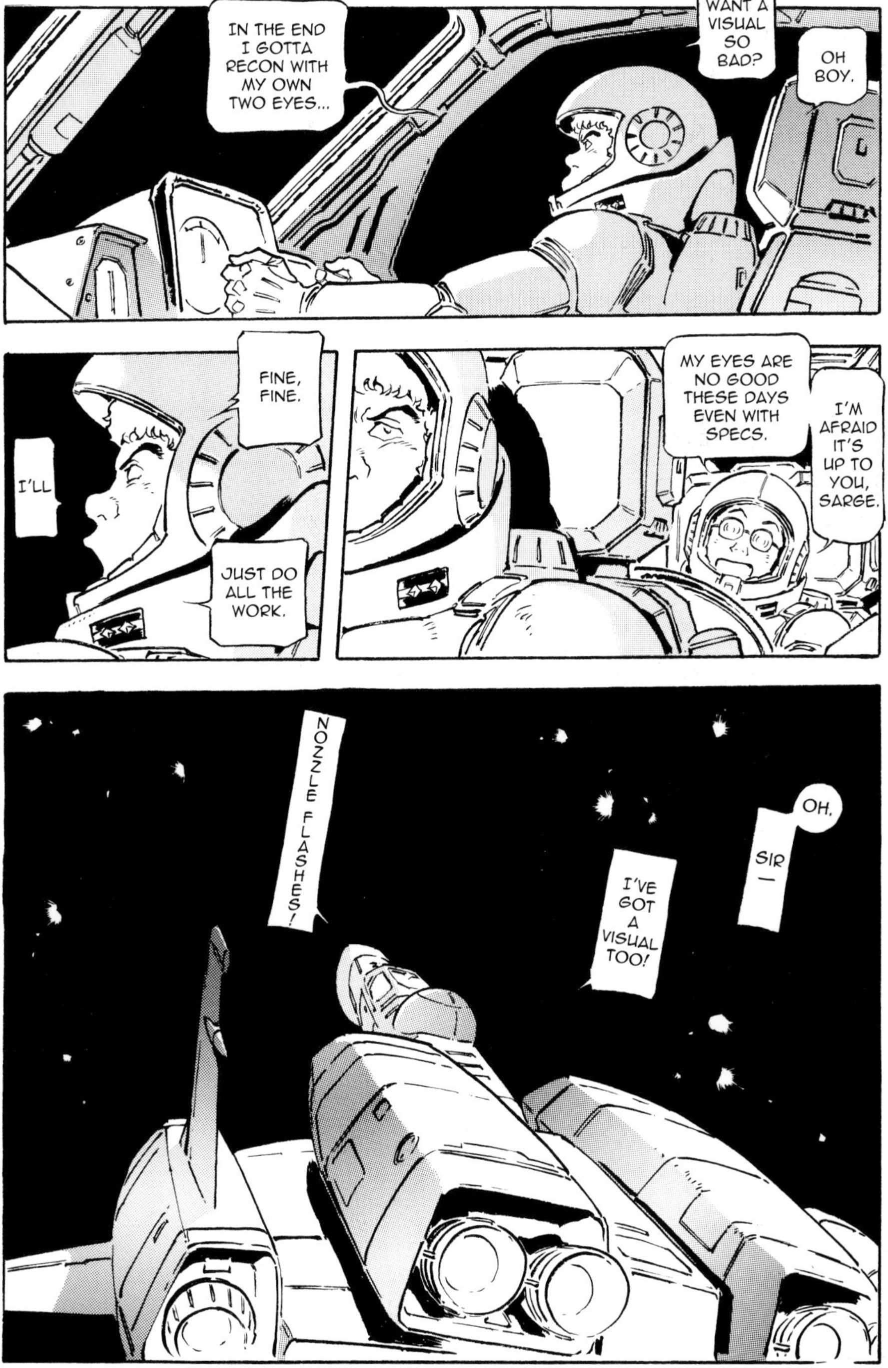
OH BOY.
THEY WANT A VISUAL SO BAD?
IN THE END I GOTTA RECON WITH MY OWN TWO EYES...
I'M AFRAID IT'S UP TO YOU, SARGE.
MY EYES ARE NO GOOD THESE DAYS EVEN WITH SPECS.
FINE, FINE.
I'LL
JUST DO ALL THE WORK.
OH,
SIR—
I'VE GOT A VISUAL TOO!
NOZZLE FLASHES!

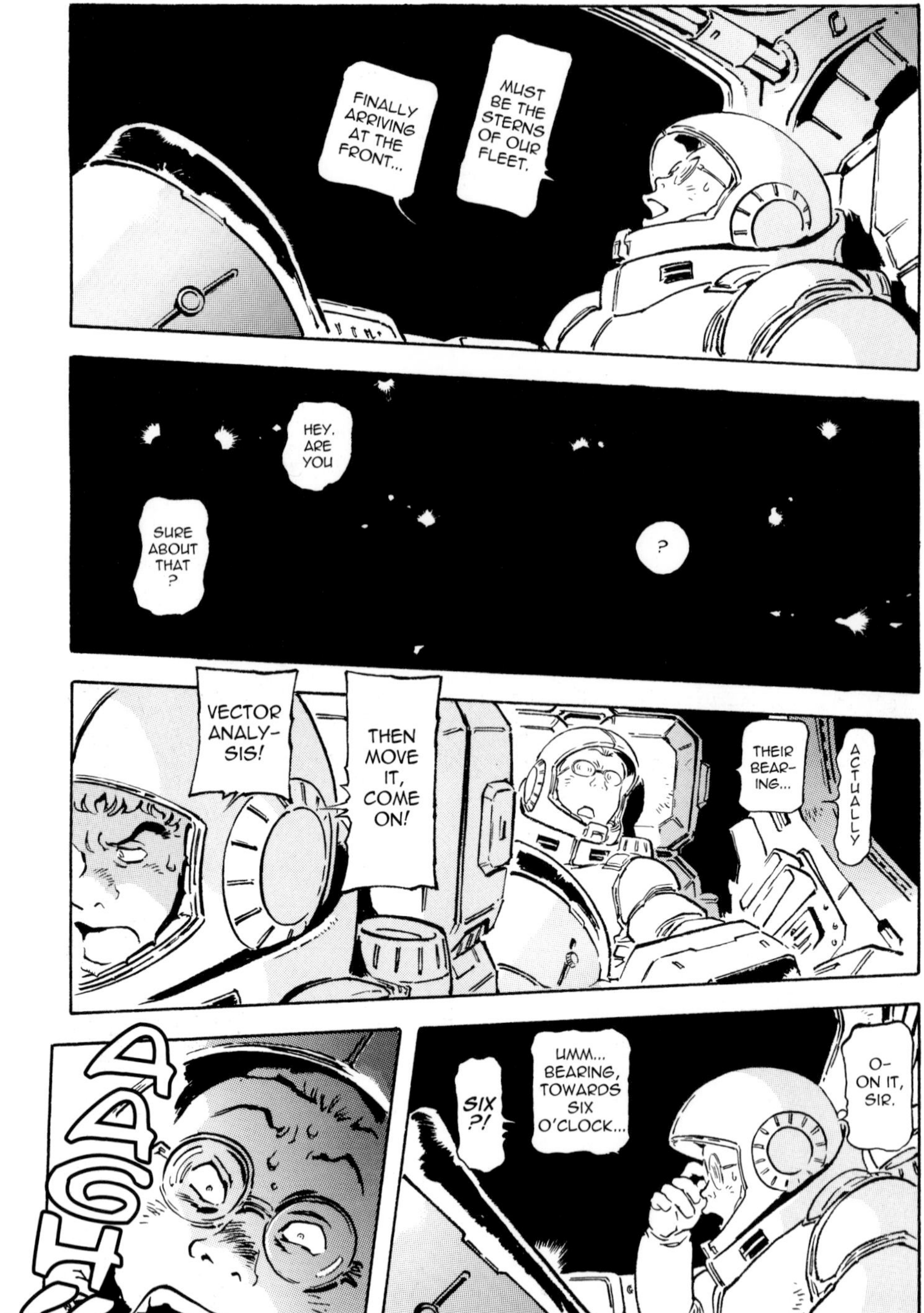
MUST BE THE STERNS OF OUR FLEET.
FINALLY ARRIVING AT THE FRONT...
?
HEY, ARE YOU
SURE ABOUT THAT?
ACTUALLY
THEIR BEARING...
THEN MOVE IT, COME ON!
VECTOR ANALYSIS!
O-ON IT, SIR.
UMM... BEARING, TOWARDS SIX O'CLOCK...
SIX?!
AAGH!!

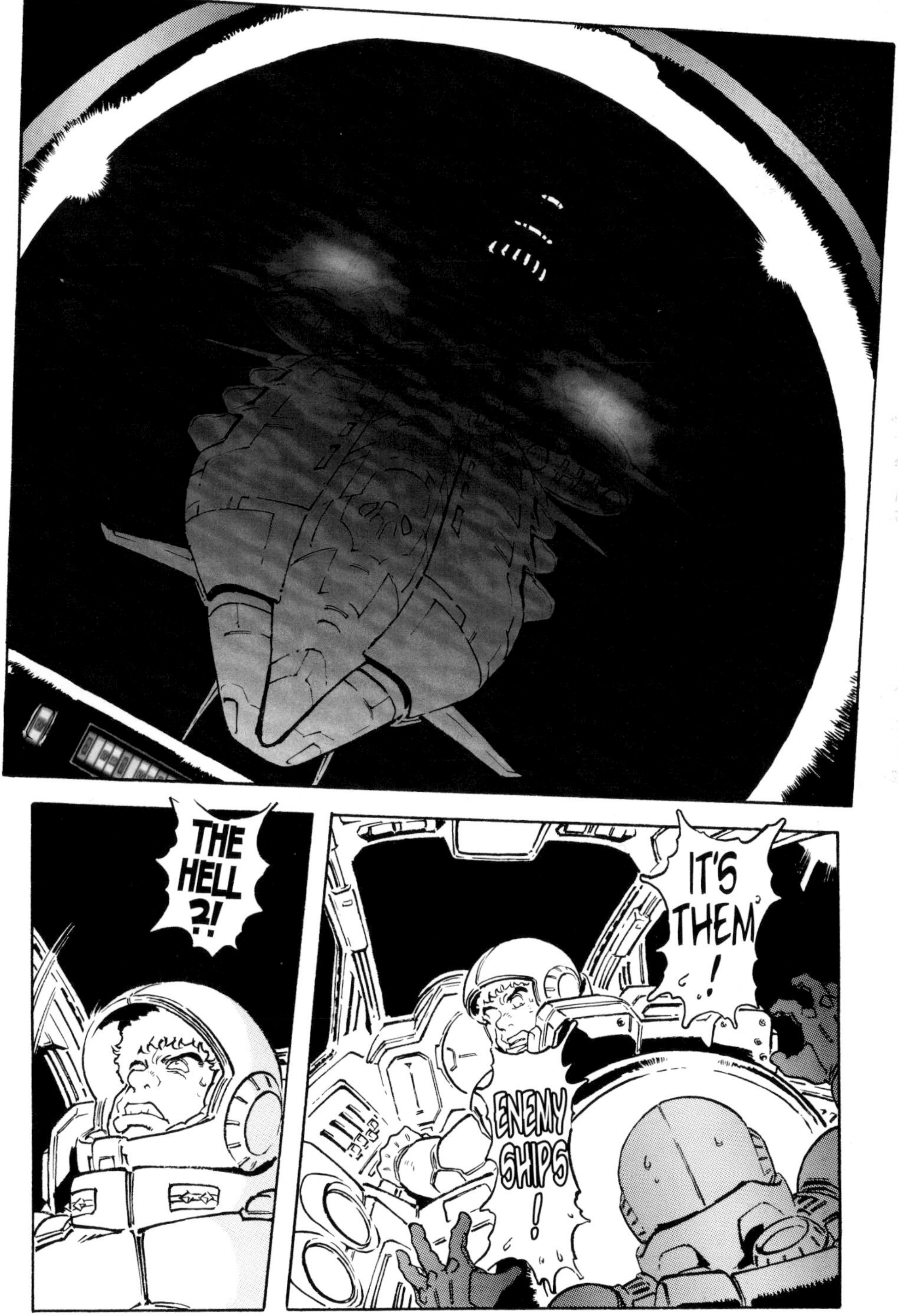
IT'S THEM...!
ENEMY SHIPS!
THE HELL?!

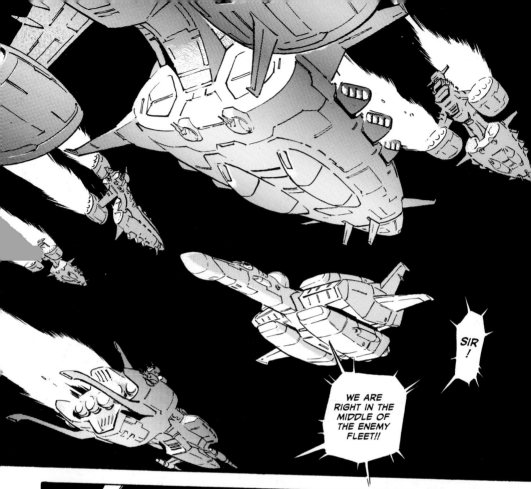

SIR!

WE ARE RIGHT IN THE MIDDLE OF THE ENEMY FLEET!!

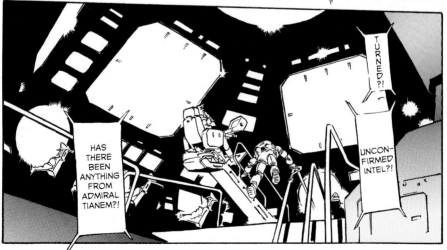

TURNED?!

UNCONFIRMED INTEL?!

HAS THERE BEEN ANYTHING FROM ADMIRAL TIANEM?!

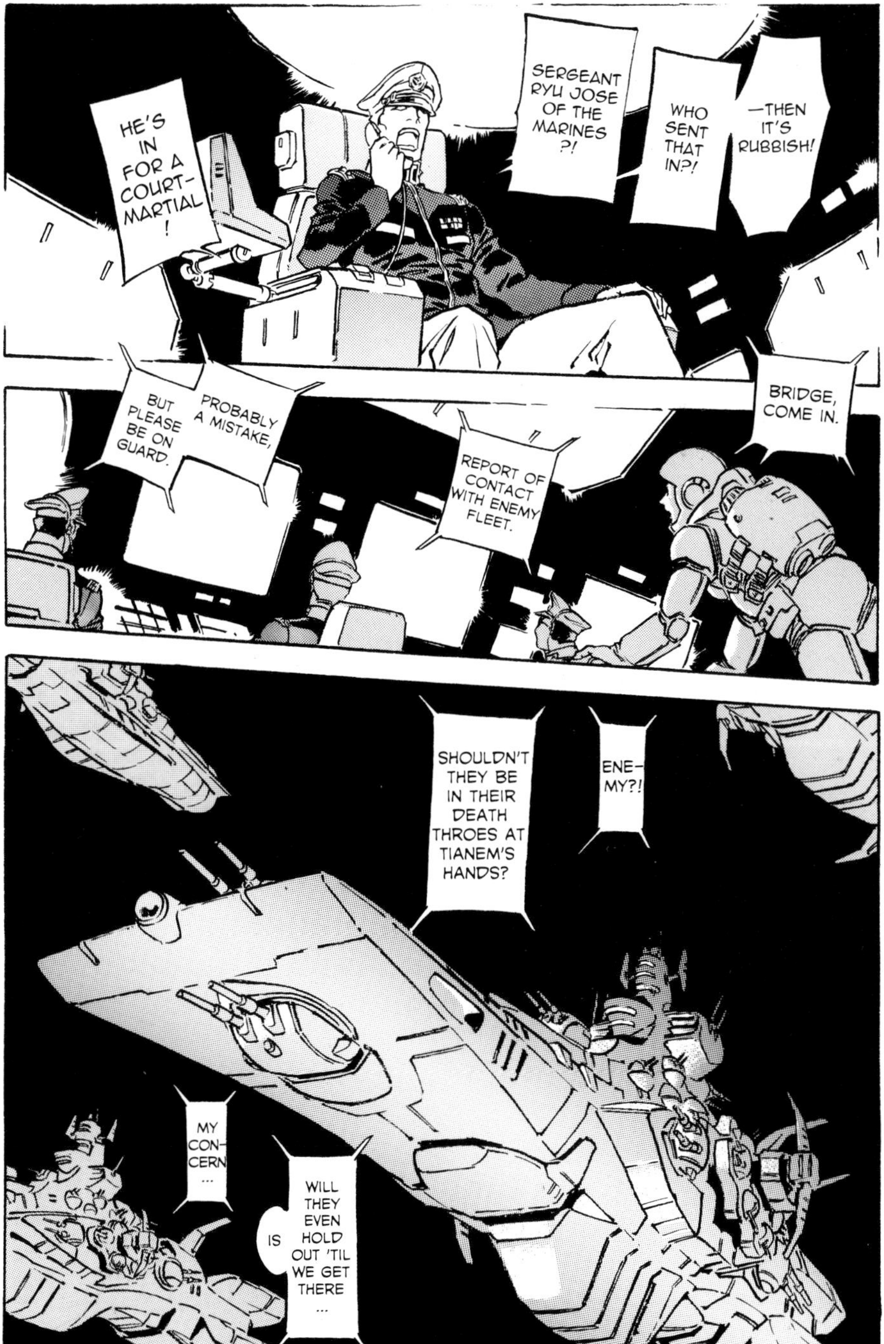
—THEN IT'S RUBBISH!
WHO SENT THAT IN?!
SERGEANT RYU JOSE OF THE MARINES?!
HE'S IN FOR A COURT-MARTIAL!
BRIDGE, COME IN.
REPORT OF CONTACT WITH ENEMY FLEET.
PROBABLY A MISTAKE,
BUT PLEASE BE ON GUARD.
ENE-MY?!
SHOULDN'T THEY BE IN THEIR DEATH THROES AT TIANEM'S HANDS?
MY CON-CERN...
IS
WILL THEY EVEN HOLD OUT 'TIL WE GET THERE...

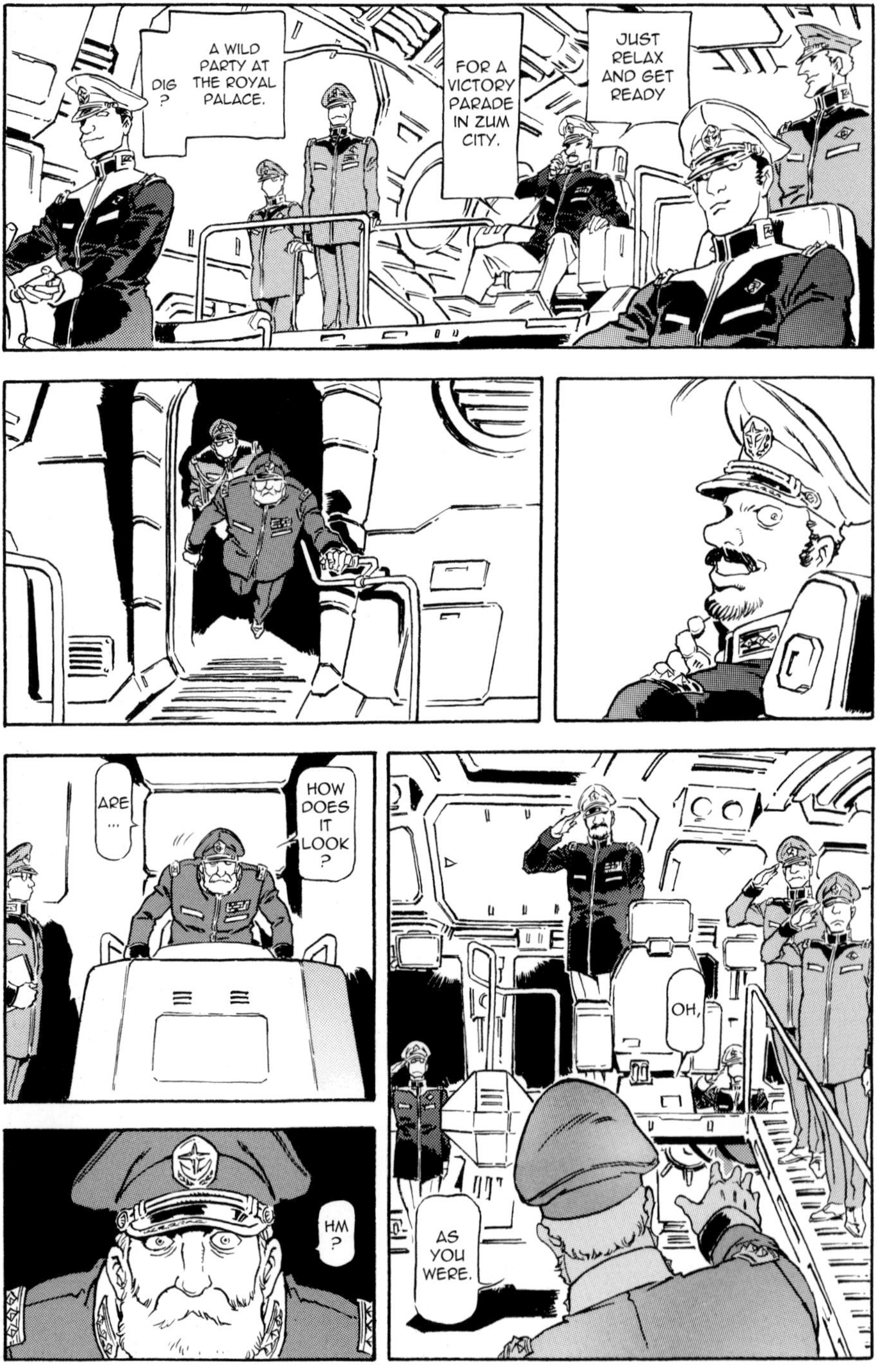
JUST RELAX AND GET READY
FOR A VICTORY PARADE IN ZUM CITY.
A WILD PARTY AT THE ROYAL PALACE.
DIG ?
OH,
AS YOU WERE.
HOW DOES IT LOOK ?
ARE ...
HM ?

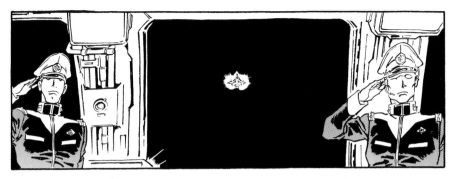

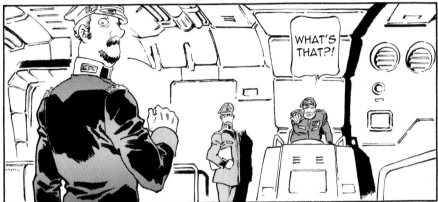

WHAT'S
THAT?!

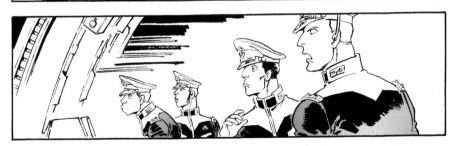

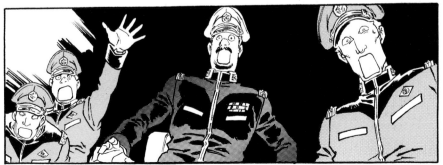

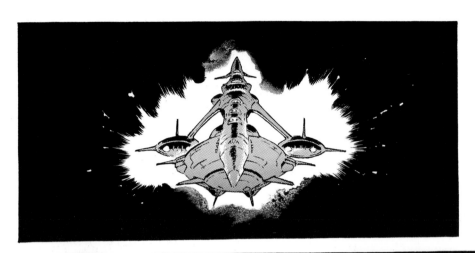

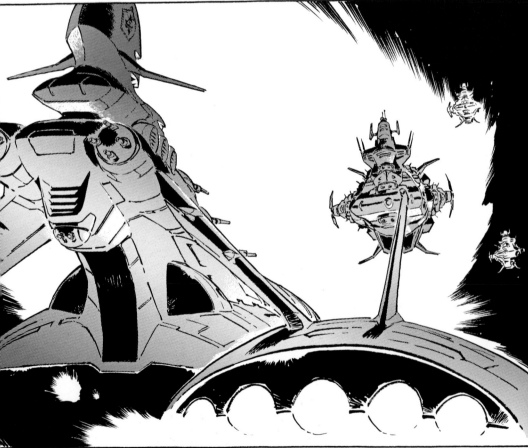

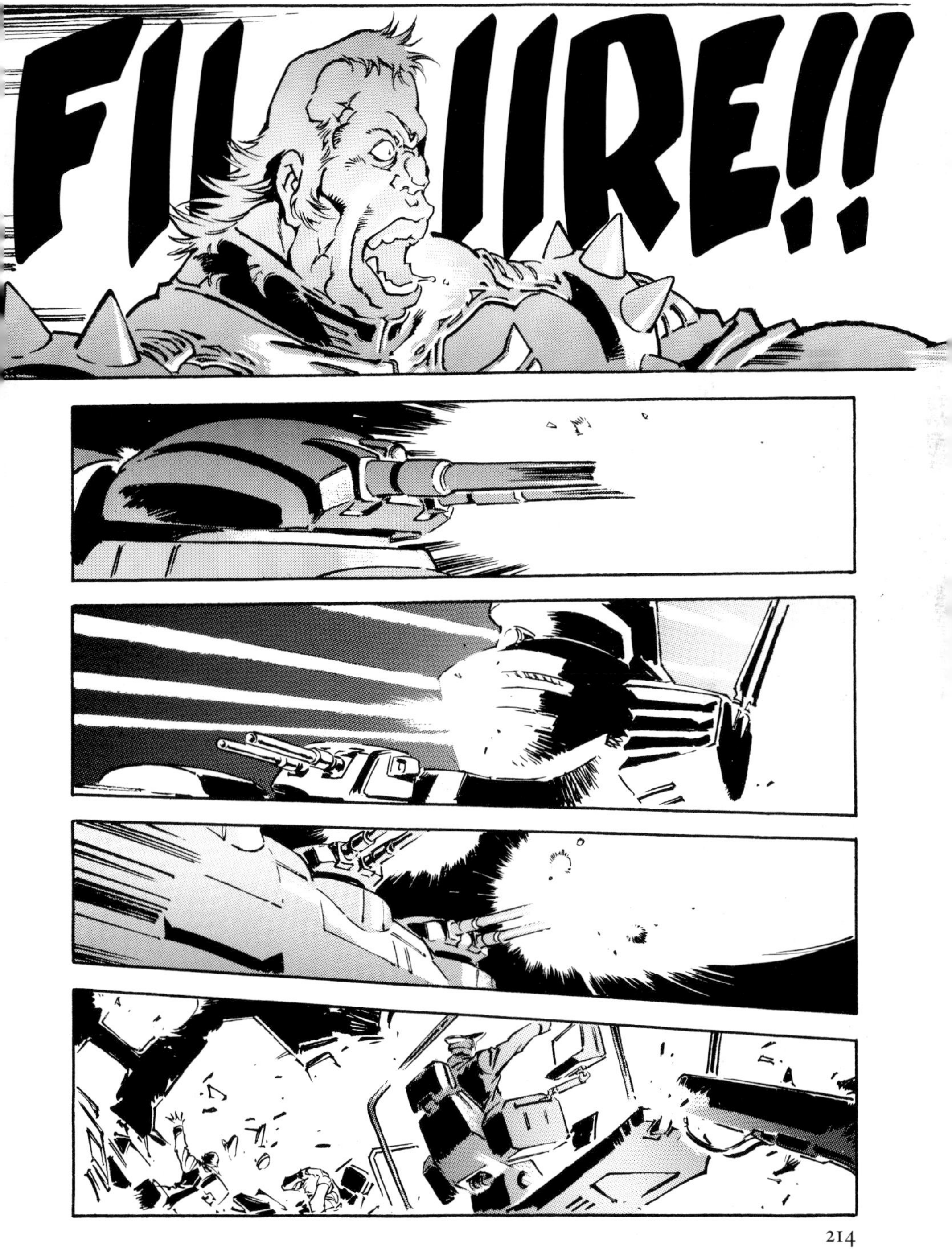
FI IIRE!!

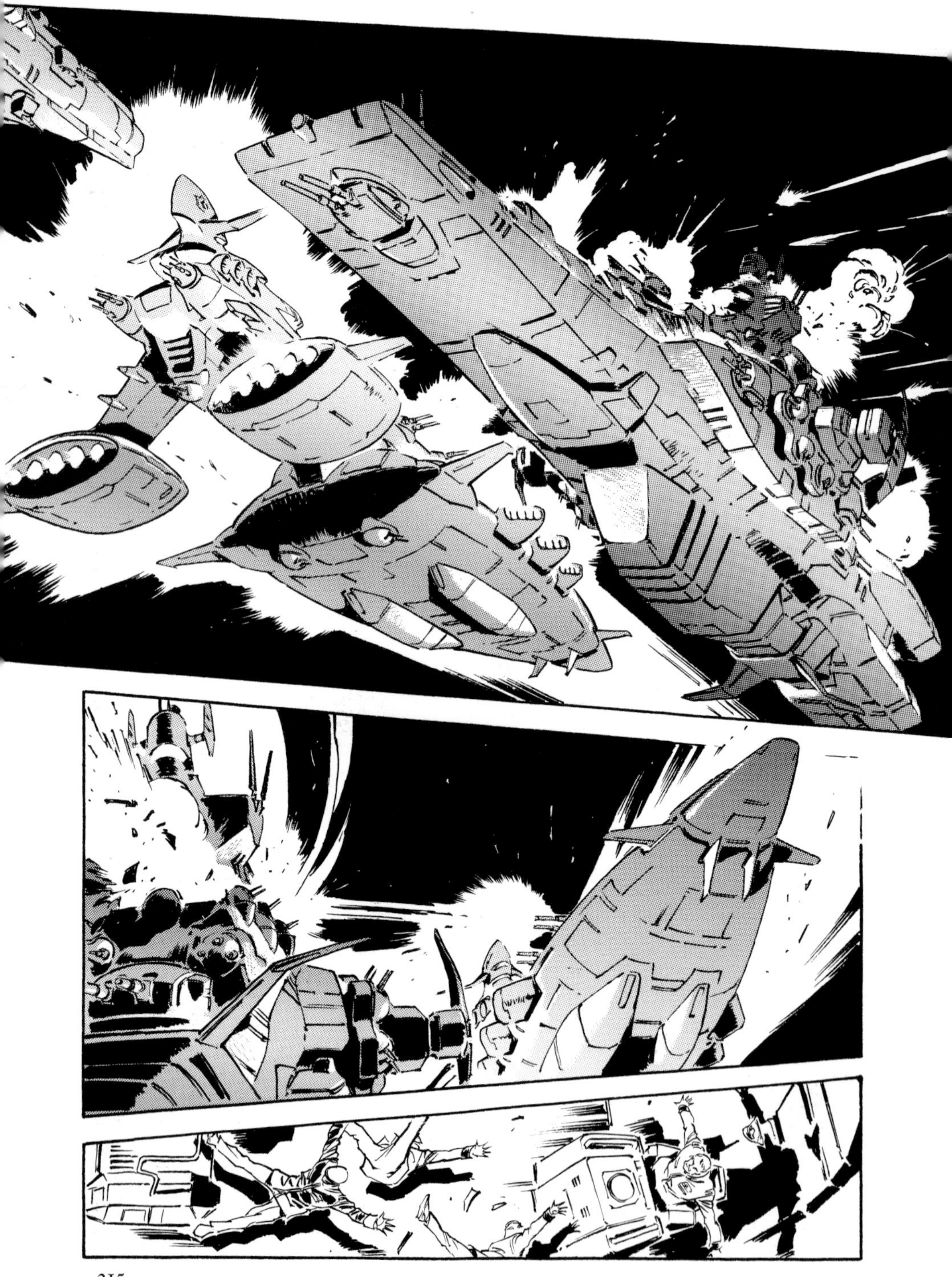

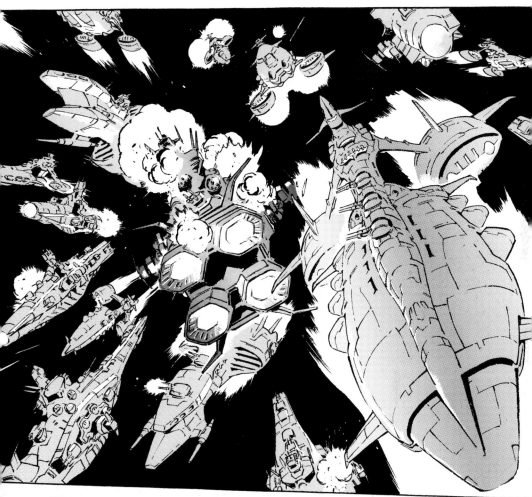

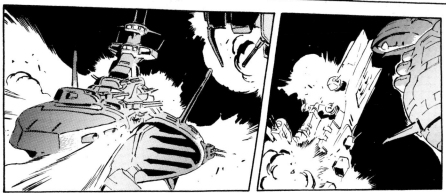

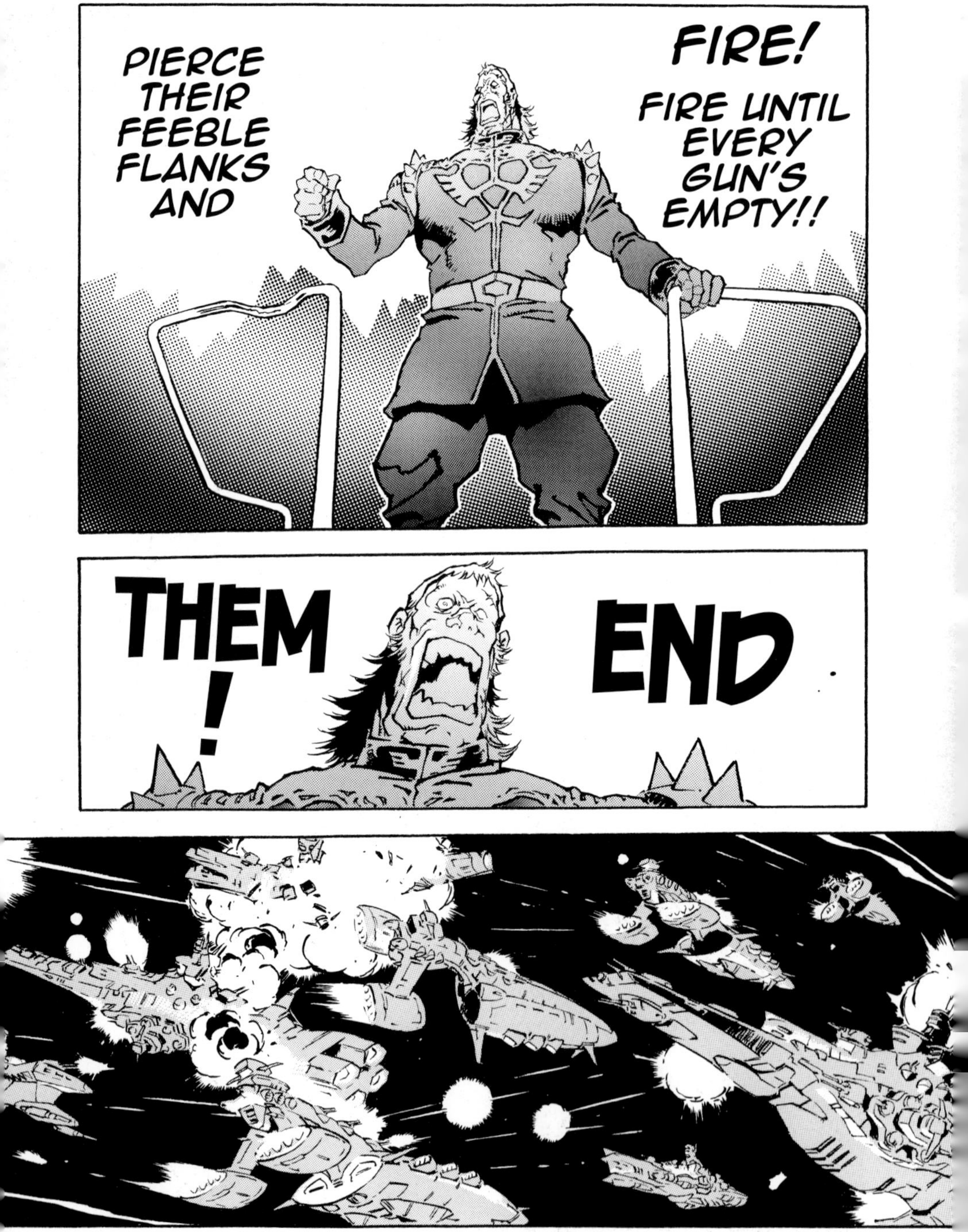
FIRE!
FIRE UNTIL EVERY GUN'S EMPTY!!
PIERCE THEIR FEEBLE FLANKS AND
END
THEM!

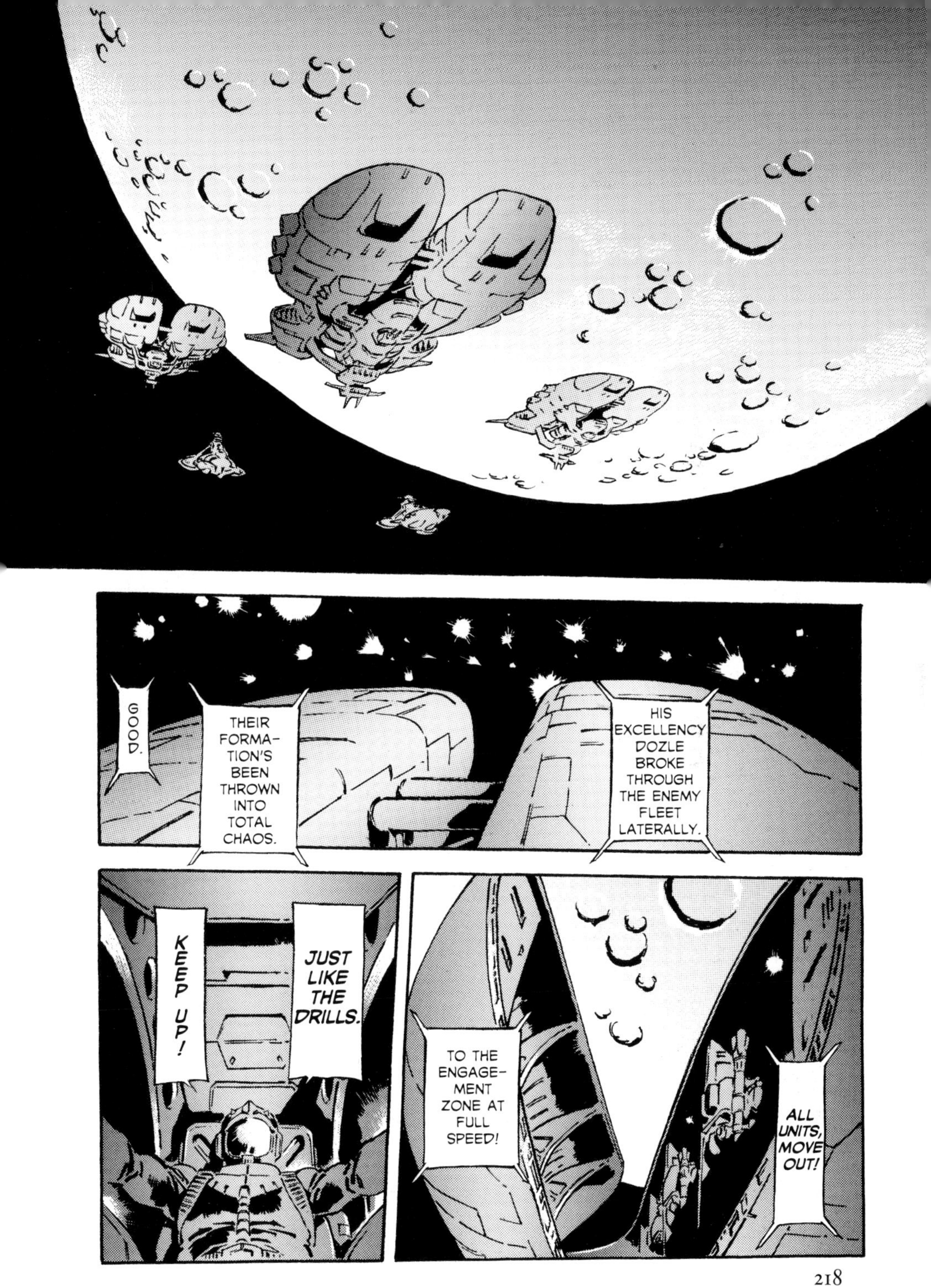
HIS EXCELLENCY DOZLE BROKE THROUGH THE ENEMY FLEET LATERALLY.
THEIR FORMATION'S BEEN THROWN INTO TOTAL CHAOS.
GOOD.
ALL UNITS, MOVE OUT!
TO THE ENGAGEMENT ZONE AT FULL SPEED!
JUST LIKE THE DRILLS.
KEEP UP!

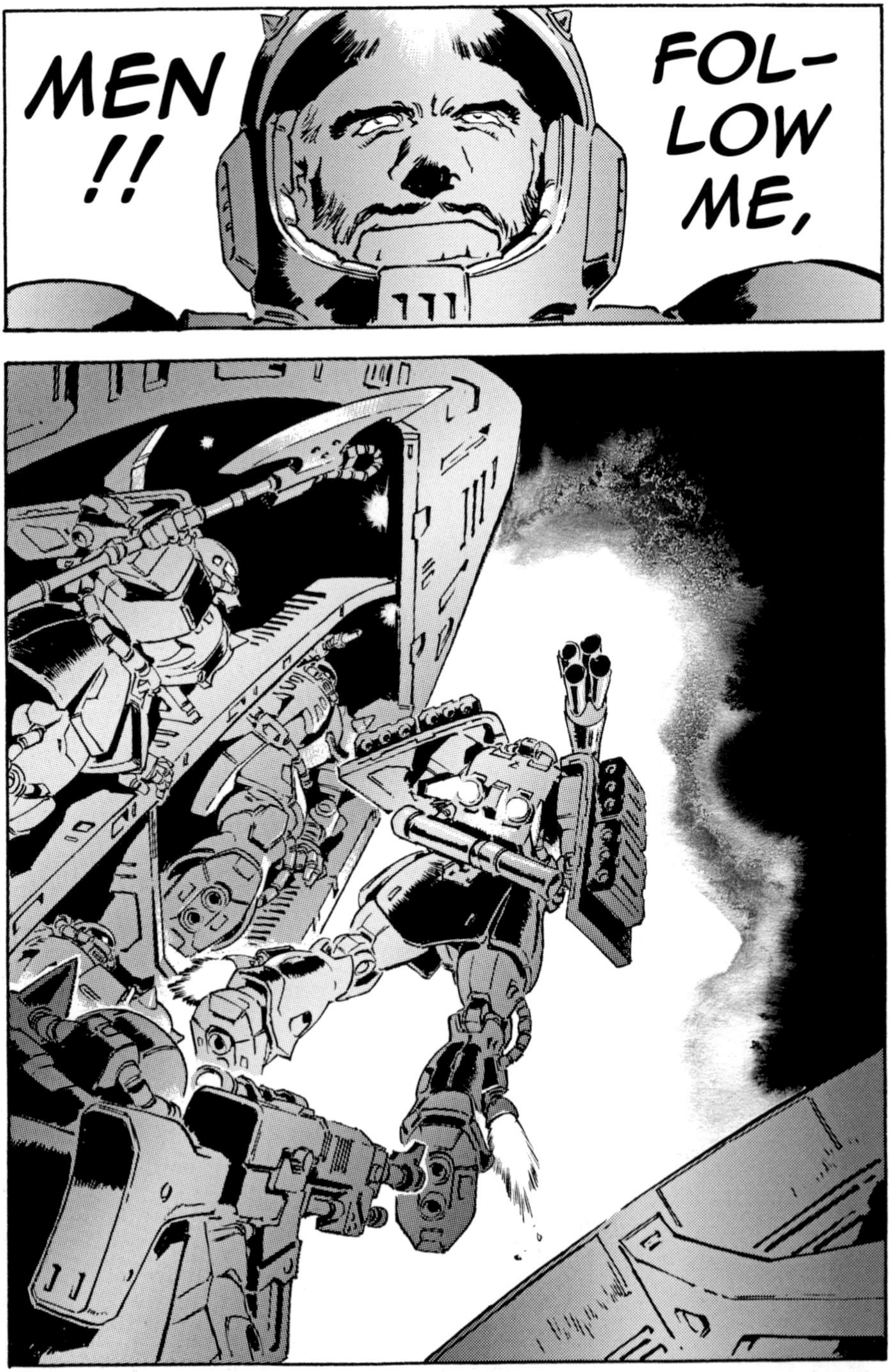
FOL-
LOW
ME,
MEN
!!

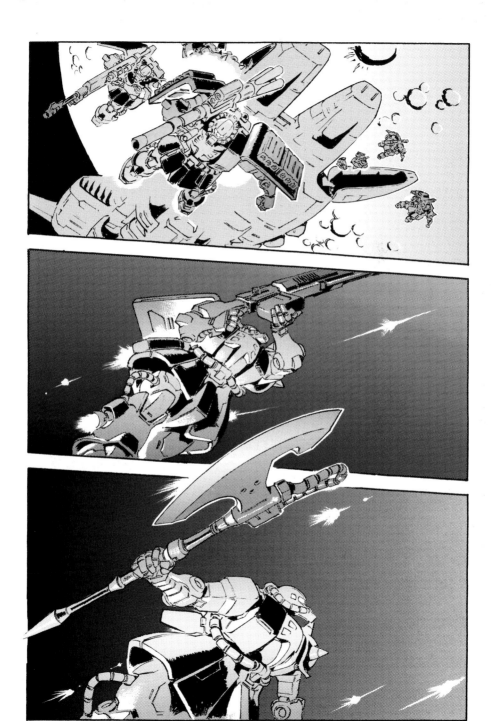

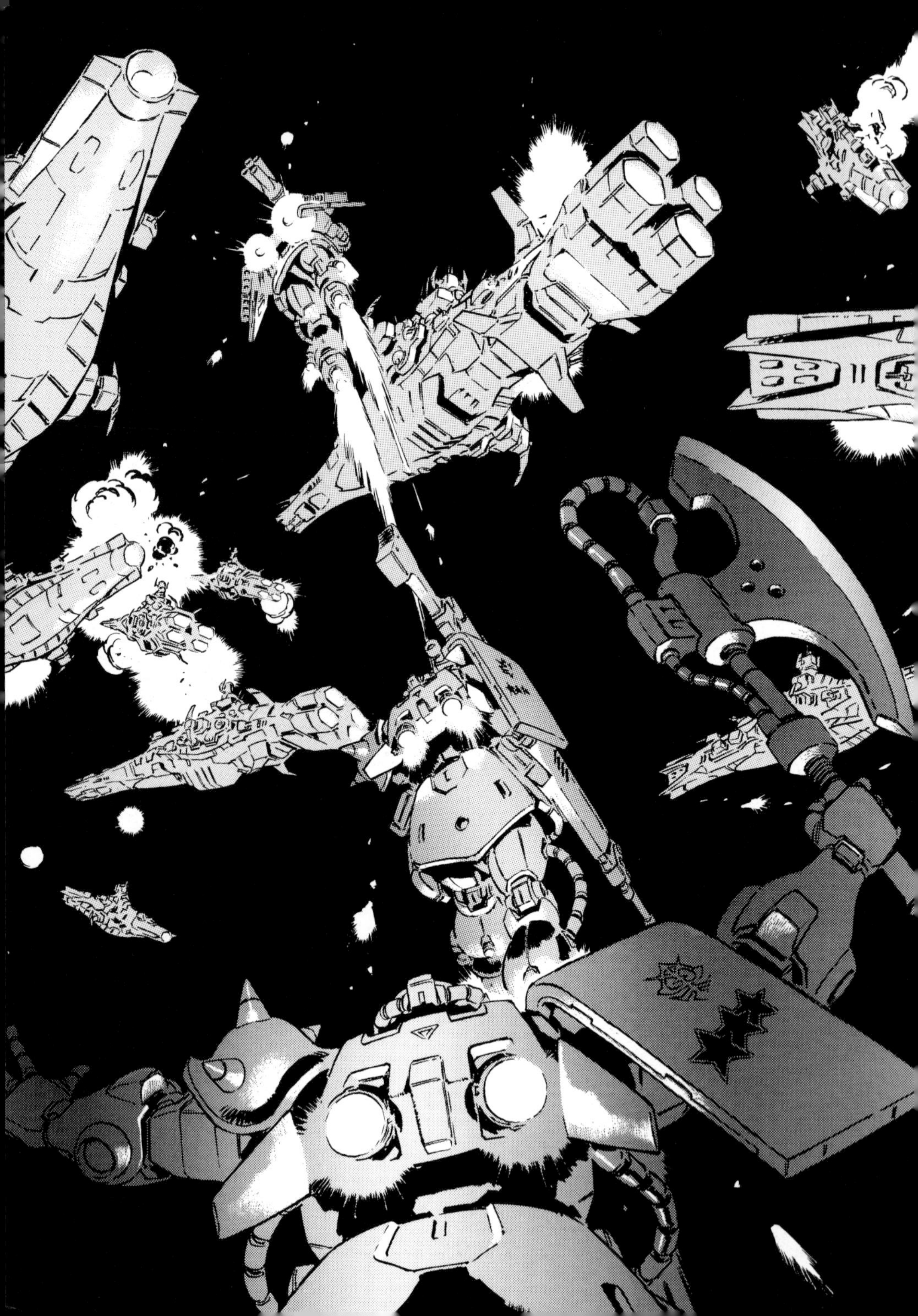

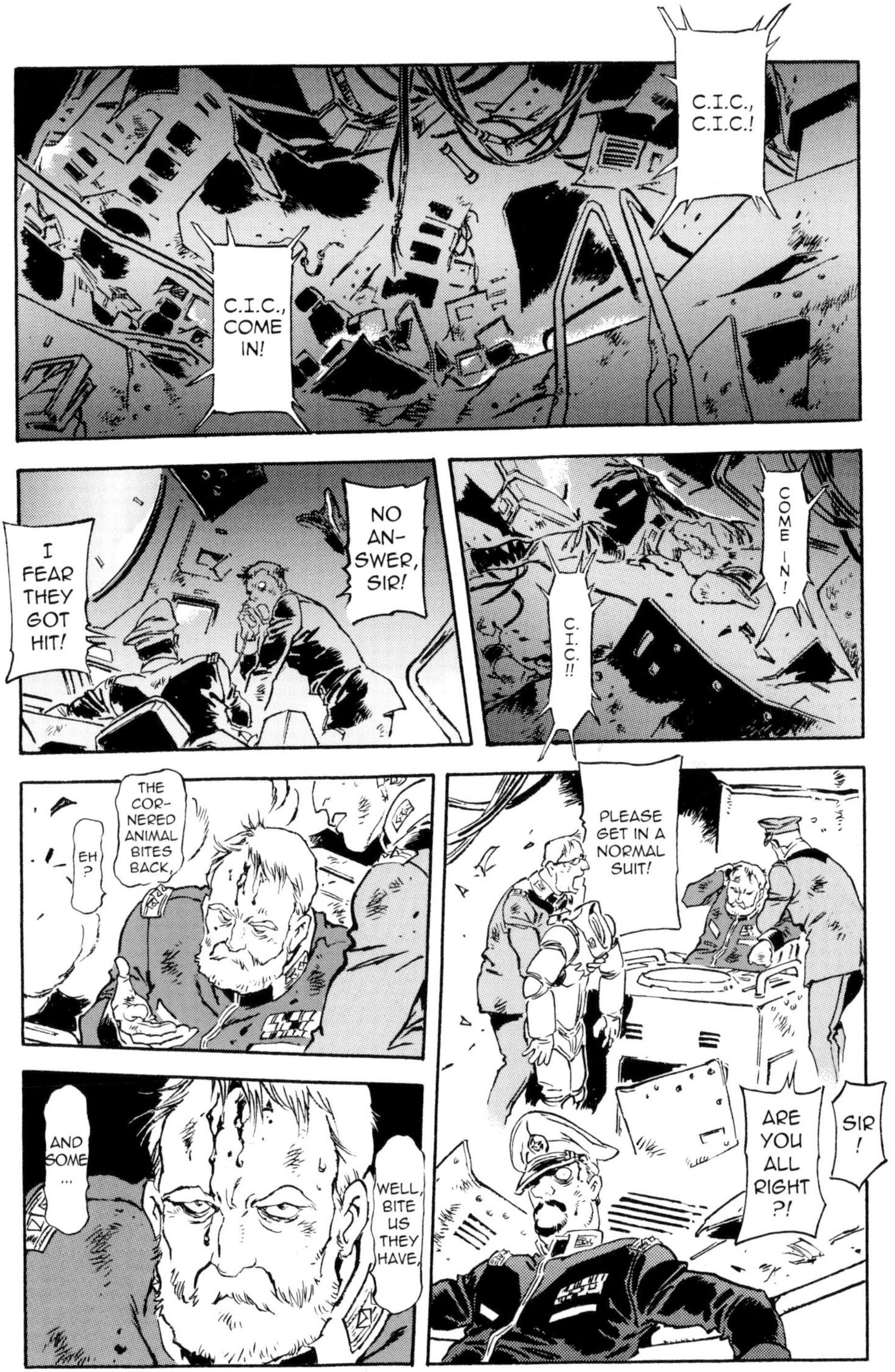
C.I.C., C.I.C.!
C.I.C., COME IN!
COME IN!
C.I.C.!!
NO ANSWER, SIR!
I FEAR THEY GOT HIT!
PLEASE GET IN A NORMAL SUIT!
SIR!
ARE YOU ALL RIGHT?!
THE CORNERED ANIMAL BITES BACK,
EH?
WELL, BITE US THEY HAVE,
AND SOME...

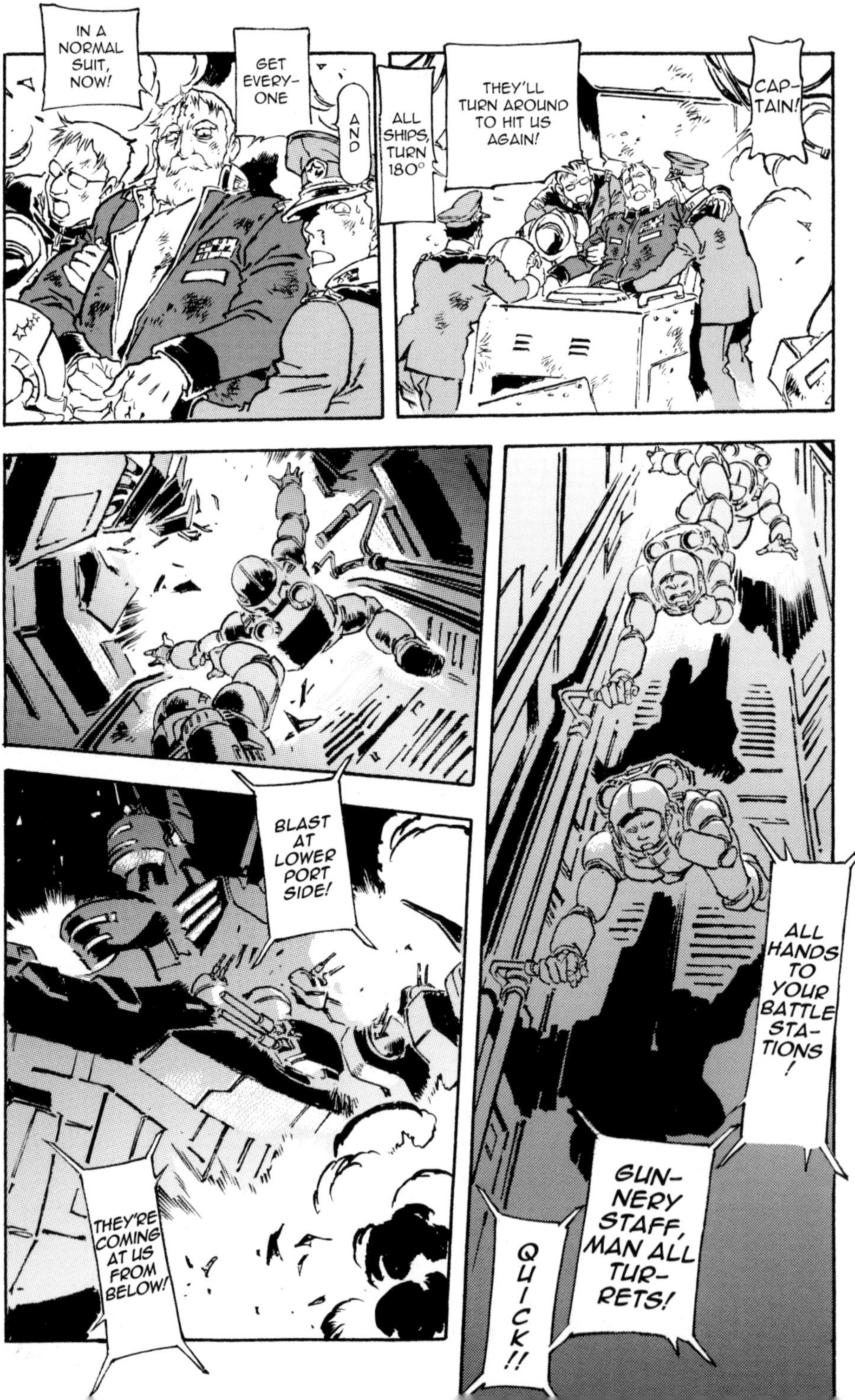
CAP-TAIN!
THEY'LL TURN AROUND TO HIT US AGAIN!
ALL SHIPS, TURN 180°
AND
GET EVERY-ONE
IN A NORMAL SUIT, NOW!
ALL HANDS TO YOUR BATTLE STA-TIONS!
GUN-NERY STAFF, MAN ALL TUR-RETS!
QUICK!!
BLAST AT LOWER PORT SIDE!
THEY'RE COMING AT US FROM BELOW!

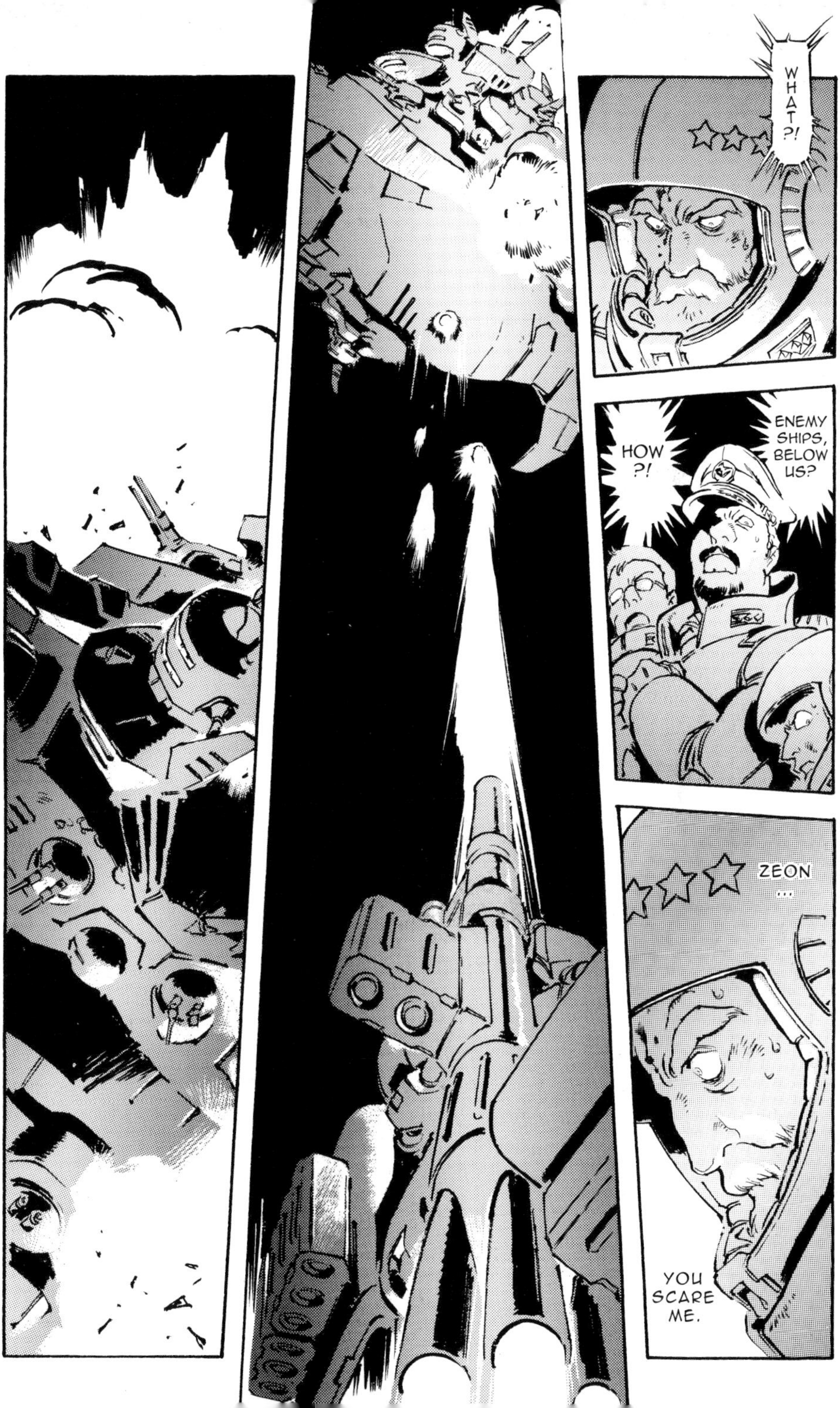
WHAT?!
ENEMY SHIPS, BELOW US?
HOW?!
ZEON...
YOU SCARE ME.

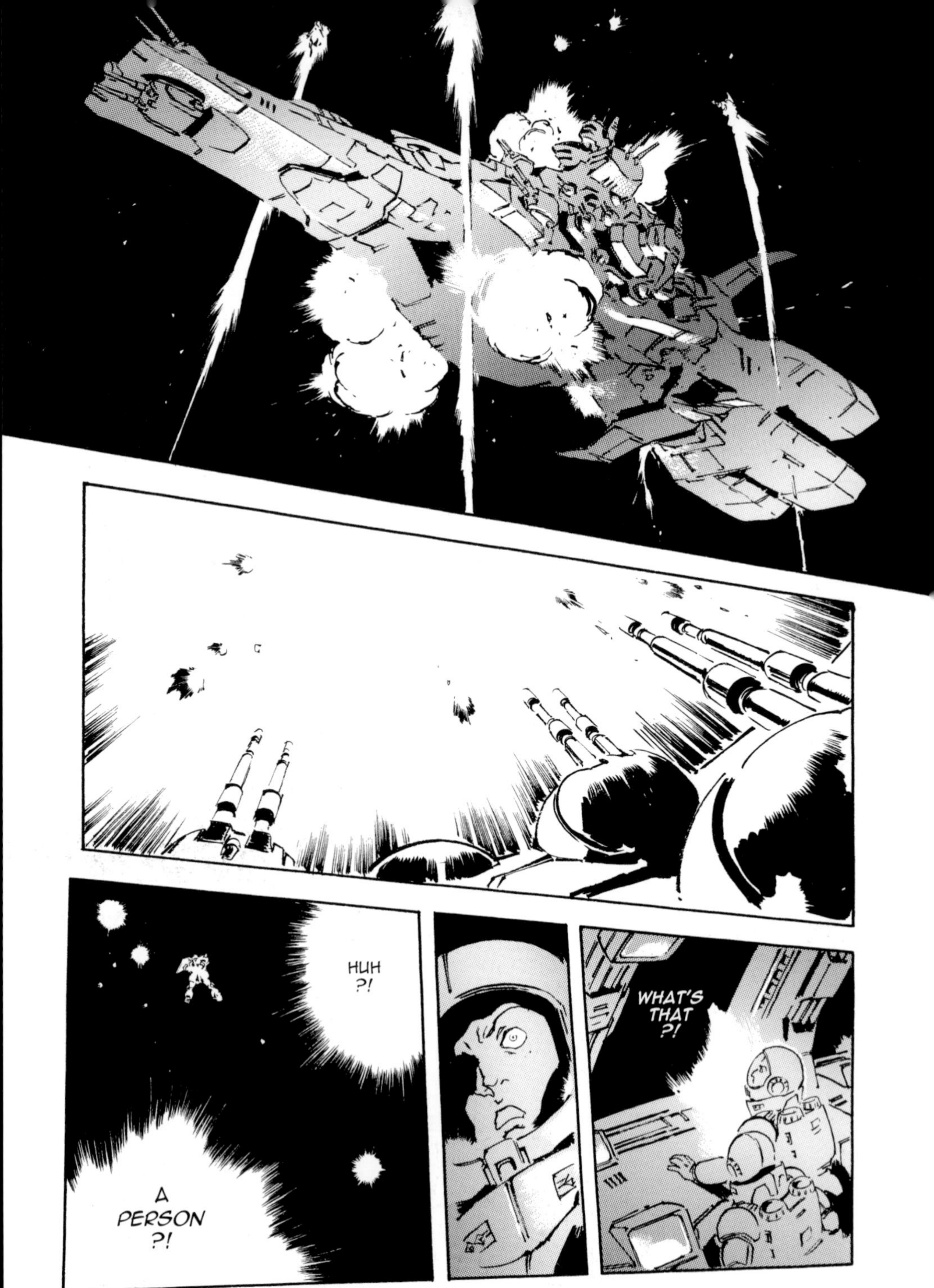
WHAT'S THAT ?!
HUH ?!
A PERSON ?!

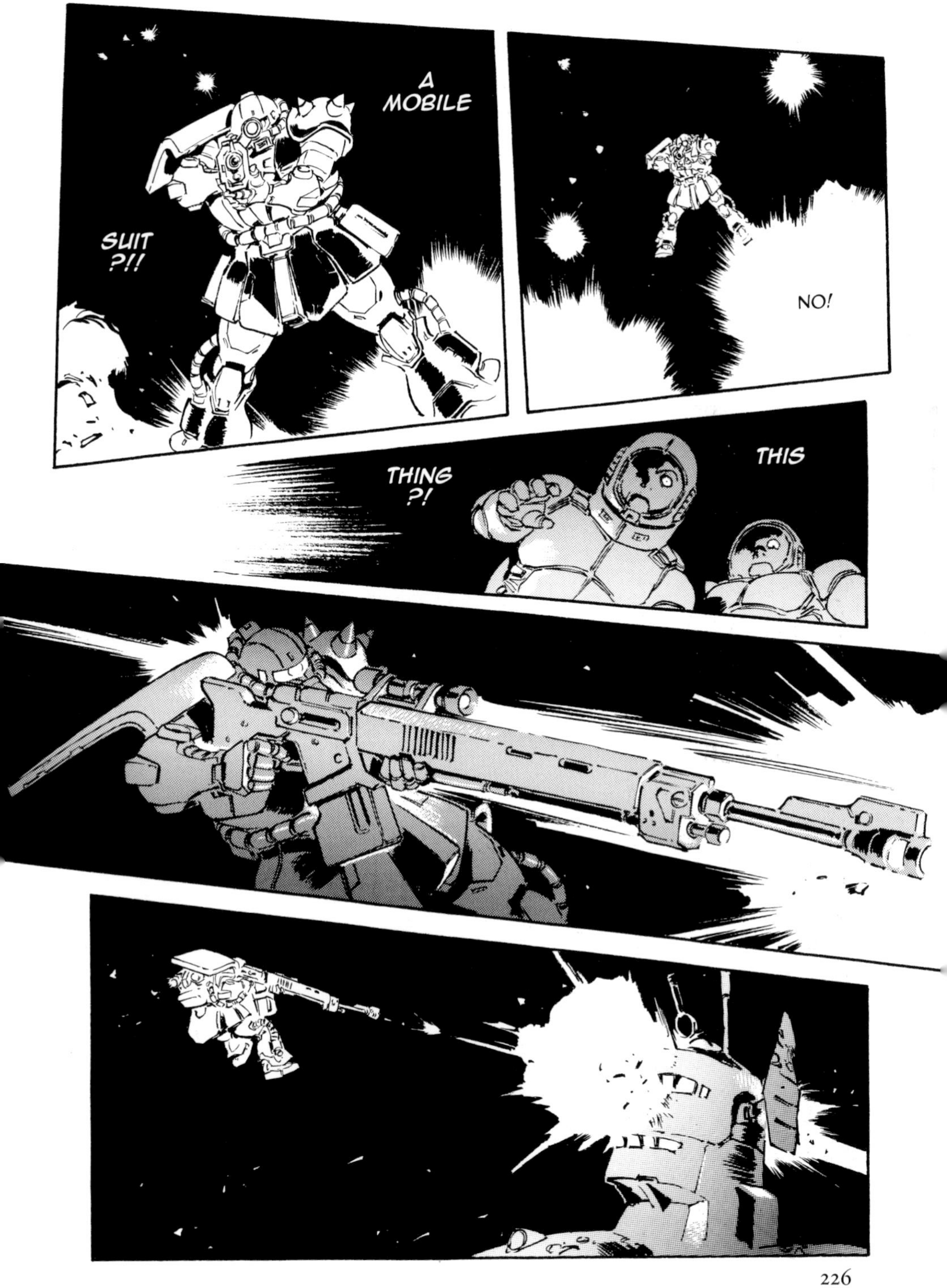
NO!
A MOBILE
SUIT ?!!
THIS
THING ?!

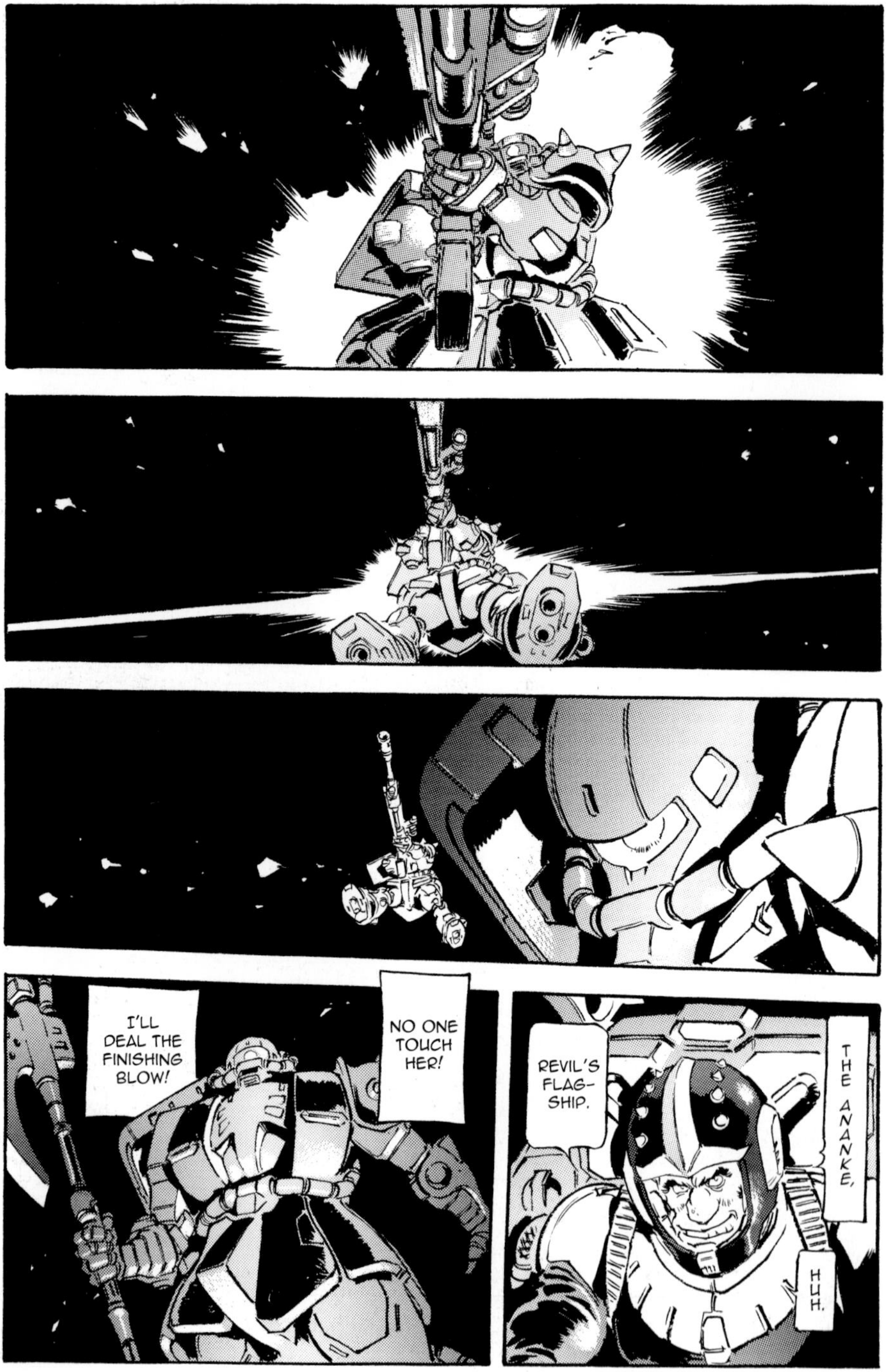
THE ANANKE,
REVIL'S FLAG-SHIP.
HUH.
NO ONE TOUCH HER!
I'LL DEAL THE FINISHING BLOW!

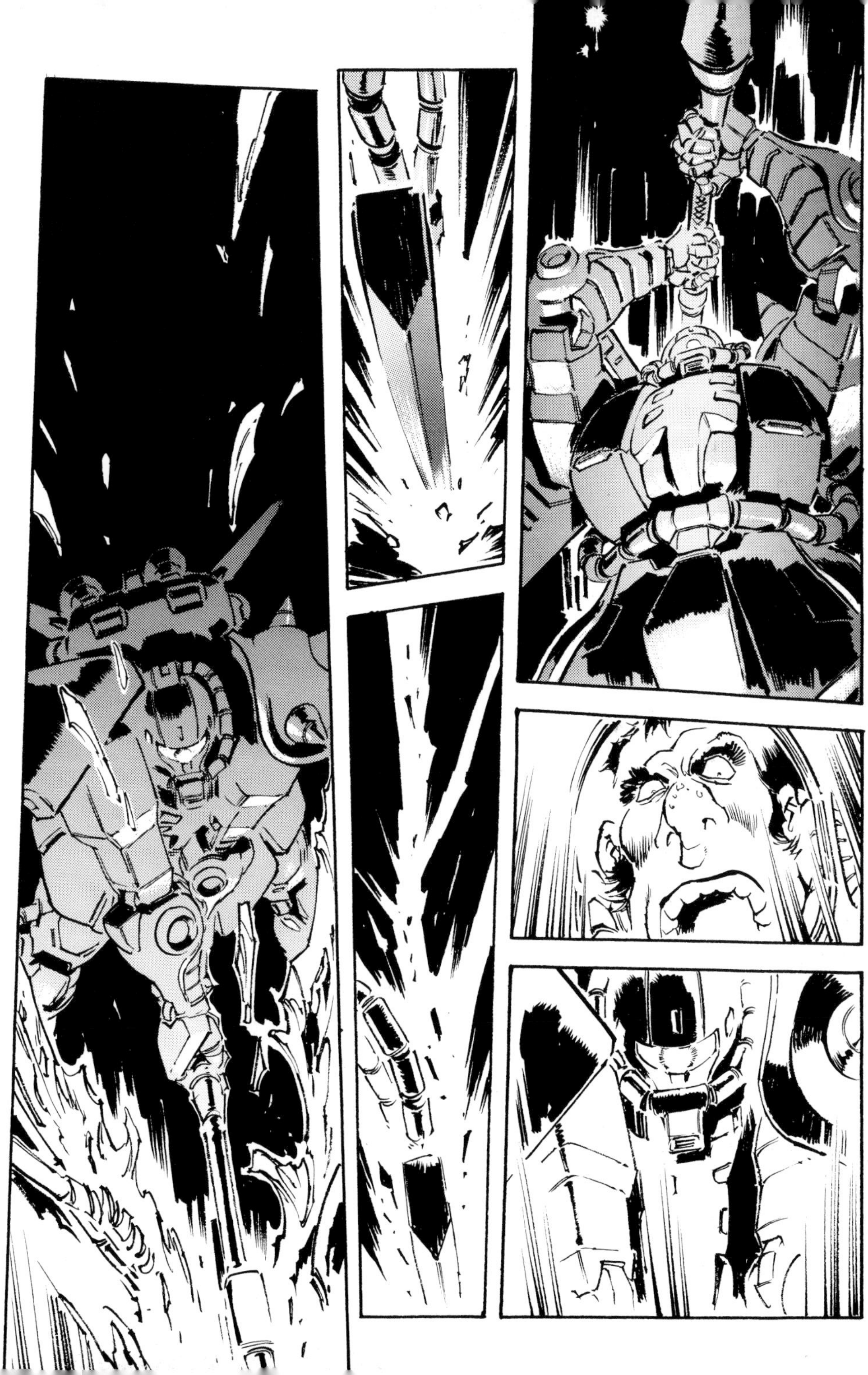

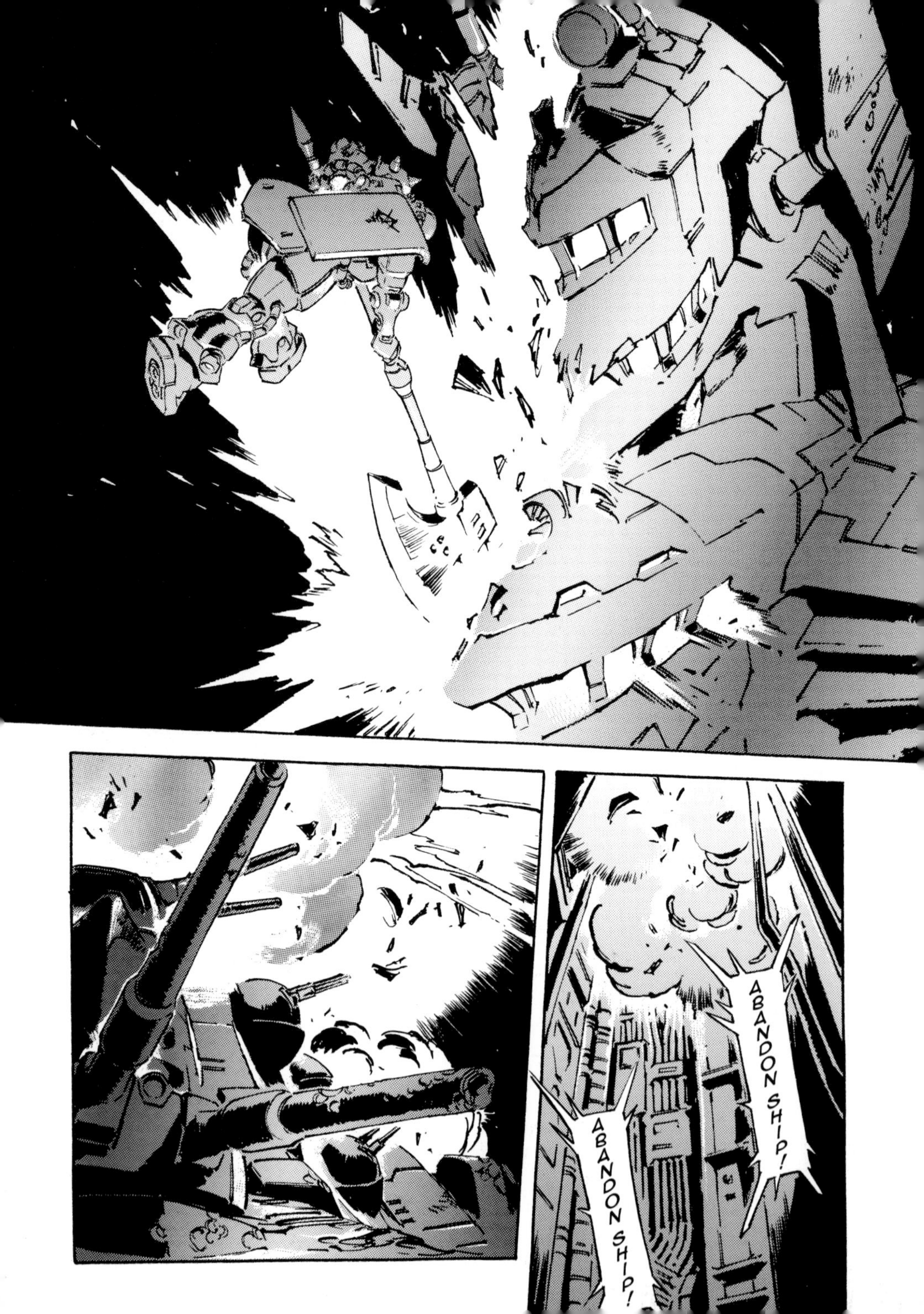
ABANDON SHIP!
ABANDON SHIP!

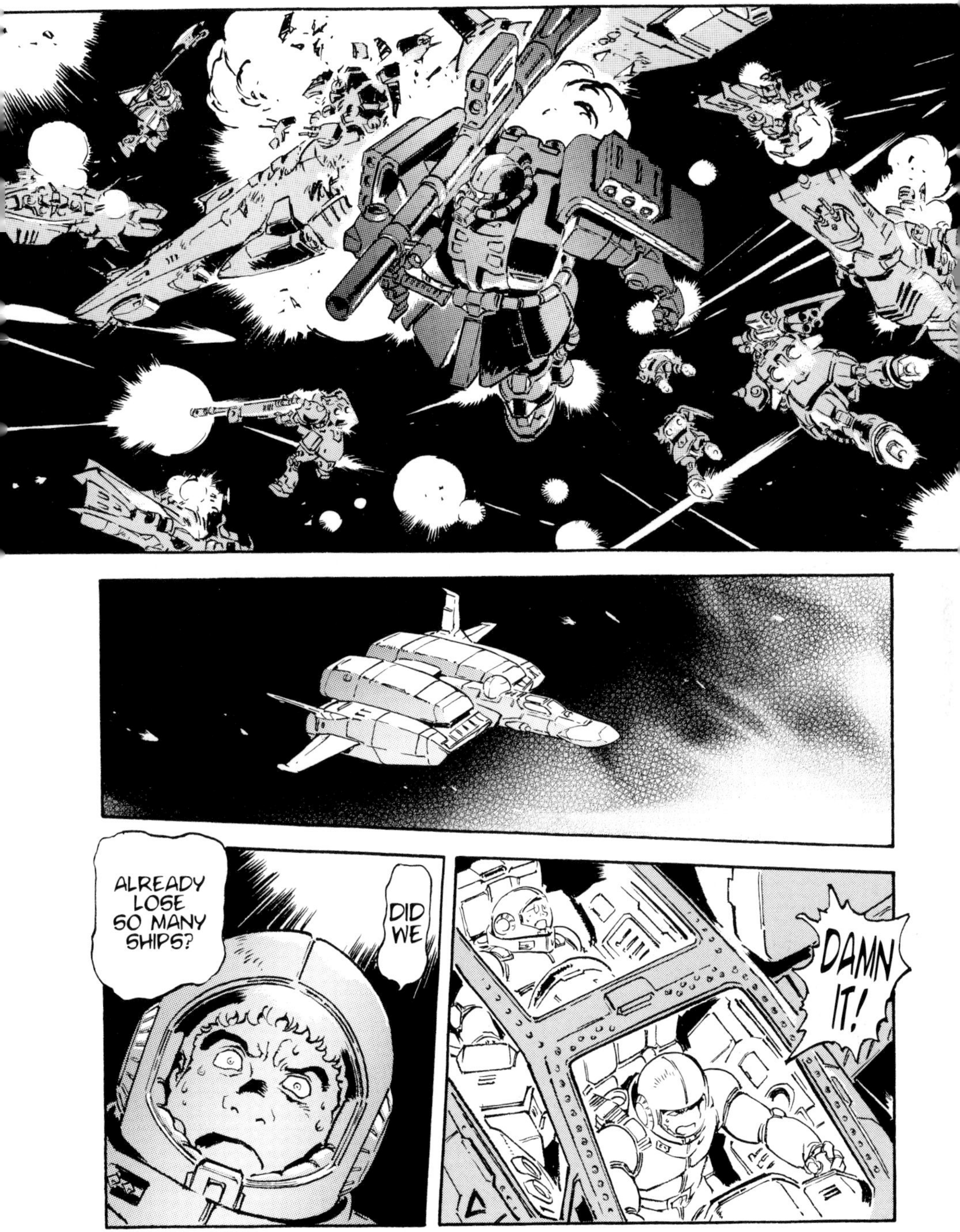
DAMN IT!
DID WE
ALREADY LOSE SO MANY SHIPS?

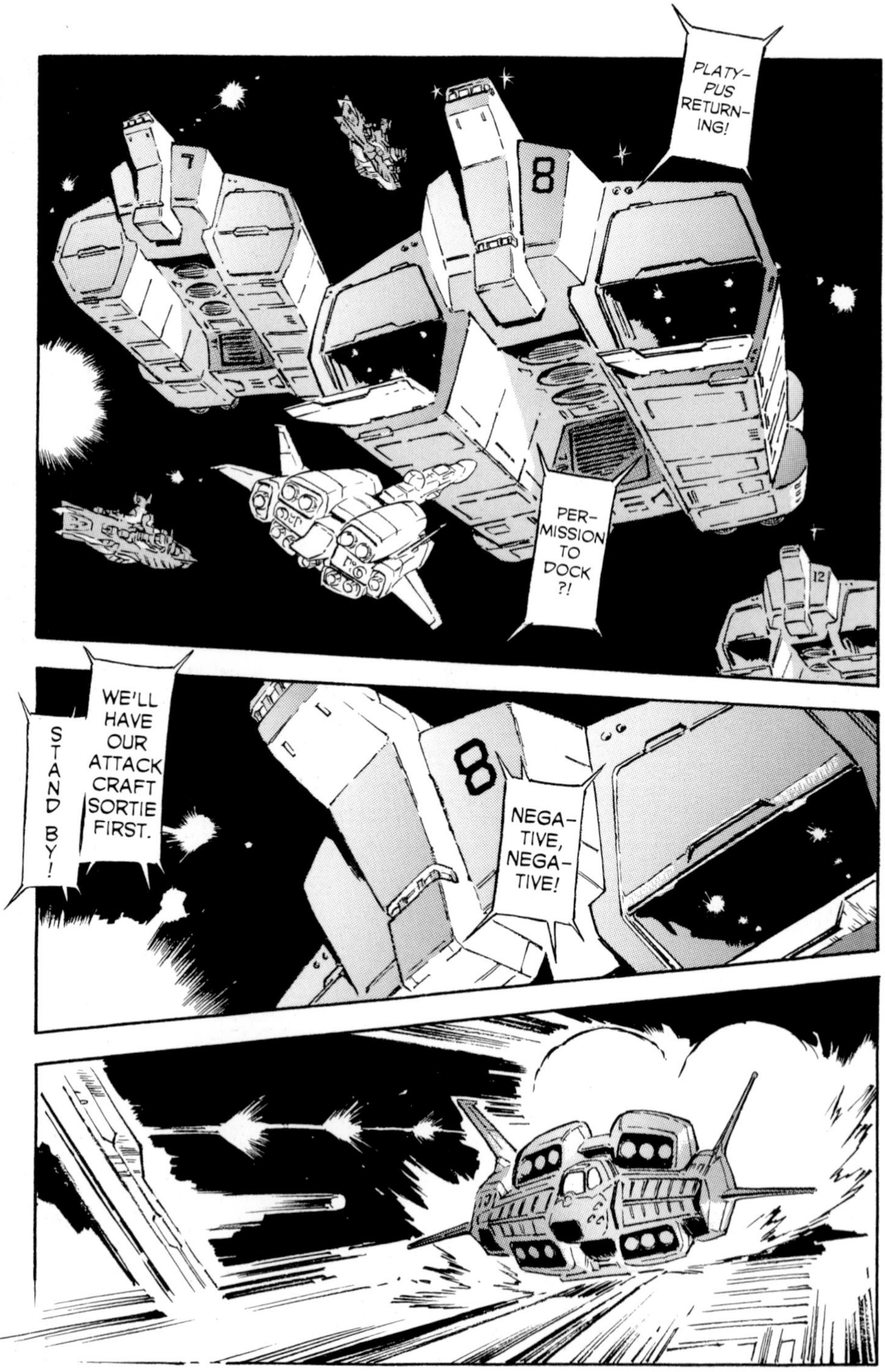
PLATY-PUS RETURN-ING!
PER-MISSION TO DOCK ?!
NEGA-TIVE, NEGA-TIVE!
WE'LL HAVE OUR ATTACK CRAFT SORTIE FIRST.
STAND BY!

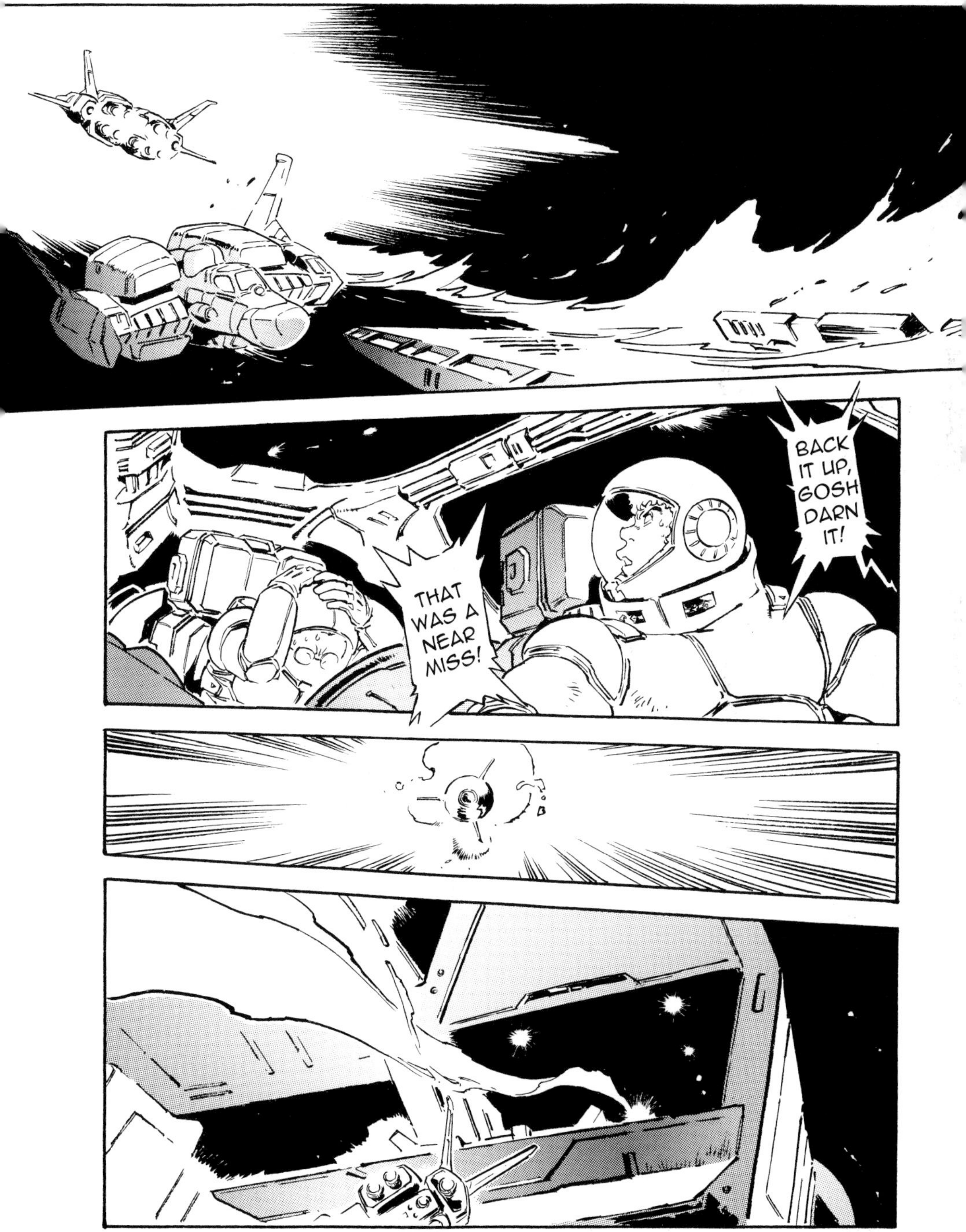
BACK IT UP, GOSH DARN IT!
THAT WAS A NEAR MISS!

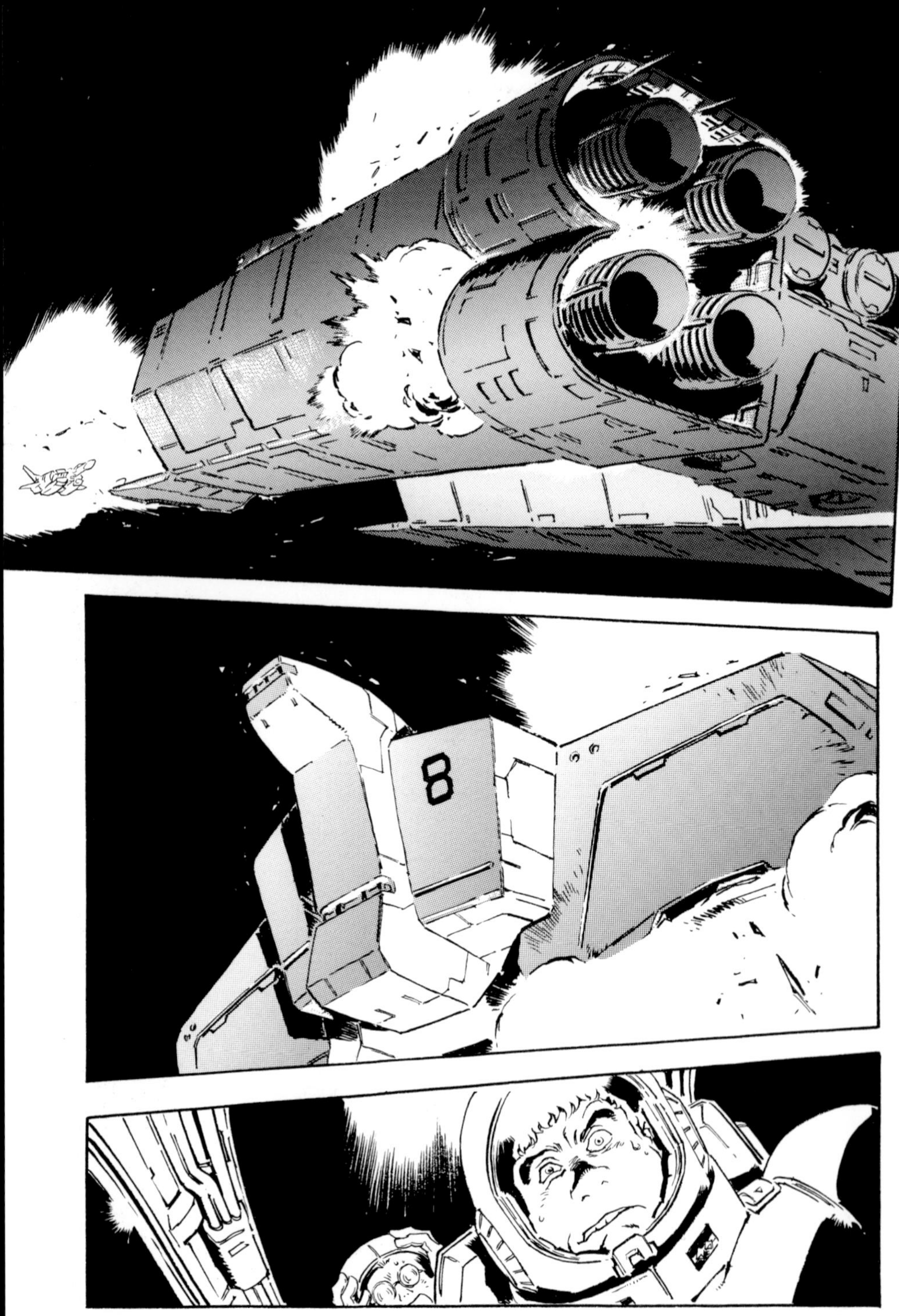
8

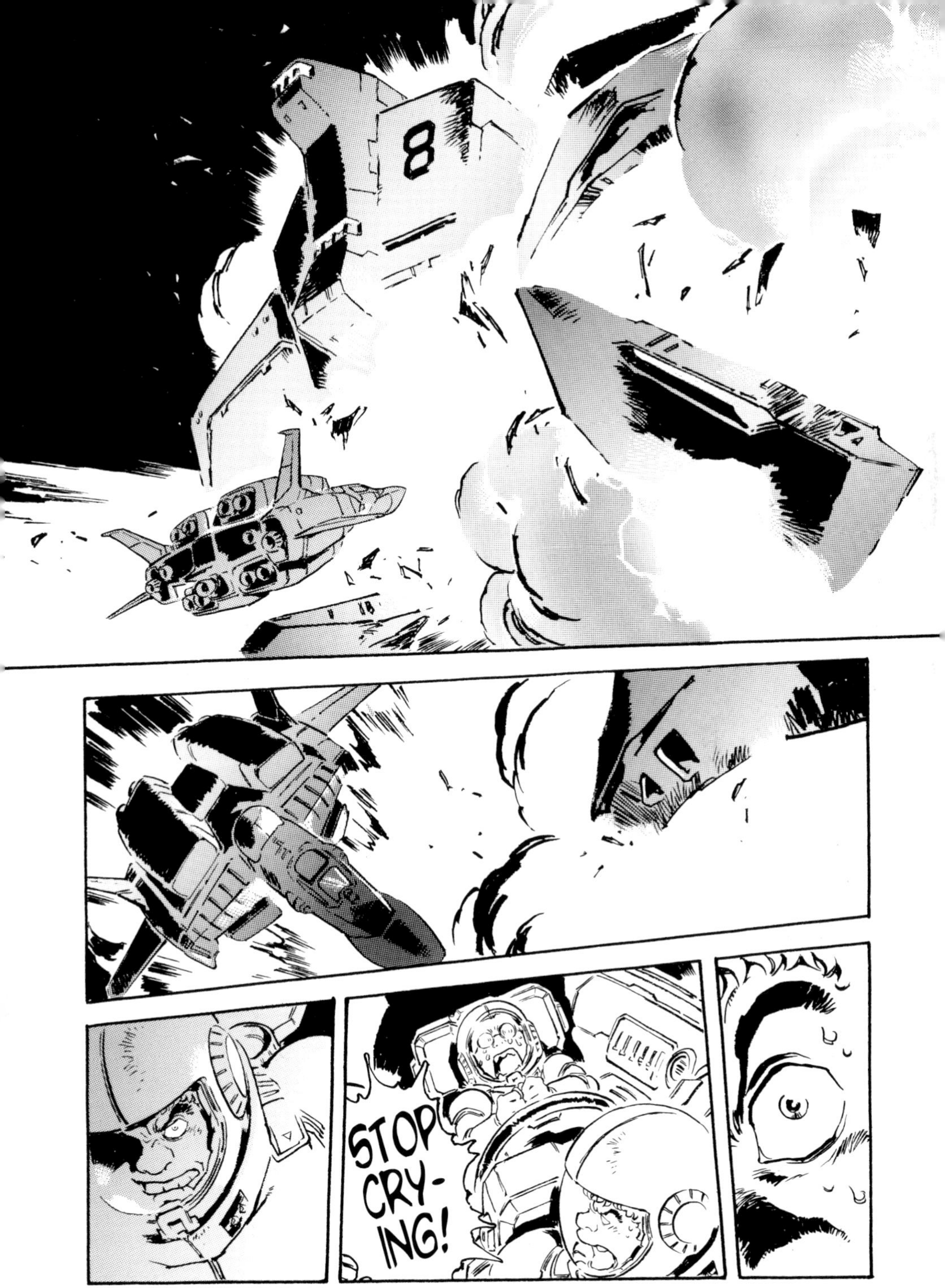
8
STOP CRY-ING!

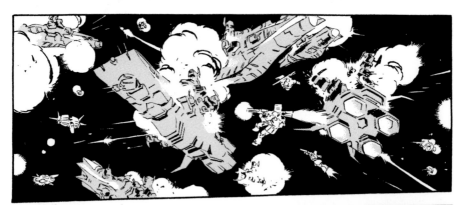

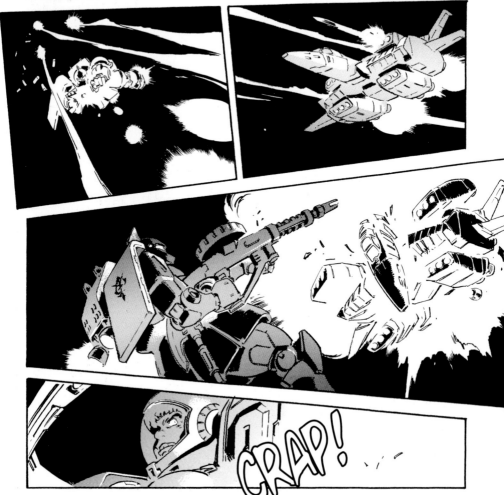

CRAP!

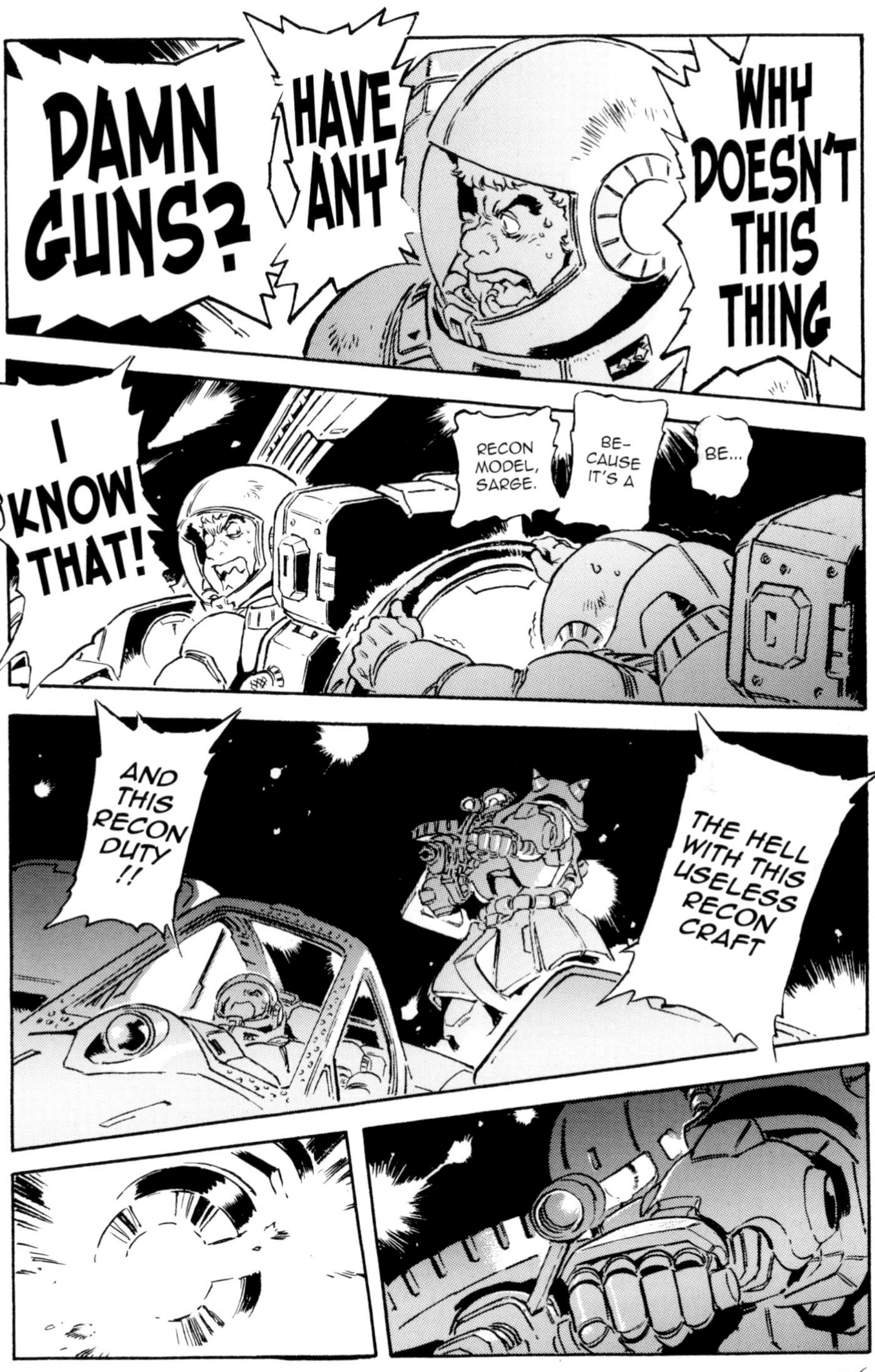
WHY DOESN'T THIS THING
HAVE ANY
DAMN GUNS?
BE...
BE-CAUSE IT'S A
RECON MODEL, SARGE.
I KNOW THAT!
THE HELL WITH THIS USELESS RECON CRAFT
AND THIS RECON DUTY!!

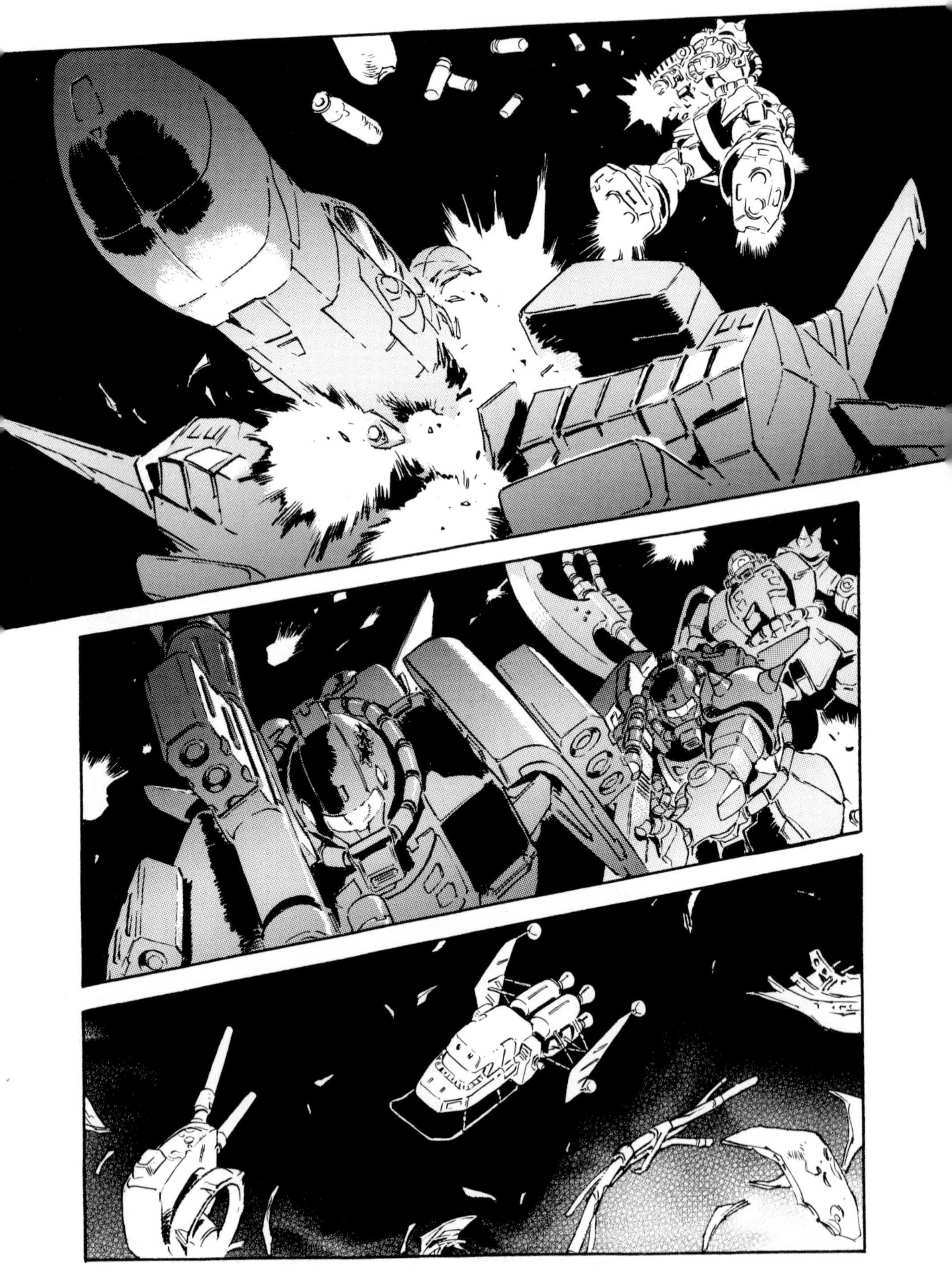

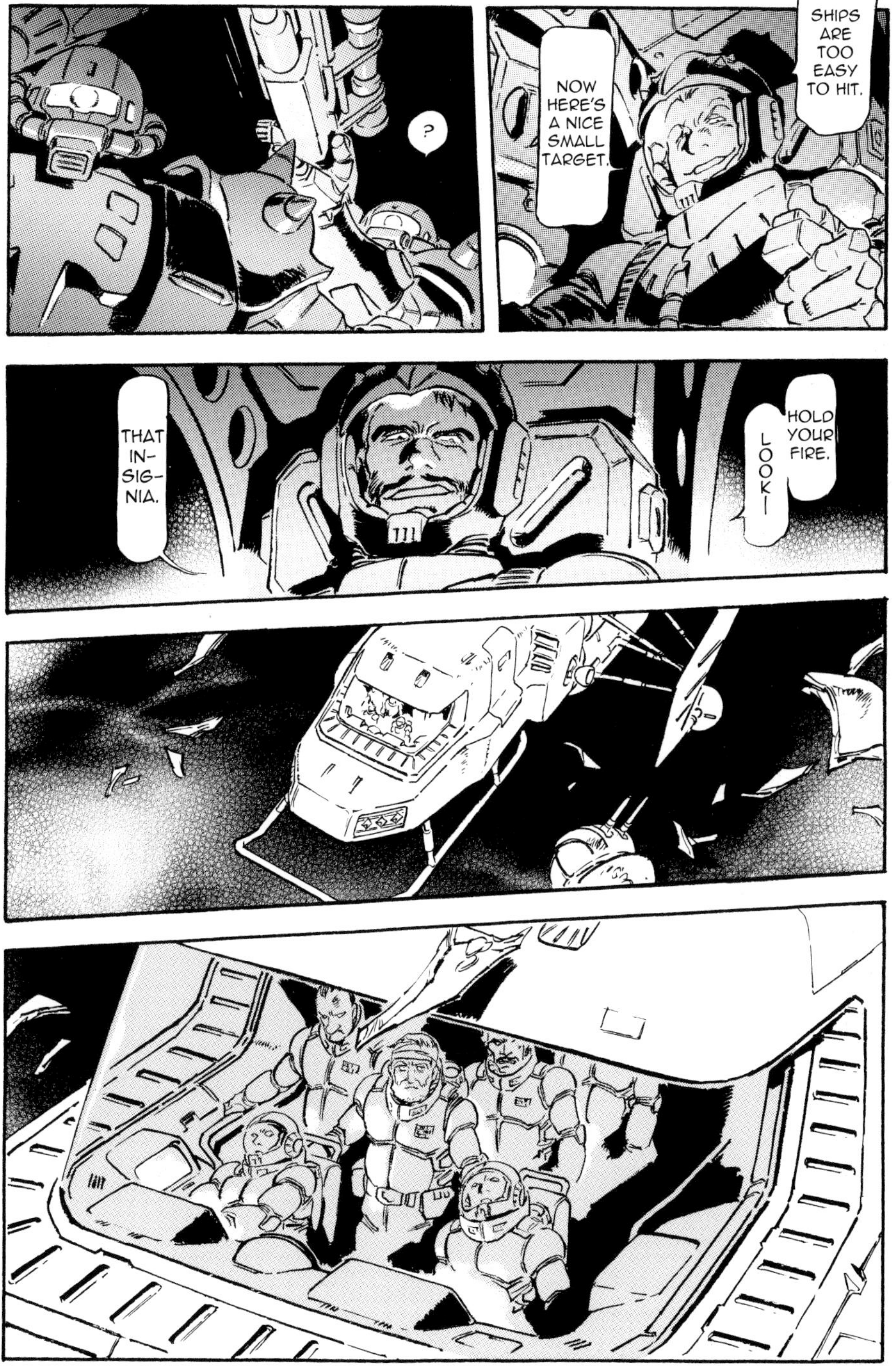
SHIPS ARE TOO EASY TO HIT.
NOW HERE'S A NICE SMALL TARGET.
?
HOLD YOUR FIRE.
LOOK!
THAT IN-SIG-NIA.

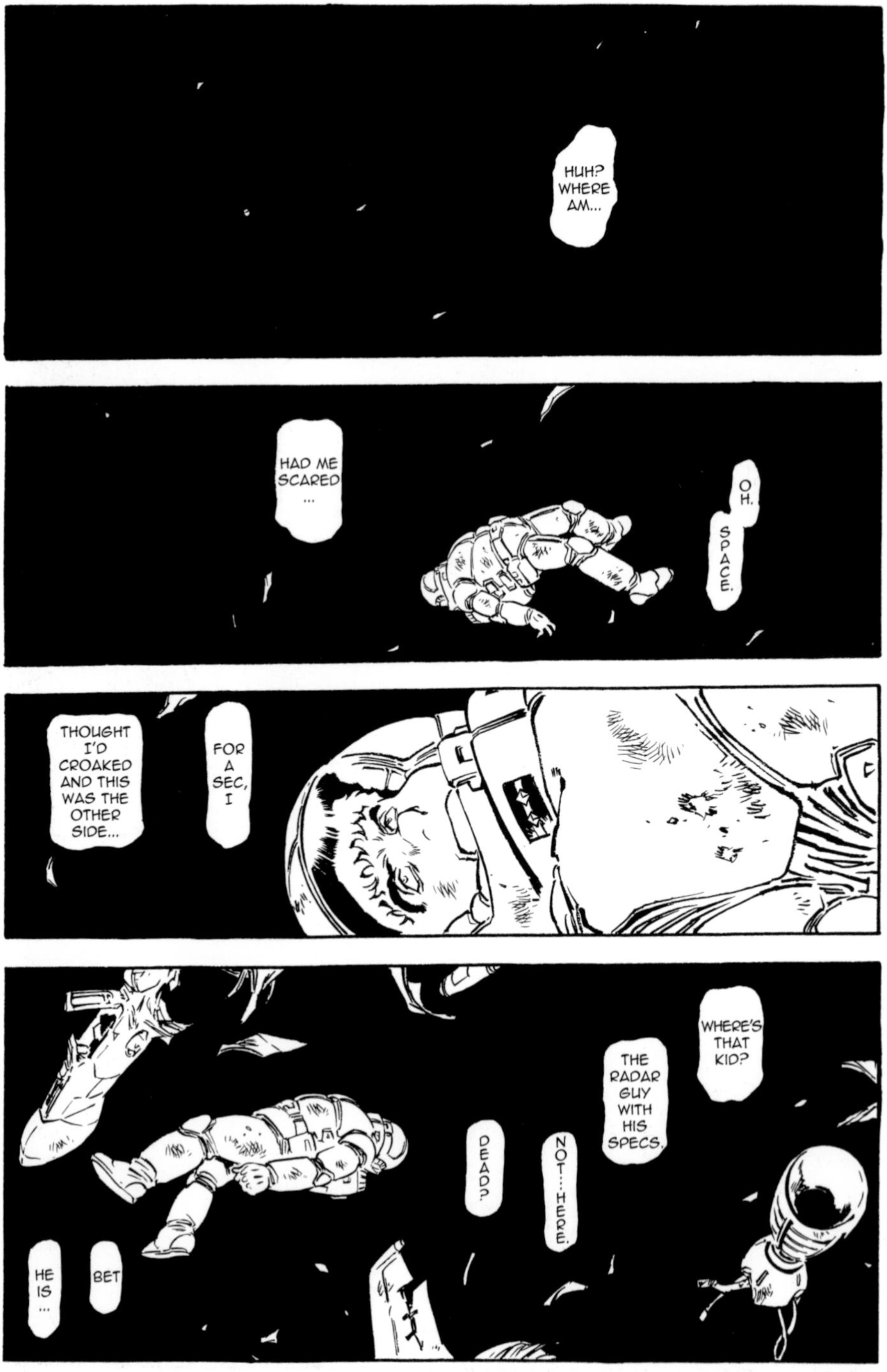
HUH? WHERE AM...
OH, SPACE.
HAD ME SCARED ...
FOR A SEC, I
THOUGHT I'D CROAKED AND THIS WAS THE OTHER SIDE...
WHERE'S THAT KID?
THE RADAR GUY WITH HIS SPECS.
NOT...HERE.
DEAD?
BET
HE IS ...

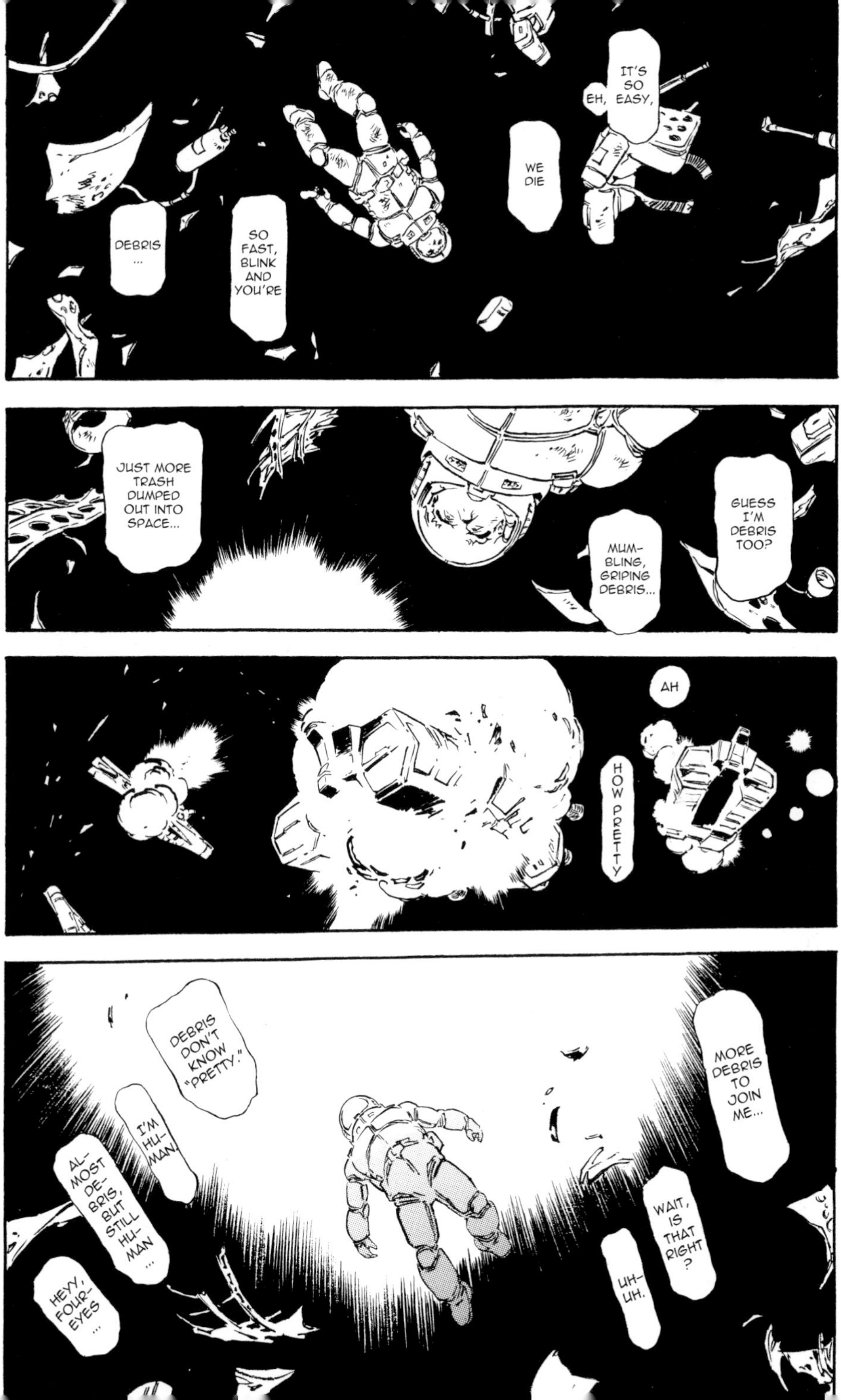
IT'S SO EASY, EH,
WE DIE
SO FAST, BLINK AND YOU'RE
DEBRIS...
GUESS I'M DEBRIS TOO?
MUM-BLING, GRIPING DEBRIS...
JUST MORE TRASH DUMPED OUT INTO SPACE...
AH
HOW PRETTY
MORE DEBRIS TO JOIN ME...
WAIT, IS THAT RIGHT?
UH-UH.
DEBRIS DON'T KNOW "PRETTY."
I'M HU-MAN.
AL-MOST DE-BRIS, BUT STILL HU-MAN...
HEYY, FOUR-EYES...

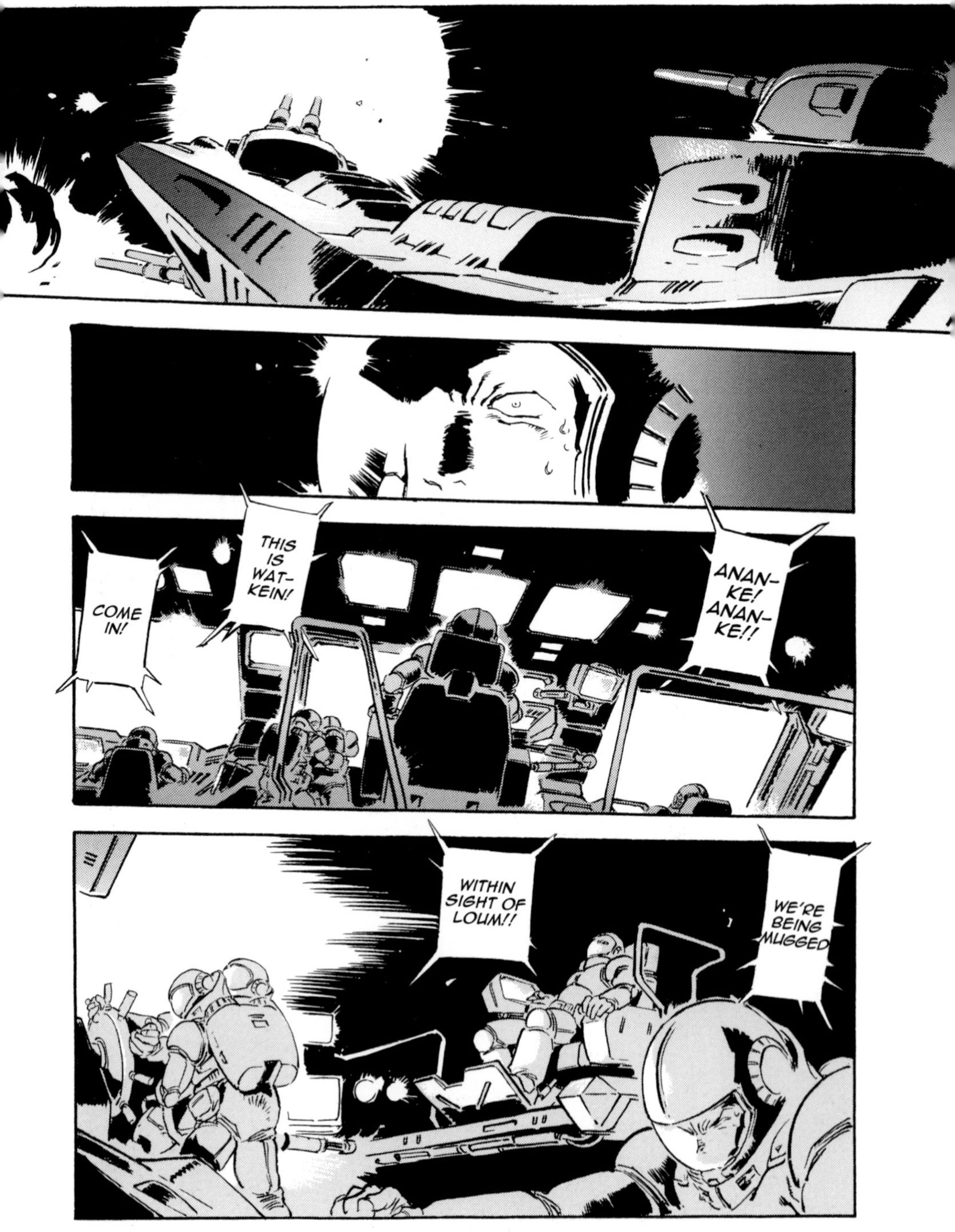
ANAN-KE! ANAN-KE!!
THIS IS WAT-KEIN!
COME IN!
WE'RE BEING MUGGED
WITHIN SIGHT OF LOUM!!

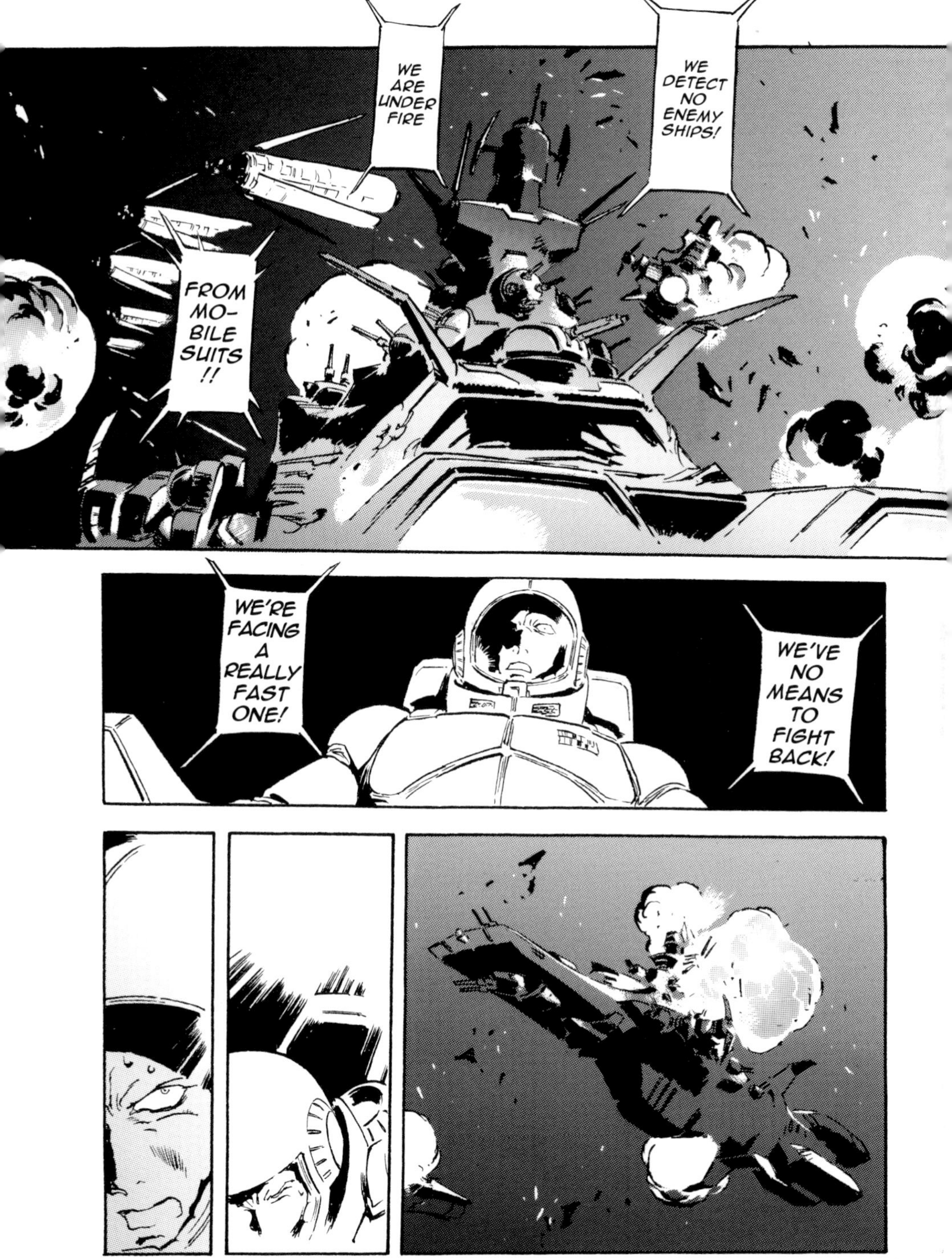
WE DETECT NO ENEMY SHIPS!
WE ARE UNDER FIRE
FROM MO- BILE SUITS !!
WE'VE NO MEANS TO FIGHT BACK!
WE'RE FACING A REALLY FAST ONE!

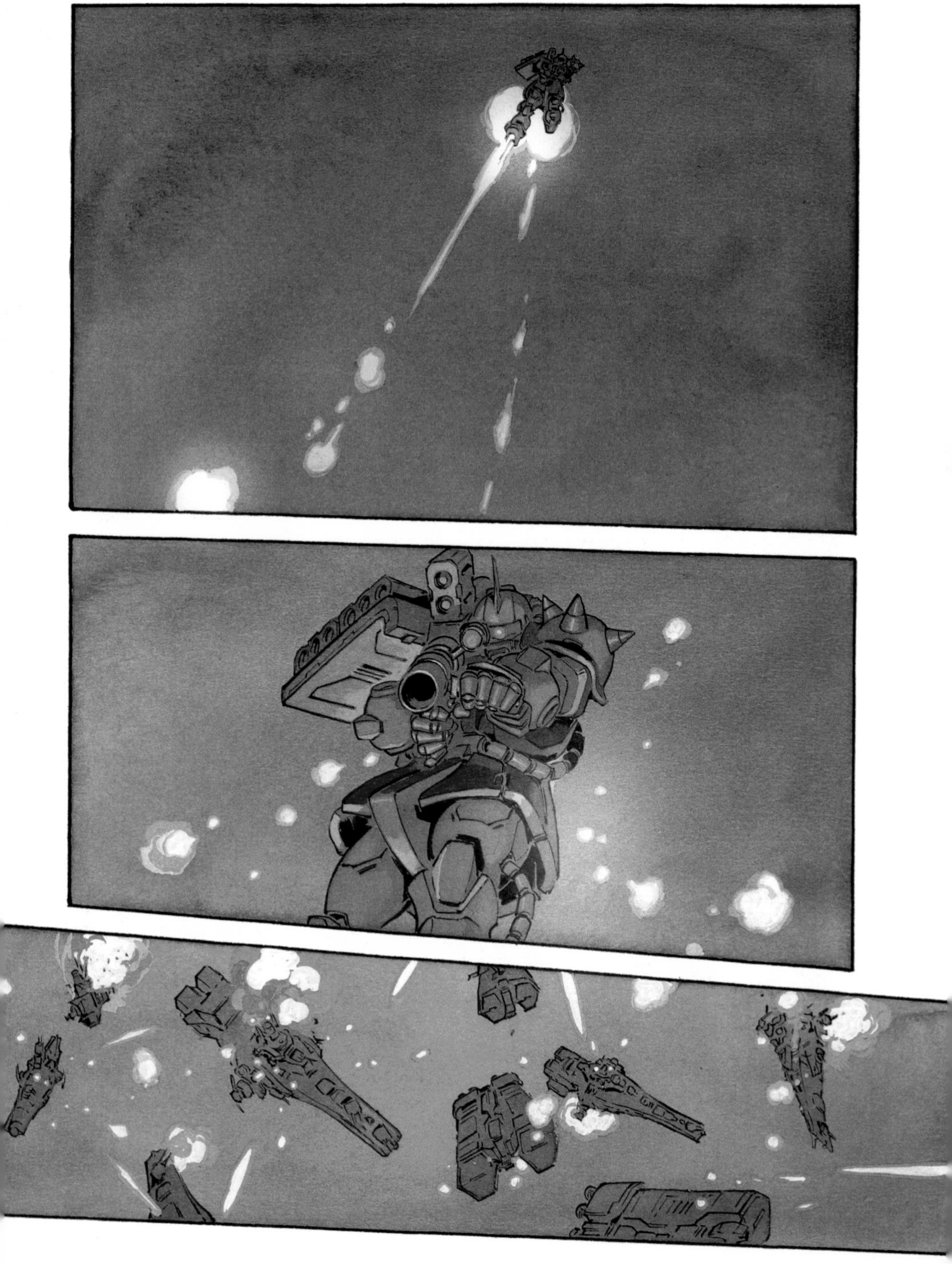

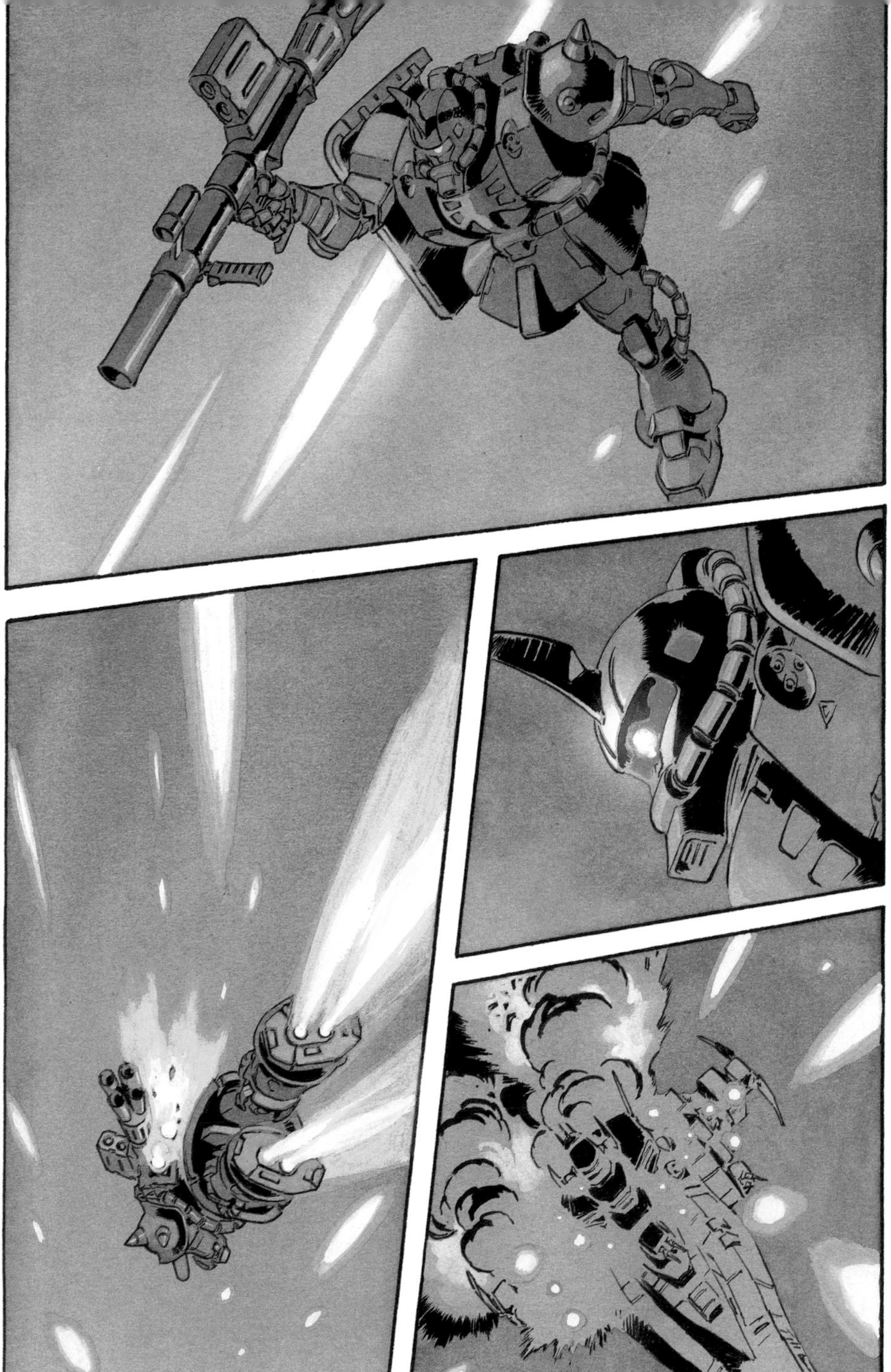

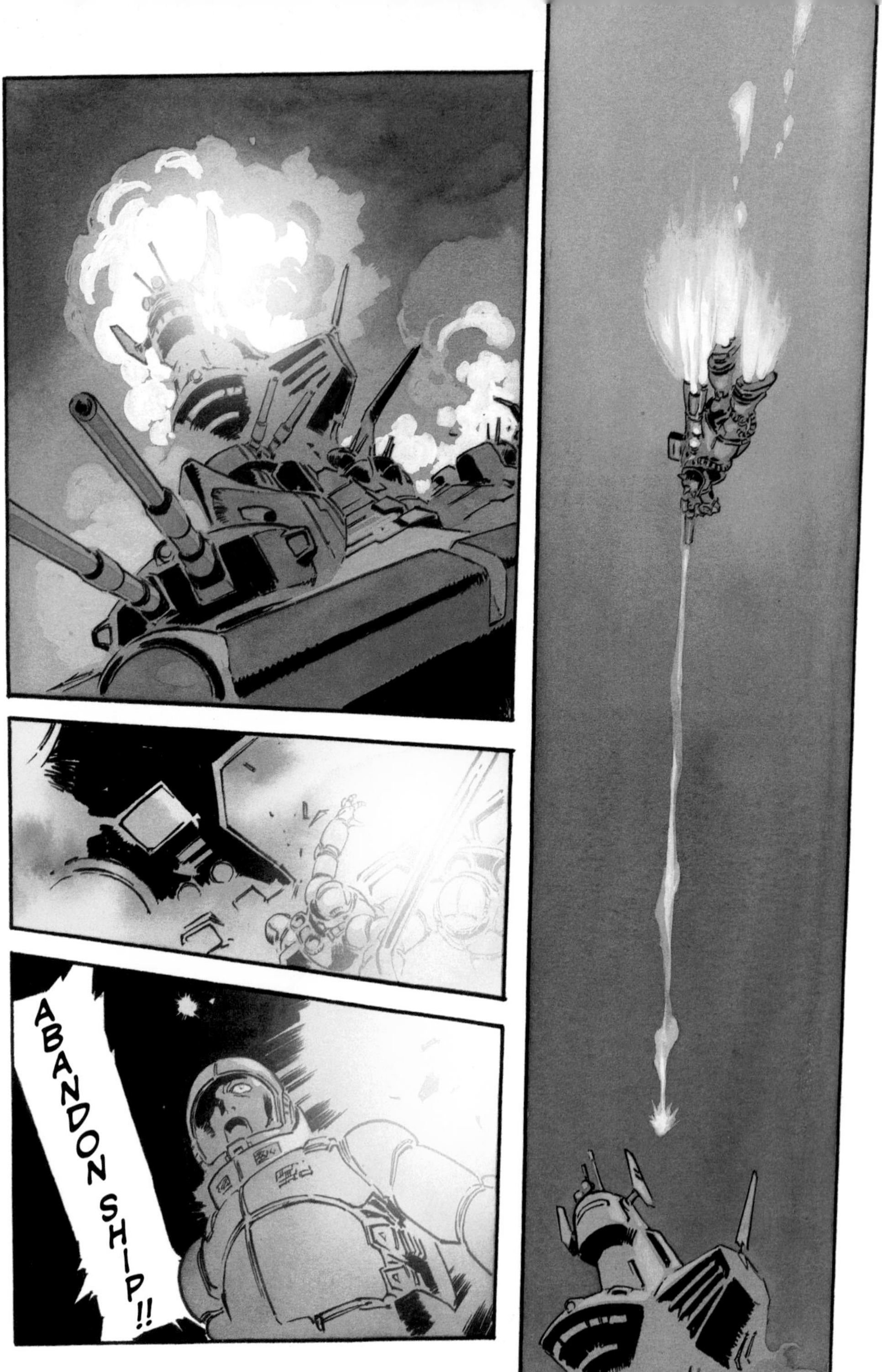
ABANDON SHIP!!

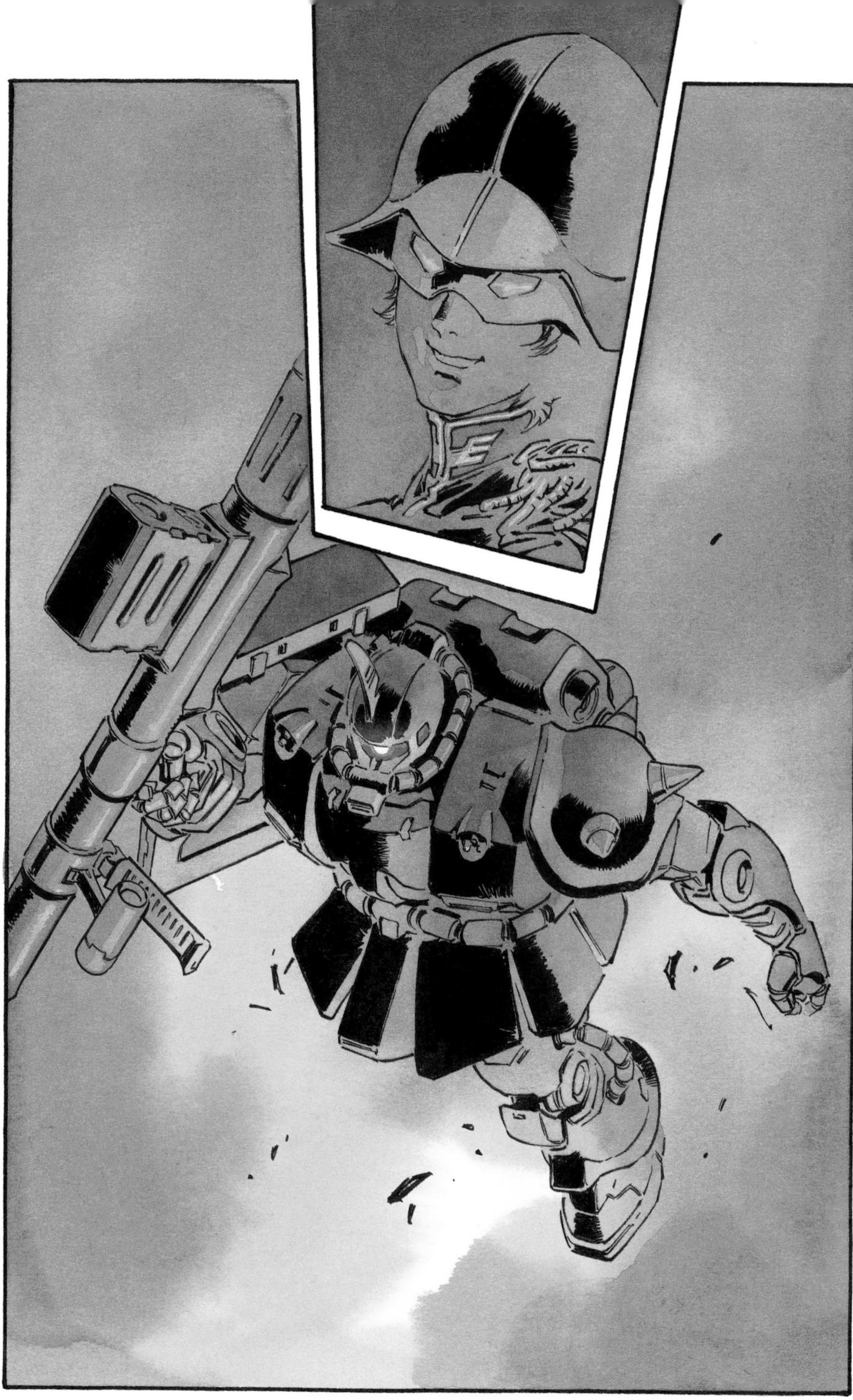

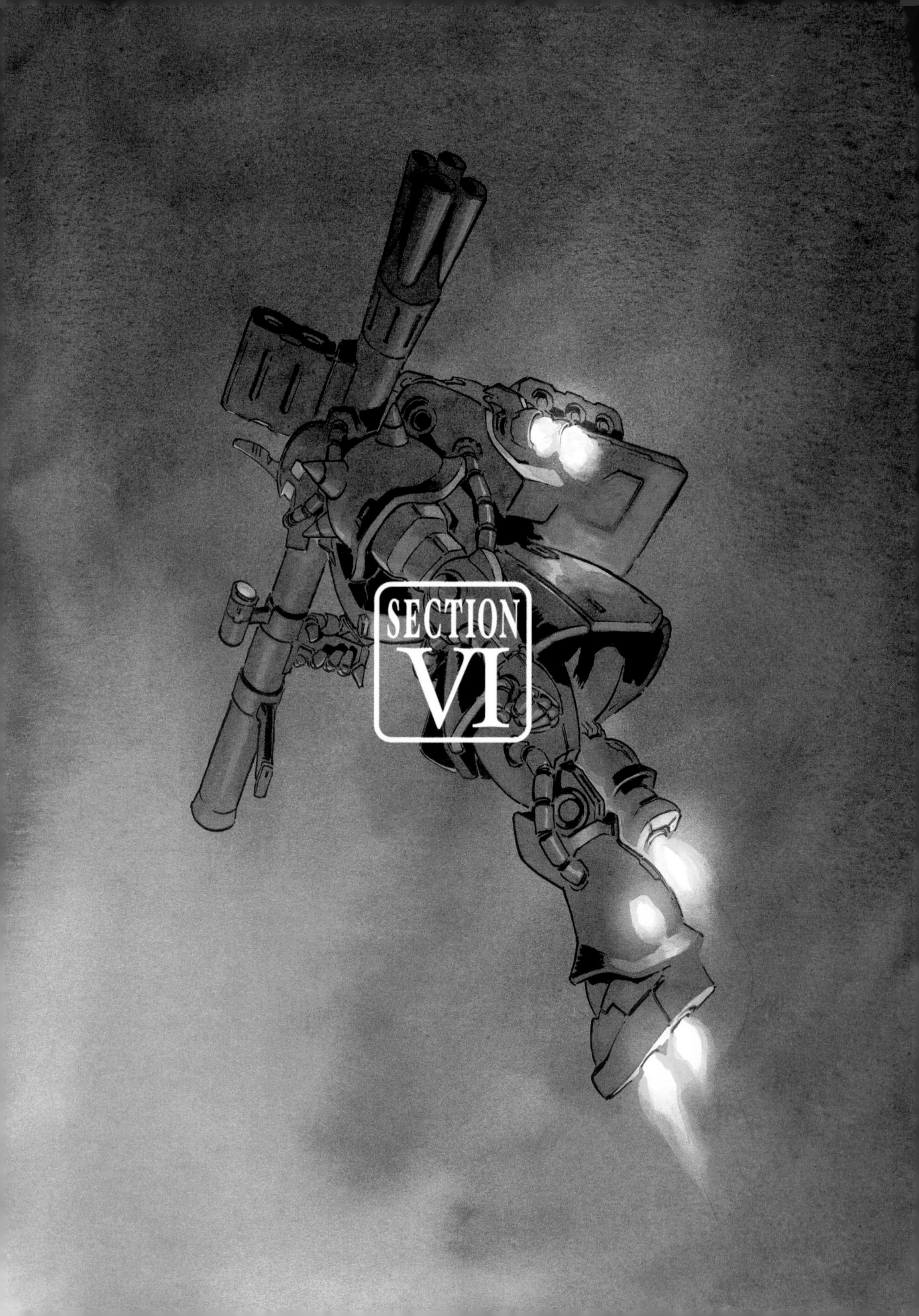

SECTION VI

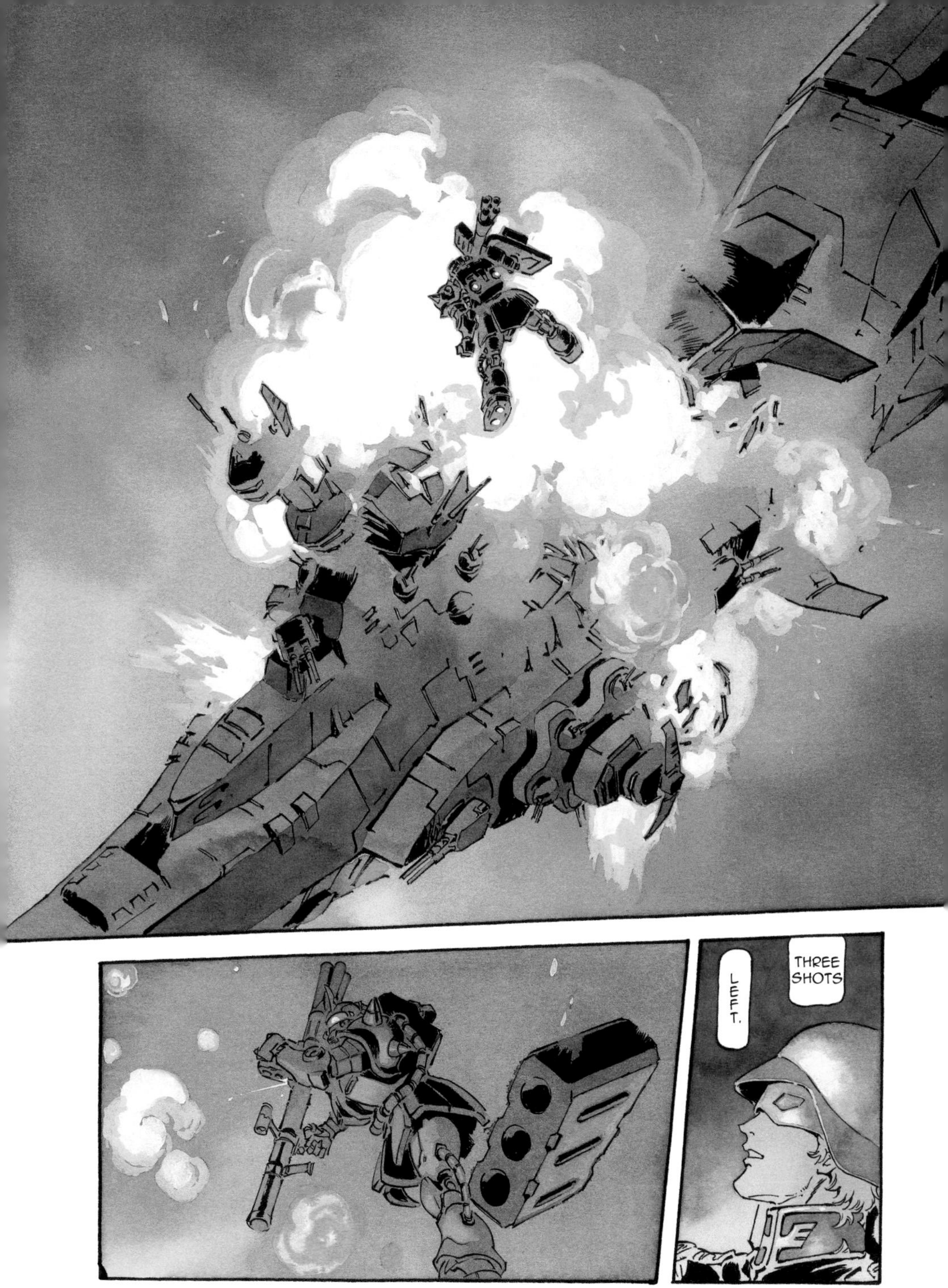
THREE SHOTS
LEFT.

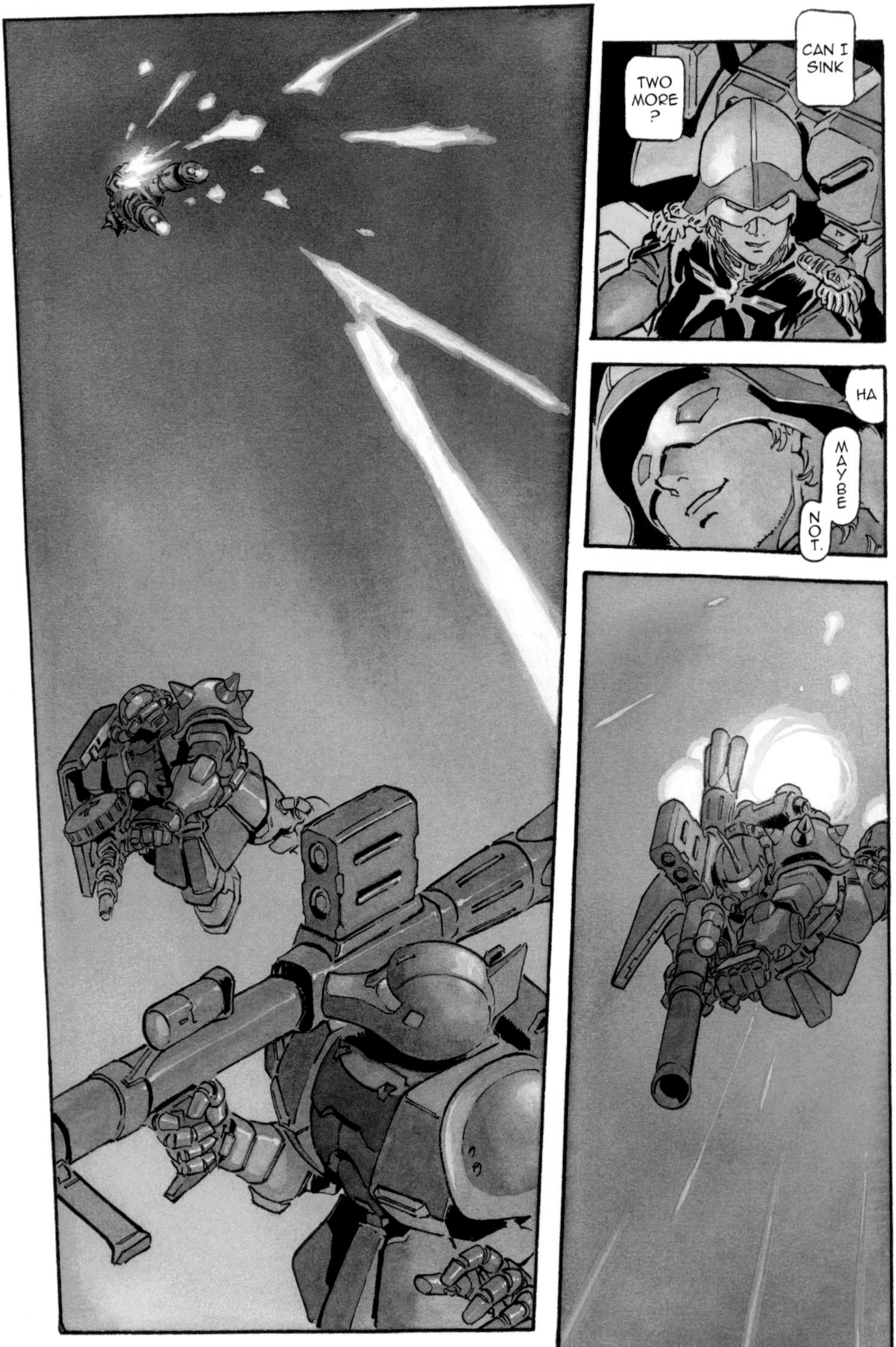
CAN I SINK
TWO MORE ?
HA
MAYBE NOT.

HE'S FAST! WHO IS THAT?
WELL, WASN'T IT RED,
OR DID YOU MISS THAT?
IT'S LT. CHAR.
AH, YOU JUST CAN'T COM-PETE WITH
A CUSTOM UNIT WITH A RAMPED-UP VERNIER.
HM?!
HEY—
LT. CHAR'S ZAKU WASN'T FITTED
WITH ANY
SPECIAL THRUST-ERS—
WAS IT...
THEN HOW THE HELL
IS HE THAT FAST?
I'D SAY THREE TIMES
AS FAST.
YUP.
TRIPLE...

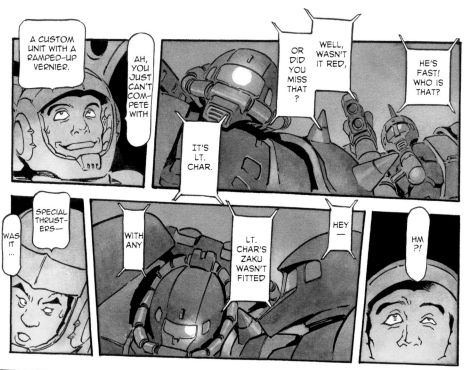

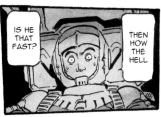

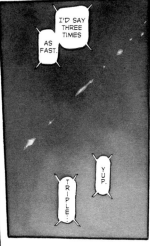

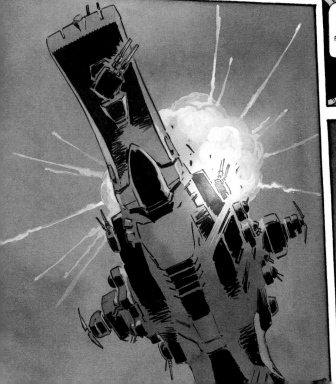

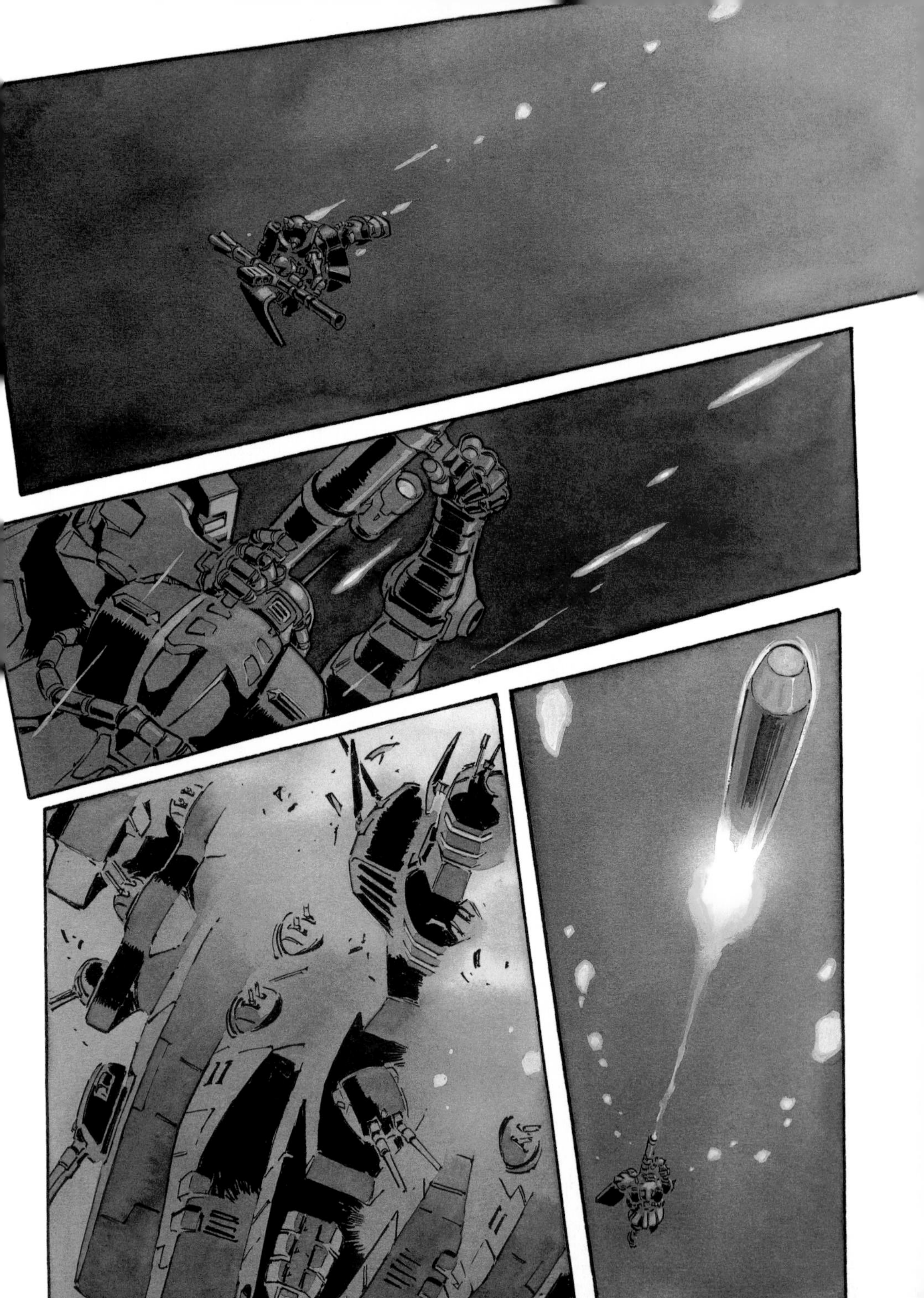

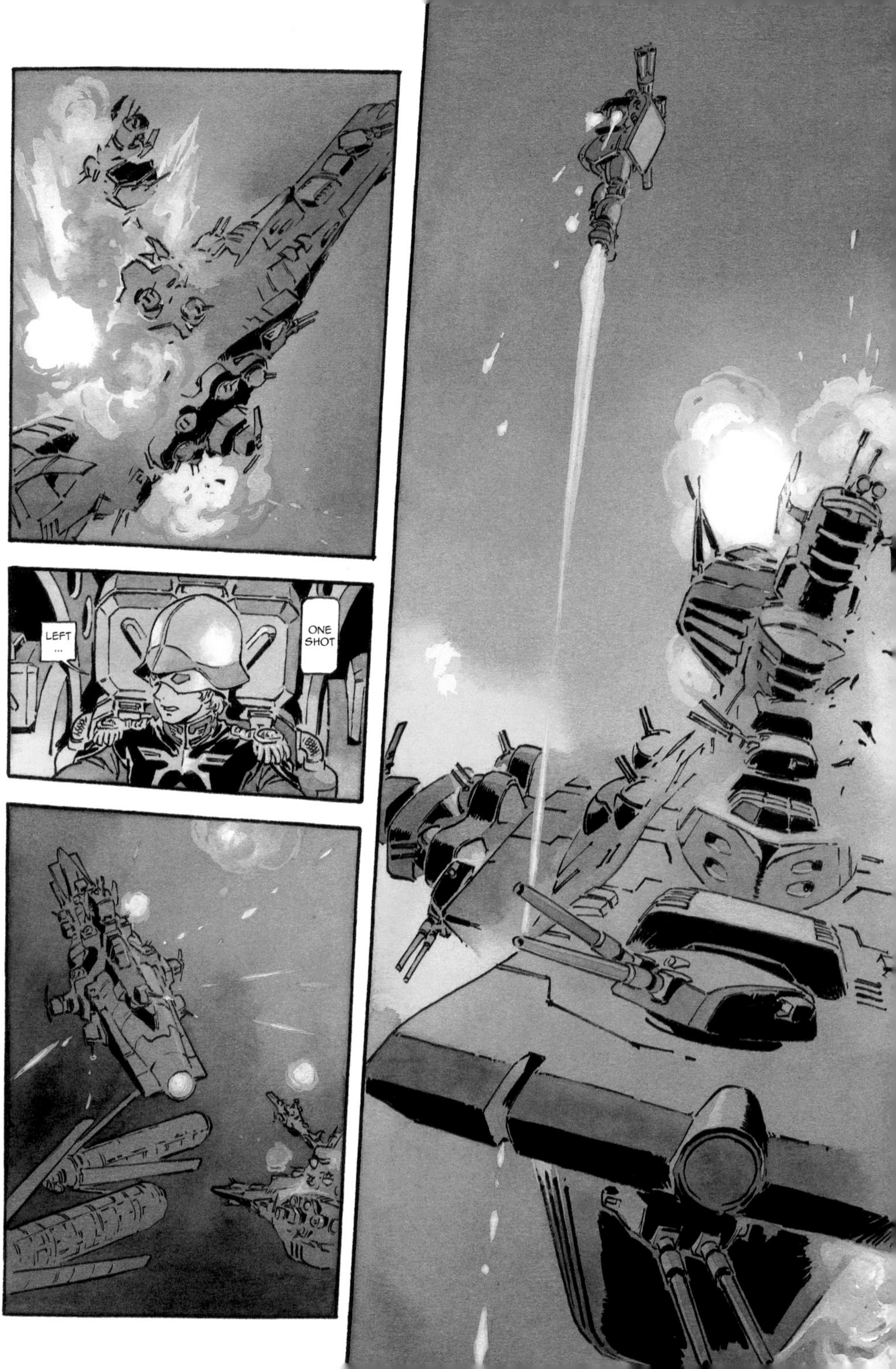
ONE SHOT
LEFT ...

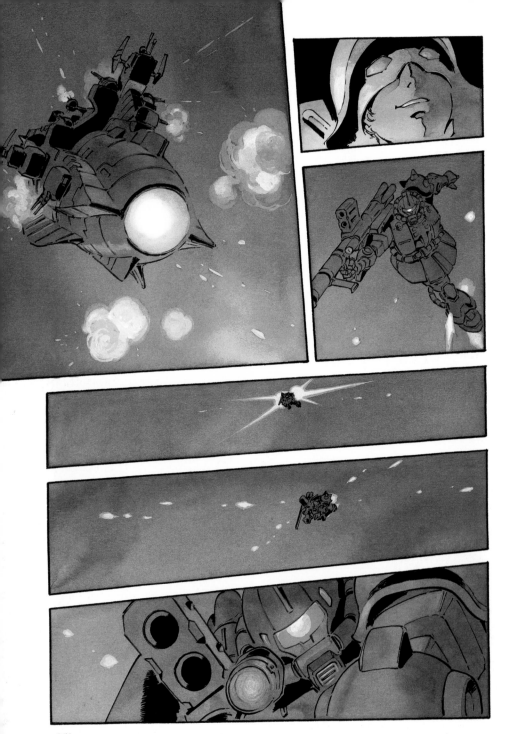

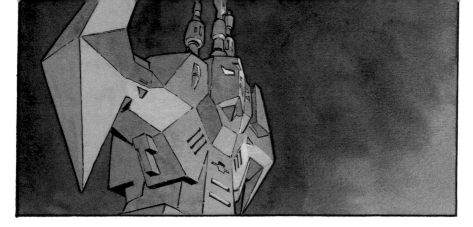

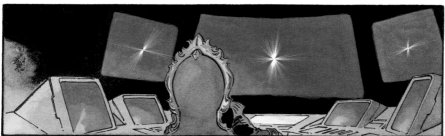

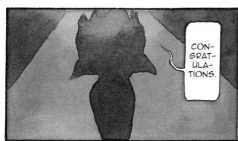

CON-
GRAT-
ULA-
TIONS.

HAH...

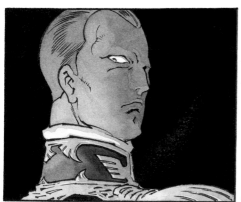

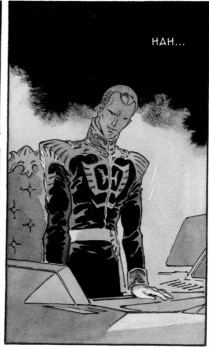

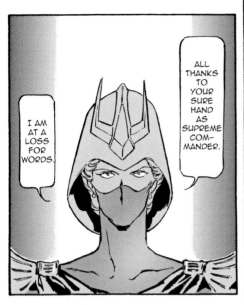

ALL THANKS TO YOUR SURE HAND AS SUPREME COMMANDER.

I AM AT A LOSS FOR WORDS.

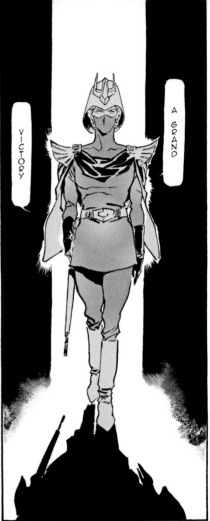

A GRAND

VICTORY

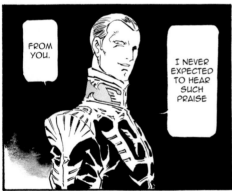

FROM YOU.

I NEVER EXPECTED TO HEAR SUCH PRAISE

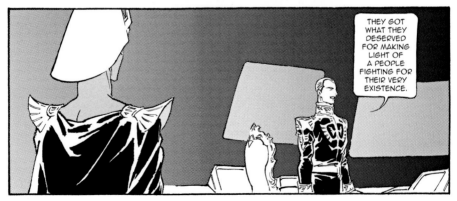

THEY GOT WHAT THEY DESERVED FOR MAKING LIGHT OF A PEOPLE FIGHTING FOR THEIR VERY EXISTENCE.

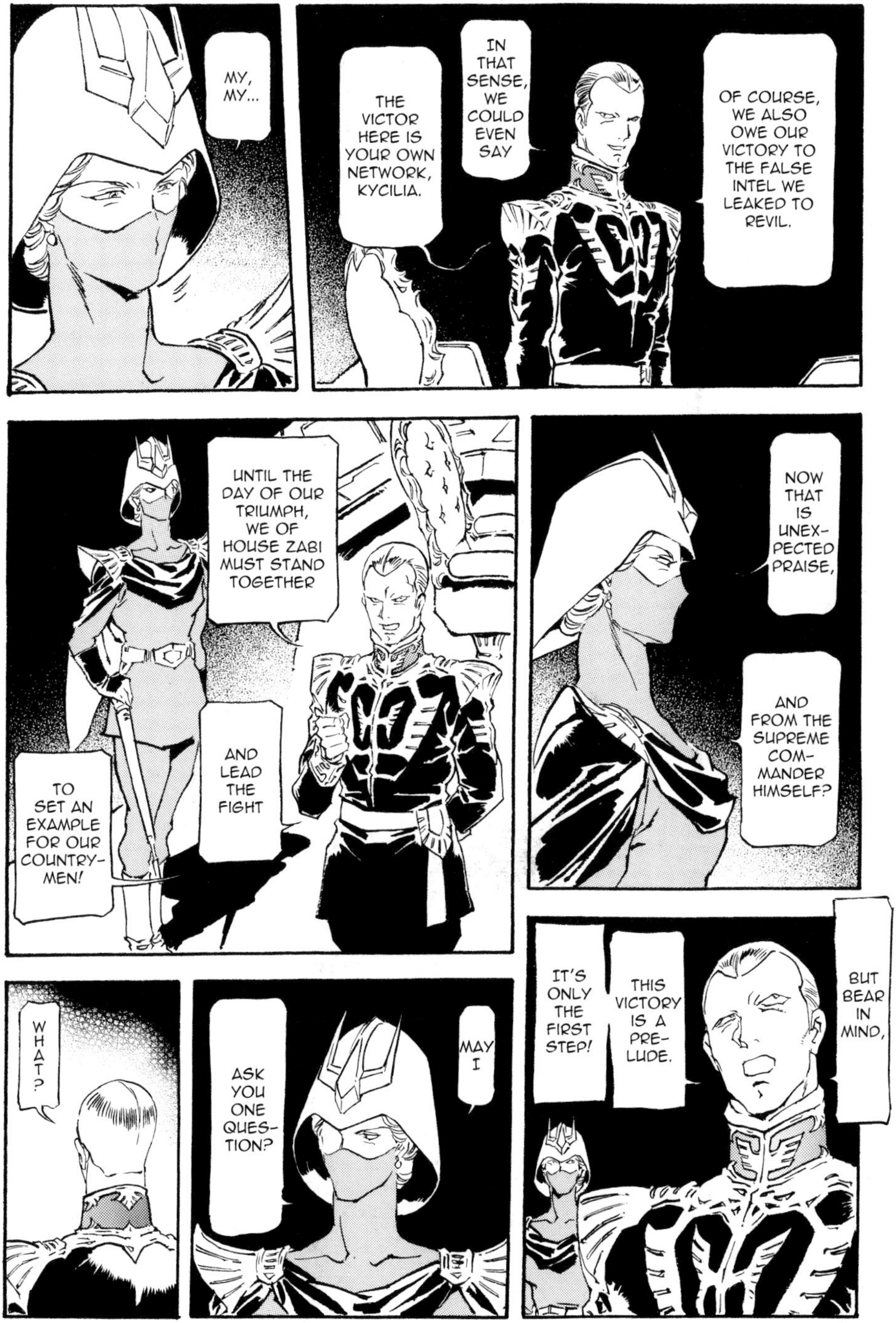
OF COURSE, WE ALSO OWE OUR VICTORY TO THE FALSE INTEL WE LEAKED TO REVIL.
IN THAT SENSE, WE COULD EVEN SAY
THE VICTOR HERE IS YOUR OWN NETWORK, KYCILIA.
MY, MY...
NOW THAT IS UNEXPECTED PRAISE,
AND FROM THE SUPREME COMMANDER HIMSELF?
UNTIL THE DAY OF OUR TRIUMPH, WE OF HOUSE ZABI MUST STAND TOGETHER
AND LEAD THE FIGHT
TO SET AN EXAMPLE FOR OUR COUNTRYMEN!
BUT BEAR IN MIND,
THIS VICTORY IS A PRELUDE.
IT'S ONLY THE FIRST STEP!
MAY I
ASK YOU ONE QUESTION?
WHAT?

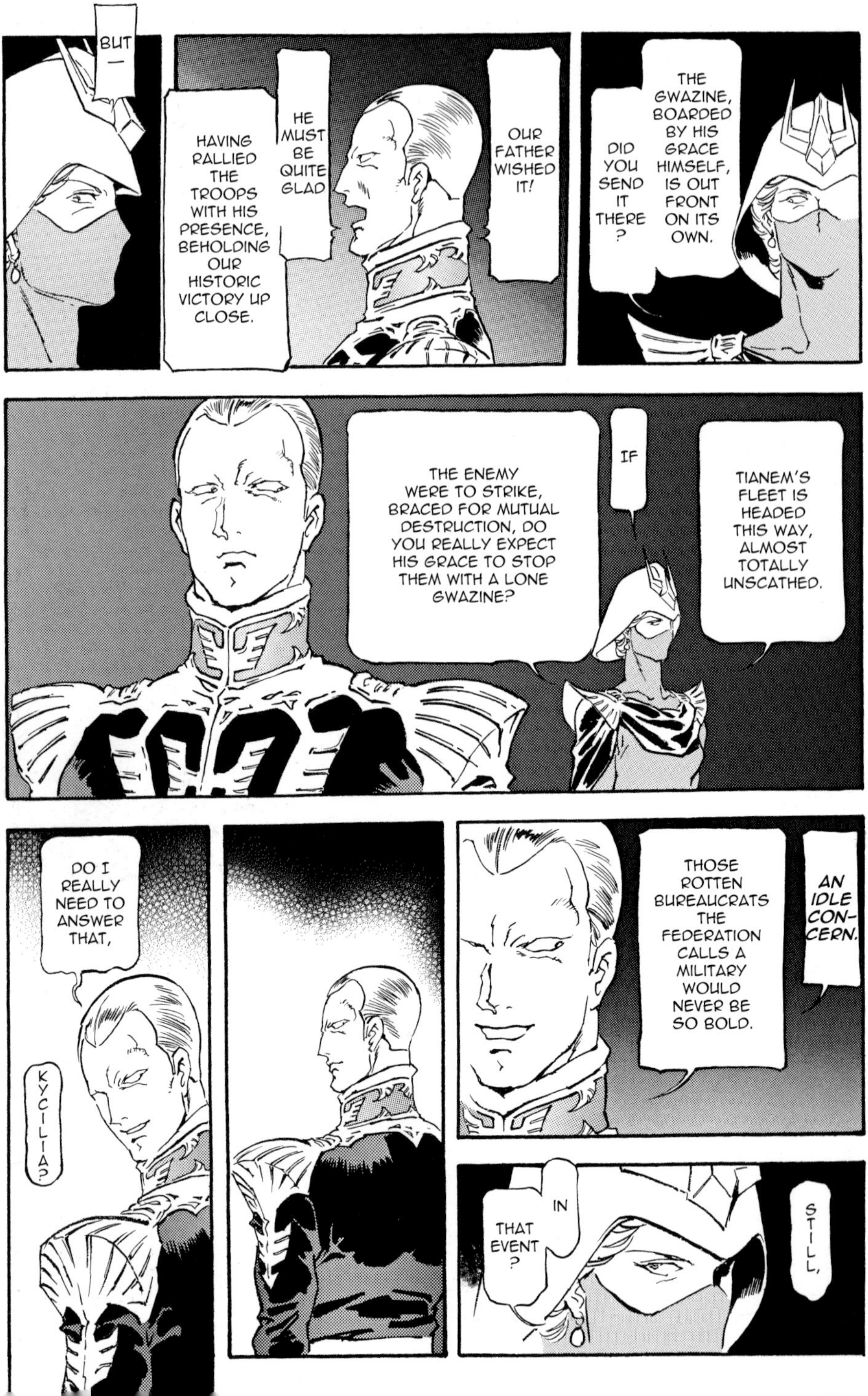
THE GWAZINE, BOARDED BY HIS GRACE HIMSELF, IS OUT FRONT ON ITS OWN.
DID YOU SEND IT THERE?
OUR FATHER WISHED IT!
HE MUST BE QUITE GLAD
HAVING RALLIED THE TROOPS WITH HIS PRESENCE, BEHOLDING OUR HISTORIC VICTORY UP CLOSE.
BUT —
TIANEM'S FLEET IS HEADED THIS WAY, ALMOST TOTALLY UNSCATHED.
IF
THE ENEMY WERE TO STRIKE, BRACED FOR MUTUAL DESTRUCTION, DO YOU REALLY EXPECT HIS GRACE TO STOP THEM WITH A LONE GWAZINE?
AN IDLE CONCERN.
THOSE ROTTEN BUREAUCRATS THE FEDERATION CALLS A MILITARY WOULD NEVER BE SO BOLD.
STILL,
IN THAT EVENT?
DO I REALLY NEED TO ANSWER THAT,
KYCILIA?

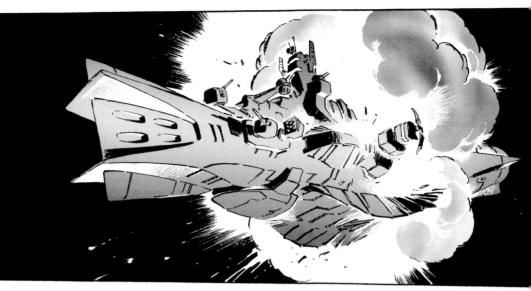

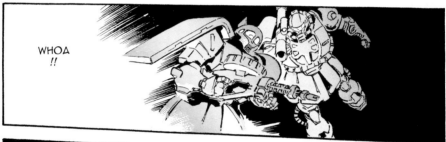

WHOA
!!

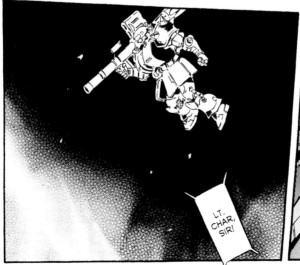

LT.
CHAR,
SIR!

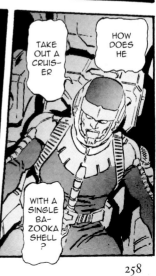

TAKE
OUT A
CRUIS-
ER

HOW
DOES
HE

WITH A
SINGLE
BA-
ZOOKA
SHELL
?

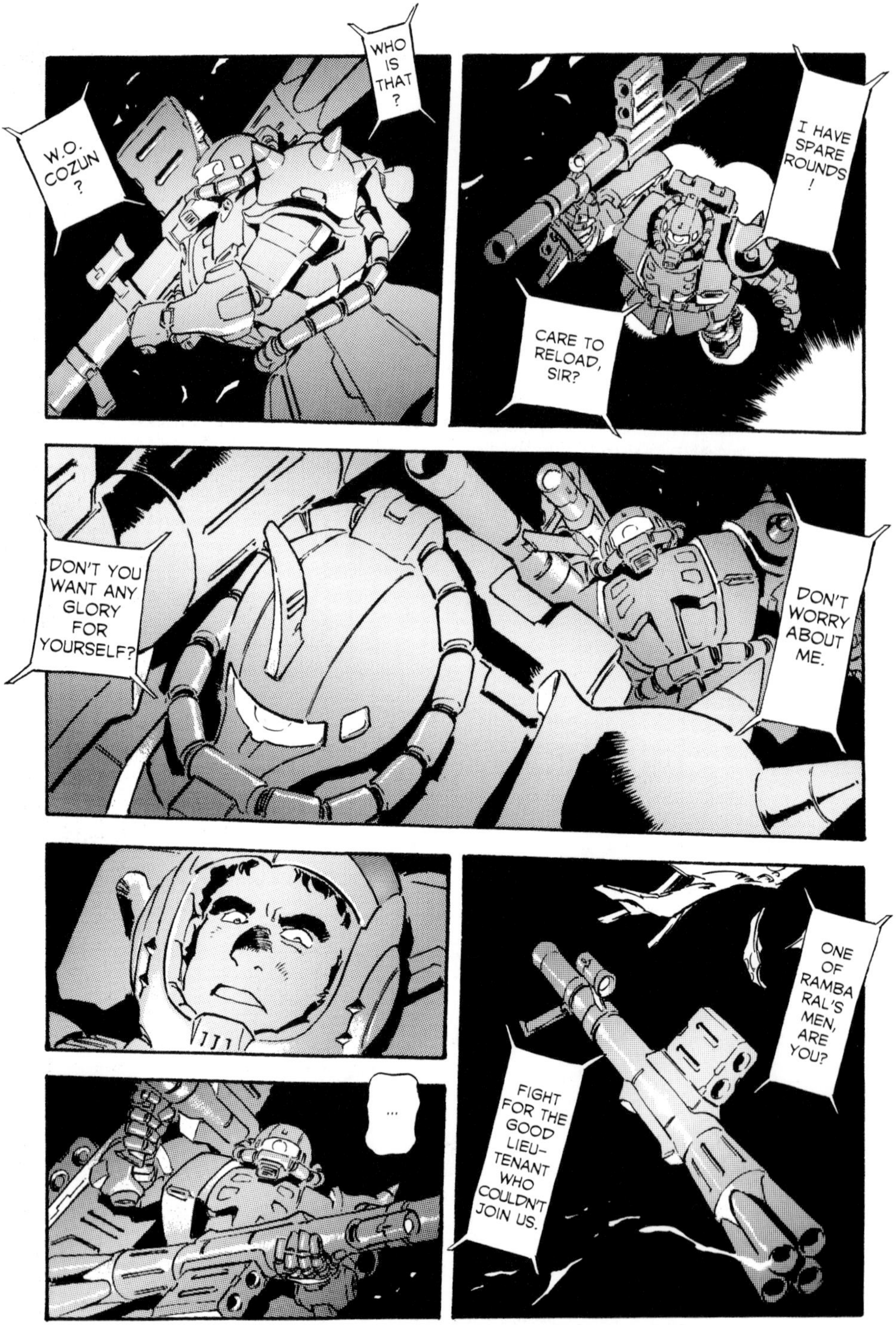
I HAVE SPARE ROUNDS!
CARE TO RELOAD, SIR?
WHO IS THAT?
W.O. COZUN?
DON'T WORRY ABOUT ME.
DON'T YOU WANT ANY GLORY FOR YOURSELF?
ONE OF RAMBA RAL'S MEN, ARE YOU?
FIGHT FOR THE GOOD LIEUTENANT WHO COULDN'T JOIN US.
...

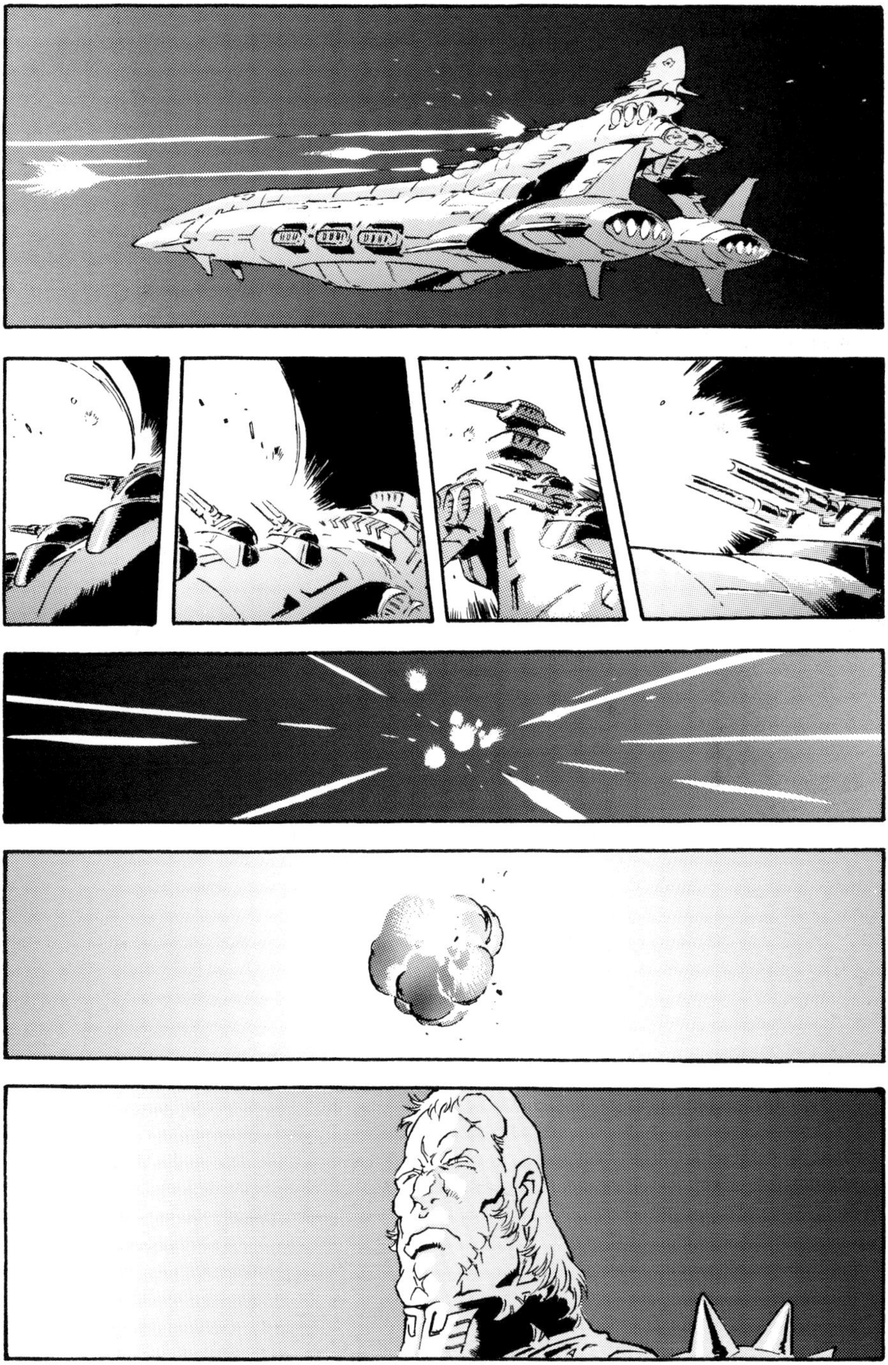

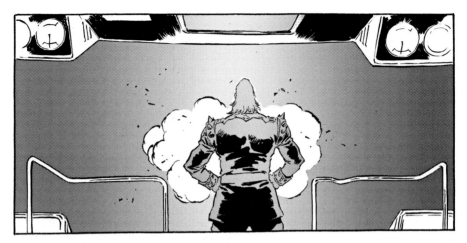

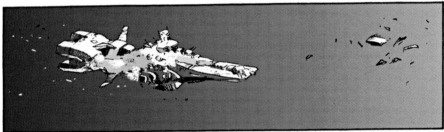

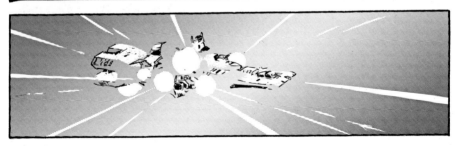

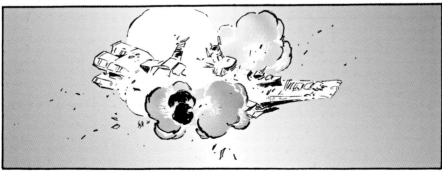

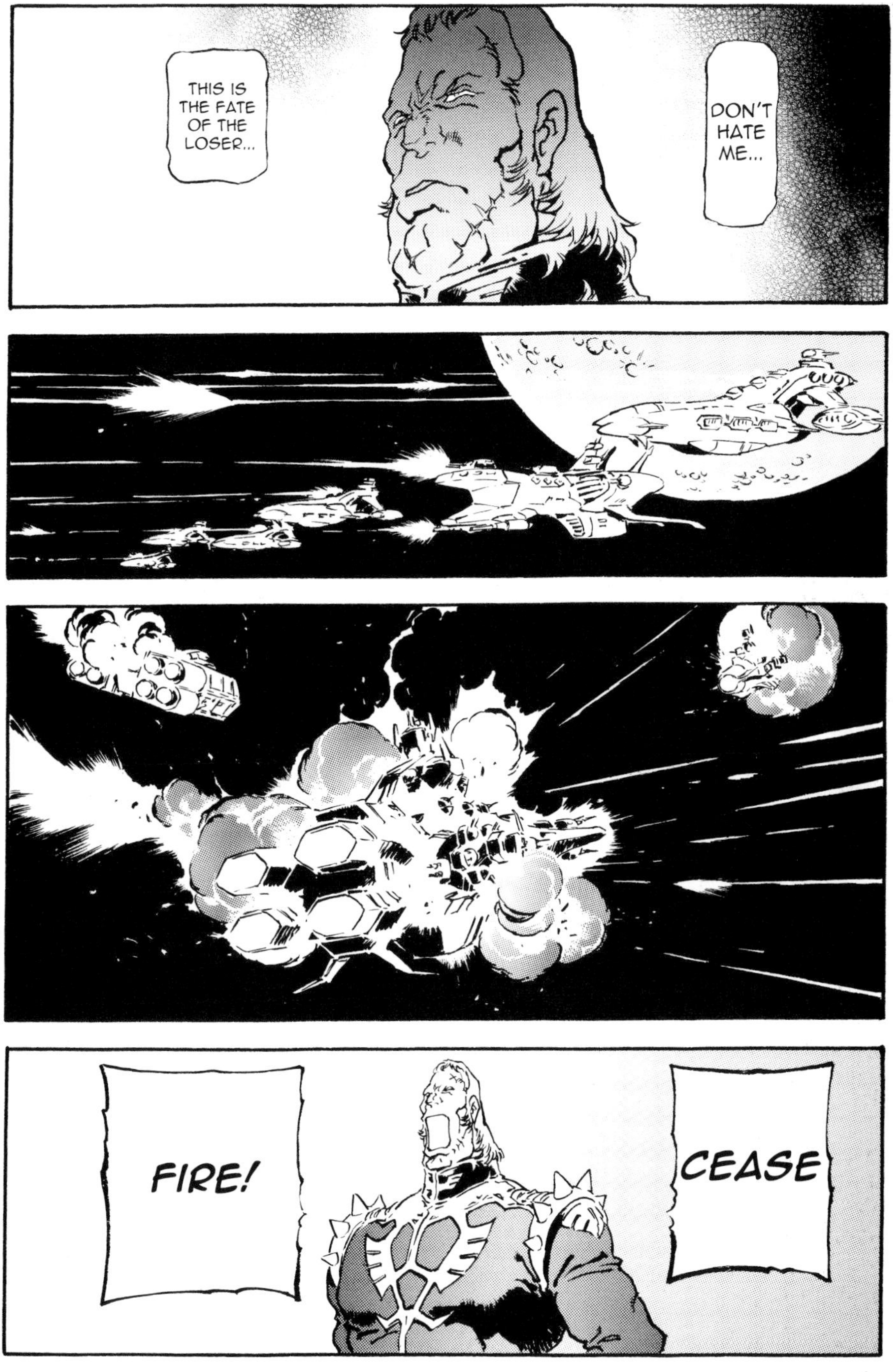
DON'T HATE ME...
THIS IS THE FATE OF THE LOSER...
CEASE
FIRE!

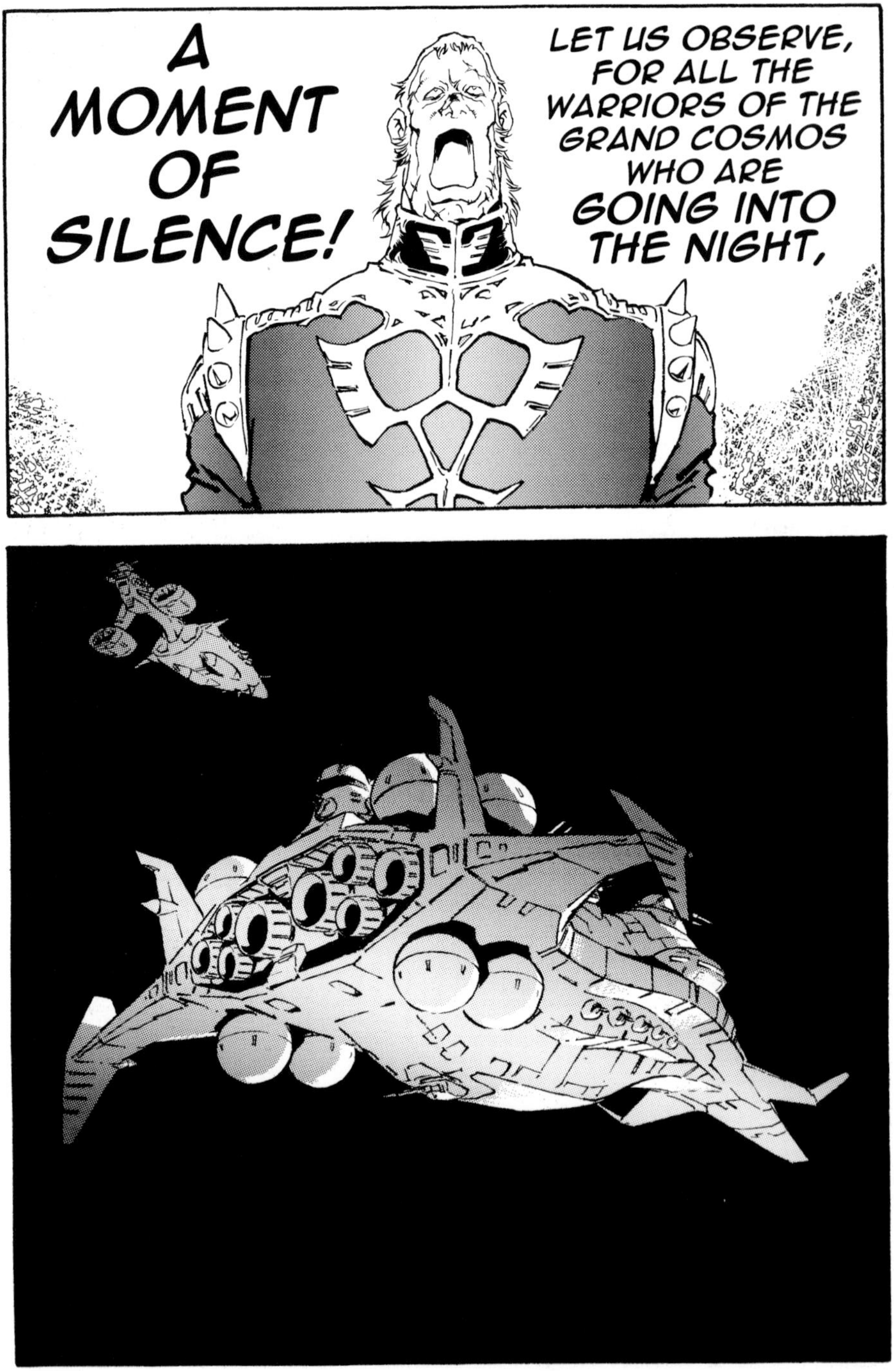
LET US OBSERVE, FOR ALL THE WARRIORS OF THE GRAND COSMOS WHO ARE GOING INTO THE NIGHT,
A MOMENT OF SILENCE!

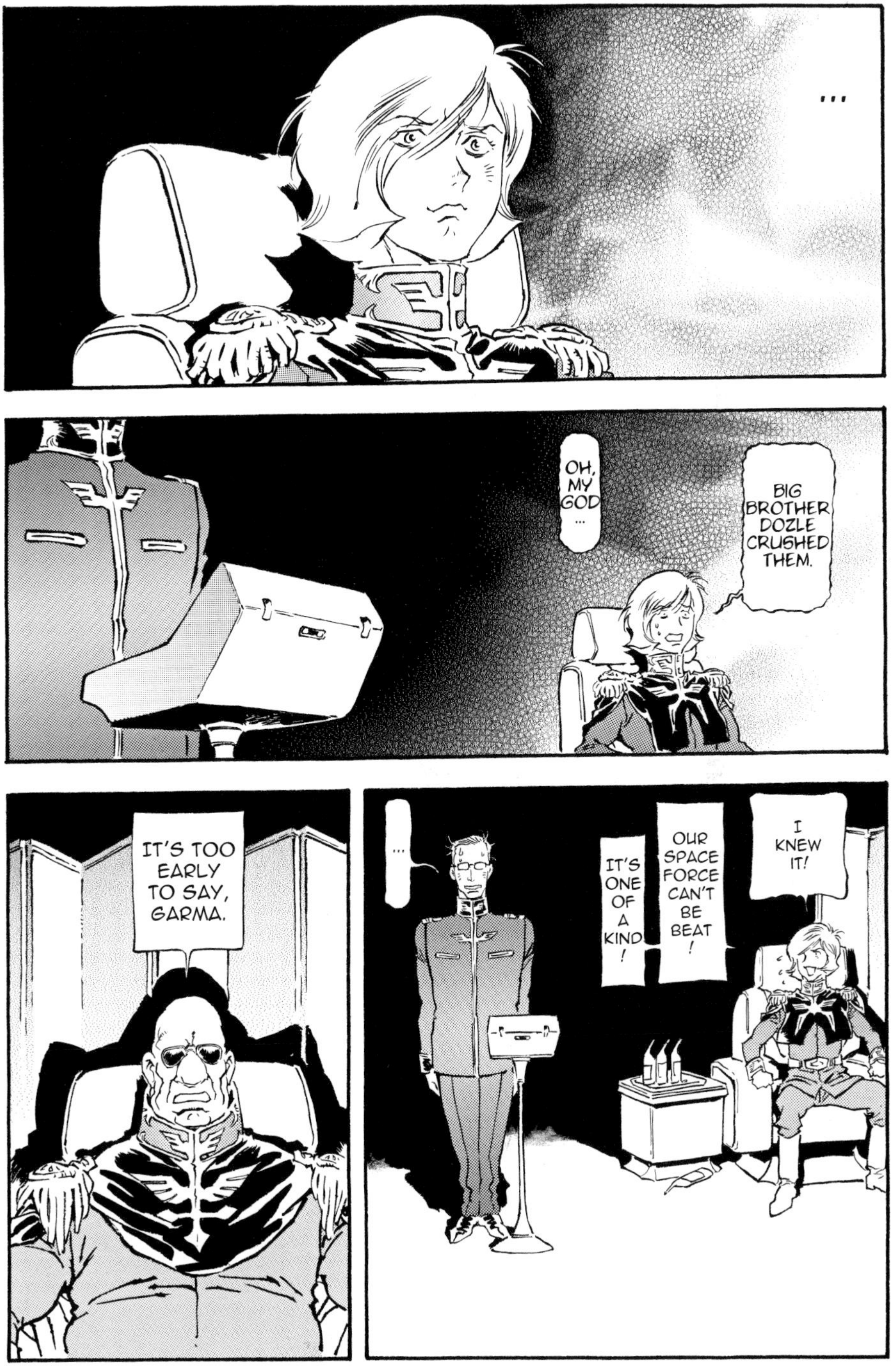
...
BIG BROTHER DOZLE CRUSHED THEM.
OH, MY GOD ...
I KNEW IT!
OUR SPACE FORCE CAN'T BE BEAT!
IT'S ONE OF A KIND!
...
IT'S TOO EARLY TO SAY, GARMA.

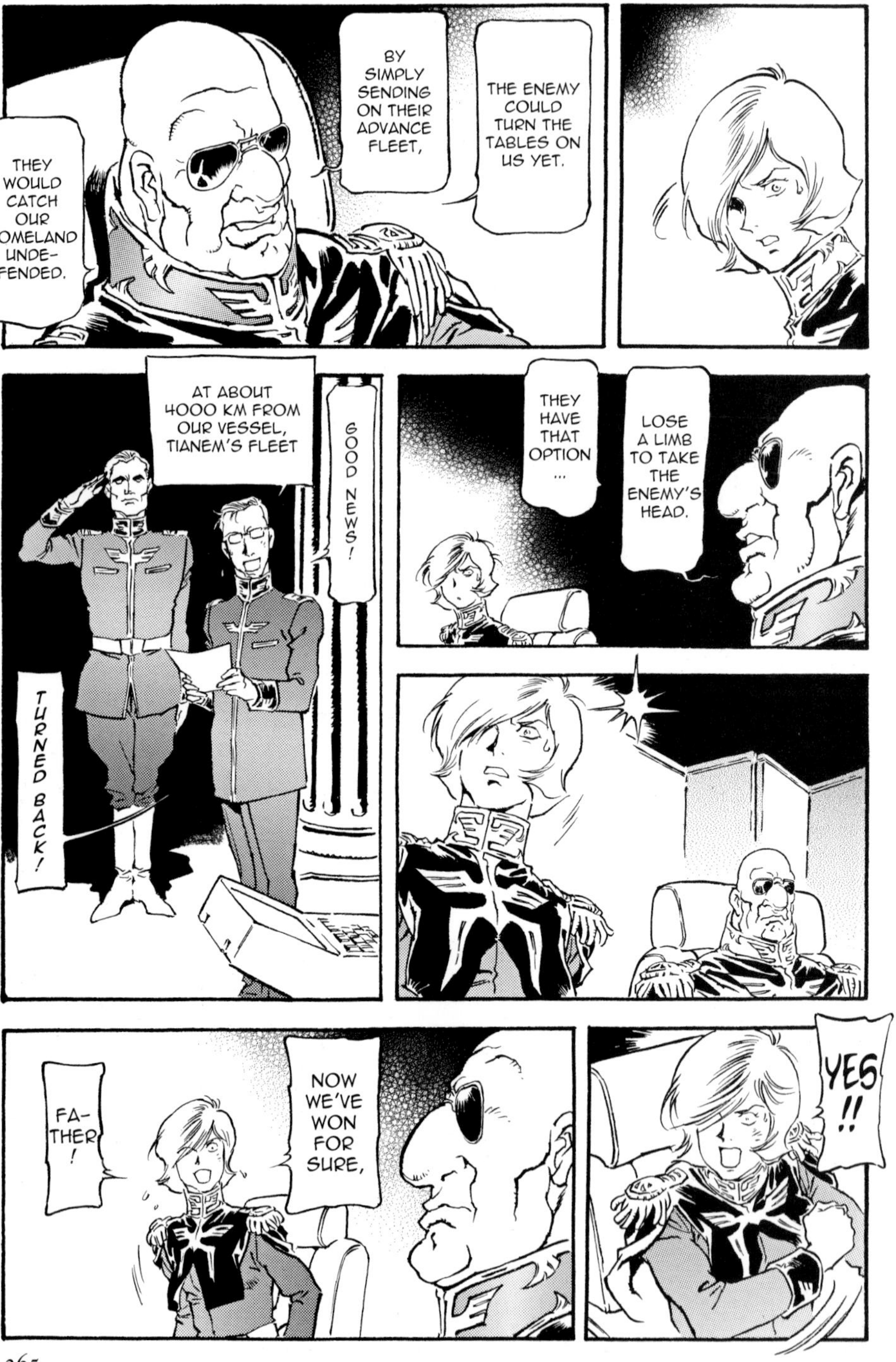
THE ENEMY COULD TURN THE TABLES ON US YET.
BY SIMPLY SENDING ON THEIR ADVANCE FLEET,
THEY WOULD CATCH OUR HOMELAND UNDE-FENDED.
LOSE A LIMB TO TAKE THE ENEMY'S HEAD.
THEY HAVE THAT OPTION ...
GOOD NEWS!
AT ABOUT 4000 KM FROM OUR VESSEL, TIANEM'S FLEET
TURNED BACK!
YES!!
NOW WE'VE WON FOR SURE,
FA-THER!

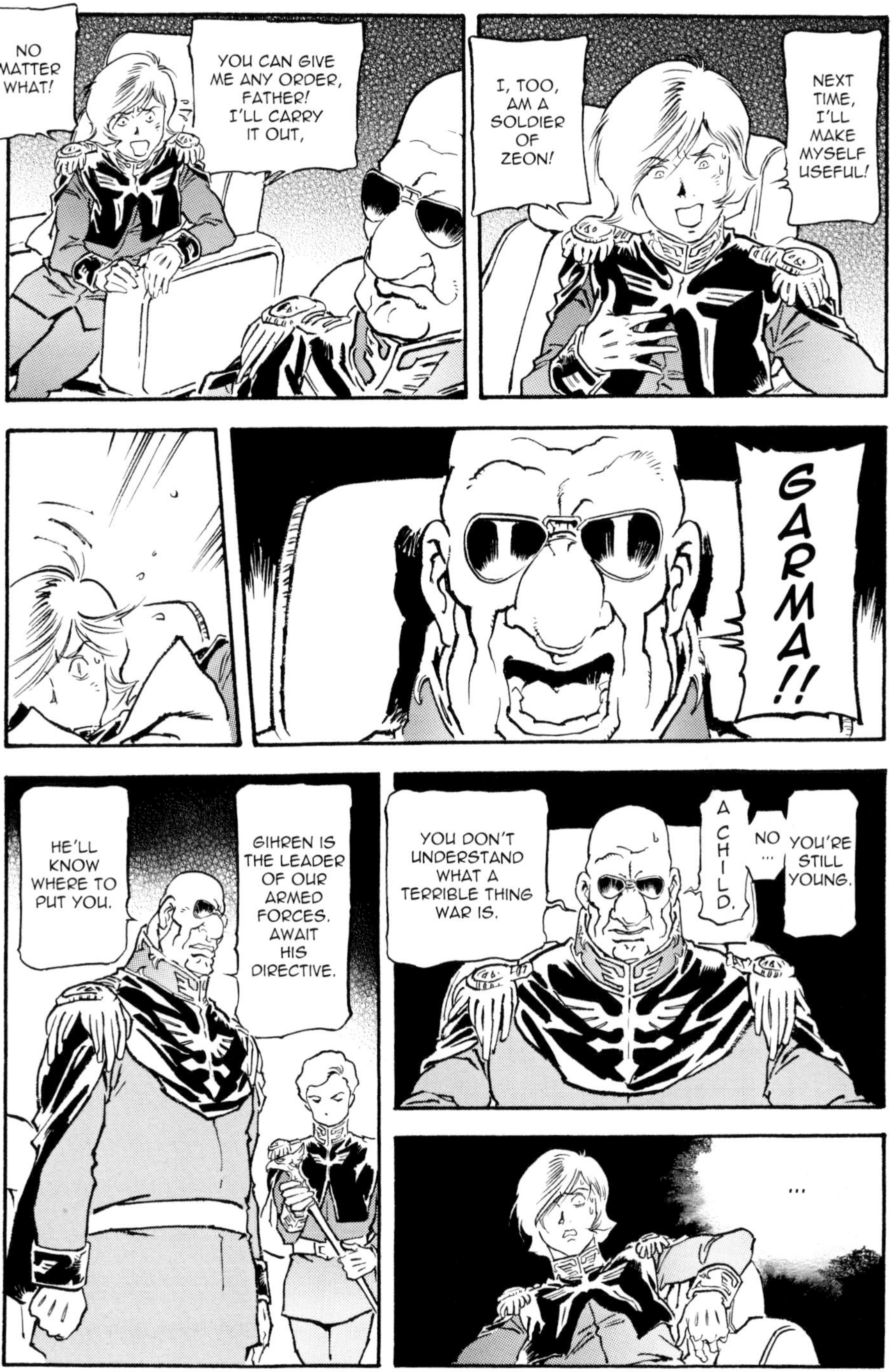
NEXT TIME, I'LL MAKE MYSELF USEFUL!
I, TOO, AM A SOLDIER OF ZEON!
YOU CAN GIVE ME ANY ORDER, FATHER! I'LL CARRY IT OUT,
NO MATTER WHAT!
GARMA!!
YOU'RE STILL YOUNG.
NO...
A CHILD.
YOU DON'T UNDERSTAND WHAT A TERRIBLE THING WAR IS.
...
GIHREN IS THE LEADER OF OUR ARMED FORCES. AWAIT HIS DIRECTIVE.
HE'LL KNOW WHERE TO PUT YOU.

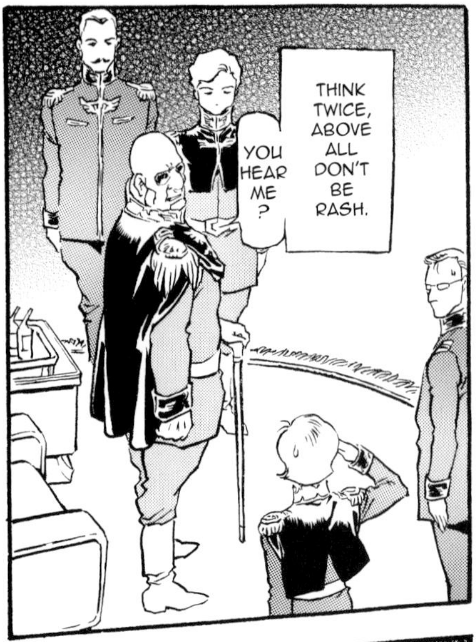
THINK TWICE, ABOVE ALL DON'T BE RASH.
YOU HEAR ME?
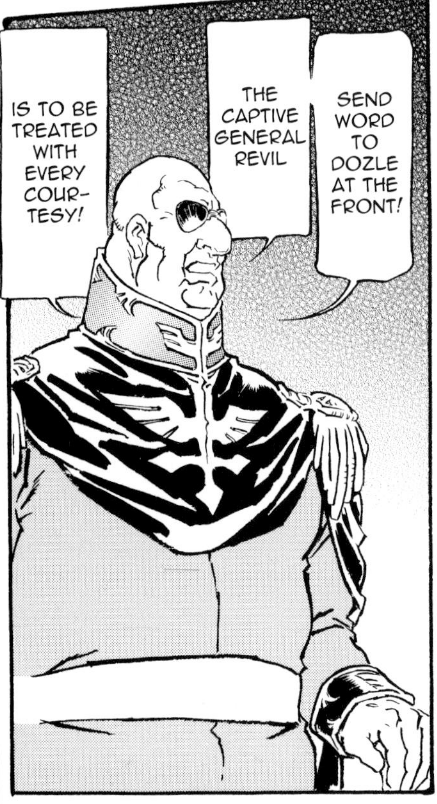
SEND WORD TO DOZLE AT THE FRONT!
THE CAPTIVE GENERAL REVIL
IS TO BE TREATED WITH EVERY COURTESY!
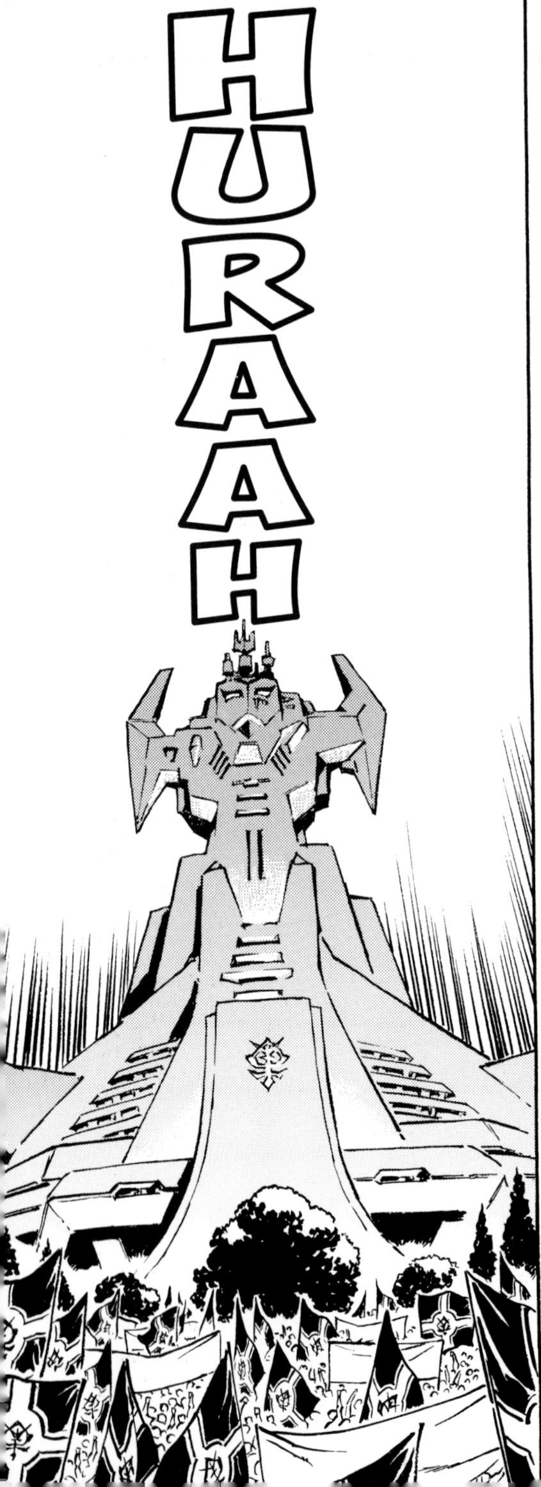
HURRAAH

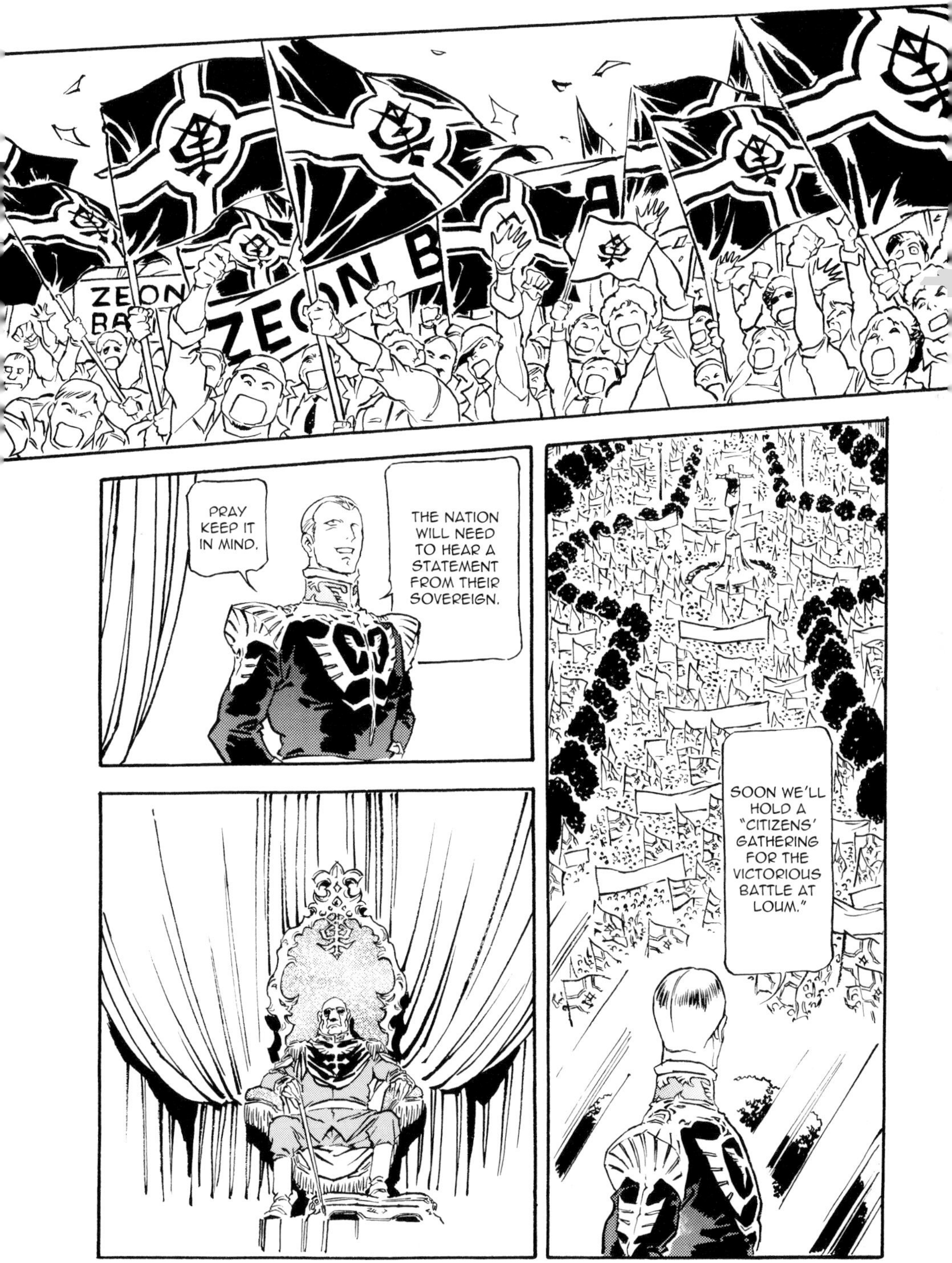
ZEON B
ZEON
SOON WE'LL HOLD A "CITIZENS' GATHERING FOR THE VICTORIOUS BATTLE AT LOUM."
THE NATION WILL NEED TO HEAR A STATEMENT FROM THEIR SOVEREIGN.
PRAY KEEP IT IN MIND.

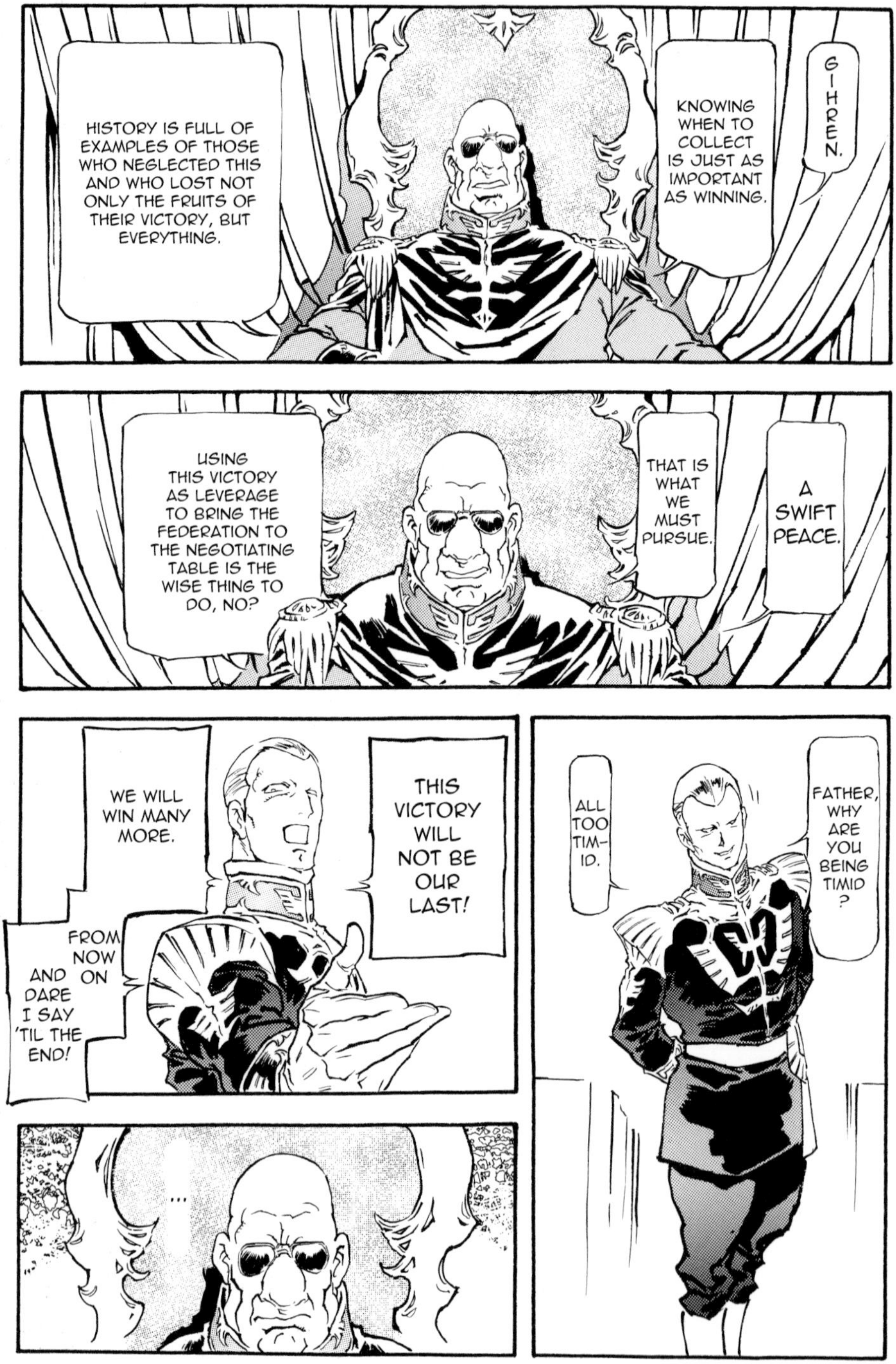
GIHREN.
KNOWING WHEN TO COLLECT IS JUST AS IMPORTANT AS WINNING.
HISTORY IS FULL OF EXAMPLES OF THOSE WHO NEGLECTED THIS AND WHO LOST NOT ONLY THE FRUITS OF THEIR VICTORY, BUT EVERYTHING.
A SWIFT PEACE.
THAT IS WHAT WE MUST PURSUE.
USING THIS VICTORY AS LEVERAGE TO BRING THE FEDERATION TO THE NEGOTIATING TABLE IS THE WISE THING TO DO, NO?
FATHER, WHY ARE YOU BEING TIMID?
ALL TOO TIM-ID.
THIS VICTORY WILL NOT BE OUR LAST!
WE WILL WIN MANY MORE.
FROM NOW ON AND DARE I SAY 'TIL THE END!
...

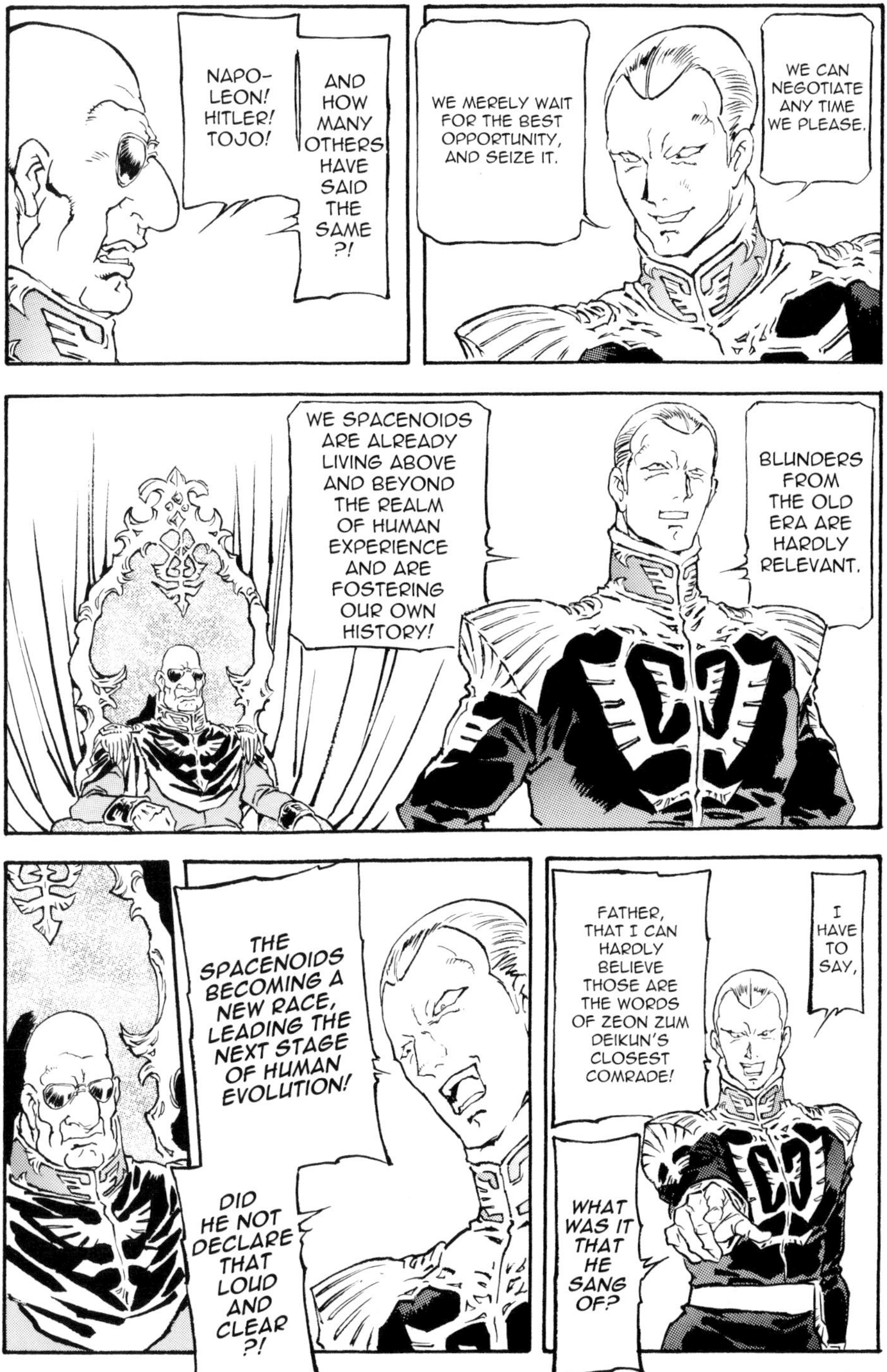
WE CAN NEGOTIATE ANY TIME WE PLEASE.
WE MERELY WAIT FOR THE BEST OPPORTUNITY, AND SEIZE IT.
NAPO-LEON! HITLER! TOJO!
AND HOW MANY OTHERS HAVE SAID THE SAME?!
BLUNDERS FROM THE OLD ERA ARE HARDLY RELEVANT.
WE SPACENOIDS ARE ALREADY LIVING ABOVE AND BEYOND THE REALM OF HUMAN EXPERIENCE AND ARE FOSTERING OUR OWN HISTORY!
I HAVE TO SAY,
FATHER, THAT I CAN HARDLY BELIEVE THOSE ARE THE WORDS OF ZEON ZUM DEIKUN'S CLOSEST COMRADE!
WHAT WAS IT THAT HE SANG OF?
THE SPACENOIDS BECOMING A NEW RACE, LEADING THE NEXT STAGE OF HUMAN EVOLUTION!
DID HE NOT DECLARE THAT LOUD AND CLEAR?!

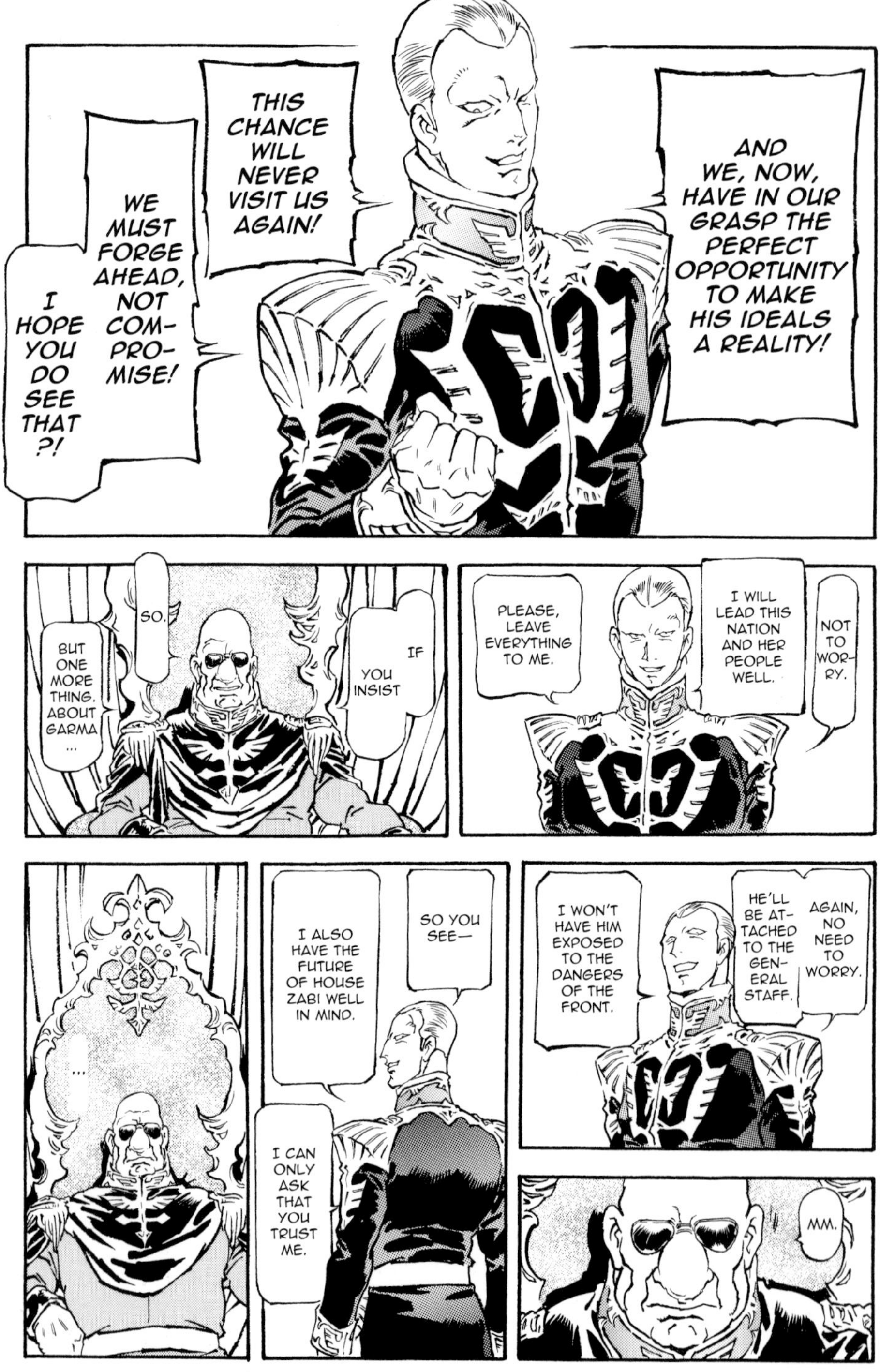
AND WE, NOW, HAVE IN OUR GRASP THE PERFECT OPPORTUNITY TO MAKE HIS IDEALS A REALITY!
THIS CHANCE WILL NEVER VISIT US AGAIN!
WE MUST FORGE AHEAD, NOT COMPROMISE!
I HOPE YOU DO SEE THAT?!
NOT TO WORRY.
I WILL LEAD THIS NATION AND HER PEOPLE WELL.
PLEASE, LEAVE EVERYTHING TO ME.
IF YOU INSIST
SO.
BUT ONE MORE THING. ABOUT GARMA ...
AGAIN, NO NEED TO WORRY.
HE'LL BE ATTACHED TO THE GENERAL STAFF.
I WON'T HAVE HIM EXPOSED TO THE DANGERS OF THE FRONT.
MM.
SO YOU SEE—
I ALSO HAVE THE FUTURE OF HOUSE ZABI WELL IN MIND.
I CAN ONLY ASK THAT YOU TRUST ME.
...

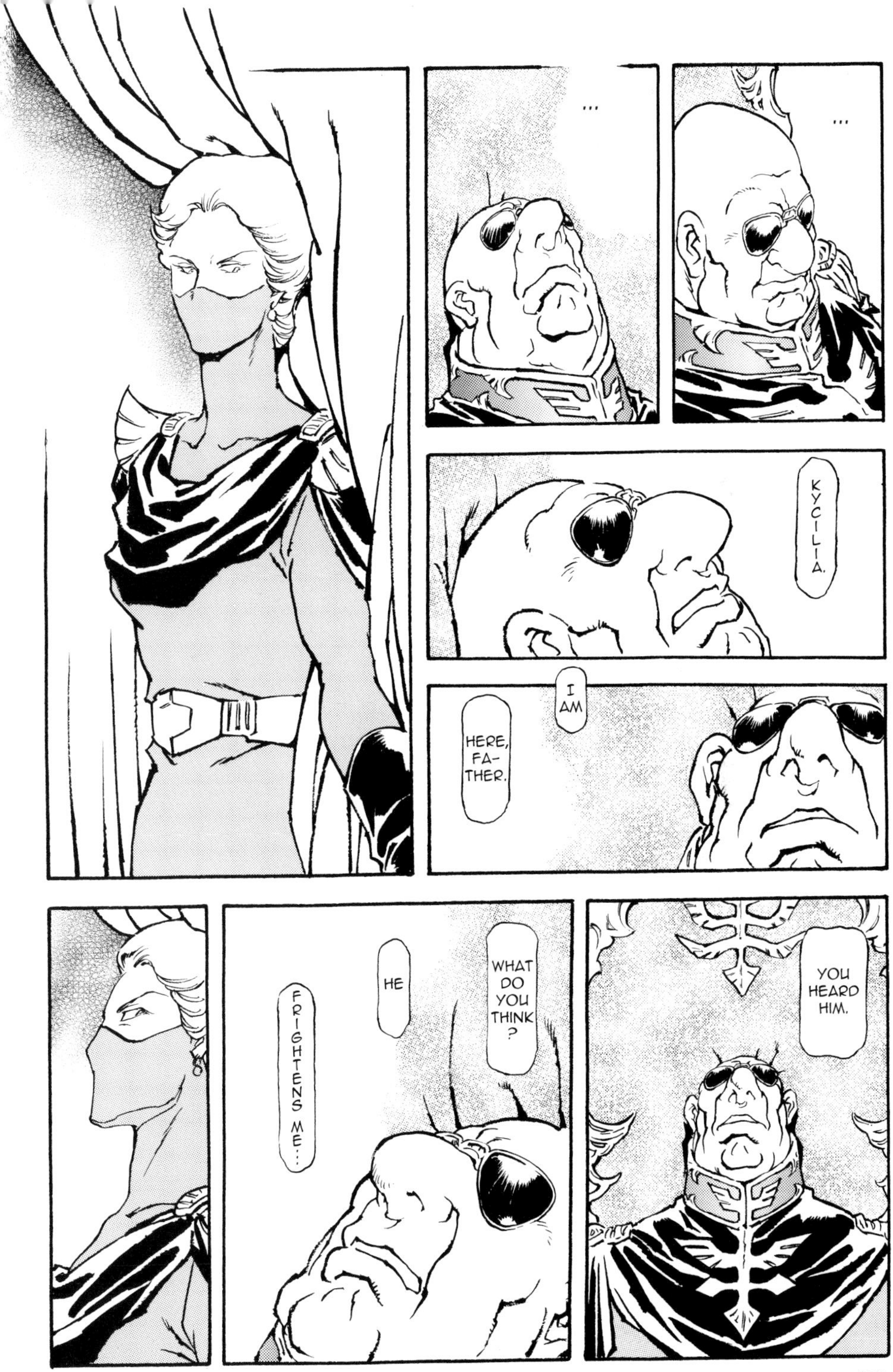
...
...
KYCILIA.
I AM HERE, FATHER.
YOU HEARD HIM.
WHAT DO YOU THINK?
HE FRIGHTENS ME...

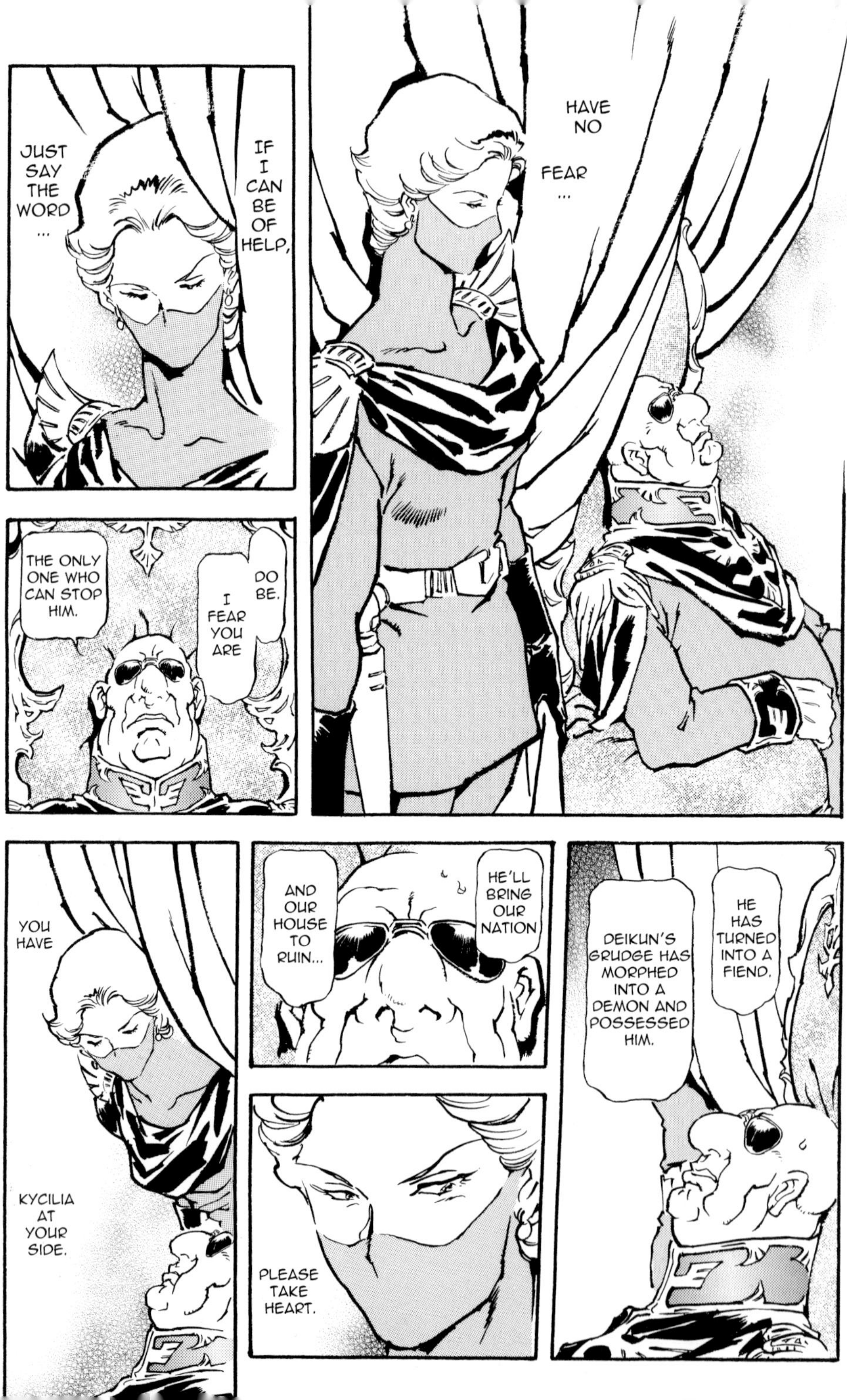

HAVE NO FEAR ...
IF I CAN BE OF HELP,
JUST SAY THE WORD ...
DO BE.
I FEAR YOU ARE
THE ONLY ONE WHO CAN STOP HIM.
HE HAS TURNED INTO A FIEND.
DEIKUN'S GRUDGE HAS MORPHED INTO A DEMON AND POSSESSED HIM.
HE'LL BRING OUR NATION
AND OUR HOUSE TO RUIN...
PLEASE TAKE HEART.
YOU HAVE
KYCILIA AT YOUR SIDE.

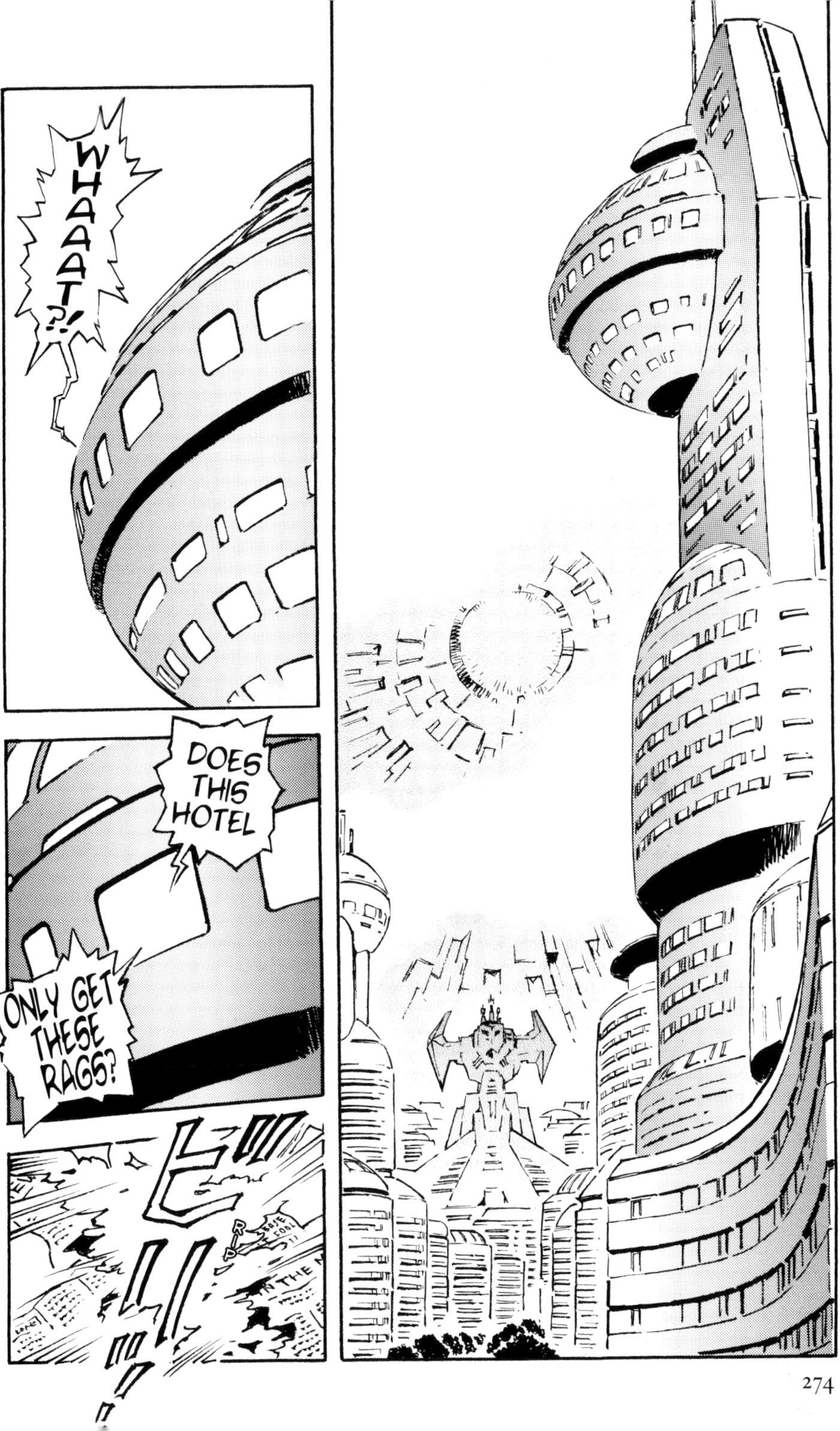
WHAAAT?!
DOES THIS HOTEL
ONLY GET THESE RAGS?
RIP

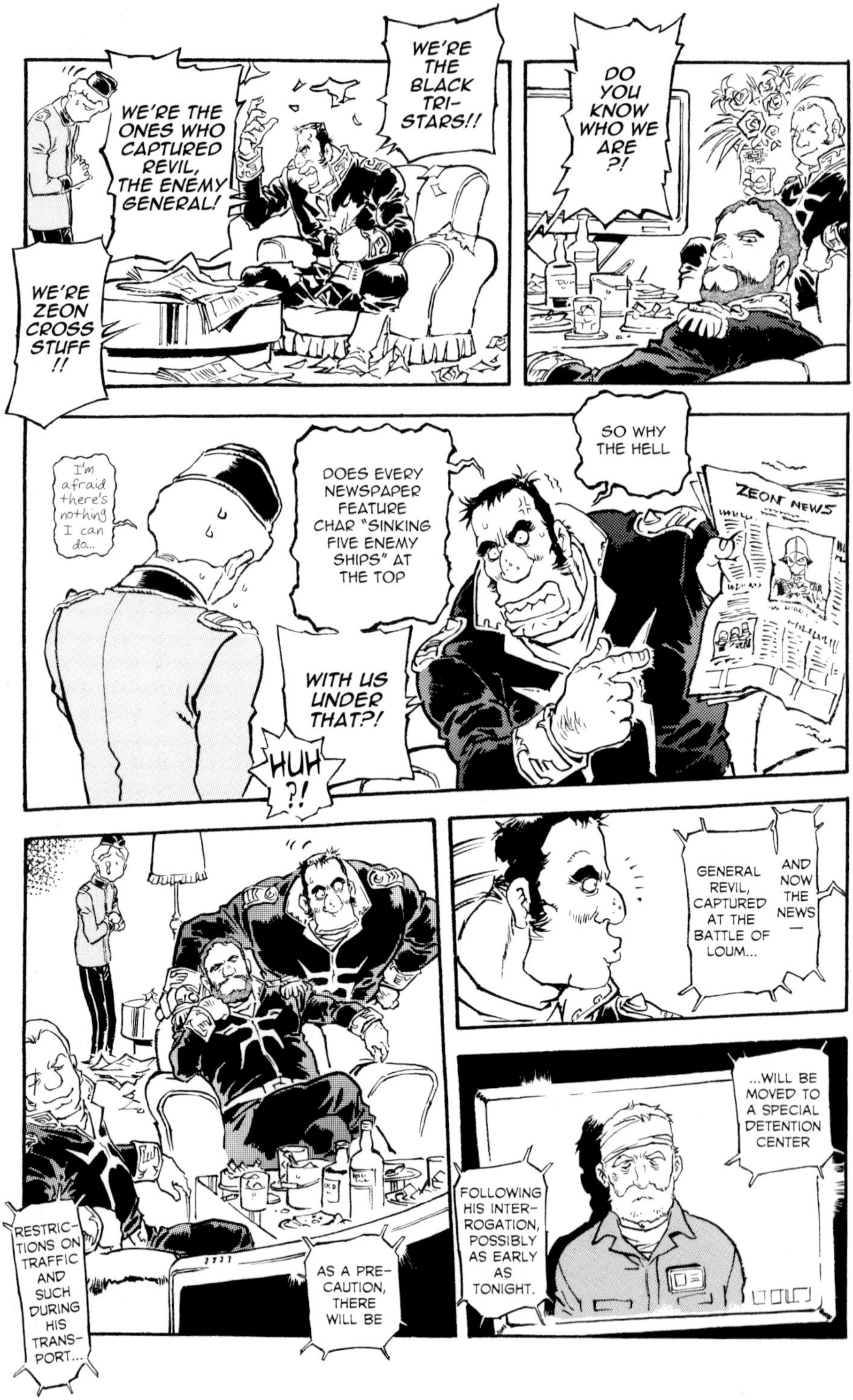
DO YOU KNOW WHO WE ARE?!
WE'RE THE BLACK TRI-STARS!!
WE'RE THE ONES WHO CAPTURED REVIL, THE ENEMY GENERAL!
WE'RE ZEON CROSS STUFF!!
SO WHY THE HELL
ZEON NEWS
DOES EVERY NEWSPAPER FEATURE CHAR "SINKING FIVE ENEMY SHIPS" AT THE TOP
WITH US UNDER THAT?!
HUH?!
I'm afraid there's nothing I can do...
AND NOW THE NEWS—
GENERAL REVIL, CAPTURED AT THE BATTLE OF LOUM...
...WILL BE MOVED TO A SPECIAL DETENTION CENTER
FOLLOWING HIS INTERROGATION, POSSIBLY AS EARLY AS TONIGHT.
AS A PRECAUTION, THERE WILL BE
RESTRICTIONS ON TRAFFIC AND SUCH DURING HIS TRANSPORT...

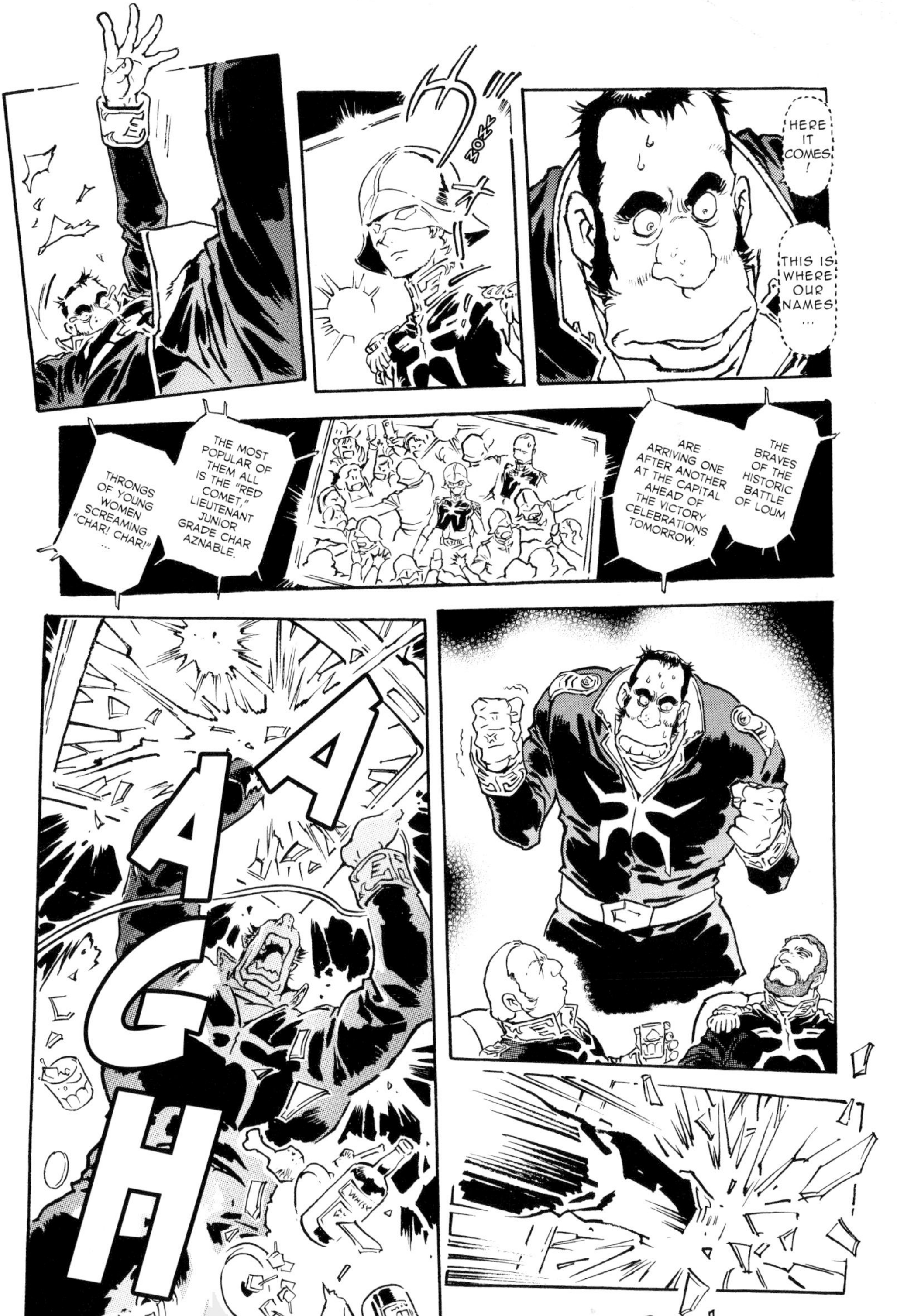
HERE IT COMES!
THIS IS WHERE OUR NAMES...
THE BRAVES OF THE HISTORIC BATTLE OF LOUM
ARE ARRIVING ONE AFTER ANOTHER AT THE CAPITAL AHEAD OF THE VICTORY CELEBRATIONS TOMORROW.
THE MOST POPULAR OF THEM ALL IS THE "RED COMET," LIEUTENANT JUNIOR GRADE CHAR AZNABLE.
THRONGS OF YOUNG WOMEN SCREAMING "CHAR! CHAR!"...
AAGH

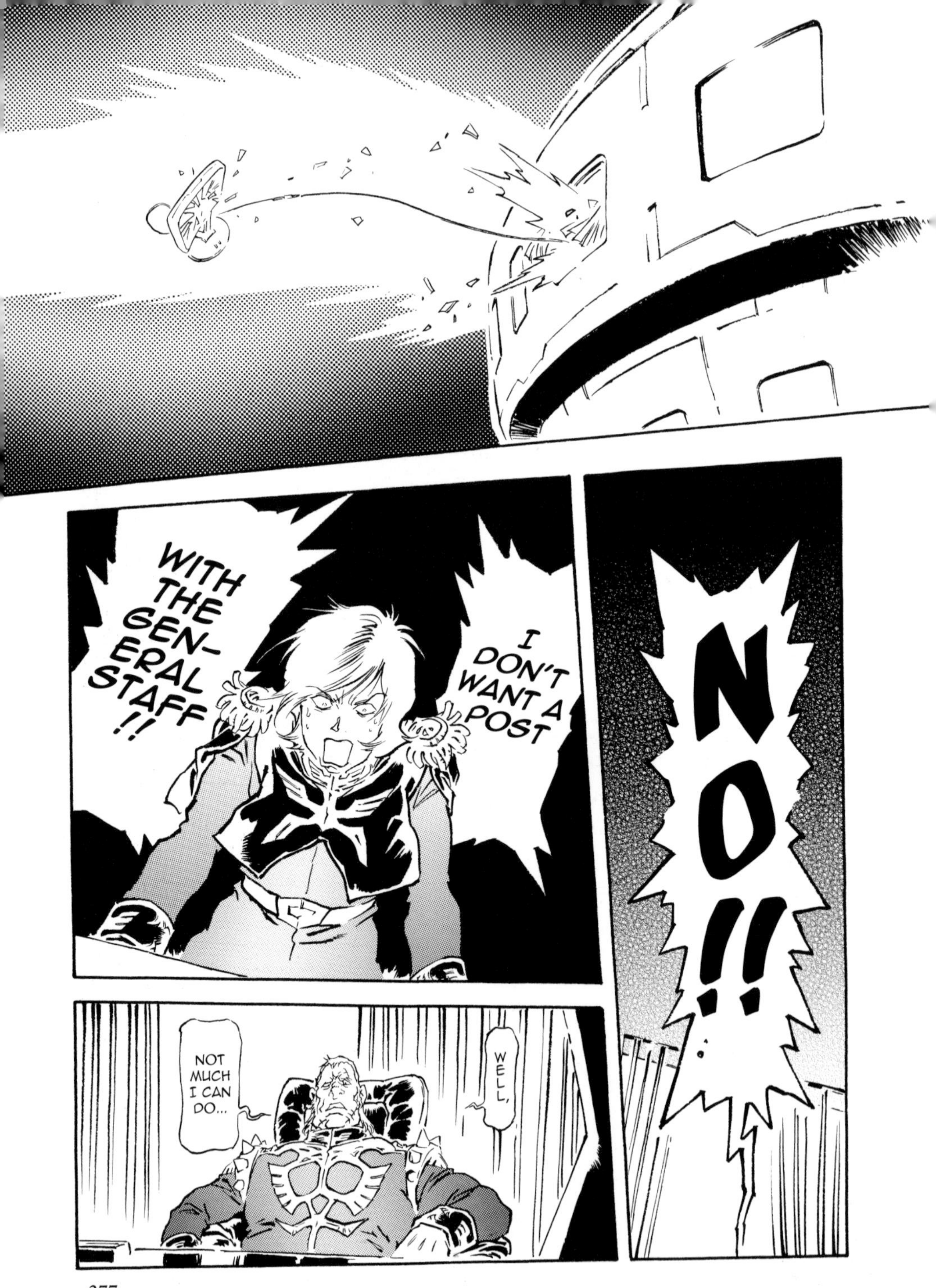
NO!!
I DON'T WANT A POST
WITH THE GEN-ERAL STAFF!!
WELL,
NOT MUCH I CAN DO...

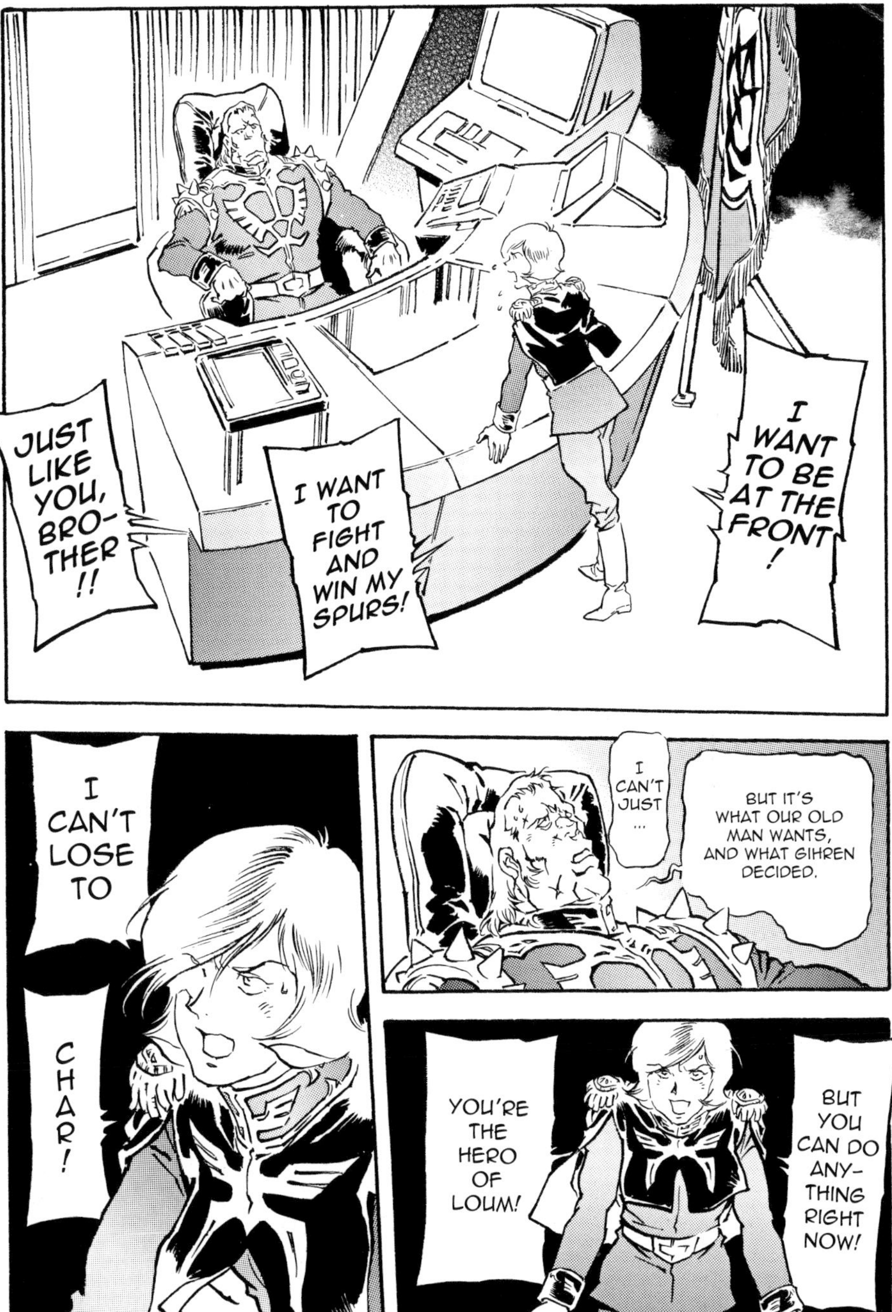

I WANT TO BE AT THE FRONT!
I WANT TO FIGHT AND WIN MY SPURS!
JUST LIKE YOU, BRO-THER!!
BUT IT'S WHAT OUR OLD MAN WANTS, AND WHAT GIHREN DECIDED.
I CAN'T JUST ...
BUT YOU CAN DO ANY-THING RIGHT NOW!
YOU'RE THE HERO OF LOUM!
I CAN'T LOSE TO
CHAR!

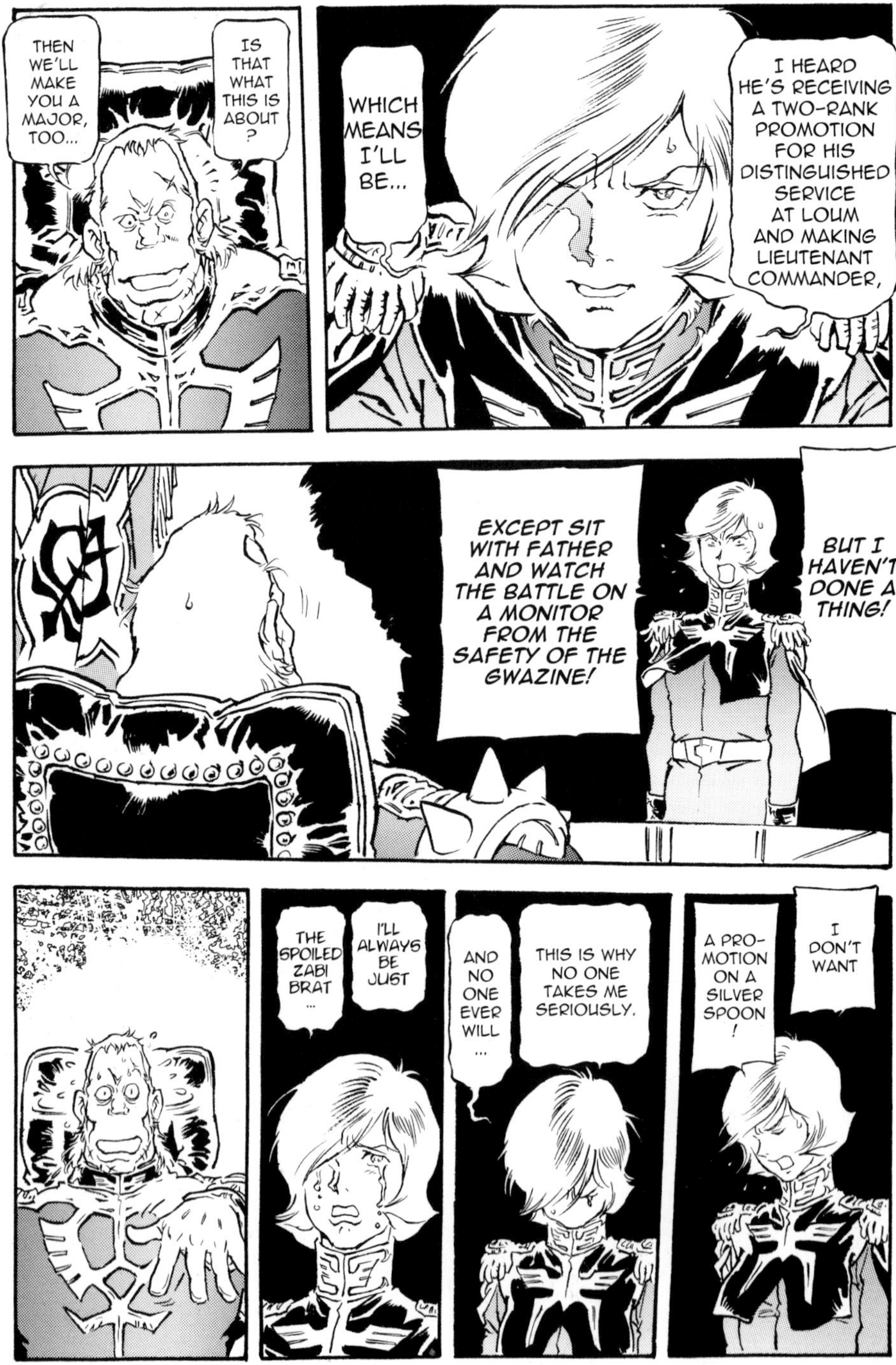
I HEARD HE'S RECEIVING A TWO-RANK PROMOTION FOR HIS DISTINGUISHED SERVICE AT LOUM AND MAKING LIEUTENANT COMMANDER,
WHICH MEANS I'LL BE...
IS THAT WHAT THIS IS ABOUT?
THEN WE'LL MAKE YOU A MAJOR, TOO...
BUT I HAVEN'T DONE A THING!
EXCEPT SIT WITH FATHER AND WATCH THE BATTLE ON A MONITOR FROM THE SAFETY OF THE GWAZINE!
I DON'T WANT
A PROMOTION ON A SILVER SPOON!
THIS IS WHY NO ONE TAKES ME SERIOUSLY.
AND NO ONE EVER WILL...
I'LL ALWAYS BE JUST
THE SPOILED ZABI BRAT...

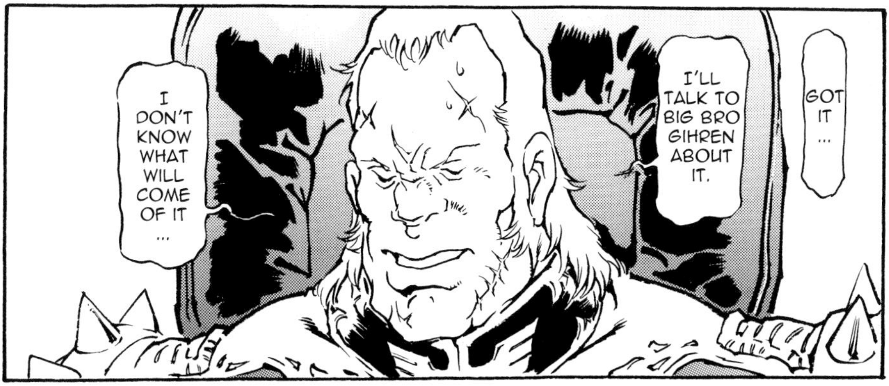
GOT IT ...
I'LL TALK TO BIG BRO GIHREN ABOUT IT.
I DON'T KNOW WHAT WILL COME OF IT ...
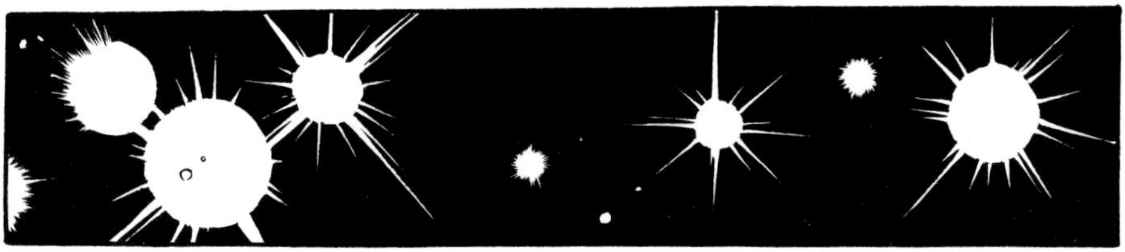
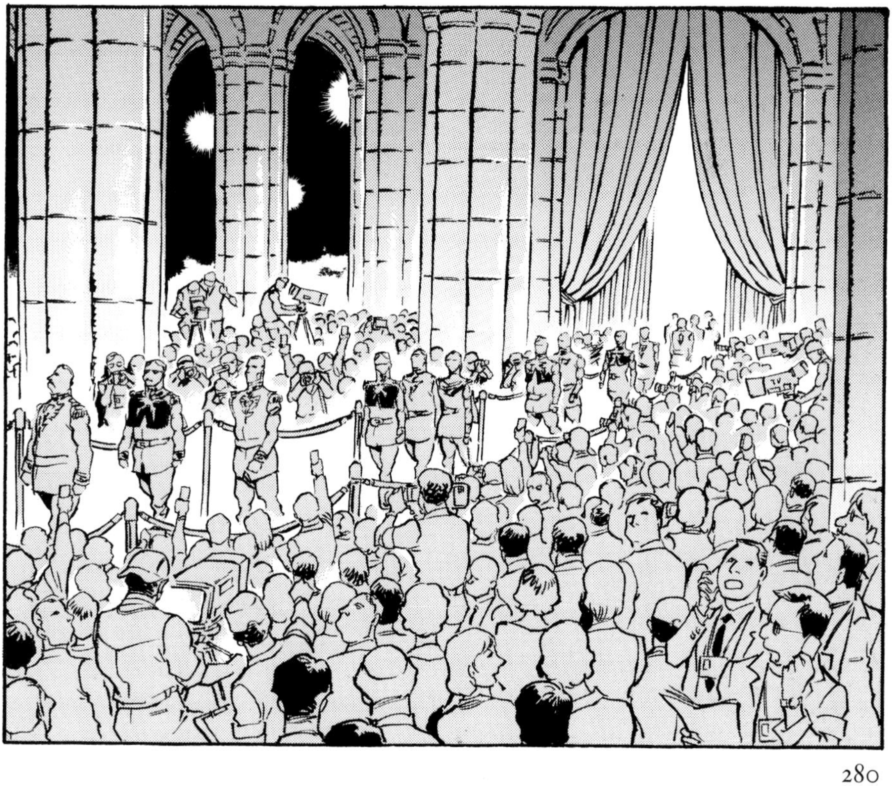

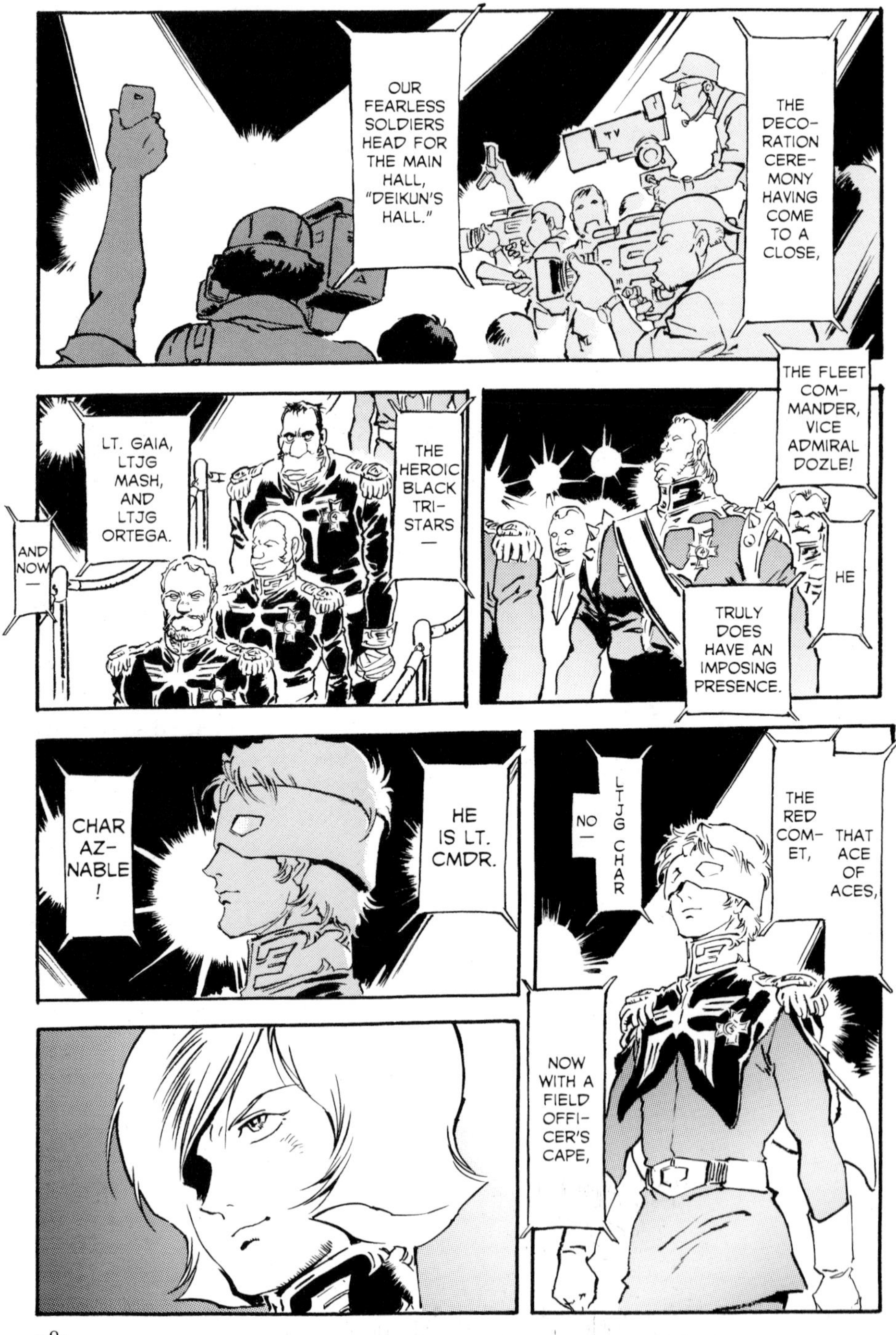
THE DECORATION CEREMONY HAVING COME TO A CLOSE,
OUR FEARLESS SOLDIERS HEAD FOR THE MAIN HALL, "DEIKUN'S HALL."
THE FLEET COMMANDER, VICE ADMIRAL DOZLE!
HE
TRULY DOES HAVE AN IMPOSING PRESENCE.
THE HEROIC BLACK TRI-STARS—
LT. GAIA, LTJG MASH, AND LTJG ORTEGA.
AND NOW—
THE RED COMET,
THAT ACE OF ACES,
NOW WITH A FIELD OFFICER'S CAPE,
LTJG CHAR
NO—
HE IS LT. CMDR.
CHAR AZNABLE!

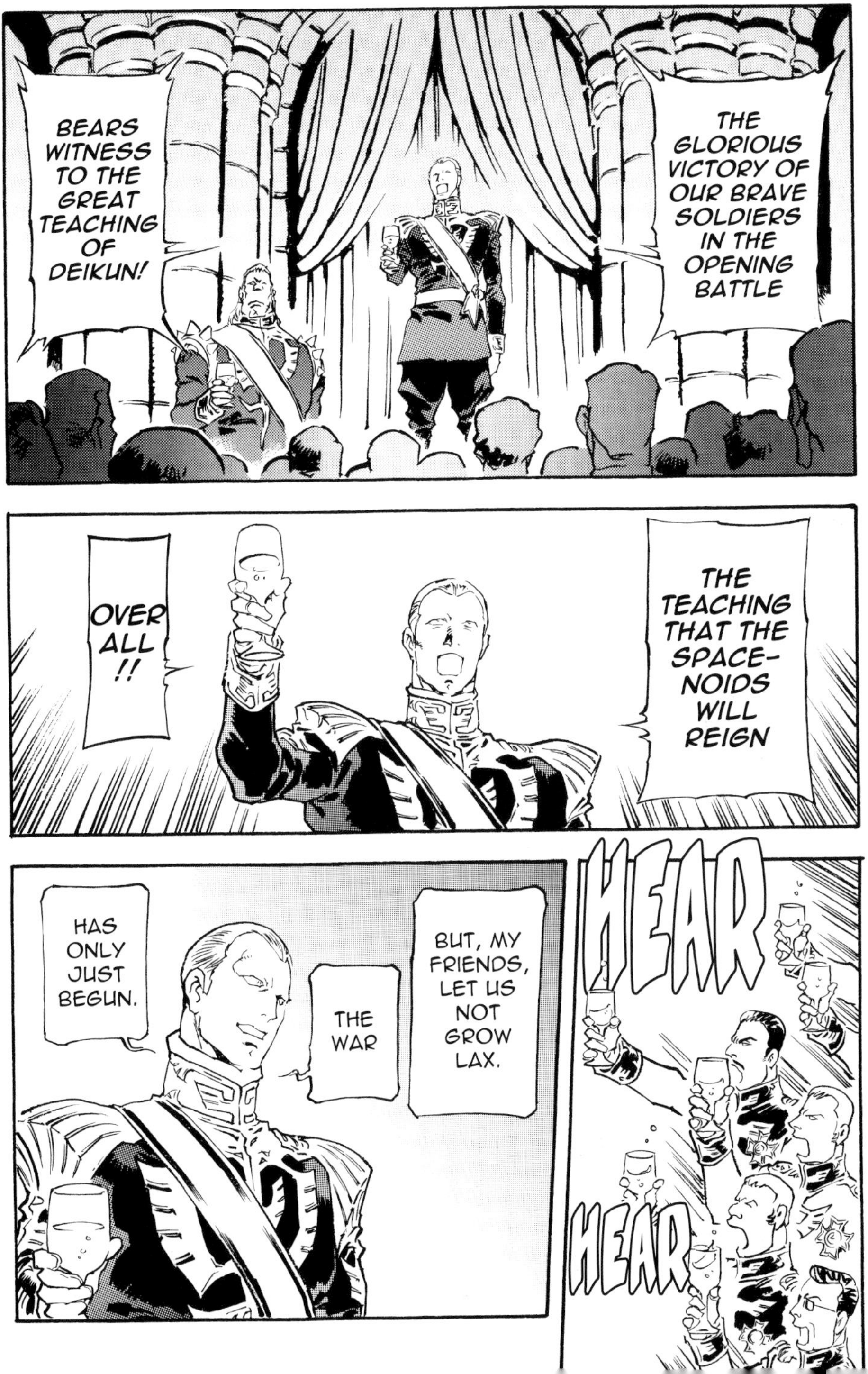
THE GLORIOUS VICTORY OF OUR BRAVE SOLDIERS IN THE OPENING BATTLE
BEARS WITNESS TO THE GREAT TEACHING OF DEIKUN!
THE TEACHING THAT THE SPACE-NOIDS WILL REIGN
OVER ALL !!
HEAR
HEAR
BUT, MY FRIENDS, LET US NOT GROW LAX.
THE WAR
HAS ONLY JUST BEGUN.

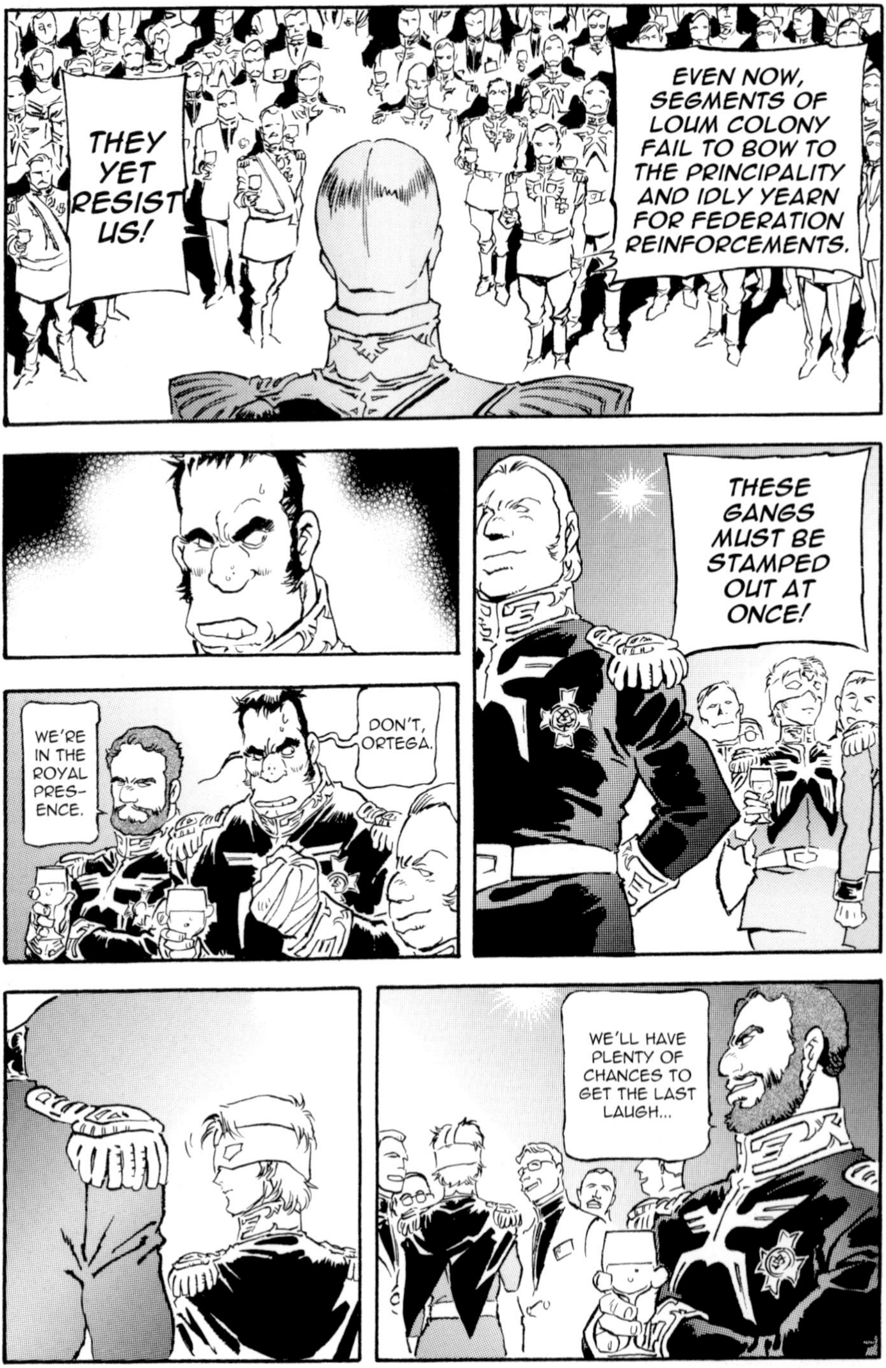
EVEN NOW, SEGMENTS OF LOUM COLONY FAIL TO BOW TO THE PRINCIPALITY AND IDLY YEARN FOR FEDERATION REINFORCEMENTS.
THEY YET RESIST US!
THESE GANGS MUST BE STAMPED OUT AT ONCE!
DON'T, ORTEGA.
WE'RE IN THE ROYAL PRESENCE.
WE'LL HAVE PLENTY OF CHANCES TO GET THE LAST LAUGH...

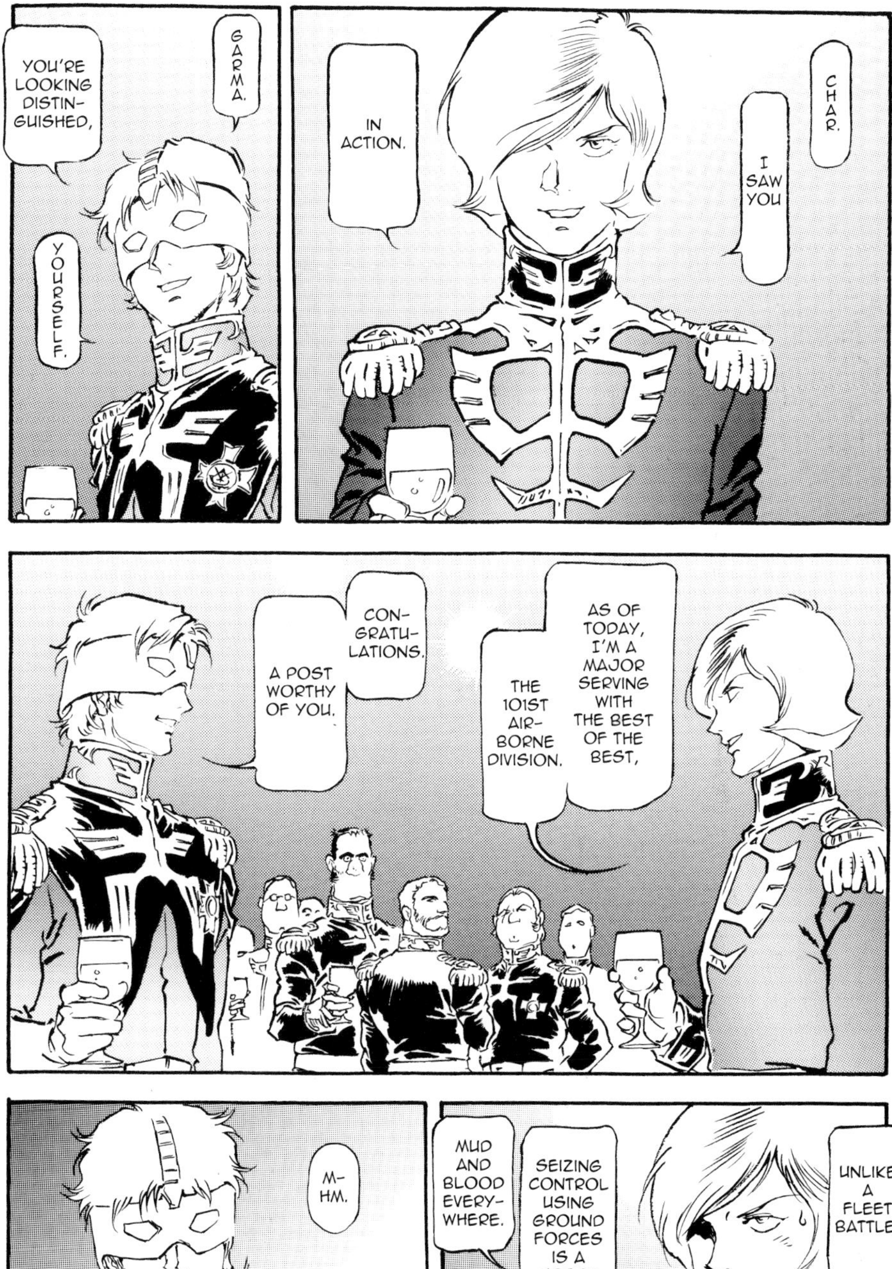
CHAR.
I SAW YOU
IN ACTION.
GARMA.
YOU'RE LOOKING DISTIN-GUISHED,
YOURSELF.
AS OF TODAY, I'M A MAJOR SERVING WITH THE BEST OF THE BEST,
THE 101ST AIR-BORNE DIVISION.
CON-GRATU-LATIONS.
A POST WORTHY OF YOU.
UNLIKE A FLEET BATTLE,
SEIZING CONTROL USING GROUND FORCES IS A MESSY AFFAIR.
MUD AND BLOOD EVERY-WHERE.
M-HM.

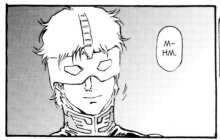

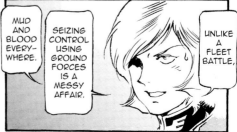

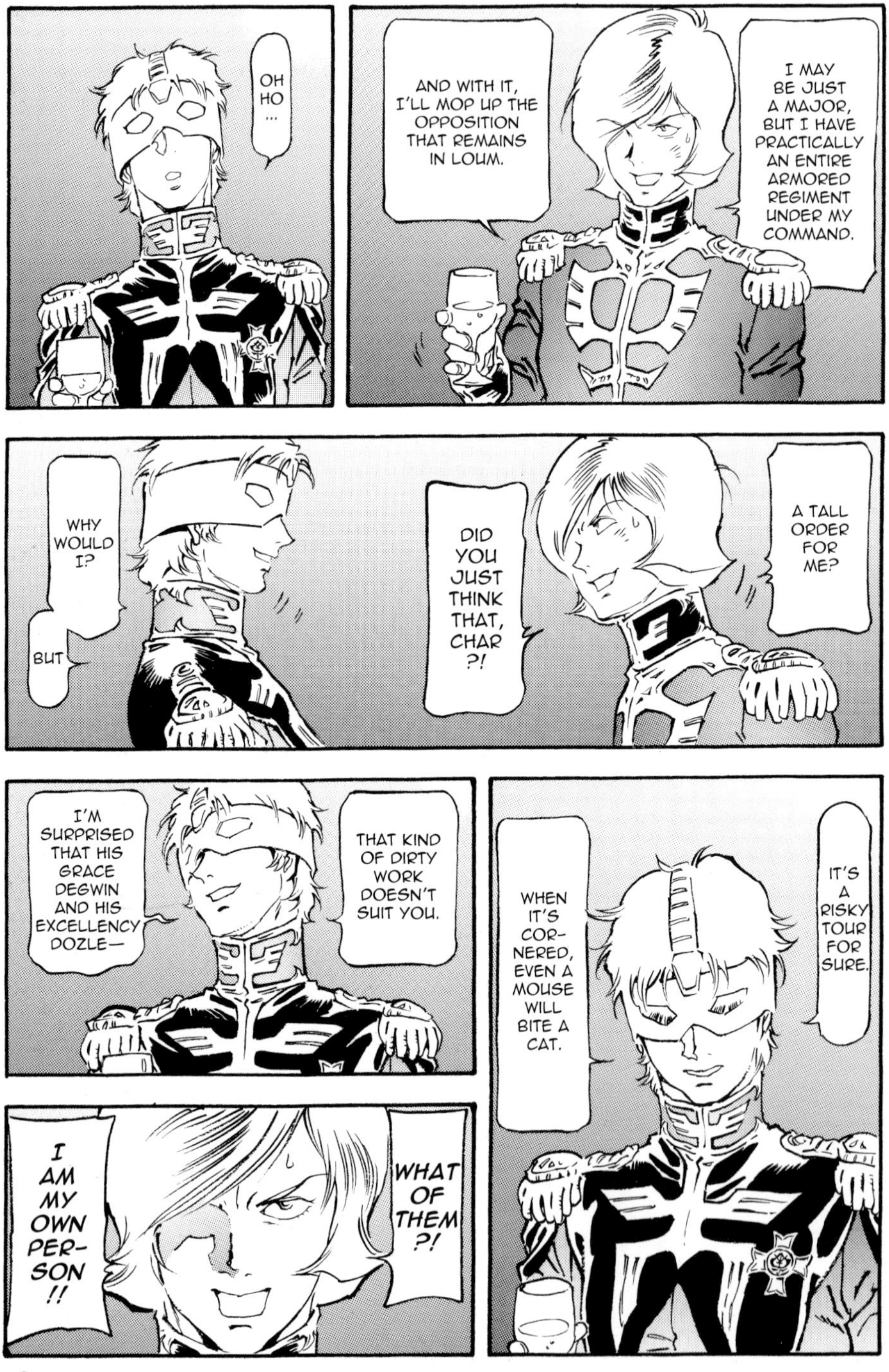
I MAY BE JUST A MAJOR, BUT I HAVE PRACTICALLY AN ENTIRE ARMORED REGIMENT UNDER MY COMMAND.
AND WITH IT, I'LL MOP UP THE OPPOSITION THAT REMAINS IN LOUM.
OH HO ...
A TALL ORDER FOR ME?
DID YOU JUST THINK THAT, CHAR ?!
WHY WOULD I?
BUT
IT'S A RISKY TOUR FOR SURE.
WHEN IT'S COR-NERED, EVEN A MOUSE WILL BITE A CAT.
THAT KIND OF DIRTY WORK DOESN'T SUIT YOU.
I'M SURPRISED THAT HIS GRACE DEGWIN AND HIS EXCELLENCY DOZLE—
WHAT OF THEM ?!
I AM MY OWN PER-SON !!

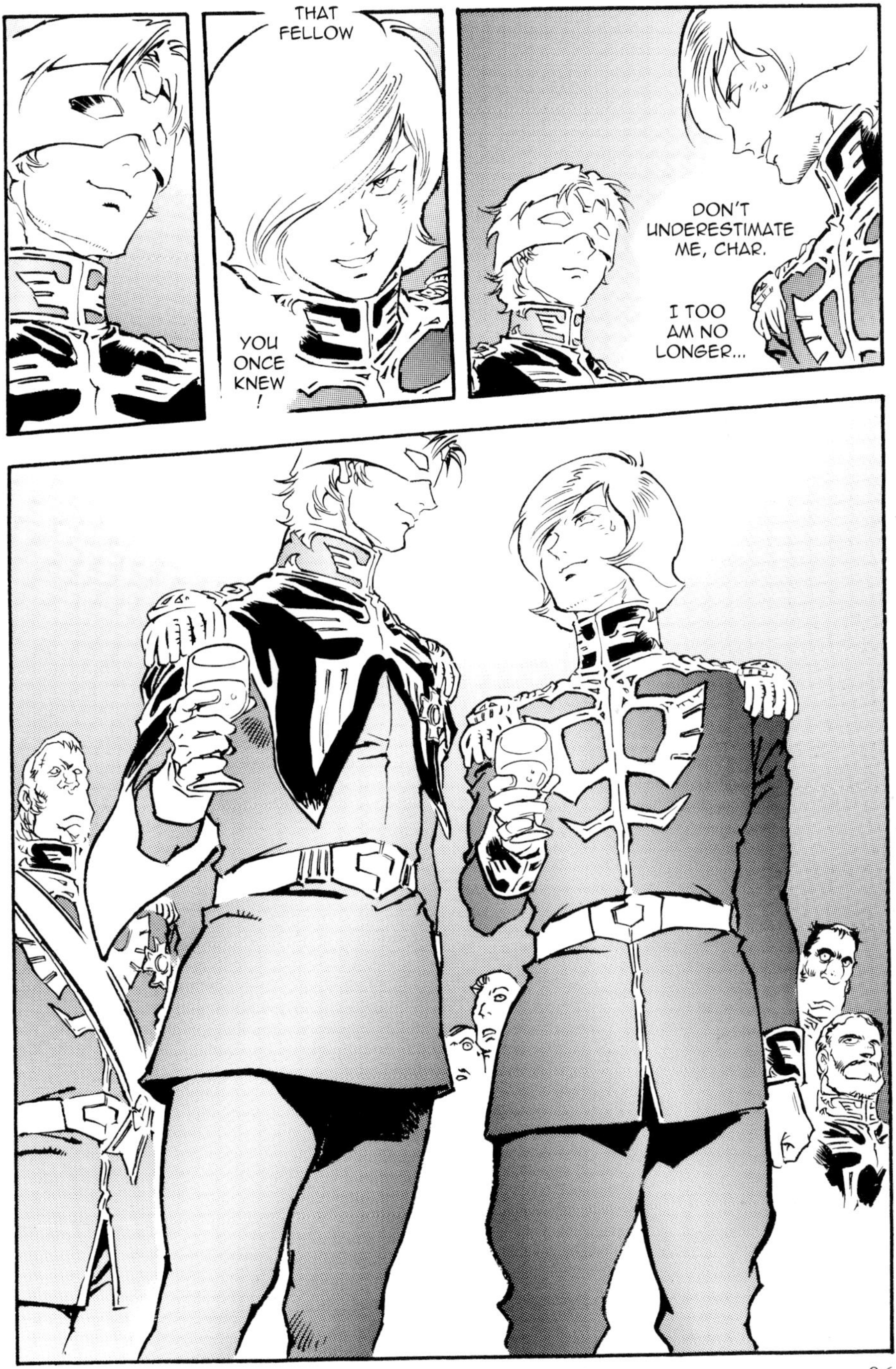
DON'T UNDERESTIMATE ME, CHAR.
I TOO AM NO LONGER...
THAT FELLOW
YOU ONCE KNEW!

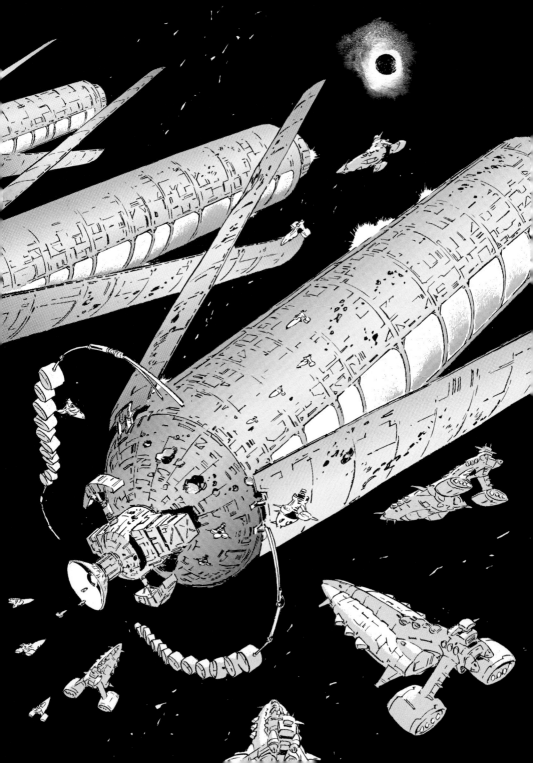

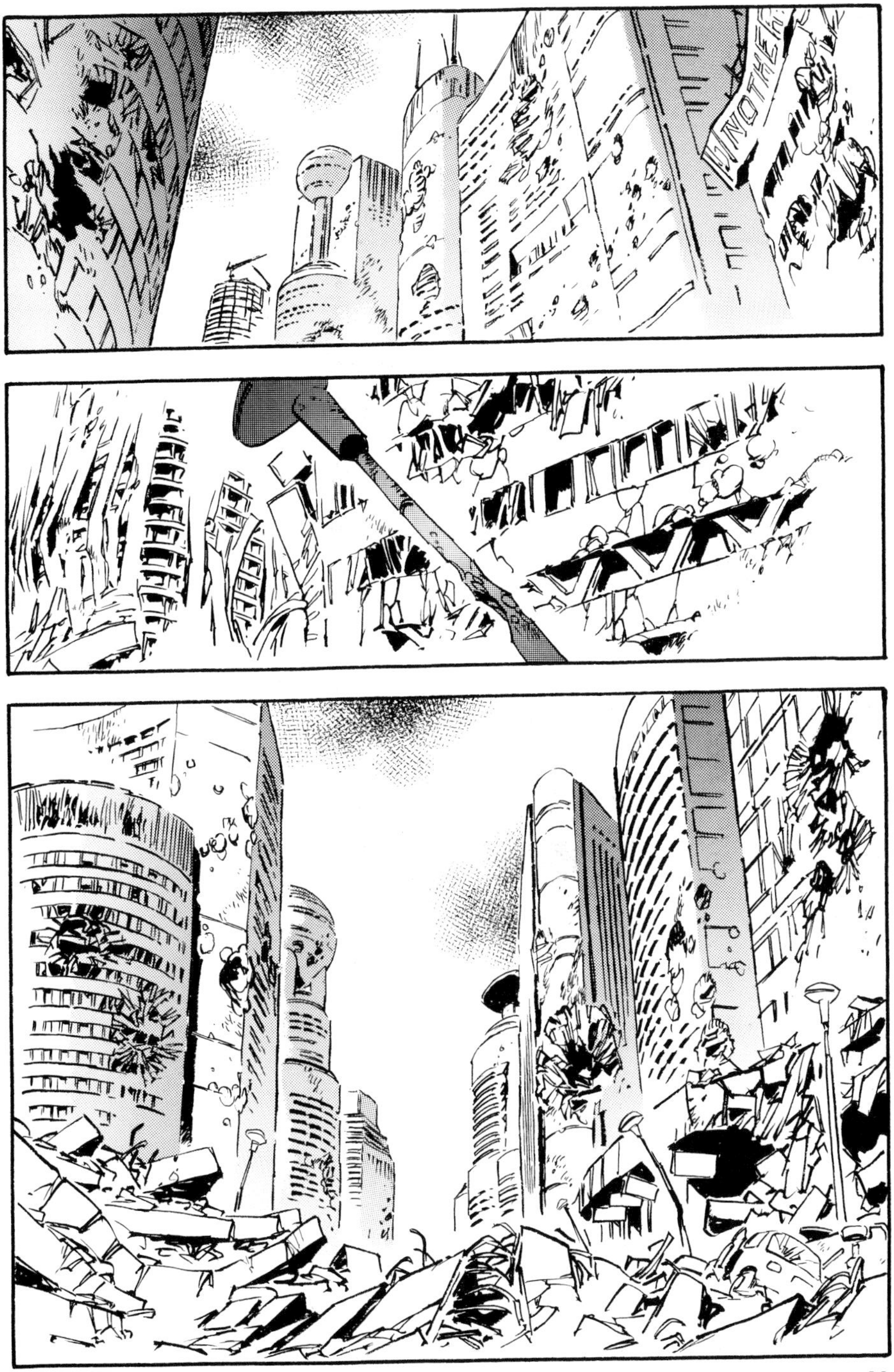

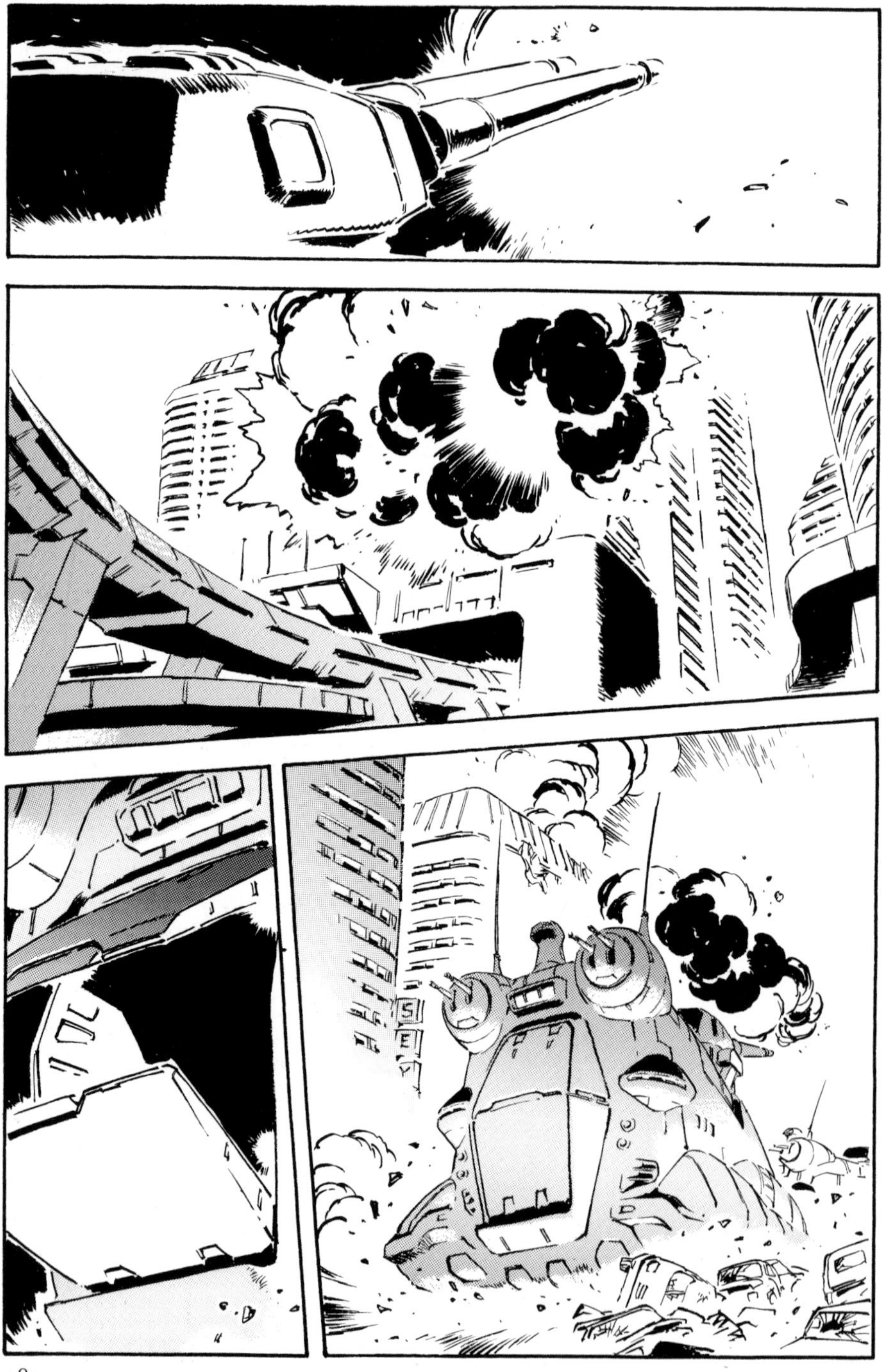
SEY

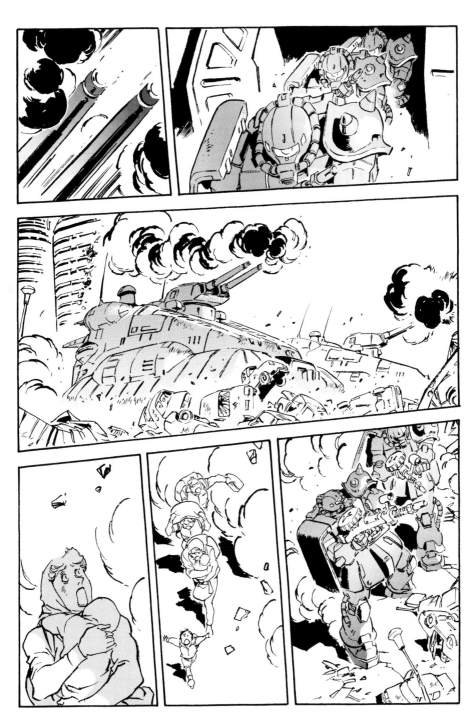

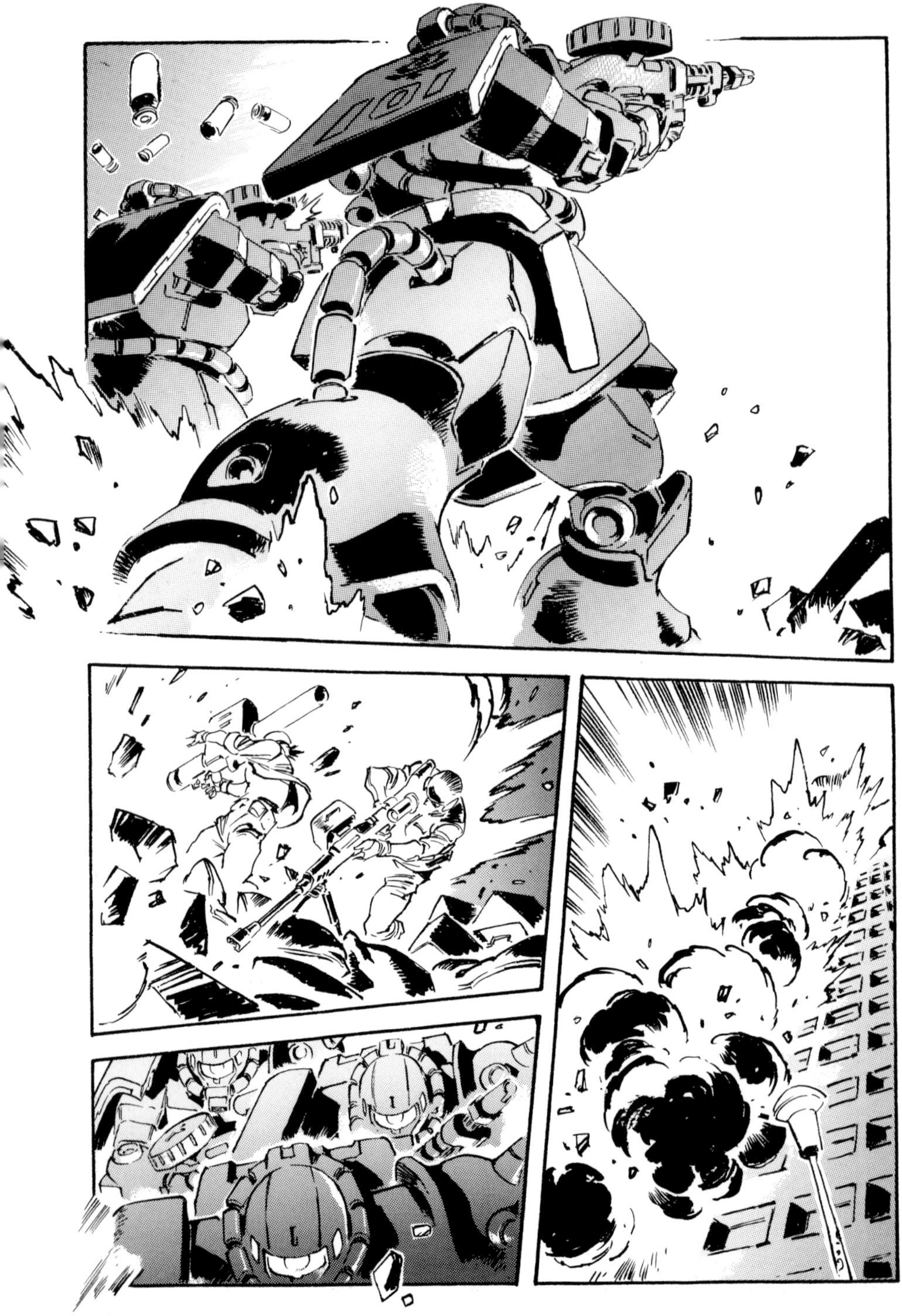

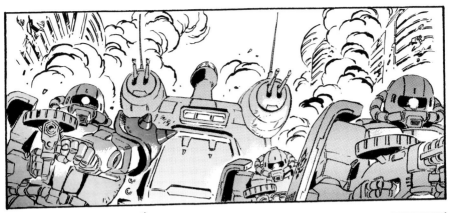

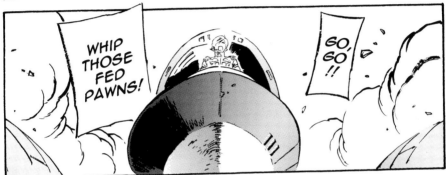

WHIP THOSE FED PAWNS!

GO, GO !!

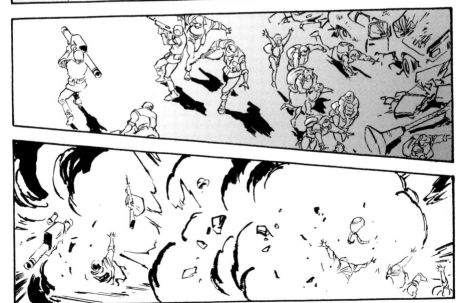

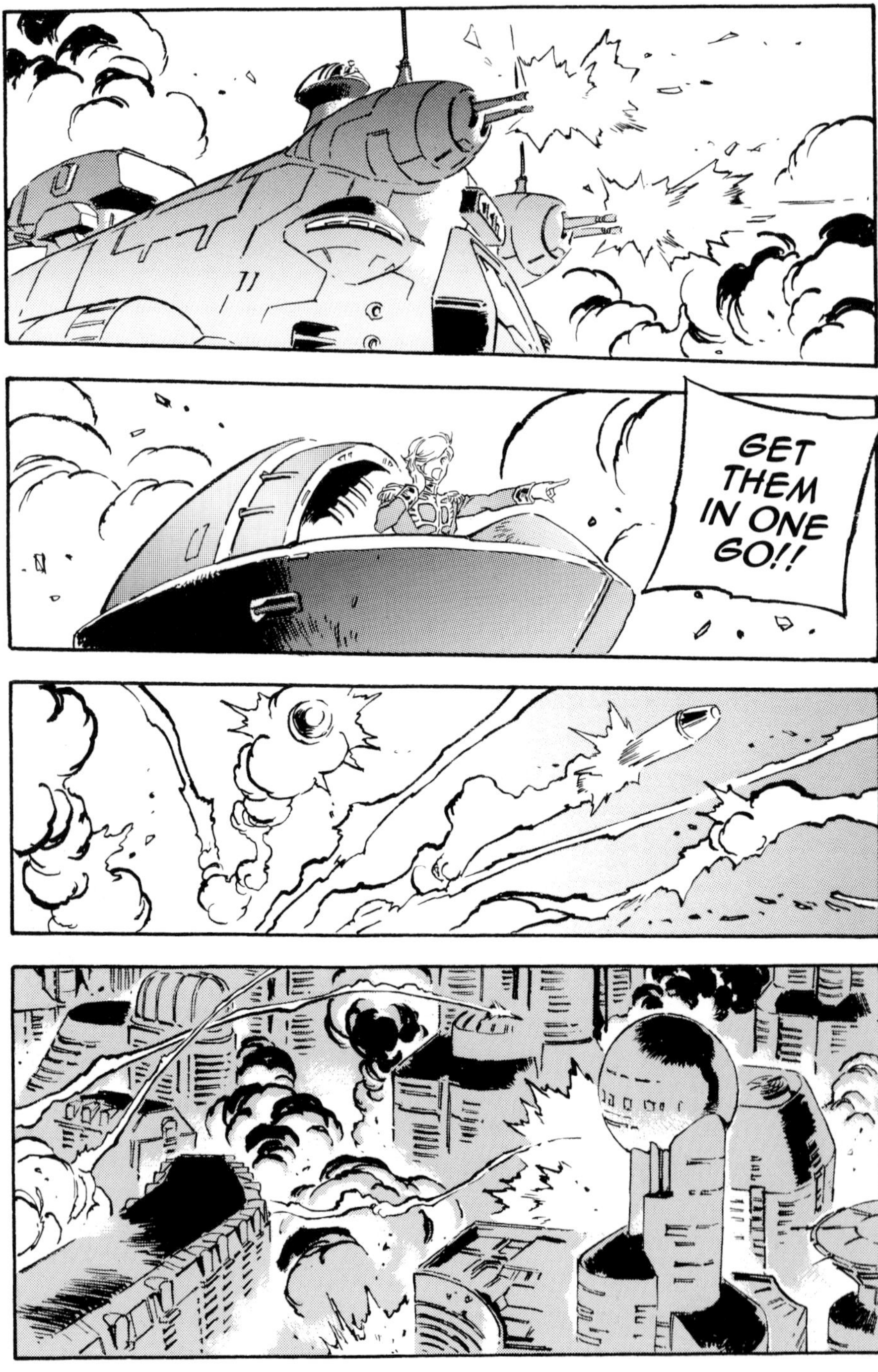
GET THEM IN ONE GO!!

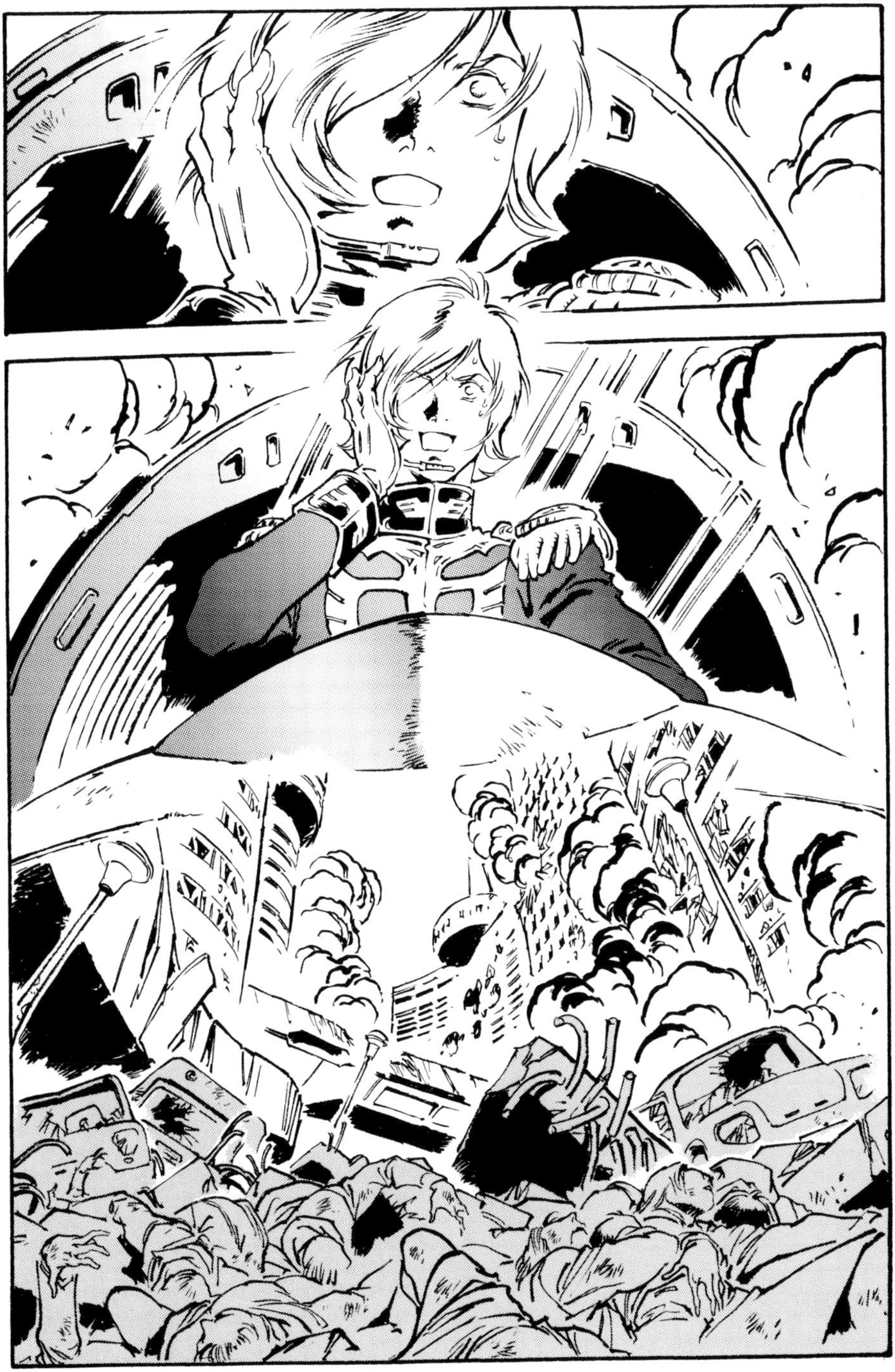

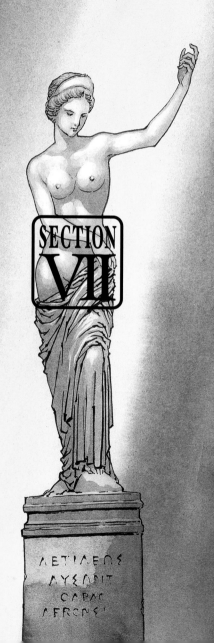

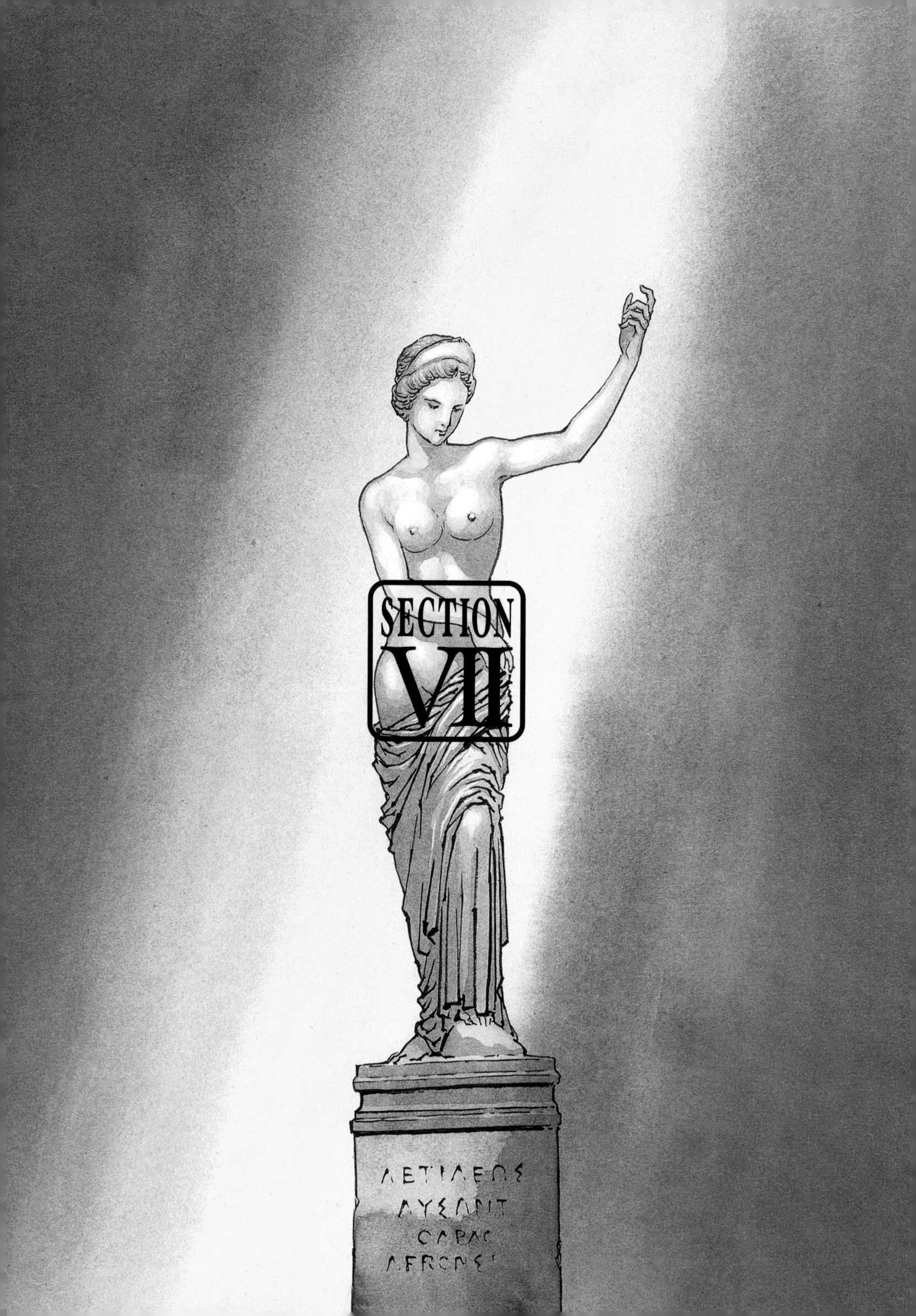

SECTION
VII

ΛΕΤΙΛΕΠΣ
ΛΥΣΛΠΙΤ
ΟΑΡΑΣ
ΛΕΓΩΡΣΙ

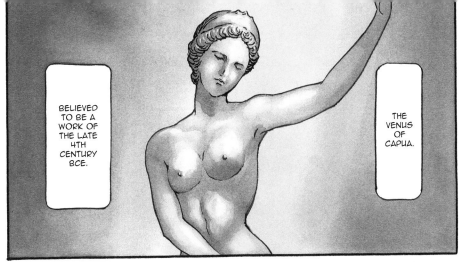

THE VENUS OF CAPUA.
BELIEVED TO BE A WORK OF THE LATE 4TH CENTURY BCE.
VENUS, OR APH-RODITE, IS THE GOD-DESS OF LOVE AND BEAUTY.
IN GREEK MYTH SHE IS THE DAUGHTER OF ZEUS, BORN OF SEA FOAM —
IT'S A
FAKE.
THE REAL ONE WAS A REPLICA MADE IN THE ROMAN ERA.
AND THIS IS A COPY OF THAT, I'D SAY RENAIS-SANCE ...

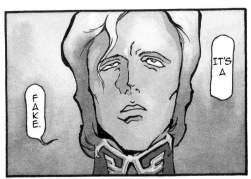

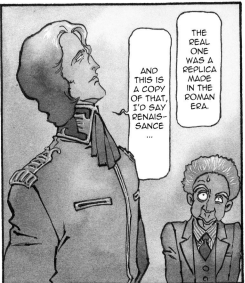

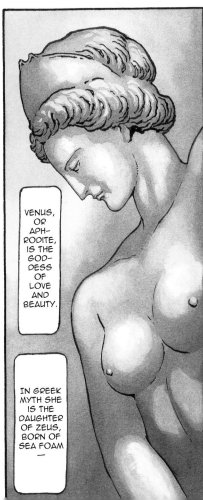

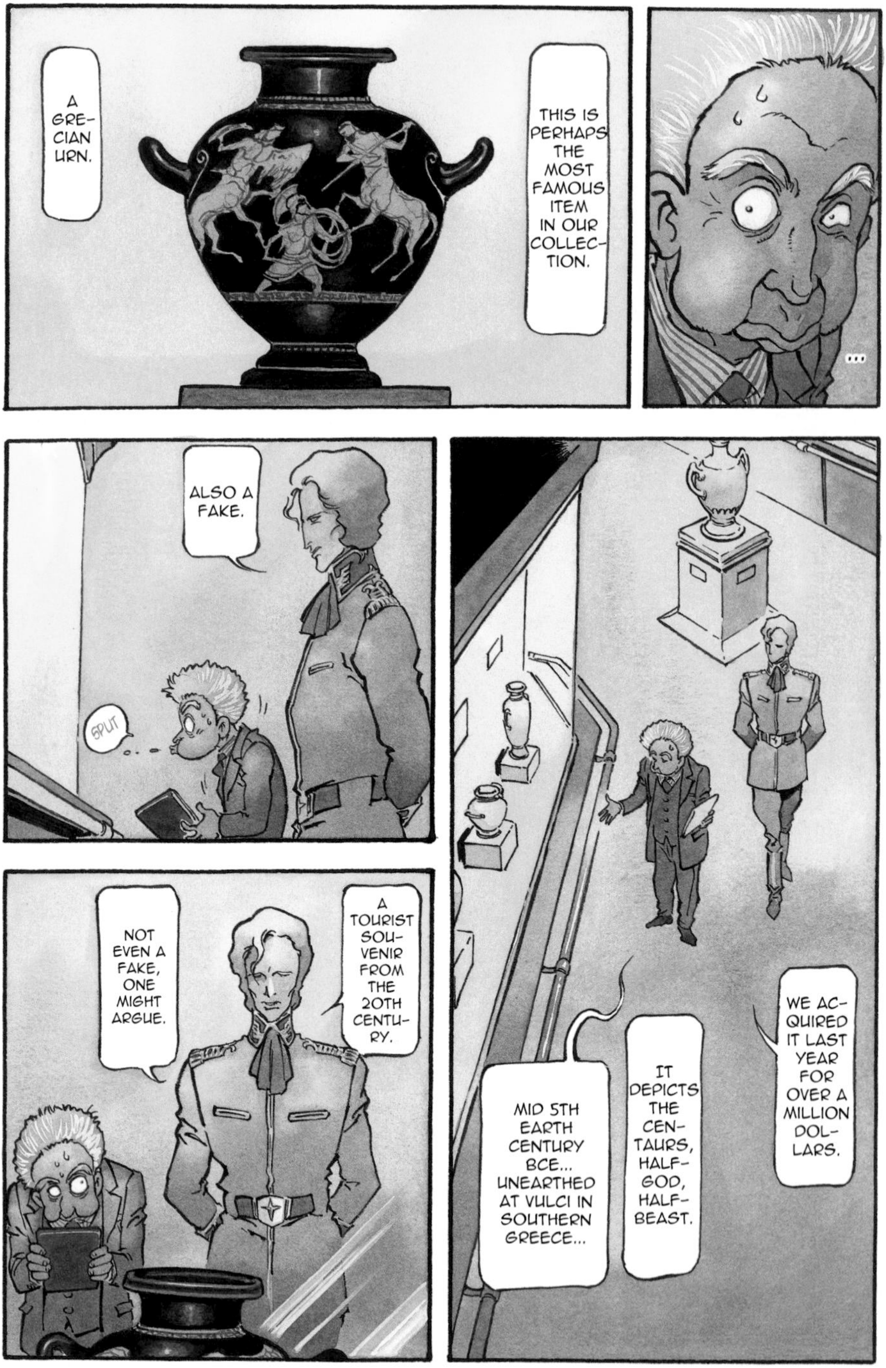
...
THIS IS PERHAPS THE MOST FAMOUS ITEM IN OUR COLLEC-TION.
A GRE-CIAN URN.
WE AC-QUIRED IT LAST YEAR FOR OVER A MILLION DOL-LARS.
IT DEPICTS THE CEN-TAURS, HALF-GOD, HALF-BEAST.
MID 5TH EARTH CENTURY BCE... UNEARTHED AT VULCI IN SOUTHERN GREECE...
ALSO A FAKE.
SPUT
A TOURIST SOU-VENIR FROM THE 20TH CENTU-RY.
NOT EVEN A FAKE, ONE MIGHT ARGUE.

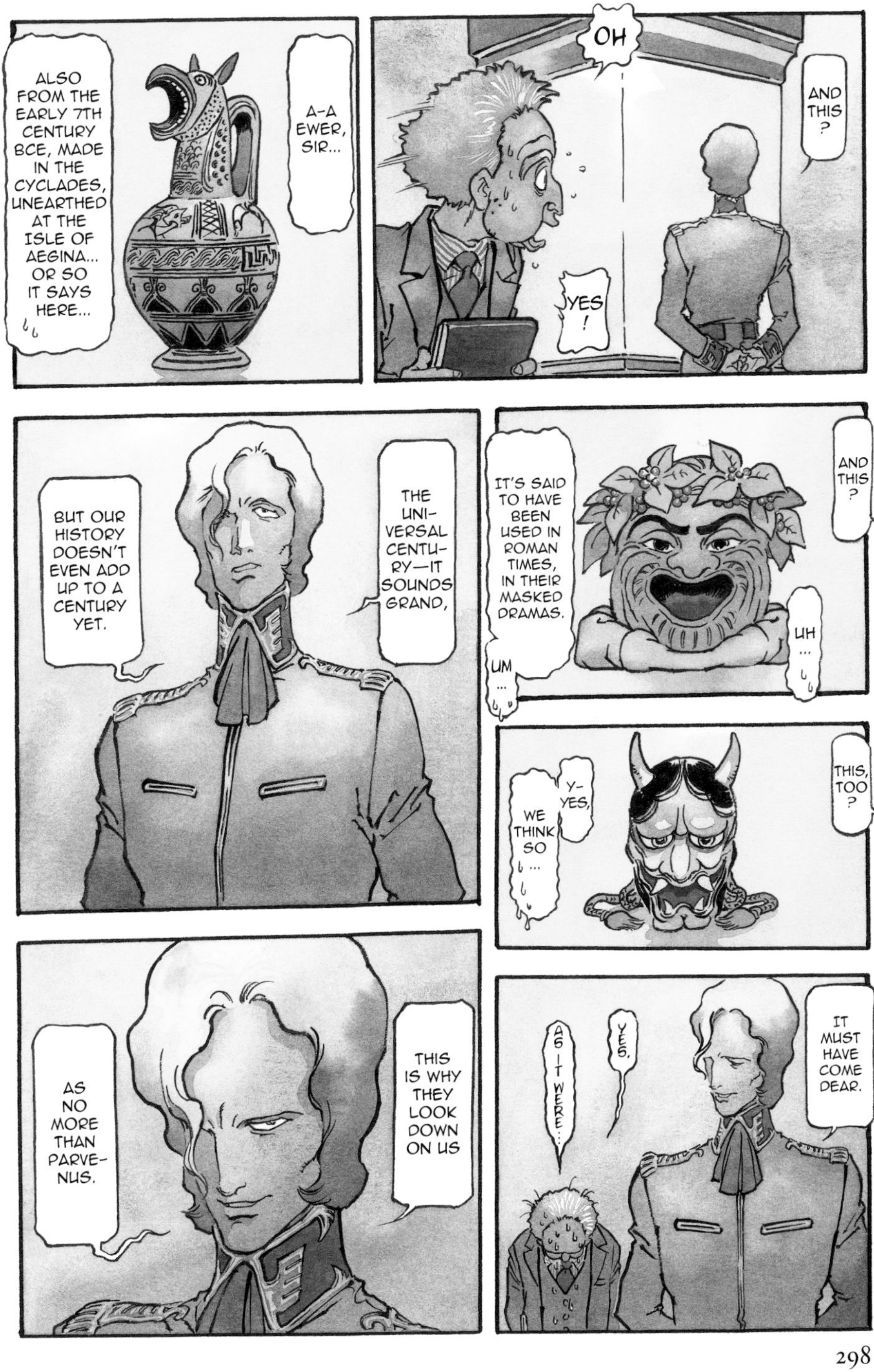
OH
AND THIS?
YES!
A-A EWER, SIR...
ALSO FROM THE EARLY 7TH CENTURY BCE, MADE IN THE CYCLADES, UNEARTHED AT THE ISLE OF AEGINA... OR SO IT SAYS HERE...
AND THIS?
IT'S SAID TO HAVE BEEN USED IN ROMAN TIMES, IN THEIR MASKED DRAMAS.
UH...
UM...
THIS, TOO?
Y-YES,
WE THINK SO...
THE UNIVERSAL CENTURY—IT SOUNDS GRAND,
BUT OUR HISTORY DOESN'T EVEN ADD UP TO A CENTURY YET.
IT MUST HAVE COME DEAR.
YES,
AS IT WERE...
THIS IS WHY THEY LOOK DOWN ON US
AS NO MORE THAN PARVENUS.

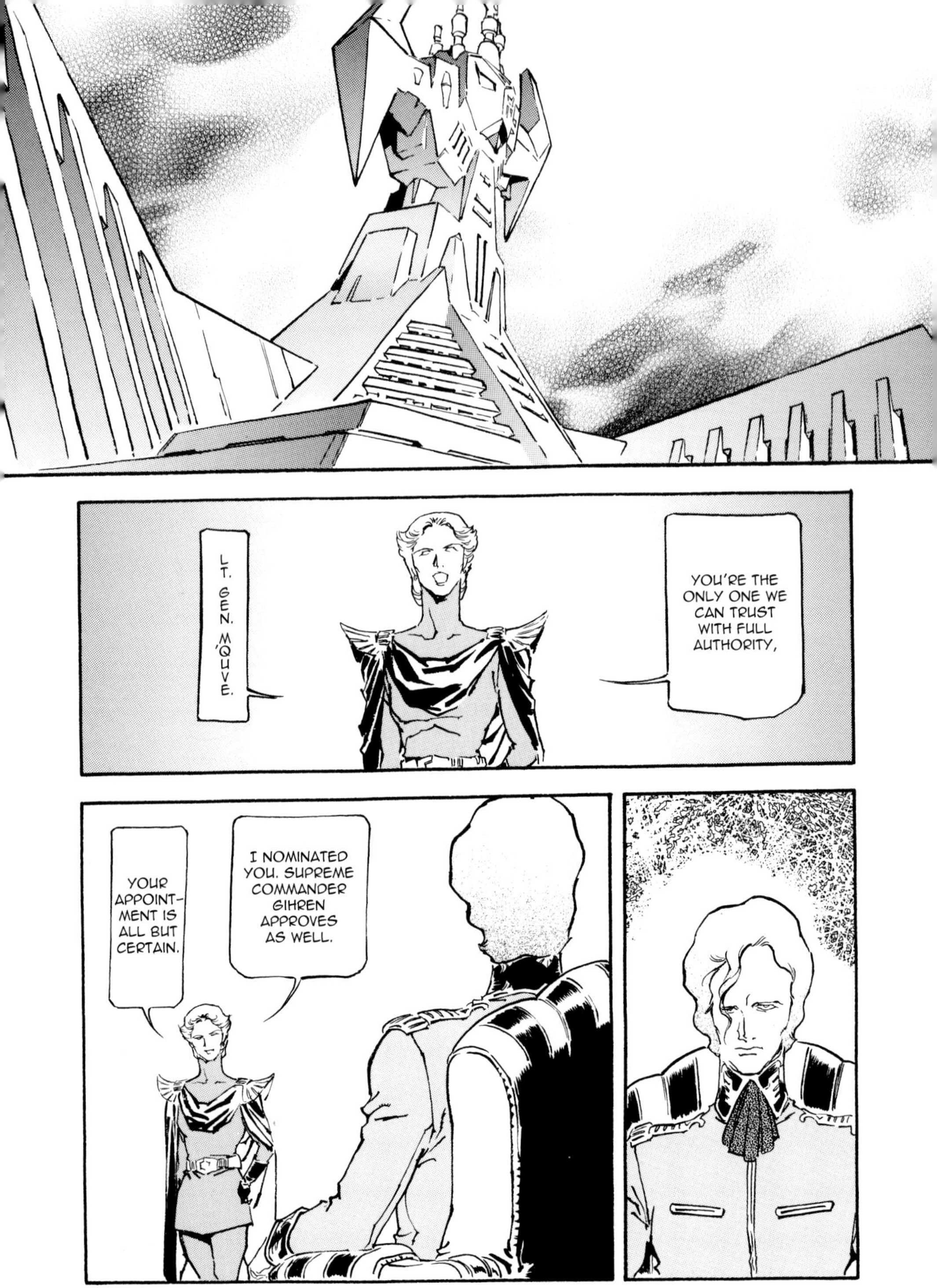
YOU'RE THE ONLY ONE WE CAN TRUST WITH FULL AUTHORITY,
LT. GEN. M'QUVE.
I NOMINATED YOU. SUPREME COMMANDER GIHREN APPROVES AS WELL.
YOUR APPOINT-MENT IS ALL BUT CERTAIN.

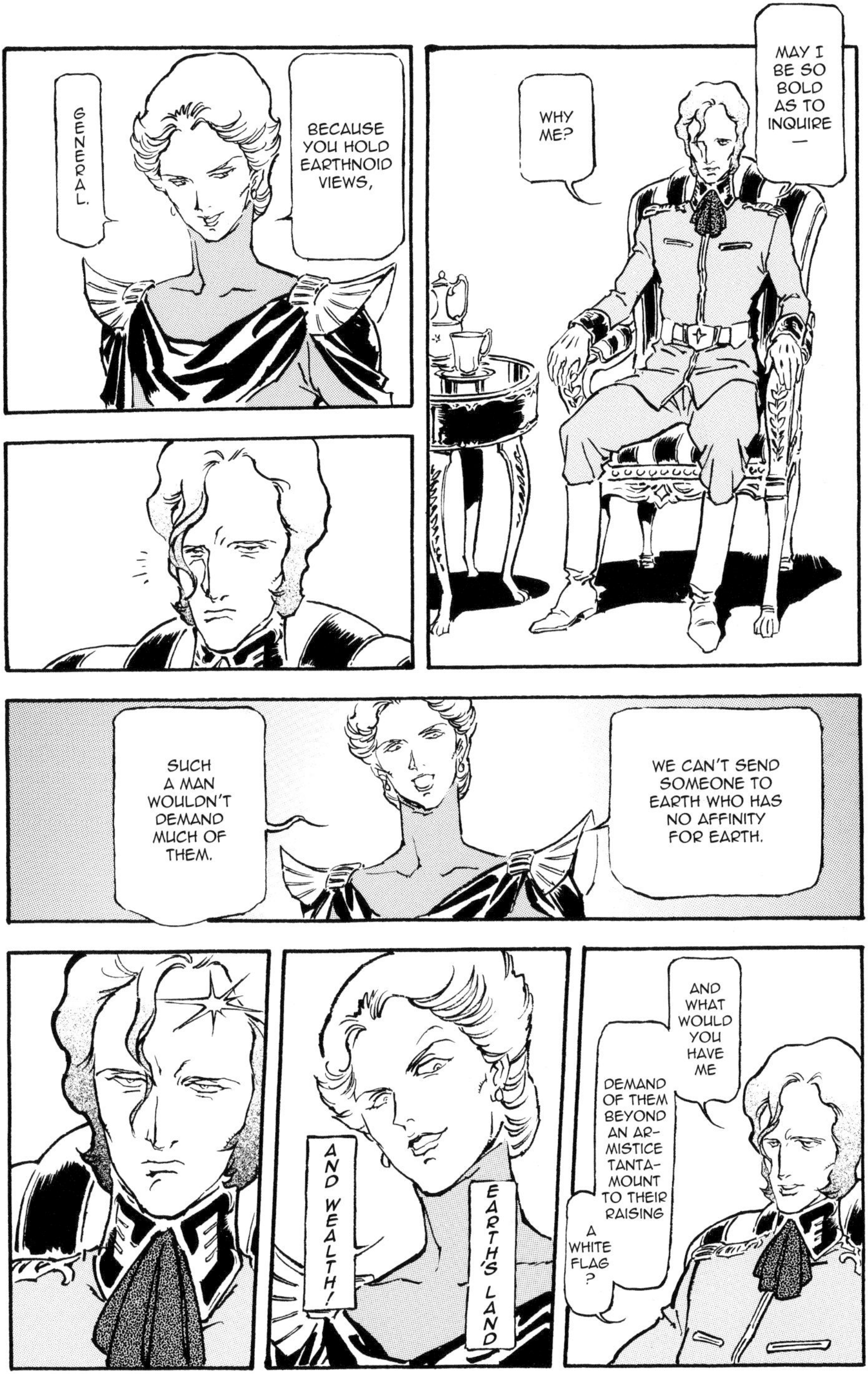
MAY I BE SO BOLD AS TO INQUIRE —
WHY ME?
BECAUSE YOU HOLD EARTHNOID VIEWS,
GENERAL.
WE CAN'T SEND SOMEONE TO EARTH WHO HAS NO AFFINITY FOR EARTH.
SUCH A MAN WOULDN'T DEMAND MUCH OF THEM.
AND WHAT WOULD YOU HAVE ME
DEMAND OF THEM BEYOND AN ARMISTICE TANTAMOUNT TO THEIR RAISING
A WHITE FLAG?
EARTH'S LAND
AND WEALTH!

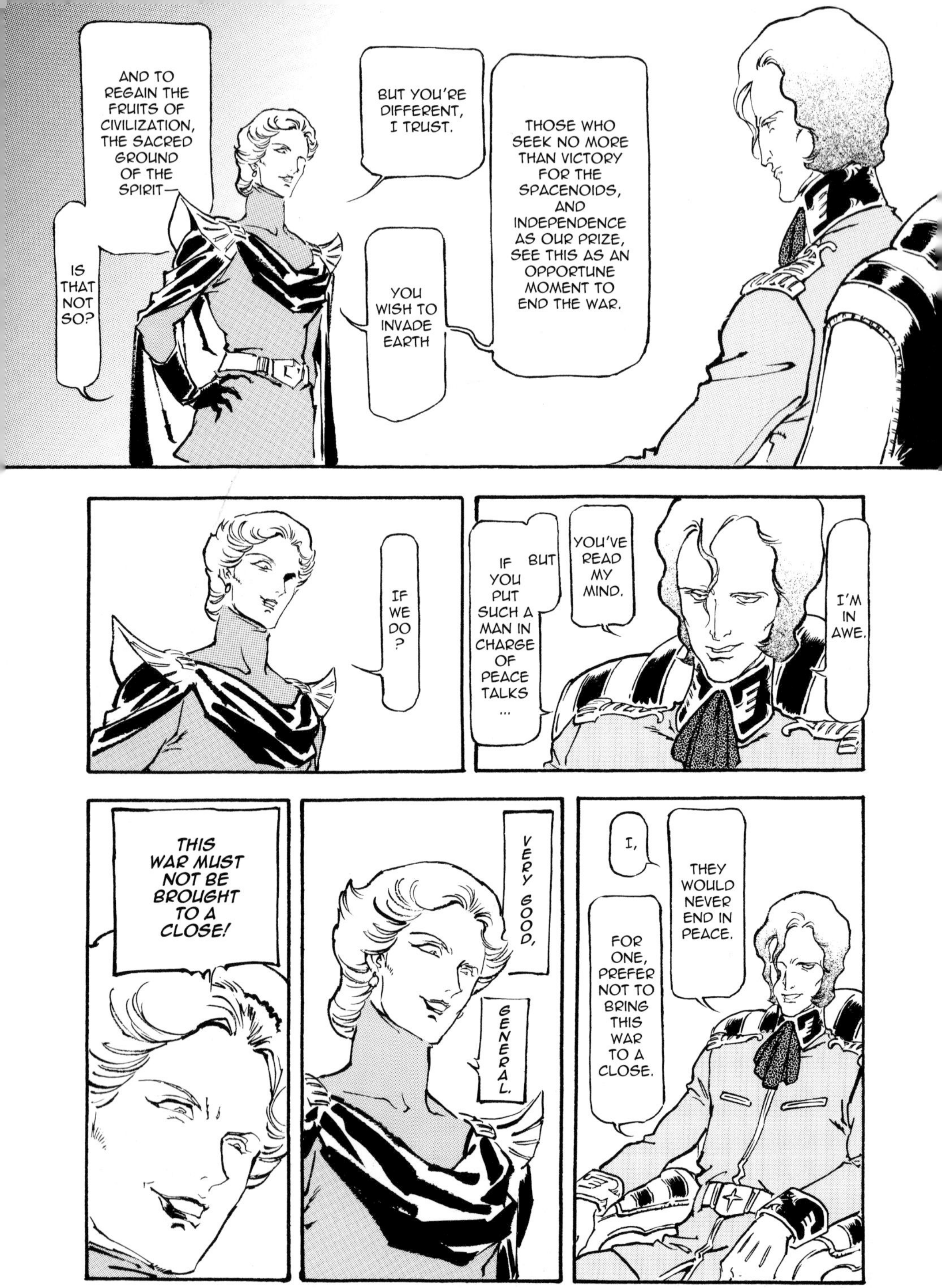
THOSE WHO SEEK NO MORE THAN VICTORY FOR THE SPACENOIDS, AND INDEPENDENCE AS OUR PRIZE, SEE THIS AS AN OPPORTUNE MOMENT TO END THE WAR.
BUT YOU'RE DIFFERENT, I TRUST.
YOU WISH TO INVADE EARTH
AND TO REGAIN THE FRUITS OF CIVILIZATION, THE SACRED GROUND OF THE SPIRIT—
IS THAT NOT SO?
I'M IN AWE.
YOU'VE READ MY MIND.
BUT IF YOU PUT SUCH A MAN IN CHARGE OF PEACE TALKS ...
IF WE DO?
THEY WOULD NEVER END IN PEACE.
I,
FOR ONE, PREFER NOT TO BRING THIS WAR TO A CLOSE.
VERY GOOD,
GENERAL.
THIS WAR MUST NOT BE BROUGHT TO A CLOSE!

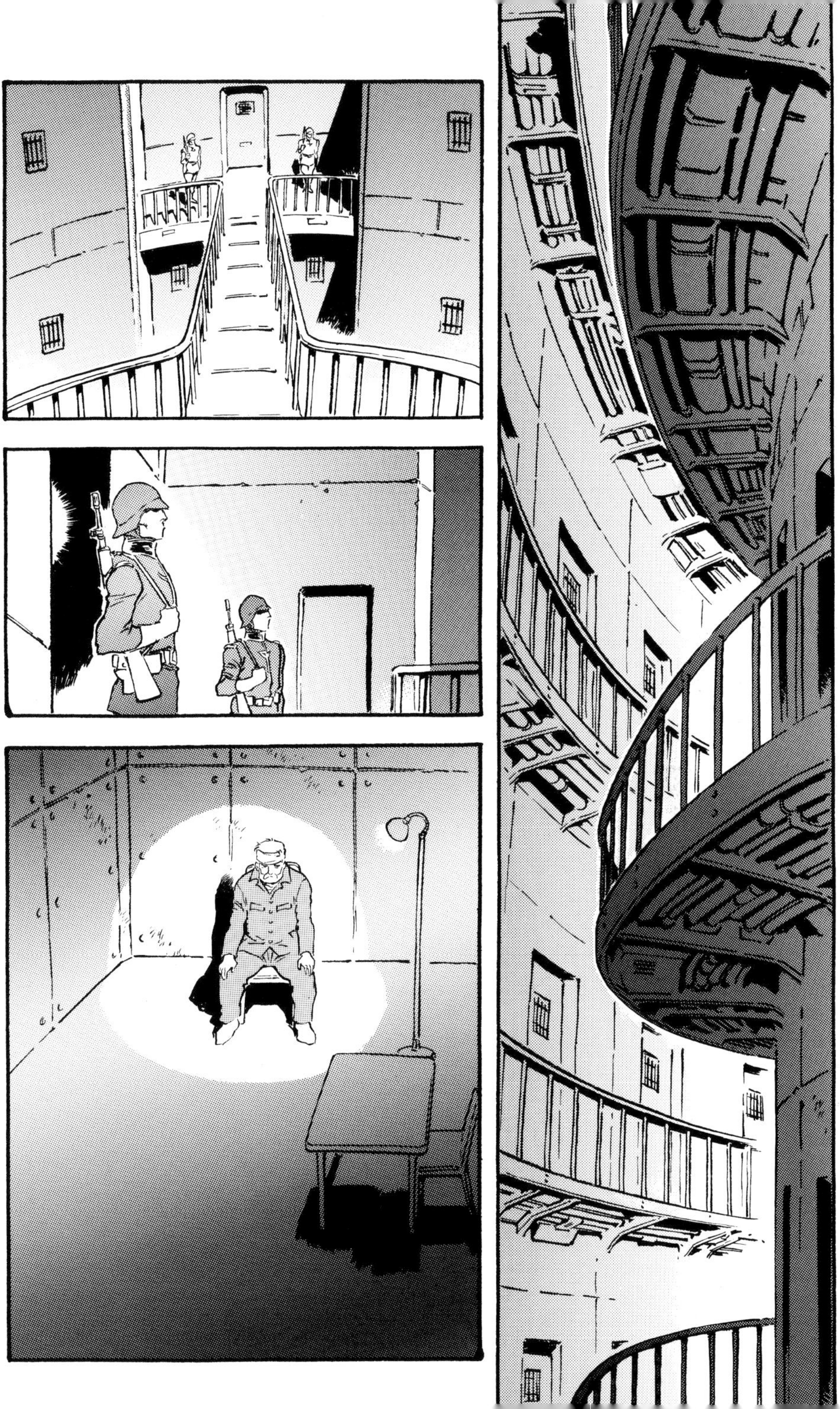

KLAK
KCHIK
KLAK
TOK
TOK
TOK
CREAK

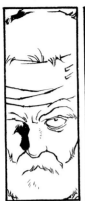

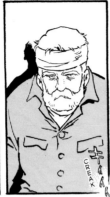

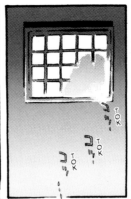

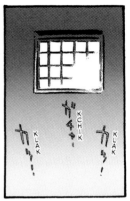

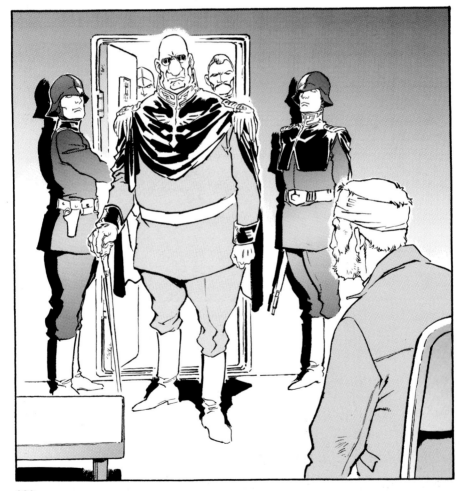

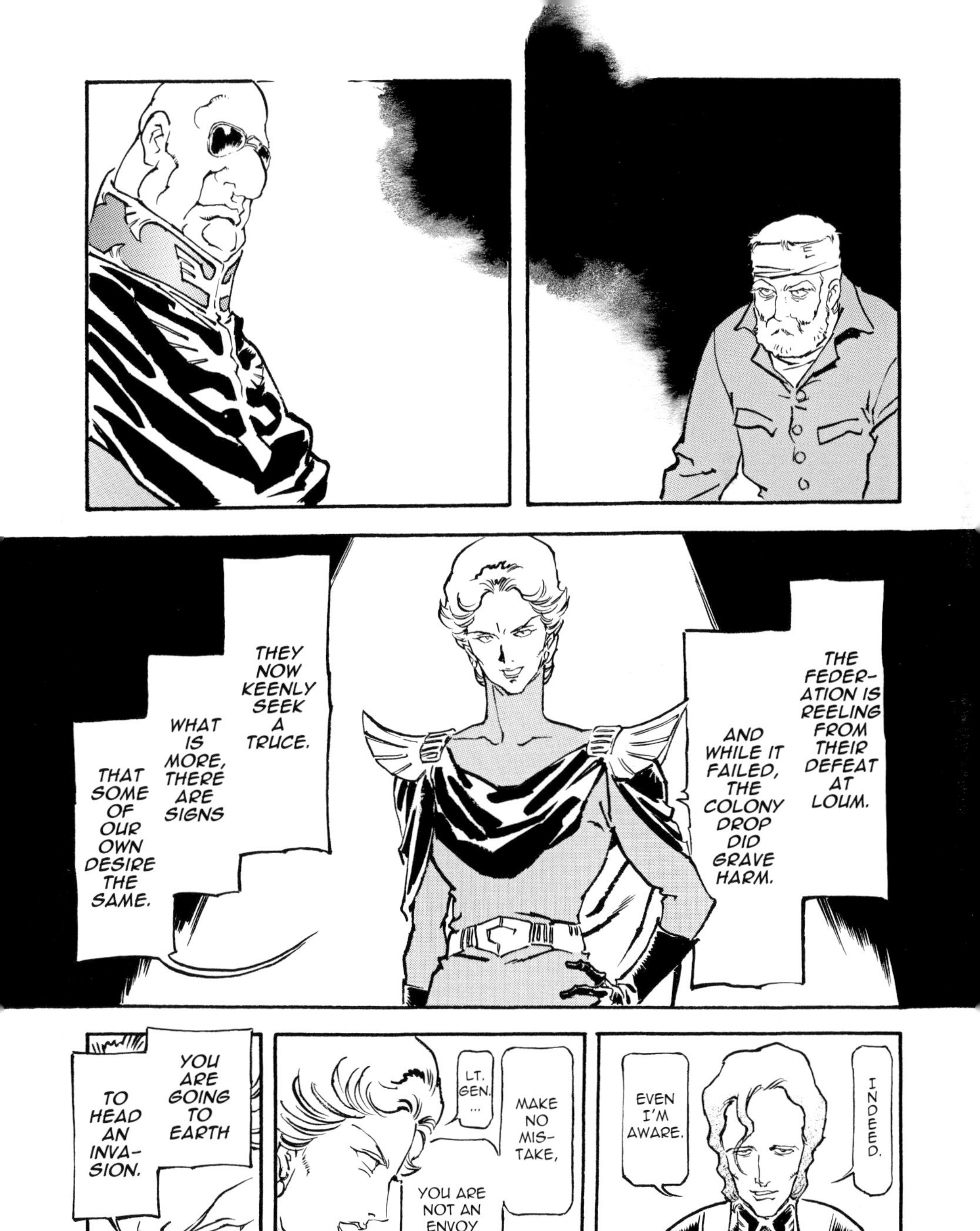
THE FEDERATION IS REELING FROM THEIR DEFEAT AT LOUM.
AND WHILE IT FAILED, THE COLONY DROP DID GRAVE HARM.
THEY NOW KEENLY SEEK A TRUCE.
WHAT IS MORE, THERE ARE SIGNS
THAT SOME OF OUR OWN DESIRE THE SAME.
INDEED.
EVEN I'M AWARE.
LT. GEN. ...
MAKE NO MISTAKE,
YOU ARE NOT AN ENVOY OF PEACE.
YOU ARE GOING TO EARTH
TO HEAD AN INVASION.

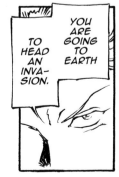

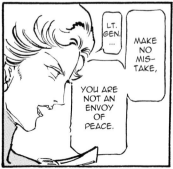

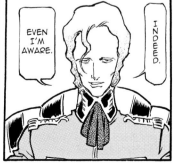

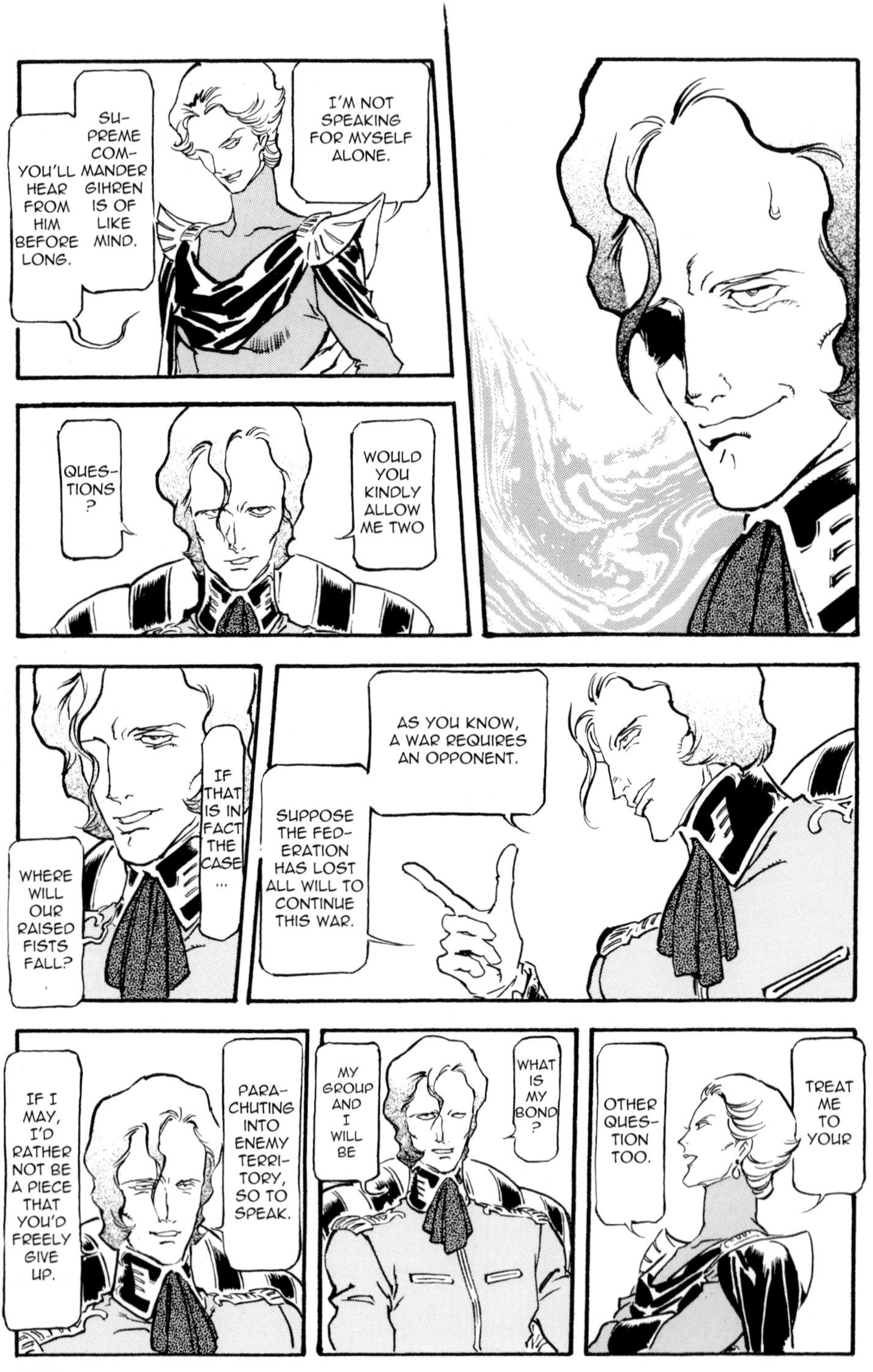
I'M NOT SPEAKING FOR MYSELF ALONE.
SUPREME COMMANDER GIHREN IS OF LIKE MIND.
YOU'LL HEAR FROM HIM BEFORE LONG.
WOULD YOU KINDLY ALLOW ME TWO
QUESTIONS?
AS YOU KNOW, A WAR REQUIRES AN OPPONENT.
SUPPOSE THE FEDERATION HAS LOST ALL WILL TO CONTINUE THIS WAR.
IF THAT IS IN FACT THE CASE...
WHERE WILL OUR RAISED FISTS FALL?
TREAT ME TO YOUR
OTHER QUESTION TOO.
WHAT IS MY BOND?
MY GROUP AND I WILL BE
PARACHUTING INTO ENEMY TERRITORY, SO TO SPEAK.
IF I MAY, I'D RATHER NOT BE A PIECE THAT YOU'D FREELY GIVE UP.

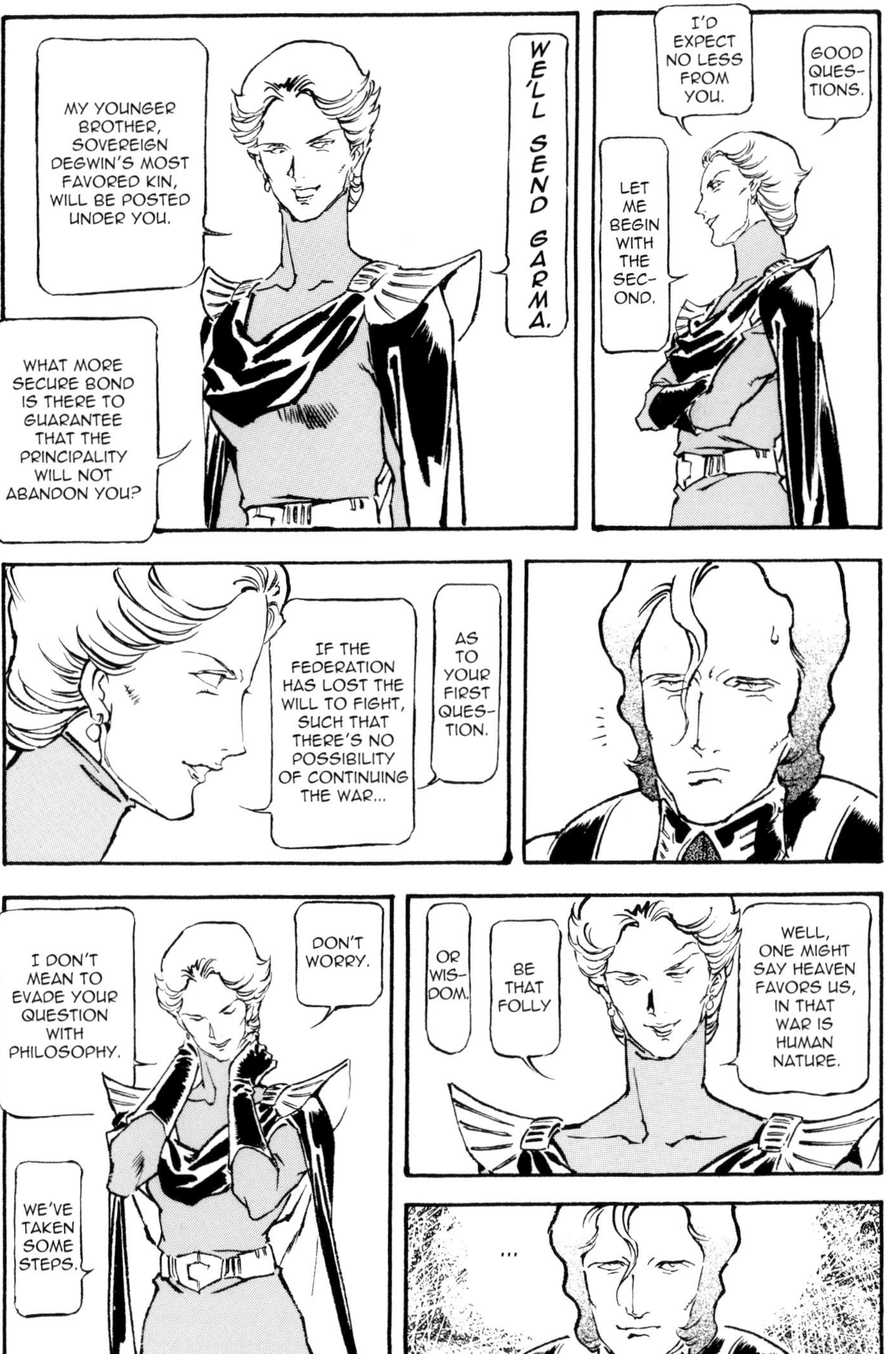
GOOD QUESTIONS.
I'D EXPECT NO LESS FROM YOU.
LET ME BEGIN WITH THE SECOND.
WE'LL SEND GARMA.
MY YOUNGER BROTHER, SOVEREIGN DEGWIN'S MOST FAVORED KIN, WILL BE POSTED UNDER YOU.
WHAT MORE SECURE BOND IS THERE TO GUARANTEE THAT THE PRINCIPALITY WILL NOT ABANDON YOU?
AS TO YOUR FIRST QUESTION.
IF THE FEDERATION HAS LOST THE WILL TO FIGHT, SUCH THAT THERE'S NO POSSIBILITY OF CONTINUING THE WAR...
WELL, ONE MIGHT SAY HEAVEN FAVORS US, IN THAT WAR IS HUMAN NATURE.
BE THAT FOLLY
OR WISDOM.
...
DON'T WORRY.
I DON'T MEAN TO EVADE YOUR QUESTION WITH PHILOSOPHY.
WE'VE TAKEN SOME STEPS.

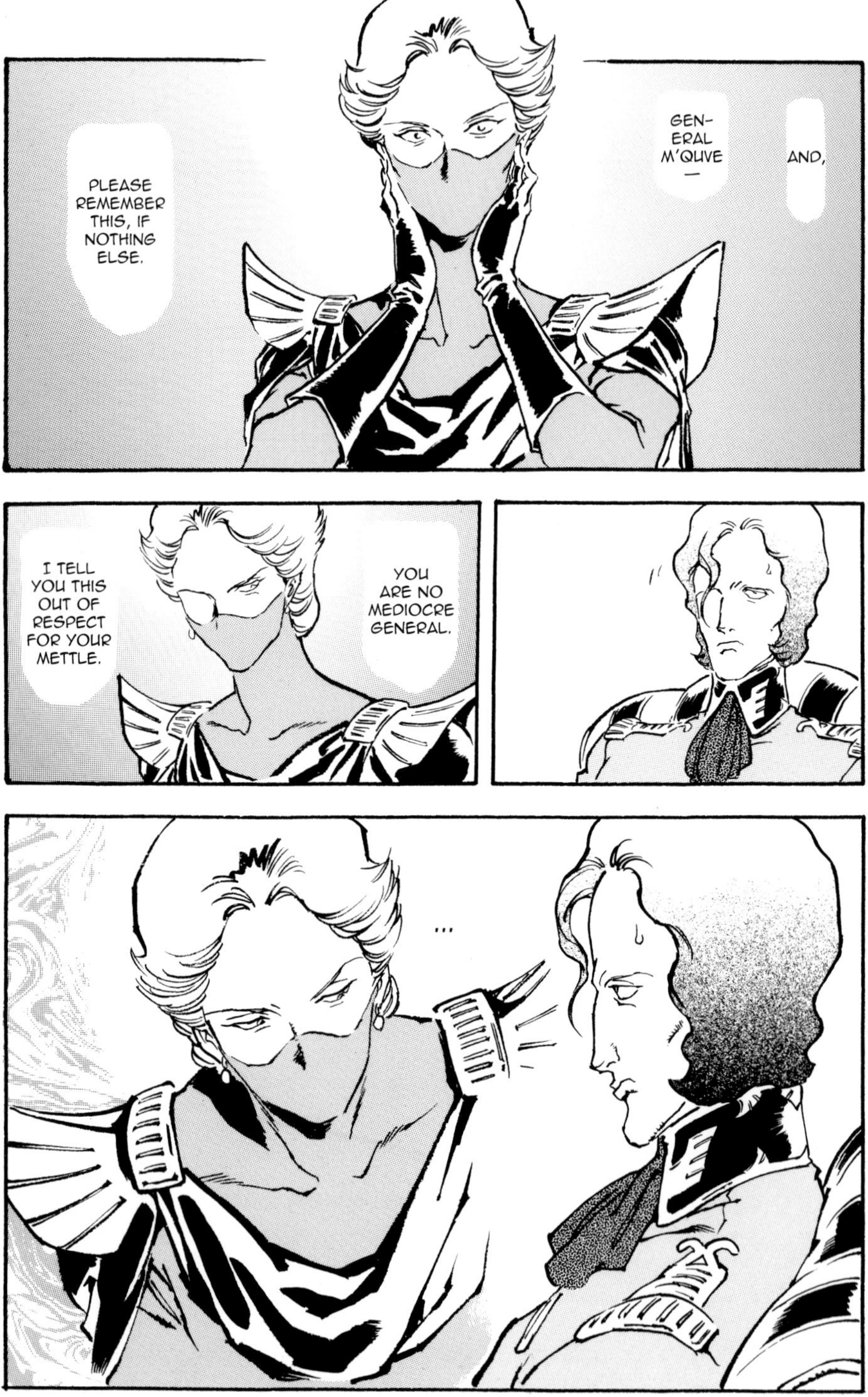
AND,
GEN-ERAL M'QUVE —
PLEASE REMEMBER THIS, IF NOTHING ELSE.
YOU ARE NO MEDIOCRE GENERAL.
I TELL YOU THIS OUT OF RESPECT FOR YOUR METTLE.
...

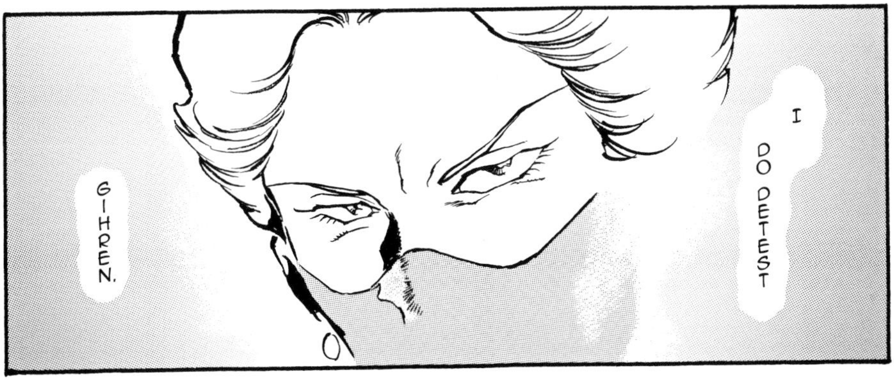
I DO DETEST
GIHREN.

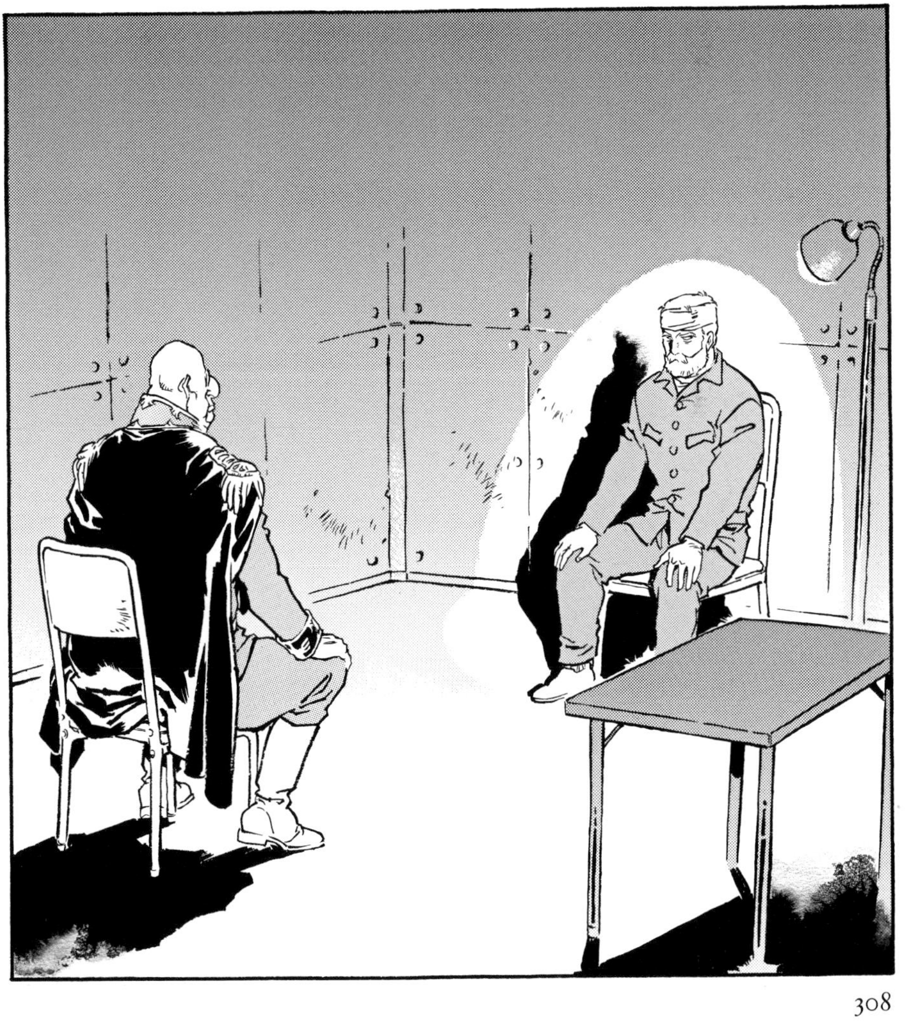

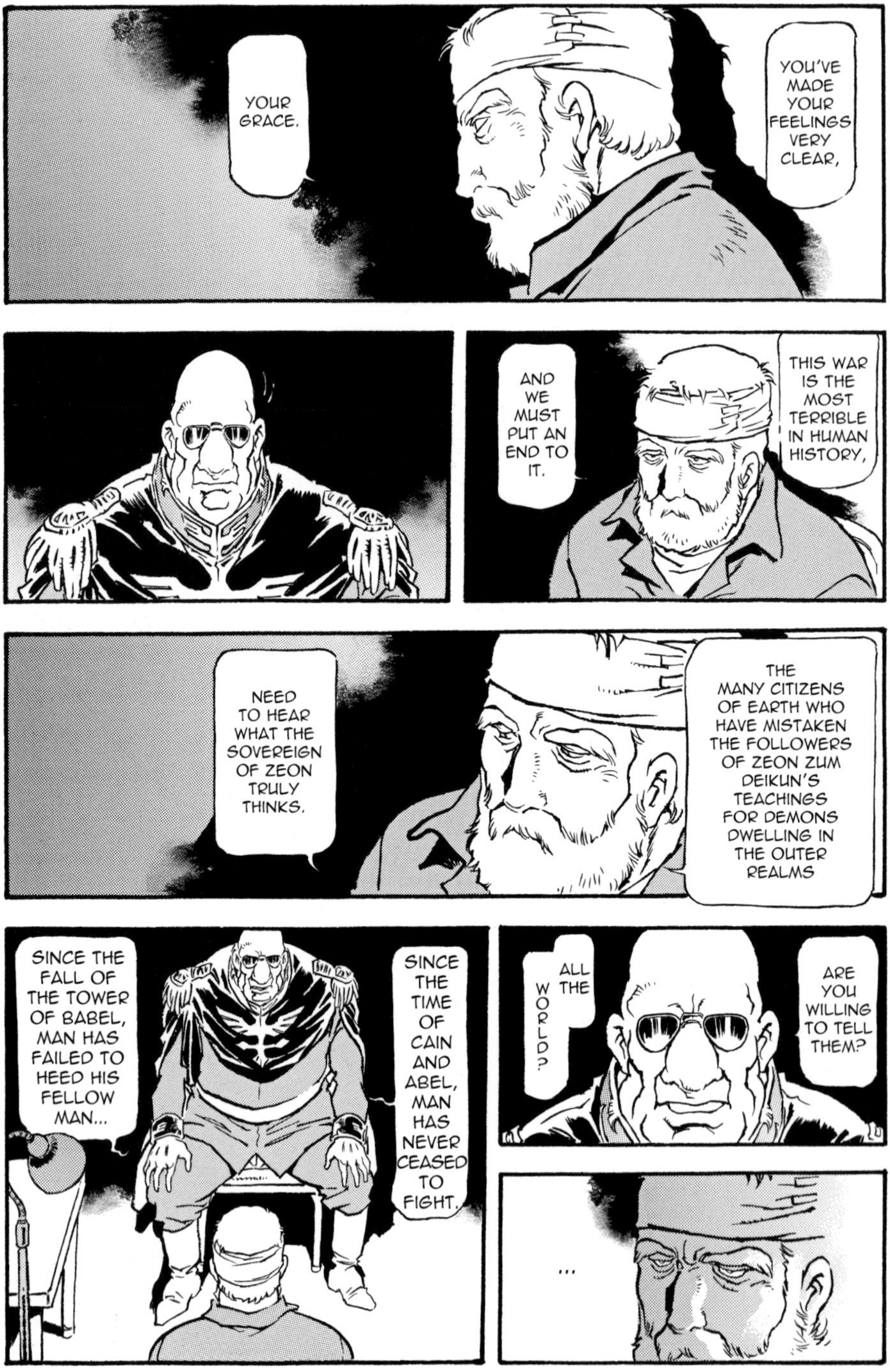
YOU'VE MADE YOUR FEELINGS VERY CLEAR,
YOUR GRACE.
THIS WAR IS THE MOST TERRIBLE IN HUMAN HISTORY,
AND WE MUST PUT AN END TO IT.
THE MANY CITIZENS OF EARTH WHO HAVE MISTAKEN THE FOLLOWERS OF ZEON ZUM DEIKUN'S TEACHINGS FOR DEMONS DWELLING IN THE OUTER REALMS
NEED TO HEAR WHAT THE SOVEREIGN OF ZEON TRULY THINKS.
ARE YOU WILLING TO TELL THEM?
ALL THE WORLD?
...
SINCE THE TIME OF CAIN AND ABEL, MAN HAS NEVER CEASED TO FIGHT.
SINCE THE FALL OF THE TOWER OF BABEL, MAN HAS FAILED TO HEED HIS FELLOW MAN...

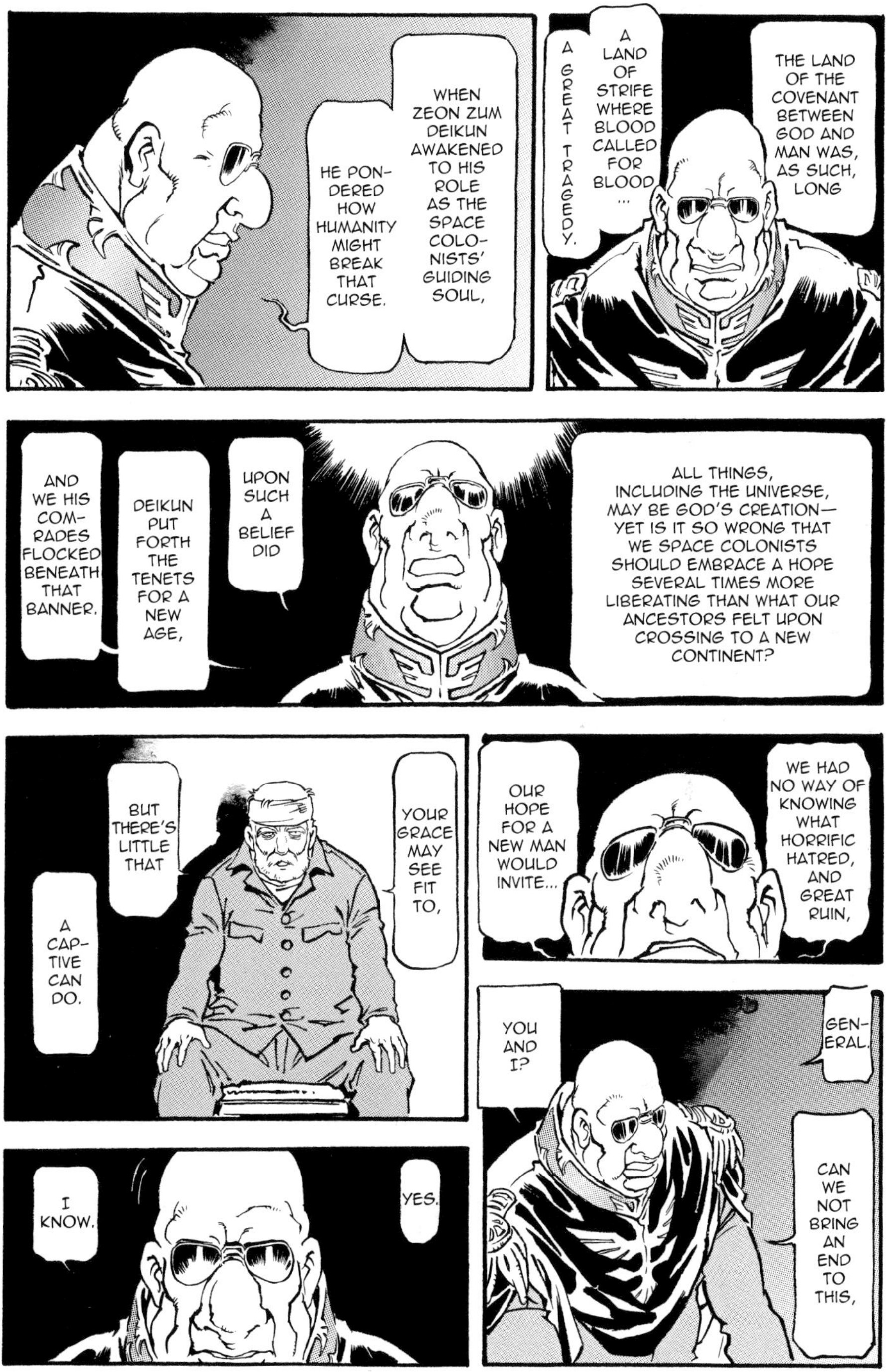
THE LAND OF THE COVENANT BETWEEN GOD AND MAN WAS, AS SUCH, LONG
A LAND OF STRIFE WHERE BLOOD CALLED FOR BLOOD...
A GREAT TRAGEDY.
WHEN ZEON ZUM DEIKUN AWAKENED TO HIS ROLE AS THE SPACE COLONISTS' GUIDING SOUL,
HE PONDERED HOW HUMANITY MIGHT BREAK THAT CURSE.
ALL THINGS, INCLUDING THE UNIVERSE, MAY BE GOD'S CREATION— YET IS IT SO WRONG THAT WE SPACE COLONISTS SHOULD EMBRACE A HOPE SEVERAL TIMES MORE LIBERATING THAN WHAT OUR ANCESTORS FELT UPON CROSSING TO A NEW CONTINENT?
UPON SUCH A BELIEF DID
DEIKUN PUT FORTH THE TENETS FOR A NEW AGE,
AND WE HIS COMRADES FLOCKED BENEATH THAT BANNER.
WE HAD NO WAY OF KNOWING WHAT HORRIFIC HATRED, AND GREAT RUIN,
OUR HOPE FOR A NEW MAN WOULD INVITE...
GENERAL.
CAN WE NOT BRING AN END TO THIS,
YOU AND I?
YOUR GRACE MAY SEE FIT TO,
BUT THERE'S LITTLE THAT
A CAPTIVE CAN DO.
YES.
I KNOW.

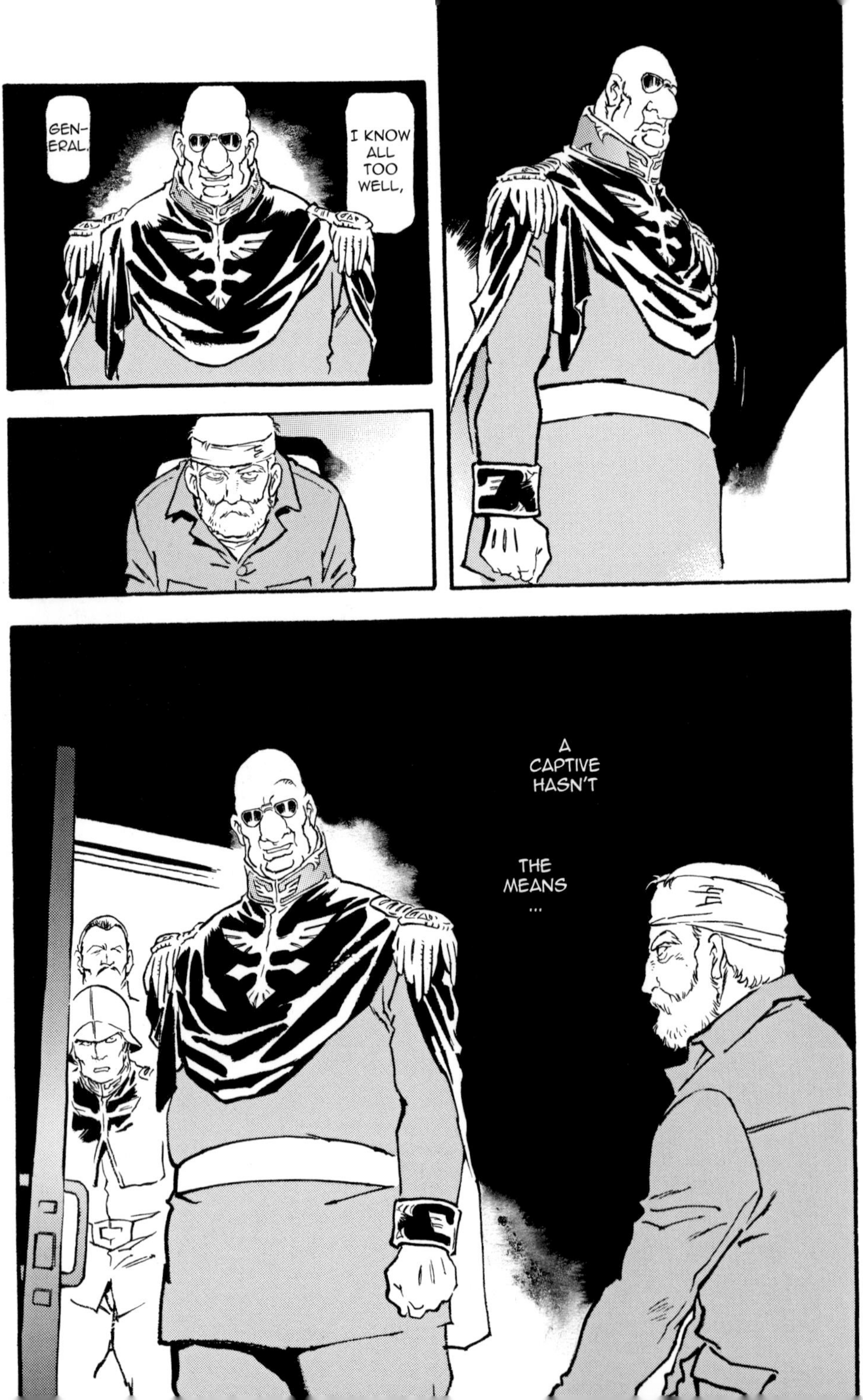
I KNOW ALL TOO WELL,
GEN-ERAL.
A CAPTIVE HASN'T
THE MEANS ...

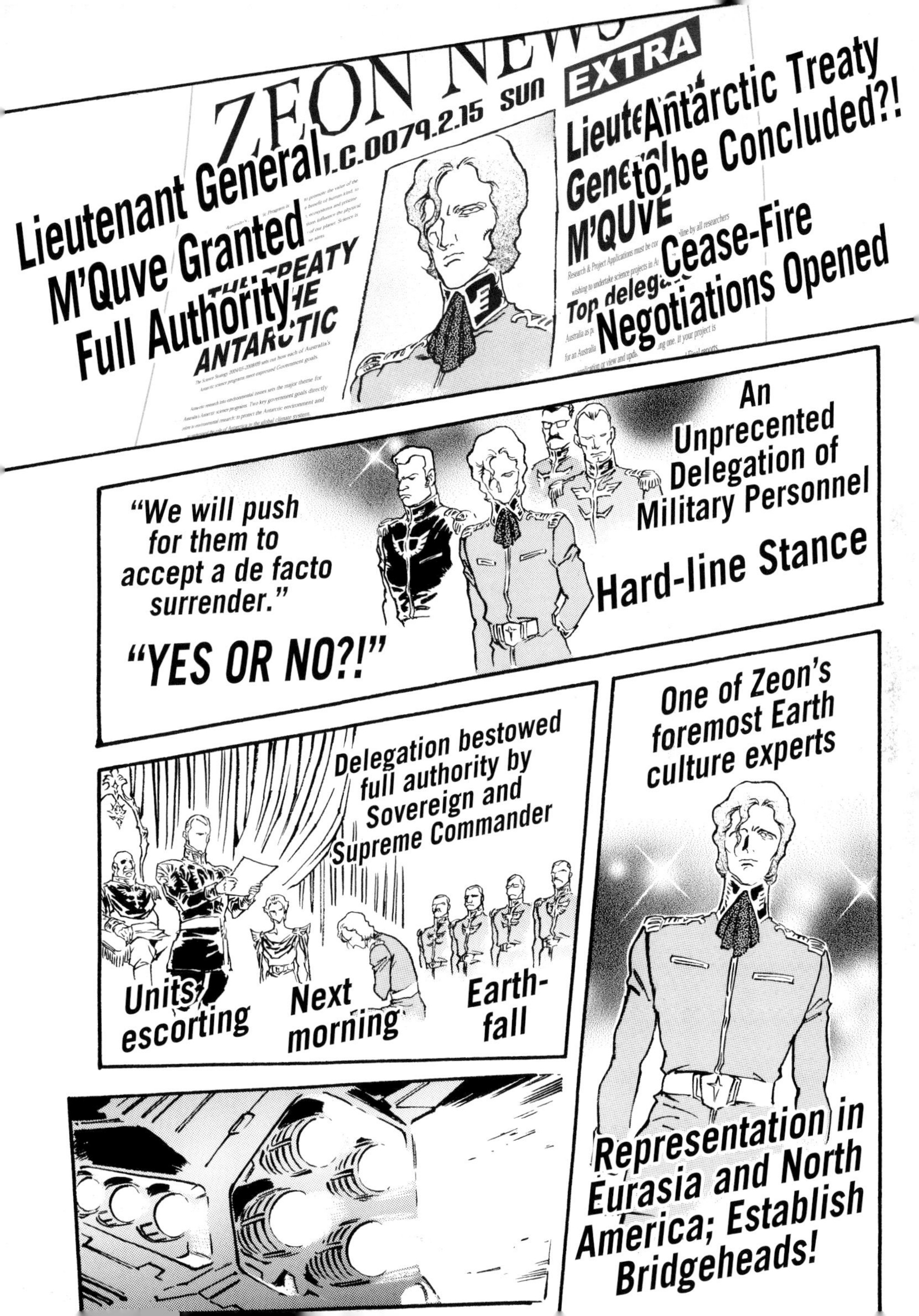
ZEON NEWS
EXTRA
U.C.0079.2.15 SUN
Antarctic Treaty to be Concluded?!
Cease-Fire Negotiations Opened
Lieutenant General M'Quve Granted Full Authority
An Unprecented Delegation of Military Personnel
Hard-line Stance
“We will push for them to accept a de facto surrender.”
“YES OR NO?!”
One of Zeon's foremost Earth culture experts
Representation in Eurasia and North America; Establish Bridgeheads!
Delegation bestowed full authority by Sovereign and Supreme Commander
Earth-fall
Next morning
Units escorting

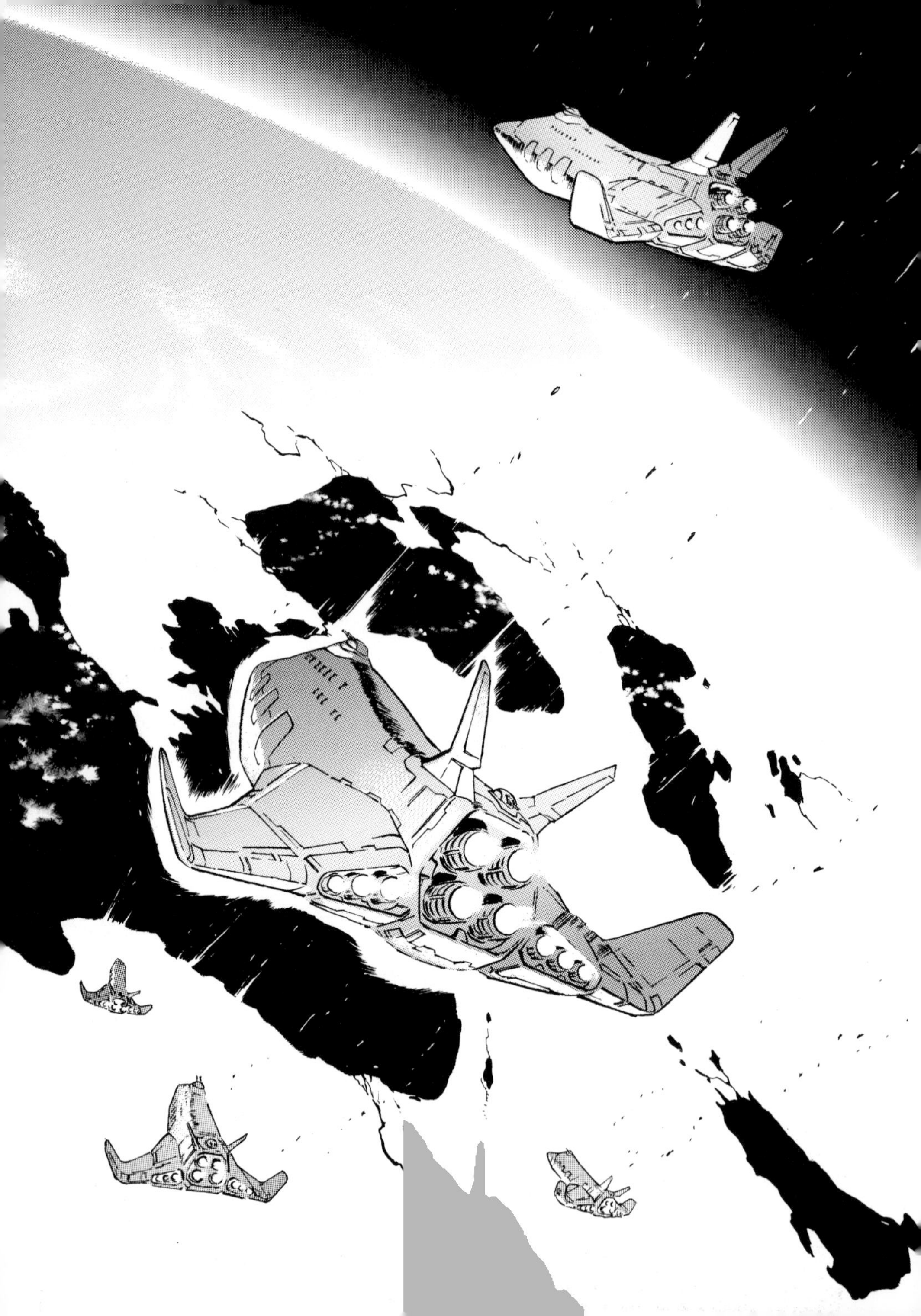

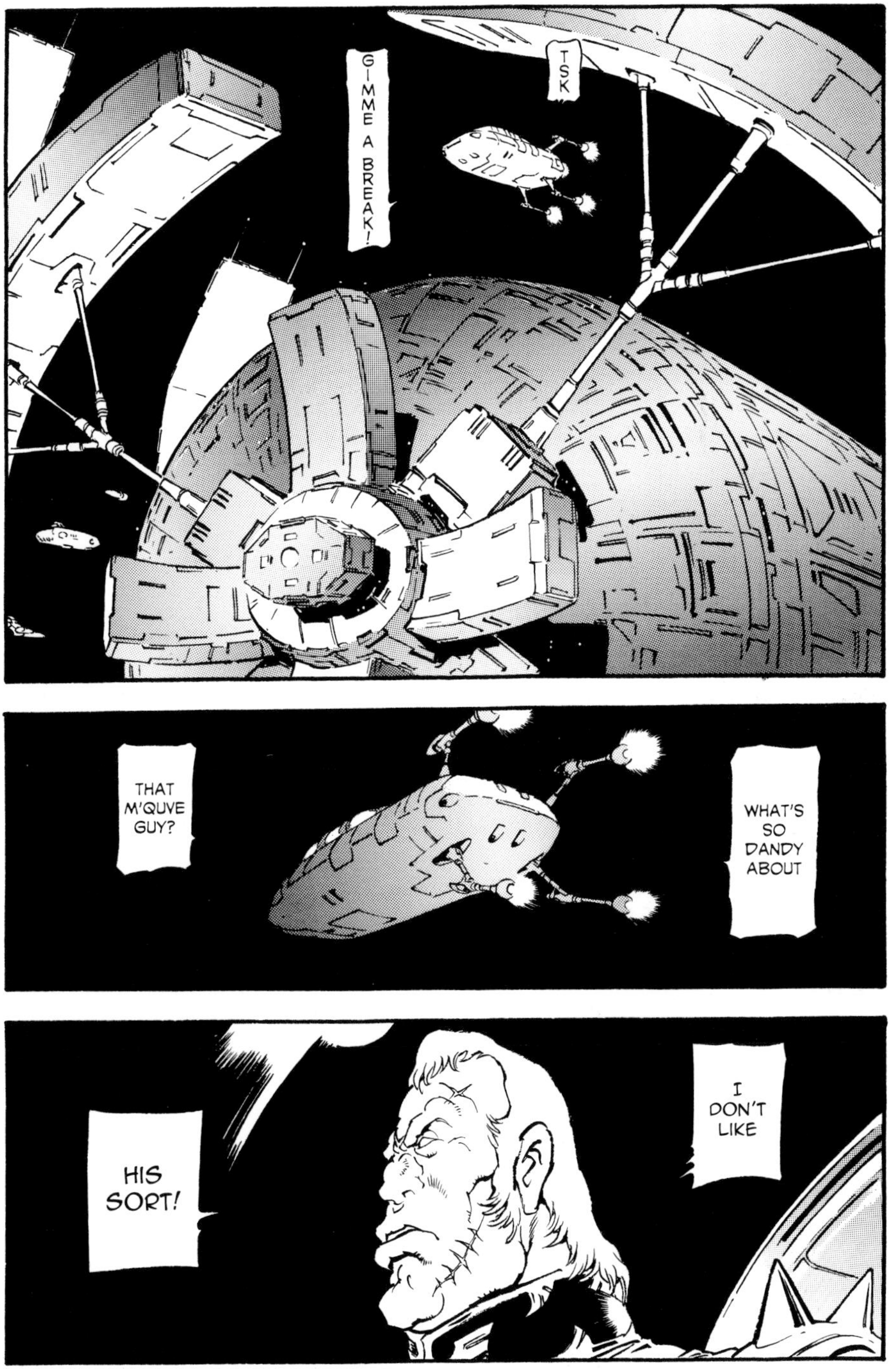
TSK
GIMME A BREAK!
WHAT'S SO DANDY ABOUT
THAT M'QUVE GUY?
I DON'T LIKE
HIS SORT!

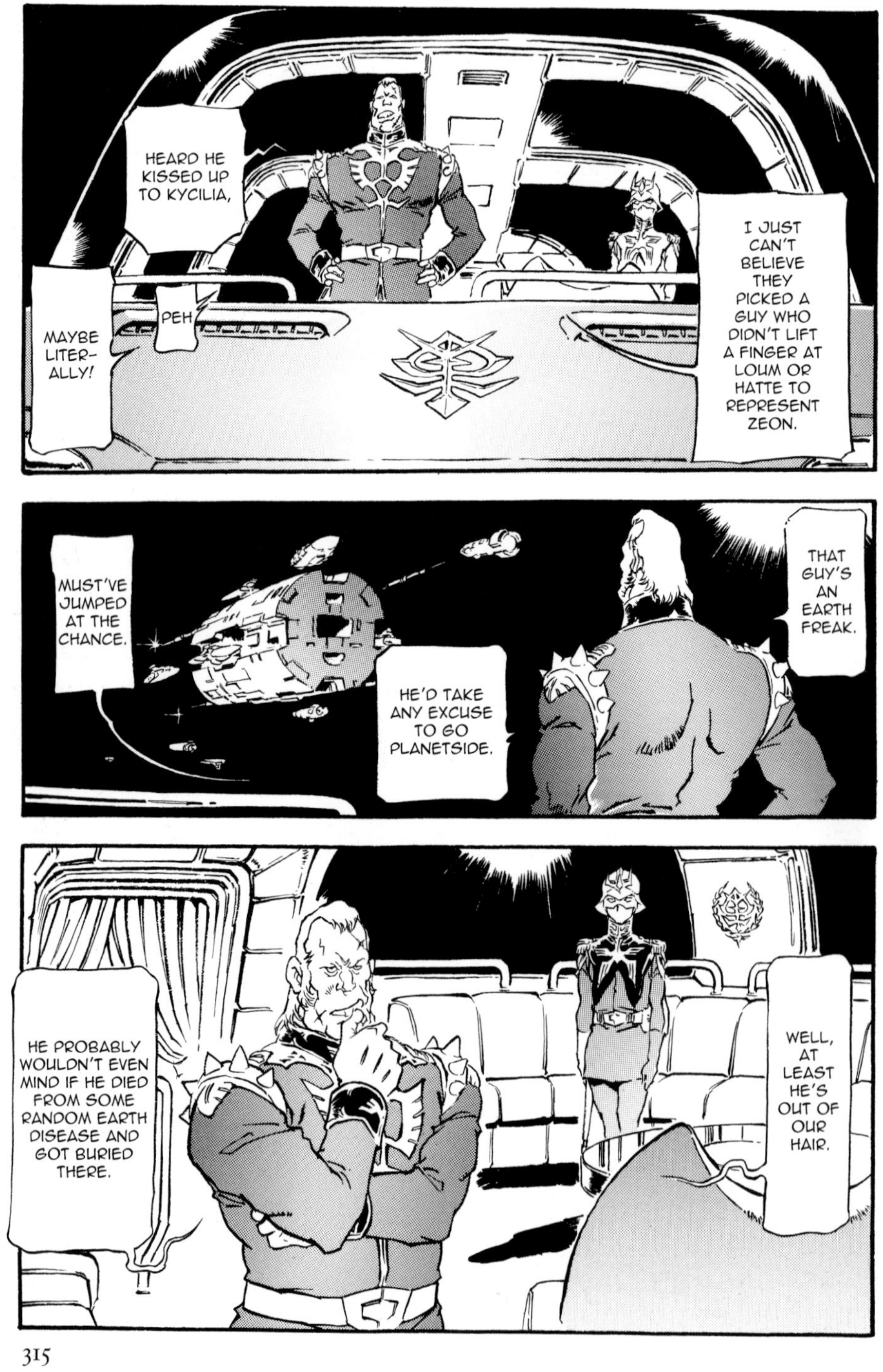
I JUST CAN'T BELIEVE THEY PICKED A GUY WHO DIDN'T LIFT A FINGER AT LOUM OR HATTE TO REPRESENT ZEON.
HEARD HE KISSED UP TO KYCILIA,
PEH
MAYBE LITER-ALLY!
THAT GUY'S AN EARTH FREAK.
HE'D TAKE ANY EXCUSE TO GO PLANETSIDE.
MUST'VE JUMPED AT THE CHANCE.
WELL, AT LEAST HE'S OUT OF OUR HAIR.
HE PROBABLY WOULDN'T EVEN MIND IF HE DIED FROM SOME RANDOM EARTH DISEASE AND GOT BURIED THERE.

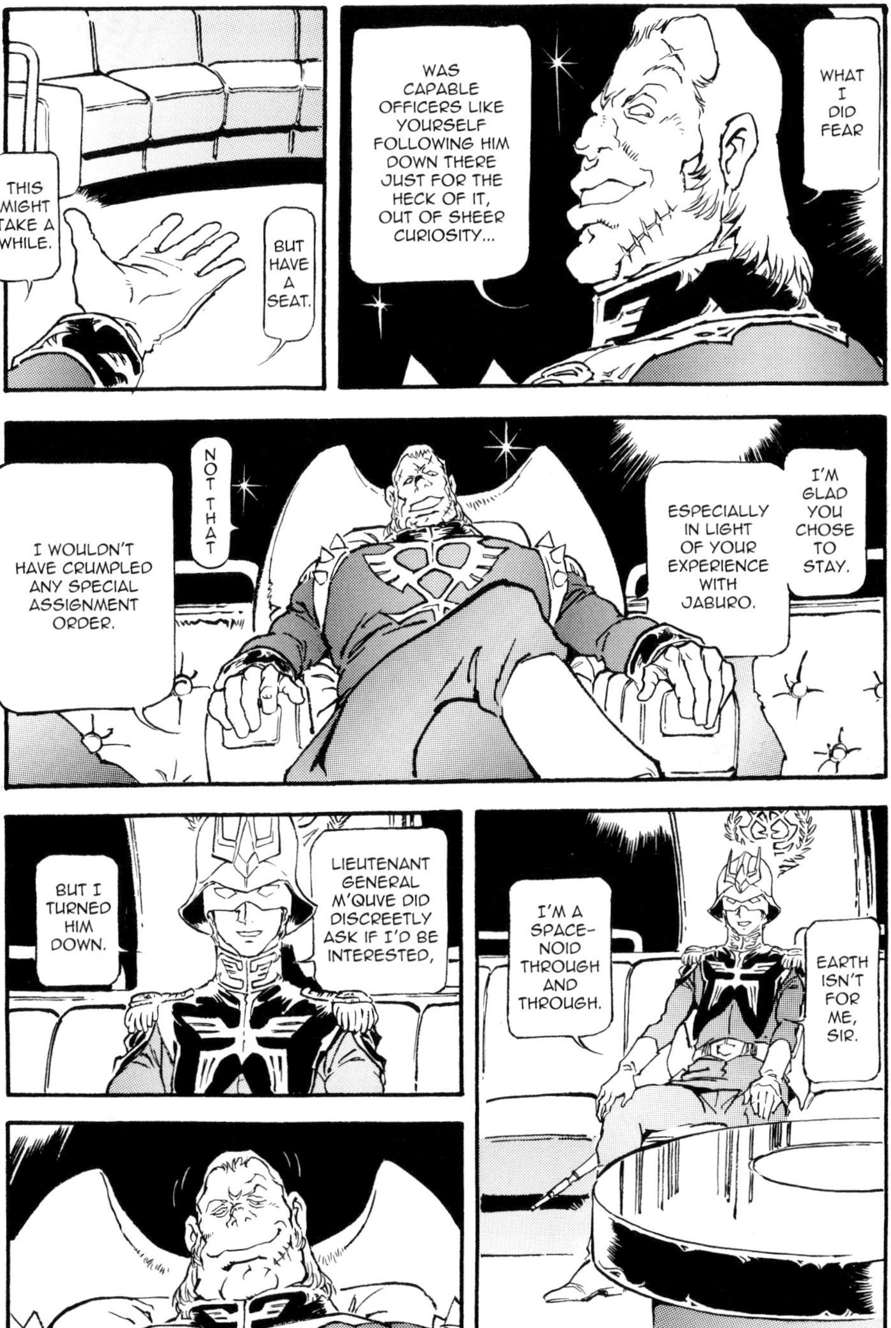
WHAT I DID FEAR
WAS CAPABLE OFFICERS LIKE YOURSELF FOLLOWING HIM DOWN THERE JUST FOR THE HECK OF IT, OUT OF SHEER CURIOSITY...
BUT HAVE A SEAT.
THIS MIGHT TAKE A WHILE.
I'M GLAD YOU CHOSE TO STAY.
ESPECIALLY IN LIGHT OF YOUR EXPERIENCE WITH JABURO.
NOT THAT
I WOULDN'T HAVE CRUMPLED ANY SPECIAL ASSIGNMENT ORDER.
EARTH ISN'T FOR ME, SIR.
I'M A SPACE-NOID THROUGH AND THROUGH.
LIEUTENANT GENERAL M'QUVE DID DISCREETLY ASK IF I'D BE INTERESTED,
BUT I TURNED HIM DOWN.

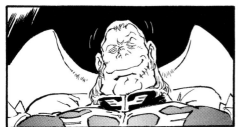

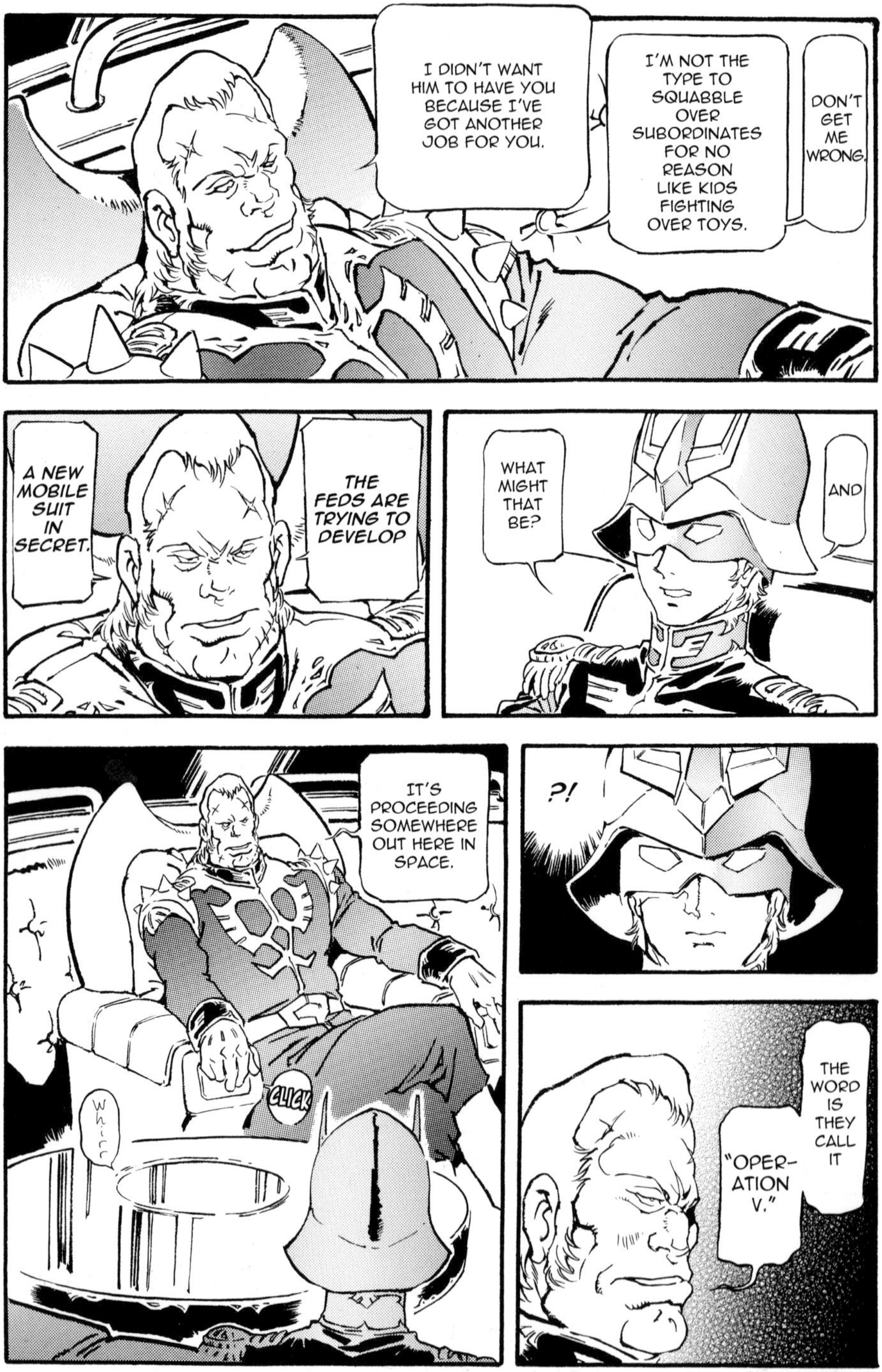
DON'T GET ME WRONG.
I'M NOT THE TYPE TO SQUABBLE OVER SUBORDINATES FOR NO REASON LIKE KIDS FIGHTING OVER TOYS.
I DIDN'T WANT HIM TO HAVE YOU BECAUSE I'VE GOT ANOTHER JOB FOR YOU.
AND
WHAT MIGHT THAT BE?
THE FEDS ARE TRYING TO DEVELOP
A NEW MOBILE SUIT IN SECRET.
?!
THE WORD IS THEY CALL IT
"OPERATION V."
IT'S PROCEEDING SOMEWHERE OUT HERE IN SPACE.
CLICK
Whirr

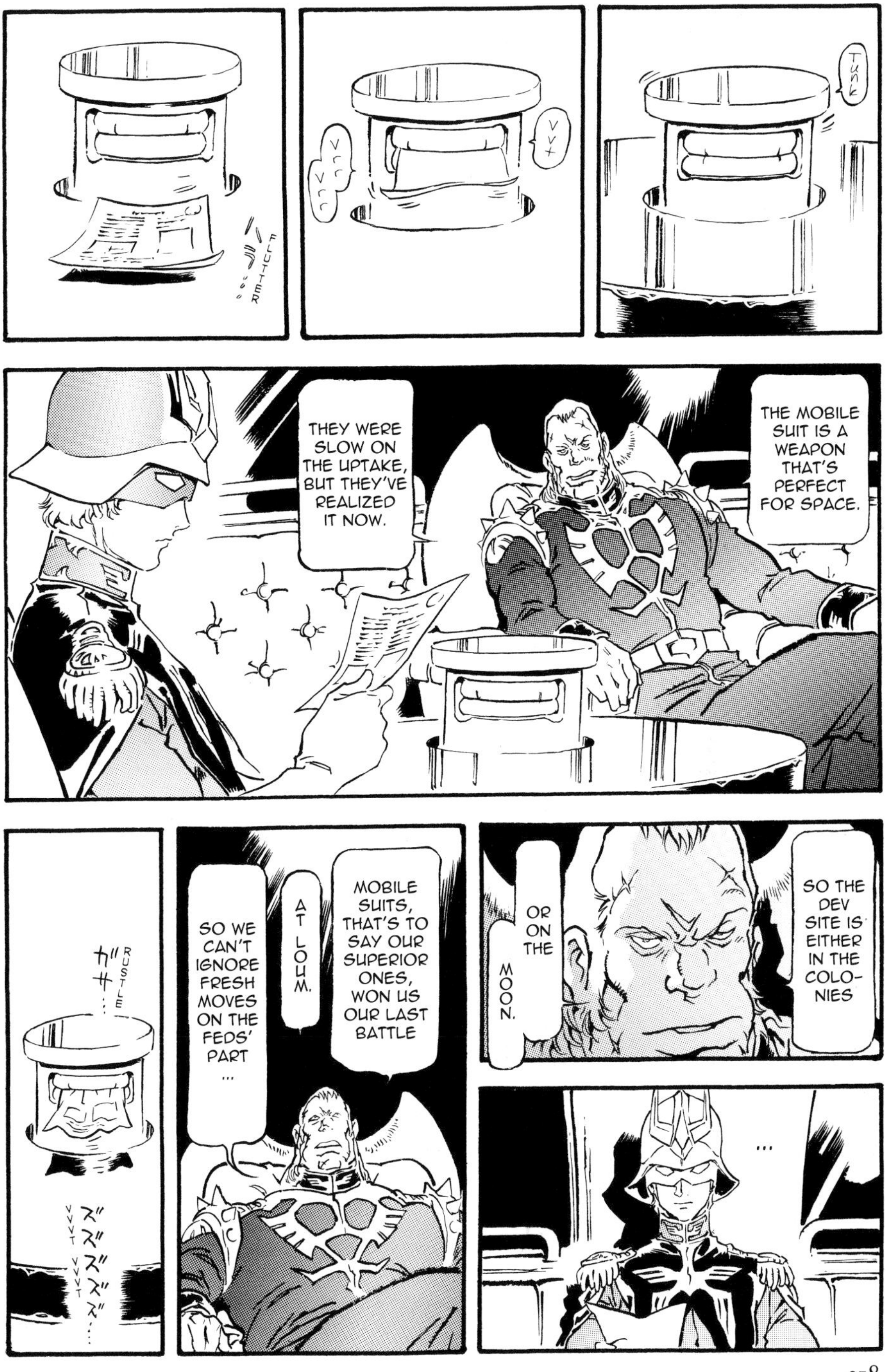
Tunk
Vvt
Vrr
Vrr
FLUTTER
THE MOBILE SUIT IS A WEAPON THAT'S PERFECT FOR SPACE.
THEY WERE SLOW ON THE UPTAKE, BUT THEY'VE REALIZED IT NOW.
SO THE DEV SITE IS EITHER IN THE COLONIES
OR ON THE MOON.
...
MOBILE SUITS, THAT'S TO SAY OUR SUPERIOR ONES, WON US OUR LAST BATTLE
AT LOUM.
SO WE CAN'T IGNORE FRESH MOVES ON THE FEDS' PART ...
RUSTLE
VVVT VVVT

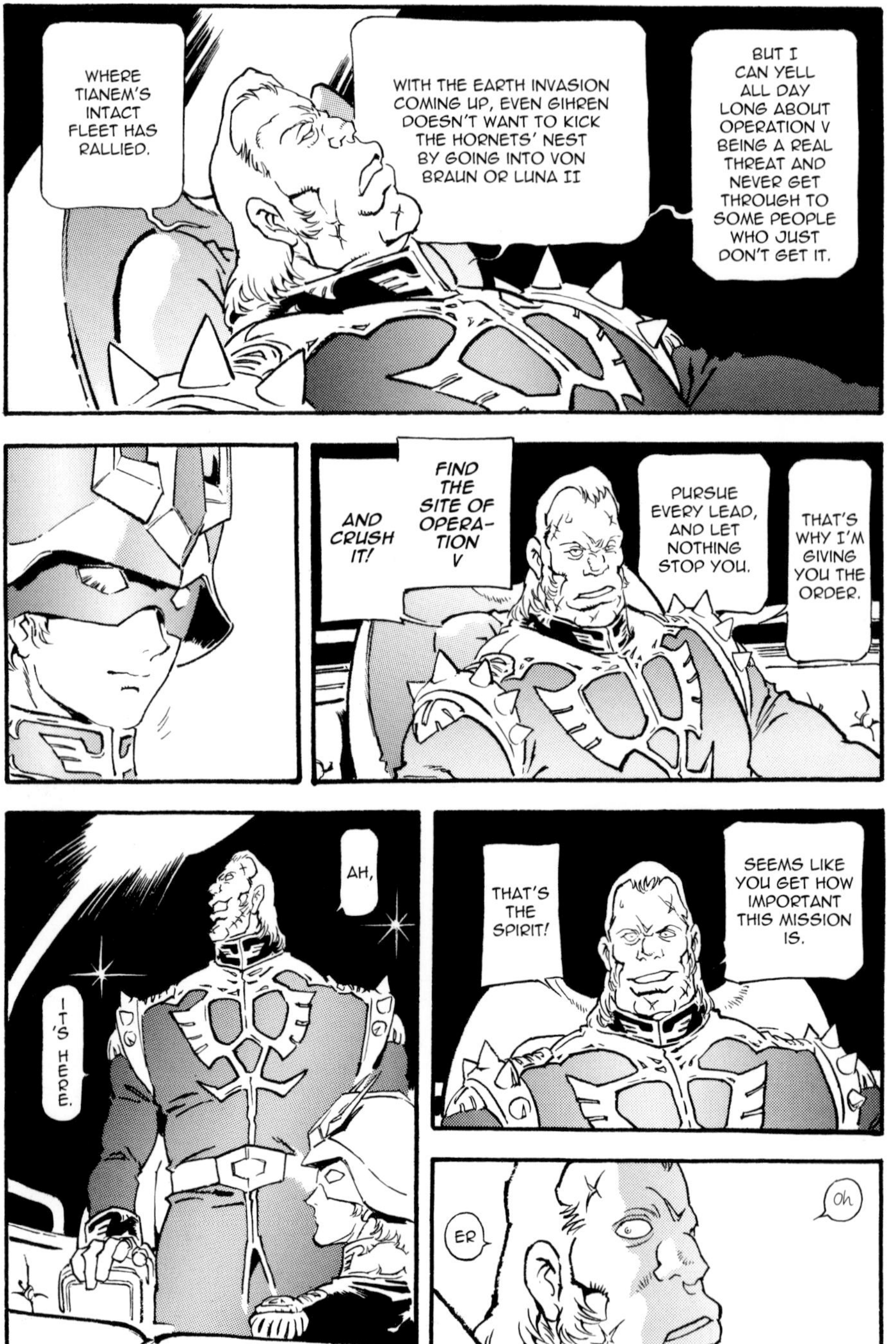
BUT I CAN YELL ALL DAY LONG ABOUT OPERATION V BEING A REAL THREAT AND NEVER GET THROUGH TO SOME PEOPLE WHO JUST DON'T GET IT.
WITH THE EARTH INVASION COMING UP, EVEN GIHREN DOESN'T WANT TO KICK THE HORNETS' NEST BY GOING INTO VON BRAUN OR LUNA II
WHERE TIANEM'S INTACT FLEET HAS RALLIED.
THAT'S WHY I'M GIVING YOU THE ORDER.
PURSUE EVERY LEAD, AND LET NOTHING STOP YOU.
FIND THE SITE OF OPERATION V
AND CRUSH IT!
SEEMS LIKE YOU GET HOW IMPORTANT THIS MISSION IS.
THAT'S THE SPIRIT!
Oh
ER
AH,
IT'S HERE.

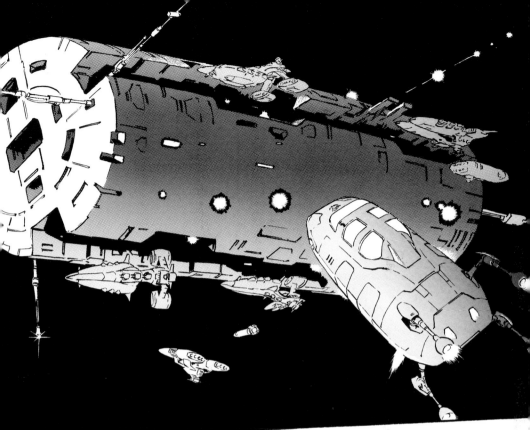

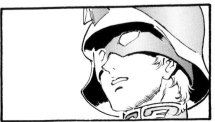

LOOK.

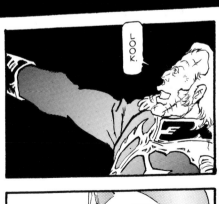

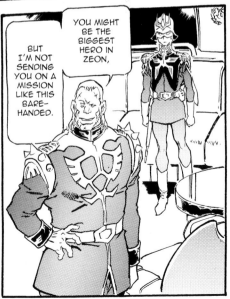

YOU MIGHT BE THE BIGGEST HERO IN ZEON,

BUT I'M NOT SENDING YOU ON A MISSION LIKE THIS BARE-HANDED.

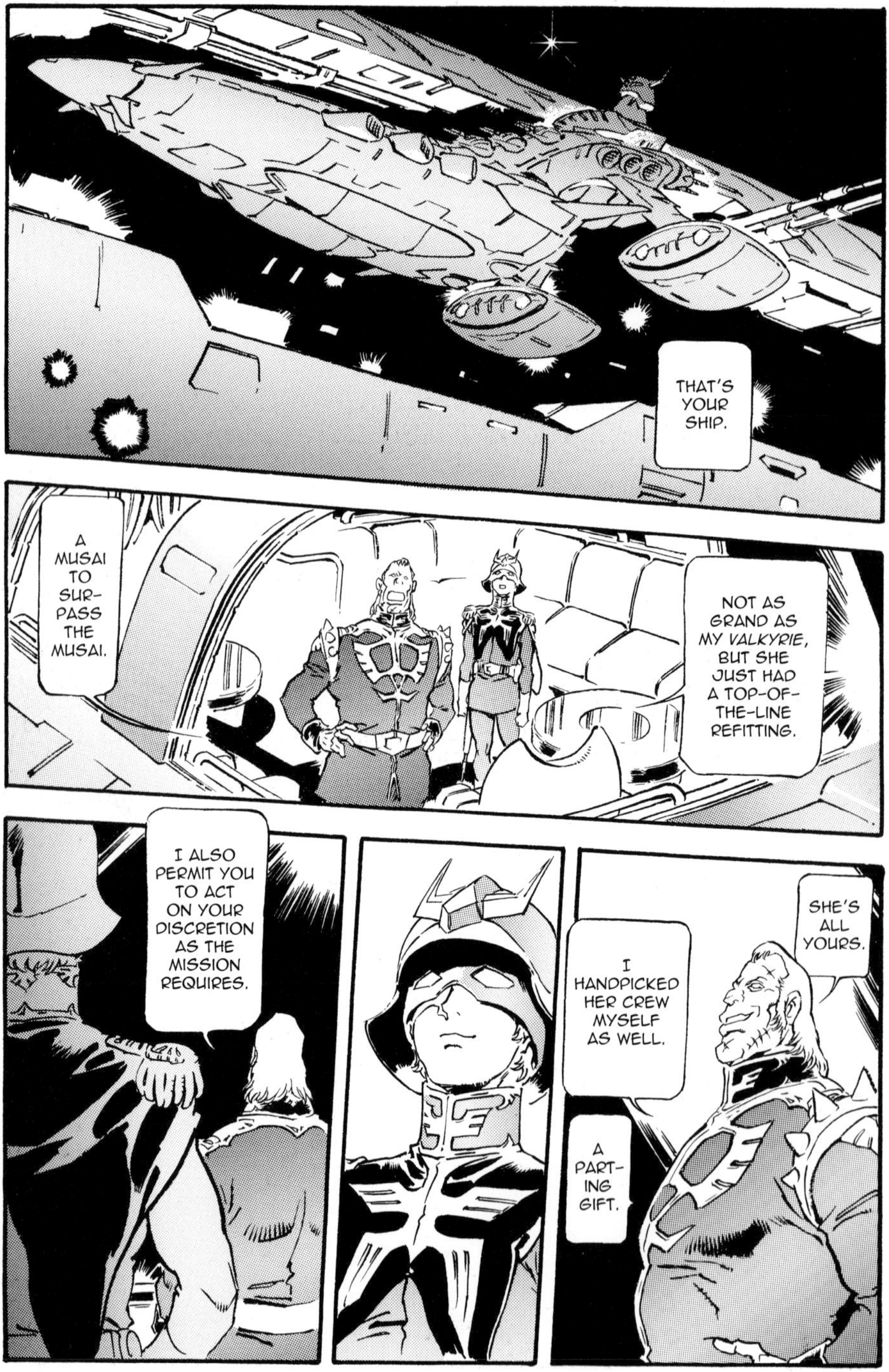
THAT'S YOUR SHIP.
NOT AS GRAND AS MY *VALKYRIE*, BUT SHE JUST HAD A TOP-OF-THE-LINE REFITTING.
A MUSAI TO SURPASS THE MUSAI.
SHE'S ALL YOURS.
I HANDPICKED HER CREW MYSELF AS WELL.
A PARTING GIFT.
I ALSO PERMIT YOU TO ACT ON YOUR DISCRETION AS THE MISSION REQUIRES.

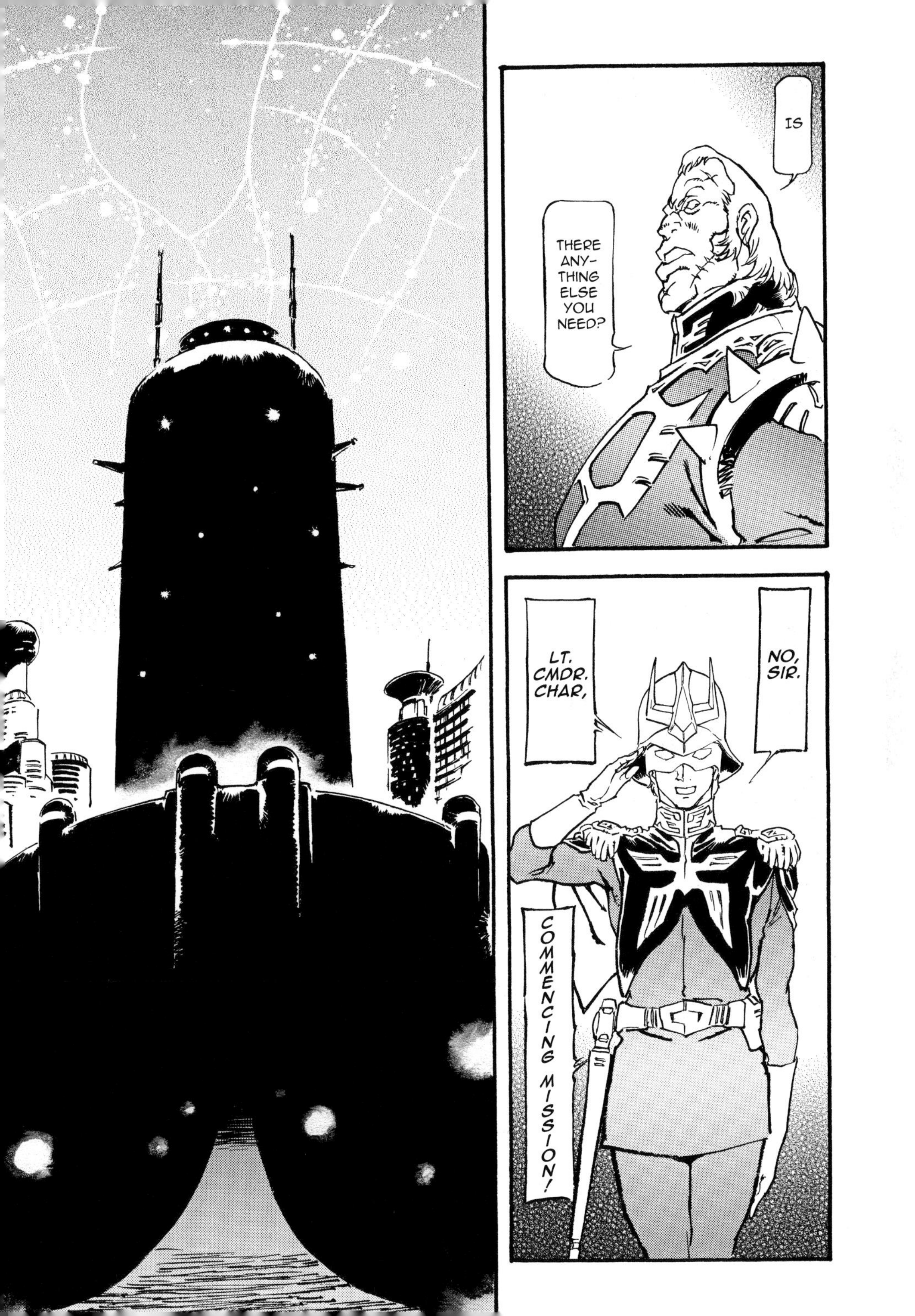
IS
THERE ANY-THING ELSE YOU NEED?
NO, SIR.
LT. CMDR. CHAR,
COMMENCING MISSION!

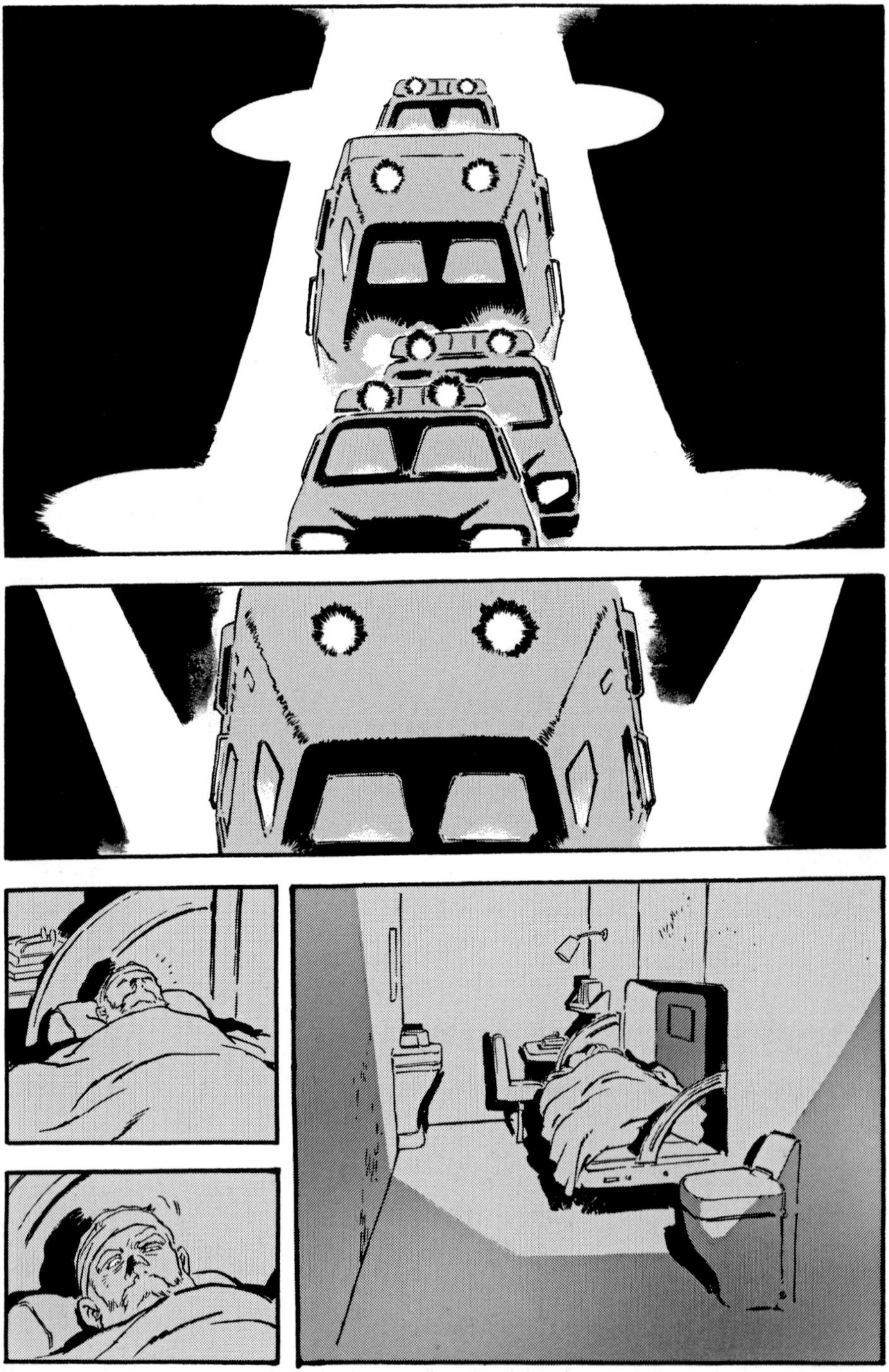

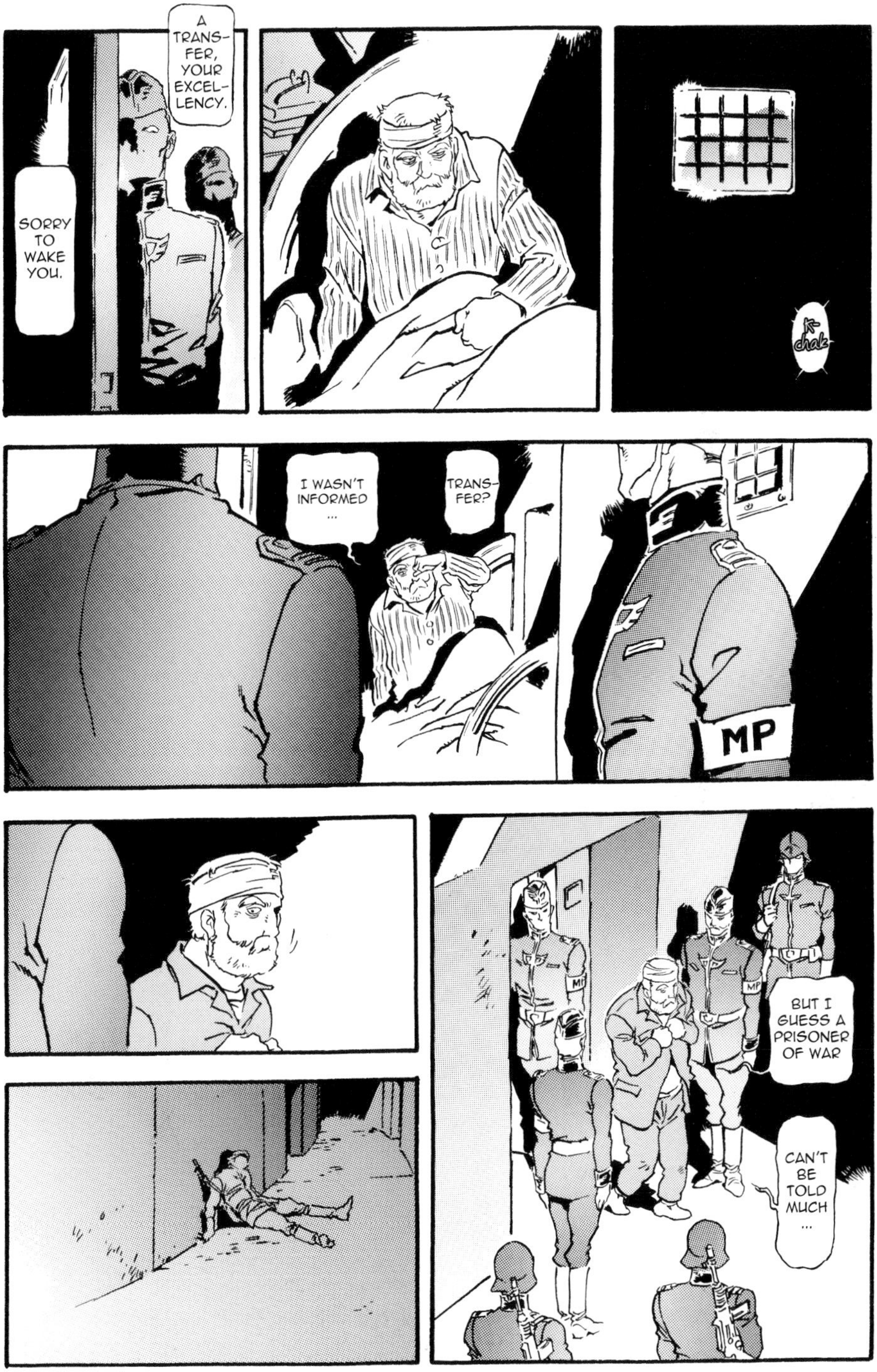
k-chak
A TRANSFER, YOUR EXCELLENCY.
SORRY TO WAKE YOU.
TRANSFER?
I WASN'T INFORMED ...
BUT I GUESS A PRISONER OF WAR
CAN'T BE TOLD MUCH ...
MP

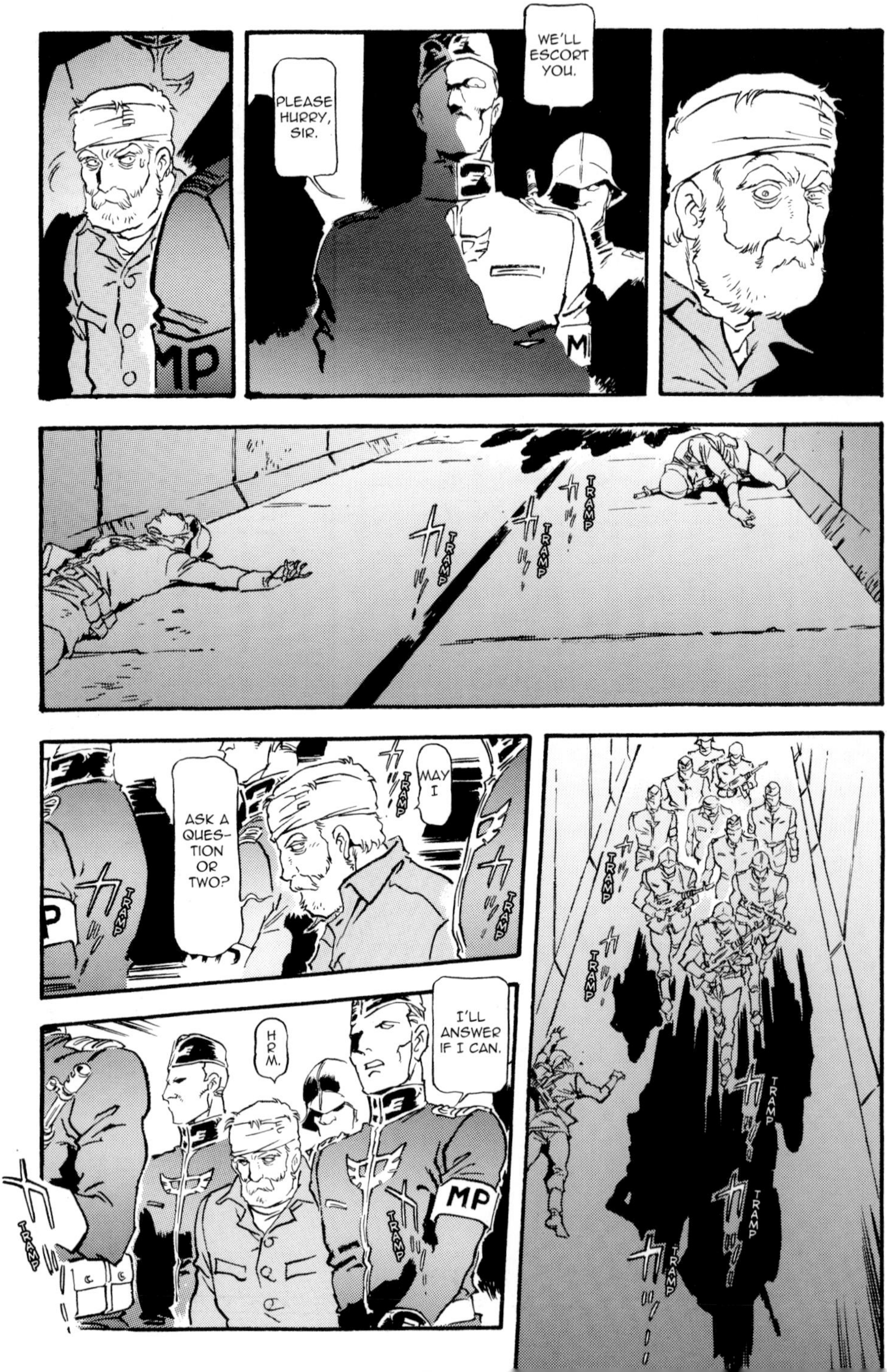
WE'LL ESCORT YOU.
PLEASE HURRY, SIR.
TRAMP
TRAMP
TRAMP
TRAMP
TRAMP
TRAMP
TRAMP
TRAMP
MAY I
ASK A QUESTION OR TWO?
TRAMP
TRAMP
TRAMP
I'LL ANSWER IF I CAN.
HRM.
TRAMP
TRAMP

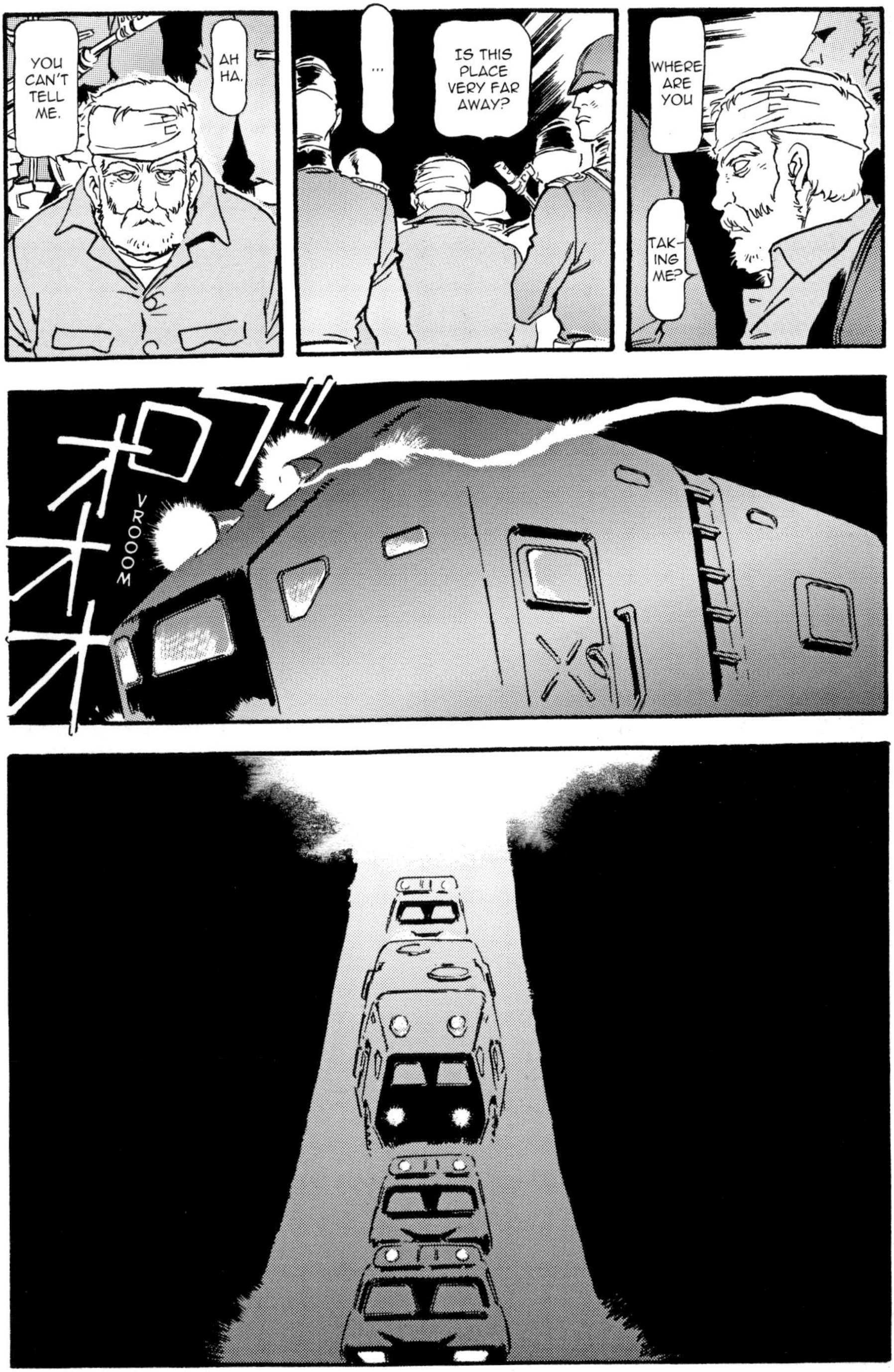
WHERE ARE YOU
TAKING ME?
...
IS THIS PLACE VERY FAR AWAY?
AH HA.
YOU CAN'T TELL ME.
ブロオオオ
VROOOM

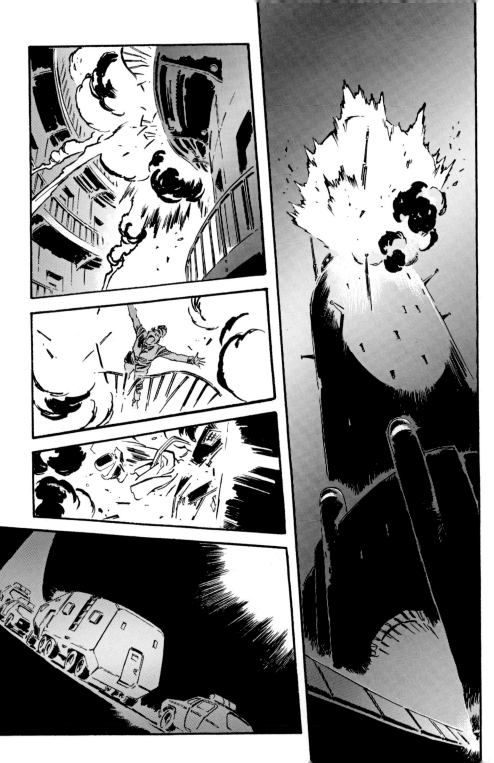

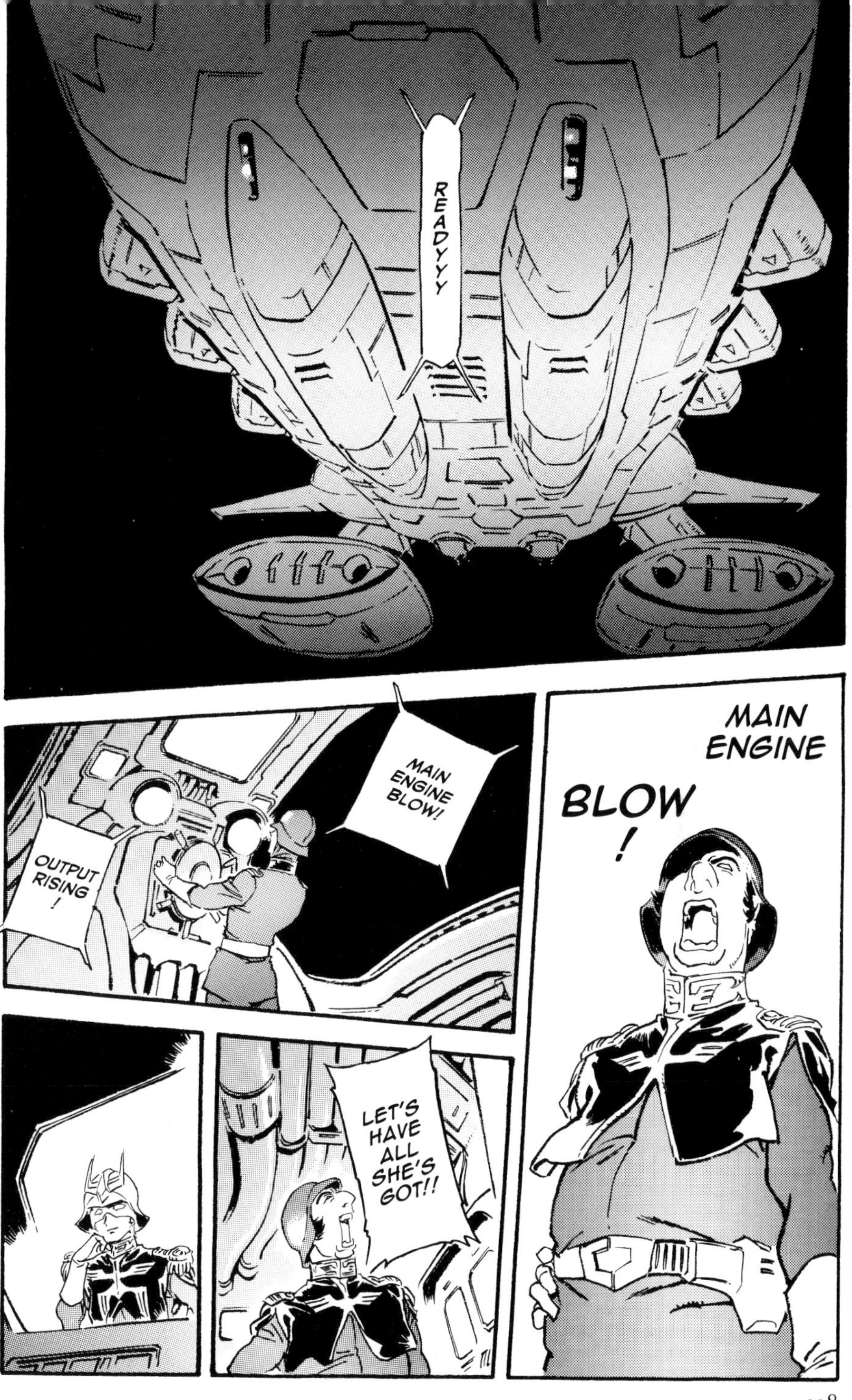
READYYY
MAIN ENGINE BLOW!
MAIN ENGINE BLOW!
OUTPUT RISING!
LET'S HAVE ALL SHE'S GOT!!

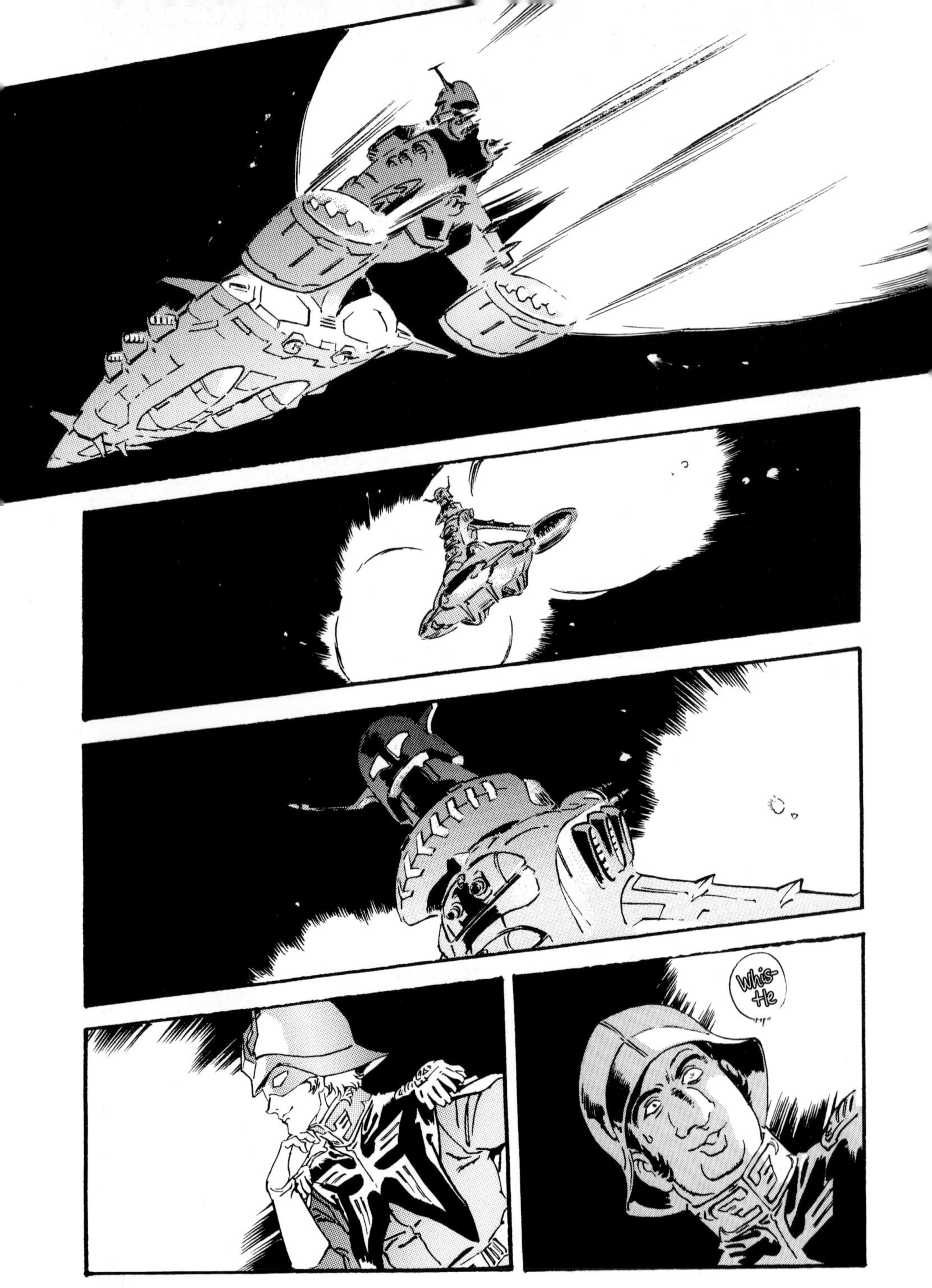
Whis-tle

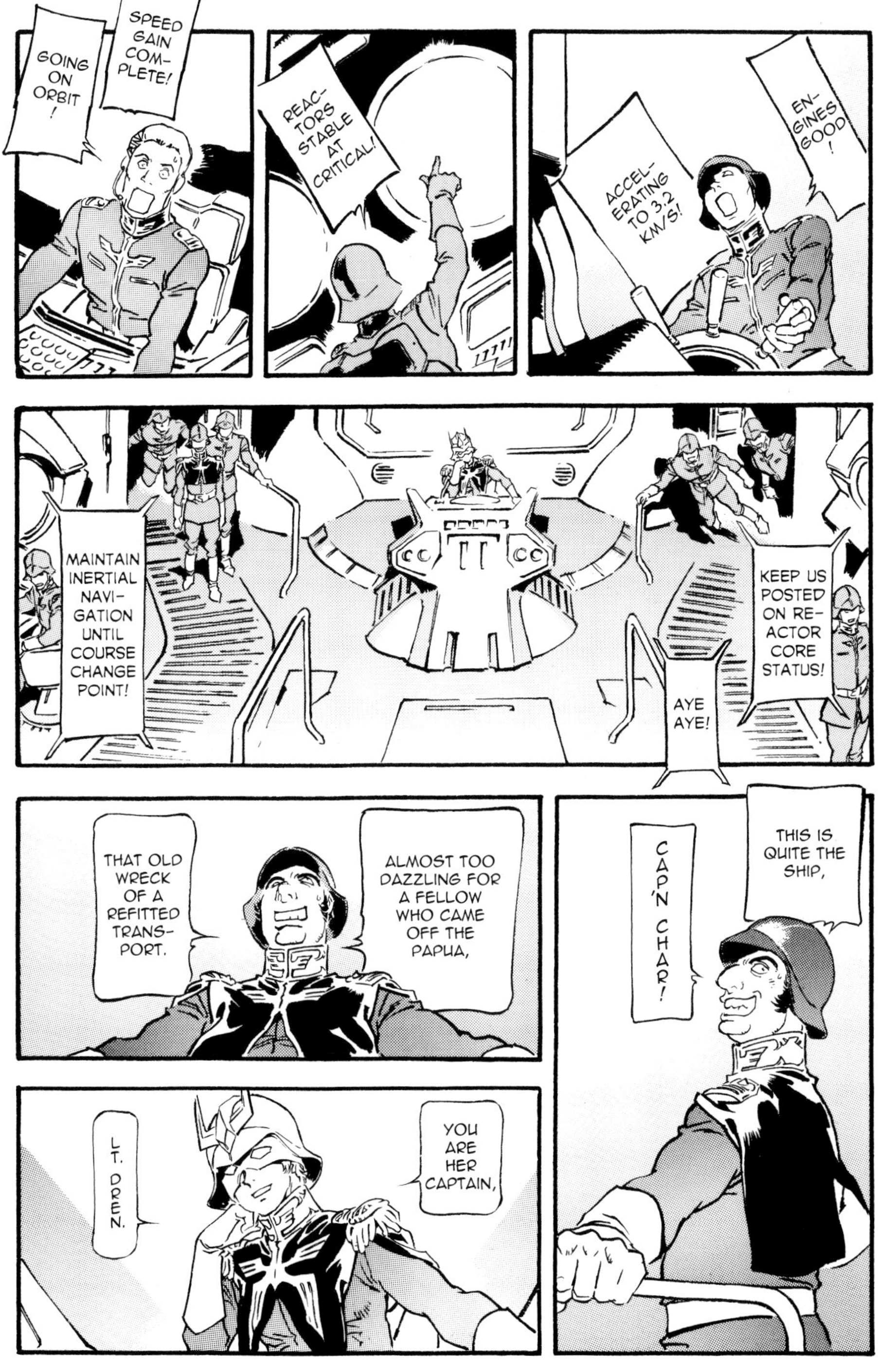
ENGINES GOOD!
ACCELERATING TO 3.2 KM/S!
REACTORS STABLE AT CRITICAL!
SPEED GAIN COMPLETE!
GOING ON ORBIT!
KEEP US POSTED ON REACTOR CORE STATUS!
AYE AYE!
MAINTAIN INERTIAL NAVIGATION UNTIL COURSE CHANGE POINT!
THIS IS QUITE THE SHIP,
CAP'N CHAR!
ALMOST TOO DAZZLING FOR A FELLOW WHO CAME OFF THE PAPUA,
THAT OLD WRECK OF A REFITTED TRANSPORT.
YOU ARE HER CAPTAIN,
LT. DREN.

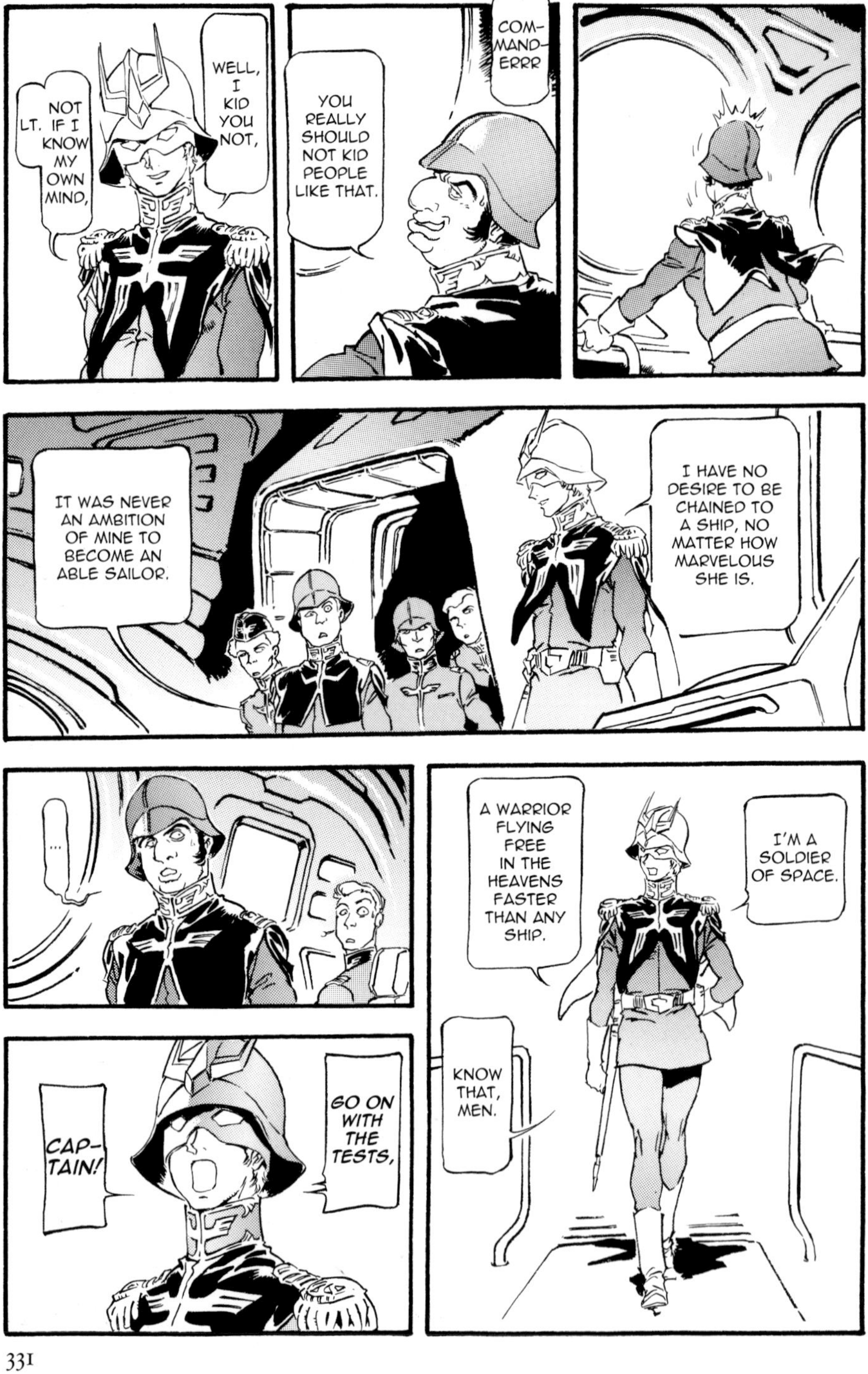
COM-MAND-ERRR
YOU REALLY SHOULD NOT KID PEOPLE LIKE THAT.
WELL, I KID YOU NOT,
NOT LT. IF I KNOW MY OWN MIND,
I HAVE NO DESIRE TO BE CHAINED TO A SHIP, NO MATTER HOW MARVELOUS SHE IS.
IT WAS NEVER AN AMBITION OF MINE TO BECOME AN ABLE SAILOR.
I'M A SOLDIER OF SPACE.
A WARRIOR FLYING FREE IN THE HEAVENS FASTER THAN ANY SHIP.
KNOW THAT, MEN.
...
GO ON WITH THE TESTS,
CAP-TAIN!

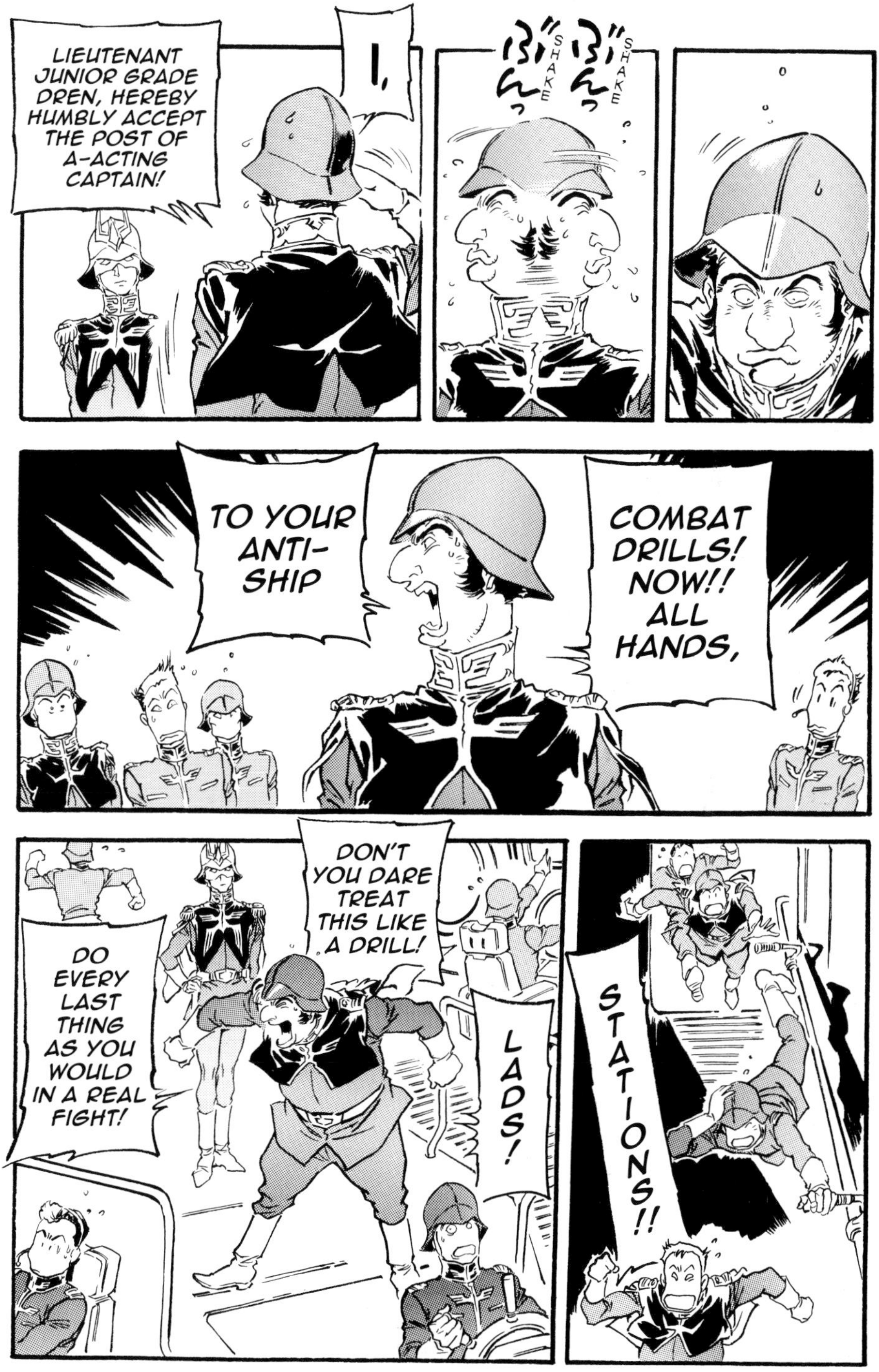
ぶんっ SHAKE
ぶんっ SHAKE
I,
LIEUTENANT JUNIOR GRADE DREN, HEREBY HUMBLY ACCEPT THE POST OF A-ACTING CAPTAIN!
COMBAT DRILLS! NOW!! ALL HANDS,
TO YOUR ANTI-SHIP
STATIONS!!
LADS!
DON'T YOU DARE TREAT THIS LIKE A DRILL!
DO EVERY LAST THING AS YOU WOULD IN A REAL FIGHT!

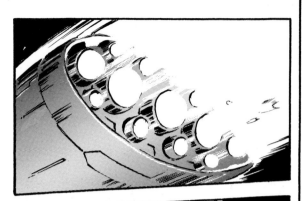

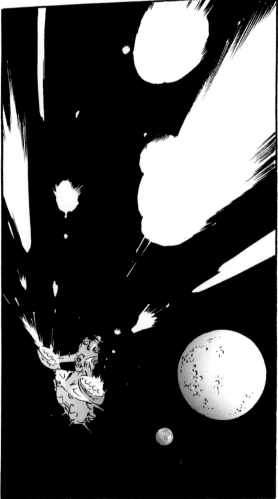

SETTING COURSE FOR THE BATTLE ZONE! TURN 90 DEGREES!

FULL SPEED AHEAD !!!

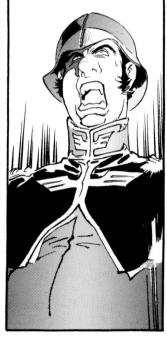

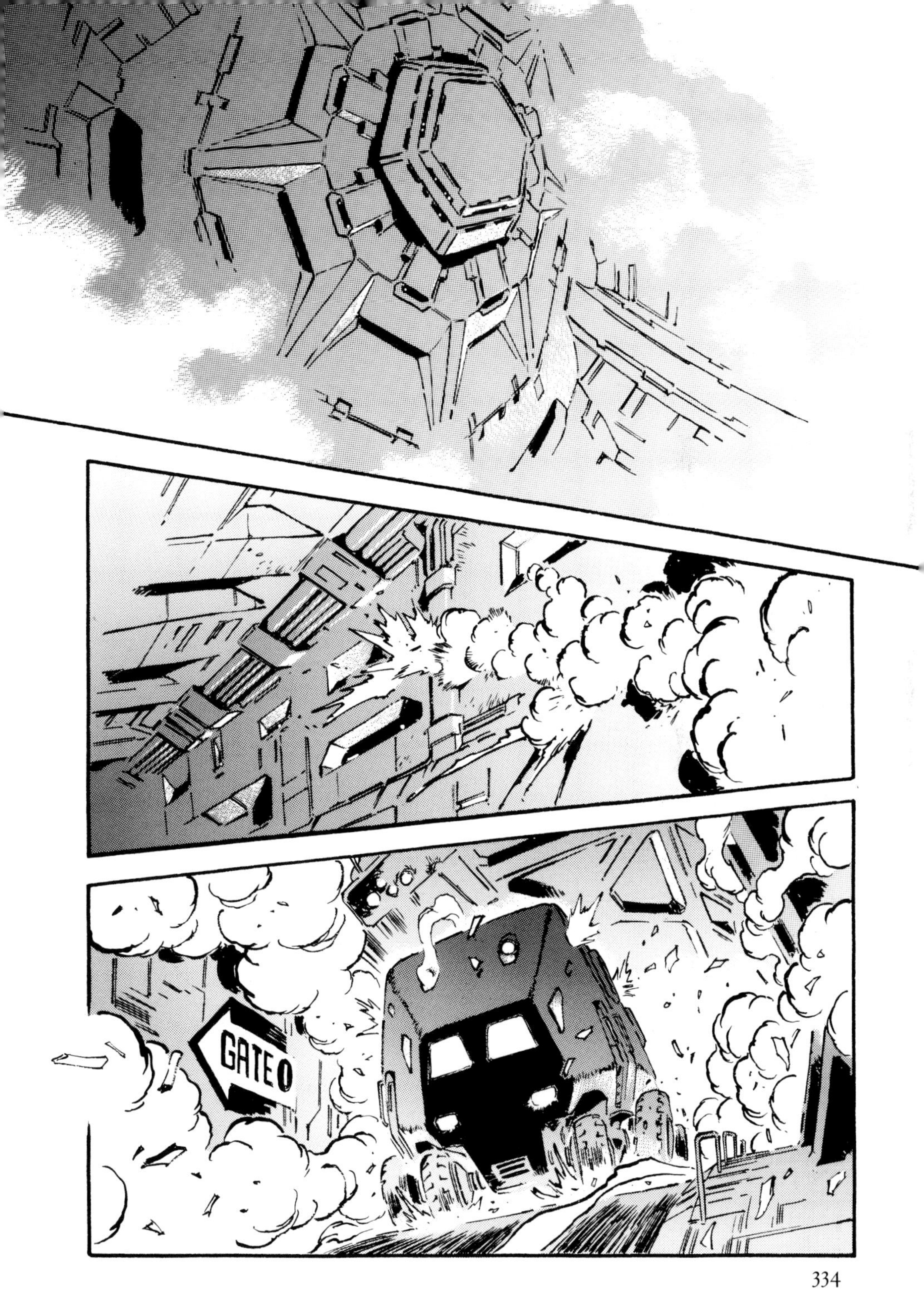
GATE 0

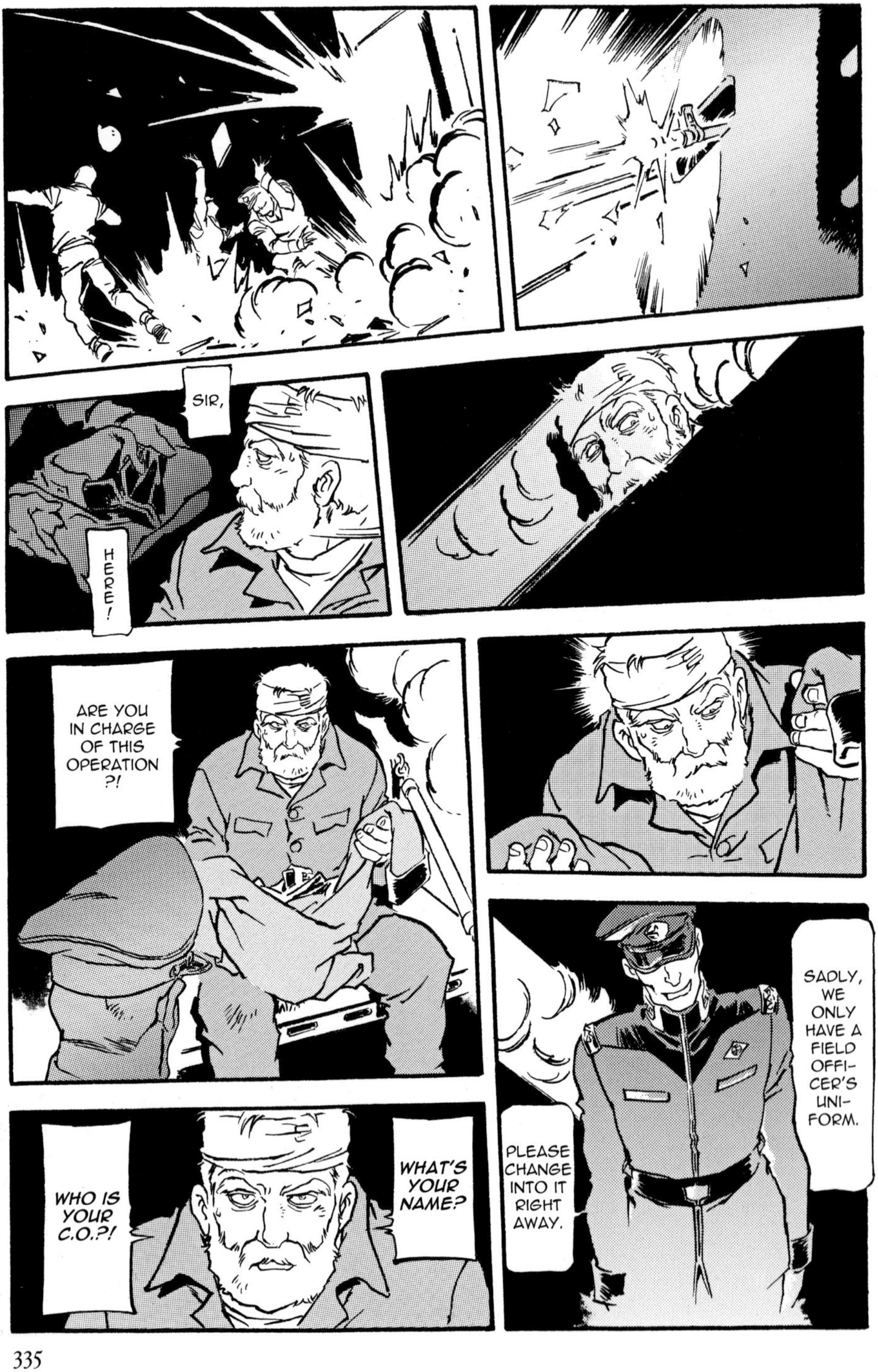
SIR,
HERE!
ARE YOU IN CHARGE OF THIS OPERATION?!
SADLY, WE ONLY HAVE A FIELD OFFICER'S UNIFORM.
PLEASE CHANGE INTO IT RIGHT AWAY.
WHAT'S YOUR NAME?
WHO IS YOUR C.O.?!

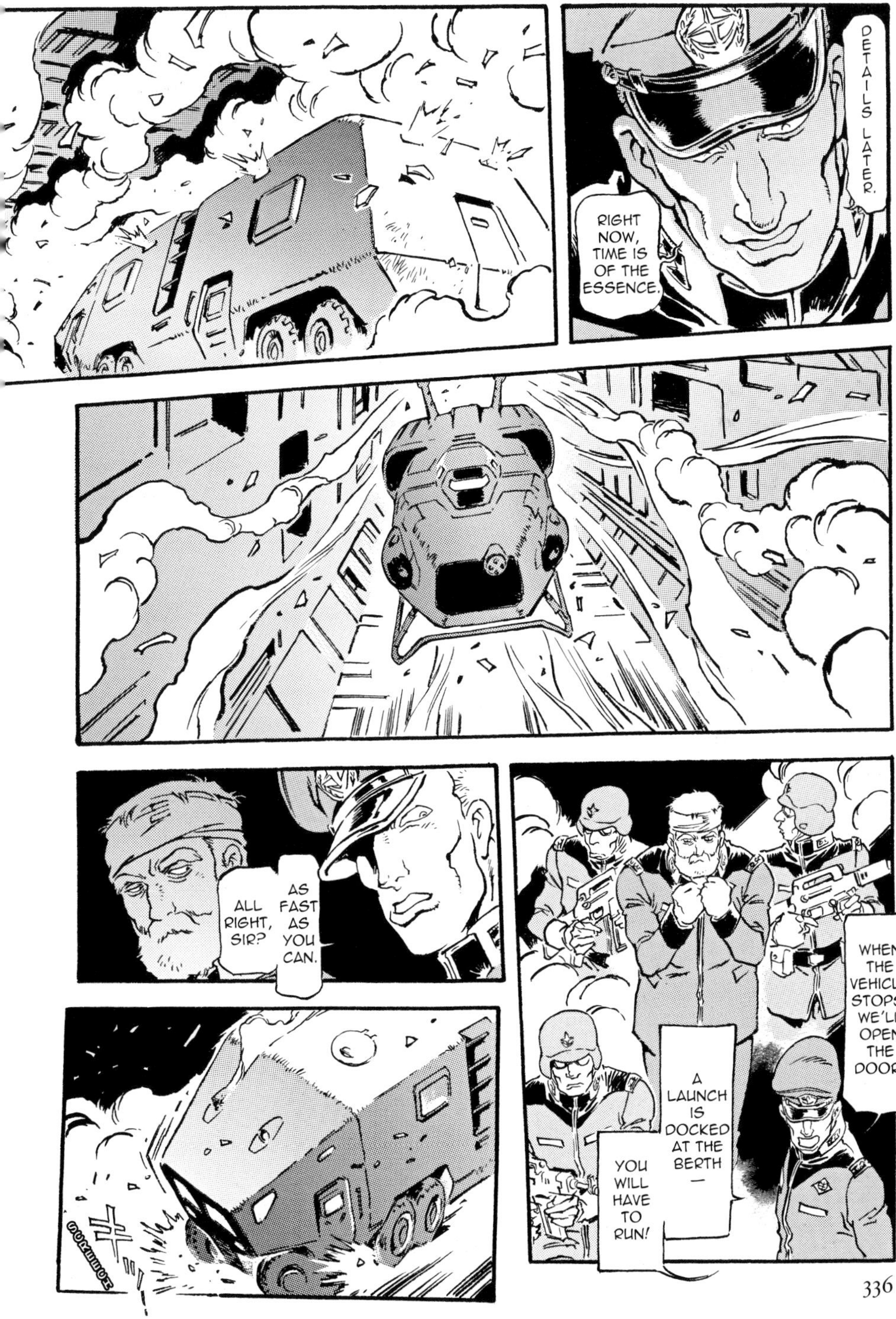
DETAILS LATER.
RIGHT NOW, TIME IS OF THE ESSENCE.
WHEN THE VEHICLE STOPS, WE'LL OPEN THE DOOR.
A LAUNCH IS DOCKED AT THE BERTH—
YOU WILL HAVE TO RUN!
AS FAST AS YOU CAN.
ALL RIGHT, SIR?

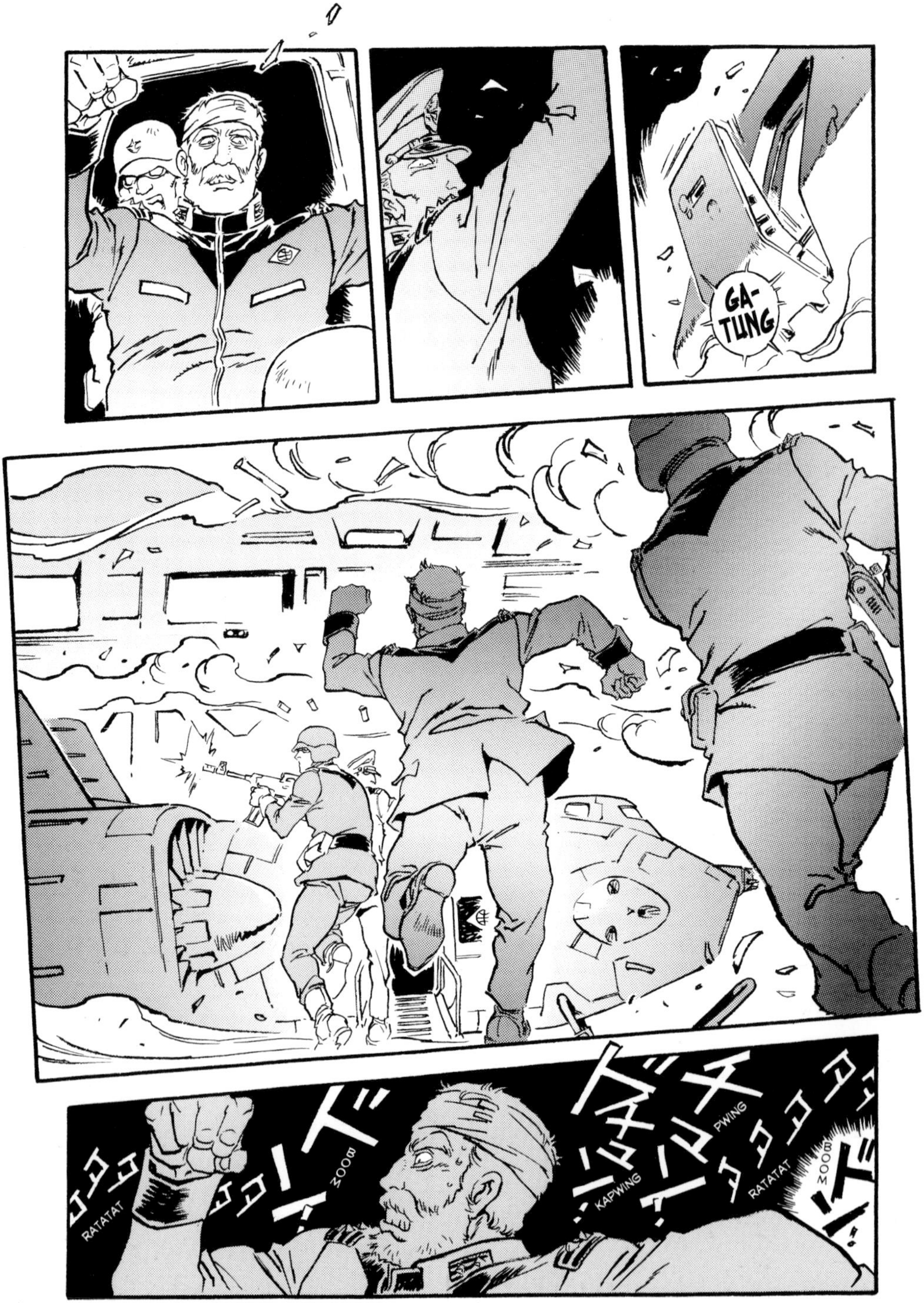
GA-TUNG
BOOM
RATATAT
PWING
KAPWING
BOOM
RATATAT

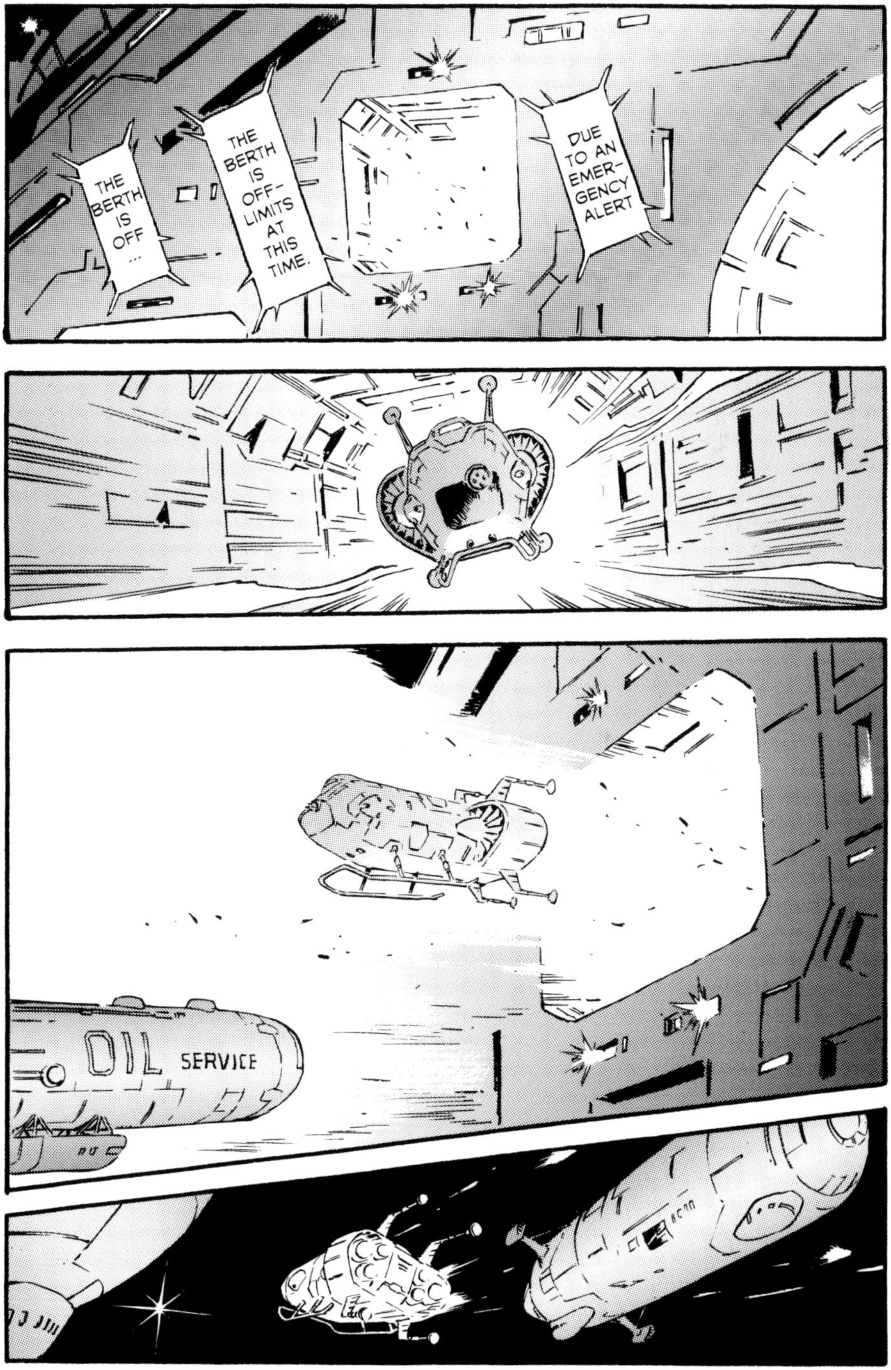
DUE TO AN EMERGENCY ALERT
THE BERTH IS OFF-LIMITS AT THIS TIME.
THE BERTH IS OFF ...
OIL SERVICE

ALL CLEAR
WE HAVE THE GEN-ERAL.
OFF TO REN-DEZ-VOUS POINT.
HUFF
HUFF
HUFF
HUFF
HUFF
HUFF ...
.....

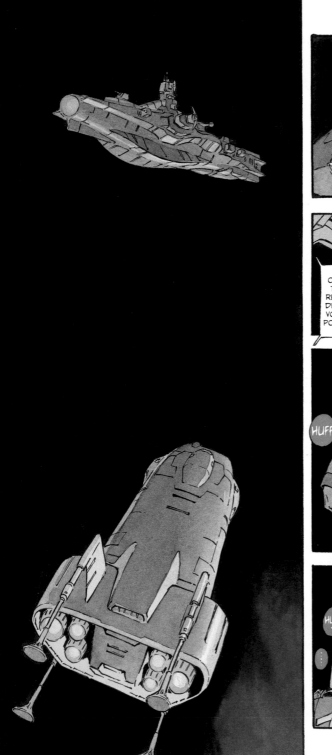

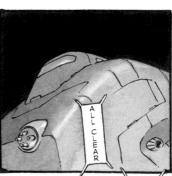

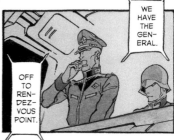

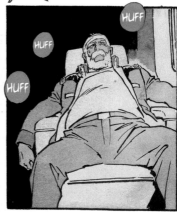

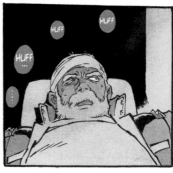

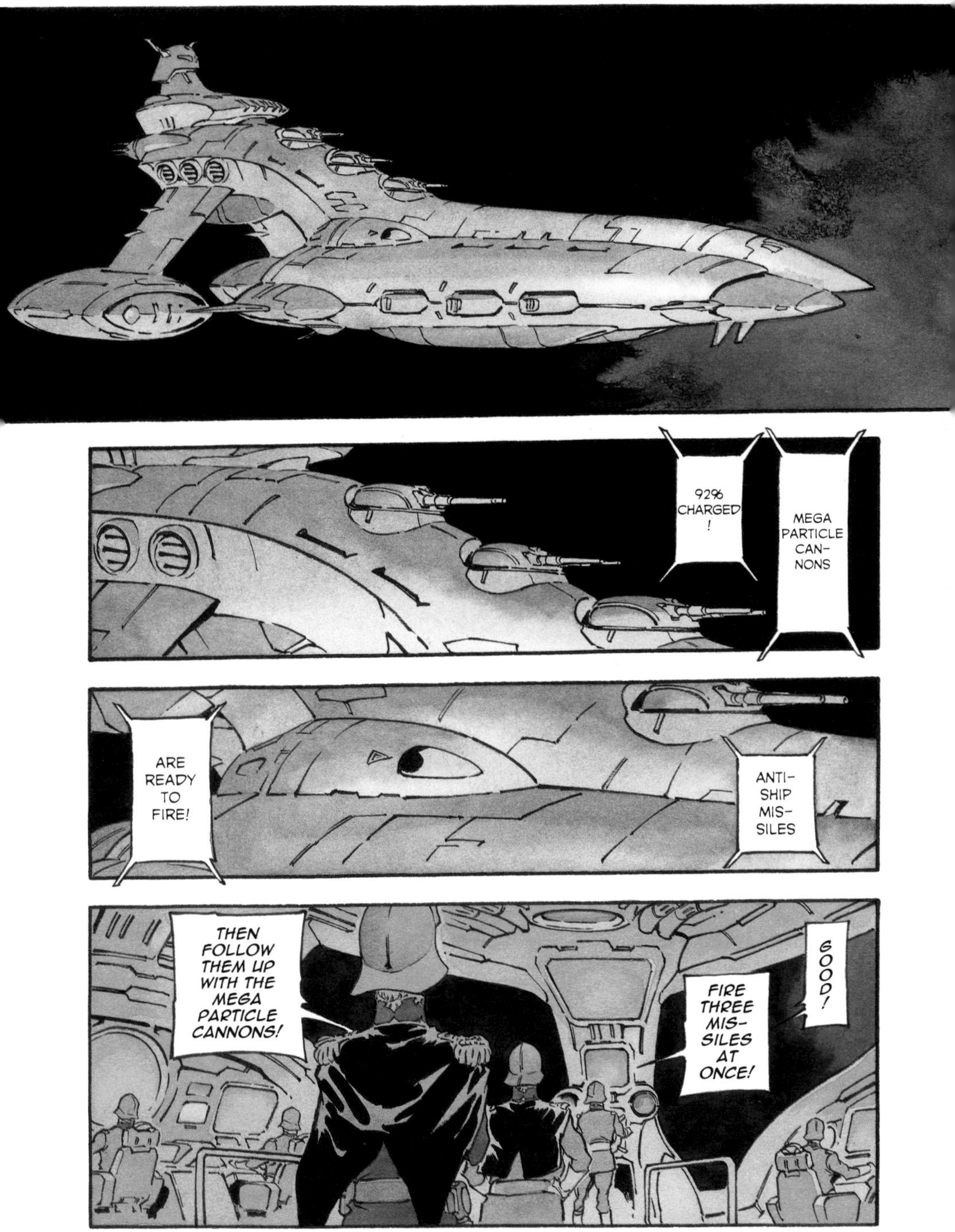
MEGA PARTICLE CAN-NONS
92% CHARGED!
ANTI-SHIP MIS-SILES
ARE READY TO FIRE!
GOOD!
FIRE THREE MIS-SILES AT ONCE!
THEN FOLLOW THEM UP WITH THE MEGA PARTICLE CANNONS!

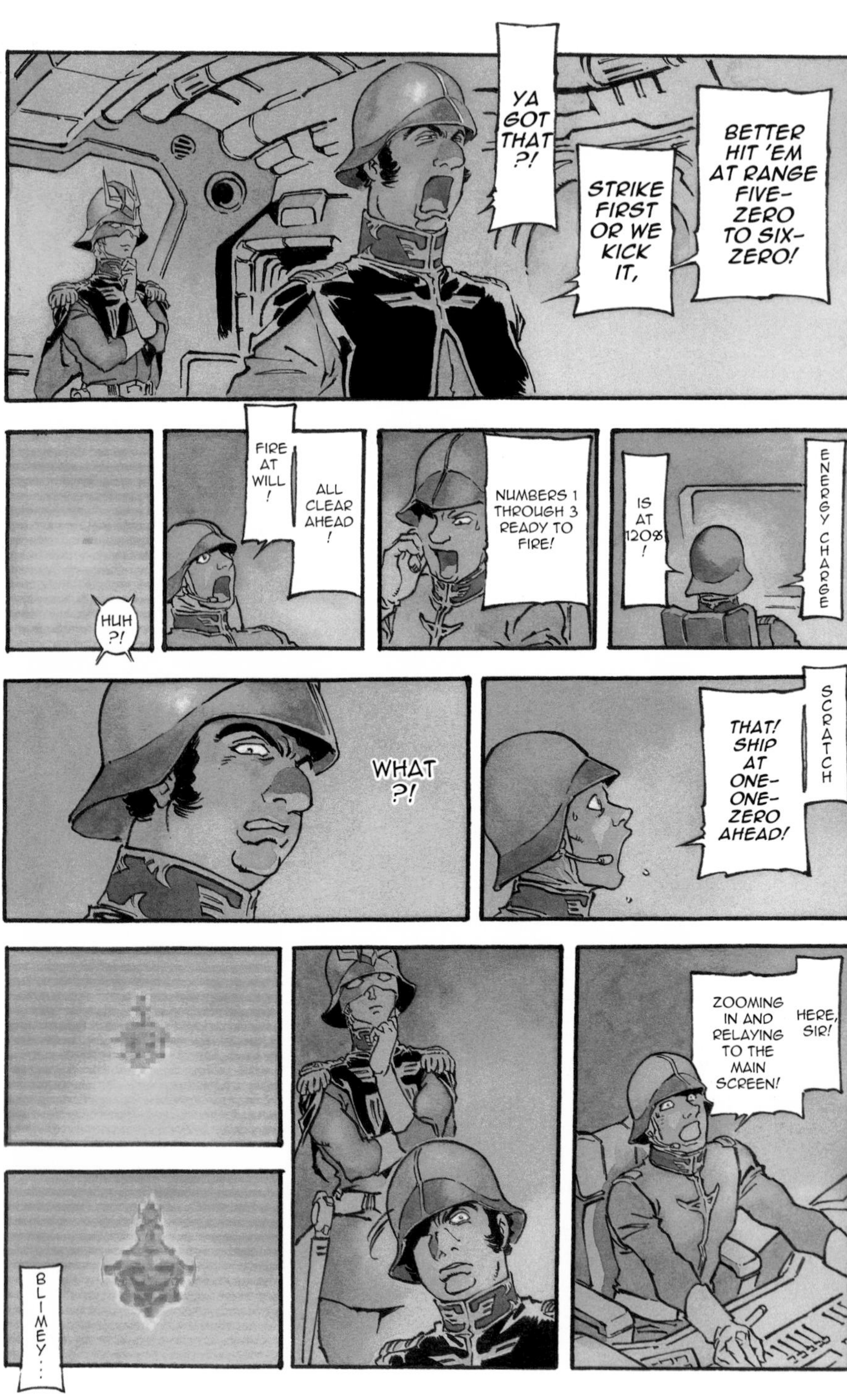
BETTER HIT 'EM AT RANGE FIVE-ZERO TO SIX-ZERO!
STRIKE FIRST OR WE KICK IT,
YA GOT THAT?!
ENERGY CHARGE
IS AT 120%!
NUMBERS 1 THROUGH 3 READY TO FIRE!
ALL CLEAR AHEAD!
FIRE AT WILL!
HUH?!
SCRATCH
THAT! SHIP AT ONE-ONE-ZERO AHEAD!
WHAT?!
HERE, SIR!
ZOOMING IN AND RELAYING TO THE MAIN SCREEN!
BLIMEY...

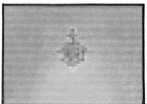

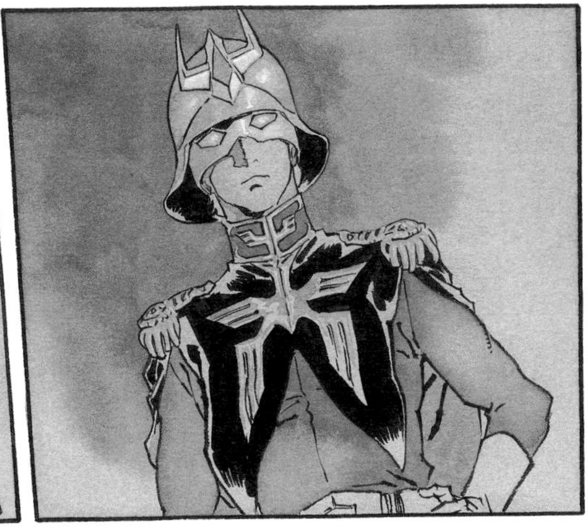

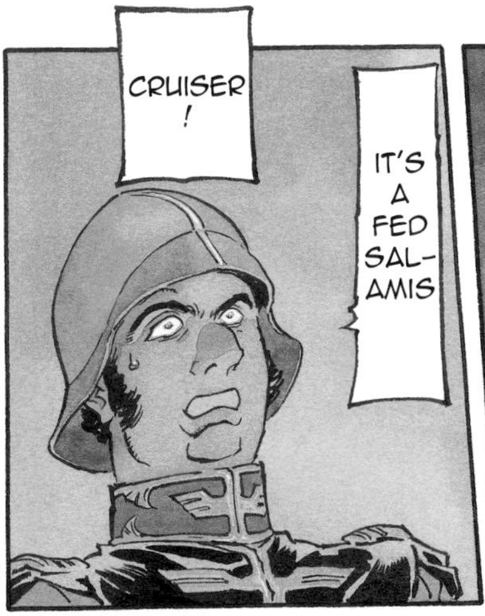
IT'S A FED SAL-AMIS
CRUISER!

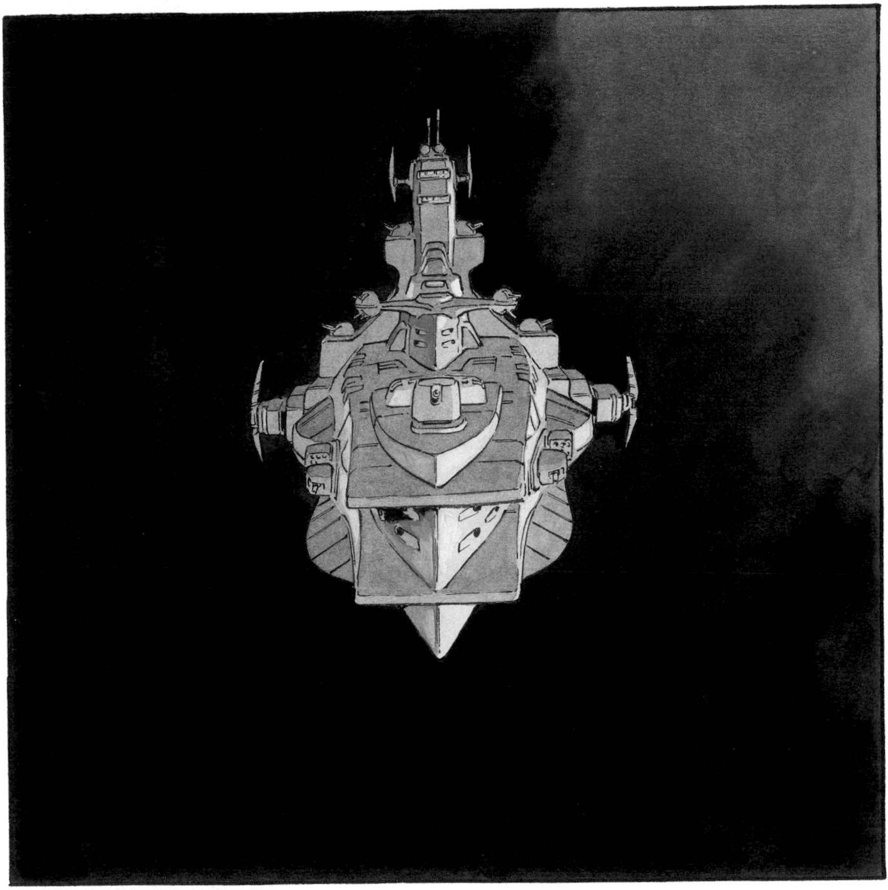

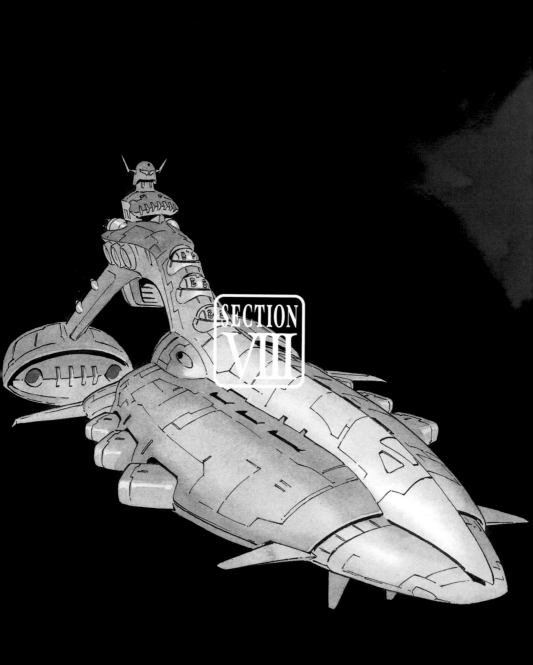

SECTION
VIII

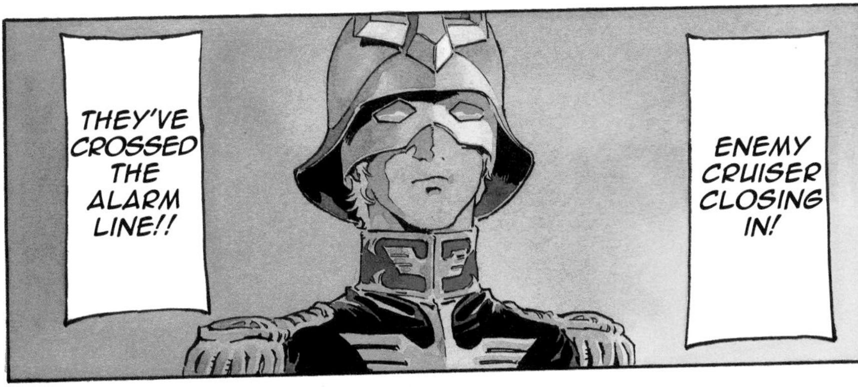
ENEMY CRUISER CLOSING IN!
THEY'VE CROSSED THE ALARM LINE!!
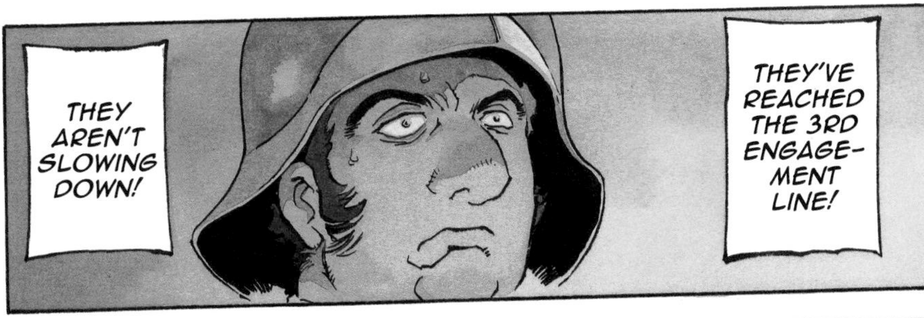
THEY'VE REACHED THE 3RD ENGAGEMENT LINE!
THEY AREN'T SLOWING DOWN!
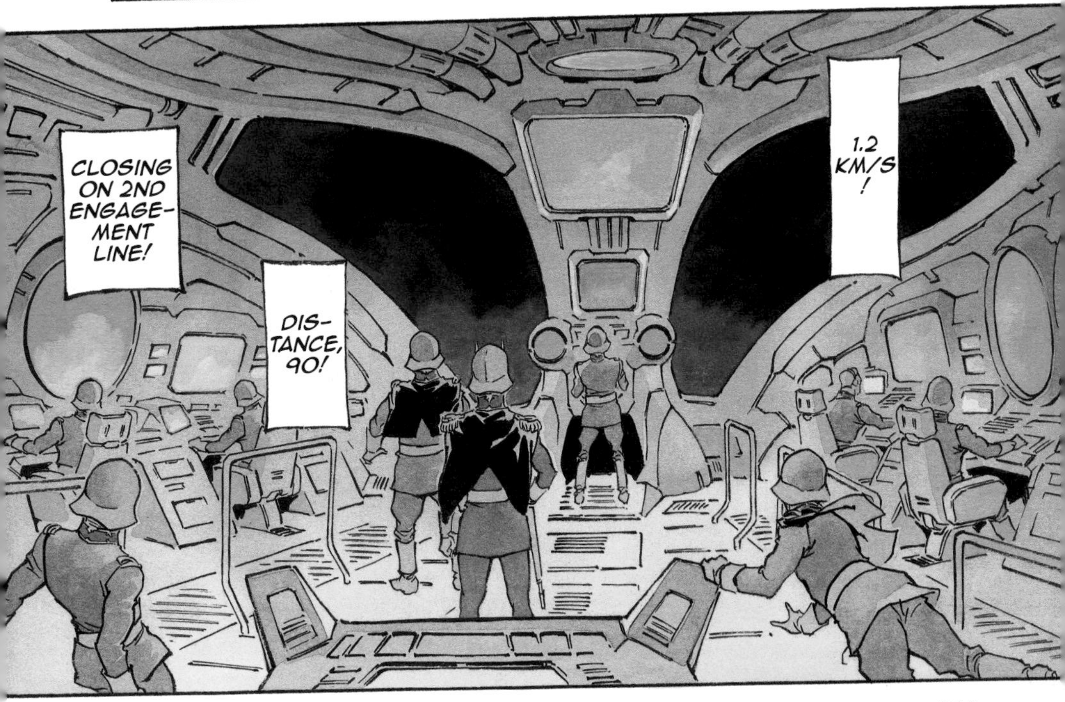
1.2 KM/S!
CLOSING ON 2ND ENGAGEMENT LINE!
DISTANCE, 90!

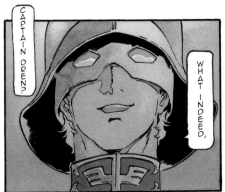

CAPTAIN DREN?

WHAT INDEED,

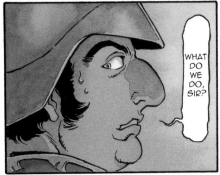

WHAT DO WE DO, SIR?

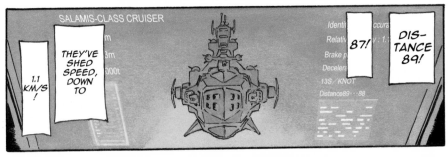

SALAMIS-CLASS CRUISER

THEY'VE SHED SPEED, DOWN TO

1.1 KM/S!

87!

DIS-TANCE 89!

Identi... ccura...
Relativ... v : 1...
Brake p...
Decelera...
13S／KNOT
Distance89…88

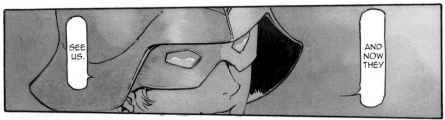

SEE US.

AND NOW THEY

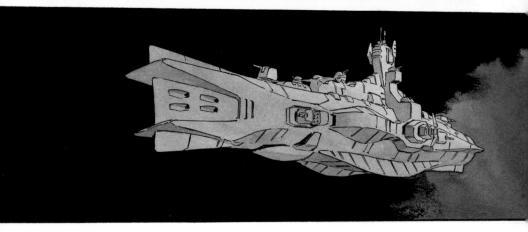

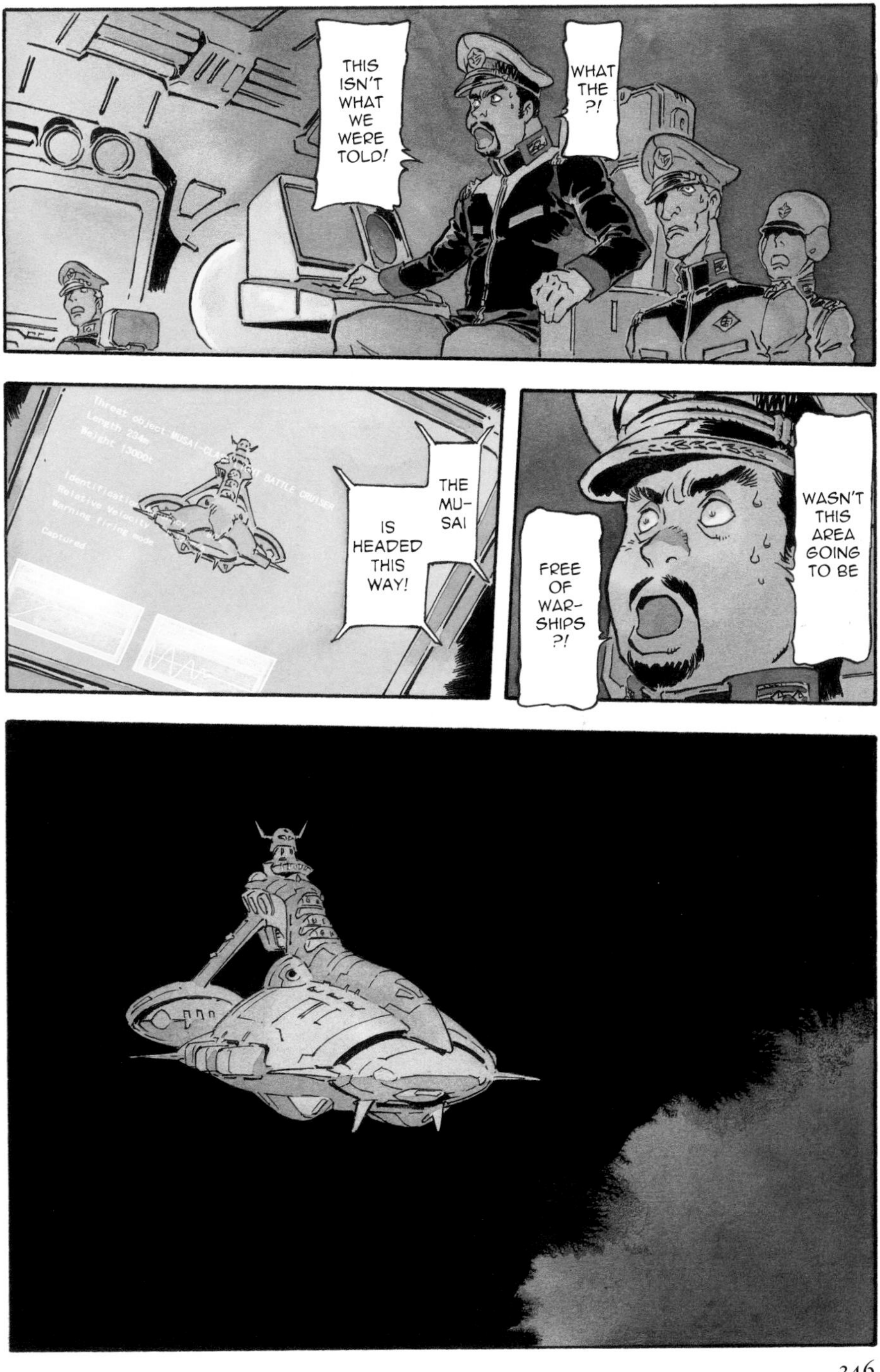
WHAT THE ?!
THIS ISN'T WHAT WE WERE TOLD!
WASN'T THIS AREA GOING TO BE
FREE OF WAR-SHIPS ?!
THE MU-SAI
IS HEADED THIS WAY!
Length 234m
Weight 13000t
Relative Velocity
Warning firing mode
Captured

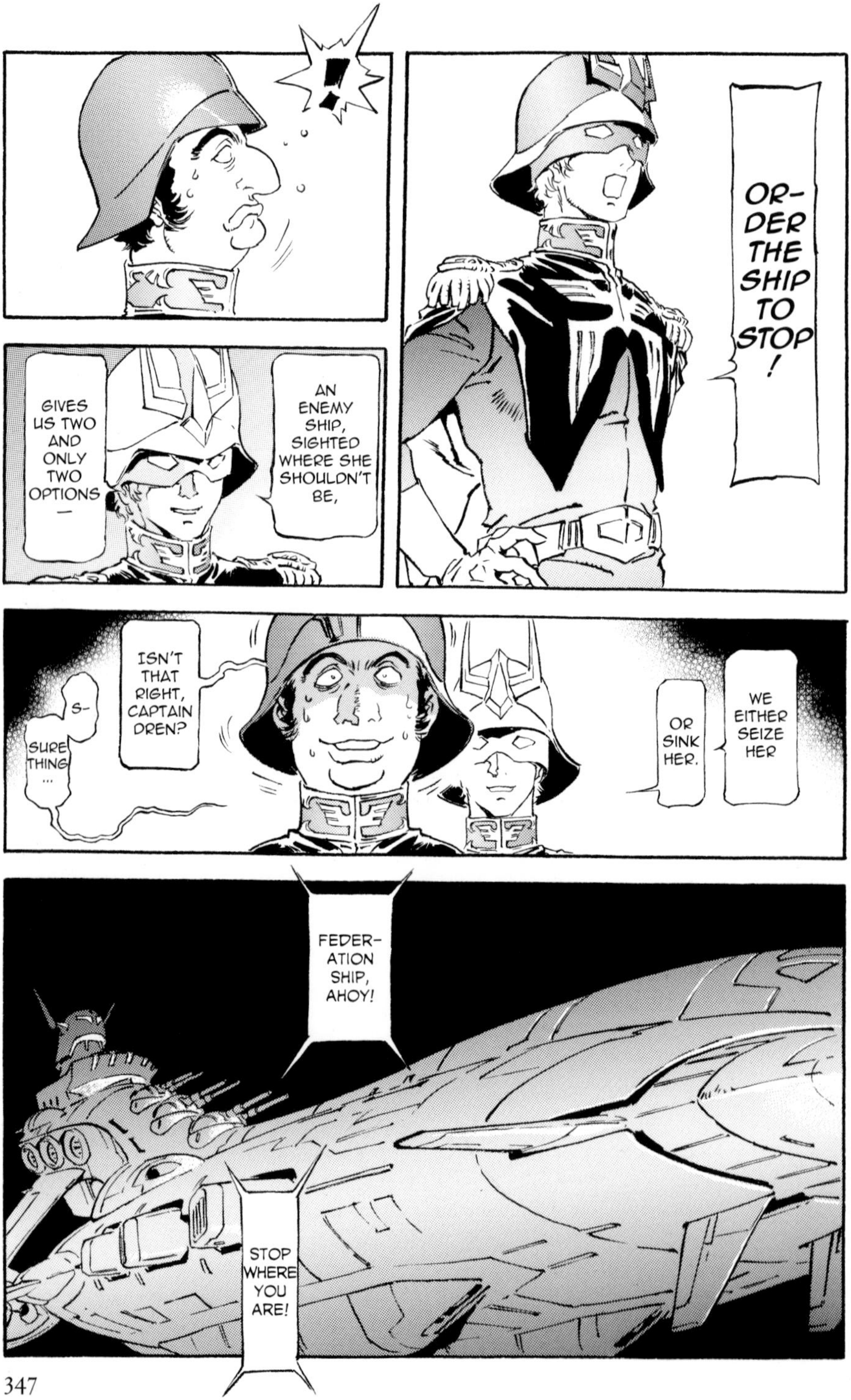
OR-DER THE SHIP TO STOP!
!
AN ENEMY SHIP, SIGHTED WHERE SHE SHOULDN'T BE,
GIVES US TWO AND ONLY TWO OPTIONS—
WE EITHER SEIZE HER
OR SINK HER.
ISN'T THAT RIGHT, CAPTAIN DREN?
S-
SURE THING...
FEDER-ATION SHIP, AHOY!
STOP WHERE YOU ARE!

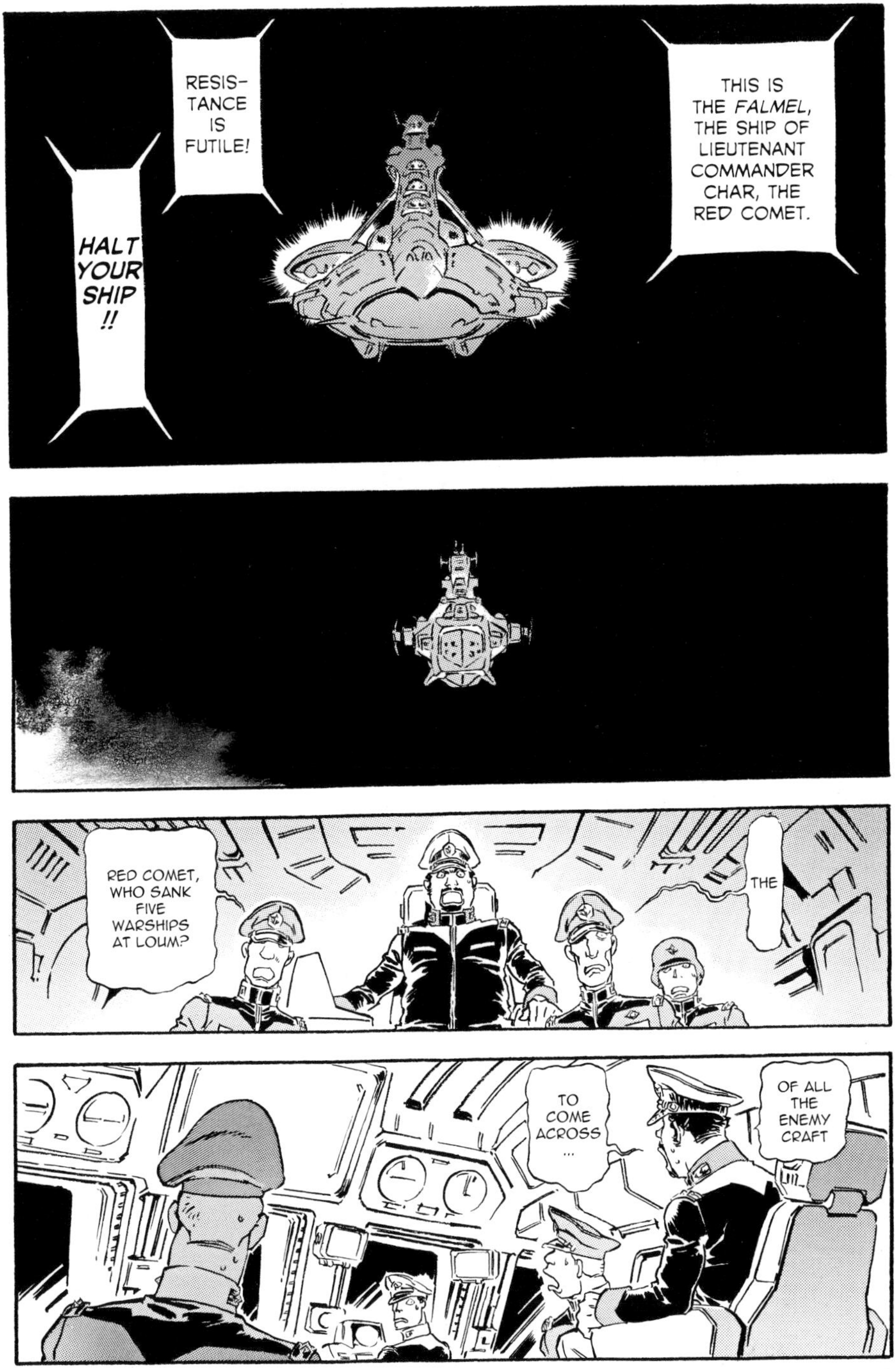
THIS IS THE *FALMEL*, THE SHIP OF LIEUTENANT COMMANDER CHAR, THE RED COMET.
RESIS-TANCE IS FUTILE!
HALT YOUR SHIP !!
THE
RED COMET, WHO SANK FIVE WARSHIPS AT LOUM?
OF ALL THE ENEMY CRAFT
TO COME ACROSS ...

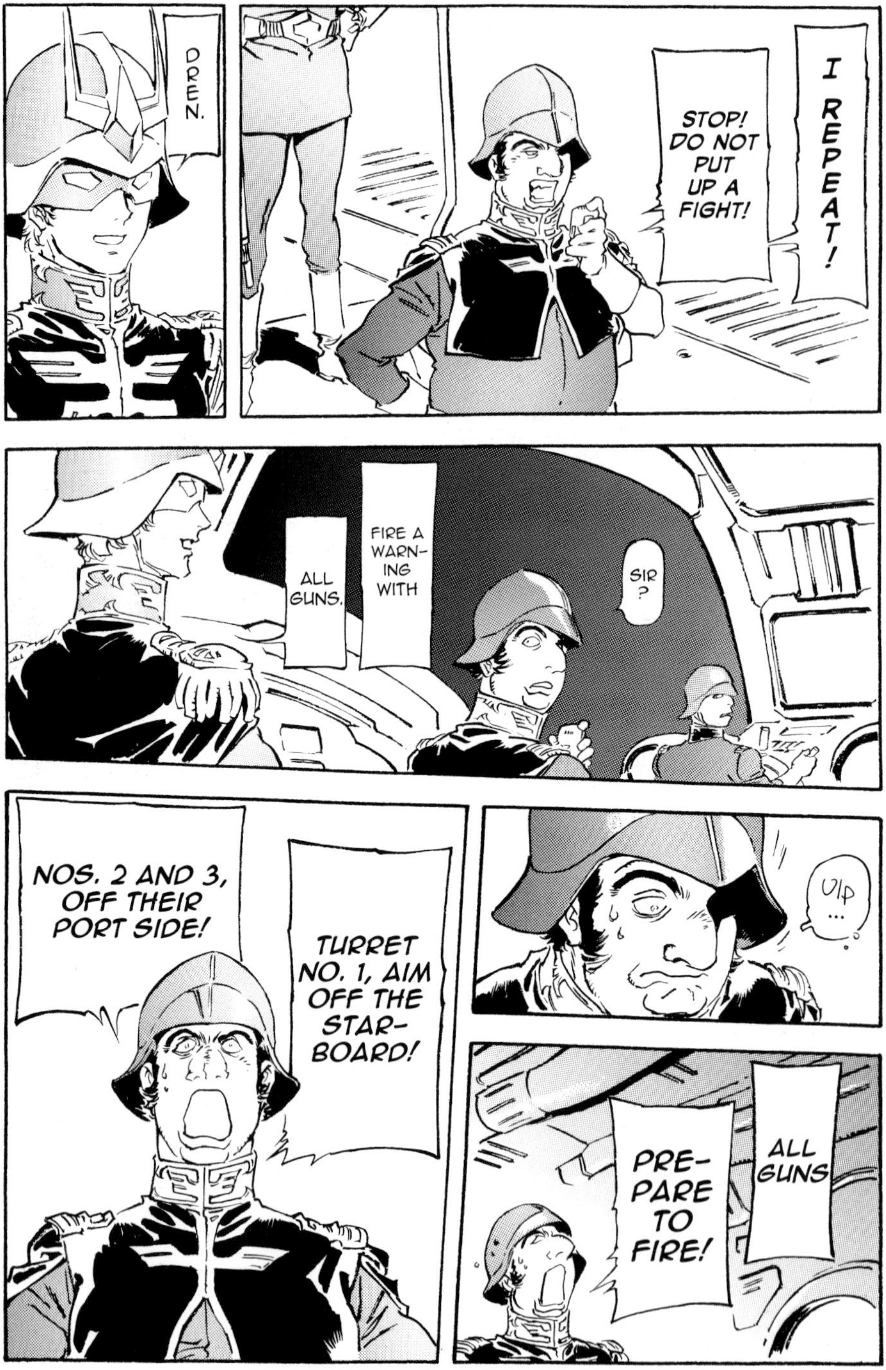
I REPEAT!
STOP! DO NOT PUT UP A FIGHT!
DREN.
SIR?
FIRE A WARNING WITH
ALL GUNS.
Ulp...
ALL GUNS
PRE-PARE TO FIRE!
TURRET NO. 1, AIM OFF THE STAR-BOARD!
NOS. 2 AND 3, OFF THEIR PORT SIDE!

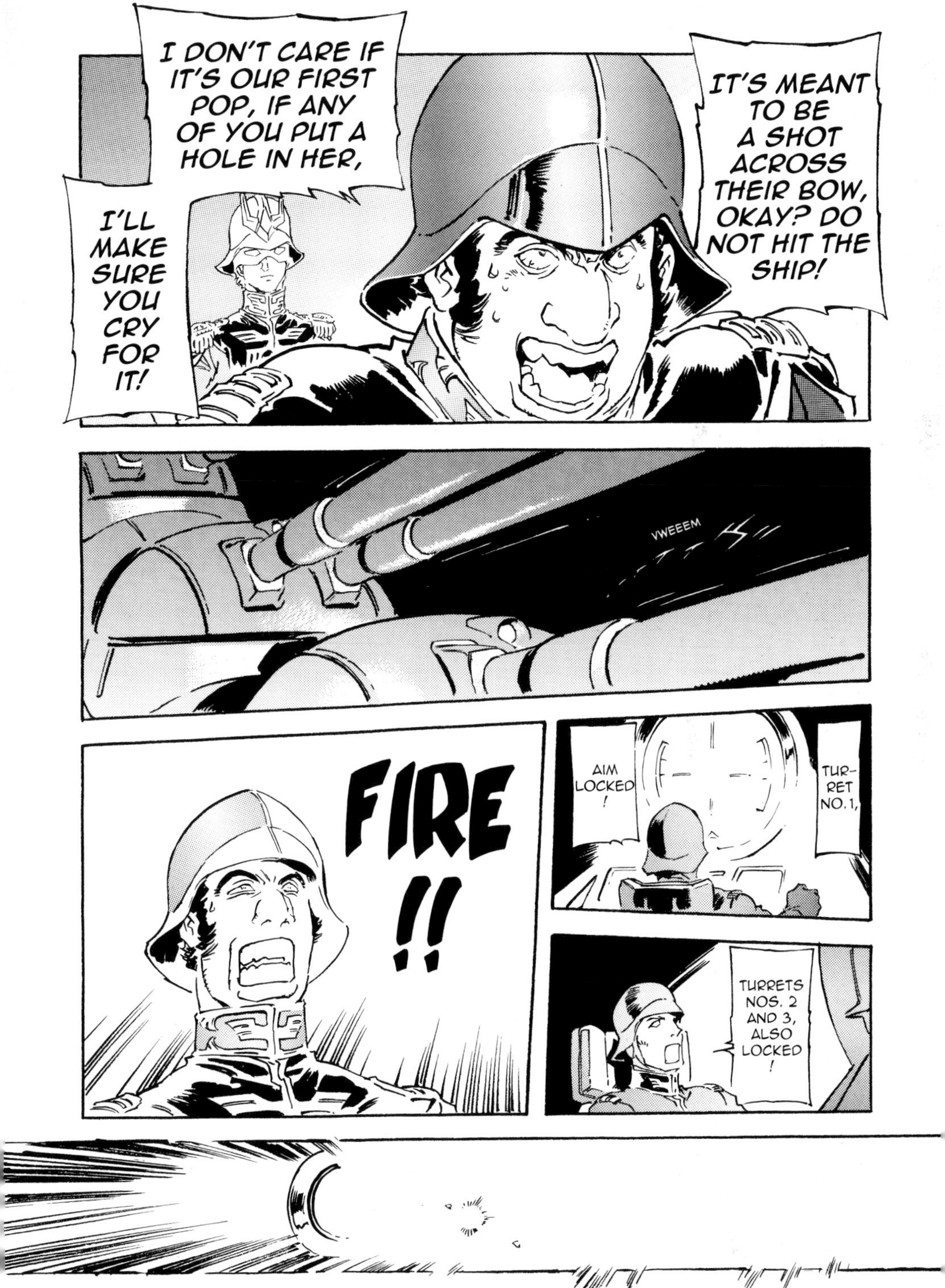
IT'S MEANT TO BE A SHOT ACROSS THEIR BOW, OKAY? DO NOT HIT THE SHIP!
I DON'T CARE IF IT'S OUR FIRST POP, IF ANY OF YOU PUT A HOLE IN HER,
I'LL MAKE SURE YOU CRY FOR IT!
VWEEEM
TURRET NO. 1,
AIM LOCKED!
TURRETS NOS. 2 AND 3, ALSO LOCKED!
FIRE!!

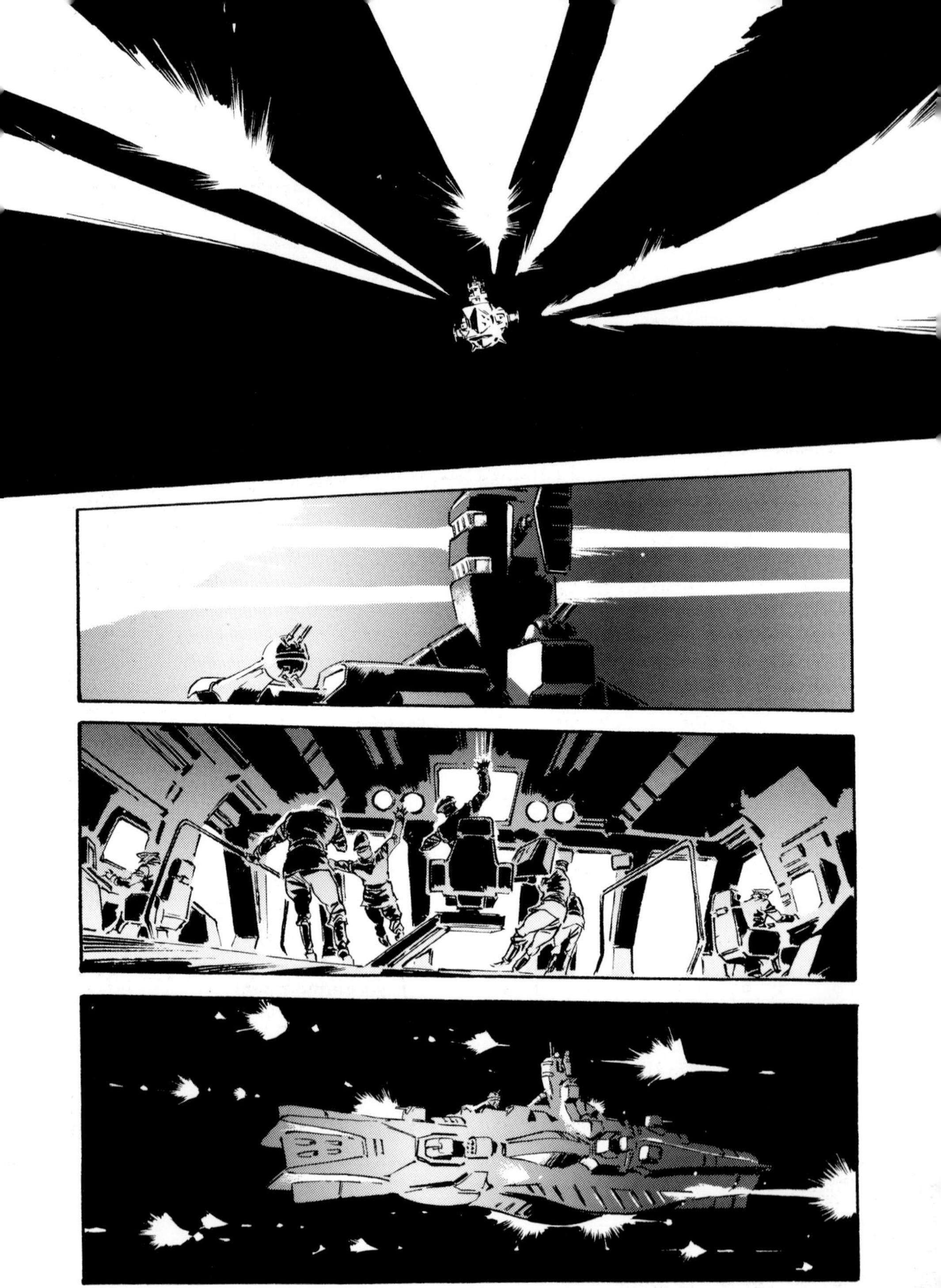

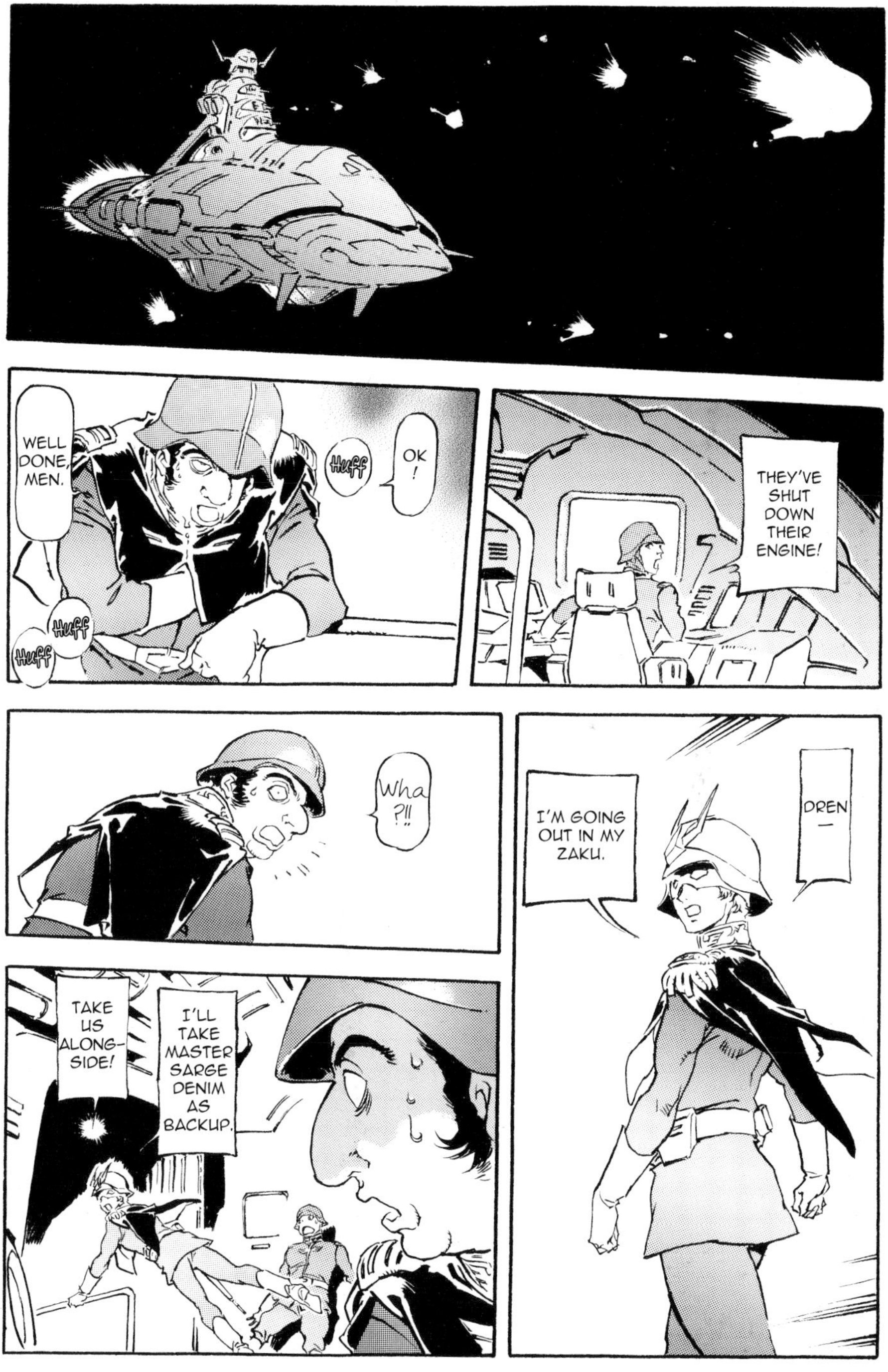
THEY'VE SHUT DOWN THEIR ENGINE!
OK!
Huff
WELL DONE, MEN.
Huff
Huff
DREN—
I'M GOING OUT IN MY ZAKU.
Wha?!!
I'LL TAKE MASTER SARGE DENIM AS BACKUP.
TAKE US ALONGSIDE!

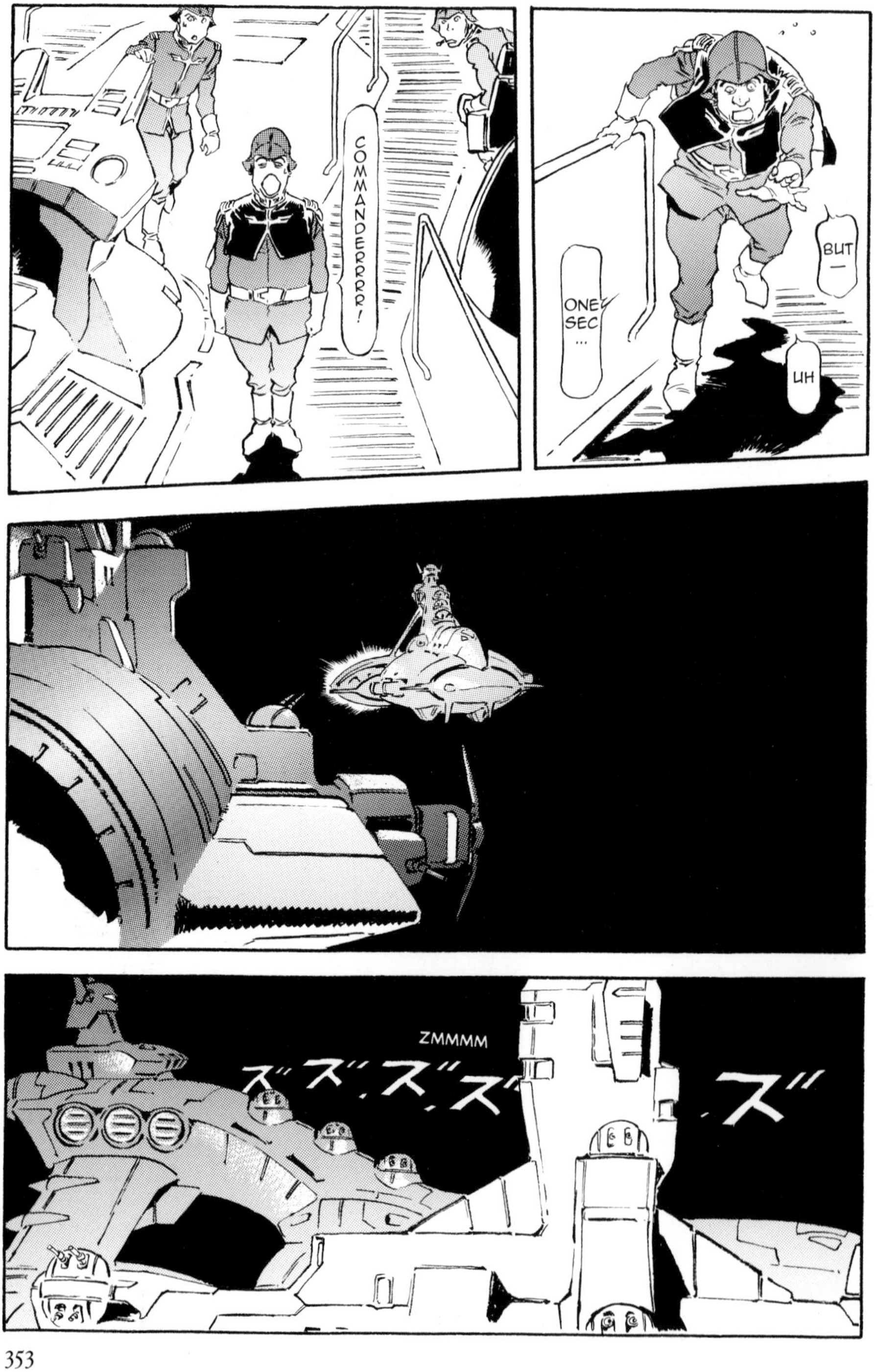
BUT—
UH
ONE SEC...
COMMANDERRR!
ZMMMM
ズズズズズ

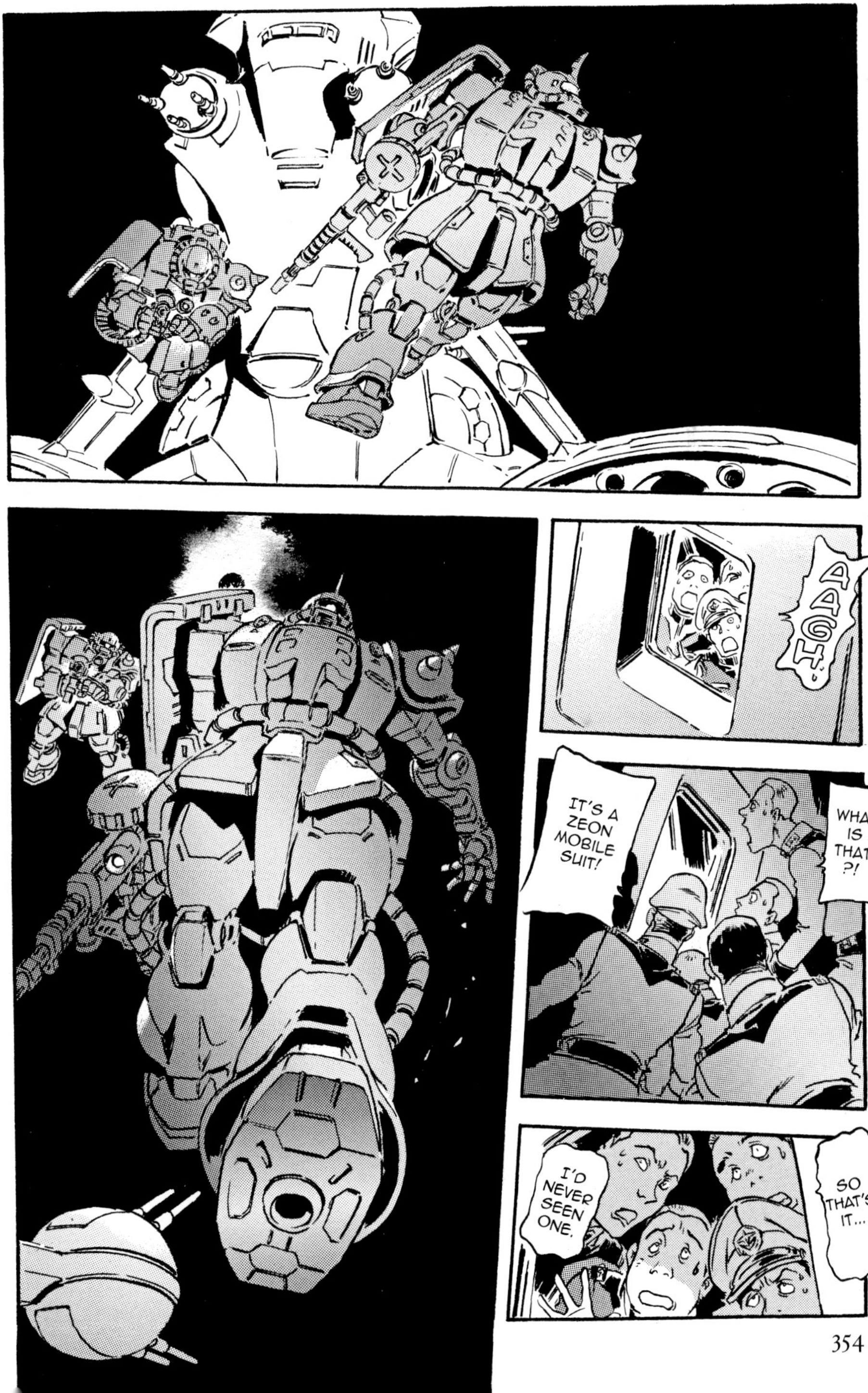
AAGH
WHAT IS THAT?!
IT'S A ZEON MOBILE SUIT!
SO THAT'S IT...
I'D NEVER SEEN ONE.

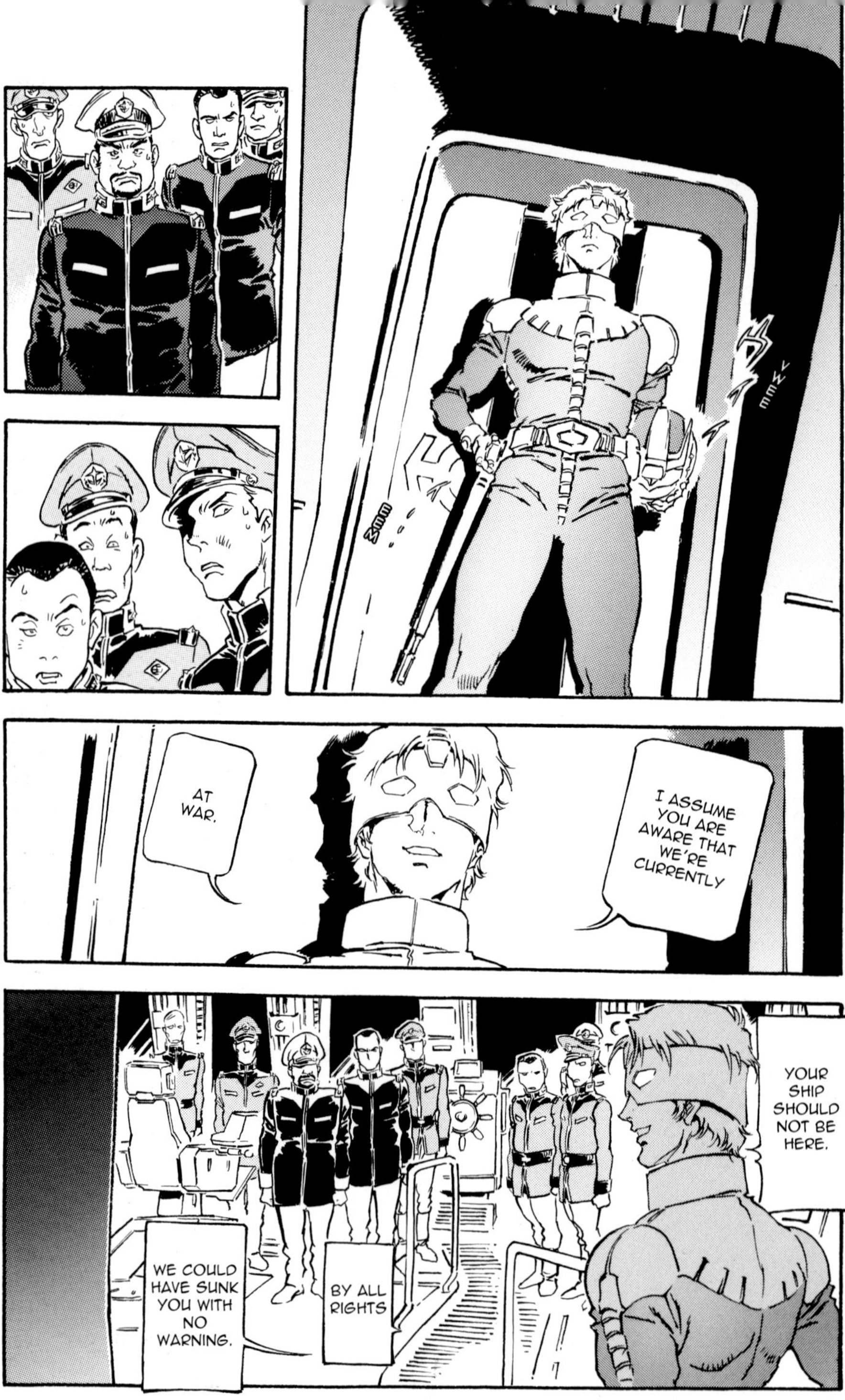
I ASSUME YOU ARE AWARE THAT WE'RE CURRENTLY
AT WAR.
YOUR SHIP SHOULD NOT BE HERE.
BY ALL RIGHTS
WE COULD HAVE SUNK YOU WITH NO WARNING.

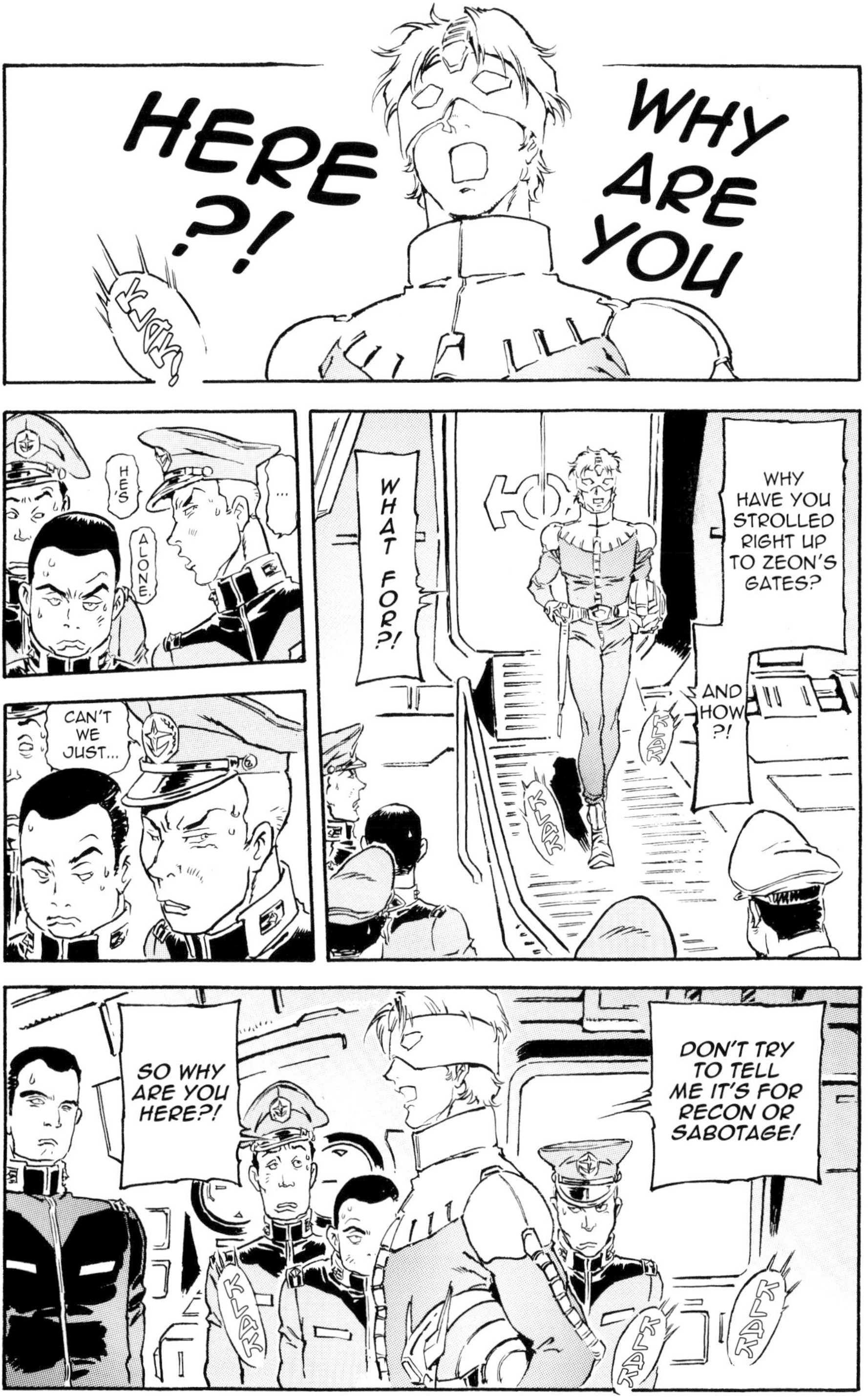
WHY ARE YOU
HERE?!
WHY HAVE YOU STROLLED RIGHT UP TO ZEON'S GATES?
WHAT FOR?!
AND HOW?!
KLAK
KLAK
...
HE'S ALONE.
CAN'T WE JUST...
DON'T TRY TO TELL ME IT'S FOR RECON OR SABOTAGE!
SO WHY ARE YOU HERE?!
KLAK
KLAK
KLAK

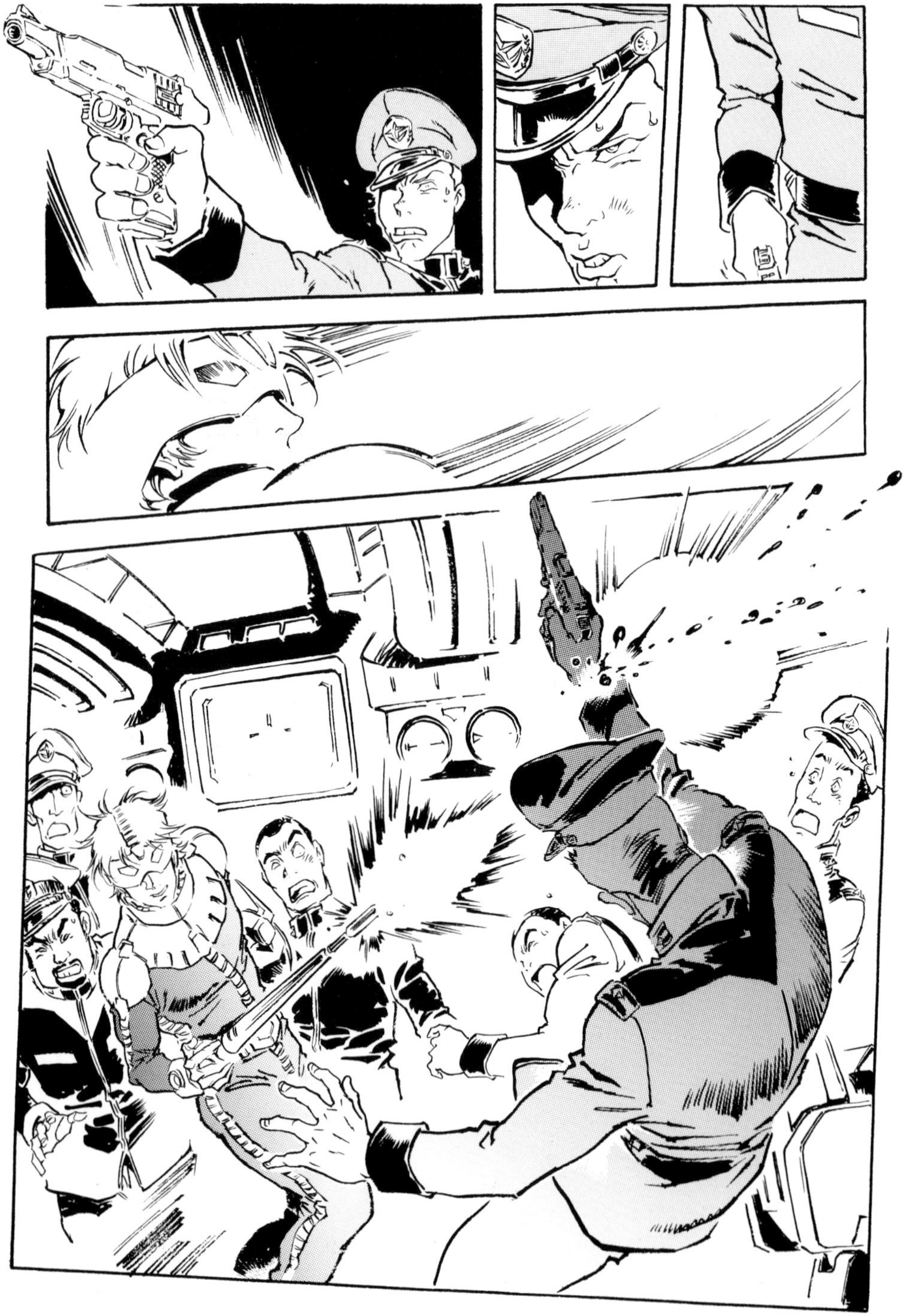

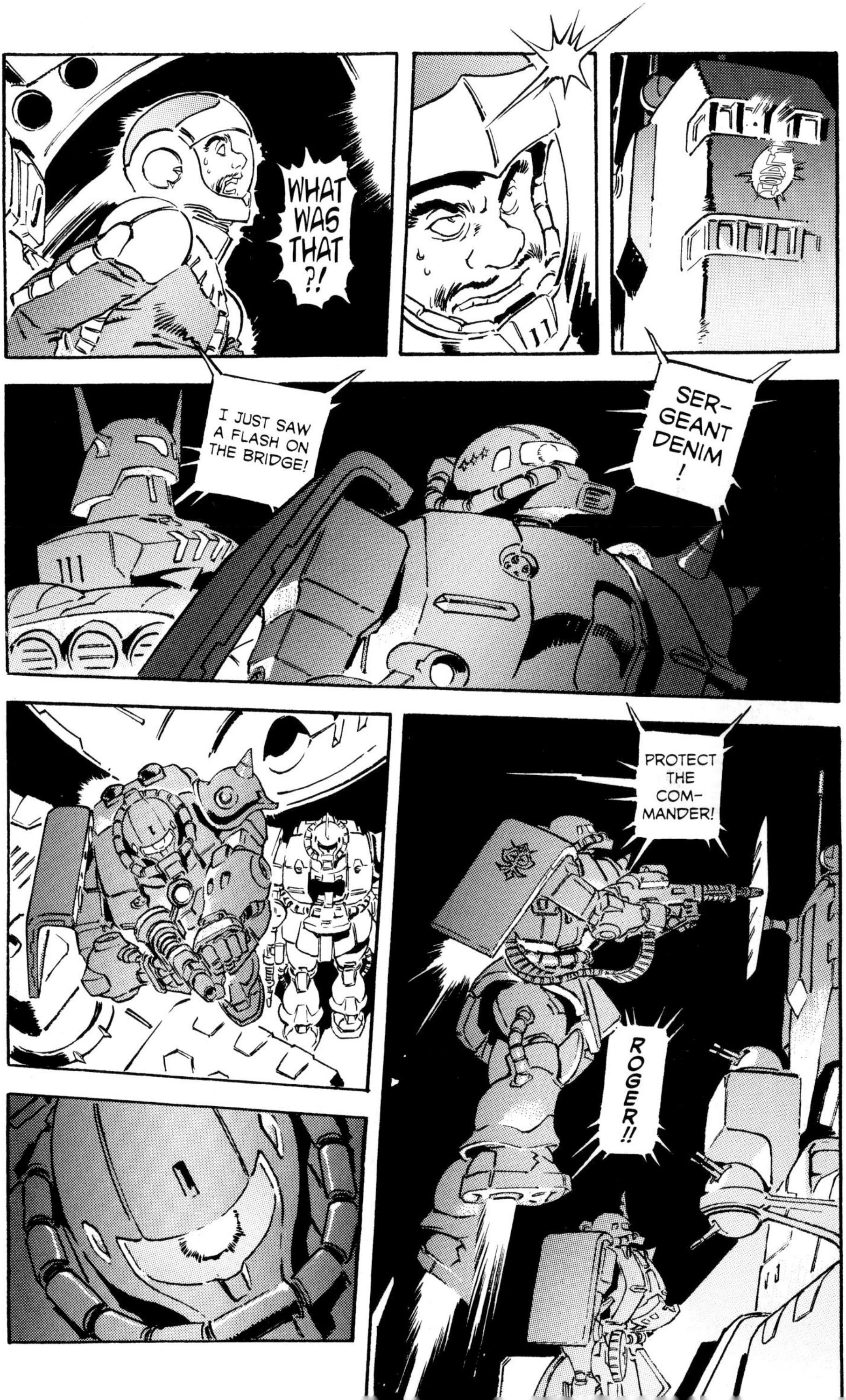
WHAT WAS THAT ?!
SER-GEANT DENIM !
I JUST SAW A FLASH ON THE BRIDGE!
PROTECT THE COM-MANDER!
ROGER!!

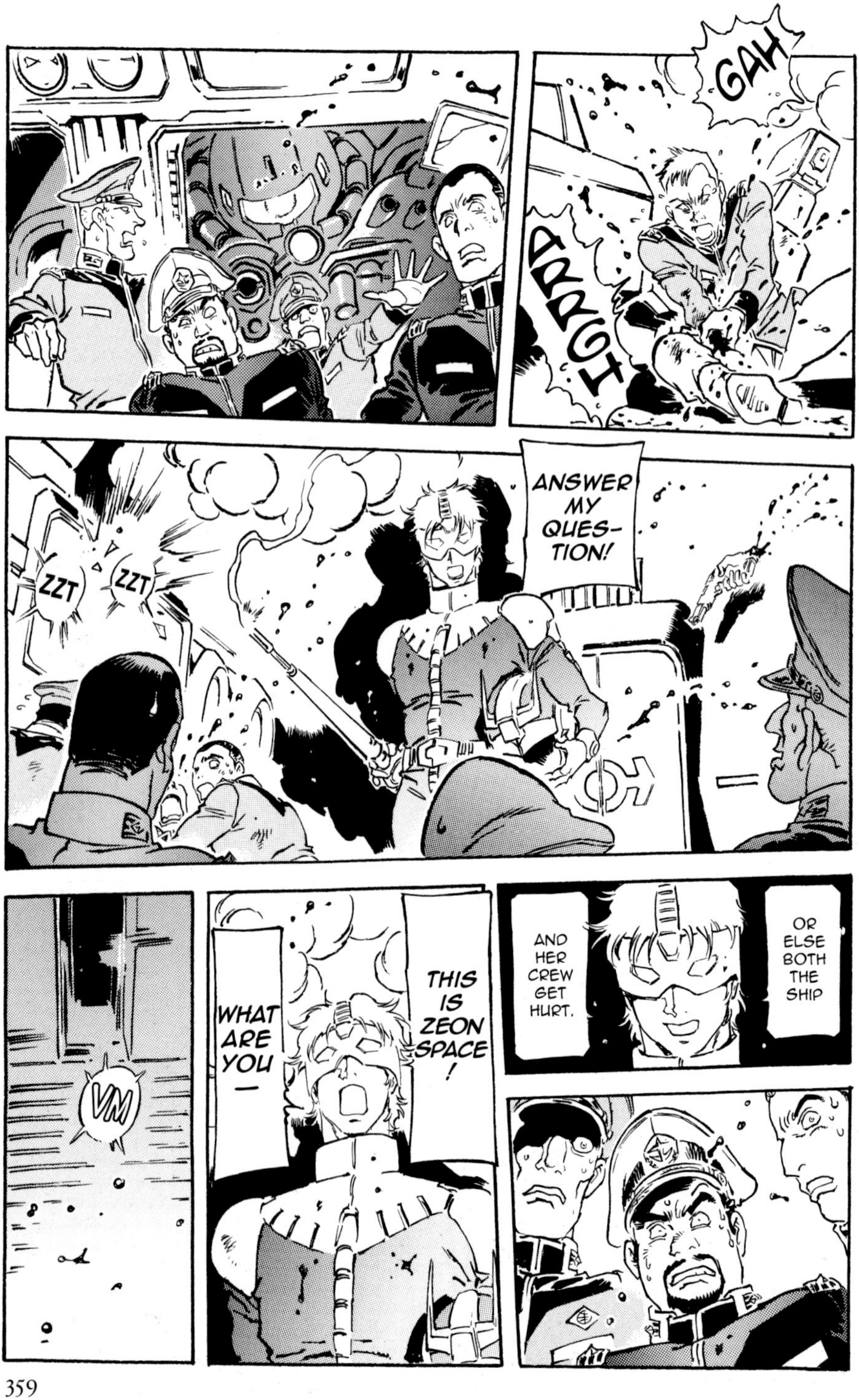
GAH
ARRGH
ANSWER MY QUES-TION!
ZZT
ZZT
OR ELSE BOTH THE SHIP
AND HER CREW GET HURT.
THIS IS ZEON SPACE!
WHAT ARE YOU—
VM

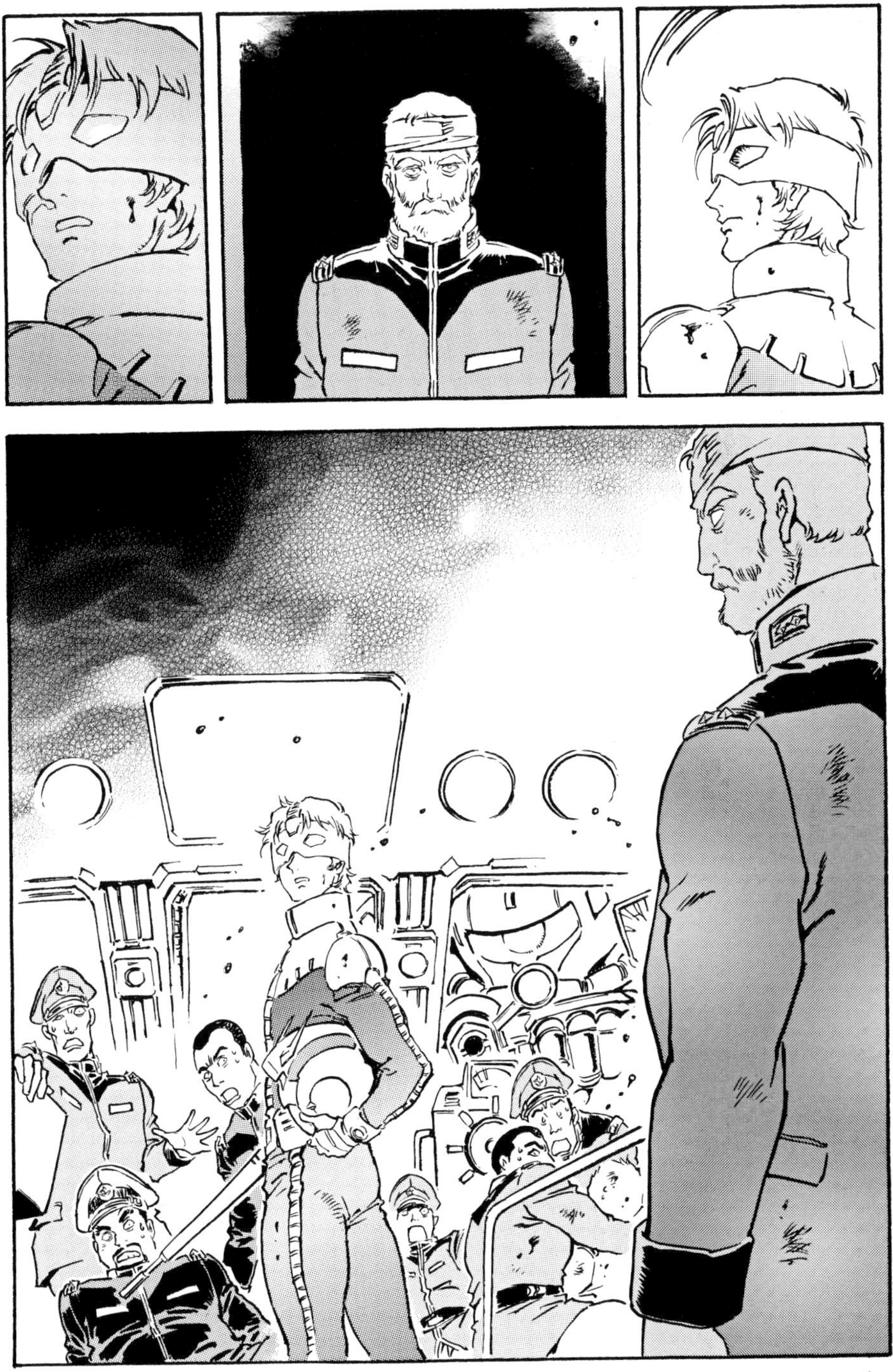

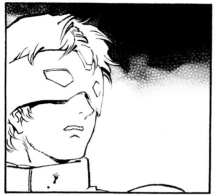

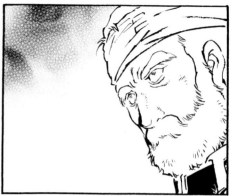

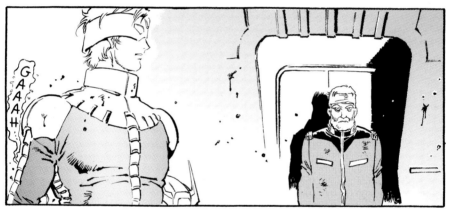

GAAAH

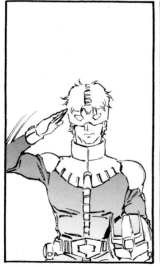

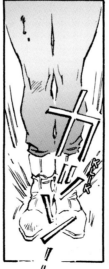

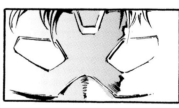

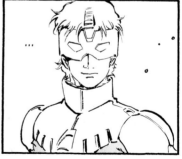

...

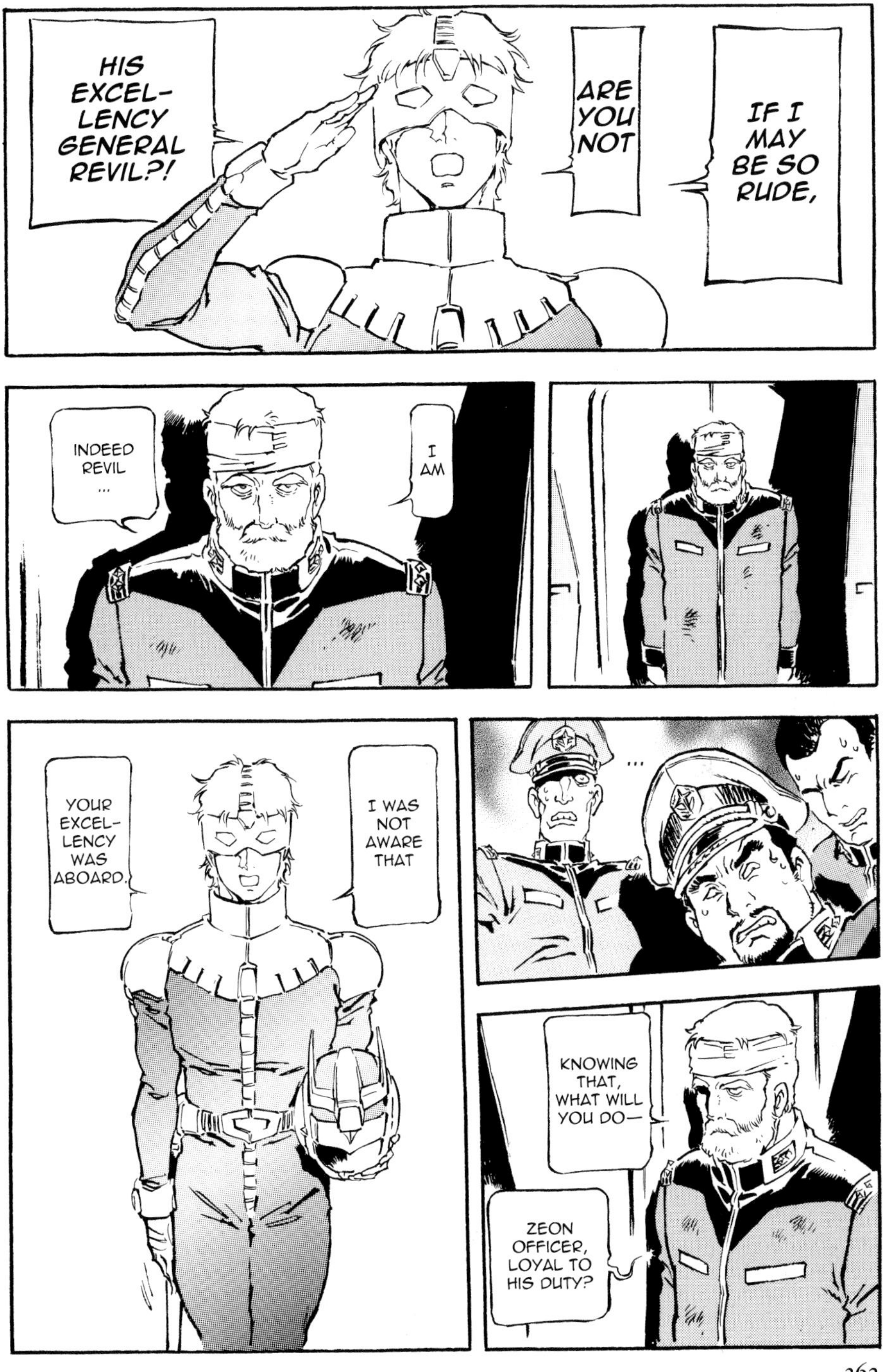
IF I MAY BE SO RUDE,
ARE YOU NOT
HIS EXCEL-LENCY GENERAL REVIL?!
I AM
INDEED REVIL ...
...
KNOWING THAT, WHAT WILL YOU DO—
ZEON OFFICER, LOYAL TO HIS DUTY?
I WAS NOT AWARE THAT
YOUR EXCEL-LENCY WAS ABOARD.

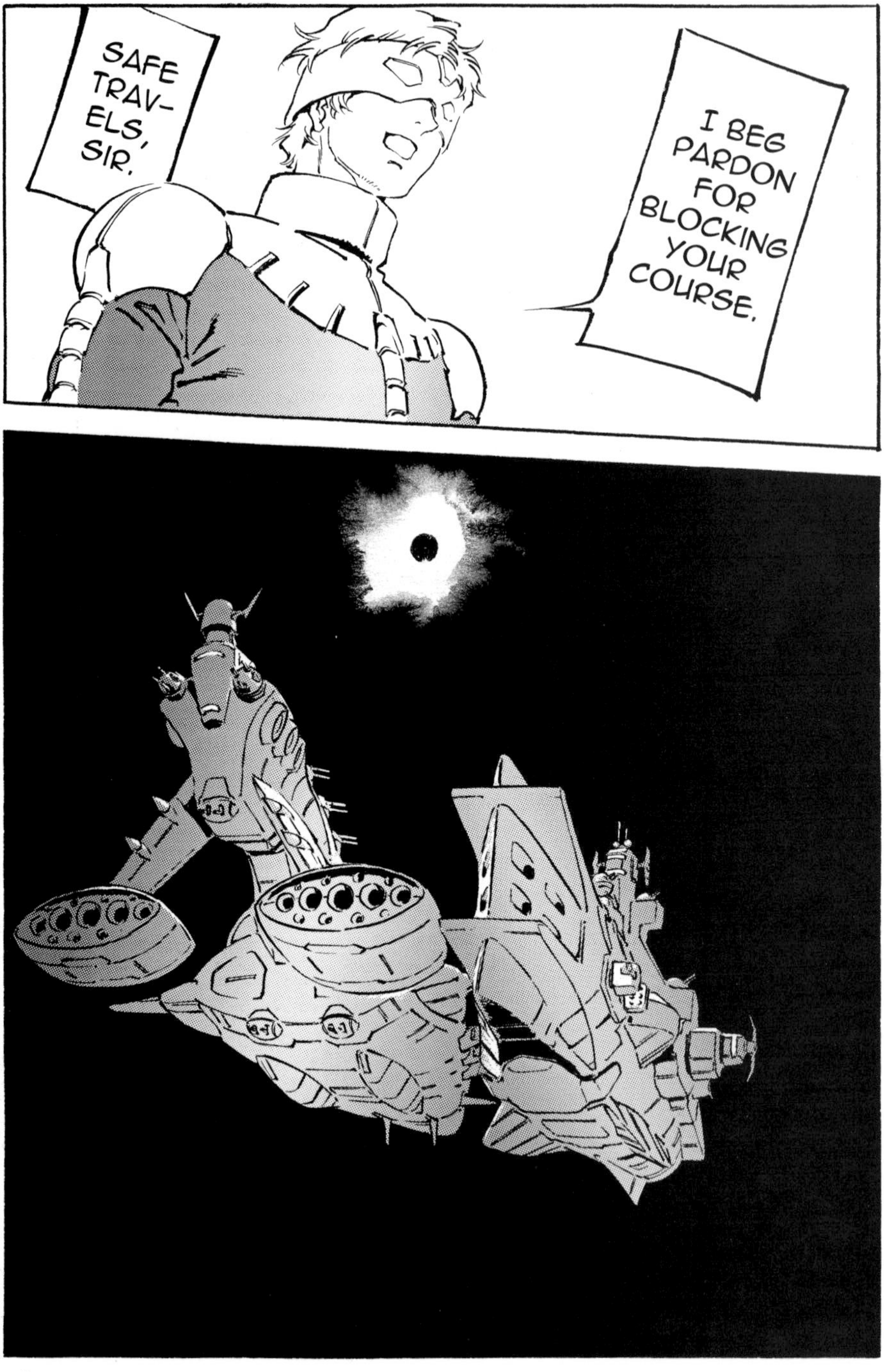
I BEG PARDON FOR BLOCKING YOUR COURSE.
SAFE TRAVELS, SIR.

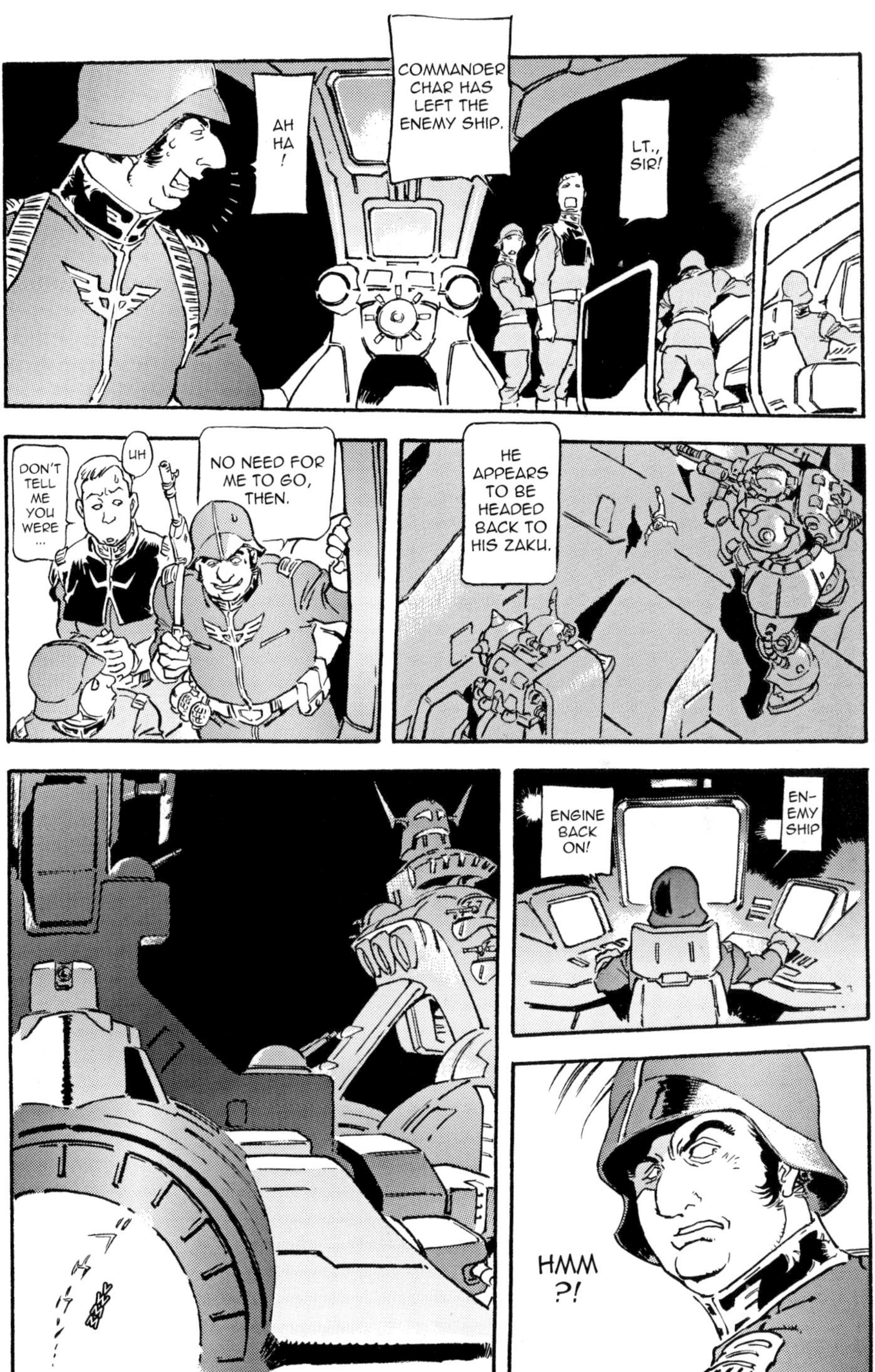
LT., SIR!
COMMANDER CHAR HAS LEFT THE ENEMY SHIP.
AH HA!
HE APPEARS TO BE HEADED BACK TO HIS ZAKU.
NO NEED FOR ME TO GO, THEN.
UH
DON'T TELL ME YOU WERE ...
EN-EMY SHIP
ENGINE BACK ON!
HMM ?!

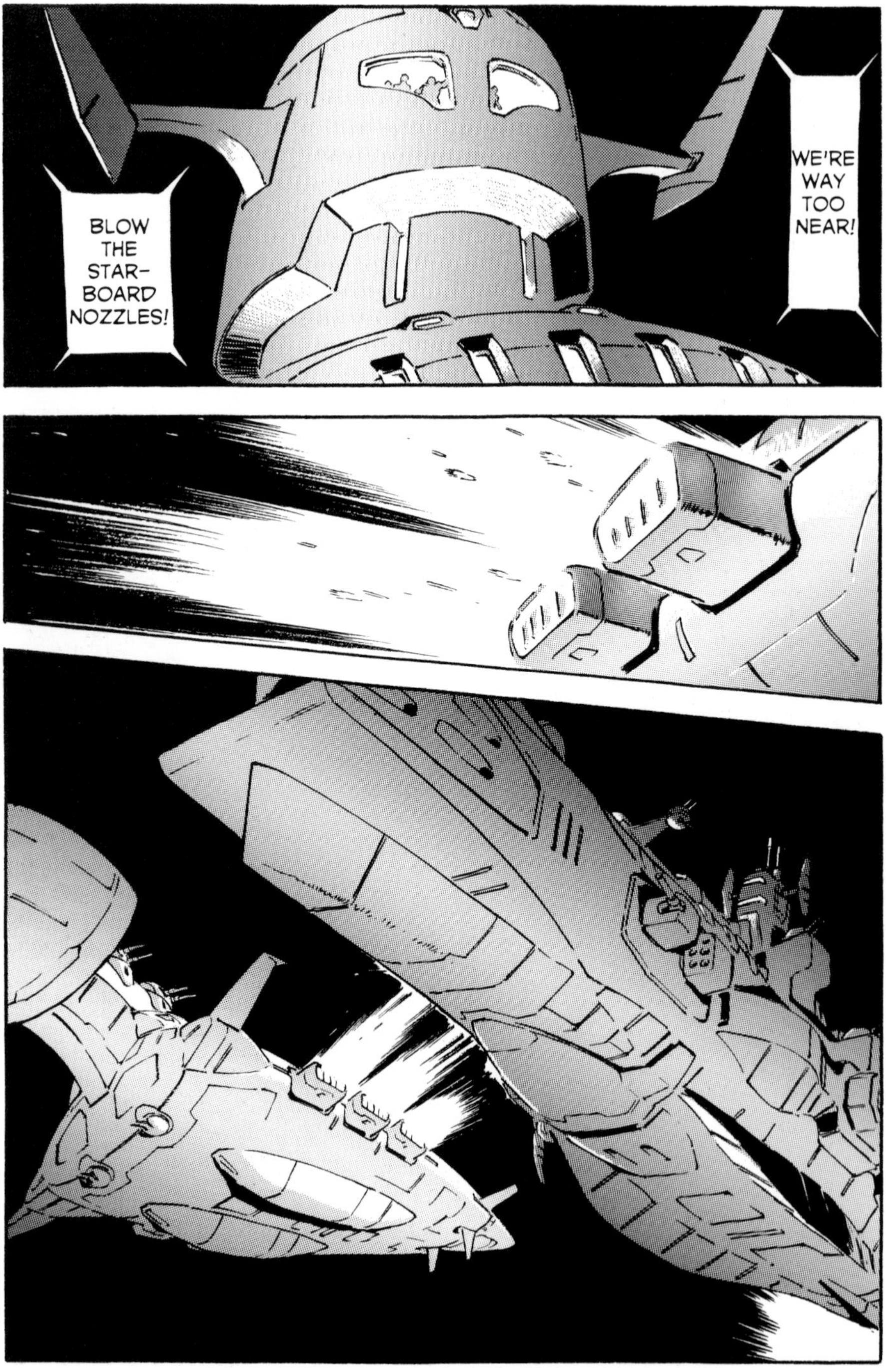
WE'RE WAY TOO NEAR!
BLOW THE STAR-BOARD NOZZLES!

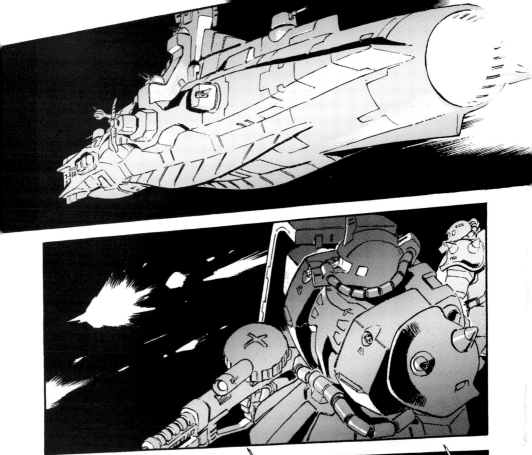

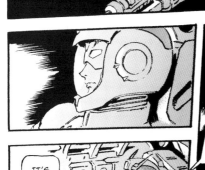

THAT SHIP TRESPASSED ON ZEON SPACE! ARE WE JUST GOING TO LET THEM SAIL OFF?!

SIR!

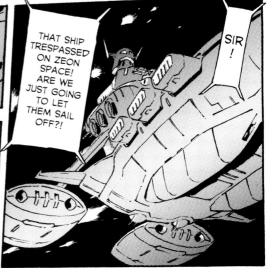

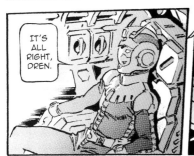

IT'S ALL RIGHT, DREN.

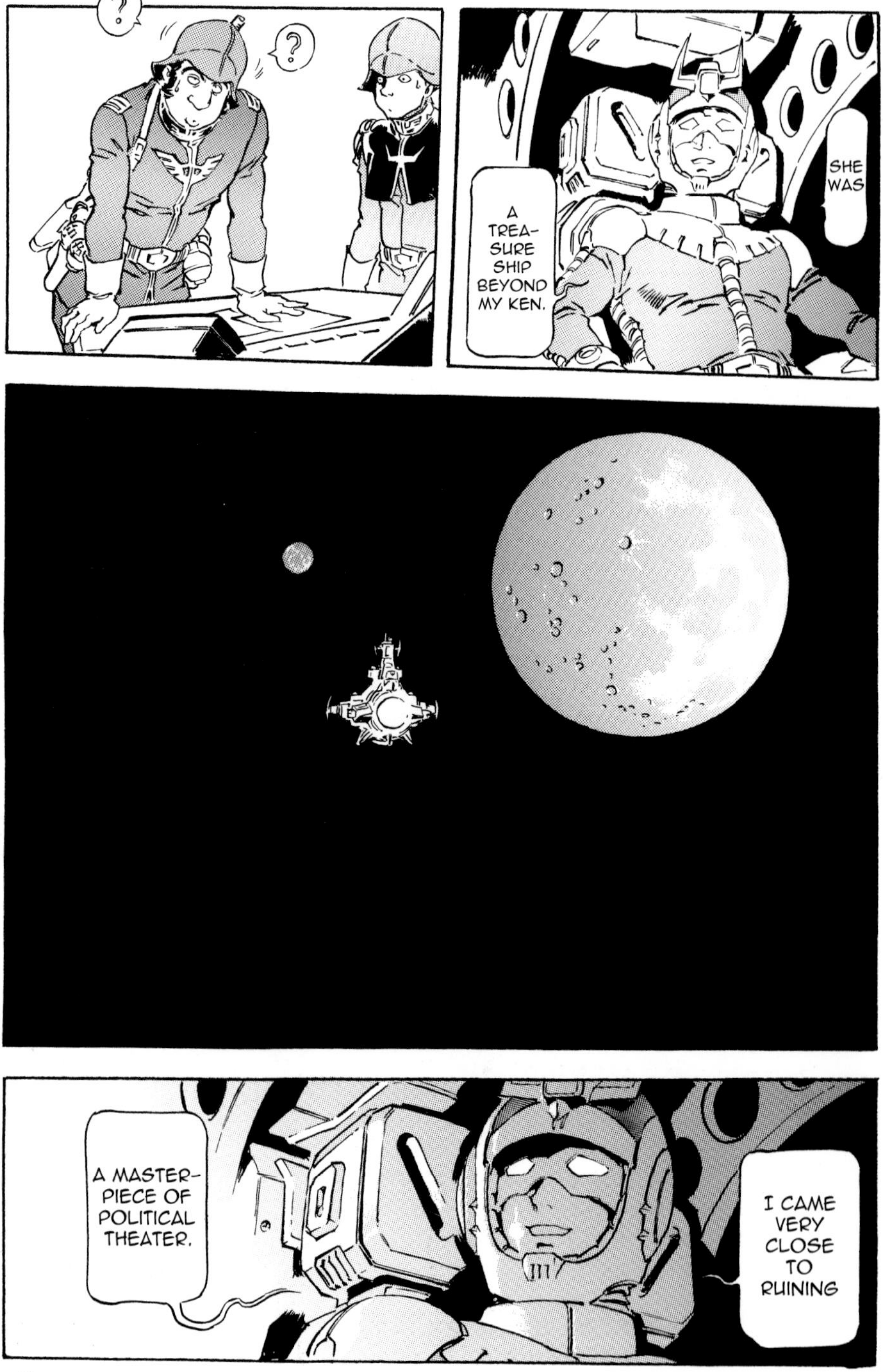
SHE WAS
A TREA-SURE SHIP BEYOND MY KEN.
?
?
I CAME VERY CLOSE TO RUINING
A MASTER-PIECE OF POLITICAL THEATER.

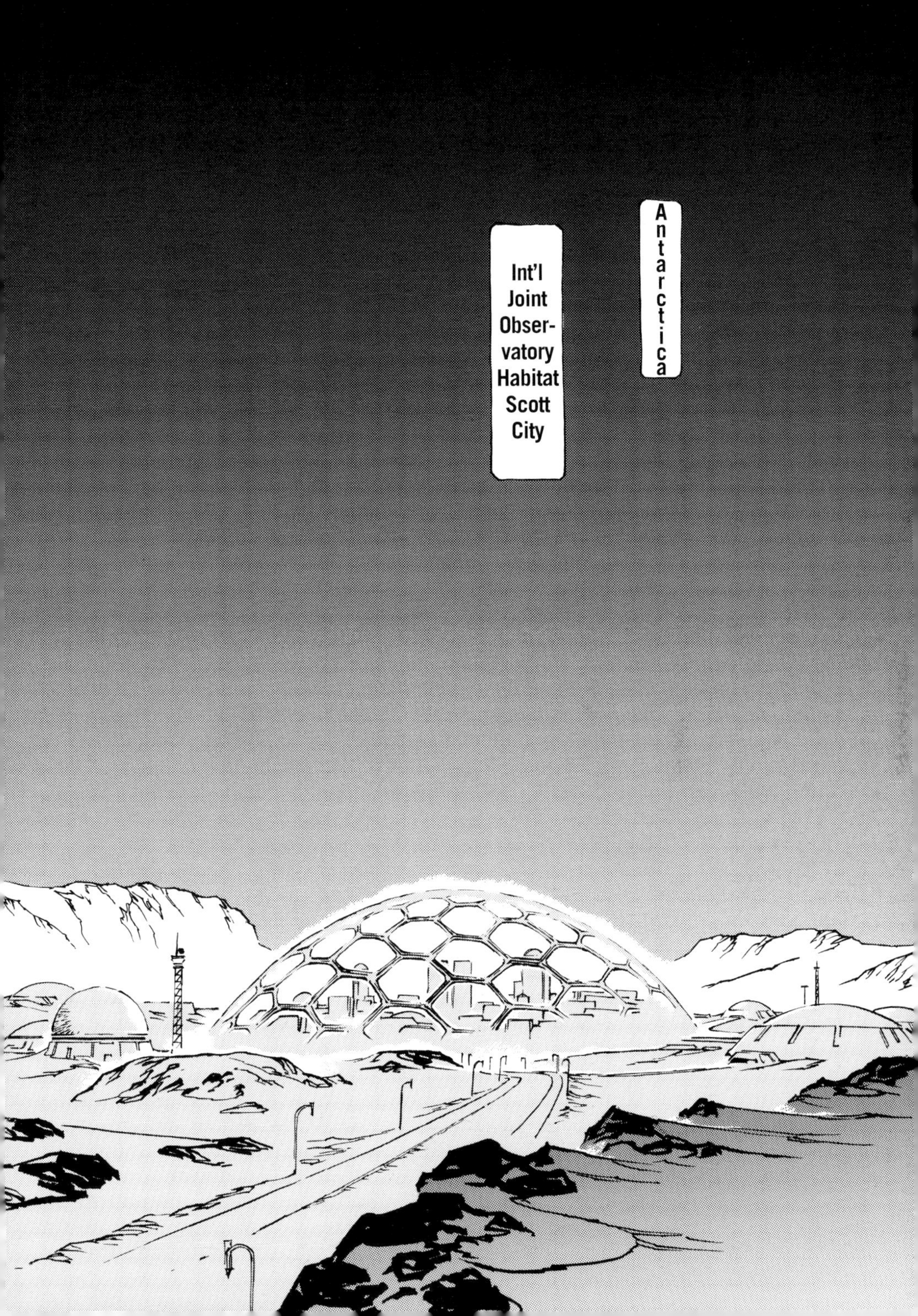
Antarctica
Int'l Joint Observatory Habitat Scott City

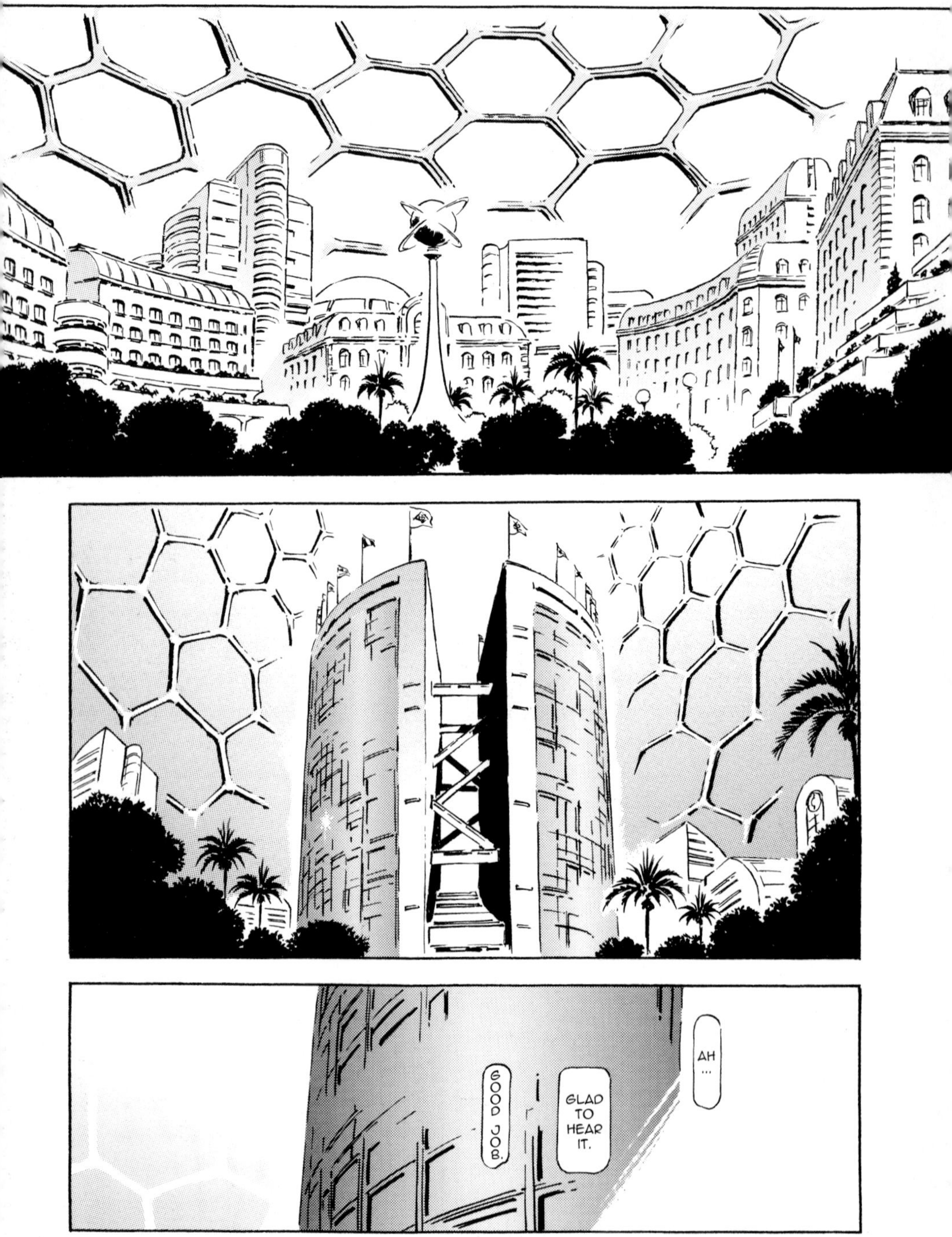
AH...
GLAD TO HEAR IT.
GOOD JOB.

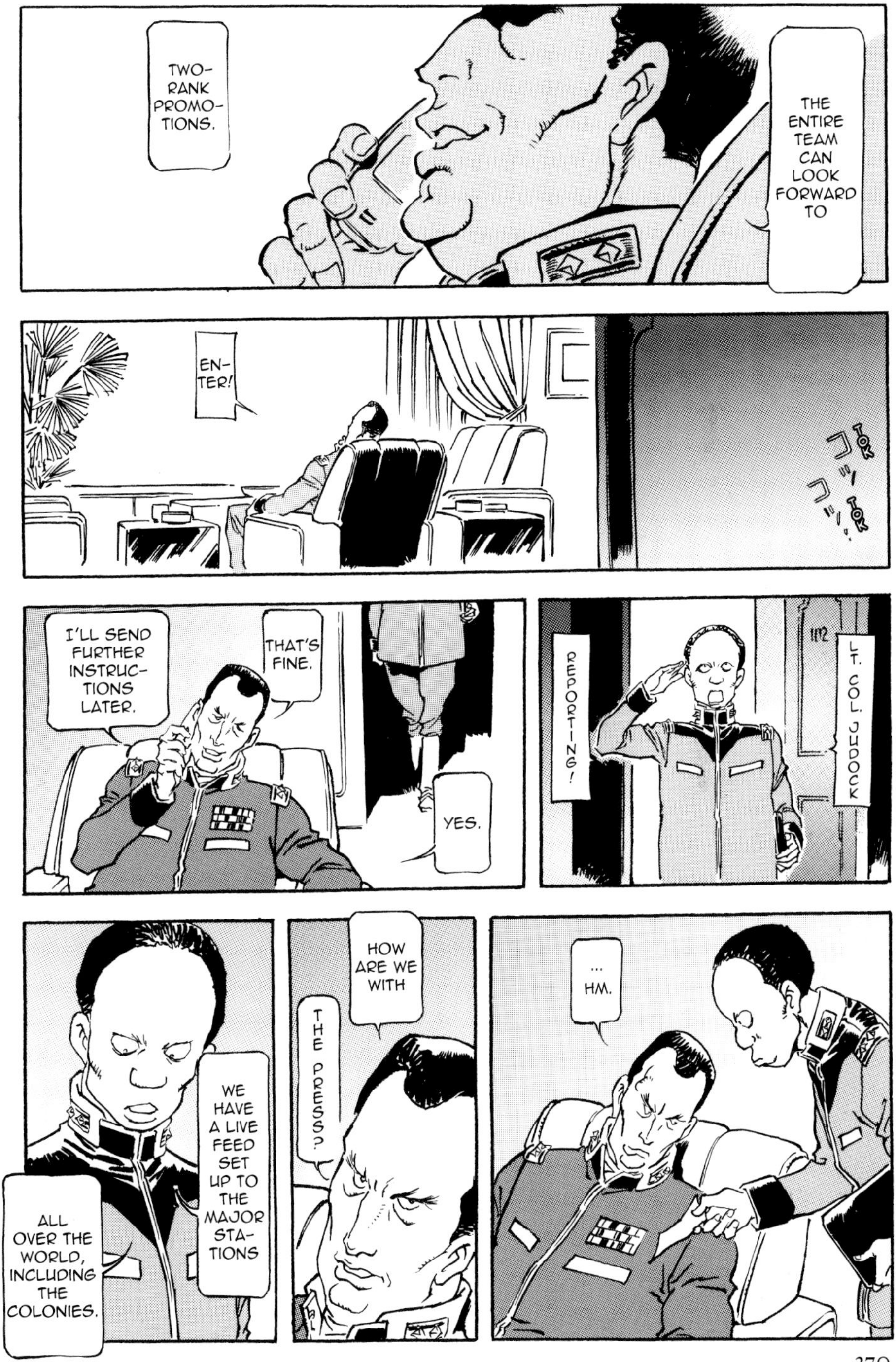
THE ENTIRE TEAM CAN LOOK FORWARD TO
TWO-RANK PROMOTIONS.
コツ TOK
コツ TOK
EN-TER!
LT. COL. JUDOCK
REPORTING!
THAT'S FINE.
I'LL SEND FURTHER INSTRUC-TIONS LATER.
YES.
... HM.
HOW ARE WE WITH
THE PRESS?
WE HAVE A LIVE FEED SET UP TO THE MAJOR STA-TIONS
ALL OVER THE WORLD, INCLUDING THE COLONIES.

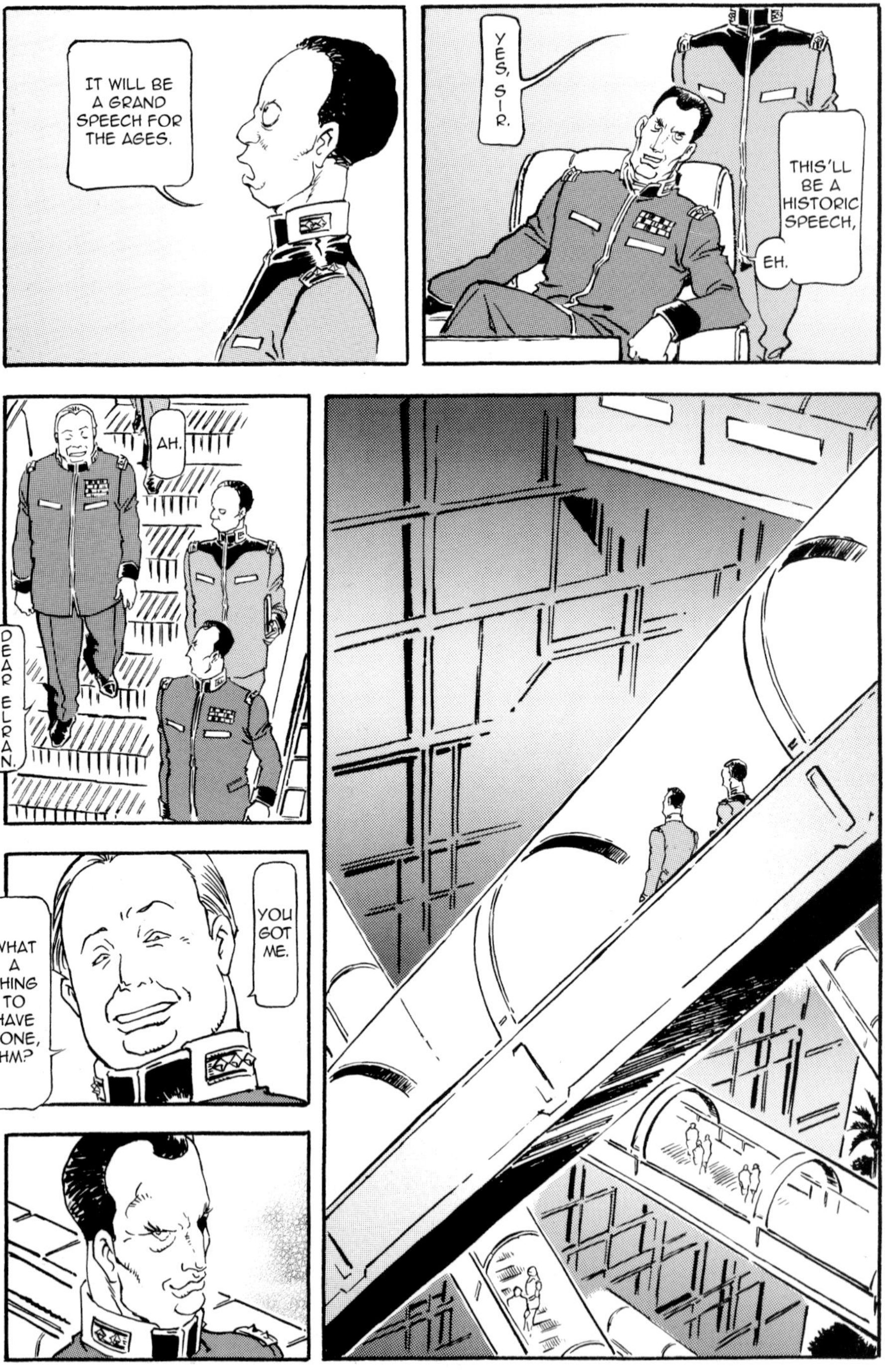
THIS'LL BE A HISTORIC SPEECH,
EH.
YES, SIR.
IT WILL BE A GRAND SPEECH FOR THE AGES.
AH.
DEAR ELRAN.
YOU GOT ME.
WHAT A THING TO HAVE DONE, HM?

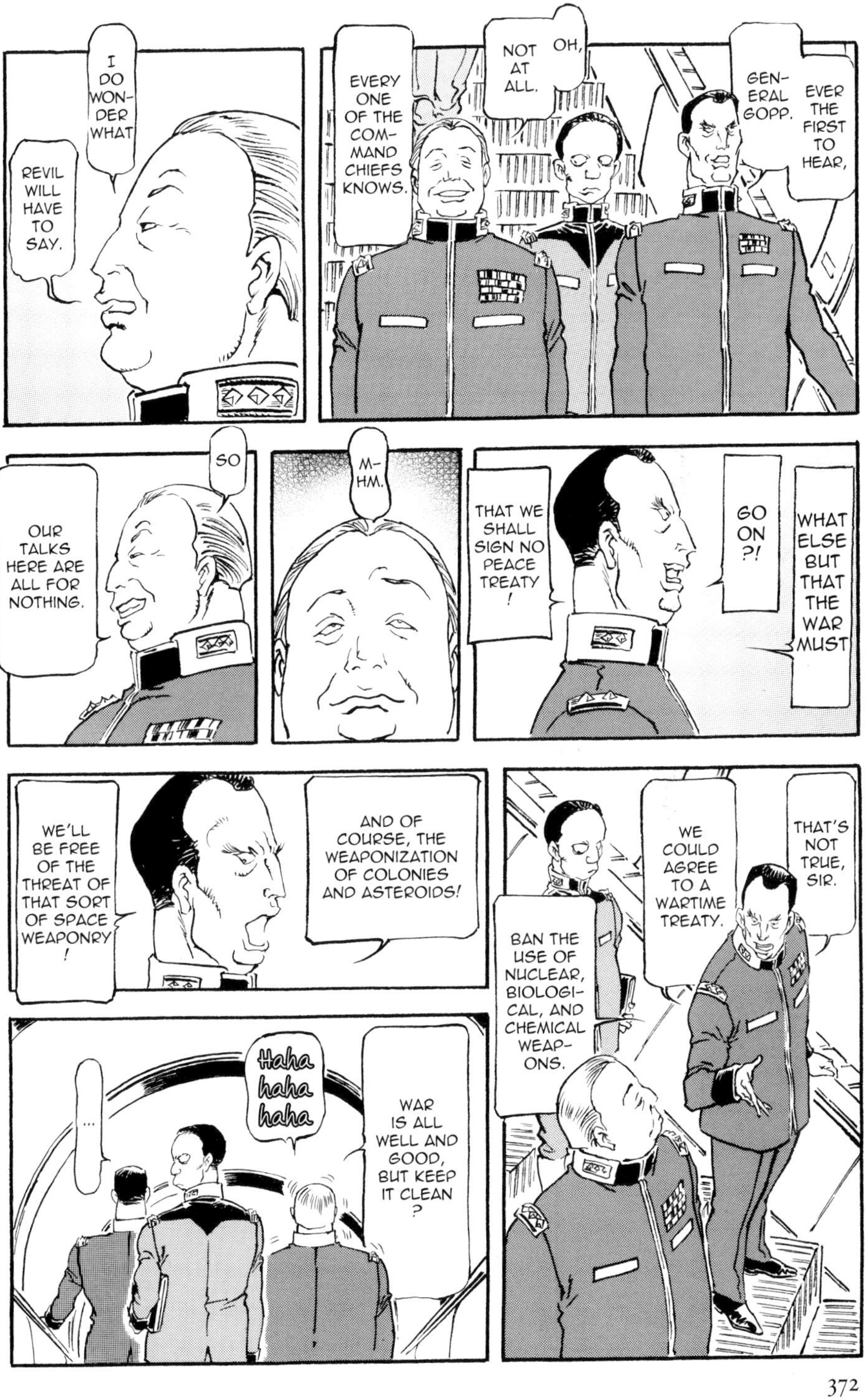
EVER THE FIRST TO HEAR,
GENERAL GOPP.
OH,
NOT AT ALL.
EVERY ONE OF THE COMMAND CHIEFS KNOWS.
I DO WONDER WHAT
REVIL WILL HAVE TO SAY.
WHAT ELSE BUT THAT THE WAR MUST
GO ON?!
THAT WE SHALL SIGN NO PEACE TREATY!
M-HM.
SO
OUR TALKS HERE ARE ALL FOR NOTHING.
THAT'S NOT TRUE, SIR.
WE COULD AGREE TO A WARTIME TREATY.
BAN THE USE OF NUCLEAR, BIOLOGICAL, AND CHEMICAL WEAPONS.
AND OF COURSE, THE WEAPONIZATION OF COLONIES AND ASTEROIDS!
WE'LL BE FREE OF THE THREAT OF THAT SORT OF SPACE WEAPONRY!
WAR IS ALL WELL AND GOOD, BUT KEEP IT CLEAN?
Haha haha haha
...

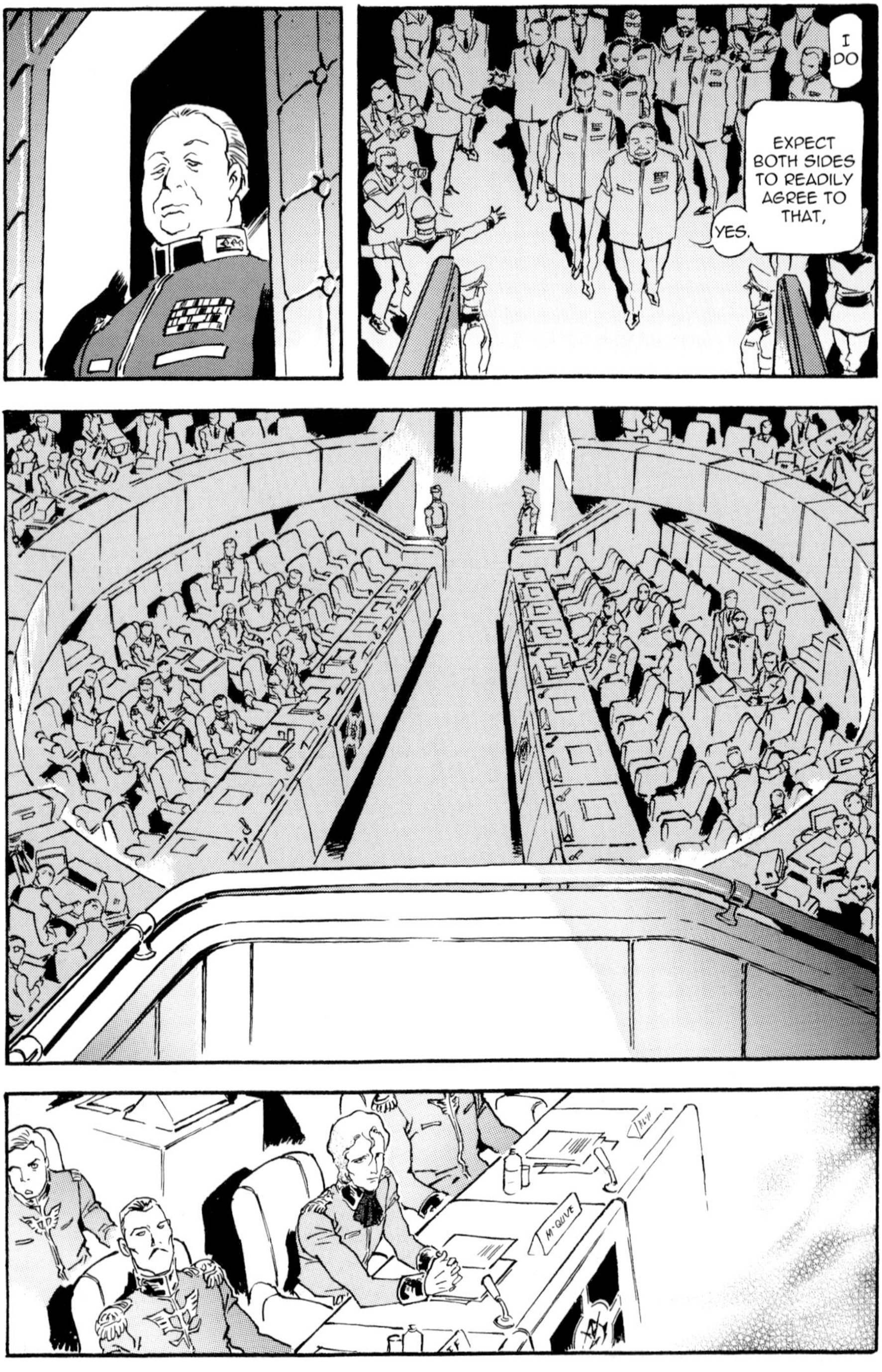
I DO
EXPECT BOTH SIDES TO READILY AGREE TO THAT,
YES.

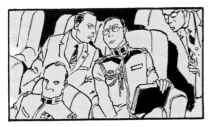

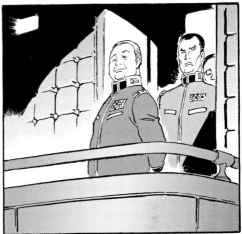

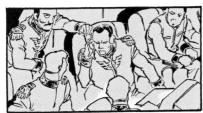

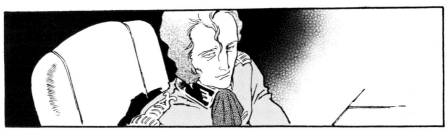

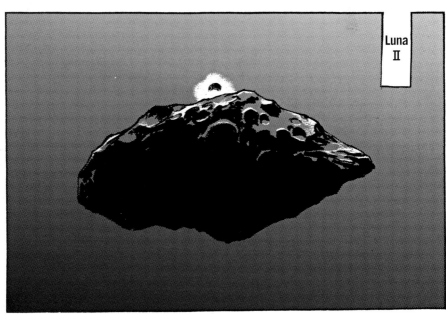

Luna
II

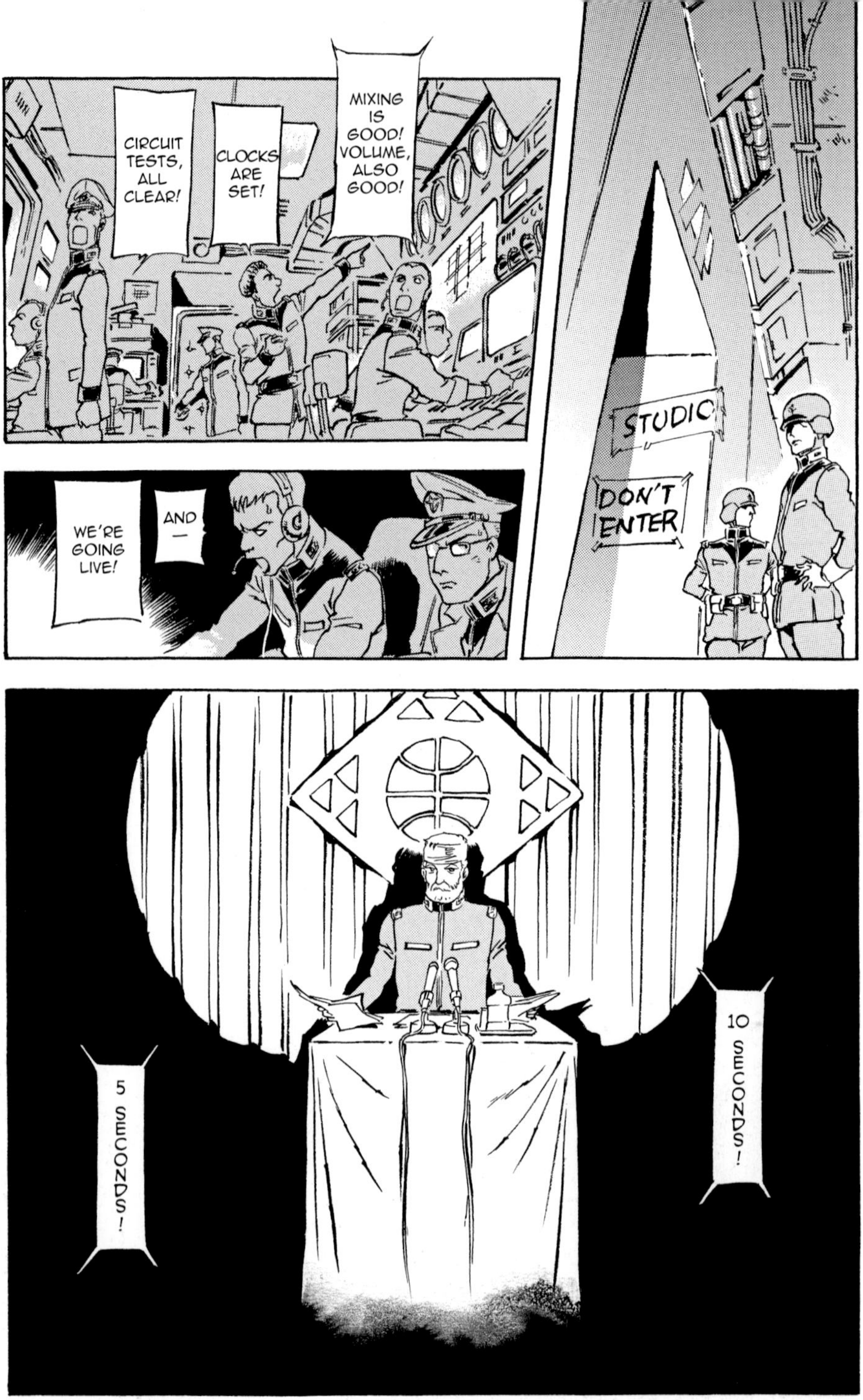
STUDIO
DON'T ENTER
MIXING IS GOOD! VOLUME, ALSO GOOD!
CLOCKS ARE SET!
CIRCUIT TESTS, ALL CLEAR!
AND—
WE'RE GOING LIVE!
10 SECONDS!
5 SECONDS!

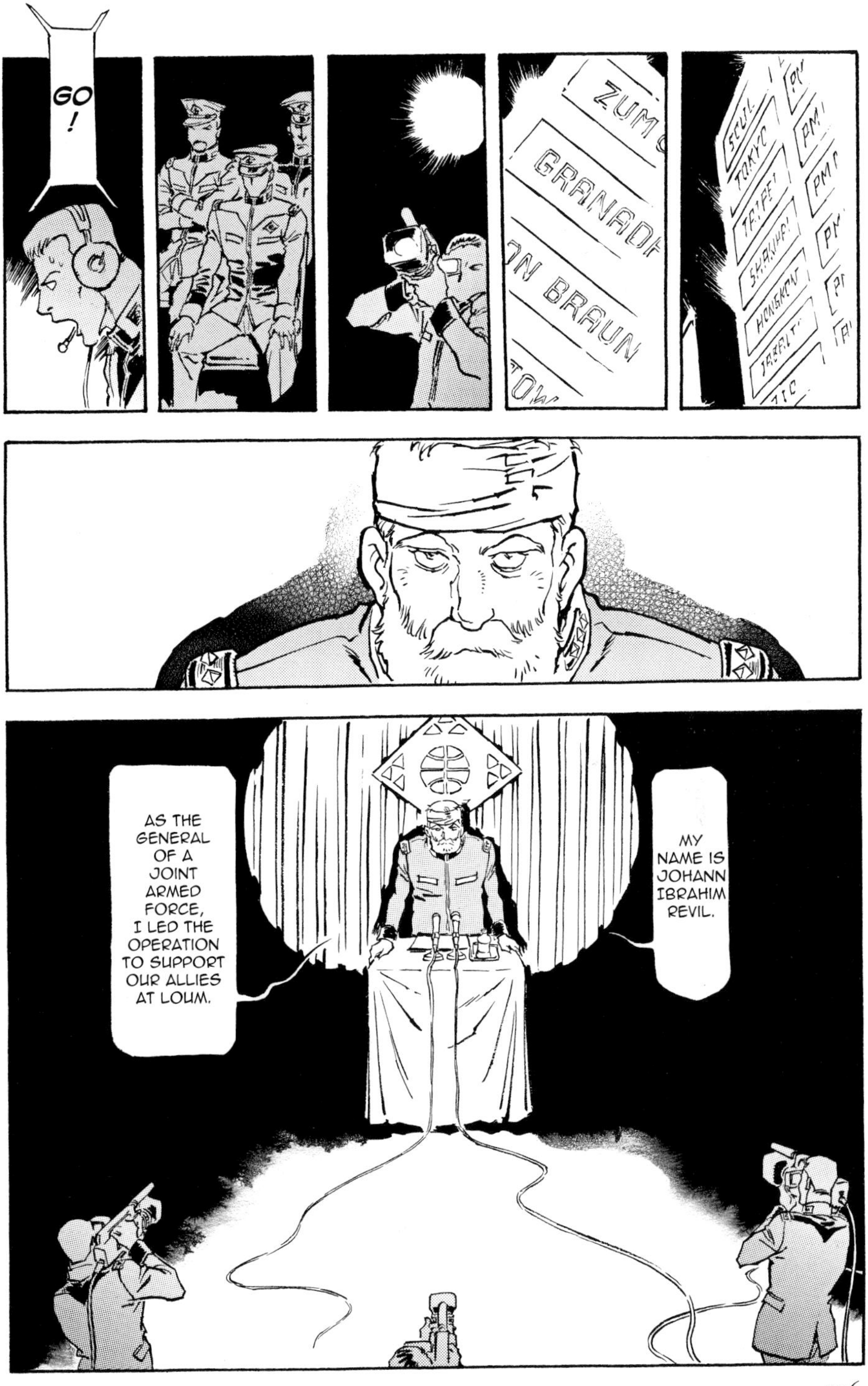
GO!
MY NAME IS JOHANN IBRAHIM REVIL.
AS THE GENERAL OF A JOINT ARMED FORCE, I LED THE OPERATION TO SUPPORT OUR ALLIES AT LOUM.

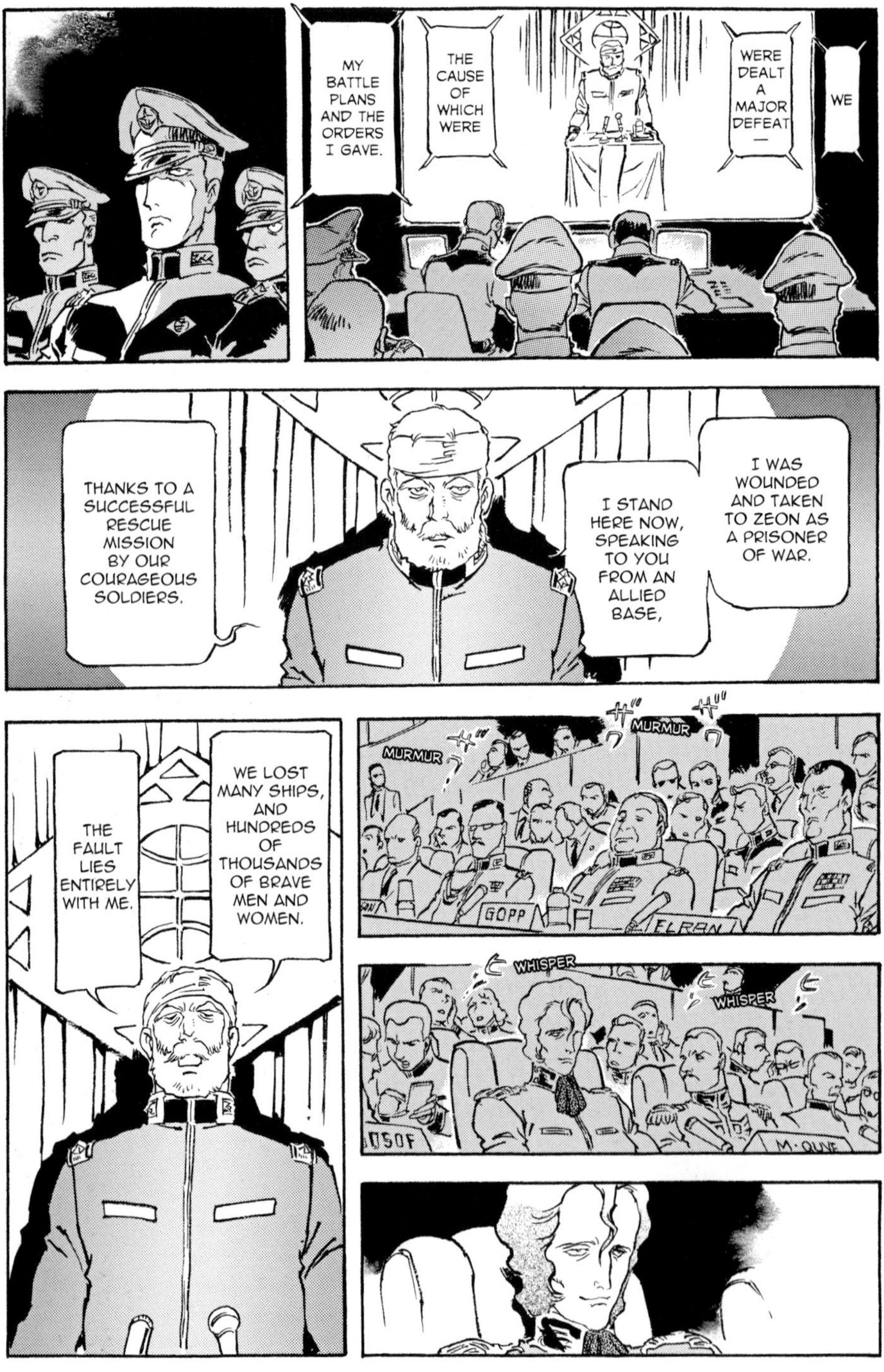
WE
WERE DEALT A MAJOR DEFEAT —
THE CAUSE OF WHICH WERE
MY BATTLE PLANS AND THE ORDERS I GAVE.
I WAS WOUNDED AND TAKEN TO ZEON AS A PRISONER OF WAR.
I STAND HERE NOW, SPEAKING TO YOU FROM AN ALLIED BASE,
THANKS TO A SUCCESSFUL RESCUE MISSION BY OUR COURAGEOUS SOLDIERS.
MURMUR
MURMUR
GOPP
ELRAN
WHISPER
WHISPER
WE LOST MANY SHIPS, AND HUNDREDS OF THOUSANDS OF BRAVE MEN AND WOMEN.
THE FAULT LIES ENTIRELY WITH ME.

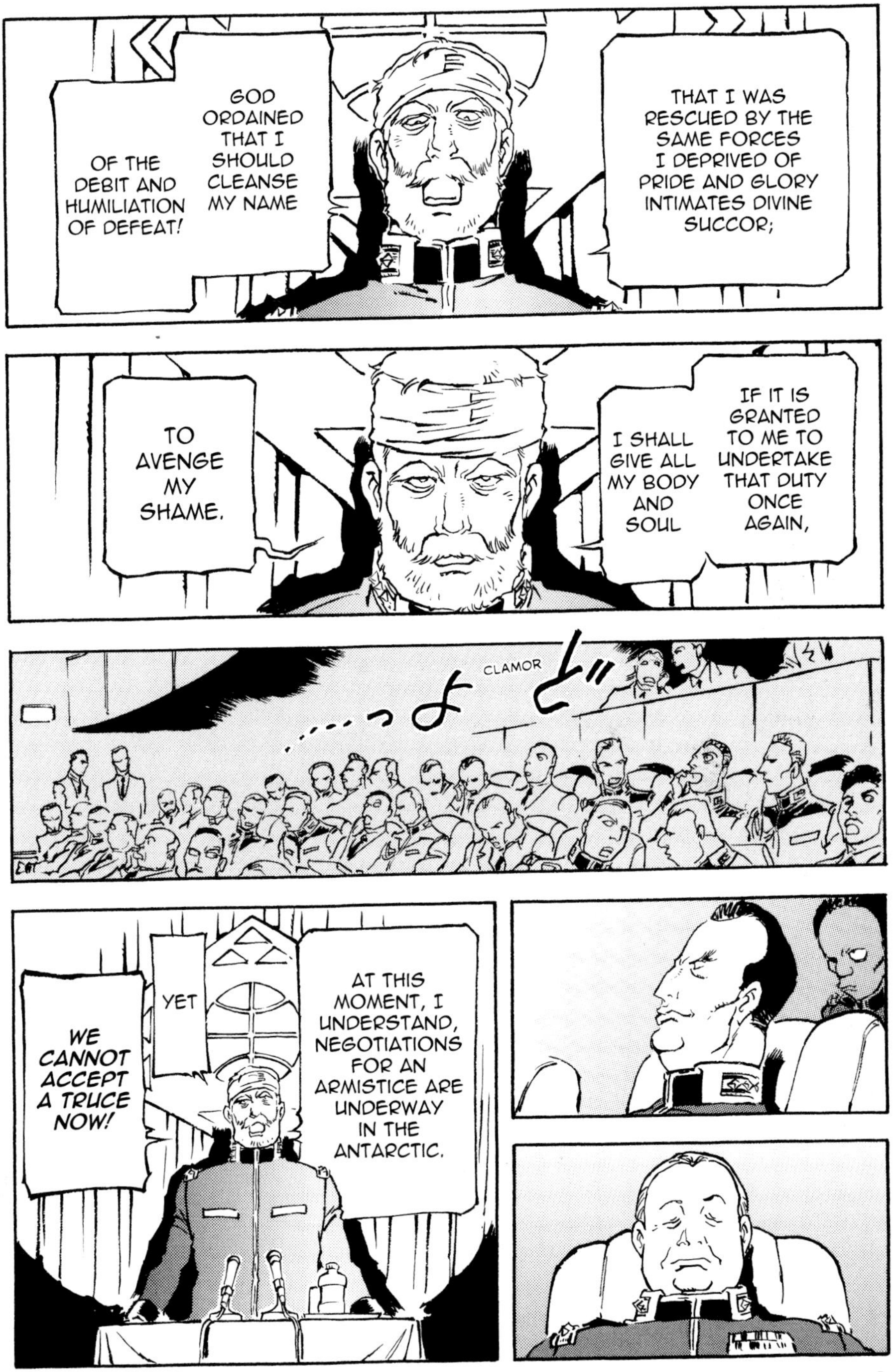
THAT I WAS RESCUED BY THE SAME FORCES I DEPRIVED OF PRIDE AND GLORY INTIMATES DIVINE SUCCOR;
GOD ORDAINED THAT I SHOULD CLEANSE MY NAME
OF THE DEBIT AND HUMILIATION OF DEFEAT!
IF IT IS GRANTED TO ME TO UNDERTAKE THAT DUTY ONCE AGAIN,
I SHALL GIVE ALL MY BODY AND SOUL
TO AVENGE MY SHAME.
CLAMOR
どよっ……
AT THIS MOMENT, I UNDERSTAND, NEGOTIATIONS FOR AN ARMISTICE ARE UNDERWAY IN THE ANTARCTIC.
YET
WE CANNOT ACCEPT A TRUCE NOW!

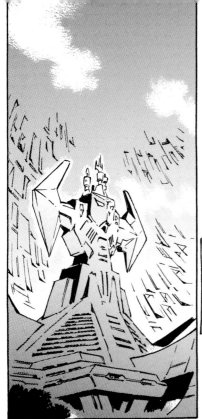

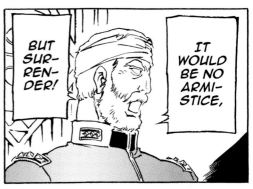

IT WOULD BE NO ARMISTICE,

BUT SURRENDER!

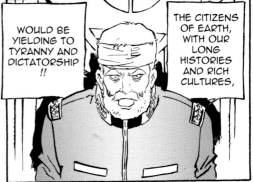

THE CITIZENS OF EARTH, WITH OUR LONG HISTORIES AND RICH CULTURES,

WOULD BE YIELDING TO TYRANNY AND DICTATORSHIP!!

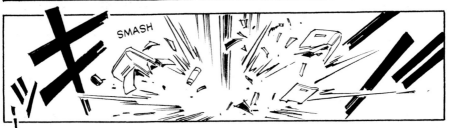

SMASH

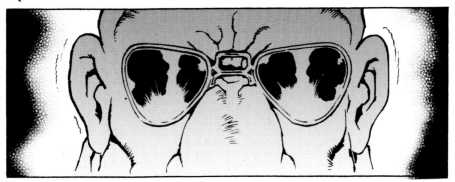

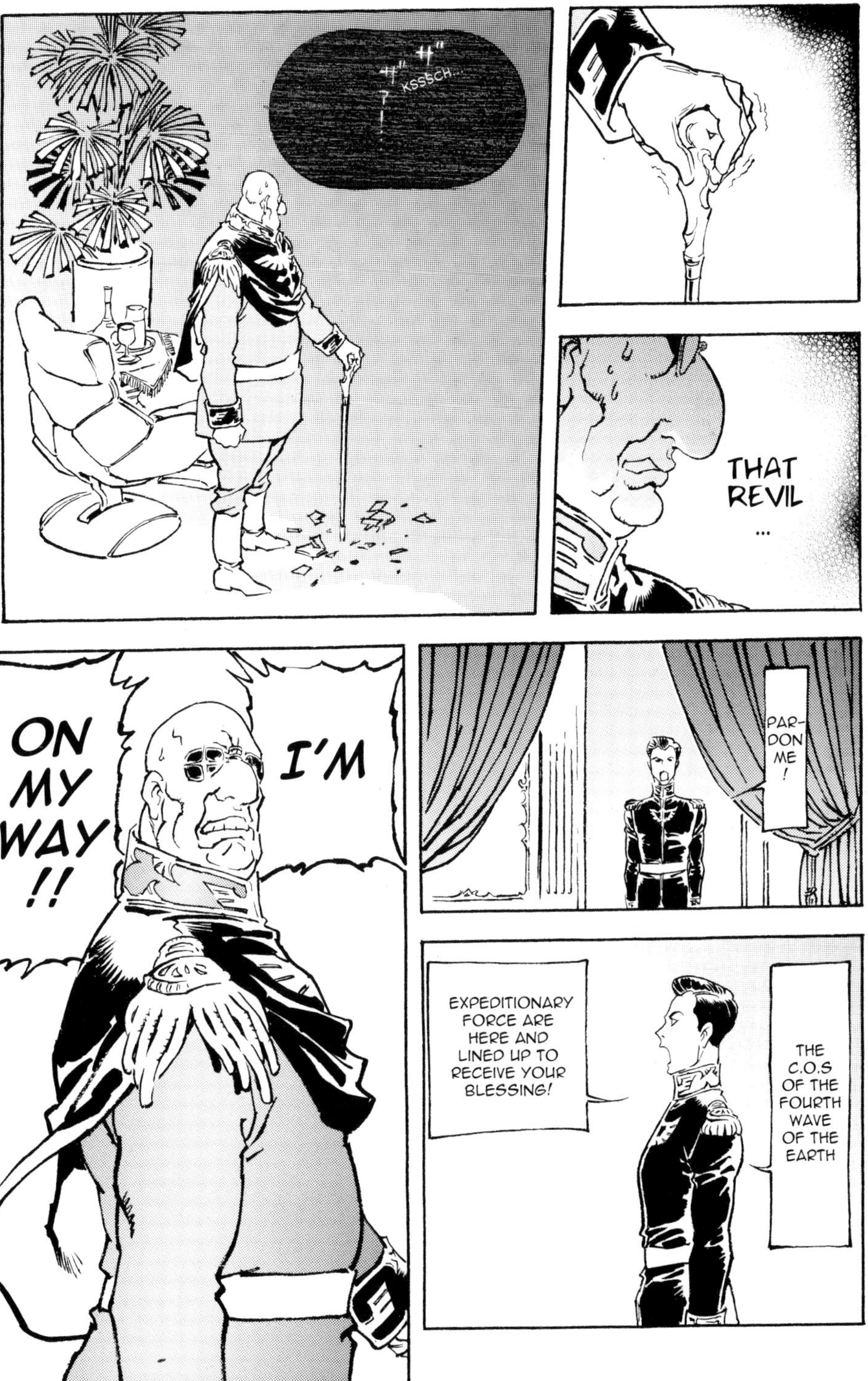
THAT REVIL ...
KSSSCH...
PARDON ME!
THE C.O.S OF THE FOURTH WAVE OF THE EARTH
EXPEDITIONARY FORCE ARE HERE AND LINED UP TO RECEIVE YOUR BLESSING!
I'M
ON MY WAY!!

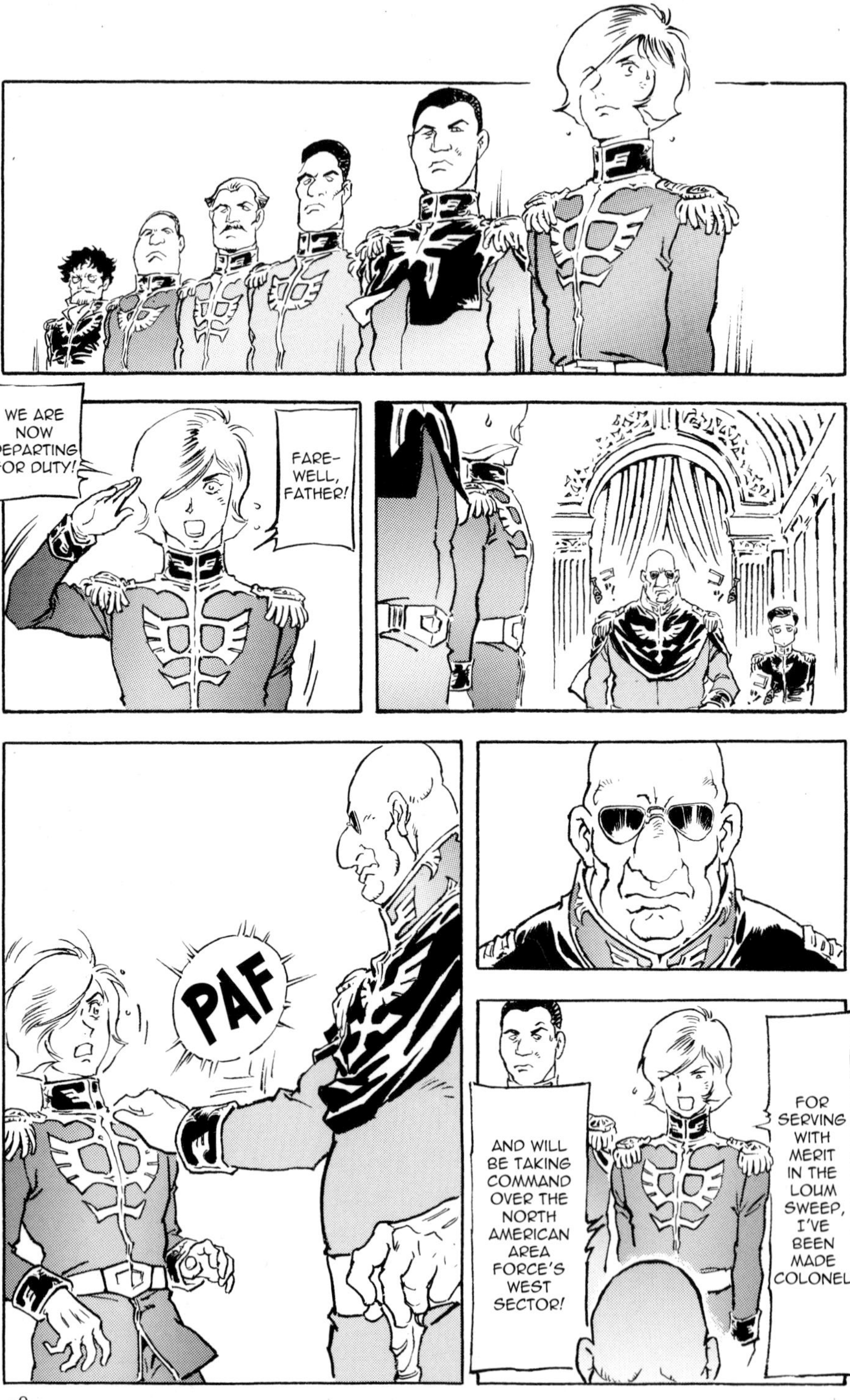
FARE-WELL, FATHER!
WE ARE NOW DEPARTING FOR DUTY!
FOR SERVING WITH MERIT IN THE LOUM SWEEP, I'VE BEEN MADE COLONEL
AND WILL BE TAKING COMMAND OVER THE NORTH AMERICAN AREA FORCE'S WEST SECTOR!
PAF

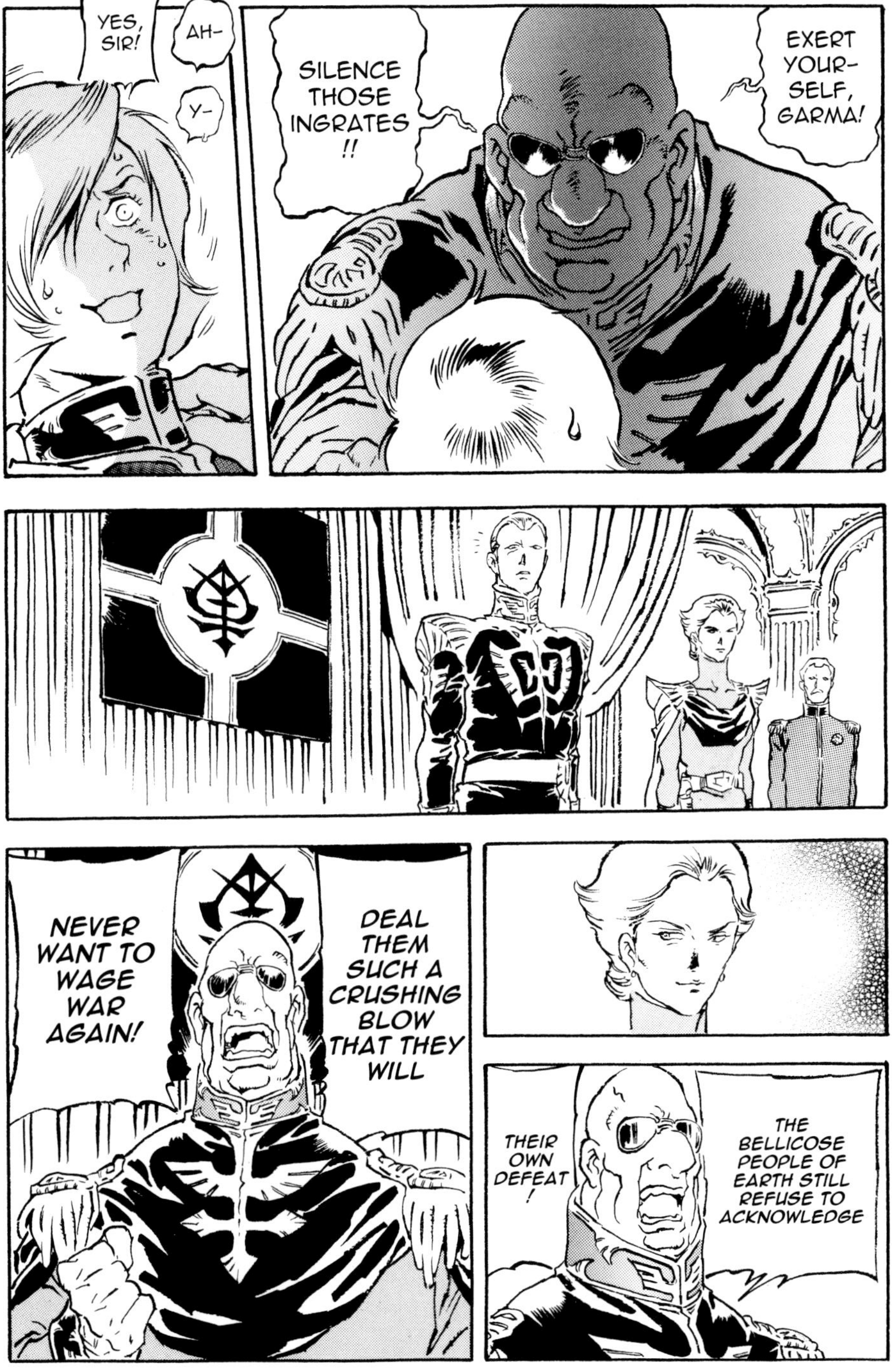
EXERT YOUR-SELF, GARMA!
SILENCE THOSE INGRATES !!
AH-
Y-
YES, SIR!
THE BELLICOSE PEOPLE OF EARTH STILL REFUSE TO ACKNOWLEDGE
THEIR OWN DEFEAT !
DEAL THEM SUCH A CRUSHING BLOW THAT THEY WILL
NEVER WANT TO WAGE WAR AGAIN!

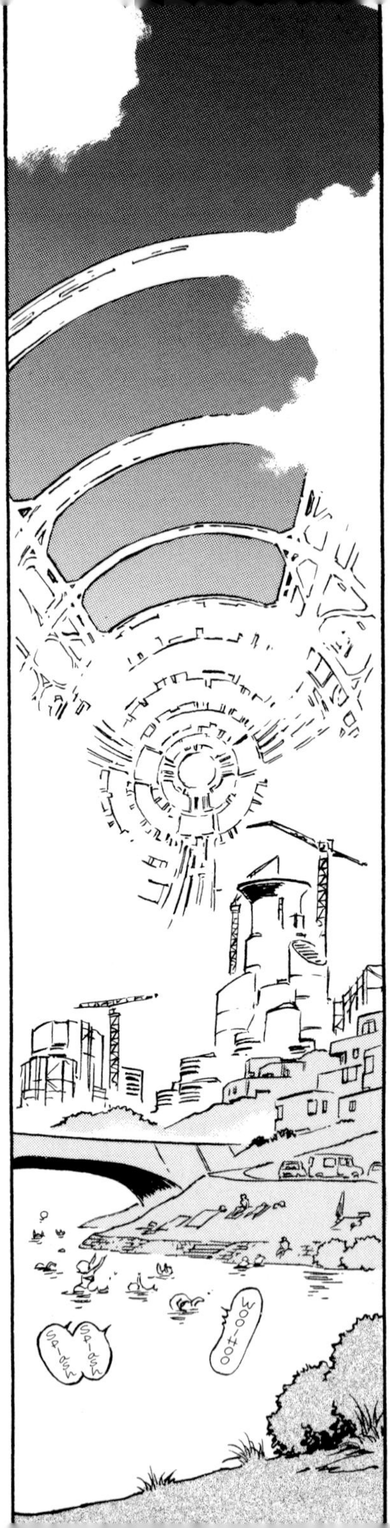
WOO-HOO
Splash
Splash

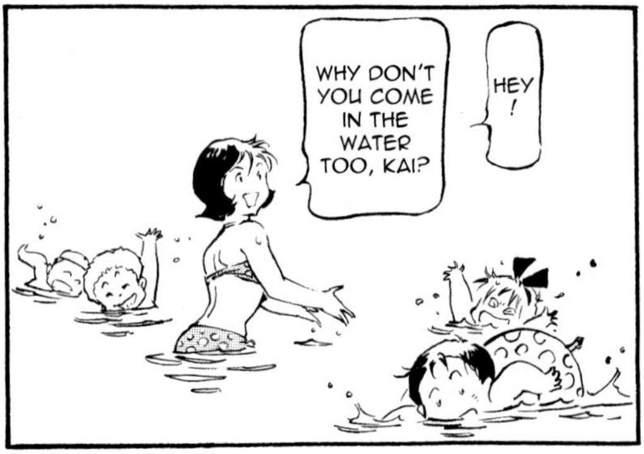
HEY!
WHY DON'T YOU COME IN THE WATER TOO, KAI?

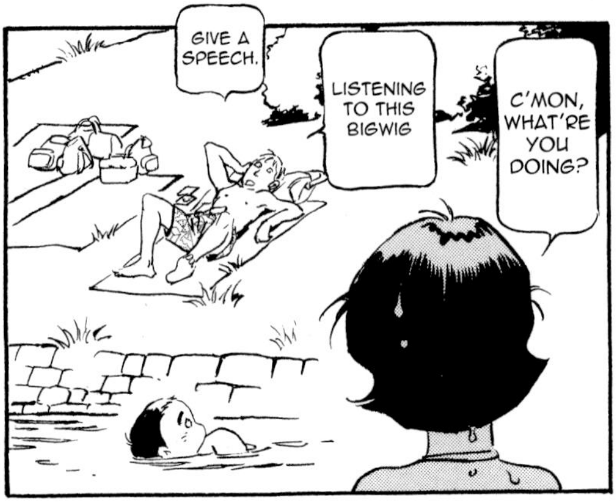
C'MON, WHAT'RE YOU DOING?
LISTENING TO THIS BIGWIG
GIVE A SPEECH.

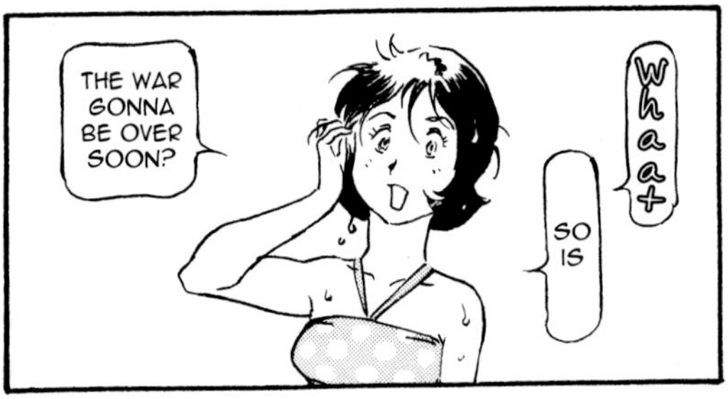
Whaat
SO IS
THE WAR GONNA BE OVER SOON?

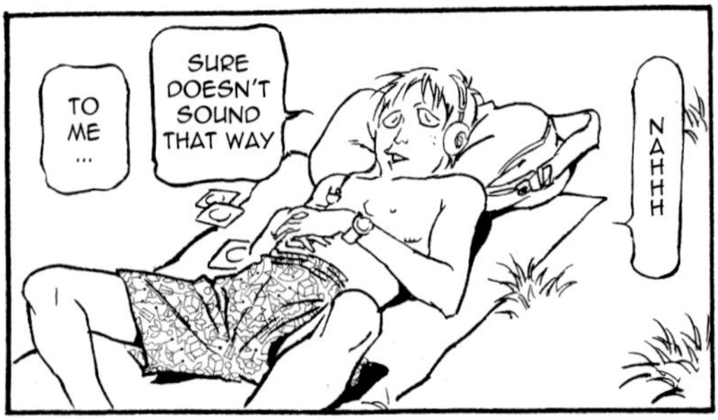
NAHHH
SURE DOESN'T SOUND THAT WAY
TO ME ...

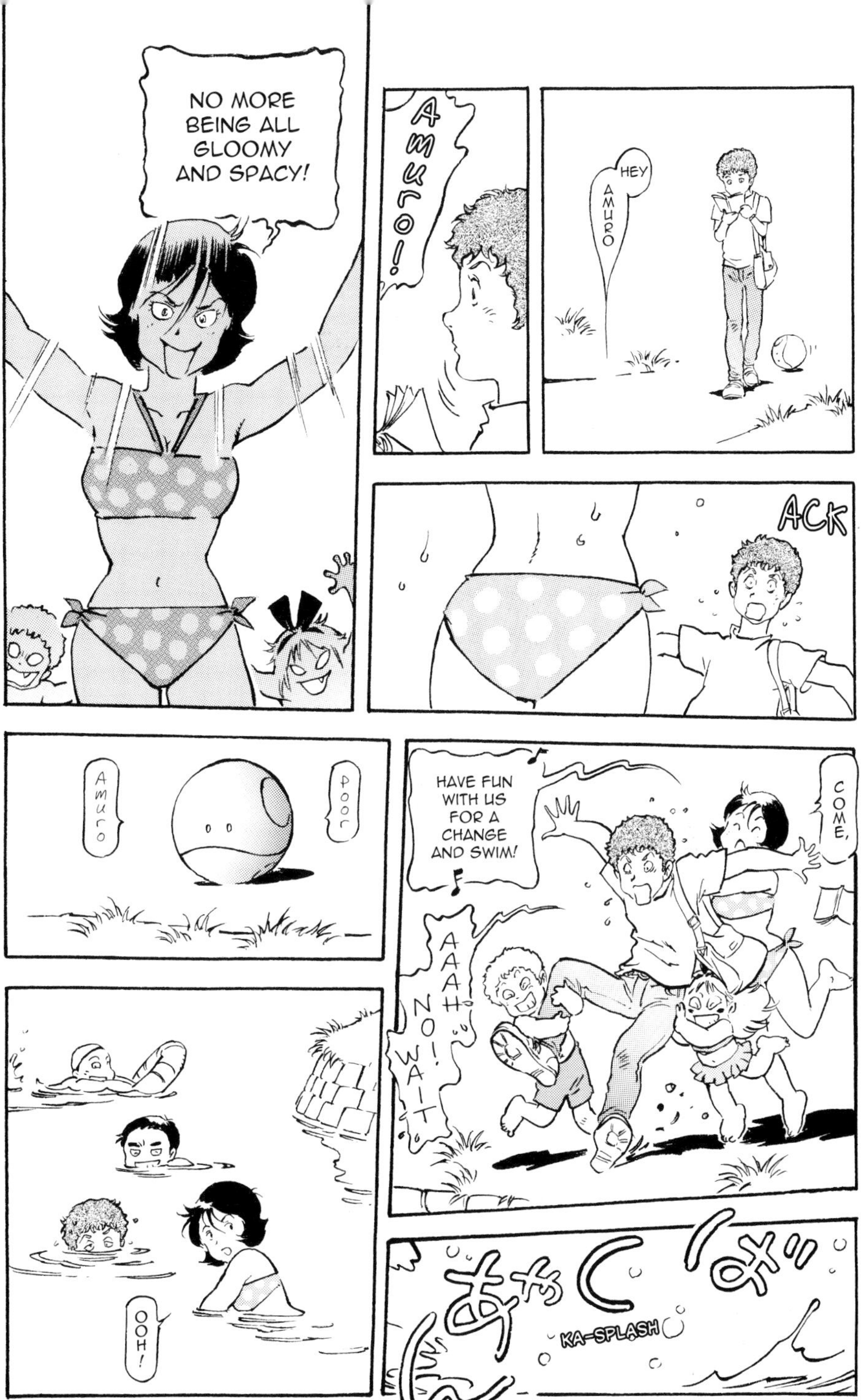
HEY AMURO
AMURO!
ACK
NO MORE BEING ALL GLOOMY AND SPACY!
COME,
HAVE FUN WITH US FOR A CHANGE AND SWIM!
AAAH
NO! WAIT
POOR
AMURO
KA-SPLASH
OOH!

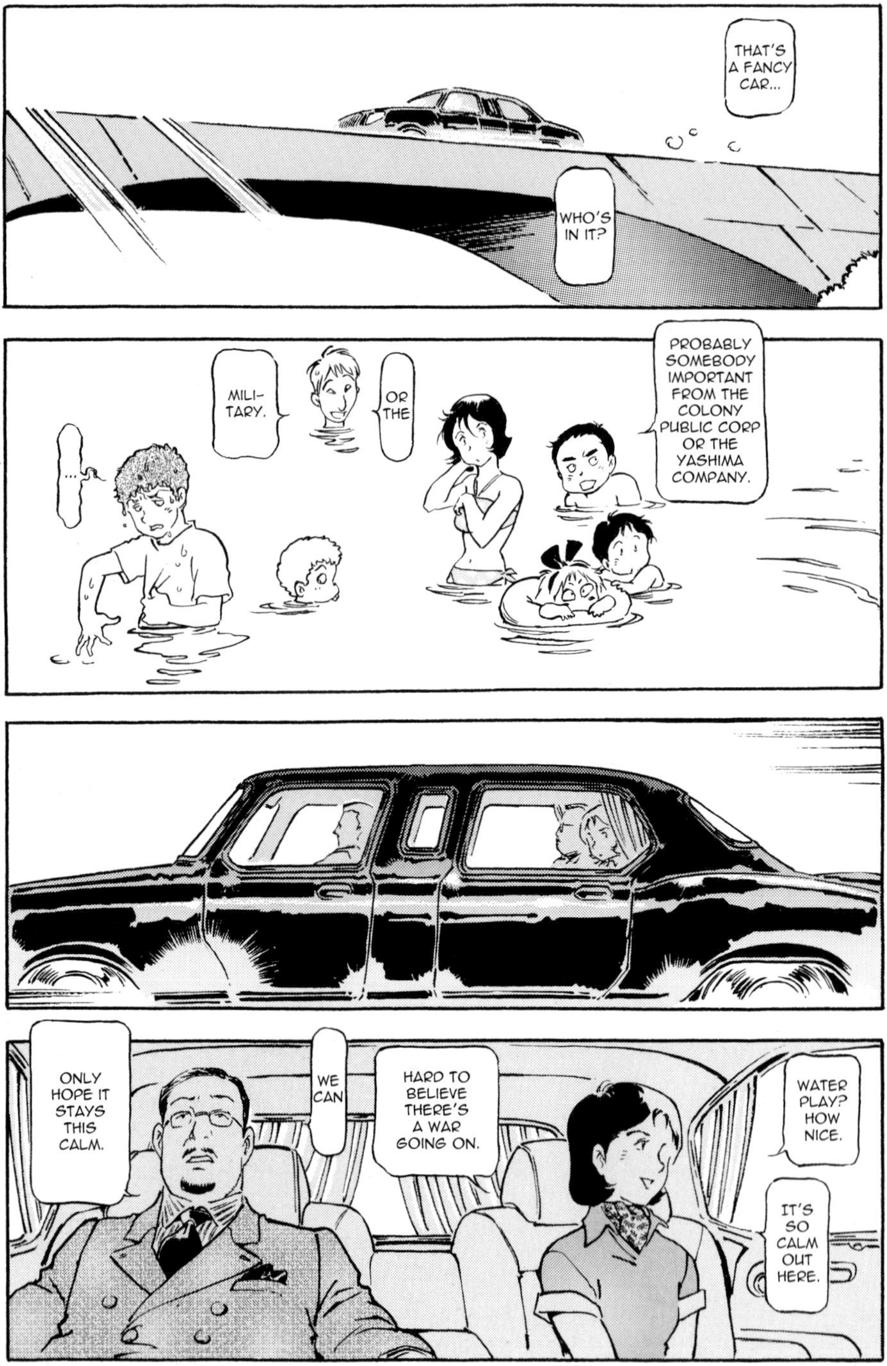
THAT'S A FANCY CAR...
WHO'S IN IT?
PROBABLY SOMEBODY IMPORTANT FROM THE COLONY PUBLIC CORP OR THE YASHIMA COMPANY.
OR THE
MILI-TARY.
...
WATER PLAY? HOW NICE.
IT'S SO CALM OUT HERE.
HARD TO BELIEVE THERE'S A WAR GOING ON.
WE CAN
ONLY HOPE IT STAYS THIS CALM.

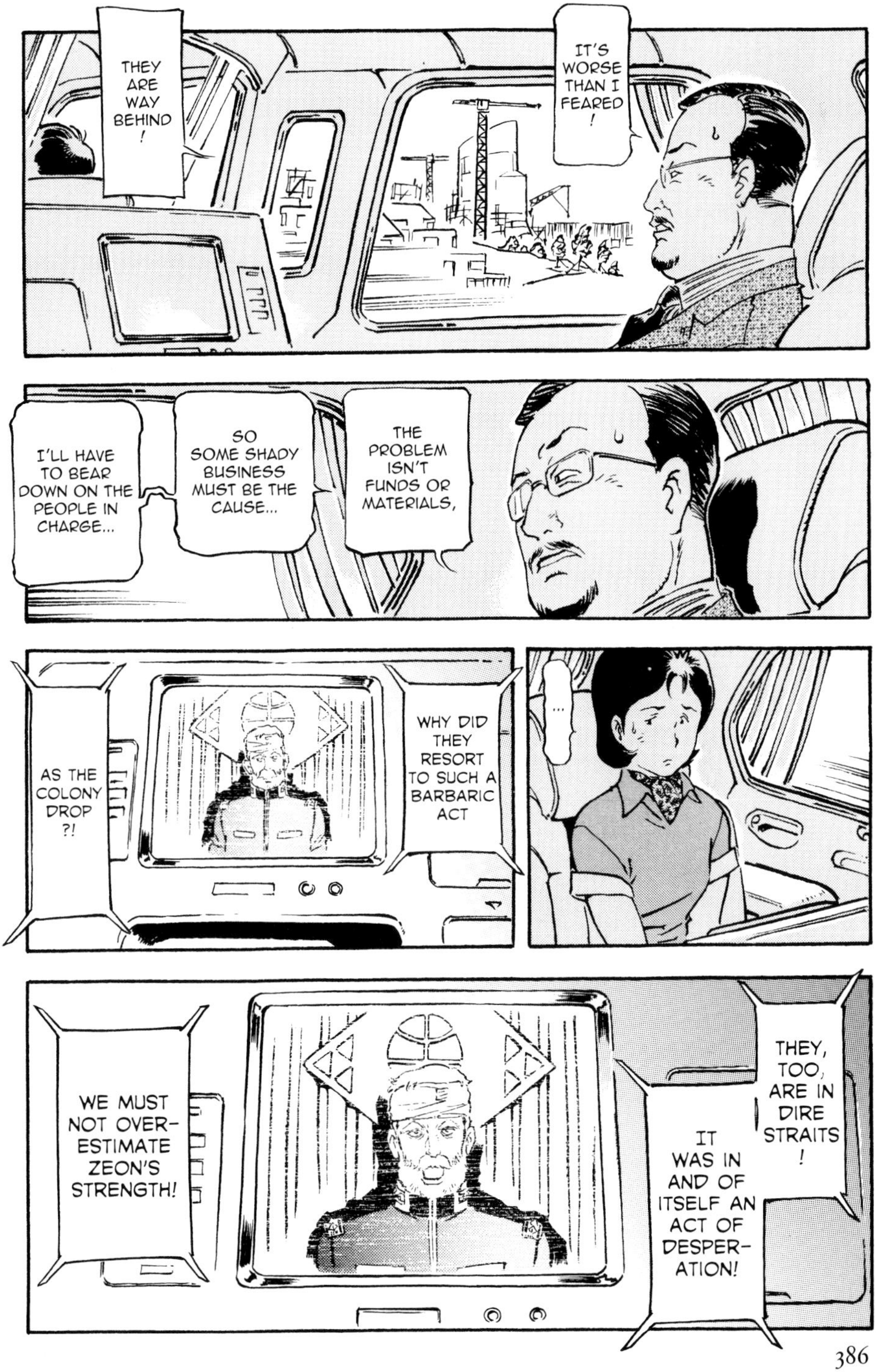
IT'S WORSE THAN I FEARED!
THEY ARE WAY BEHIND!
THE PROBLEM ISN'T FUNDS OR MATERIALS,
SO SOME SHADY BUSINESS MUST BE THE CAUSE...
I'LL HAVE TO BEAR DOWN ON THE PEOPLE IN CHARGE...
...
WHY DID THEY RESORT TO SUCH A BARBARIC ACT
AS THE COLONY DROP ?!
THEY, TOO, ARE IN DIRE STRAITS!
IT WAS IN AND OF ITSELF AN ACT OF DESPER-ATION!
WE MUST NOT OVER-ESTIMATE ZEON'S STRENGTH!

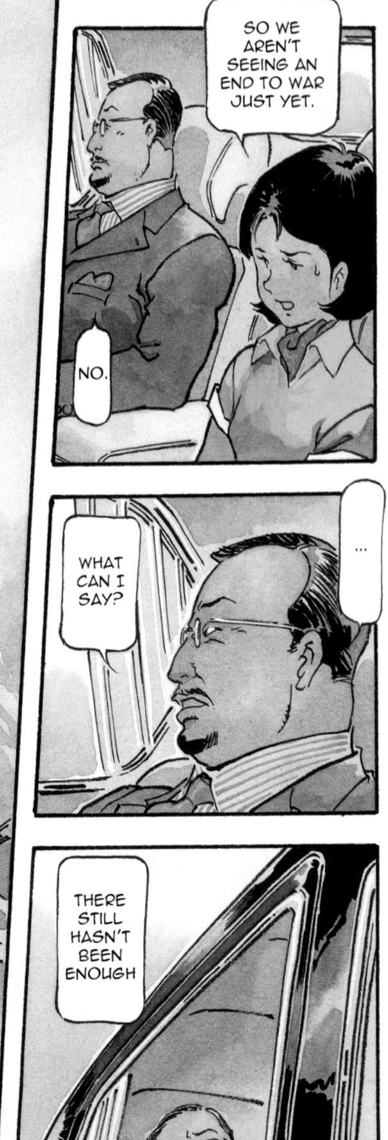
SO WE AREN'T SEEING AN END TO WAR JUST YET.
NO.
...
WHAT CAN I SAY?
THERE STILL HASN'T BEEN ENOUGH
RUIN!
HUMANS HAVEN'T PUSHED THINGS AS FAR AS THEY CAN GO.
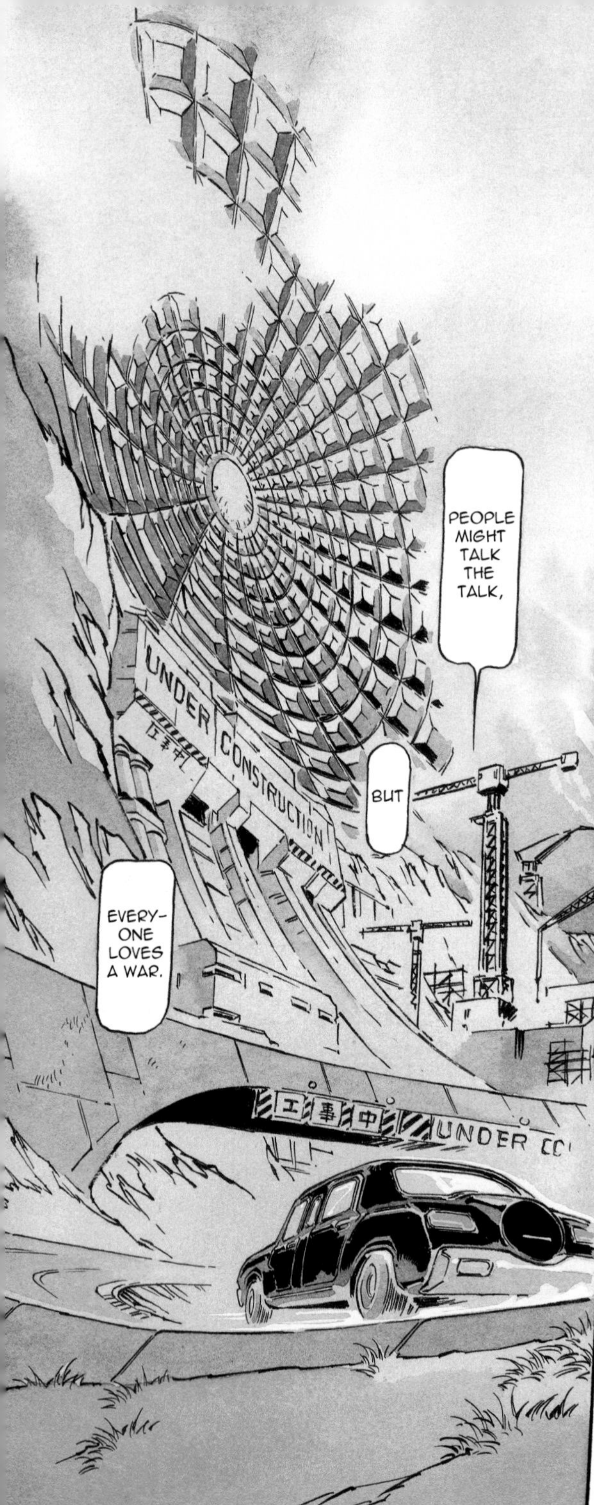
PEOPLE MIGHT TALK THE TALK,
BUT
EVERY-ONE LOVES A WAR.
UNDER CONSTRUCTION
工事中
UNDER CO

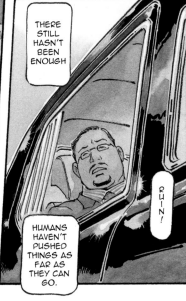

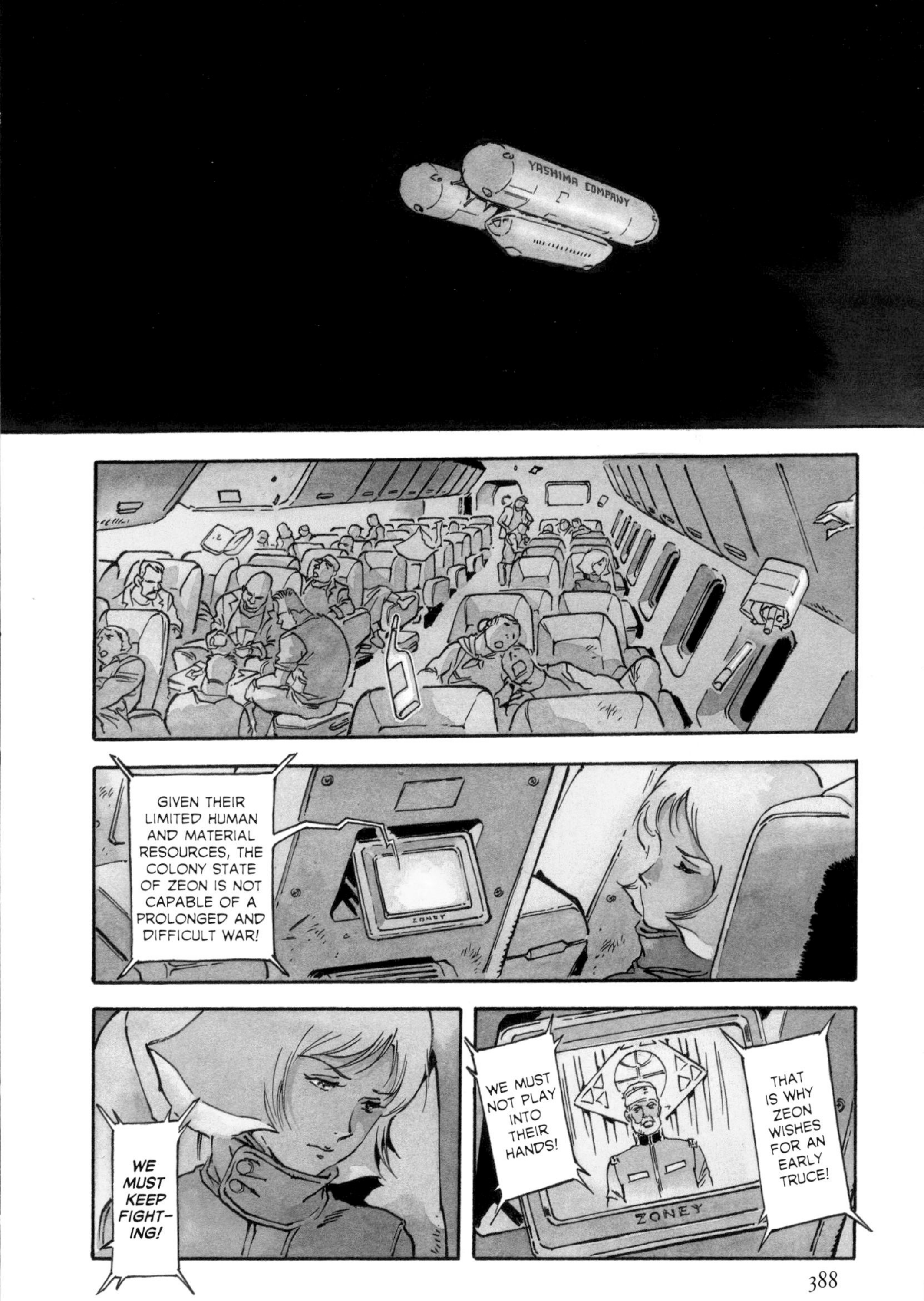
YASHIMA COMPANY
GIVEN THEIR LIMITED HUMAN AND MATERIAL RESOURCES, THE COLONY STATE OF ZEON IS NOT CAPABLE OF A PROLONGED AND DIFFICULT WAR!
ZONEY
THAT IS WHY ZEON WISHES FOR AN EARLY TRUCE!
WE MUST NOT PLAY INTO THEIR HANDS!
ZONEY
WE MUST KEEP FIGHT-ING!

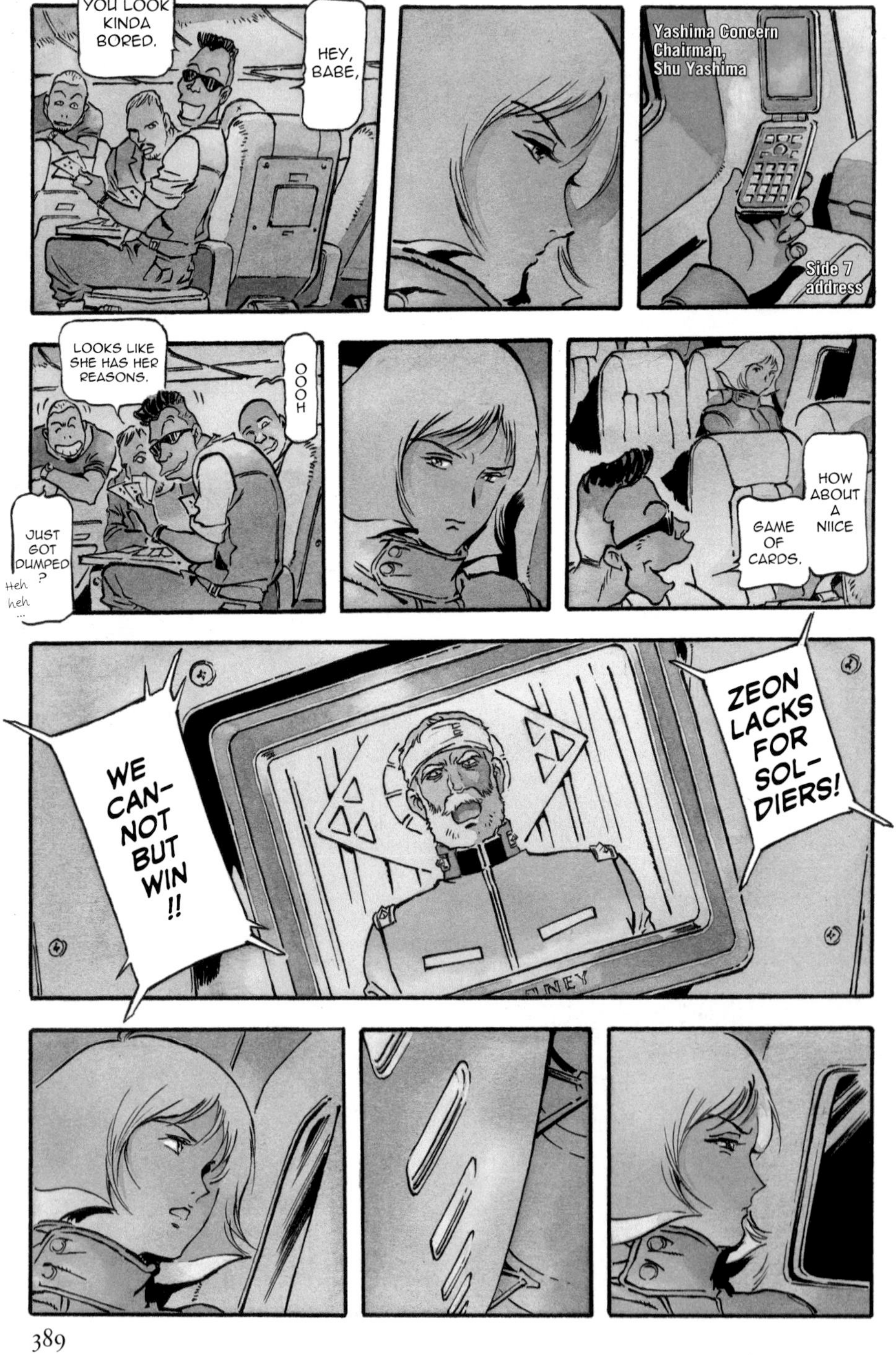
Yashima Concern Chairman, Shu Yashima
Side 7 address
HEY, BABE,
YOU LOOK KINDA BORED.
HOW ABOUT A NIICE
GAME OF CARDS.
OOOH
LOOKS LIKE SHE HAS HER REASONS.
JUST GOT DUMPED?
Heh heh ...
ZEON LACKS FOR SOL-DIERS!
WE CAN-NOT BUT WIN!!

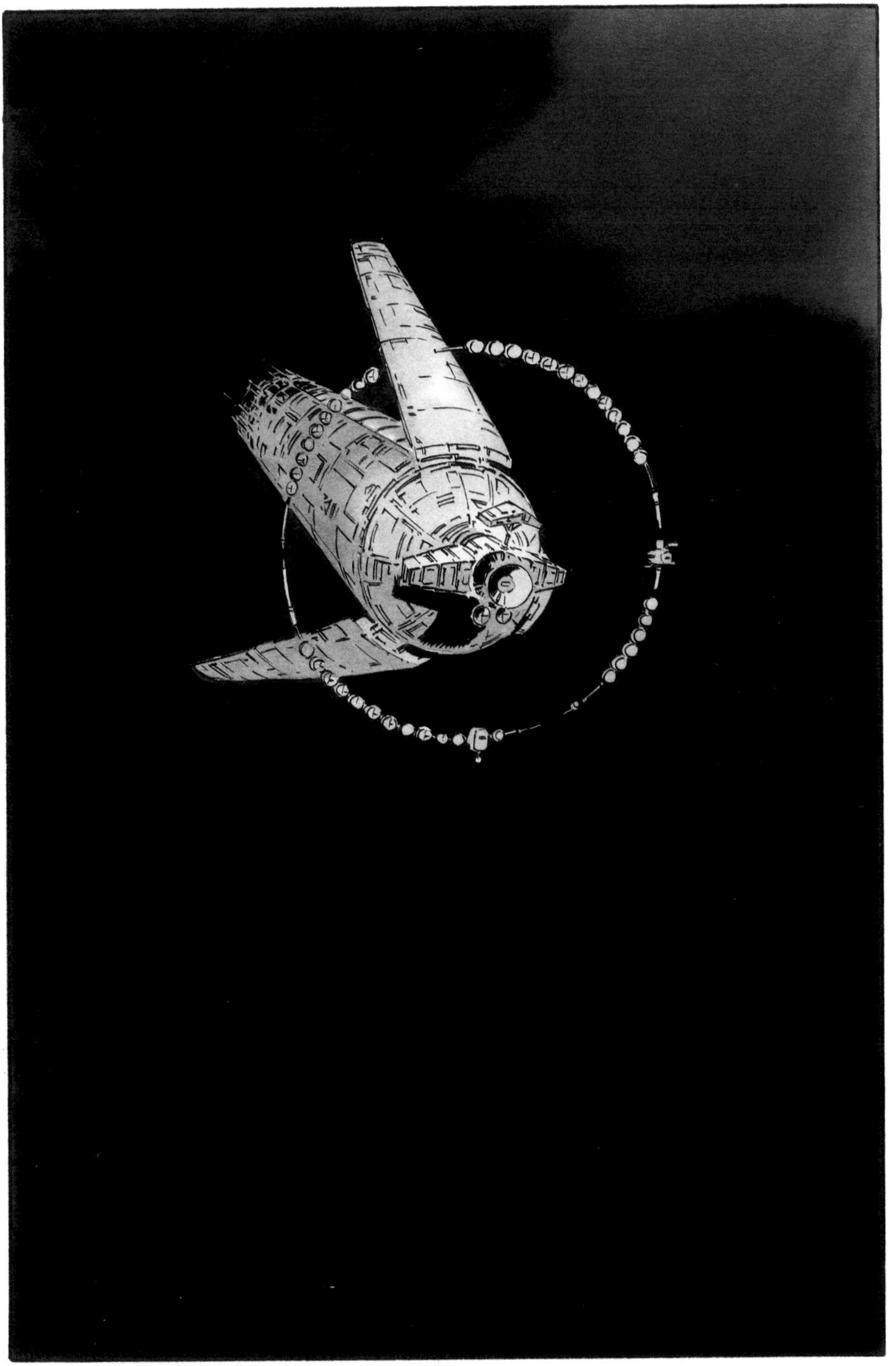

to be continued...

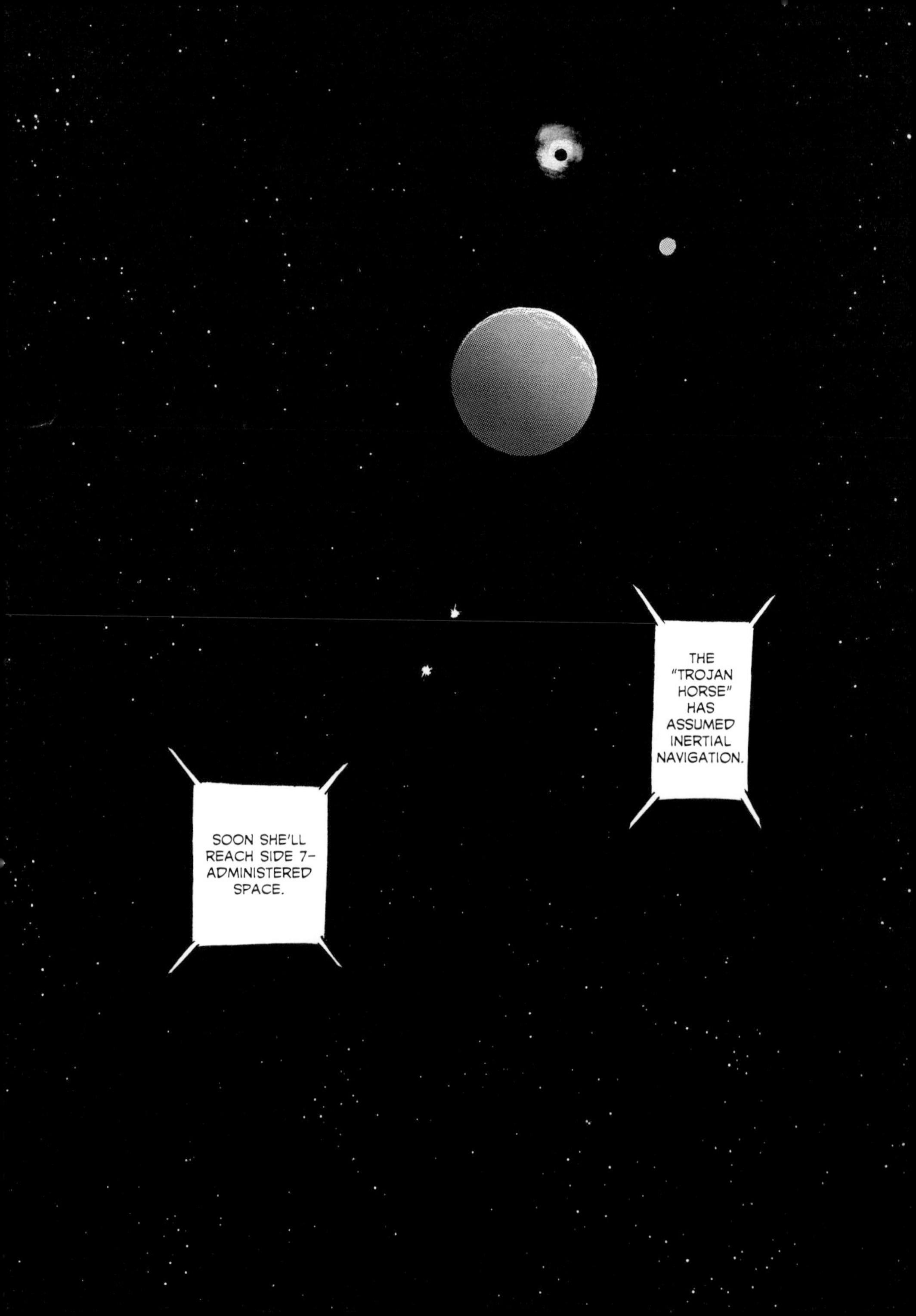
THE "TROJAN HORSE" HAS ASSUMED INERTIAL NAVIGATION.
SOON SHE'LL REACH SIDE 7-ADMINISTERED SPACE.

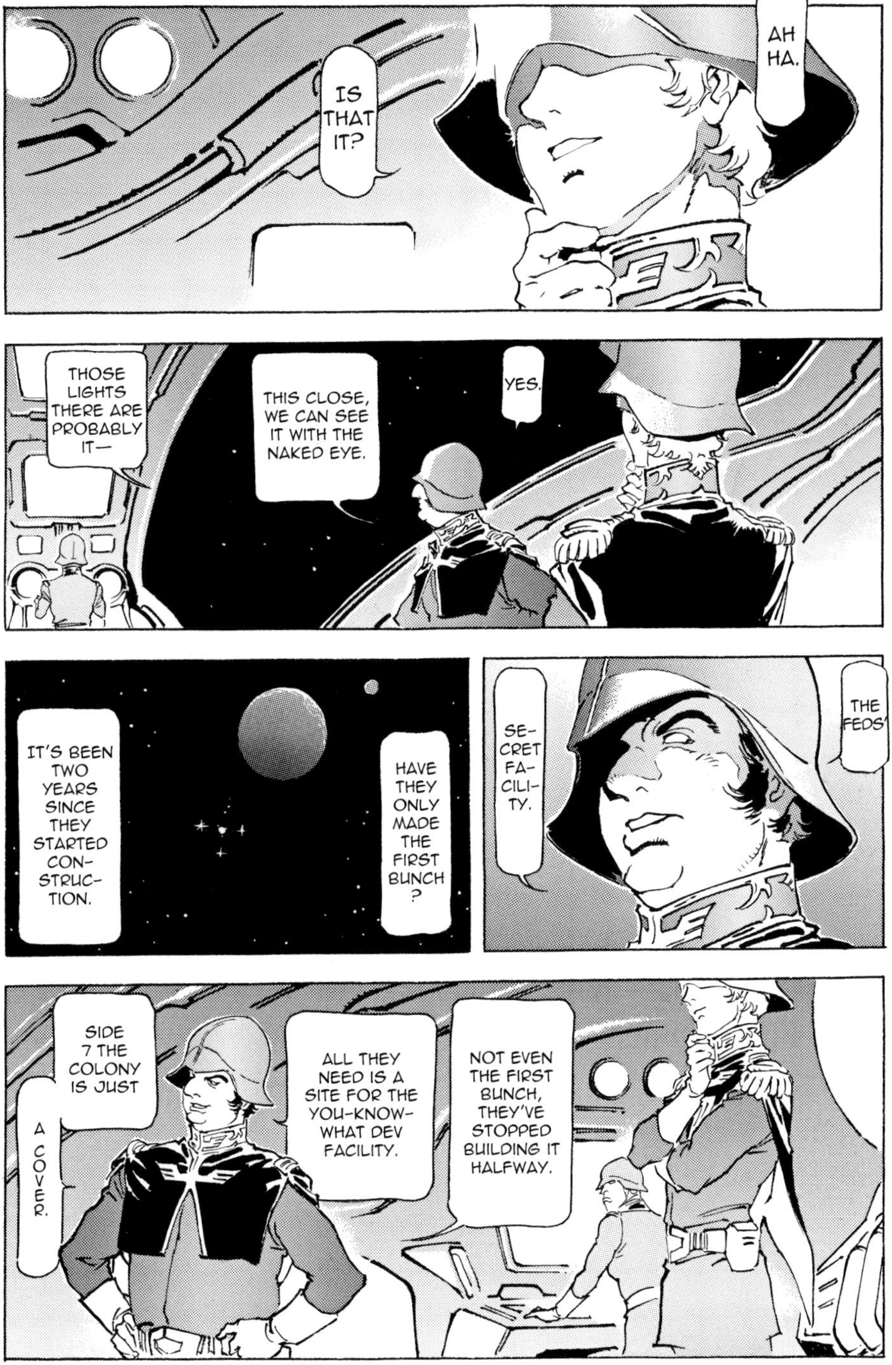
AH HA.
IS THAT IT?
YES.
THIS CLOSE, WE CAN SEE IT WITH THE NAKED EYE.
THOSE LIGHTS THERE ARE PROBABLY IT—
THE FEDS'
SE-CRET FA-CILI-TY.
HAVE THEY ONLY MADE THE FIRST BUNCH?
IT'S BEEN TWO YEARS SINCE THEY STARTED CON-STRUC-TION.
NOT EVEN THE FIRST BUNCH, THEY'VE STOPPED BUILDING IT HALFWAY.
ALL THEY NEED IS A SITE FOR THE YOU-KNOW-WHAT DEV FACILITY.
SIDE 7 THE COLONY IS JUST
A COVER.

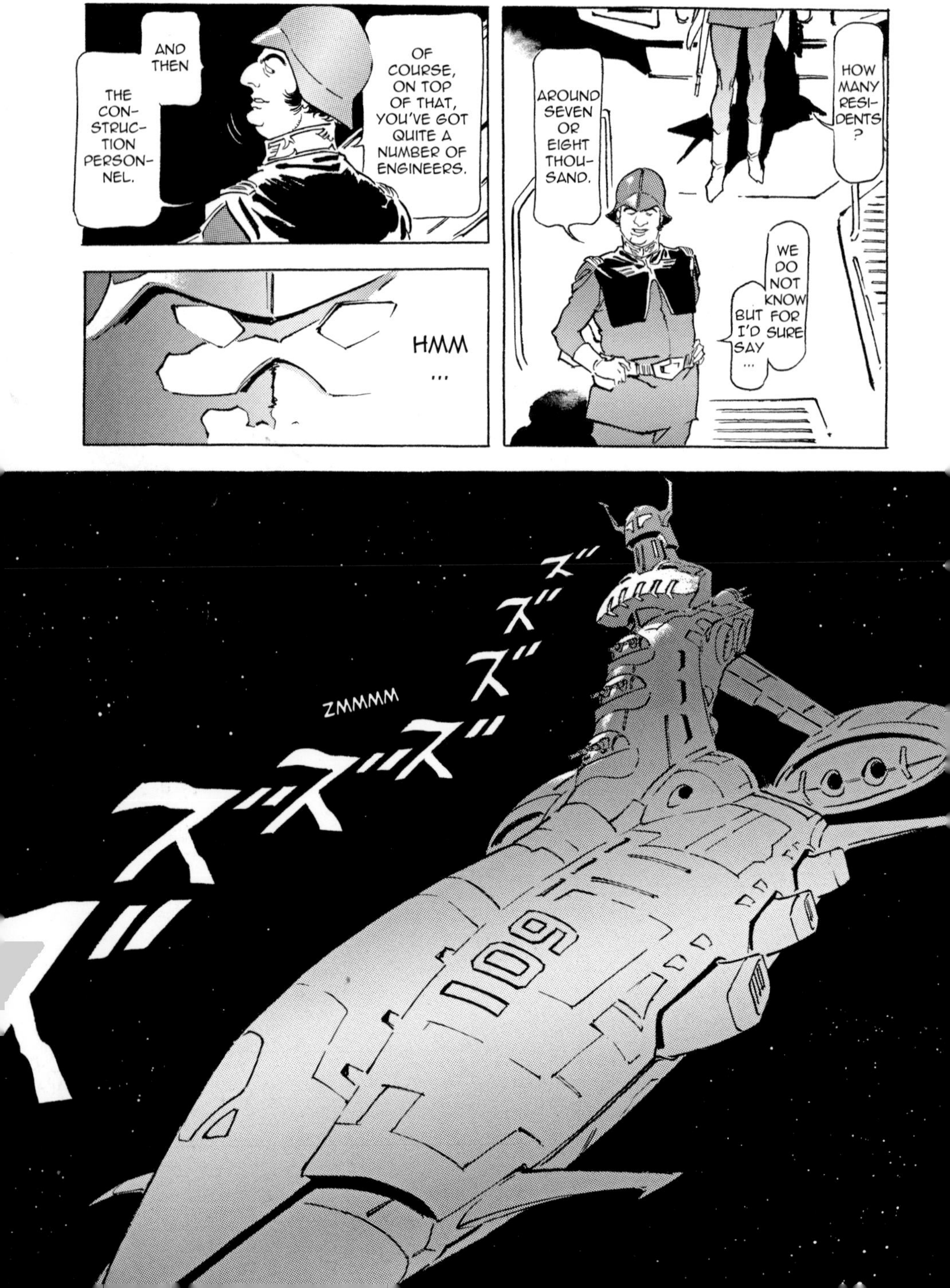
HOW MANY RESIDENTS?
WE DO NOT KNOW FOR SURE BUT I'D SAY ...
AROUND SEVEN OR EIGHT THOUSAND.
OF COURSE, ON TOP OF THAT, YOU'VE GOT QUITE A NUMBER OF ENGINEERS.
AND THEN
THE CONSTRUCTION PERSONNEL.
HMM ...
ズズズズズズ
ZMMMM
109

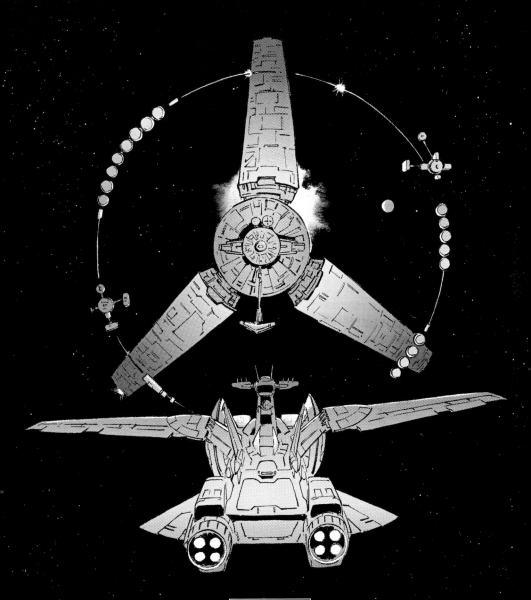

Special Feature

On the Eve

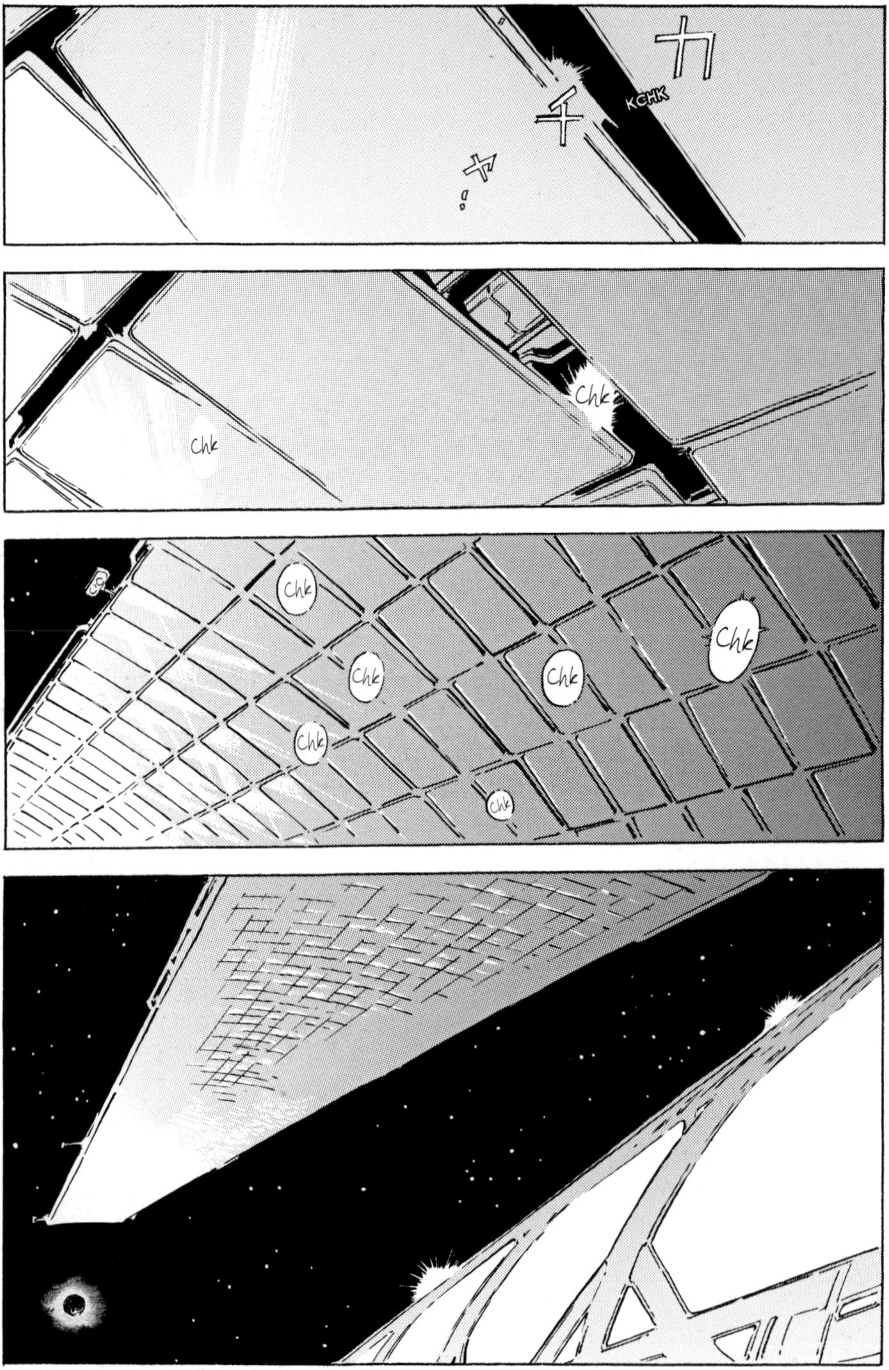
カチャ!
KCHK
Chk
Chk
Chk
Chk
Chk
Chk
Chk
Chk

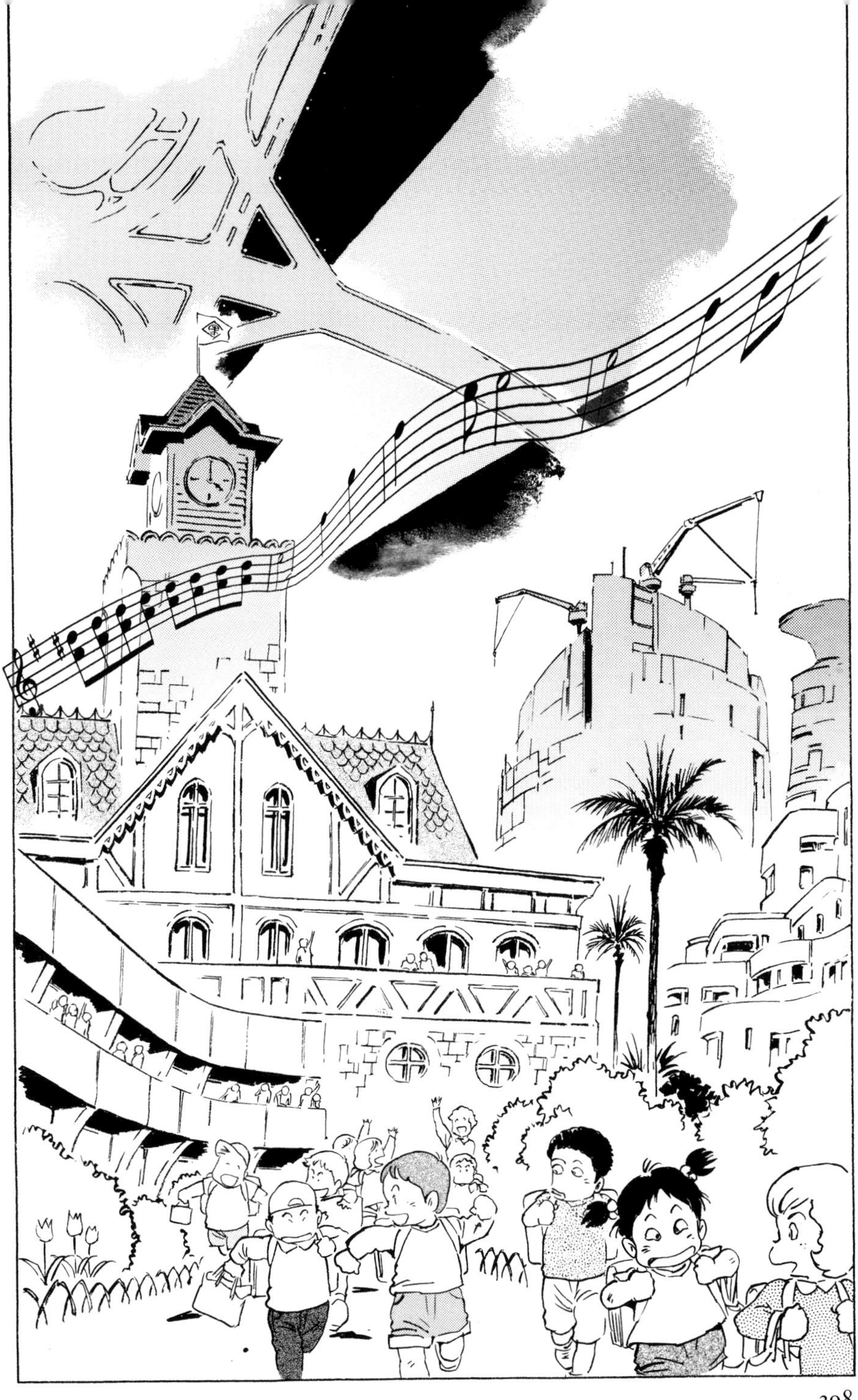

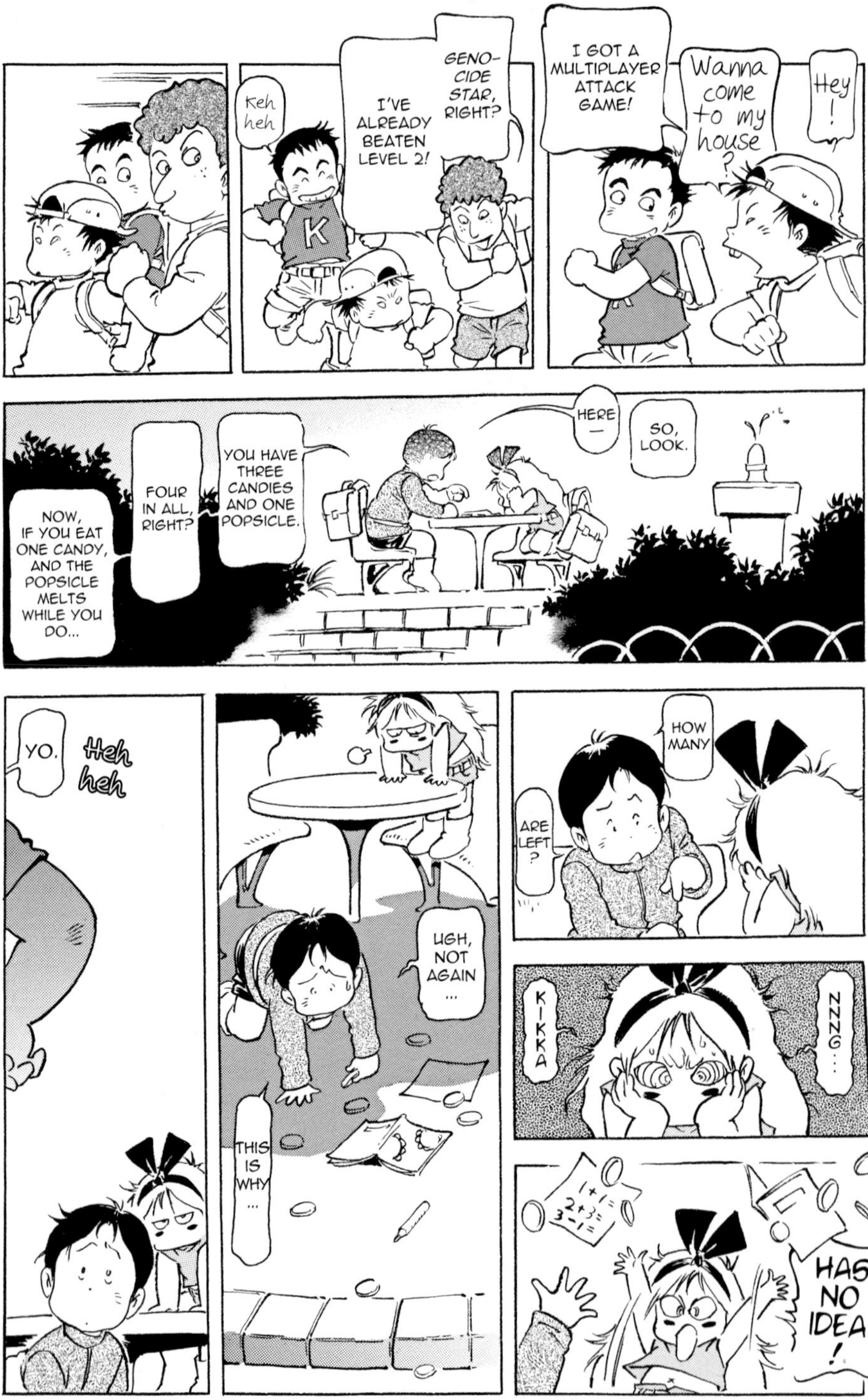
Hey!
Wanna come to my house?
I GOT A MULTIPLAYER ATTACK GAME!
GENO-CIDE STAR, RIGHT?
I'VE ALREADY BEATEN LEVEL 2!
Keh heh
SO, LOOK.
HERE—
YOU HAVE THREE CANDIES AND ONE POPSICLE.
FOUR IN ALL, RIGHT?
NOW, IF YOU EAT ONE CANDY, AND THE POPSICLE MELTS WHILE YOU DO...
HOW MANY
ARE LEFT?
NNNG...
KIKKA
1+1=
2+3=
3−1=
HAS NO IDEA!
UGH, NOT AGAIN...
THIS IS WHY...
YO.
Heh heh

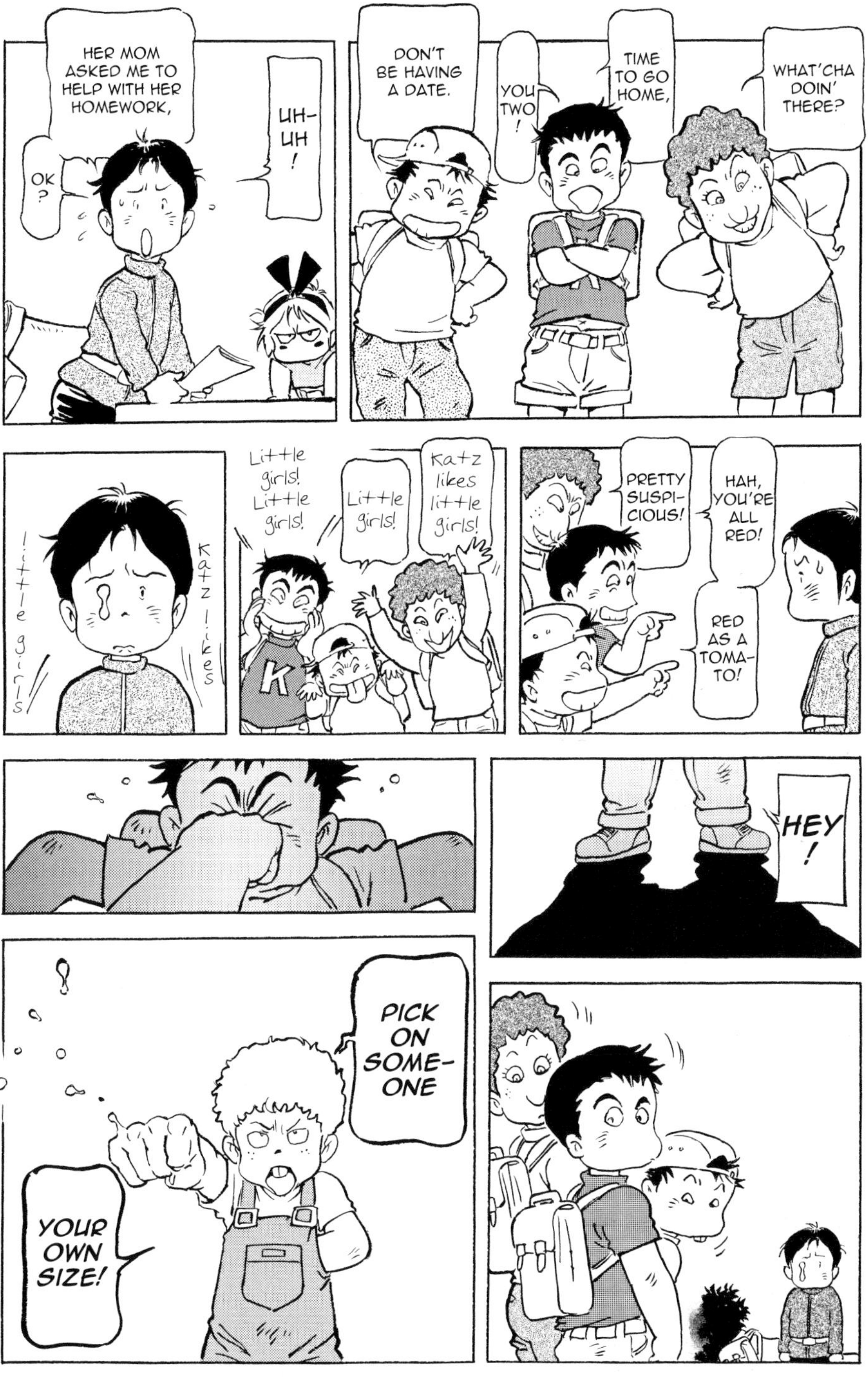
WHAT'CHA DOIN' THERE?
TIME TO GO HOME,
YOU TWO!
DON'T BE HAVING A DATE.
UH-UH!
HER MOM ASKED ME TO HELP WITH HER HOMEWORK,
OK?
HAH, YOU'RE ALL RED!
PRETTY SUSPICIOUS!
RED AS A TOMATO!
Katz likes little girls!
Little girls!
Little girls! Little girls!
Katz likes little girls
HEY!
PICK ON SOME-ONE
YOUR OWN SIZE!

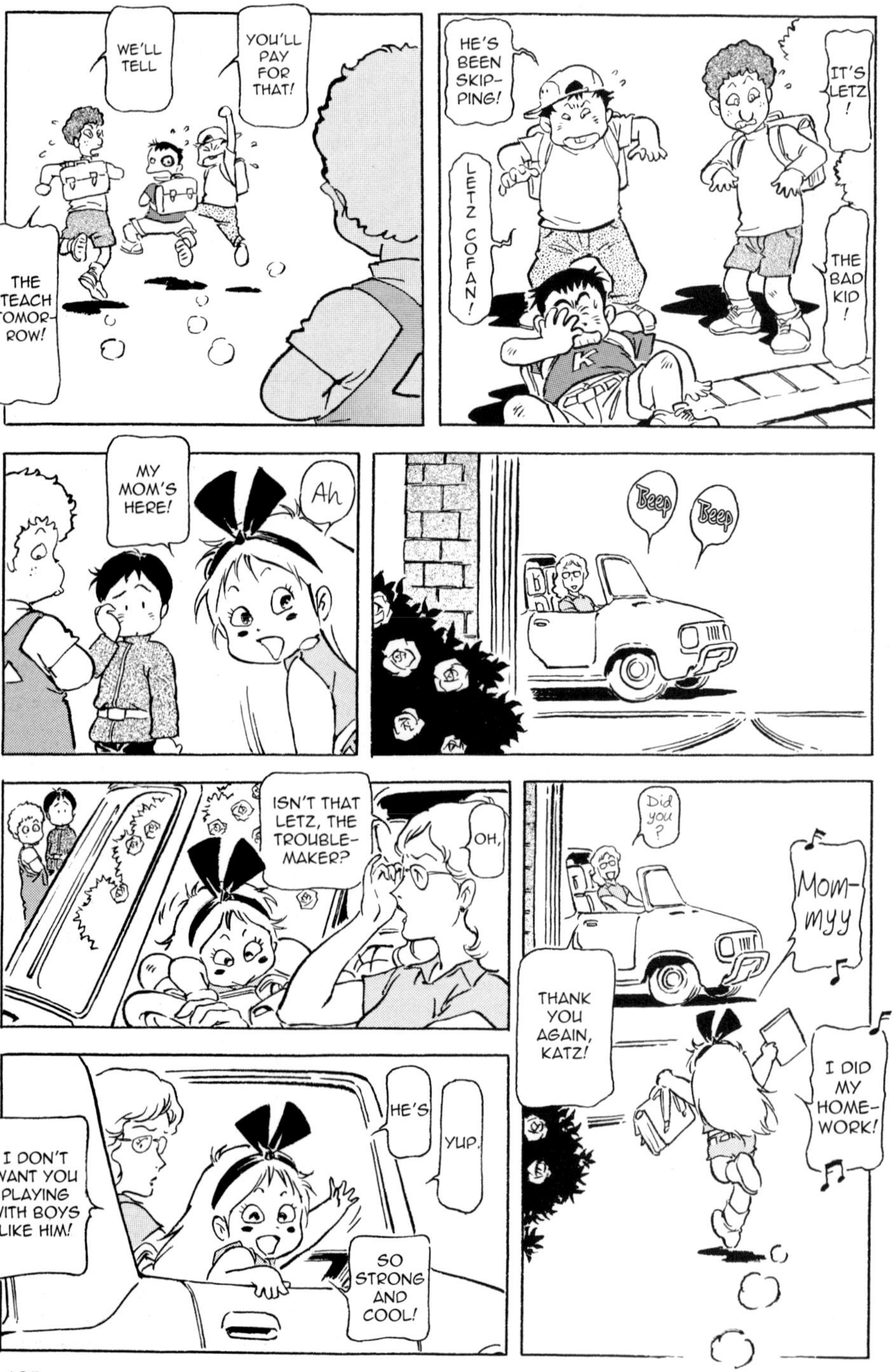
HE'S BEEN SKIP-PING!
IT'S LETZ!
LETZ COFAN!
THE BAD KID!
YOU'LL PAY FOR THAT!
WE'LL TELL
THE TEACH TOMOR-ROW!
Beep
Beep
Ah
MY MOM'S HERE!
Mom-myy
Did you?
I DID MY HOME-WORK!
THANK YOU AGAIN, KATZ!
OH,
ISN'T THAT LETZ, THE TROUBLE-MAKER?
YUP.
HE'S
SO STRONG AND COOL!
I DON'T WANT YOU PLAYING WITH BOYS LIKE HIM!

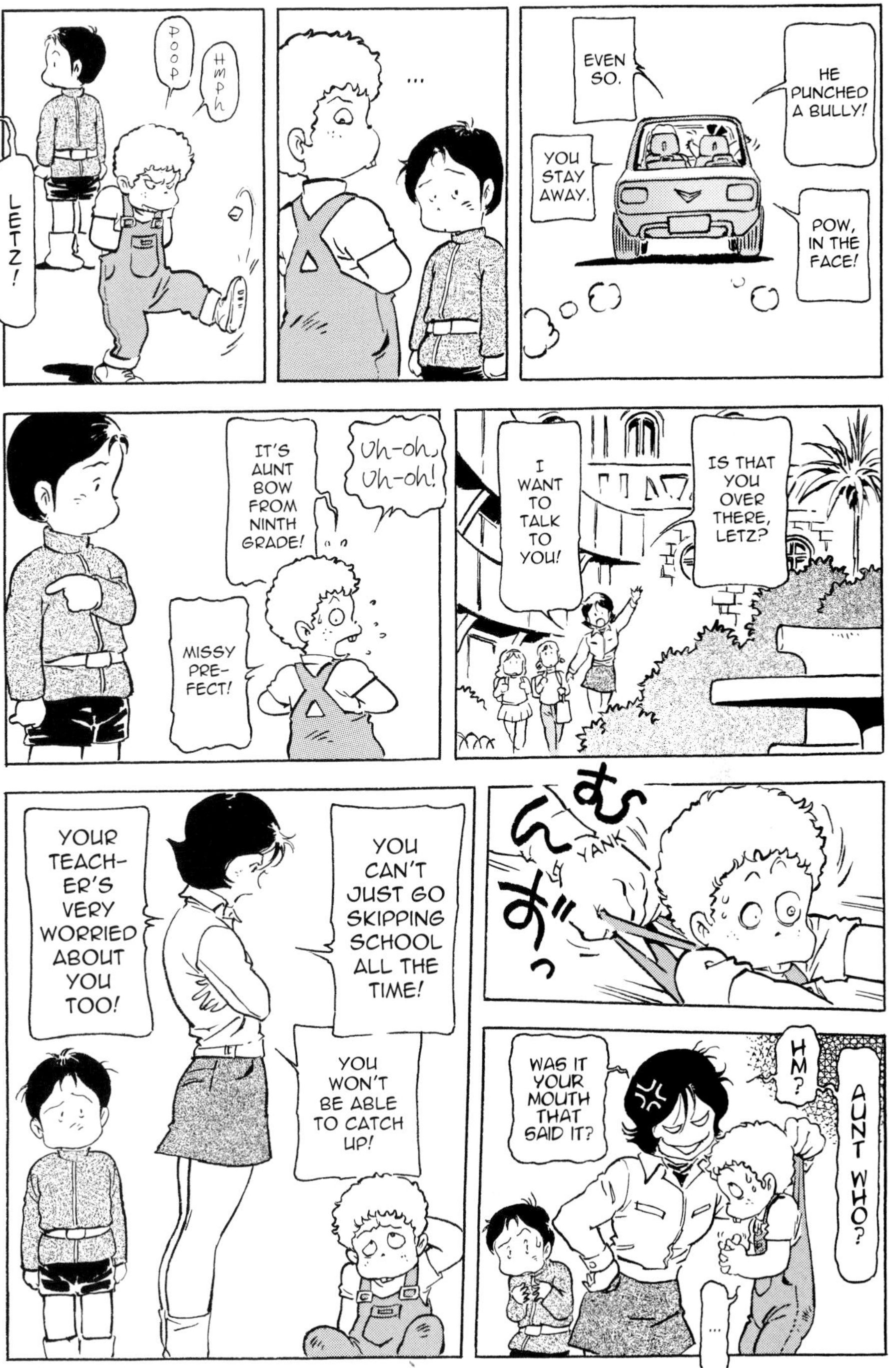
HE PUNCHED A BULLY!
POW, IN THE FACE!
EVEN SO.
YOU STAY AWAY.
...
HMPH
POOP
LETZ!
IS THAT YOU OVER THERE, LETZ?
I WANT TO TALK TO YOU!
Uh-oh, Uh-oh!
IT'S AUNT BOW FROM NINTH GRADE!
MISSY PRE-FECT!
むんず
YANK
AUNT WHO?
HM?
WAS IT YOUR MOUTH THAT SAID IT?
...
YOU CAN'T JUST GO SKIPPING SCHOOL ALL THE TIME!
YOUR TEACHER'S VERY WORRIED ABOUT YOU TOO!
YOU WON'T BE ABLE TO CATCH UP!

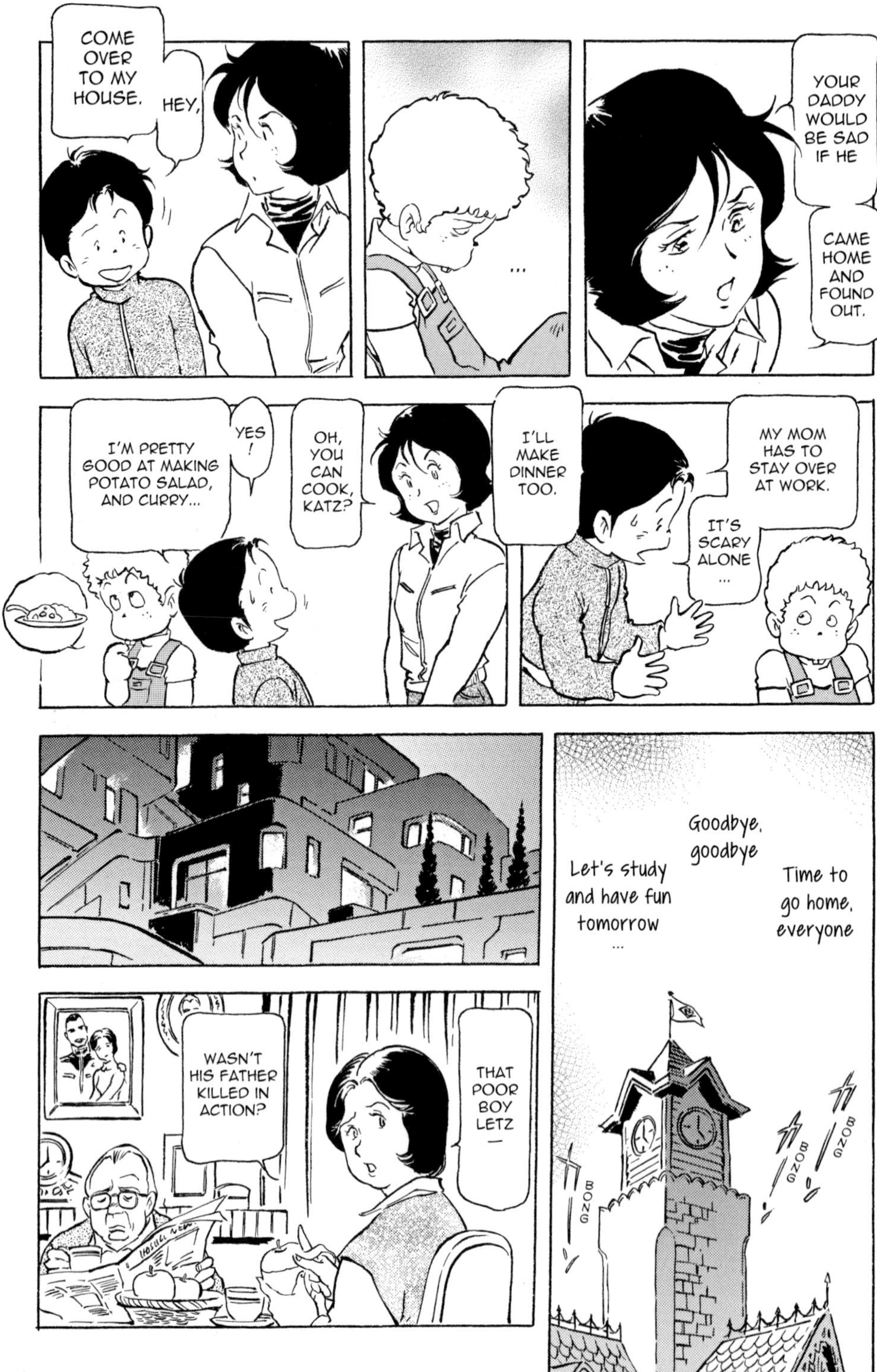
YOUR DADDY WOULD BE SAD IF HE
CAME HOME AND FOUND OUT.
...
HEY,
COME OVER TO MY HOUSE.
MY MOM HAS TO STAY OVER AT WORK.
IT'S SCARY ALONE ...
I'LL MAKE DINNER TOO.
OH, YOU CAN COOK, KATZ?
YES!
I'M PRETTY GOOD AT MAKING POTATO SALAD, AND CURRY...
Time to go home, everyone
Goodbye, goodbye
Let's study and have fun tomorrow ...
BONG
BONG
BONG
THAT POOR BOY LETZ —
WASN'T HIS FATHER KILLED IN ACTION?

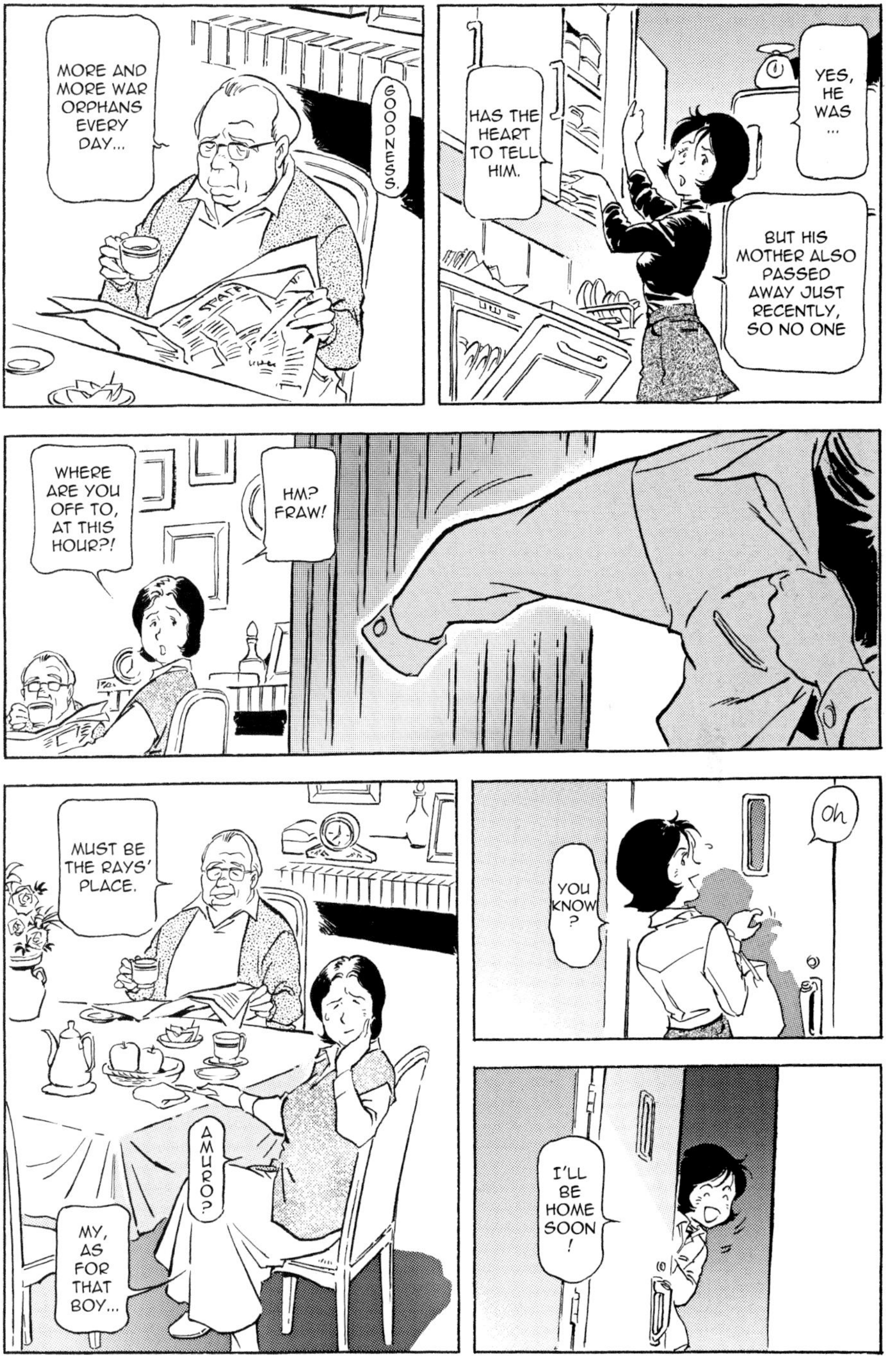
YES, HE WAS ...
BUT HIS MOTHER ALSO PASSED AWAY JUST RECENTLY, SO NO ONE
HAS THE HEART TO TELL HIM.
MORE AND MORE WAR ORPHANS EVERY DAY...
GOODNESS.
HM? FRAW!
WHERE ARE YOU OFF TO, AT THIS HOUR?!
Oh
YOU KNOW?
I'LL BE HOME SOON!
MUST BE THE RAYS' PLACE.
AMURO?
MY, AS FOR THAT BOY...

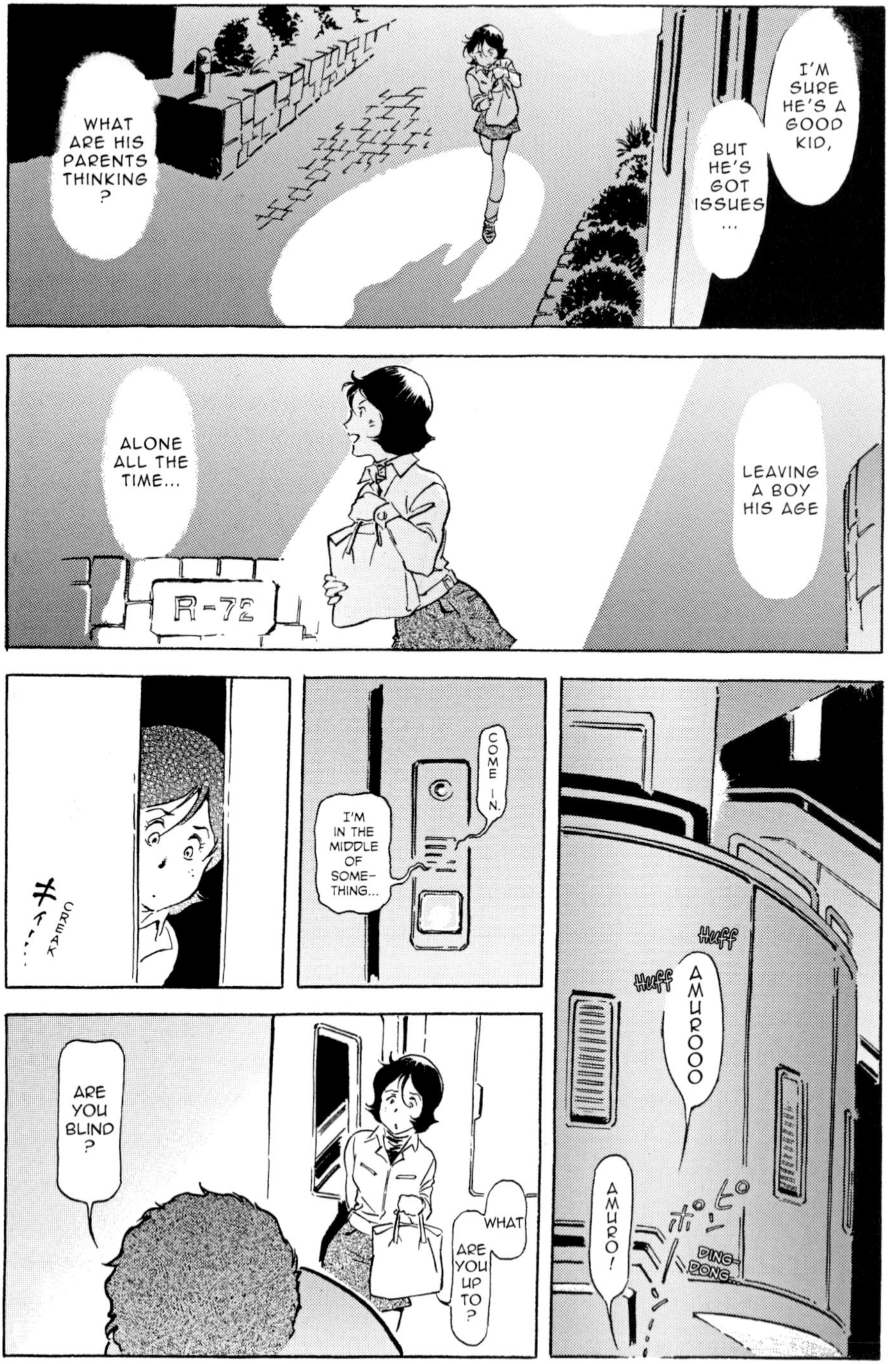
I'M SURE HE'S A GOOD KID,
BUT HE'S GOT ISSUES...
WHAT ARE HIS PARENTS THINKING?
LEAVING A BOY HIS AGE
ALONE ALL THE TIME...
Huff
Huff
AMUROOO
AMURO!
DING-DONG...
COME IN.
I'M IN THE MIDDLE OF SOME-THING...
CREAK
WHAT ARE YOU UP TO?
ARE YOU BLIND?

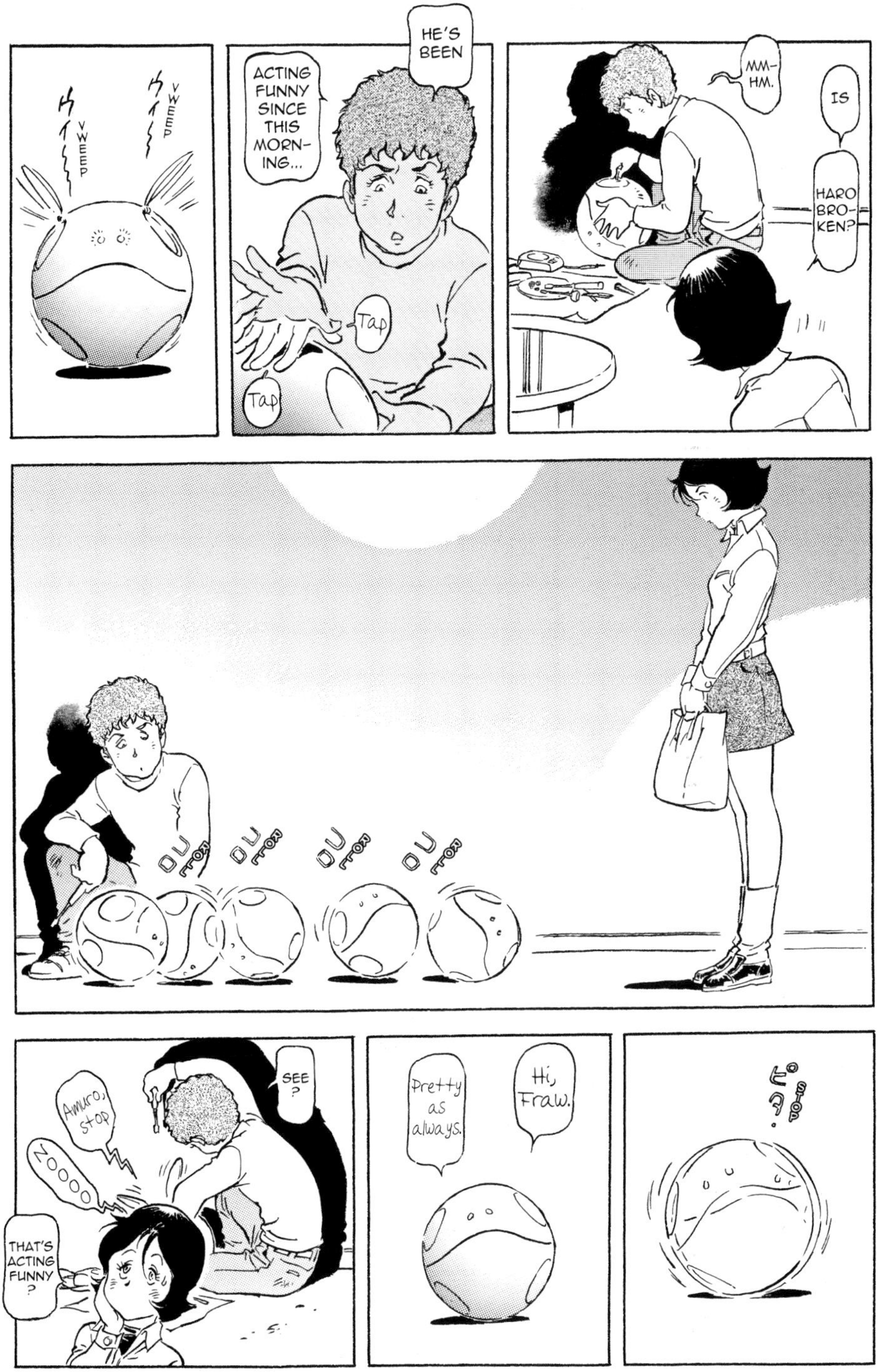

IS HARO BROKEN?
MM-HM.
HE'S BEEN
ACTING FUNNY SINCE THIS MORNING...
Tap
Tap
ウィ～
VWEEP
ウィ～
VWEEP
ROLL
ROLL
ROLL
ROLL
STOP
Hi, Fraw.
Pretty as always.
SEE?
Amuro, stop
ZOOOO
THAT'S ACTING FUNNY?

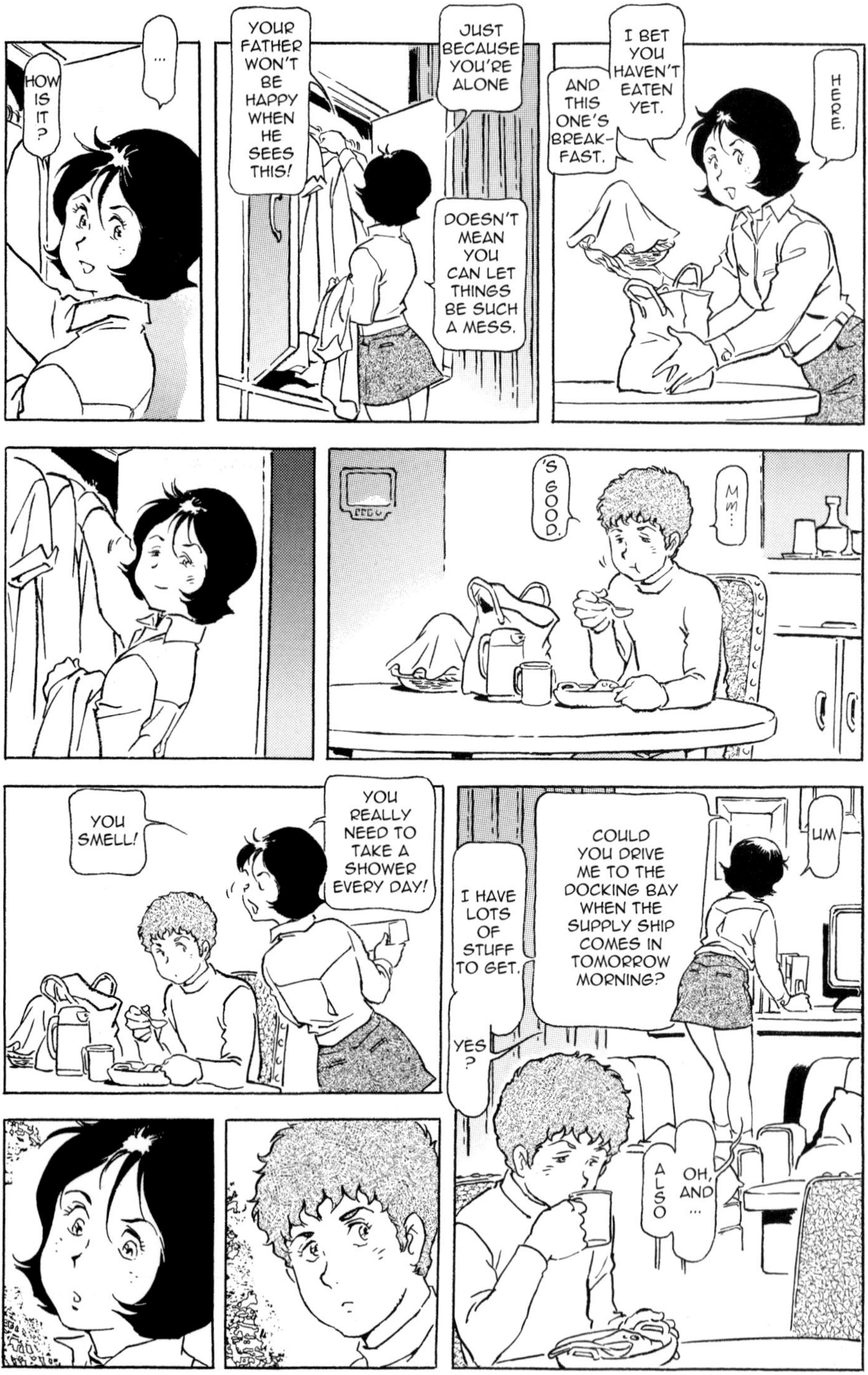
HERE.
I BET YOU HAVEN'T EATEN YET.
AND THIS ONE'S BREAKFAST.
JUST BECAUSE YOU'RE ALONE
DOESN'T MEAN YOU CAN LET THINGS BE SUCH A MESS.
YOUR FATHER WON'T BE HAPPY WHEN HE SEES THIS!
...
HOW IS IT?
MM...
'S GOOD.
UM
COULD YOU DRIVE ME TO THE DOCKING BAY WHEN THE SUPPLY SHIP COMES IN TOMORROW MORNING?
I HAVE LOTS OF STUFF TO GET.
YES?
OH, AND...
ALSO
YOU REALLY NEED TO TAKE A SHOWER EVERY DAY!
YOU SMELL!

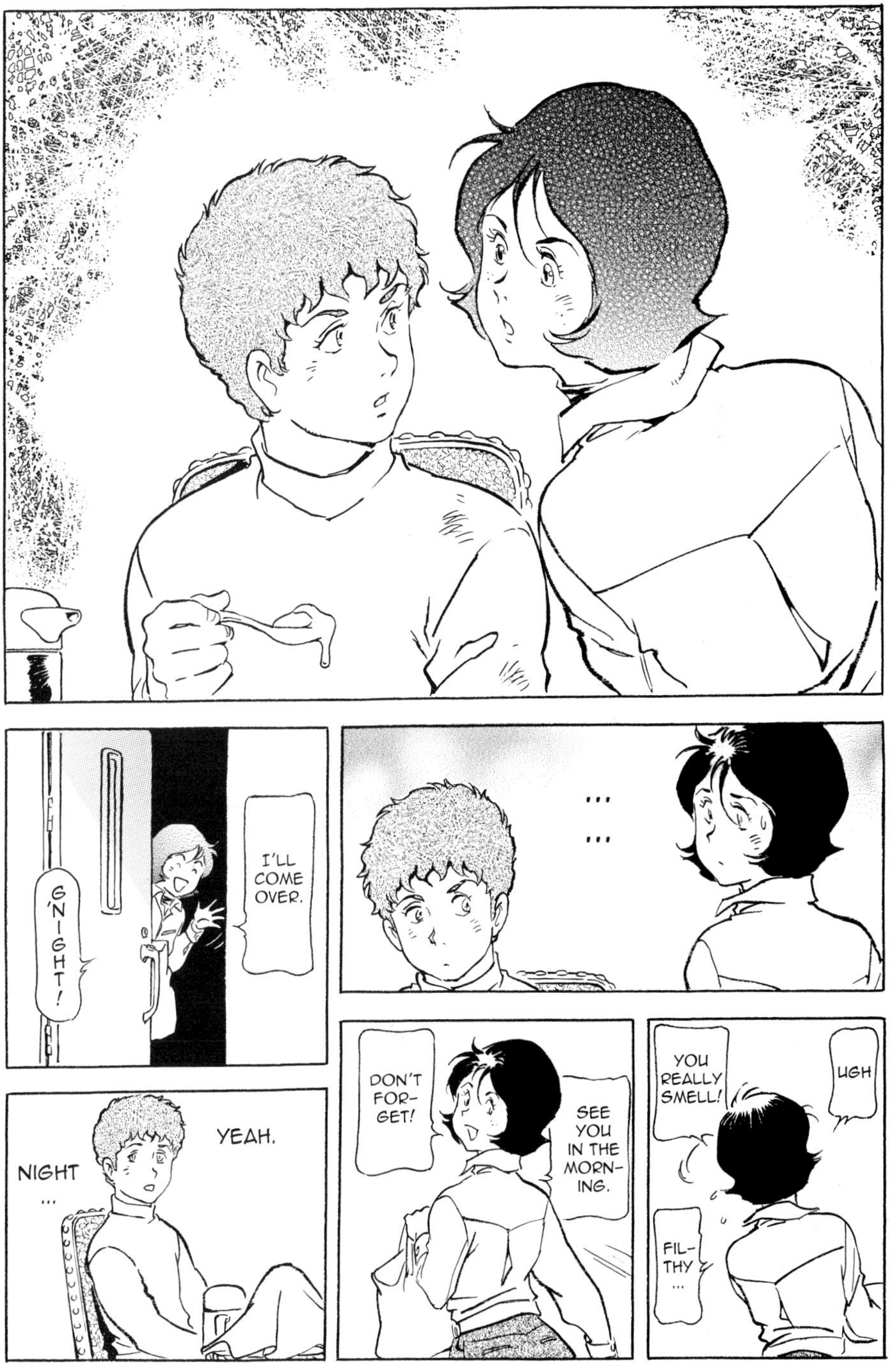
...
...
I'LL COME OVER.
G'NIGHT!
UGH
YOU REALLY SMELL!
FILTHY ...
SEE YOU IN THE MORNING.
DON'T FORGET!
YEAH.
NIGHT ...

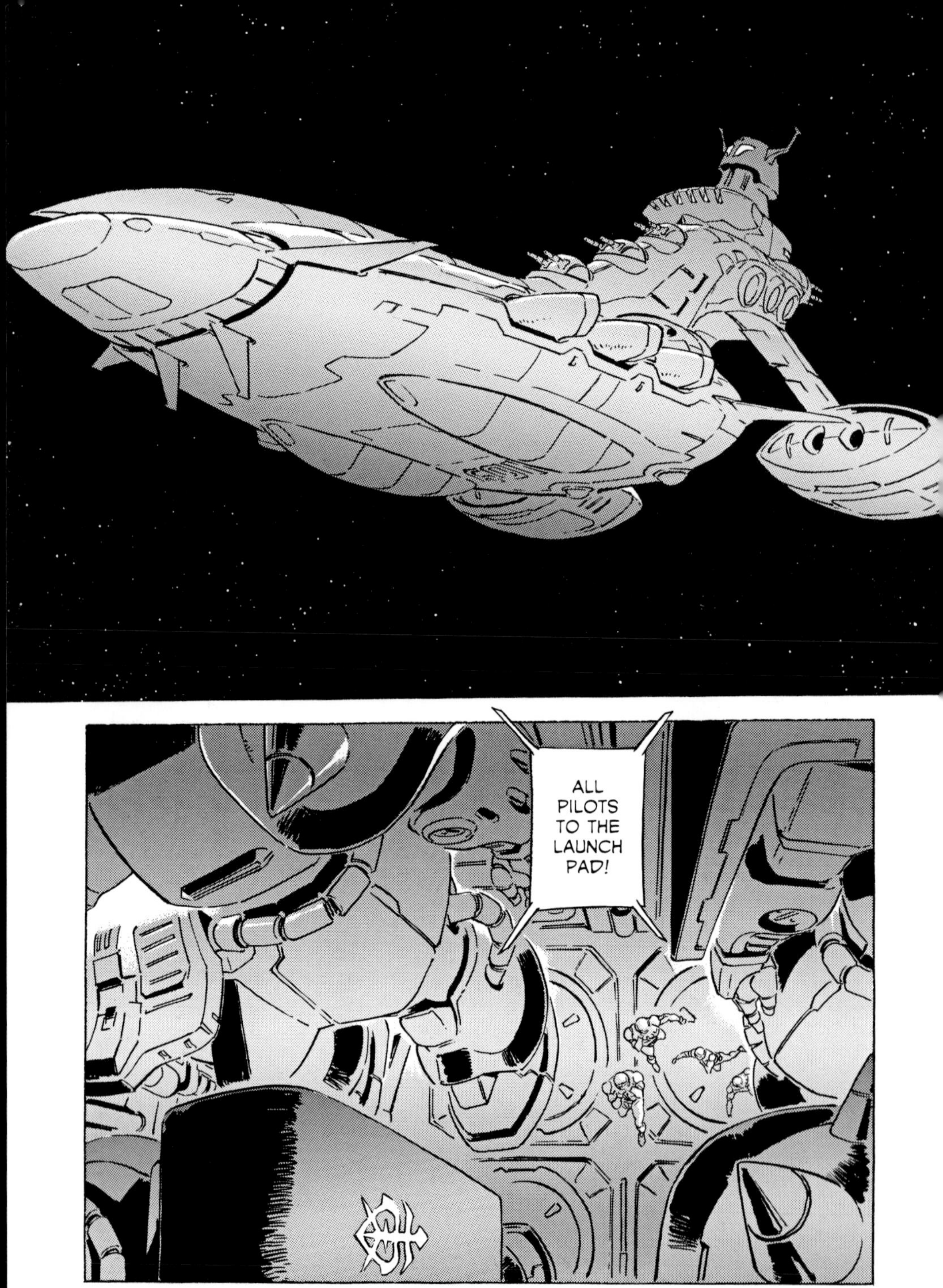
ALL PILOTS TO THE LAUNCH PAD!

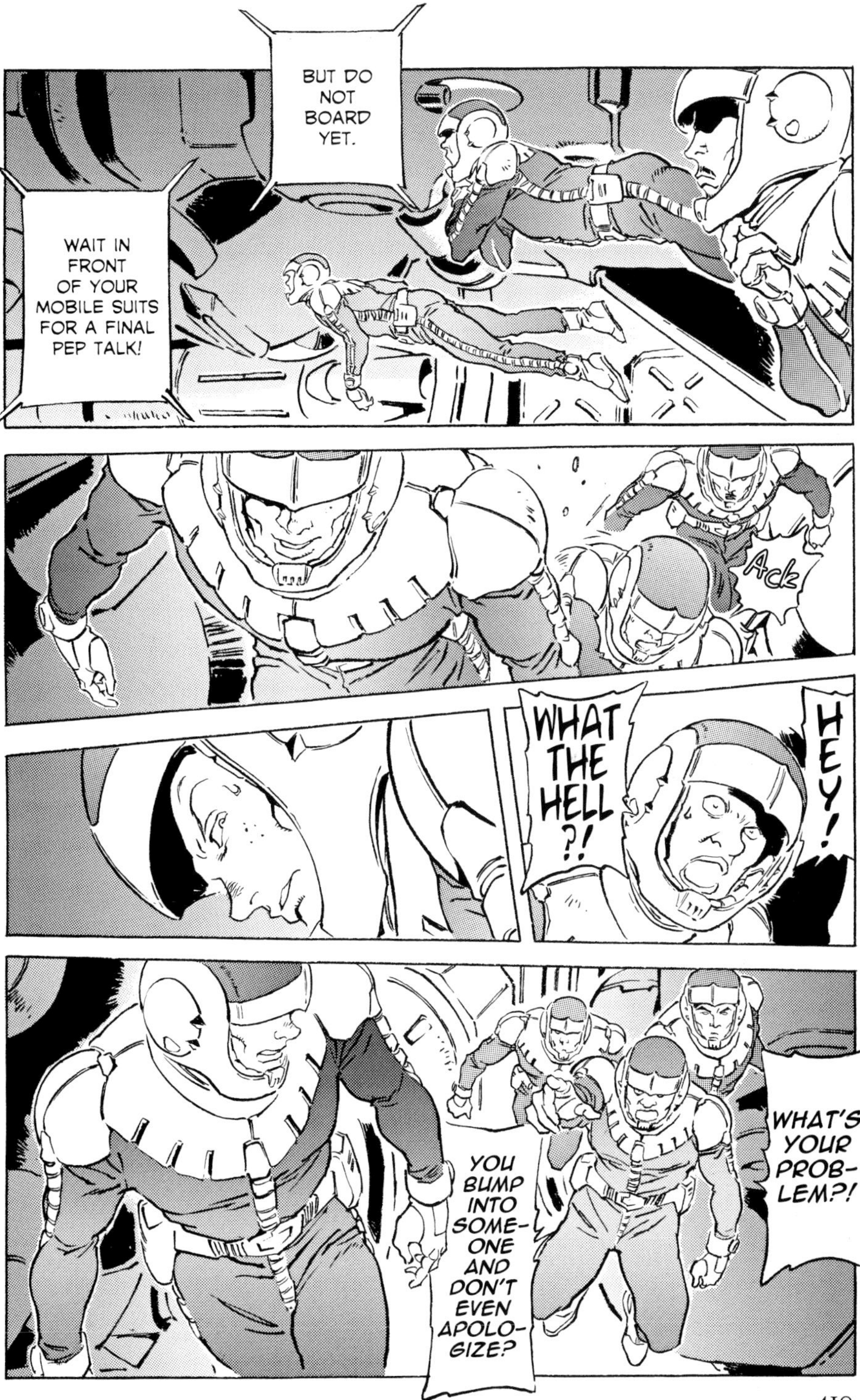
BUT DO NOT BOARD YET.
WAIT IN FRONT OF YOUR MOBILE SUITS FOR A FINAL PEP TALK!
Ack
HEY!
WHAT THE HELL?!
WHAT'S YOUR PROB-LEM?!
YOU BUMP INTO SOME-ONE AND DON'T EVEN APOLO-GIZE?

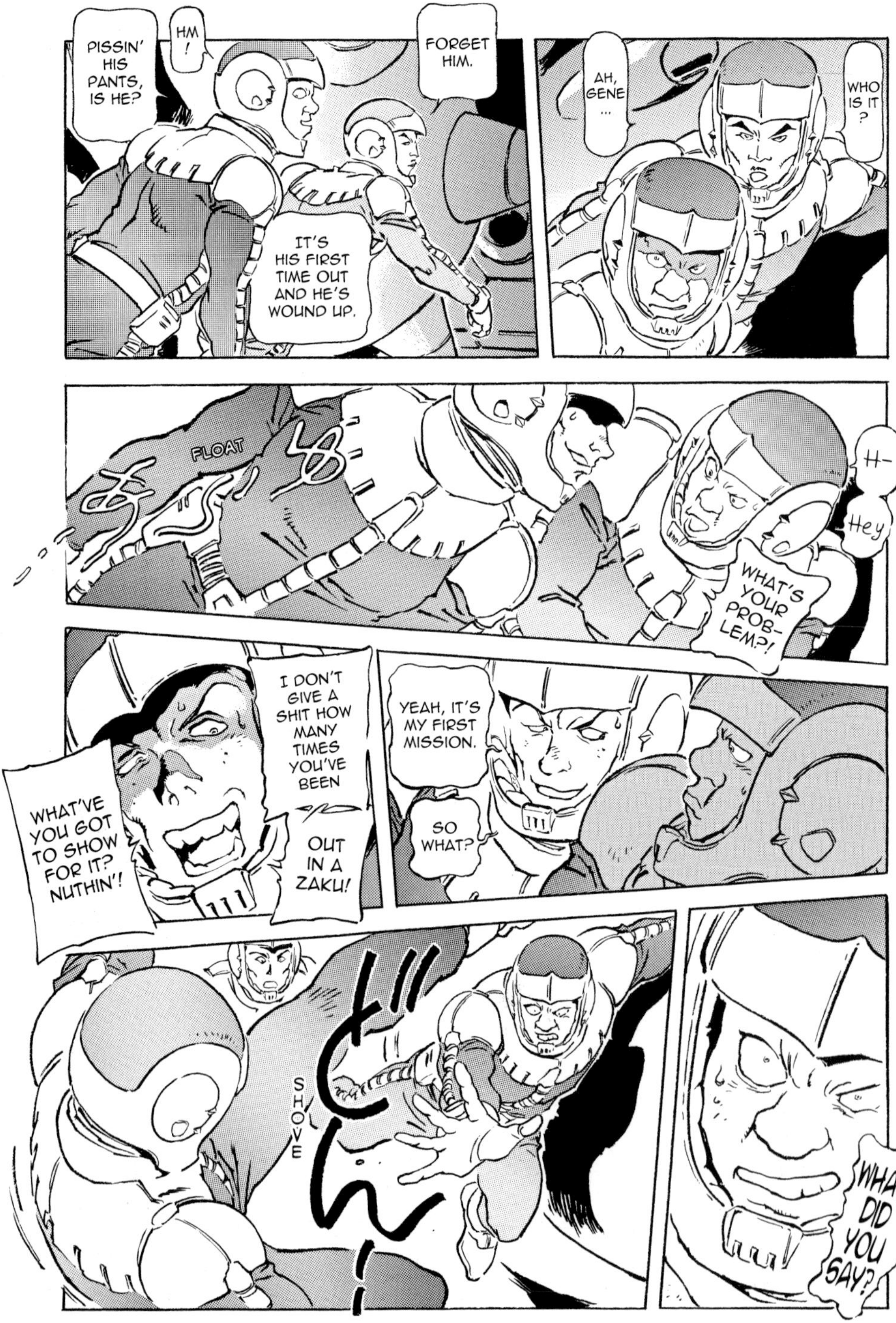

WHO IS IT?
AH, GENE...
FORGET HIM.
HM!
PISSIN' HIS PANTS, IS HE?
IT'S HIS FIRST TIME OUT AND HE'S WOUND UP.
H-
Hey
WHAT'S YOUR PROB-LEM?!
FLOAT
YEAH, IT'S MY FIRST MISSION.
SO WHAT?
I DON'T GIVE A SHIT HOW MANY TIMES YOU'VE BEEN
OUT IN A ZAKU!
WHAT'VE YOU GOT TO SHOW FOR IT? NUTHIN'!
WHAT DID YOU SAY?
SHOVE

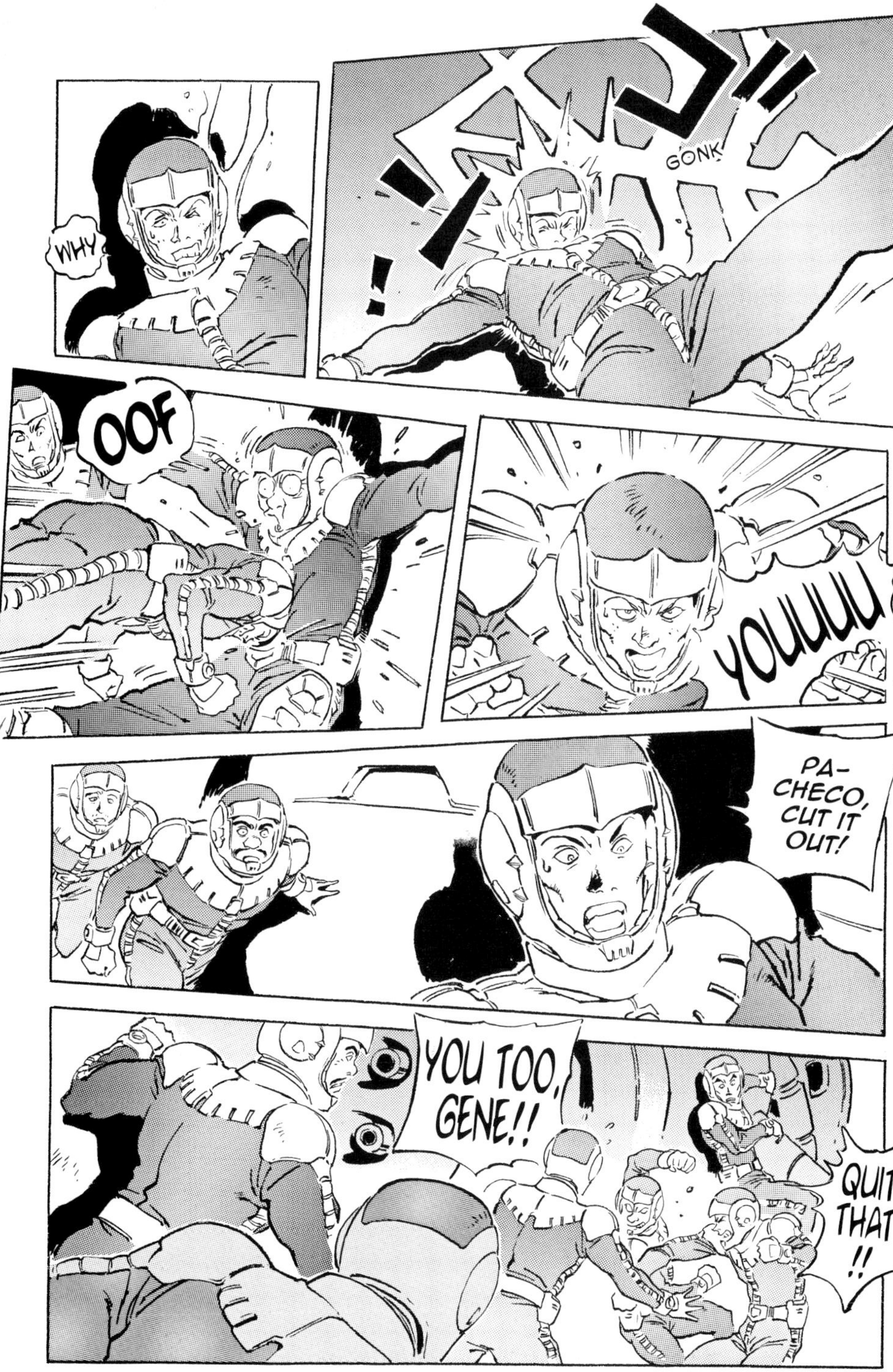
GONK
WHY
YOUUUU
OOF
PA-CHECO, CUT IT OUT!
QUIT THAT!!
YOU TOO, GENE!!

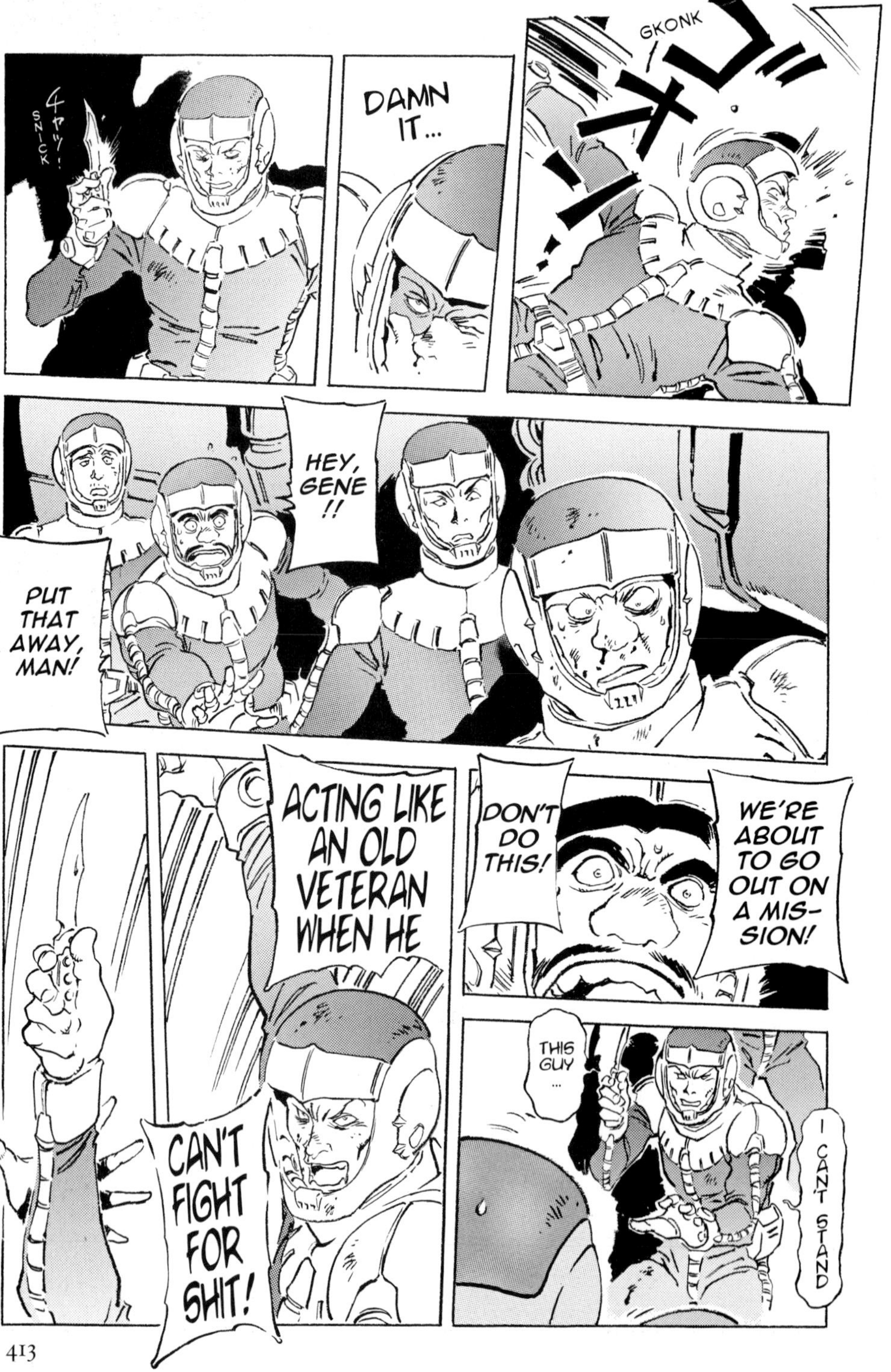
GKONK
DAMN IT...
SNICK
HEY, GENE!!
PUT THAT AWAY, MAN!
WE'RE ABOUT TO GO OUT ON A MIS-SION!
DON'T DO THIS!
I CAN'T STAND
THIS GUY...
ACTING LIKE AN OLD VETERAN WHEN HE
CAN'T FIGHT FOR SHIT!

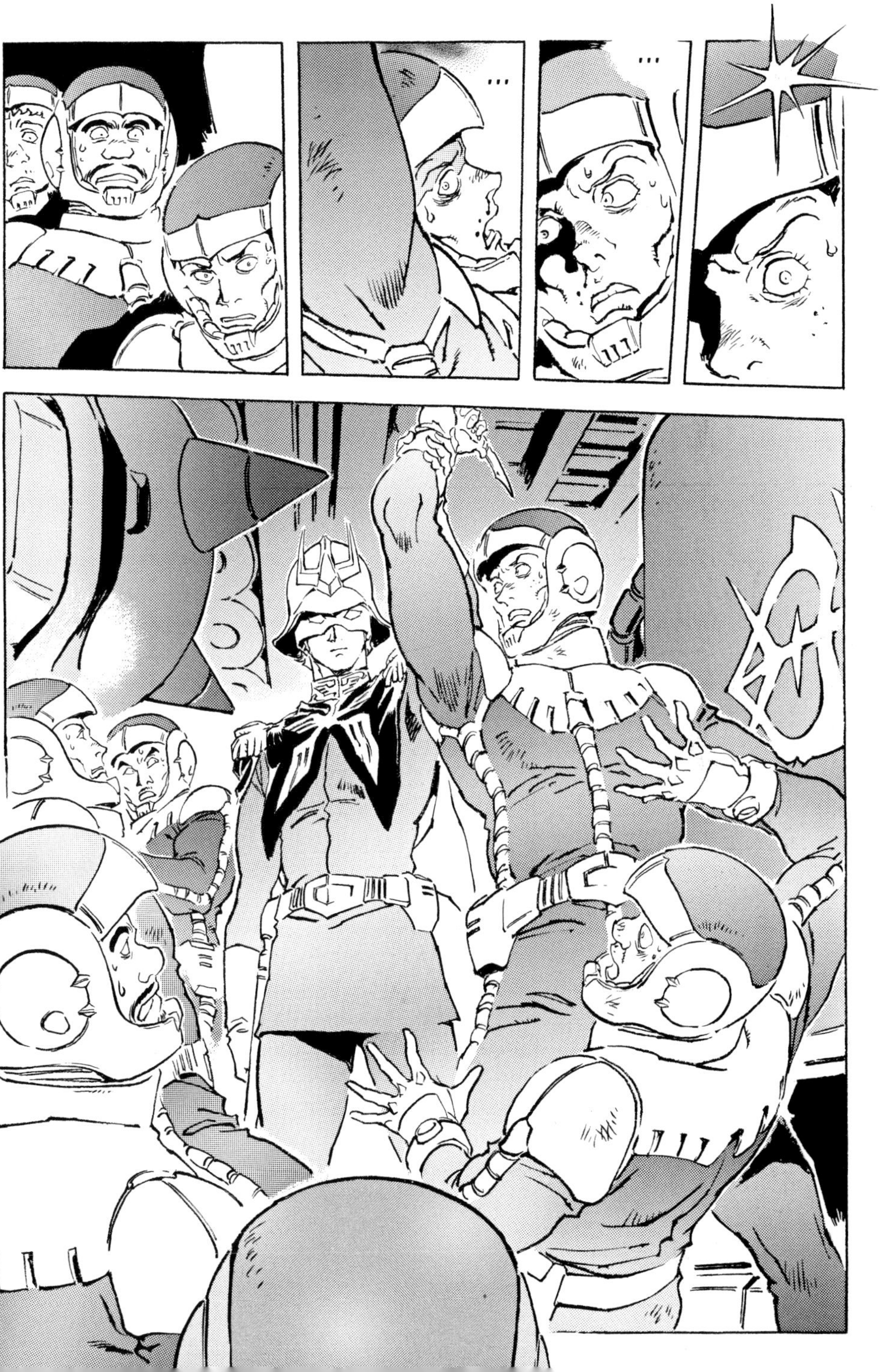
...
...

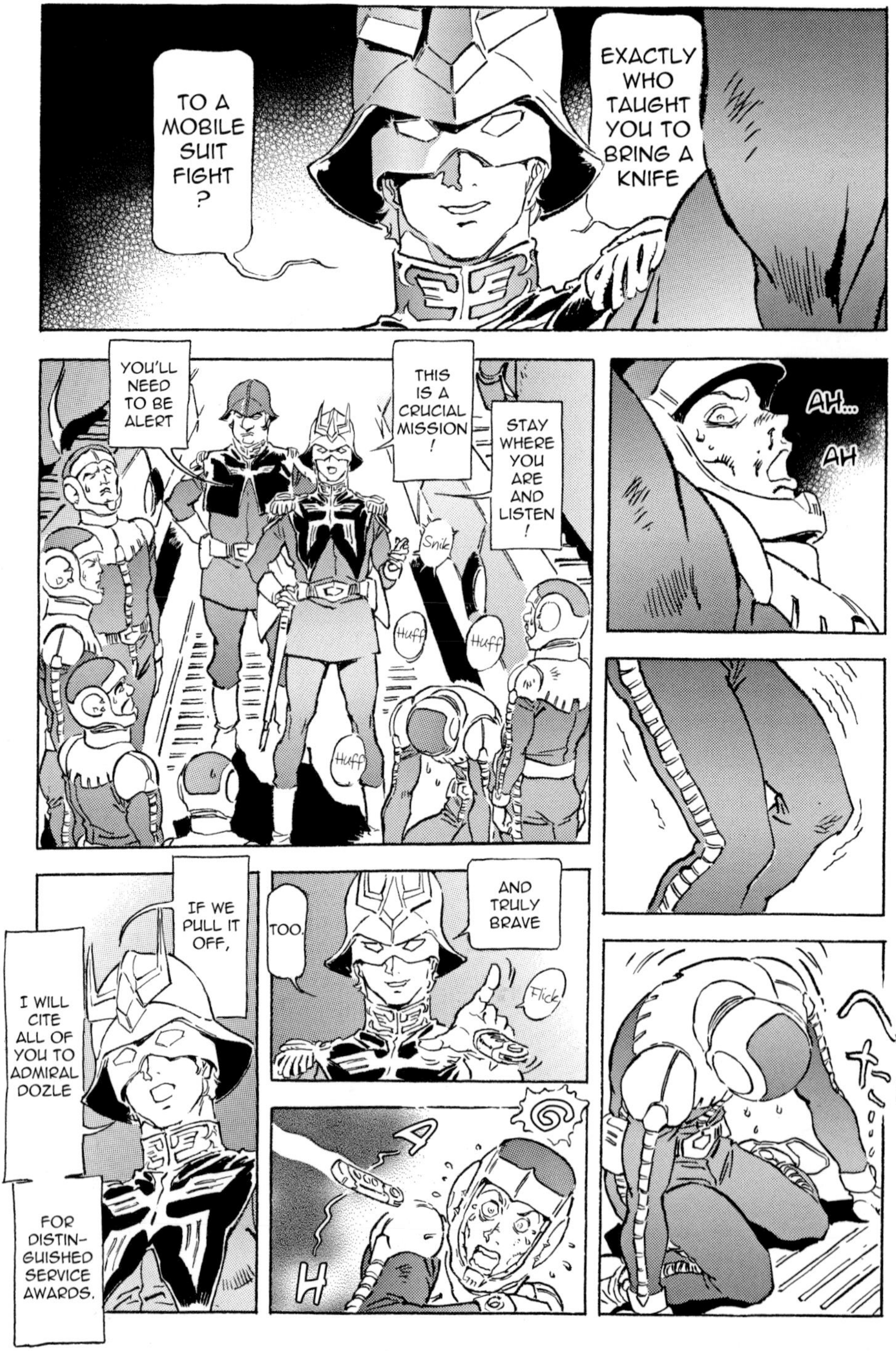

EXACTLY WHO TAUGHT YOU TO BRING A KNIFE
TO A MOBILE SUIT FIGHT ?
AH... AH
STAY WHERE YOU ARE AND LISTEN !
THIS IS A CRUCIAL MISSION !
YOU'LL NEED TO BE ALERT
Snik
Huff
Huff
Huff
SLUMP
AND TRULY BRAVE
TOO.
Flick
A H
IF WE PULL IT OFF,
I WILL CITE ALL OF YOU TO ADMIRAL DOZLE
FOR DISTINGUISHED SERVICE AWARDS.

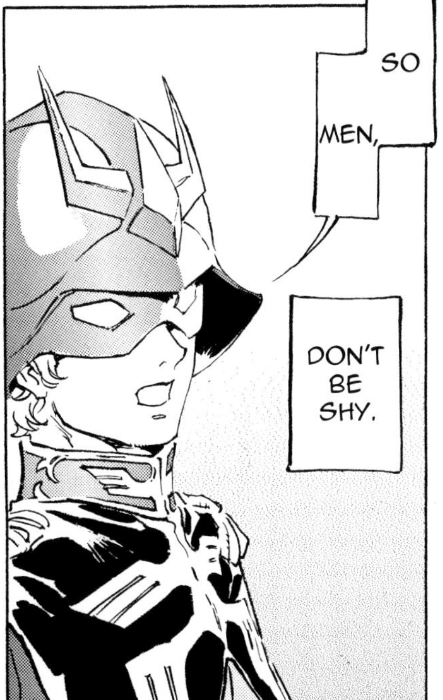
SO MEN,
DON'T BE SHY.

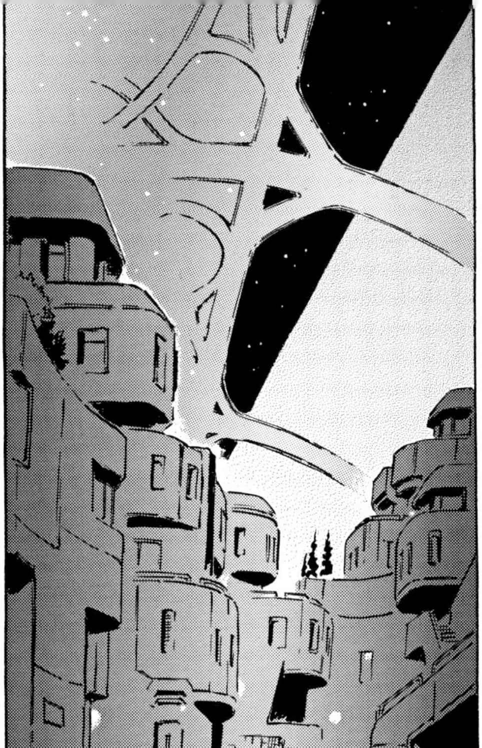

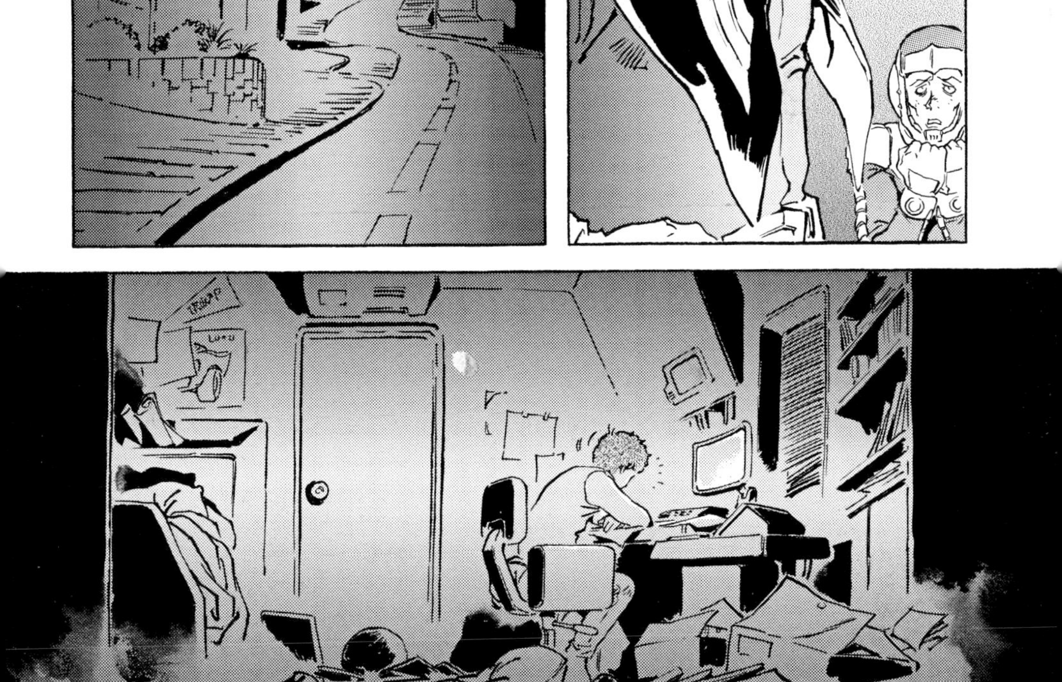

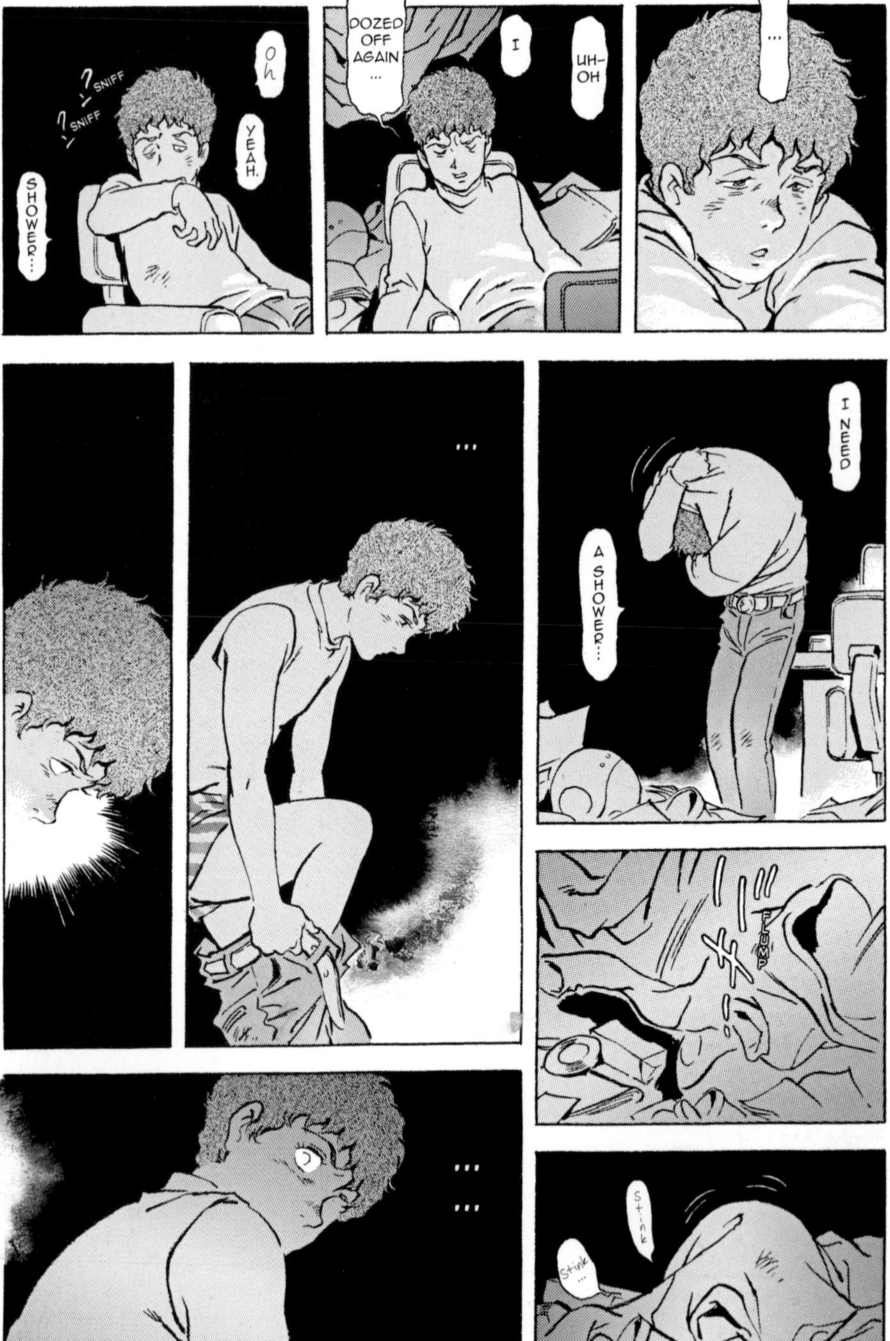
...
UH-OH
I
DOZED OFF AGAIN...
Oh
YEAH.
SNIFF
SNIFF
SHOWER...
I NEED
A SHOWER...
FLUMP
Stink
Stink...
...
...
...

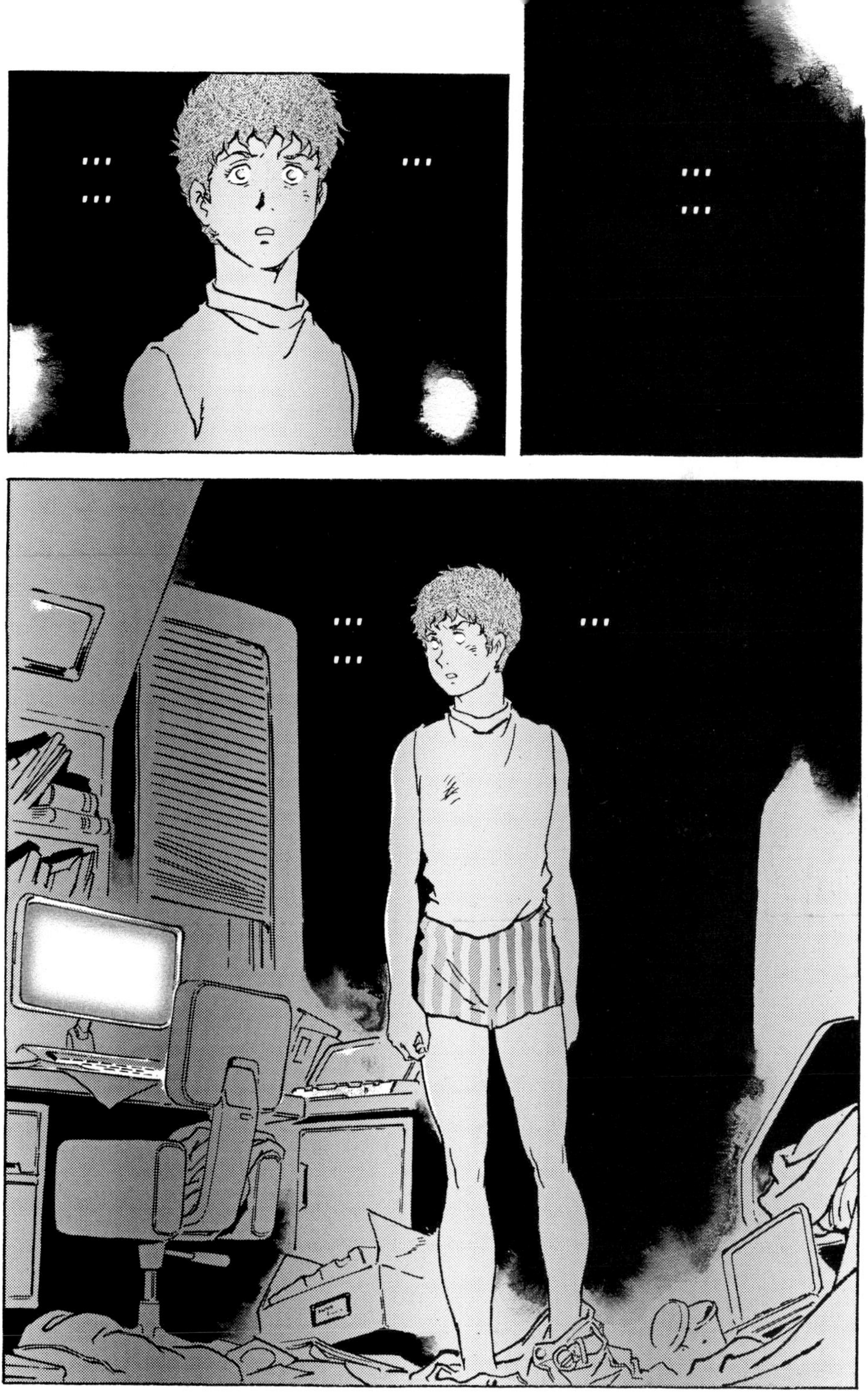
...
...
...
...
...
...
...
...

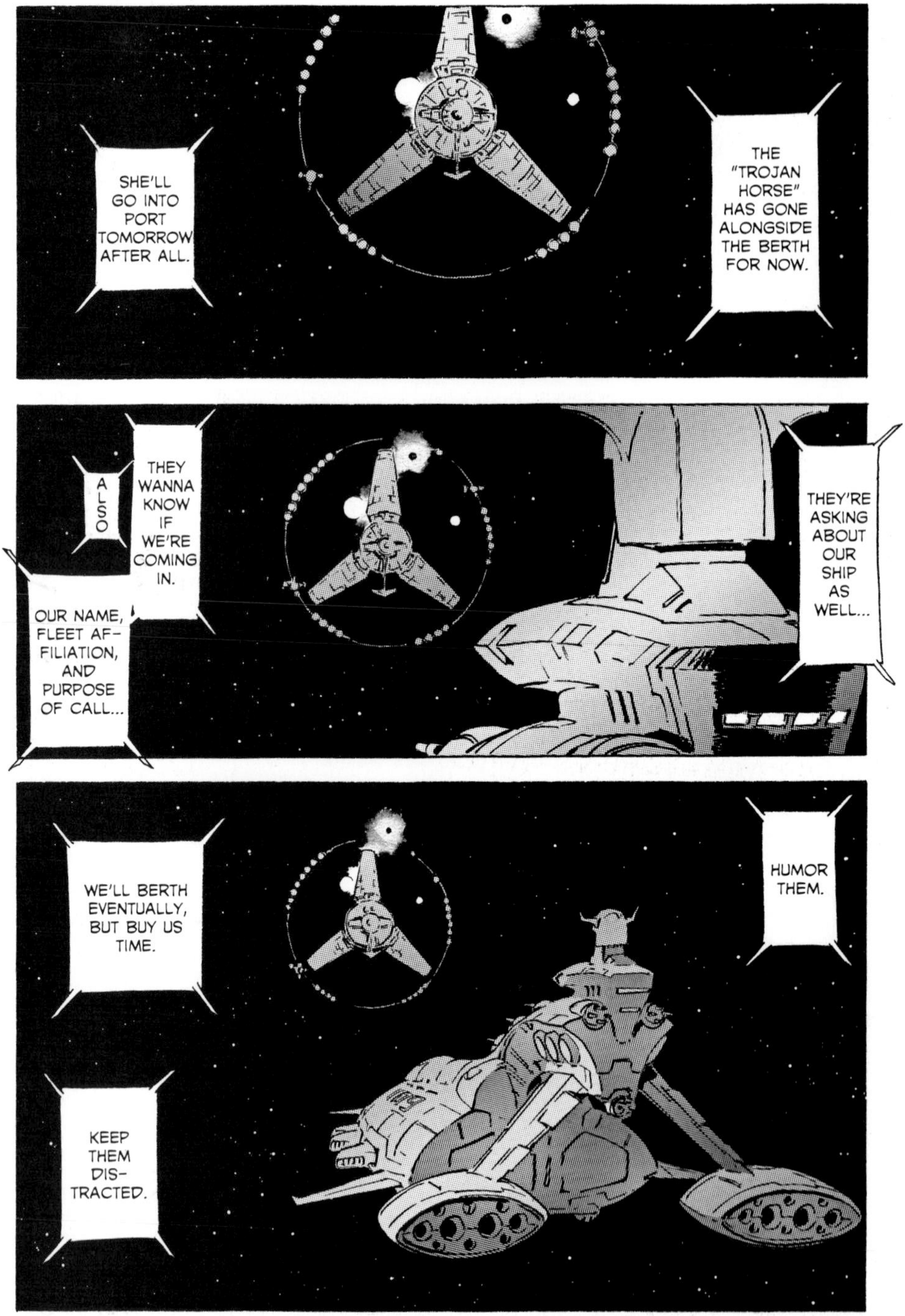
THE "TROJAN HORSE" HAS GONE ALONGSIDE THE BERTH FOR NOW.
SHE'LL GO INTO PORT TOMORROW AFTER ALL.
THEY'RE ASKING ABOUT OUR SHIP AS WELL...
THEY WANNA KNOW IF WE'RE COMING IN.
ALSO
OUR NAME, FLEET AF-FILIATION, AND PURPOSE OF CALL...
HUMOR THEM.
WE'LL BERTH EVENTUALLY, BUT BUY US TIME.
KEEP THEM DIS-TRACTED.

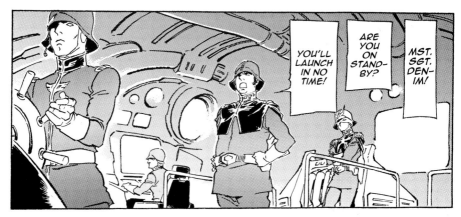

MST. SGT. DENIM!
ARE YOU ON STANDBY?
YOU'LL LAUNCH IN NO TIME!
FOLLOW A GREAT-CIRCLE ROUTE TO GET TO THE ANTIPODE!
GOT THAT?
MAINTAIN RADIO SILENCE UNTIL YOU REACH THE TARGET!
AND NO VERNIER THRUST! ONLY AIR!
THE BLIND SPOT IS STRAIGHT OUT FROM THE COLONY'S CENTRAL AXIS!
THINK OF IT AS A NARROW TUBE!
STAY INSIDE IT!!

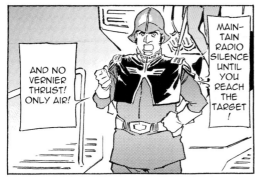

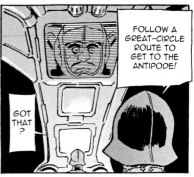

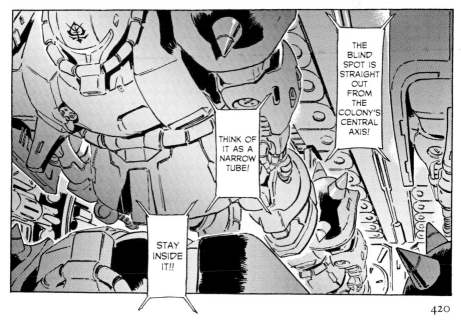

HATCH OPENING IN 5 SECONDS.
4
3
2
1
GATUNNNG
MST. SGT. DEN-IM UNIT
SHOONT
LAUNCH

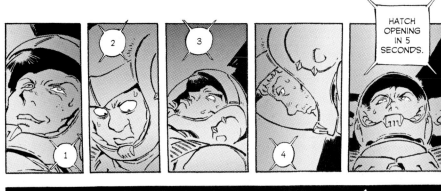

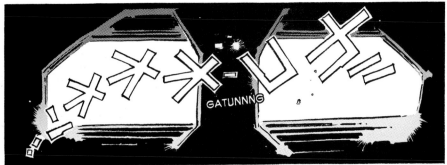

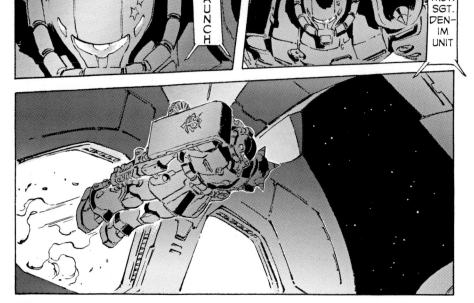

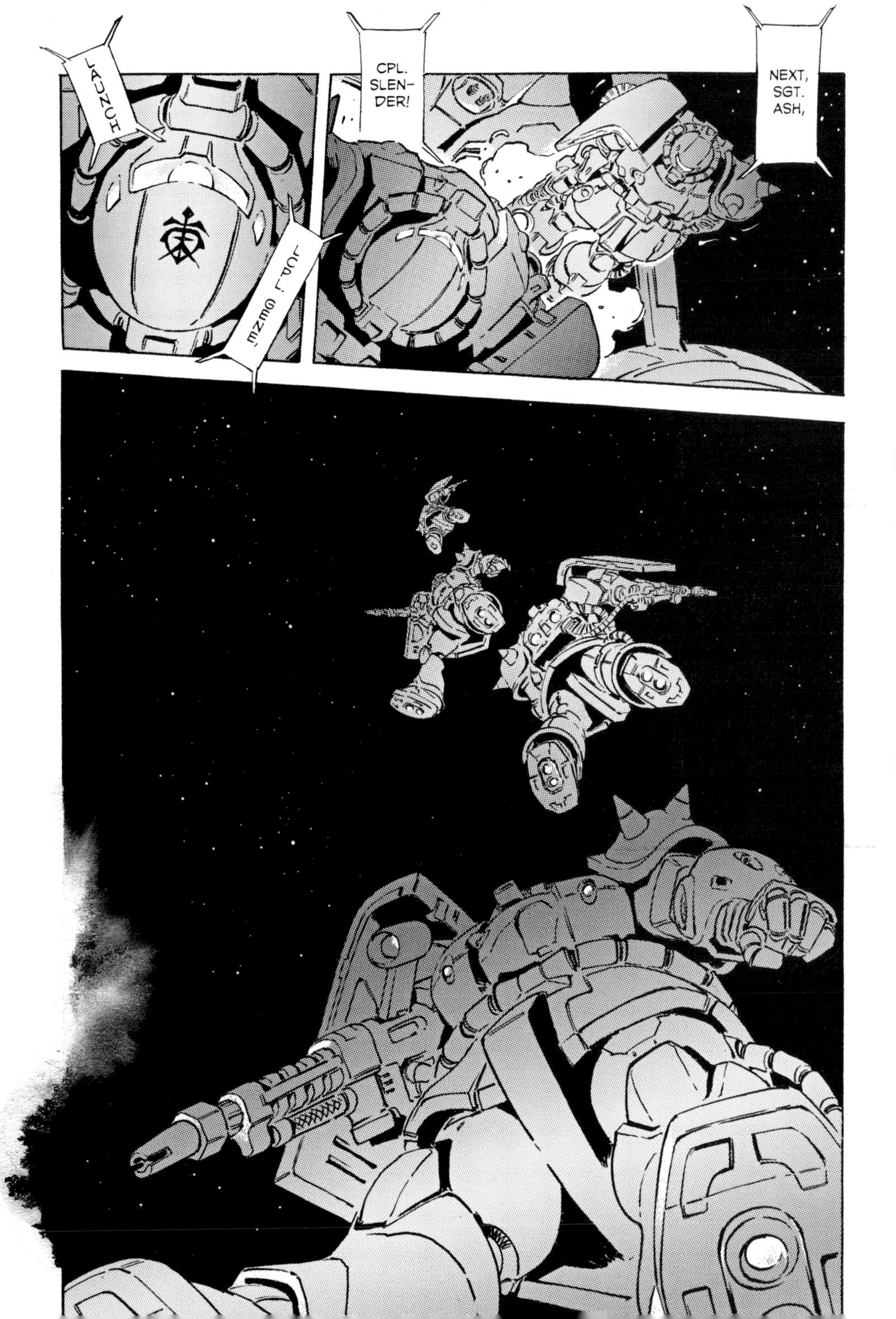
NEXT, SGT. ASH,
CPL. SLENDER!
CPL. GENE,
LAUNCH

This Special Feature "On the Eve" was originally included in the *Mobile Suit Gundam The Origin: Official Guidebook* (Kadokawa, 2004).

yet," you might say. Still, this connects the story…connects it directly to *Zeta Gundam*. Connected, just like that, on a fundamental level. Maybe I'm reading too much into it. That's fine if I am. Mr. Yasuhiko left behind this for our sake, understanding our passionate feelings at the time of the original broadcast better than anyone else.

Here is to hoping his dropped item leads to something.

Here is to hoping that Sayla lives on. In the storytelling realm.

I can't be the only one who feels that kind of love for Sayla?

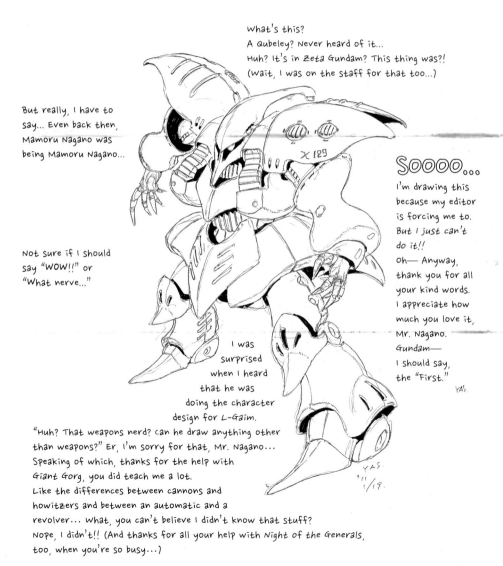

What's this?
A Qubeley? Never heard of it...
Huh? It's in *Zeta Gundam*? This thing was?!
(Wait, I was on the staff for that too...)
But really, I have to say... Even back then, Mamoru Nagano was being Mamoru Nagano...
SOOOO...
I'm drawing this because my editor is forcing me to. But I just can't do it!!
Oh— Anyway, thank you for all your kind words. I appreciate how much you love it, Mr. Nagano. Gundam— I should say, the "First."
YAS.
Not sure if I should say "WOW!!" or "What nerve..."
X 129
I was surprised when I heard that he was doing the character design for *L-Gaim*.
"Huh? That weapons nerd? Can he draw anything other than weapons?" Er, I'm sorry for that, Mr. Nagano...
Speaking of which, thanks for the help with *Giant Gorg*, you did teach me a lot.
Like the differences between cannons and howitzers and between an automatic and a revolver... What, you can't believe I didn't know that stuff?
Nope, I didn't!! (And thanks for all your help with *Night of the Generals*, too, when you're so busy...)
YAS.
'11 1/19.

4. Artesia!!

Sayla Mass. How many people burned with passion for this character? *Mobile Suit Gundam* gave rise to a "Team Sayla" on a totally different level from Char.

I'm mean, fans at the time would speak of her respectfully, only using a honorific for her: "Sayla-san." You can immediately tell whether someone watched the first TV run and how much they really loved *Gundam* by whether or not they call her "Sayla-san."

Sayla, though, is a character Mr. Tomino really embraced and ran off with. I think everyone would agree that she's another no-fair character that an original creator simply took off with. But even knowing that she belongs to Mr. Tomino, who could handle her other than Mr. Yasuhiko…or so I would declare if not for the fact that Mr. Tomino would say, "You're dead to me now!"

But now we can only see her in Mr. Yasuhiko's art. Because that wonderful, truly wonderful lady, the possessor of Sayla's sweet voice, has departed for the great beyond.

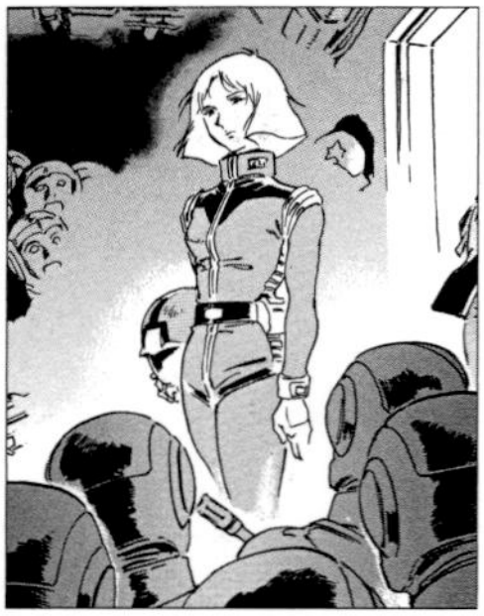

Reading *The Origin* casually every month, by the time of the final battle I'd let my guard down. I was not—NOT—expecting that! So many readers must have let their guard down, thinking that all that remained was the battle between Amuro and Char, the Gundam and the Zeong—and then he drops the bomb.

Sayla went and identified herself as "Artesia." Or rather, Zeon forces discovered that she's really "Artesia Som Deikun." Of course they would split into Deikunists and Gihren supporters! Is *this* why all hell broke loose and A Baoa Qu fell? Strategically speaking, the way it looked in the TV series, Zeon definitely should have won.

Or more precisely, just as Kycilia says, Zeon had no hope of winning a prolonged war, and it was their chance to negotiate a truce on their terms. With Gihren's death and Char's betrayal, House Zabi fell.

That's how the Federation was able to win the Battle of A Baoa Qu. That's how it went in the TV series. Mr. Yasuhiko must have wanted to show not only that, but the internal collapse of Zeon itself, from a different viewpoint. Because that way, a new drama emerges.

Well, I don't know because I haven't read it to the end yet, but once they know that "Artesia" is Deikun's daughter—what could Zeon soldiers do having learned that??? They'd be loyal to her, and follow her after the battle ends. Or they find out about Casval too, and follow him.

And what about Axis, far away at Jupiter? "Huh, what's that? That doesn't exist

2. Lalah!!

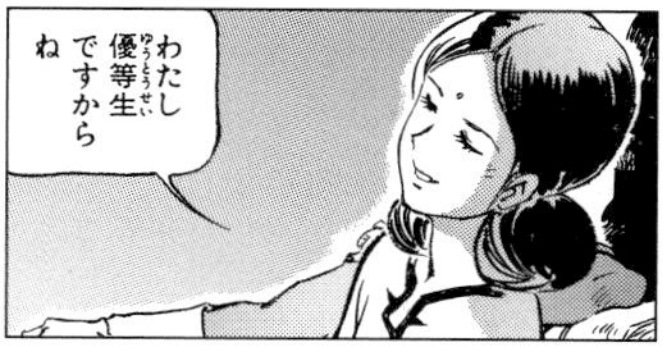
わたし優等生ですからね

I wonder if people remember being shocked that *Gundam* had an Indian character. In an interview for an anime magazine, Mr. Tomino commented that "we're about to introduce a character who will become very important to the latter half of the story," and the fans got pretty excited. Of course they did, because in *Gundam* every single character to make an appearance was amazing. The fans would get hyped every time a new character appeared, and even side characters who were only in a single episode gained an avid following. And then, everyone was bewildered when this new character turned out to be a dark-skinned girl. *Gundam* being what it was, people asked each other, "So *that's* important?" Because at that point, nobody knew that the late stages of the story would revolve around Newtypes.

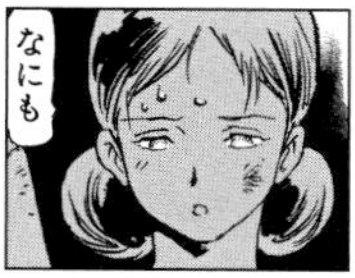
なにも

3. Hamon!!

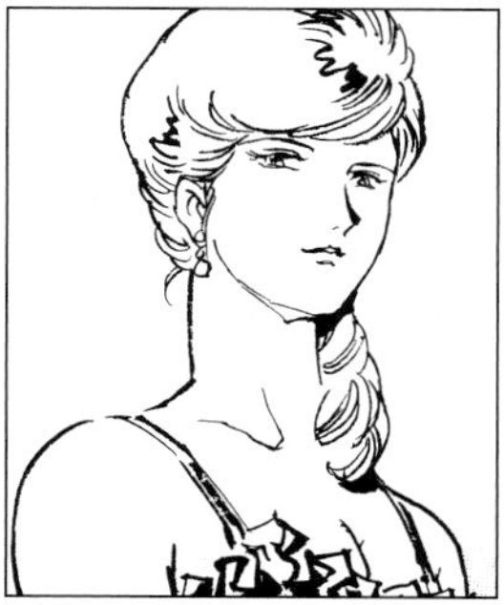

As I've said time and time again, the awesome thing about *The Origin* is that the characters really are just the same as they were in the anime. It's something that absolutely no one but Mr. Yasuhiko could have pulled off. It's almost not fair. And he does it with such nuke-grade-unfair skills that the reader can do nothing but nod, "Yeaaahhhh." She comes into the story around when the Gouf does. (My computer hasn't been recognizing the mobile suit names at all here. It shows how rarely I actually type them out. Anyway…) There she is, boom, in Zeon itself! Ral and Hamon have been popular since the anime originally aired, but I think Mr. Yasuhiko must have had a lot of fun writing those scenes—it's like, boom, here's a character we know and love coming on stage in a totally different setting from what we remember, just like that! Not only does Hamon appear in various outfits, but all those wardrobe changes flow naturally with the story. Mr. Yasuhiko draws from a vast knowledge of costume, which puts him in a whole different dimension from an artist who just buys a bunch of fashion magazines and tries to dress characters from there.

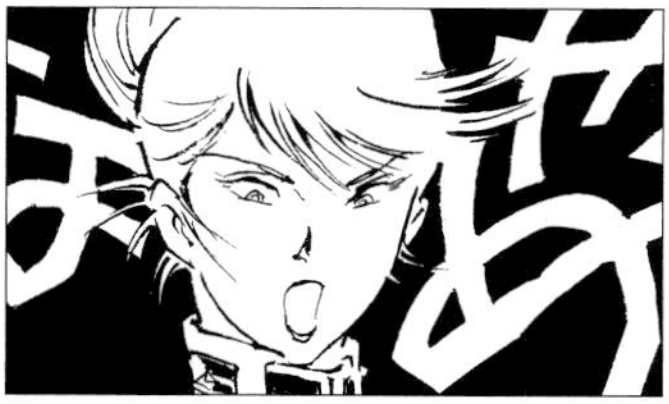

Spilling the beans!! *Gundam* commentary by Mamoru Nagano? Unprecedented, you wouldn't come across one anywhere else. New information, stories from the time of broadcast. Things long buried, things everyone else forgot—it's all here!!

1. Zaku!!

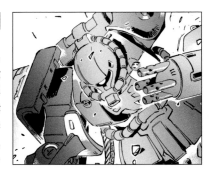

The mobile suit Zaku. At the time of its debut, never had a giant robot made such a shocking appearance. Designed by Mr. Okawara, and refined by Mr. Yasuhiko, the version that made it to the screen conveyed a feeling of enormous size and mass. Right after the first episode aired, Director Tomino's rival at Sunrise, the late director Nagahama, congratulated him saying, "You did it, Tomi-chan!" And it won even higher praise from viewers.

While the fans were all blown away by the Zaku that Mr. Yasuhiko drew, the manufacturers of plastic models fought an uphill battle to bring it into three dimensions. The "Stream Base" modeler cabal of Hobby Japan at the time—Oda, Kawaguchi, and Takahashi—complained one and all about the difficulty of modeling the Zaku; the challenge partly lay in negotiating between the pictorial design and the impression imparted on screen.

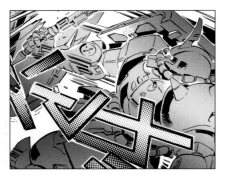

Soon after the first episode aired on TV, some particular fans—the regular customers of a coffee shop called Manga Garou [Gallery] in the Egota neighborhood of Tokyo, and the editors of the magazine *Gekkan [Monthly] OUT* who were writing there—were gossiping that "Zaku" was actually ZAC, standing for Zeon Air Command. Later, I had an opportunity to ask Mr. Tomino whether the rumor was true. "Is that right? That's not actually so bad, is it?" he told me. I also tried asking Mr. Iizuka, who was in charge of content continuity at Sunrise then, but never received a straight answer. Somewhere along the line, though, people stopped talking about the "Zeon Air Command" appellation.

But at the time, I thought it was a really cool way to name the mobile suit.

I just genuinely like *Mobile Suit Gundam*.

Without that great masterpiece, there's no way I would be what I am today. I love it, just as the new fans who got caught up in the Gundam boom a few years ago love the Zaku just as much as the older fans do.

It's a sentiment that appears to be distinct from working on *Gundam*. Unless I get a direct request from Sunrise as a designer, I can't bring myself to draw Zakus and Gelgoogs. Because those are the creations of the people who originally made *Mobile Suit Gundam*.

And don't the other people who've worked on Gundam feel the same way? It's like, "You can't draw Gundam with *respect*! Respect doesn't even cut it!" Maybe this is a conflict unique to those who get involved in the production of something they love.

But it doesn't make me more important for having worked on it. That's not what this is about.

Why? Because, "Hyaku Shiki?? Qubeley?? What the heck? That ain't no mobile suit that ever showed up in *Gundam*!!"

Yuuuuup!! They're not in the original *Gundam*! At all!! The last one to appear in *Gundam* was the Zeong!! I totally agree!!

People like me, who designed the mobile suits in the later series and Char's outfits, and people building Gunpla models and drawing Zakus for fun rather than for anyone else to see—in the face of *Mobile Suit Gundam*, we are all the same. Each one of us, in our own way, loves *Gundam*. The original "Johnny Ridden Zaku" that appeared as a plastic model, the Gundams that transform or have tons of extra spikes, or come in all different colors like the Power Rangers—they're all *Gundam*.

I'm grateful that the whole gamut of us can simply enjoy Mr. Yasuhiko's *The Origin* as a manga and that *Mobile Suit Gundam* is living on into the 21st century. And to think—*the manga and anime have the same art and the same storyyyyyy!* I'm very grateful, as a *Gundam* fan.

Mamoru Nagano
Worked as a designer on projects such as *Heavy Metal L-Gaim*, then started serializing *Five Star Stories* in 1986. In celebration of its 25th anniversary, *Five Star Stories: Reboot* volumes 1 through 7 have been issued bimonthly starting February 10, 2011. The feature-length animation *Gothicmade*, directed by Nagano, was released in 2012.

As you're reading, it really is easy to just take it in like any other manga, but when you pause to think for a moment, a flood of emotions comes welling up.

Like the character whose appearance I'd been anticipating, and dreading, since the beginning of the serialization—yes, Lalah Sune—even Lalah is drawn so naturally, without affectation, like Amuro and company at the outset. That gave me an indescribable feeling.

"Ah, it's Lalah!" "Note: The Real Thing." "Yup." "I can't even handle this."

"Lalah, though—Lalah should have thicker hair, and a unibrow, and—and heavyset legs—"

"She *should*…"

"But now the real thing's here and no one cares about my dumb fantasies… *Slump*."

Still, there was one thing that had me worried. One thing that I wondered how Mr. Yasuhiko, as the animator and character designer, would handle. Yes, that. "How will Yoshikazu Yasuhiko interpret and show the characters whose creation he wasn't involved in?" Lots of people worked on *Gundam*. He may have been the lead designer and the visual director, but I felt a bit uneasy over the arrival of the characters from when he wasn't working on it. I was even thinking that maybe he wouldn't include them, but then, one showed up right on the cover of *Gundam Ace*.

Challia Bull.

"So there he is, without ado." Yes, that was what Mr. Yasuhiko had decided to do.

Think about it for a second.

Challia Bull. A new character appearing in the original *Gundam* thirty years after the initial broadcast. *C'mon, get more excited about it!! Why are you all so calm?! Have you even seen the show?!* That's how much of an impact it had on me. You could say it, too, is something Mr. Yasuhiko just dropped behind him.

I think *Gundam* is a work that turns frightening the moment you find yourself on the makers' side, the side that needs to deliver. The only ones who truly know how frightening it is are the creators of the original *Mobile Suit Gundam* and the people who've worked on the related merchandise. There was a time when, knowing how frightening it could be, I took on *Gundam* again and again, only to be shattered in defeat. But…

…But Mr. Yasuhiko, I think, will understand this—*Gundam* has loved me. And I feel as if it's been protecting me all this time, even after I threw myself into the core of the development of later series. That is because despite my involvement, I am still pretty blessed. Even though I have taken on *Gundam* three times, and failed three times. Because after three such spectacular failures I shouldn't even be in the industry.

Well, *I* think it must love me.

that make me want to say, "But Mr. Yasuhiko, you're dropping things all over the place!"

Right, it's probably deliberate, but I find myself thinking as I read, "These things that keep falling off here and there, only Mr. Yasuhiko could ever pick up!" The one that sticks out the most is the scene where Artesia reveals her identity at A Baoa Qu—"If Sayla became Artesia here, it could only carry over into a setup for Zeta Gundam!!" "But Mr. Yasuhiko is the only one who could follow through with that setup!!"

So it's a one-two punch of lost and found. Gaaah! If I start giving more examples, I'll never stop. But there's a lot of that going on.

The anime *Mobile Suit Gundam* tells the story of all these characters—Amuro, the crew of *White Base*, Sayla, Lalah, Mirai—with Amuro fixed at the center. But *The Origin* is clear about Zeon's side of the story—not just Char, but the people who come under the big tent called Side 3 with Zeon Zum Deikun as a central presence. House Zabi, as well as Casval and Artesia as children, and Ral and Hamon, are depicted as main characters in their own right, apart from the story of *White Base*.

This probably has something to do with how much time has gone by since the production of the original anime. But it seems like more than just an attempt to cater to the popularity of the Zeon side or Char. Is it that Mr. Yasuhiko is writing this in the same way as the many historical manga series he's penned after taking a step back from the anime industry?

"Write the antagonists just like everyone else." It must be as simple as that.

Mr. Yasuhiko is recounting the excellent narrative broadcast in 1979 that is *Mobile Suit Gundam* in the same way as the historical manga he's worked on in the meantime.

Maybe he approached it with an attitude like, "Oh, so this is the next thing you want me to make into a manga? This thing called 'Gundam,' huh?" And doesn't he write it so calmly, even *coldheartedly*, that you just want to yell, "But Mr. Yasuhiko, *you* were the original designer!"

Of course, I imagine that when he was approached about writing a Gundam manga, he was exploding with a million times more emotion than me, and it must have been hard to contain all those feelings. But I don't really get that sense from the manga itself, which I think must be due to such a stance.

And that's why the first episode of *The Origin* made me realize: "This man isn't worked up about it or preening about this being originally his. He manages to write *this* story—Gundam—placidly, like it's nothing?"

Amuro, Char, Sayla—they haven't changed a bit. To a frightening degree, they are the same characters as they were in 1979. Even Hamon and Miharu, Tim and Watkein—they appear in the story just as they did on TV so many years ago, and it's so wonderful it hurts.

Thoughts on *Gundam: The Origin*

Mamoru Nagano

When I first read *The Origin*, memories from my childhood came flooding back. As elementary school kids, we were raised on anime and manga. But even at that age, we noticed things, and there was something to criticize—the manga we were reading and the anime on TV were not the same. With series like *Tiger Mask* and *Devilman*, the original manga and the derivative anime were radically different with respect to both visuals and story. Kids at the time must have all recognized that the anime and the manga were totally separate. Naoki Tsuji's illustrations in *Tiger Mask* were more evocative of *gekiga*, but in the anime, Mr. Kubo gave us a refined-looking, handsome Naoto Date who looked nothing like his manga counterpart. Devilman had a beastly aspect in the original manga but looked more like an American comics character in the anime. Still, I think both the original manga and derivative anime of *Tiger Mask* and *Devilman* are masterpieces.

So, my point is, I think kids kind of had a critical expectation that when the opposite happens—when there is a derivative manga based on an original anime—it'll also end up completely different.

Tatsunoko Production and Sunrise, for instance, have a lot of franchises for which the anime was the original work. The manga versions often appeared in magazines for small children, and while they resembled the anime at first glance, something always seemed different. Of course, with animators drawing one, and manga artists drawing the other, differences were inevitable no matter how much they tried to keep the visuals consistent. The "feeling" inherent to animated works can't quite be conveyed on a page, so there will always be that sense that something is a little off.

Ever since I noticed this as a kid, it was a little disappointing to me. But when I read *The Origin*, my mind went right back to that time, and I felt such a simple rush of joy: *The anime and the manga are the same!*

I have no idea why, but Mr. Yasuhiko has been friendly enough to put up with me over the years. So I know for a fact that he won't care one bit if I were to tell him all the things about *The Origin* that I find so amazing. We've known each other so long that obviously, I should write things that would make him go, "What, *that's* the thing you want to nitpick?!"

Well, it's Mr. Yasuhiko we're talking about, so of course he's probably just drawing all of it effortlessly—be it a Zaku, or Gihren—but as an author there are a ton of things

AIZOUBAN MOBILE SUIT GUNDAM THE ORIGIN vol. 7

Translation: Melissa Tanaka

Production: Grace Lu
Hiroko Mizuno
Anthony Quintessenza
Risa Cho

© Yoshikazu YASUHIKO 2011, 2012

© SOTSU · SUNRISE

Edited by KADOKAWA SHOTEN
First published in Japan in 2011, 2012 by KADOKAWA CORPORATION, Tokyo

English translation rights arranged with KADOKAWA CORPORATION,
through Tuttle-Mori Agency, Inc., Tokyo

Translation copyright © 2014 Vertical, Inc.

Published by Vertical, Inc., New York

Originally published in Japanese as *Kidou Senshi Gundam THE ORIGIN*
volumes 13 and 14 in 2006 and re-issued in hardcover as *Aizouban Kidou Senshi Gundam
THE ORIGIN VII -Ruumu-* in 2011, by Kadokawa Shoten, Co., Ltd.

Kidou Senshi Gundam THE ORIGIN first serialized in *Gundam Ace,*
Kadokawa Shoten, Co., Ltd., 2001-2011

ISBN: 978-1-939130-67-9

Manufactured in the United States of America

First Edition

Vertical, Inc.
451 Park Avenue South
7th Floor
New York, NY 10016
www.vertical-inc.com